Denise Robins

Denise Robins has touched the lives of millions
of readers with her novels of romance and love-
inspired intrigue. Ballantine Books is pleased to
present the stories of Denise Robins, collected
and published in twelve enchanting volumes of
three or four novels. Each omnibus volume
will be an enthralling experience of the human
heart because . . .

**"RARELY HAS A WRITER DELVED
SO DEEPLY INTO THE SECRET PLACES
OF A WOMAN'S HEART."**
Taylor Caldwell

LOVE BY DENISE ROBINS
Volume VI

Over half a million copies of these new
editions in print

Also by Denise Robins
Published by Ballantine Books:

LOVE VOLUME I

LOVE VOLUME II

LOVE VOLUME III

LOVE VOLUME IV

LOVE VOLUME V

Love

VOLUME VI

BY
DENISE ROBINS

BALLANTINE BOOKS • NEW YORK

Library of Congress Catalog Card Number: 79-90240

ISBN 0-345-28520-4

This edition published by arrangement with
Hodder and Stoughton

Originally published as three volumes: *The Other Side of Love;
Sweet Cassandra; Climb to the Stars.*

Manufactured in the United States of America

First Edition: August 1980

CONTENTS

BOOK I

The Other Side of Love

"I hated now with a hatred more vital than indifference because it was the other side of love."

STRINDBERG

FOR MONICA

NIRA AND DES

Chapter 1

NIRA WAS ONE of those people who wake up early and she was at her best in the morning, and more inclined to feel sleepy at the end of the day. On this particular April morning she woke at seven. Instead of getting straight out of bed to switch on the electric kettle and make the early tea, she lay quietly in the big double bed beside her still-sleeping husband and contemplated him—and life. Their life and those of their two children. Jonathan and Renira (her mother's name in full) were not yet stirring. No sounds came from the two rooms at the end of the corridor.

Nira stretched her long slender limbs, luxuriating in the warmth of the bed and of the masculine body beside hers.

Desmond Curtis lay on his side facing her. At times, when she first opened her eyes she would find his head on her shoulder, and he would be snoring very gently, though not loudly enough to disturb her. Sometimes he opened an eye and blinked sleepily at her then with sudden longing would draw her close and begin to make love to her.

Nine times out of ten she responded. She was still in love with Des. Their relationship had been a very happy one. The close association of eleven years had not yet extinguished the fire of the early days. Neither had parenthood destroyed the romance, even though it sometimes made it a little more difficult for them to be romantic. Tricky was, perhaps, the word. Not so easy to exchange passionate embraces while a crying infant, or inquisitive child, disturbed them.

Little Jonathan had suffered from night terrors from

3

the time he was two. He often ran into their room for comfort. So it wasn't easy to feel relaxed and enjoy completely the ardours of the year before the first baby came.

Nira looked at her husband's face with fond approval. She was lucky to be married to a man like Des and he seemed well satisfied with her. Of course they both had their faults and moments of disagreement *and* there had certainly been one or two blazing rows. On the whole they tolerated each other's discrepancies and the infrequent quarrels were soon over, and followed by what Des called 'fun and games' in the marriage bed.

In sleep he looked very handsome, she thought. She put out a hand to touch the thick brown hair which he wore longer than he used to do; not too long. She wouldn't stand that. But he allowed a nice tail to grow down at the nape of the neck and he had recently cultivated a small moustache. She had hated that to begin with, now she liked it. He was a tall athletic man and at his best in country clothes. She liked to see him in pullover and slacks striding over the golf course or driving off a tee with his tremendous vigour. He was a good golfer. They spent most of their week-ends on the local course which had pleasant surroundings and an attractive club house. They were fifteen miles from Brighton. Sometimes they played up on the Dyke. Nira played mainly to please Des—and to be with him. She dreaded becoming what they called a golf-widow. But she didn't really care for the game, and she wasn't very good. Des both teased and encouraged her and had been glad when she stopped using the children as an excuse for not leaving them. Now Susan, a local girl, came daily to take care of Jonathan and Renira when they were not at school, or in the evenings when Nira wanted to go out.

Des has a lovely straight nose, thought Nira, and she adored his large, dark-brown eyes, long lashes and rather full sensual lips. Asleep, he looked young despite that moustache. He had marvellous points. He was kind and attentive and a wonderful lover. Of course he had his weaknesses—for wine and women. He almost always beat it up at a dinner party and he was a frightful flirt. But Nira was not a jealous person. She was sure of his deep affection and certain of his fidelity. But she did wish sometimes that he wouldn't be quite so noisy when he'd had a couple of drinks or that he wouldn't make such outrageous passes at the good-looking girls who were all too anxious to say snap. However, she was fairly sure that the fun didn't go too far. Des always derided both the girls and himself once he was alone with his wife again.

"Attractive females amuse me, but you are the one I love," he'd say.

She had nothing to complain of, she reflected happily as she lay dreaming, watching the sun filter through the slats in the Venetian blinds. It filled the room with little golden slivers of light. It was going to be a lovely morning. It was Saturday, too. That meant Susan would be here early to take Jonathan and Renira off her hands. Golf, and lunch at the Club, and tonight they were going out to a dinner party.

A very pleasant day.

She began to think about what she would wear tonight. If it stayed fine she'd try out that new violet dinner-dress with the silver collar. She'd had her hair done yesterday—the way Des liked it best. It just needed a comb-out. Her hair was dark and silky. The best of the local hairdressers, an Italian, shaped it well. She wore it brushed back from her forehead high on top.

Suddenly she sprang out of bed. She wanted to take off her shortie nightgown and stand naked in front of her mirror. She did so, and contemplated her reflection. With the blinds still down and in that dusty gold sunlight, she stood a moment, staring.

She had always been on the tall side—four inches shorter than Des, who was six foot. She had kept her small waist and her smallish, rounded breasts. People told her she had a lovely figure. She could have been a model.

She was the same age as Des but looked younger. She had limpid eyes, greyish-blue, narrowing to slits when she laughed, and a slightly tip-tilted nose. Her mouth was moist and sweet. She had a pale fine skin and high cheek-bones. When she was made up she could look quite stunning.

She slipped into a white candlewick dressing-gown, tied the belt, then switched on the kettle. She was going to make tea and wake Des.

Now she could hear the children's voices. They were not allowed to come in here till half-past seven. Possibly by this time young Jon was out of bed and sitting beside his little sister. They got on very well, which was fortunate. Nira disliked brothers and sisters who were hostile to each other. It was usually out of jealousy. But she and Des had made a point of not causing this by showing favouritism. They prided themselves on being ideal parents.

Yawning, Nira dug a spoon into the tea-tin and made sure she hadn't forgotten Des's sugar. She didn't take it. She had a strong will and stuck to a reasonable diet. Des was putting on weight and she was cross sometimes when he refused to deny himself an extra slice of bread or lump of sugar, or those foaming tankards of beer he liked so much, and which were so fattening.

As soon as the kettle hissed and boiled she made the tea and called her husband.

"Wake up, lover."

He groaned and buried his face in the pillow.

"Too early."

"It isn't."

"Darling, it is. It's only quarter-past seven," his muffled voice slurred back. "Not a working day. Why wake? Come back to bed."

She leaned over him, shook the broad shoulders gently then dropped a kiss on his hair. She liked the odour of his hair tonic and after-shave lotion, and the faint rich smell of cigar smoke that still clung to him. A business friend had come back for a drink last night and given Des a cigar. He had enjoyed it. He liked expensive things. He meant to forge ahead in his business and eventually lead a life of luxury, and give her and the children all they wanted. That was one of the things

Nira liked about him. He was so generous—too much so at times—inclined to be extravagant.

He was a business executive in an advertising firm, and after six years he was doing well and looked like making steady progress. They were always hard up—most young couples with children in their income group found it hard to manage—what with the steady rise in prices and disheartening taxation. But they were luckier than their friends the Hallings, whom they saw more of than anyone else in the district. Boyce Halling was a research engineer and he didn't seem to get either the salary rises or opportunities that gave Desmond an aura of success, yet Boyce worked just as hard. But his wife and small son had to economise and sometimes Mrs. Halling—known as Cricket, because of her petite figure and twittering voice—envied Nira.

Desmond gave a prodigious yawn, cleared his throat and sat up, running his fingers through tousled hair. He licked his lips and scowled.

"I drank too much last night. Why in God's name must you be so bright so early, woman?"

"Darling, you know we're having early golf, and that first of all we've got to drive Susan and the kids into Brighton and settle them with Gandy." (The children's nickname for old Mrs. Curtis was Gandy.)

"What a bore!" said Des.

"Well, your mother's taking Susan and the kids off our hands for the whole day, and you ought to be grateful."

Desmond swung his legs over the bed and rubbed his palms over his naked torso. He had a habit of wearing pajama trousers but never the coat. The hairs on his chest were curly—chestnut brown like the thick hair on his head.

Nira looked at him with pride and pleasure. Her handsome Des! No wonder all the girls fell for him.

"You never remember anything and you're never grateful and you're hopeless!" she complained, and fell into his arms and was nearly smothered. Then he pushed her away, protesting, "I refuse to be seduced at seven fifteen a.m., so go and get the tea and behave yourself."

"You're one to talk! And it's seven twenty-five now and the tea's been ready for ten minutes."

"Well, make some more," said Desmond. He walked to the window and pulled up the Venetian blinds, letting in the delightful warmth of the Spring sunshine. He whistled. "Crikey, what a day! It'll be super up on the golf course."

She put some more water into the tea pot, poured out two cups and handed him one.

"Super. Out in the open all day—then the party to-night."

"Who's giving a party?"

"Honestly! You never remember anything," said Nira for the second time, "You've got such a ghastly memory. I've got to remember everything for everyone in this house including Susan, and I'm much older than she is."

"You don't look it," he said and threw an appreciative glance at Nira's graceful figure and the face that he used to tell her in their early days of wooing could easily have launched a thousand ships had she lived at the same time as Helen of Troy. He had a sincere admiration for his wife.

"Surely you remember it's Rob Bessiford's dinner."

"What, old Rob? What's he throwing the party for? I forget."

"*Comme toujours*," said Nira whose French accent was poor but she made the foreign words sound withering.

Des was now in the bathroom. She could hear the whirr of his electric razor. He called to her, "Okay—I remember now. It's for his birthday and it's at The Richmond."

Richmond Hall was one of the brightest spots in the otherwise unremarkable suburban town of Ponders Heath. Forty years ago, before the war, the Hall was private property—a beautiful Georgian building in a fine garden which nobody now could afford to keep up to anything like its old glory. But it made a superb hotel with the additional restaurant, dance room and a good bar which had been built on by the successful Brighton restaurateur who now ran the place.

They avoided ageing residents and catered for the general public. The gates opened on to what was now the main Ponders Heath Road from London to Brighton. There was much to attract passing trade, and the Saturday night dinner-dances at Richmond Hall Hotel had become very popular. There was a good band and the excellent cuisine encouraged the most elegant and monied among the local inhabitants.

"It is old Rob's birthday, isn't it?" Des called out to his wife.

"Yes, his forty-ninth, and he says it's the last he'll ever celebrate because he refuses to be fifty."

"You can't stop the march of time," came from Desmond, followed by a great splashing as he sponged his face.

Nira walked into the bathroom and grimaced at him.

"So speaks my thirty-year-old playboy."

"I wish I were a playboy, and I must say I've had a few chances of being one since I came here. I thought it was pretty ghastly, the life we led in Brighton. You never really got to know anybody. But they've all been very friendly in this little place. I suppose belonging to the local golf club has helped, and they've mostly turned out to be rather a smart go-ahead lot, haven't they?"

Nira began to brush her dark silky hair, shaking it back from her face. For the moment she was silent. She loved parties and good times and enjoyed everything with Des, but personally, she had rather liked Brighton. True, their flat had been far too small and once Renira was born they had simply had to find a house and garden. Besides, it was countrified in Ponders Heath—they thought it good for the kids, and they were not too far from Reigate where they could shop if they didn't find what they wanted here, but all kinds of new big stores and supermarkets were opening up in The Heath as they called it.

Brighton appealed only to Nira's love of culture, art

and beauty. There were good concerts, art exhibitions, and the Theatre Royal. She enjoyed all three. It was a part of her which had never really found response in the man she had married. They could get together—and did—in all kinds of other ways, but Des never wanted to stroll through the Lanes and look for treasures, or go to concerts or galleries. He only took her to the Theatre Royal to see the amusing shows. He didn't really like serious things. Because she was so much in love with him, and his influence over her was considerable, she did as he wished, and shrugged off the sad fact that her idol was fundamentally a selfish man. She loved him. It didn't matter that she was really much better educated than he. He was first and foremost a businessman. Because he was a gay companion and good lover when he was at home, she had so far felt he was all she needed.

They had had another important reason for wanting to leave Brighton—Des's mother. She lived in one of those attractive Regency squares near Black Rock. Since her husband, a chartered accountant, had died, she had devoted herself to charitable pursuits. She was a dedicated do-gooder. She spent most of her spare time helping the helpless, attending committee-meetings, opening bazaars and helping the Church. She had been left enough money to live in comfort. Although she loved her only son, she openly disapproved because he was not a churchgoer, and Nira had admitted that neither was she.

The only time the young couple entered a church these days was to attend a wedding, a christening or a funeral. While they lived in Brighton, Mrs. Curtis was too often on their backs, and had a genius for upsetting Des and making him irritable. Nira quite liked her mother-in-law but was relieved when Des decided to move to their present home in The Heath. Fortunately Nira was placid and tolerant enough to avoid falling out with her mother-in-law, but the one real point of contact between them now was the children. Gandy adored them. She was much better with them than she had been with her own son. Neither Nira nor Des could forget that they owed a lot to Gandy. She paid for Jonathan's and Renira's private school education, bought quite a lot of their clothes, and occasionally financed a special holiday for the whole family.

It was Nira who coaxed Des into going to see Mrs. Curtis more often than he would have done without her influence. Sometimes she accused him of lacking gratitude and affection for his mother. But it was not her business, as she often told herself, and she had to admit that the rather smug little white-haired woman, now in her sixty-seventh year, could be very irritating. However, they had all been better friends since they put a few miles between them.

Des was successful in his business life but one had to have more salary than he could provide to run an establishment like this one in The Heath. It was a sevenroomed house with a small garden. They could only just afford Susan (Mrs. Curtis helped them to pay her wages). And whatever Des said or however much he clashed with his mother, he couldn't deny that the rather gay and free life they were leading now, they owed to her generosity.

Susan was Nira's greatest help and joy. Not only was she the babywatcher, but dealt with all their washing, ironing and mending. Nira had had to do it herself in the old Brighton days. What a difference the allowance from Gandy had made! There remained the cooking. But Nira rather liked her kitchen, and trying out new dishes, and she watched the television chefs avidly. She shared the housework with Mrs. Tulk, a plump, cheerful daily who came three mornings a week to clean. Everything was organised. For the moment, Nira felt that she was so lucky—she feared something must go wrong.

Chapter 2

THEY RAN INTO Rob Bessiford as they walked into the golf club.

"Hi!" Des said cheerfully to the older man and grinned the schoolboy grin which Bessiford never felt was quite in character with the moustache, or the pseudo-American slang. Being essentially English and rather conventional, Rob returned with a more ordinary "Hello!" Then turning to Nira, he added, "And good morning to you, Nira. You're looking as fresh as the Spring morning, if I may say so."

"You may say so," said Nira happily. "I feel rather Springlike. It's quite warm. I shall shed my pullover any moment now."

"Don't forget you're my guests tonight."

Nira put the tips of her fingers against her lips.

"Oh, *of course,* it's your birthday. Many happy returns, dear Rob."

"Let's skip that," he smiled, "I'm only using the anniversary as an excuse to throw a party."

"Well, you can be sure we won't forget to come."

"And if I may add," put in Desmond, "you don't look a day over eighty, Rob!"

They all laughed. That sort of quip was typical of Des. It did in fact suddenly annoy Nira. She knew that Des meant to be just jolly, but she thought it rather a tactless joke. After all Rob was pretty well the oldest of them all in their circle.

"I *feel* eighty sometimes, my dear Desmond," he said. He was the one person who never shortened the name to Des. Some of Nira's friends thought Rob a bit on the staid and sober side. Des jeered and called Rob a flag-raiser, the type to get up and stand smartly to attention when The Queen was played; to do the right thing on all occasions; unfailingly courteous. The sort of chap Des wouldn't tell a dirty story to in front of the girls. He was interesting, well-informed and friendly to all. Worthy, of course. Nobody could possibly dislike Rob.

"I rather enjoy his old-fashioned manners," Nira had said on one occasion when she had heard Rob being criticised. "It's refreshing."

Des had qualified this by saying, "So are you at times. I don't know why you married a coarse brute like myself."

She had denied fiercely that he was either coarse or brutal. He was, she said, just—a devil at times. But she liked that. She adored him. Everyone had their little ways. Take Cricket Halling, who was tiny and looked fragile, but was never ill. She had huge limpid blue eyes and a silver-bell voice. That spurious air of innocence and childish laugh seemed to fascinate the men. But she was far from what she appeared to be. Nira had heard her tell a story in front of the boys which made her blush. Cricket prided herself on being with it, and frank about intimate subjects. Nobody could dislike her. She was as affectionate and cuddlesome as a kitten. There seemed to be no real malice in Cricket, but somehow Nira didn't trust her. She made her feel that although they were the same age, she, Nira, was a good deal older.

Nira had grown up in a rather dull conventional home—the kind that seemed to be rapidly disappearing. Undoubtedly it had left a mark on her. She had a reserved, dignified side, but fundamentally she was warm, impulsive and passionate. Her father had been a Regular Army Officer, killed in the last year of the War. A fine soldier, but not as strong a character as Nira's mother. The most important legacy he had left his daughter was his sense of humour and an honest approach to life.

This morning, Rob Bessiford looked down at Nira with greater pleasure than he knew he ought to feel.

He was in love with her.

He had fallen in love just like that, when they first met at a drinks party given by Anthony and Grace Conniston who lived at the Manor House—the oldest and most attractive place in Ponders Heath.

The Connistons—Anthony was a baronet—entertained on a large scale. He was at the head of all the Conservative activities. Her ladyship upheld the traditions. They had a teenage family. The eldest daughter, Vanessa, had become a model, which fact Grace Conniston was always trying to excuse. Grace was quite unable to cope with this permissive age. Vanessa seldom wore shoes and despite her parents' disapproval, appeared on most occasions wearing shorts and shirts (often her brother's), and with naked feet. Her beautiful face was usually half hidden behind two curtains of long red hair.

When Rob was first introduced to the Curtis family, he felt at once that Nira was different from the other young married women he met in Ponders Heath. Nira on her part, was impressed by Rob's exceptional height, and the attractive combination of suntanned face and silver hair. He had seemed old to her at first glance—then quite young—and Nira never again felt that he was elderly, in any sense of the word. His eyes were pure, piercing blue, but he had had trouble with his sight, and wore tinted glasses.

During the Conniston party they sat together, talking. She heard about his life in Nairobi and his subsequent illness. They talked animatedly. They were on the same mental wave-length. They discussed everything and everybody, including Vanessa, their host's daughter. She drank a lot of champagne and never left the side of a teenage youth whose fair hair was almost as long as hers, and who wore a crimson velvet suit.

It was a cold November day. The Connistons were celebrating their Silver Wedding. Desmond and Nira had been invited because when the Curtis family first came to town, Lady Conniston's youngest—a boy of ten—had made friends with Jonathan who was at the same prep school. So the two mothers had met and liked each other, although Anthony, like Rob, admired Nira but was not particularly impressed by Desmond Curtis.

By the time the party ended, Nira felt she had known Rob all her life and decided to ask him to dinner.

She made him talk about himself.

He lived in The Hollies, an enormous Victorian double-fronted house, not far from the Curtis home. It backed on to the park which was also the local cricket ground. It was the sort of house that Rob secretly liked, although it was badly planned, rambling and draughty, but recently improved by the newly-installed central heating.

As a bachelor Rob might have been better in a flat, but the big house spelt home to him. It belonged to his eighty-nine-year-old aunt—Ida Bessiford—a maiden lady who had been part of Rob's life ever since he could remember. The oldest of his father's unmarried sisters and the only one left living, Aunt Ida was devoted to Rob and had made a will in favour of him. Not that she had much to leave now except The Hollies and its contents, but there was considerable value in the beautiful furniture, the Georgian silver, and one or two of the paintings. Rob had shared the house with her since his return from Kenya.

He told Nira that he had spent twenty-two years in Nairobi. He had become quite well known out there as a photographer of wild animal life. He even made money out of his movies, and regularly sold them in England, America and France. He had other business interests in East Africa but it all came to an end after Independence Day. Even then, because Rob adored Nairobi—the splendid rolling mountains and great lakes and rivers—the place had become dearer to him than England. He stayed out there until a sudden rare illness struck him down and finished his career. After a year in hospital, he was forced back to the old country. He could no longer go on safari nor lead the wandering life that had required so much stamina when living under difficult conditions.

The virus that struck him down had affected his eye-

sight. During the last year his eyes had improved sufficiently to allow him to golf again, but he still suffered
from headaches. It had all been a tragedy for him. He
had given so much to his work in Kenya. He had hoped
to end his days there. Now that he was rising fifty, the
doctors had advised him to stay home in a more tem-
perate climate. Fortunately he had saved enough money
to make it possible for him to lead his present quiet but
comfortable life without working other than for charity
organisations in the locality.

He went away sometimes for weekends to friends.
Talking to Nira he told her what a grand old lady his
aunt was—marvellous for her age and with a mind still
young. She was now almost totally crippled by arthritis,
and spent most of the time in a wheelchair. When Nira
herself first saw The Hollies, she was amused and interested by Rob's personal possessions—his elephant-foot
table, his ivories, his leopard-skin rugs, and the other
trophies he had added to Aunt Ida's collection.

Rob—the confirmed bachelor—from the first moment he had looked down into Nira's fine grey-blue
eyes, knew she was the one woman he could have, and
would have, married, if he had been given the chance.
But it was far too late. She was Mrs. Desmond Curtis—
very much so—and there were those two nice children—and that was that. As time went on and he saw
more of her, he was determined that she should never
guess he felt this way about her, and tried to be content
with her friendship.

They got on very well. He hoped and believed that
she liked him. He was usually included in her dinner
parties, and often played bridge at Nylands, their home.
He was glad, too, that he and Desmond were good
friends, despite the fact that they had little in common
save golf and bridge. Mentally, they were poles apart.

He tried to be grateful for the fact that he seemed
welcome in Nira's home, and to stamp on more dangerous feelings. He was nearly twenty years her senior, and
she must surely look on him as the children did—as an
uncle, or elder brother. Nira was only just thirty.

He admired her when she was dressed up for occasions, but he found her even more attractive as she was in the Club this morning in that soft yellow pullover, grey ski-trousers and suède boots. Her grace and charm, as always, pulled at his heart-strings.

He was so tall that he stooped slightly. He made Nira feel short, but he gave her a curious feeling of security.

Rob and Desmond exchanged friendly comments. But Rob did not particularly care for Desmond. He was not the type he could ever have made a close friend of—too boisterous and self-satisfied. But at least he seemed to keep Nira happy. That was important to Rob. They appeared a devoted couple. Obviously the sex side must be satisfactory between them. Rob's jealous eyes now and again noticed the way Nira stood close to her husband or how they suddenly held hands, or their eyes would meet in delightful appreciation of each other. But why she had fallen in love with him in the first place puzzled Rob. They were so different. She had been very young then—reserved—perhaps inexperienced, Desmond Curtis, so charming and self-assured must have swept her off her feet. He was immensely popular with all the females around here, Rob had to admit that. He definitely had what was called animal magnetism.

But for Rob, all the magnetism in the world lay in Nira's eyes. They fascinated him as she looked up at him this moment. Her lashes were dark like her hair, and luxuriant. Hers was an Irish type of beauty. The curve of her lips enchanted him. She used an attractive pink lipstick, and he had grown familiar with her perfume. He had asked her, once, what it was and she told him Paco Rabanne's *Calandre*. Flower-fresh, like the graceful girl herself, he thought. Nira always seemed so well groomed and smelt so good. He had bought her a bottle of the *Calandre* for Christmas, and given it to her at the party the Curtis family always held on Boxing Day.

While Desmond chatted to another golfer in the bar, Rob and Nira walked out on to the verandah. There was a light breeze—cool but not cold. They gazed across the green course—it looked beautiful, with the fringe of dark fir trees on one side and a long row of hawthorn bushes, already in bud, warmed by the Spring sunshine. Nira loved it up here. One of the attractions that had led Des and herself to settle in Ponders Heath had been this eighteen-hole golf course, recommended in the first place by a business friend who had been a Ponders Heath resident for some years.

"How are the offspring?" Rob was asking Nira. She rewarded him with the bright proud smile which always lit up her face when her children were discussed. That was another thing he admired—her pride in these two children, and the way she handled them. Desmond was a permissive father, lavish with pocket-money and treats and it was not always because he loved to spoil them, but because it was the easy way of getting them out of his way when he wanted to be free of them. More than once Nira had argued that it was bad to spoil the children. She told Rob that she disliked what she saw going on around her. The way the young controlled their parents. It should be the other way round. Nira disliked pampered children and disobedient animals. Rob agreed.

"The babes are fine," she answered his question, "rather too energetic. I assure you I'm glad to have Susan."

"But you're with them a lot yourself."

"I used to be more so until we came here. We couldn't afford either Susan or a daily in the old days. I'm very lucky to have Des's mother to help with finance now."

Rob nodded. But he was not sure Nira was all that lucky. He could never bring himself to believe that Desmond Curtis was right for her. Physically, Nira was a splendid mature young woman, but Rob, who prided himself on being a psychologist, and also because he was so deeply attracted by her, had watched and listened and at times thought that she was immature in other ways. She was almost like a child in her frank enjoyment of things. She seemed to accept life as it was and ask no more. Just as she accepted that pretentious husband of hers. Women were wonderful, and a bit frightening to Rob. When they loved they seemed so blind to the man's faults, and even in these days of woman's liberation, still slavishly devoted to the one of their choice. Or did they accept what was really unacceptable and gloss it over? Whichever way it was with Nira, Rob found her touching and adorable. But he often worried about her.

Desmond was not worth her adoration, and Rob feared the day would come when Nira would wake up to this fact. She would, with her nature, expect fidelity from a man. *Did she get it from Des?*

Even during this short time that he had known the Curtises, Rob had heard a few things said at the Club about Des that he found disturbing. A week or two ago he had been having a drink at the bar and heard a man named Robinson—an estate agent who was a noted gossip—discussing Desmond with Lieut.-Col. Moffatt—a retired Army man now working for a Conservative organisation, and married to a nice dull woman. Typical Army wife, Des called her—tweed coat and hair-net, flag-waving, hearty and organising.

"Lover-Boy's going to upset old Boyce Halling soon if he doesn't watch out," Robinson had said, apropos of Desmond.

Someone else asked for an explanation of this. The answer was, "He's got this thing about Cricket."

"Hasn't everybody?" the plump and affable Colonel put in, laughing. "She's—what is the word they all use?—dishy!"

"Oh, definitely," said Robinson, "While Boyce was away on that business trip in the U.S.A. someone I know ran into the pair in town, and they were staying in some hotel together."

Rob had walked out feeling uneasy and suddenly troubled for Nira. Even more so when Robinson's rather loud voice, still gossiping with the Colonel, followed him.

"There's quite a bit of this and that going on in our little town, old boy. Ponders Heath will be in the wife-swopping class before long."

Laughter and a few mild protests followed, all in

good fun no doubt, but Rob felt an active dislike of
Desmond at that moment. Where there was such talk
there was always a modicum of truth. Why did Desmond Curtis want to pursue Cricket Halling?

Afterwards Rob had thought a lot about the Robinson gossip. He was no prig. It was just that word *wife-
swopping* that offended him. He might even have been
amused by that if it hadn't been aimed at Des Curtis.
Why should Des, with a wife like Nira, want another
girl, even for a few hours' fun? As for Cricket Halling,
Rob had no regard for her whatever. She and Boyce
had long since seemed a bit too fond of that word permissive.

But of one thing he was certain—if Desmond was actually having fun with Cricket, Nira didn't know it. If
she had done, there wouldn't be that contented glow in
her eyes, nor would she be so vividly pleased with life—
and Des.

Rob thought, *I hope to God she never hears what's
being said.*

He felt fiercely protective and embarrassingly old.
He was, of course, older than any of them in this young
set. But Rob felt uneasy because he *minded* about Nira.

He heard her speaking now. He liked her voice. It
was quiet and there was music in her laughter, unlike
Cricket Halling's shrill squeals of delight.

"You've got a brooding sort of look this morning,
Rob. Anything wrong?" she asked him.

He snapped out of the darkness of his thoughts and
smiled down at her benevolently.

"Not a thing. How are we playing today? You and
Desmond against Maggie and myself?"

"I imagine so," she nodded.

Here was Maggie now, coming towards them with
her golf clubs slung over her shoulder and Desmond at
her side. They were both laughing. They made rather a
nice-looking pair, Nira thought, with the tiniest stab of
jealousy which quickly passed. She despised jealous
wives. If one loved a man, one must trust him. Still—
Maggie was a very attractive creature. About Nira's
age, she had been a widow for the last two years. Her

husband was once a doctor in one of the local syndi-
cates. Poor Bill Wilson—a general favourite—had been
killed in a car smash, and Maggie's world had crashed,
too. She lived now in a bungalow near the golf course
with her mother and a small daughter of seven. She had
been devoted to Bill, but everyone expected her to
marry again. As she walked toward them, Nira generously admired the grace of the slim figure and the
beauty of hair that held the bronze lights of beech
leaves in the autumn sun. Her large red-brown eyes
were beautiful. Nira knew that Maggie was one of Des's
favourites. She was nice and at the same time fun. They
had all been pleased here when she decided to stay on
in the town. Recently she had taken up golf and proved
herself exceptionally good. With a handicap now of
twelve she was almost on a level with Nira, who had
played much longer. Des was erratic, Rob was the best
of them all. But they made a good foursome.

"Hi!" Maggie greeted them.

Her mother was American and Maggie had been
brought up in Baltimore. As they discussed the fine
weather and the approaching game, Des looked not at
his wife but at Maggie. The creamy texture of her skin
and her big sensual mouth usually excited him. As the
conversation died, he put in, "Maggie's been telling me
there's a film we must see, on next week, Nira my darling."

"What?" she asked, and linked her arm affectionately
with his.

"What's it called, Maggie?" he asked the other girl.

*"The Virgin and The Gypsy."*__

"D. H. Lawrence," said Rob, and pulled a pipe from
his pocket and began to fill it. "I'm in two minds about
that fellow, you know. I was never a Chatterley fan but
I admit he writes well at times."

"Mum and I saw this film in London," said Maggie.
"I assure you it's worth a go, Rob. Lovely scenery—
old-fashioned village scenes—lots of beautiful colour—
I'm sure you'd like it."

"And what about the purple passion, you mentioned," Des asked with a laugh. "Plenty of that, isn't there?"

Maggie's creamy skin grew pink for a second but she laughed back.

"Yes, plenty of that, and awfully well done."

"Let's all go and see some purple passion next week," said Nira.

But suddenly for some unknown reason she moved away from Des and her eyes clouded very slightly. It was that sudden flush on Maggie's charming face that had troubled her. Maggie was not really a shy person. Nira had always found her rather sophisticated and with plenty of that free-thinking impetuous American blood running through her veins. She was not one to *blush,* and Nira had also caught the sudden swift glance that had passed between her and Des.

Then Nira reproached herself.

Don't be a fool, Nira, it didn't mean a thing. You're slipping.

As if she didn't know that Des was a born flirt. He was candid enough to admit it. But he loved *her.*

She forgot all about that exchange of glances and thoroughly enjoyed the game. But she played badly and disgraced herself at the eighteenth hole. She had taken five to deal with the little ball. She and Des lost the game to the other two.

While they were having drinks in the bar before lunch, the Hallings walked in.

Boyce was a man of medium height, on the thin side, his light brown hair growing rapidly back from a high forehead. He was not good-looking but all the women thought he had handsome eyes—hazel-green, magnetic, arresting. His movements were quick and nervous. He had definite charm. Personally, Nira had never really cared for him although she had to admit now and again that he was attractive. He was amusing, too, and she liked a witty man, more especially if he wasn't coarse. He had a son, Simon, the same age as Nira's boy, and the whole family was musical. Boyce played a guitar and was in great demand at parties. But there was just something about him that made Nira feel that she

should be on her
"Those eyes of his
he looks at me."

To which Des ha
pancy, "Long live the

If she was ever cr
could so rarely make
when she showed a tend

Now Cricket rushed t
on her cheek. From this,
didn't really like being k
Cricket was always too lavi
less, this morning Nira adm . . . was
enchanting to look at in her . . . blue trouser-
suit. She used too much mak . . . p, but pretty she cer-
tainly was, and only two things in Nira's opinion spoiled
her. The too-full, petulant lips (that silvery glistening
lipstick intensified their sensuality), and her high, al-
most falsetto, voice. But definitely she did not look her
age, which was in the late twenties. They talked to-
gether, exchanged drinks and arranged to meet in the
dining-room for lunch.

Rob had seated himself in a basket chair, alone. He
was in what he called his looking-on mood. He didn't
particularly want to join in the banter and general chat-
ter. Through his tinted glasses, he watched when
Cricket seized hold of Nira and kissed her. He puckered
his lips, remembered what he had heard, and turning
from Cricket to Desmond Curtis, he *wondered*.

It might have been the kiss of Judas or it might just
all be malicious gossip that Rob had heard. Secretly, in
defence of his beloved Nira, he continued to wonder.

During lunch he found himself still watching those
two—Desmond and Cricket—but he gradually grew
ashamed of his suspicions and began to feel that any-
thing he had heard might be grossly exaggerated. Ger-
ald Robinson himself, possibly had a thing about
Cricket. So many men were amused and sexually ex-
cited by that wicked mixture of the adolescent and ex-
perienced female in Cricket. *Not me,* Rob thought
grimly, *I'd run miles from our semi-demi-local Lolita.*

lunch Rob saw that Des-
Cricket, quite careless of the
opposite and could hear and see it
put out a hand and caressed the
hair which Cricket had just had cut
to hang like a curtain over her eyes.

all for the new styles," he said. "Put you in a
ck and surplice today and you'd look like a choir-
y, dear."

Cricket giggled.

"Ah—men!" she intoned the words, and pressed
pointed finger-tips together in mock supplication.

"We might ask the Vicar if he'd like you to replace
one of his tribe at any time. What do you say, Boyce?"

Boyce cast an ironic glance at his wife and put his
tongue in his cheek.

"Great! And I daresay she'd get away with it."

Rob thought, *I don't think he cares a damn what his
wife does. And Desmond seems not to mind broadcast-
ing his feelings, so why do I worry? Only about Nira,
and perhaps none of it is important. They're all on the
surface this lot. I mustn't start growing really old.*

He made an excuse to leave the Club early.

His ears might have burned if he had heard the few
comments that were made after he left.

He returned home depressed—suddenly lonely.

The feeling of what's the good about anything, that
had lately been attacking him, returned. His own fault,
he thought moodily. What was the use of being in love
with another man's wife?

As his tall thin figure disappeared from the club
house, Nira looked at her husband and said, "Something's gnawing at our Rob. He seems very fed up—on
his birthday, too. Have you noticed it?"

"No," answered Des, and nudged Cricket's knee with
his very gently under the table. She had enchanting legs,
and he knew all about the dimples in her knees which
couldn't be seen at this moment, since she was wearing
slacks. He was rewarded by a gentle answering pressure
from her hand.

Boyce cut in, "I think Rob's beginning to show he's

pushing fifty. These chaps who spend their lives in darkest Africa and such places, are seldom fit when they retire, do you think?"

"Well, I'd scarcely call Nairobi darkest Africa," Nira protested.

Boyce shrugged and pierced a cigar which he had just bought from the bar. He was rather partial to cigars, and being slightly health-conscious, believed they were better for the lungs than cigarettes. He was not a pipe-smoker. He adored women and he didn't think they on the whole cared for pipes. He could remember his mother saying how she loved to see Dad smoking his, but that was a bit outdated.

Returning to the question of Rob, Boyce gave Nira what she called his lecherous look. It made her feel uncomfortable. When he flicked that critical, smouldering gaze up and down her body it was so *obvious*. He said, "Well, didn't Rob go in for all that wild animal stuff—safaris and so on? They must have been de-energising. Then he had that session in hospital and his eye-operation and a lot of fever, hadn't he?"

"He's a hell of a nice chap. I like Rob," said Desmond suddenly.

Nira threw him a grateful look. She was so fond of Rob herself. She believed that she and Des had established a good sound friendship with him. Nira sometimes made a point of going to see Aunt Ida. The dear old lady was an awful bore because she always told the same story two or three times. But she loved to see young people and Nira was one of her great favourites.

Now Nira looked at her watch and decided that it was time to go home. They must fetch Renira and Jonathan from Brighton. Gandy would have had enough of them by now, little doubt. Nira clapped Des on the shoulder.

"Home, James!"

Reluctantly he drew his knee away from Cricket, whispered, "See you, pet," and drew smartly to attention, saluting his wife. "At the ready, ma'am."

They went off arm in arm.

"Nice pair," said Boyce.

"Isn't Des *handsome*?" Cricket sighed blissfully.

"Isn't Mrs. Des *lovely*?" said Boyce, mimicking her, and drew on his cigar, his eyes half closed, "There's something about our Nira that gets me right in here—" he tapped his chest.

Cricket burst out laughing.

"You and your lovely Nira!"

"Well, there's one thing, you're not the jealous type, my love."

"No," she said, "and neither are *you,* my love!" She mocked his voice.

"We see eye to eye, which makes for a happy marriage." He gave her a sidelong smile, then returned to his thoughts about Nira. He added, "Ring up the Curtises and arrange a nice little dinner with those two for next weekend. I won't stint the cash. We'll have champagne and you can play some of those new records, and we'll roll the rugs back in the lounge and dance. Not too many lights on either."

Cricket laughed again.

"I really do dig you, Boyce, when you start making arrangements for a big seduction. But go easy with the spending, *and* the showing off. You used to have a success with Maggie, but you seem to have lost her now. She's after Des. I won't let her get him. *I* want him and he's after *me*!"

"Is he indeed!" said Boyce and yawned and stretched his legs out. "I'll have to be careful, won't I?"

"What for, may I ask, if you're rooting for my boyfriend's wife?"

Boyce grinned at the rows of bottles behind the bar and at the bored face of the barman. It must be grim to be bored. He never was. He enjoyed his job, and although he had to be careful, now, he intended to make money in the future. But certainly he spent more than he should. Women were his downfall—any girl he made love to seemed to enjoy it and asked for more. And he wanted more. Cricket was, so far, the ideal wife for him because she had very few morals and liked to fool around with other men. That suited *him*. He knew all about her little sessions with Des and why should he care? Cricket no longer attracted him except as a sort of sister, and on occasions she was an amusing little companion. But she was damned bad-tempered. Let those who found her so alluring find that out in time. Once again, why should he care? He wanted Nira. He wanted to break down that aloofness, that cool poise. To make her soft and pliant in his arms.

He found her tall graceful body and exquisite camellia skin so maddeningly attractive. All the more so because she had never once shown him the green light. It had been the red, right from the start, as though she didn't really like him.

His thoughts travelled further while Cricket combed back her blonde curls and tied a chiffon scarf over her head. Boyce paid the bar bill. As he waited for his chit he turned his thoughts to his ten-year-old son, Simon. Rather a pathetic little boy who unfortunately had his mother's fragile limbs and baby-face. He didn't like games, preferred animals, and was Mum's pet. Boyce and Cricket were always fighting about the way Simon should be treated.

Boyce had wanted a daughter, but after Simon's birth, Cricket had decided that she would never what she called 'go through it again'. Simon had improved since he went to his prep school as a day-boy and it was satisfying to Boyce to know that he had chummed up rather thickly with Jonathan. Jonathan was big and strong for his age and promised to be a first-class soccer-player. He was good for Simon and the friendship between the two boys brought the parents into frequent contact.

Boyce was altogether satisfied with the charmed circle in which he moved nowadays. The golfing crowd were a bit stuffy but there were the others, particularly the stockbrokers—Boyce called them *the king commuters*. Boyce cultivated them. But greater than all other desires was his longing for Nira. *I'll make her respond to me,* he thought, with a maddening vision of those strangely beautiful eyes with their long silky lashes. *I'll make her somewhere—somehow—and soon.*

Chapter 3.

ROB'S BIRTHDAY PARTY at the Richmond Hall Hotel was a success. The dinner was specially ordered and excellent, and he did not stint the champagne. He was by no means a heavy drinker but he allowed himself as much as he could stand that evening, and was touched by the warmth of the applause that followed his few words after the guests had called for a speech.

"Good old Rob!" Robinson called out, raising his glass. Rob acknowledged these few words from his *bête noire* with a more friendly smile than usual, but he wasn't really happy as the evening wore on.

He couldn't quite cure himself of his habit of sitting back and being the looker-on. He didn't dance. An old accident out in East Africa when he was much younger, had left him with slight trouble in one foot. He disliked dancing, anyhow. He sat back and watched his adored Nira on the floor with the other men. God, she looked gorgeous this evening, he thought. That model-girl figure was perfect in the dark violet silky dress, high Russian collar embroidered with tiny pearls, long chiffon sleeves. Her waist was firm and small for a woman who had had two children. She had beautiful arms, and moved gracefully. He always admired the elegance of her clothes. On most occasions she stood out among the others. Tonight she wore pearl earrings and a small but beautiful pearl and gold brooch pinned against one shoulder. Des had had it made for her, shaped like an open fan.

Rob followed the slim violet figure with his hungry gaze through the glasses that magnified her beauty. He felt he could never see enough of it. She was trying to

follow a new modern dance step with Boyce Halling.
The band was playing a new T. Rex theme. The rhythm
was stimulating. Cricket, glittering in a white and gold
evening suit, was dancing with Desmond. Her movements were wild and skittish and she giggled loudly.
Desmond seemed to be enjoying her antics and produced a few of his own.

Rob looked back at Nira and Boyce. The languorous
movements of Nira's body made the blood rush to his
head. He signalled the waiter and asked for more black
coffee. *I've drunk too much,* he thought sombrely.

Boyce suddenly caught his partner round the waist
and drew her nearer to him.

"What a pity we don't do this more often, Nira.
You're a great partner."

"You don't do so badly yourself," she said, in the
mood to be gay and totally unaware of Rob's unhappy
gaze following her round the floor.

For her it had been a very gay party so far. It was
rather fun behaving like a teenager—she, the mother of
a ten-year-old son and a five-year-old daughter. Rob
had done them well and this new band was good. Not
that she cared much for the place. It had been spoilt by
the new company that took it over last summer. This
dance-room, built on recently, was ugly and ultra-
modern—the lights too bright and the colour scheme
too psychedelic.

Des called it amusing—but he and Nira didn't always
share the same taste. He was, however, usually amena-
ble and let her choose the things she wanted. But she
had to admit there had been one ghastly moment when
he had brought her a table as a present which she had
disliked at sight. It wasn't even *nice* modern. It was
new—varnished—and an ugly shape. She had tried to
admire it and the words had stuck in her throat, then
for the first time he had taken offence and said, "We
never seem to agree on this sort of thing. I know you
say your old home was marvellous, and I suppose your
father was a collector and knew about antiques and
all that, but I don't see anything wrong with my table
or my taste."

She had tried to put things right by telling him that she loved him so she would love the table, but he had sulked. The table was still there in her room because she didn't want to offend him by not using it, but now and again she did feel that it spoiled her décor. She realised, of course, that it was not important. Just one of those small disputes that can arise between husband and wife and make them both suddenly conscious of certain discrepancies in taste. Anyhow, that had been years ago, before Jonathan was born, and forgiven—if not forgotten.

"Look at my wife and your husband. They're gyrating like tops," Boyce said suddenly, his lips rather close to her ear. She could feel his hot, wine-laden breath, and drew away. She glanced towards Des and Cricket.

"They're thoroughly enjoying themselves."

"Are you?"

"Of course."

"We make a good foursome, don't you think?" murmured Boyce. "You and Des and Cricket and me."

She hesitated. She didn't particularly admire Boyce. He wasn't her type but she was feminine enough to respond now and again to his flattery. He was never slow to show that he admired her. Des, in fact, had said the other night that old Boyce had a thing about her.

These *things*! she had thought at the time. She had never come across such a place as The Heath. Someone was always having *a thing* about someone else. Amusing, but she remained content with her own husband.

"Don't you agree—we make a good foursome?" repeated Boyce, and curved his fingers more tightly about her long slim hand.

"I'm sure we do," she said lightly. "Our golf, our bridge, our children."

"My trouble is that I never see you alone."

"You might get bored with me if you did. I'm not nearly as amusing as your wife."

Boyce looked slantway through the crowd at his wife's petite sparkling figure. He could hear her high-pitched laughter above the beat of the music and shuffle of feet.

"Cricket's a lot of fun—when she isn't nagging."

"All wives nag their husbands at times."

"I've never seen you out of tune with Des. He's a lucky guy."

"I'm lucky, too."

"You wouldn't mind if he was attracted by another girl?"

Now Nira opened her grey-blue eyes very widely, and flicked the long lashes that were darkened with mascara.

"If you mean do I mind his cavorting around with other girls—women—whatever they are—of course not! I'm not jealous and I don't think wives ought ever to chain their husbands. It's asking for trouble."

"Very wise. One of the things I admire about you, Nira, is your wisdom. I adore my wife but she's incredibly silly at times, and please don't think me disloyal for saying so."

Now a sudden impish wish to lash out at Boyce made her say, "I'm sure you *are* disloyal, Boyce dear, and discontented—a restless sort of man. I always feel that. You never sit still, and I've heard Cricket say you're always searching for fresh excitement."

"*She* can talk!" he protested.

"Well—do you look on yourself as a good loyal type of man?"

"Oh, I say!" Boyce protested again, laughing. "You're not being very complimentary. Anyhow, what about your own husband—I should have thought he was as restless as I am."

"Perhaps, but I know and understand him. I don't really know you, Boyce."

"That's because we're never alone and have never really communicated. I'd like us to get to know each other better. I won't deny that I find you very *very* attractive."

The red blood showed suddenly under the creamy skin of Nira's face.

"Boyce dear, *really*!"

He tightened his hold of her.

"I mean it. I know you're devoted to Des and I'm

sure he is to you, but there are moments when I think he'd get on very well for an hour or two with Cricket. And wouldn't you—get on with me? Couldn't I meet you somewhere, sometime and take you out—or take you in," he added jokingly, and his eyes suddenly seemed to her to be more desirous than usual.

"Boyce, you're being an idiot. Let's stop dancing and have a drink."

Her voice was no longer friendly. He was astute enough to realise that he must be careful with Nira or he would get into her bad books and *that* he didn't want. But the blood was racing through his veins and he had to use all his control not to lean forward and kiss that wide sweet mouth of hers. He managed to release her—and to laugh.

"It's the champagne, dear, sorry."

"We've all had our quota," she said, relieved. "Let's join Rob. He's all alone."

"I'm not at all sure poor old Rob isn't your type really. He's always on his good behaviour."

"Well, not many people are, and it's rather nice for a change," said Nira a trifle coldly. "But I assure you, *Des* is my type."

Damn, Boyce thought, as he followed her off the dance floor, *I've boobed! I'll have to be much more subtle if I'm to get anywhere with her.*

He could see that the best thing he could do was to make it easier in future for Cricket to see more of Des. It might in time upset Nira. Then perhaps she'd turn to *him.*

Before they reached their table, he spoke lightly.

"Don't be cross with me. It's not my fault you're so attractive."

She melted and gave him one of her warm smiles.

"Okay. I'm not cross. Thanks for the dance. It was super."

But her thoughts ran in a different vein. *He's too blatantly sexy—the sort of man who thinks he can get any girl he wants. I don't really like him.*

He had nevertheless had one moment of truth— unconsciously—when he had said that Rob was her type. In his way, Rob was just that. But when she looked at Des who had just finished dancing with Cricket and sat down again, she caught his significant smile and the familiar droop of the eyelids—a habit of his when they exchanged glances—intimating that he was all hers and that he adored her. He said so—often. He was definitely attractive compared to the other men—her darling Des!

She reached his side and laid a hand on his shoulder.

"Hello, there!"

"Hello, there, honey—"

They mimicked American voices—another of their habits when the mood was festive and spirits high. It was fun being married to Des. Nira glowed.

Rob looked toward that glowing loveliness and was sad. He had never before known such acute loneliness as on this, his birthday. *Fifty next year,* he thought, *I'm middle-aged with a vengeance. I never imagined it would matter.*

Why did it? Just because Nira was so much younger—or because he was the old man of the party?

Boyce, who had moments of being generous-hearted, had asked Joyce Moffatt to dance. He had an eye on Maggie but she was already on the floor with the Colonel.

Nira took the chair beside Rob.

He had half risen as she approached, then signalled to a waiter.

"You'll want a drink."

"Yes, thanks, it is rather hot in here and I've been much too energetic," she laughed and fanned her flushed cheeks.

"I saw you and Halling doing fantastic steps. I rather envy you all. I wish I could dance."

"I wish you could," she said with that sweet sudden smile which narrowed her eyes and brought little creases around them.

"Don't sit here if you'd rather go on dancing, my dear. Where's your husband?"

"In the bar with Cricket. I must tell him to ask poor

Joyce to dance. Boyce is the only one so far—except the Colonel—to ask her."

"I was talking to her just now," said Rob, "and she's really quite interesting. Everyone finds her unattractive just because she's a bit angular and dried-up, but she's spent a lot of time in the Far East when she was following the flag, and Army wives out there get like that."

"You're always kind to everyone," said Nira, and lifted the champagne which had just been poured out, towards him. "Cheers, Rob, and Happy Birthday again."

She isn't a bit jealous, he thought. *Doesn't seem to mind that that husband of hers has spent most of his time with Cricket this evening. Perhaps she feels invulnerable and safe, as well she might! He'd be crazy if he went after any other woman in the world.*

Aloud Rob said, "It's strange that we none of us really know much about the other people. How they live—what they are like in their private lives. You've got to get right under the skin in order to understand them."

"You're the sort of person people want to talk to," she said, and looked affectionately at the thin tanned face with its crown of thick silver hair. She understood exactly what little Renira had said to her the other day, "Uncle Rob's a *cosy* man, isn't he, Mummy? You sort of feel that when he talks to you."

Renira was perceptive. It was exactly what one did feel with Rob Bessiford—warm and secure. He was 'a cosy man'.

"Has poor old Joyce been confiding in you?"

"No special confidence, nothing one couldn't repeat, but did you know that the Moffatts once had two children—twin girls? They died in an accident when they were stationed in Singapore—awful tragedy."

"Oh, how grim! No, I didn't know. I *am* sorry. She's never spoken about it to me. She's obviously the kind that doesn't talk a lot about herself."

"But I can see that it has affected her whole life. They're pretty lonely, that pair. Old Moffatt gasses a lot, and does the hearty Colonel stuff, but Joyce was telling me he's never been the same man since the accident. Now he smokes and drinks too much; she admits it."

"I must ask her round. I've never thought about it before."

He eyed Nira, his eyes tender behind the tinted glasses. "Typical of you to suggest it. I'm sure she'd be most appreciative. She was saying how much she admired you."

But he didn't add that Joyce had also said that she didn't trust Desmond Curtis one inch. He was much too good-looking and slick for her. She liked the more serious-minded and honest-to-God type. *And* she didn't think Des good enough for Nira.

Now Des came out of the bar, walked to Nira's chair, and laid a familiar hand against the back of her long slender neck.

"Nirry, would you mind if I leave you for ten minutes or quarter of an hour. Cricket's developed one of her migraines. I said I'd run her home. Boyce seems occupied with the Colonel's lady, and I wouldn't mind a spot of fresh air."

"But, of course, darling," said Nira happily. "How nice of you. Poor Cricket—she gets these migraine attacks quite often."

"Nasty things," put in Rob. "The medical profession doesn't seem to have got to the root of them."

Cricket appeared, looking in Rob's estimation, not at all ill, but she had put on her white fur jacket and was cuddling herself in it, pouting her full pink lips. She said to Nira, "Isn't it *sweet* of your Des, he's offered to take me home. I promise not to keep him."

"If you mean that, I won't take you home. I like to be kept," said Des with his usual sparkle.

Nira shook her head at her husband.

"The things you say!"

They moved away. Boyce, engrossed in trying to teach Joyce Moffatt to dance in modern style, did not even see his wife go.

Rob lit another cigar and looked at the ash speculatively. *I reckon she'll keep him longer than ten minutes,* he thought. *I wonder if she's got migraine at all. I wonder what Desmond is really up to.*

But if Nira didn't mind—why should anybody else?

He decided in any case to distract Nira's mind from her husband. He began to talk to her about the children, and the summer holidays.

"Are you going down to Cornwall, like you did last year, plus mama-in-law?"

"Not with Mrs. Curtis," Nira grimaced, and leaned forward to light her cigarette from the match Rob struck for her. "The weather was super and Cornwall gorgeous, but we had to mind our p's and q's because of Gandy who, poor soul, means so well. The children adore it. The sands and rocks are terrific and I love Mawgan Porth, but Gandy is not the best companion to have on a holiday. She loves the children but she narks at them if they do anything she doesn't think right. *Don't sit on the wet sand or you'll get cold, Renira. Jon, keep your hat on. The sun's so hot today.* And so on. She didn't like my bikini much. She likes to think she's modern but she's still shaken by the unclad bodies she sees around the beaches today."

Rob smiled.

"Some don't bear criticism, but I rather agree with your mother-in-law there's far too much nudity. A few more veils as there were in the old days, add to a girl's attraction, don't you think?"

Nira nodded. "Yes, but I do rather like my bikini when there's any sun."

Rob found himself picturing Nira in her bikini and was more than a little disturbed by his reaction to the thought. What the hell was he doing, letting this sort of note creep into their relationship which was a good and friendly one. He must never spoil things. He would be the loser.

"What are you going to do this year, then?" he asked her.

"Oh, we've made all sorts of plans. Des doesn't want to be away from the office too long so I am going to take the children down to Mawgan Porth again. We know it and they love the place and the surf-bathing

and so on. That will be in July or August. Then we've
got plans to take a proper holiday with the Hallings later in Majorca. They went last year to the Formentor
Hotel and said it was super. It's expensive, but we all
thought we'd be extravagant. So we've booked for the
last week of August and the first week in September. I
know everyone says it will be hot then and crowded, but
we all like the heat and we'll have to put up with the
crowds. The Formentor has its own little private beach,
anyhow."

Rob smiled at her with the tenderness he found it
hard to conceal. She really was such a darling. He
wouldn't have minded a crowded beach and certainly
not the heat; in fact he would give anything to go on
that holiday with her. But why the Hallings? Cricket
was pretty and engaging, but such a little *poseuse,* and
Boyce irritated him. What did Nira see in them? Or was
it Des who had arranged it?

Nira enlarged on her plans. She, herself, admitted
that it wasn't the foursome she was really after. She
would rather have gone away alone with Des, but he
was so sociable and loved a party and got on well with
Boyce *and* Cricket, she added laughing, they'd never
been away in a foursome before and thought it would
be nice to have someone they knew and could play
bridge with if it rained.

Rob sighed quietly. God, he thought, he couldn't understand a fellow like Desmond Curtis wanting someone
else on his holiday as well as this wonderful girl. But
not for the first time he began to wonder if he was idiotic to think along these lines and not realise that the
world was changing. Thousands of couples today liked
crowds and fun and 'beating it up' and that sort of
thing, whatever their walk of life. He, Rob, should have
been born a hundred years ago. He was at heart a Victorian. Suddenly to his immense delight, Nira gave him
a warm friendly look from her lovely eyes and asked
him if he would like to join them on their holiday in
Majorca.

"I don't know whether you know it, but the Hallings
say Majorca offers such a lot and for so much less than

you have to pay in the South of France. Do come with us, Rob. I'm sure the others would like you to. I know Des would."

"It's sweet of you both," Rob said, his cheeks colouring, "absolutely sweet. But I'd vaguely wondered if I could go up to Scotland for some fishing in June—"

"Well, do that," she broke in, "then join us later on for the Majorcan holiday. I'm sure it wouldn't be too late to get you a booking."

"I think it might be tricky. I've never been to Majorca but I hear it's absolutely top favourite, and some chap I met thought the Formentor pretty good."

"We could try for a room for you. Shall I phone our travel agent? Des goes to one in Town. He's on the ball."

She spoke quite eagerly.

Rob turned away from that beautiful face. He wanted to fall in with her suggestion and yet—he wondered if he could take the Hallings for a whole fortnight. Suddenly he spoke with frankness.

"Cricket and Boyce are all right, of course, but I'm not sure I want to spend a whole holiday with them. With you and Des—yes, indeed."

"You wouldn't have to be with the Hallings all that much. We shall all go our own ways, and I'm sure we'd find you a gorgeous girl," said Nira gaily.

"I don't want any gorgeous girls," Rob said shortly.

"Well, think it over, Rob."

"Thank you," he said, and now behind the tinted glasses his eyes were warm and grateful, "I'm very touched. I will indeed think it over. You must make sure first that the Hallings and your husband won't object. I'd be spoiling the foursome."

"You wouldn't!" she protested.

But they dropped the subject for the moment. Nira half forgot that she'd made the invitation. But Rob remembered it and was tempted.

Chapter 4

"OH, GOD, THE kids are awake!" said Des.

He had just let Nira into the house. The light had been left on over the porch and there was one on in the hall. Nira slipped off her short fur jacket. Soft, brown, silky and rather like mink—but not mink, which was something that Des had promised but never been able to afford to buy her.

Now she saw what he saw—two small figures in dressing-gowns, sitting at the top of the staircase. Renira holding her best doll. Jonathan clutching a model aeroplane which he had just made and from which he refused to be parted.

Nira went to the foot of the stairs and called up rather crossly, "What *are* you two doing out of bed?"

They ran down the stairs. For all her crossness she opened her arms and gathered them to her. But she spoke severely.

"Go on—tell me why you aren't both fast asleep tucked up in your beds?"

Renira giggled. She had a slight lisp.

"My dollie couldn't thleep, either."

Jonathan, the beloved son who was the apple of Nira's eye, tall, rather grave-faced, with his father's chestnut, springing hair, and her soft grey-blue eyes, said, "I did go to sleep, Mummy, but I woke up, and Rennie came into my bed because she'd had a nightmare and she was crying."

Desmond, not waiting to listen to this, had walked into the dining-room and was pouring himself out a whisky and soda, which Nira noticed with disapproval. He had had quite enough champagne at the party—

more than enough, and she wasn't at all sure she was feeling friendly towards him. She addressed her children, "Nightmare or no nightmare, do you realise that it's half-past two in the morning?"

"I know it's half-patht two," said Renira, "because I heard the grandfather clock and Jonnie told me what it said."

"Why didn't you call Susan? She's sleeping here tonight, you know it."

The children looked at each other. The mother, her thoughts wandering away from them because she was still looking through the open door at Des, drinking that whisky, tried to concentrate on the children again. Renira's blue woolly dressing-gown, with the white appliquéd rabbit on each pocket, was getting far too small. The child was growing fast—would be leggy and tall like her brother. All Des's family were tall. Renira wasn't as angelic as Jonathan, but very attractive with her *retroussé* nose, her enormous dark eyes, like Des's, and straight fair hair which in the daytime was tied back in a pony tail but at this time of night fell charmingly across her face.

Jonathan began to explain that they hadn't called Susan because they heard her snoring and decided not to wake her up. They then both giggled about the snoring, and suddenly Nira felt she couldn't cope with all this fun at such an hour. She felt cold and tired. She clapped her hands and ordered the children off to bed.

"This minute, the pair of you, up you go and not another word, or I'll tell Daddy no pocket money tomorrow."

"Oh, Mum!" Jonathan began to protest loudly. "He owes it to me. You told me you've always got to pay people what you owe them. Besides, Simon says we ought to have a union and strike if we don't get what we want."

"Yes, we'll stwike," said Renira, after which she became convulsed with laughter. But Nira felt that she had no sense of humour just for the moment. Unrelenting, she lectured and threatened, and finally the children went up to bed, grumbling. There was silence. Nira joined Des in the dining-room.

"Aren't *you* coming up?"

"Have a drink—" he began affably, and she thought he tottered very slightly and this so aggravated her that she spoke with more irritation than she had ever shown him before.

"I don't want a drink and you're not going to have another one either. You've had quite enough." She marched up to him, took away the whisky bottle and banged it down on the sideboard.

He laughed and rather thickly began to protest. "Steady on, ducky, it's two pound-something a bottle these days. Don't break it."

Nira stood glaring at him quite aware of the fact that he was taking not the slightest notice either of her attitude or tone of her voice. He even made an attempt to kiss her. Then she lost her temper, which was very rare because as a rule he could do no wrong, and it took a lot to upset her. She pushed him away.

"I've just had about enough of you for one night, Des. If you don't sober up and come to bed I'll—I'll—" she broke off, her face flushed, her eyes bright with angry tears.

"But darling, I'm not drunk. What's got into you?"

"Well, if you're not drunk, you're certainly not sober. You've been swilling champagne the whole evening, and—"

"Oh, rubbish," he broke in rather rudely, and his affability vanished. If she could glare at him, he could glare, too, and he did.

Her heart sank low. She could never remember them looking at each other like this before. In the past, the nearest they had ever come to a real row was when he had been particularly hard on Jonathan for not liking games and she had been up in arms on the side of her sweet, sensitive little son. Yes, they had been angry with each other that day but not quite like this, and she had soon melted and they had been reconciled. But this was different and Nira, who did not like to keep anything locked away, and wanted to stay close to her husband, let loose the anger that had been consuming her since they left the party. She had taken great pains not to show it while they were still Rob's guests.

"And how much champagne did your friend Rob order anyhow?" Des spoke again, "I don't think any of us had more than we could take. It wasn't all that much of a party."

"How *could* you? It was a super party and he must have spent a fortune on the drinks. He's the last man on earth you'd call mean and he isn't all that rich."

Des shrugged. He kept a longing eye on the whisky bottle.

"Oh, I know he's your pet."

"You're being ridiculous! He's nobody's pet. He's not that sort of man. But what I'd like to know is how much Cricket gave *you* to drink once you got her home."

"I didn't go into the house."

Suddenly Nira felt frozen. It was as though a cold hand had been laid on her heart. *She didn't believe him.* Some strong intuition told her that he was not telling the truth.

"Des," she said, "whatever happens, don't let's start telling each other lies, *please*. I just couldn't bear it. I don't mind what you do but you *mustn't* lie to me. I didn't mind you taking Cricket home. You know I didn't. I've never been jealous, now have I?"

His eyes, not focusing very well, swivelled away from her. He gave a stupid laugh.

"No need to be, honey. You're my wife and—" he cast a glance upwards and added dramatically, "the mother of my children."

She could see that he was trying to be funny, and take the edge off their argument, but something drove her to continue it.

"Des—will you please sober up and tell me the truth. Did you or didn't you stay with Cricket and have drinks in her house? When you came back you were flushed and talking very loudly and *quite* unlike yourself."

Now he scowled.

"For God's sake don't start nagging me in the early hours of the morning. I couldn't take it."

"But you're going to tell me the truth," she persisted.

He put his hands in his coat pockets and swayed a very little from heel to toe.

"And what if I did spend a few minutes with Cricket? Is it a crime?"

Nira drew a breath. All her colour had gone. She looked suddenly very pale. The cold feeling of fear seemed to be clutching her heart a little more tightly.

"Des, I fully realise that you took her home because you wanted to be alone with her and not because she had a migraine or any such nonsense. Why don't you own up to it? You've got a thing about Cricket, haven't you? I've never taken it very seriously until tonight, but—"

"Well, if you take my advice you won't take it seriously now," he broke in and patted his lips to stifle a yawn. "Honestly, sweetie, I'm getting a bit bored with this. Let's go upstairs."

She said, "I thought it was very odd you offering to take her back like that—because she had a perfectly good husband of her own to look after her."

Des laughed.

"He'd had a ball all evening and was doing the good-boy act with Joyce Moffatt when Cricket folded. I wouldn't have disturbed him for worlds."

"That's nonsense."

"Anyhow, what are you so steamed up about? You were pretty engrossed with old Rob."

"I did not go home to Rob's house and have a drinking session alone with him," said Nira coldly.

"I wouldn't have bawled you out if you had."

She stared at him open-mouthed.

"Then *you* aren't at all jealous? You wouldn't mind what I did with other men?"

"Oh, really, Nira, you're being very dramatic. Why this attitude? Why the inquisition? You've always said you had no use for possessive wives."

"I've never been possessive, but there are limits."

He gave that stupid laugh again. Suddenly she found

him singularly unattractive. She never remembered him being in this state before. What was happening to Des? Frantically she wondered where all the warmth and understanding that had existed between them had gone. What *had* happened tonight to make her feel so suspicious, so alarmed? Her eyes suddenly filled with tears which spilled over and rolled down her cheeks.

"I don't like possessive wives and I never wanted to be one, but I do think you've got to be able to trust your husband," she said.

"So you don't trust me."

"I always have done."

"But not tonight."

Now the colour rose in her cheeks and she turned away and brushed the tears from her lashes.

"I didn't exactly say that. It's just that—oh, I don't know, forget it!" she added with sudden violence. "I'm being tired and silly. I am sure you did nothing more than crack a bottle of champagne with dear little Cricket."

Des turned from the alluring sight of the whisky. He was sobering up fast and he didn't like to see Nira's face stained with tears. It was such an unusual sight. Besides which, he had a very definite conscience. He knew perfectly well that it hadn't been just a question of 'cracking a bottle'. Cricket had been a little devil, and not for the first time if it came to that. There had been other occasions. She had a way with her; that flute-like voice and those big eyes; and the innocent nymphet-side she used as a cover-up for the sensual little cat she really was. Hell to it, a man was only flesh and blood, and he certainly was no saint. When she had turned her back to him and said archly, "Unzip me, darling—I'm going to bed as soon as you've gone," he had responded with alacrity—and didn't go. He found her an exciting change—with her petite curves and petal-soft rosy skin and dimples—a complete contrast to Nira's tall slenderness, her narrow hips and fine long legs.

Cricket played the little girl very prettily, and made him feel fine and strong. He was grateful too because she showed such blatant pleasure in him and kept saying, "You're *terrific*, Des—why can't we have fun like this more often?"

When he had asked her with some curiosity whether she had any qualms about being unfaithful to Boyce, she had laughed and said gaily why have a conscience when she knew Boyce was unfaithful to her. Then she had suggested that Des must find life a bit dreary at times because darling Nira was inclined to be serious and possessive—yes, she had used that word—and it had annoyed Des. He had told Cricket that he didn't want to discuss Nira, but it had all ended with more champagne and more passionate kisses and then he had left her and gone back to the hotel to rejoin Rob's party. He had been a bit sloshed by then and knew it. In his overheated imagination he looked back and thought it had all been a lot of fun with Cricket and could go on being so if he could get away with it. Cricket had quite convinced him that Boyce wouldn't mind and from what he had seen of old Boyce's behaviour, Des thought it true. But what about Nira? She was not the promiscuous type. He could hardly count on her to turn a blind eye to his conduct *if* she found out. It wasn't as though she fooled around with other men as Cricket or Maggie did or any of that lot. In one way it pleased him. He was proud of Nira. She had a damned fine character. But it would have been a bit more fun, perhaps, if she'd wanted fun and games now and then with, say, Boyce or even old Rob Bessiford. Of course Rob was a bit of a dry stick—she surely wouldn't fall for him, even for an hour or two. But she seemed to like him a lot. It could happen . . . here Des's thoughts broke off. All this was very much in his mind and he hadn't the least wish to crack up his marriage, or start anything awkward with his wife. They'd always been very pleased with each other. Why ask for trouble now? He loved her and his kids and his home. It was just, he told himself, that he hadn't got it in him to be as perfect as Nira might wish.

He was sufficiently sober now to review the whole evening's entertainment with more caution, and with a

revival of the old tenderness for Nira. He walked up to
her and pulled her into his arms.

"Hey! What's this all about, honey?" he asked, and
put out a finger and touched the tear that was just rolling down her cheek. Then he kissed her like a lover.
"This is ridiculous," he whispered. "I love you. Don't
for God's sake jump to wrong conclusions just because I
took Cricket home. I've never seen you so upset. You
must be round the bend to be jealous of *her,* darling.
Pull yourself together."

Nira responded quickly and with her whole heart.
She relaxed in his arms and buried her face against his
shoulder, hugging him tightly.

"Oh, I do love you, Des. I couldn't share you with
anybody."

"Who's asked you to?" He laughed easily and
brushed aside the memory of the exciting way Cricket
had of driving a fellow crazy. He was content to hold
Nira's cool loveliness and caress her, but without the
same sort of passion. With one hand he stroked the bent
dark head and kept telling her how much he loved her
and that she wasn't to be so suspicious. Finally she
apologised for her outburst and they went up the staircase with their arms around each other. Once in bed
they almost at once fell into the sleep of sheer exhaustion.

In the morning neither of them made allusion to the
Cricket incident. Des felt off-colour—Nira took him
Alka-Seltzer, then left him to sleep it off and relieved
Susan of the children. It was her Sunday off.

Nira couldn't quite forget last night, but she felt sure
in the cold light of day that there was no need for her to
have been so upset.

The sun was shining, Des suggested that if it stayed
fine he'd drive them to Chanctonbury Ring. They'd
climb up to the top of the Downs to see the beautiful
Hammer Ponds. Then he'd give them lunch at Storring-
ton.

All seemed right with Nira's world. Jonathan and Renira were in high spirits and had only one quarrel and
that was about who should sit beside Daddy. Nira al-

ways let one of them do this while she sat at the back with the other child.

It appeared to be Renira's turn, which brought protests from Jonathan who was sure it was his. It ended as usual with Nira having to threaten to cancel the whole party unless they stopped quarrelling.

Nira knew she ought to be in great spirits and yet for some reason, which she had no intention of analysing, that cosy happy secure little world in which she had lived with Des and the children so long did not seem *quite* the same as it had done yesterday. A discordant note had crept into the song they usually sang together. The rhythm was spoilt. Des had denied that there was any cause for her jealousy and she had accepted his word. But she couldn't quite recapture the old sensation of complete trust. She even began to wonder if she was being silly and old-fashioned even to expect complete fidelity these days.

Bit by bit her fears settled down. By the time Des appeared and went out to the garage to fetch the car, she was happy again but one thing became apparent. She could not like Cricket any more. She might trust Des but she did not trust Cricket. They were all supposed to be going away together this summer. That seemed a pity now. She didn't want that foursome. Particularly as she was beginning to dislike Boyce. She wished she could work her way out of that little circle, and go away with Des alone.

Then she remembered that she had suggested that Rob might join them. He hadn't seemed averse to the idea even though he had been afraid that he would make an unwanted fifth.

All the same, before that Sunday ended Nira had silently made up her mind to broach the Rob idea to Des, and if he didn't mind, she'd urge Rob to join them. She believed he'd enjoy it—lonely and bored as he was. And to her, somehow, he stood for safety (why she really didn't know) but she would like to have him along with them this summer. Perhaps his mere presence would put a brake on the flirtatious, and irrepressible Cricket—and, still more so, damp down Boyce!

On the bright warm April day the family enjoyed Chanctonbury Ring. It was windy, but sunny on the high Downs which gave them such a remarkable view of the Sussex Weald.

The children had fun. Des who had started out by complaining of a headache, felt better as the day wore on and was only short-tempered when the lunch turned out to be a failure. The food was half-cold and not as good as usual, and the service was poor. By the time they got home Jonathan and Renira, who had rushed madly over the Downs, were over-tired. Jonathan teased his little sister and made her cry. Des snapped and reduced his son to tears. In the end Nira was glad to get the children off to bed, then settle down to a quiet hour watching television with her husband.

Des went to sleep in the middle of the Sunday night play which rather annoyed Nira as she was enjoying it and liked to have someone to be observant and critical with her. She stared at Des who was slumped back in his chair and thought suddenly that he looked much older. The heavy drinking of last night seemed to have hit him harder than usual. Inevitably her thoughts returned to Cricket and the champagne Des had surely shared with her in her house.

Nira tried to concentrate on the television again, but once Des stirred and yawned and exhibited some signs of life, she brought up the subject of the forthcoming holiday in Majorca.

She drew a tapestried stool close to his chair and sat there smoking a cigarette. She was not a dedicated smoker but liked one after her meals, and one last thing at night. Turning her head, she looked at Des with the warm smile that narrowed her eyes, and which most people found so delightful.

"Des—I want to talk to you about Majorca."

He ran his fingers through his hair, gave her a sleepy smile, and looked down at the hand she had laid on his knee. It was rather long, fine-boned and slightly tanned. He had always admired her beautiful nails. She was careful of them and wore rubber gloves when she washed up. Tonight they were especially attractive because she had had a manicure for the party. They were varnished a deep rose. He patted the lovely hand and tried not to yawn. He was still feeling the worse for last night.

"What about it?"

"If we could get a room for Rob, would you object to him coming along with us?"

Now Des felt more wide awake. He sat up and reached for a cigarette. She lit it for him. His immediate reaction to her suggestion was to reject it.

"What on earth do we want him for? There are the four of us—the Hallings and us—why a fifth?"

"Darling, we can still play our bridge or cut in if Rob wants to play, and quite frankly we're not going to the Formentor to play cards. We only said it would be useful to have a bridge-four in case it was bad weather, but everyone says it should be gorgeous in Majorca in early September."

He frowned slightly. "Why ask old Rob? He doesn't sort of fit in, does he?"

"Oh, I don't see why not. Everybody likes him. Even Cricket said the other day that he was very good-looking really, and had a lot of charm in his quiet funny way."

"Darling, we don't really need quiet charm, do we? I mean, it will spoil the foursome," Des grumbled again.

Suddenly Nira drew her hand away from his knee. She found that she wanted in a stubborn way to defeat Des on this issue.

"I think it would be a great kindness to Rob. He was the first to say that surely he wouldn't be wanted, but I don't agree. He's always so amiable. Everybody likes him. The kids adore him, and he *is* a bachelor."

"So you've often said. I like old Rob too—but I don't see why we should suddenly include him in our foursome. Besides, we mightn't even be able to get a room for him."

"Okay—if we don't, he can't come."

She was smiling at him again, but it struck him suddenly that Nira really *wanted* Rob on this holiday. He ruffled her hair and laughed—his humour restored.

"Sweetie—is this just because you're sorry for the lone bachelor, or because you've suddenly got a bit sentimental about him and want him to cherish yourself?"

"Don't be silly. I don't want to cherish any man but you."

"You're a darling," said Des, but he said it rather mechanically, and was finding it difficult to control that desire to yawn. He didn't really mind if Rob did join them in Majorca. It just seemed an odd idea. But he knew his wife. She was always particularly nice to lame dogs, and Rob in his opinion was one. To his mind the friendship between his wife and Rob was just that.

"What would the Hallings say?" he asked.

"I don't think they can say anything. It's really our party. We asked them to join us and *I* booked the rooms."

"Have you any particular reason for altering the plans, honey? Of course I'm only teasing you about old Rob. I expect you find him a bore really."

She didn't and was honest enough to say so, but now that innate honesty led her to add something that she had been wanting to say for a long time.

"If you want to know, Des darling, I just can't take Boyce the whole time. I mean, quite frankly, *you* enjoy Cricket's company; most men do, and she's attractive and amusing, but Boyce—well—I don't know what it is about him but there's something which rather shakes me at times."

"Has he tried anything on with you?"

"Not definitely, but when he dances with me he gets as close as he can and he flatters me all the time and—oh, I don't know, he just makes me feel that he's wanting to sort of get-together with me, and I just don't want it."

Des got up, moved away from her, walked to the mantelpiece and looked at his reflection in the gilt-framed antique mirror. He scowled, put out his tongue, didn't like what he saw, and put it back. He was slightly worried by what Nira had just told him. He knew Boyce was a bit of a bastard, but he had half hoped that Nira liked him sufficiently to enjoy being paired off with him on this holiday. It would have left him, Des, more time and freedom for pretty Cricket. He ought to be ashamed of himself for having such ideas and he adored Nira, but dammit, a man did sometimes need the stimulus of a new face, a fresh passion, after eleven years of marriage.

He liked to believe he'd been a devoted husband because his wife was ignorant of his lapses from fidelity. Then Cricket fell for him. He found her irresistible—she roused all that was most sensual in him. He knew that he would get tired of her as he had done of other promiscuous love affairs. He would have been alarmed at the mere idea of Nira finding out, and wanting to leave him, or any such thing. Nothing was further from his mind. He just wanted to eat his cake and have it. He knew a lot of other men who managed to do that. He wasn't the only one. But he did think it a pity, perhaps, that Nira was quite so single-minded about him, and so disinclined to enter into any kind of flirtation with any other man, no matter how light or meaningless it would be. He wouldn't of course, want her to be actually unfaithful to him, but it was a pity she was quite so reserved. It would just have fitted in with his schemes a bit more, for instance, if she had found Boyce attractive. He had been mistaken in imagining that was so. She had made it quite obvious tonight that Boyce annoyed and even alarmed her.

"You do understand what I have been telling you, don't you darling?" Nira asked him.

"Of course, of course. Why not cancel the whole holiday if Boyce upsets you? I don't want you upset."

"I don't want to cancel Majorca, darling. That's absurd. Don't let's exaggerate the situation. It's just that I know you could have a lot of fun with Cricket, but I don't want to have fun with Boyce."

"Of course not," said Des with a heartiness he was far from feeling. "And you needn't think I'm out to spend all my time with Cricket, either."

Now Nira blew a ring of smoke into the air and gave him an impish look.

"No, dear, I'm sure you're not!" Her friendly laughter redeemed the sarcasm but it was not lost on him, and he began to feel that he would have to be more careful. He remembered the little devil Cricket had told him last night that she was going to make him take her to some lonely uninhabited beach, right away from the others, *and* she had enlarged on what could happen on the lovely lonely beach!

"Darling," Nira's voice interrupted his thoughts. "Let's forget about Rob. We'll stick to our old plan and I'm not all that averse to Boyce so long as he's sensible, otherwise I wouldn't have agreed to it in the first place. We've always got on well together—all four of us. I even find Cricket fun when she doesn't drink too much or be so coquettish. Our kids like each other—I don't know what Jonathan would do without Simon. They're going to have a big get-together while the parents are away. We mustn't cause ill-feeling. It would be wrong. Besides, it's all arranged. Don't let's give it another thought."

But this was where Des changed his mind. Why not let old Rob be included in the party? At least he knew that Nira was fond of him. He'd distract her attention a bit from Cricket, perhaps. As for Boyce, there were sure to be one or two unattached dolly-birds in a big hotel like The Formentor, and once he found Nira engrossed with Rob, Boyce would soon seek an alternative.

"I think I was wrong about old Rob," Des said briskly. "By all means let's include him in the party. Ring up the agents in the morning and see if you can get him a room."

Nira was pleased though anxious not to get her own way at the cost of annoying her husband. But when he made it clear that he really didn't object and even agreed that it might be doing a great kindness to Rob, Nira stopped talking. It was all fixed.

Once in bed, Des, who was nothing if not greedy, decided that he had better pull himself together and stop thinking about Cricket. He made love to his wife with a sudden hot flash of passion that took her breath away, and left her completely satisfied.

All was well again between them. She told herself that nothing was of real importance except the fact that they loved each other. They always would.

Des accepted his wife's total surrender and response—without conscience. After all, he decided yet again that the average man needed not one woman in his life, but two. That being so, he excused his attitude of mind and was as pleased with Nira's devotion as with Cricket's attentions. He could manage them both. He was nothing if not a diplomat, he told himself gaily and went to sleep holding a happy and contented Nira in his arms.

Chapter 5

BOYCE AND CRICKET had a row about Rob's inclusion in the summer holiday.

With vast indignation Cricket broke the news to her husband when he came home from the office a week after Rob's birthday party.

"I think it's the end. When I saw Nira this morning— we both happened to be in Sainsbury's—she told me she'd suggested that Rob should go with us, and said Des didn't mind and they were hoping to get a room for Rob at The Formentor. That means there'll be *five* of us. Don't you think it's an absolute bore?"

Boyce privately thought rather more than that. He actually changed colour, and poured himself out a stronger gin than usual. Everything had gone wrong for him at the office today. One of the projects they were working on had proved unsuccessful. His partner's blonde secretary, whom he had rather stupidly kissed one day, had taken him more seriously than he intended. She was now writing amorous notes and he really didn't want her on his hands. He had certain money problems—he was always spending above his income and although he was making more money these days, there was Cricket with her overdraft and constant extravagances and the general rising cost of living. *And* that new petulant cry from her: "Everything's going up. You ought to give me more for housekeeping."

Now his little schemes for softening Nira up while they were abroad looked like being thwarted. Rob was a first-rate fellow but he wasn't, in Boyce's opinion, quite one of the Ponders Heath charmed circle. Somehow he always stood outside it, and he'd be outside it in Majorca. How were they going to pair off as Boyce had pleasurably anticipated with Rob as a fifth.

Rather viciously, Boyce poured a half-bottle of tonic into his gin, then banged it down on the table.

"Really! I've never heard of such a thing. It's a god-damned silly idea. Is it a certainty?"

"Yes, if the agency can get him a room and I bet just because we don't want them to, they will."

"Who engineered this? You? I thought you were all out for moonlight on the seashore alone with our Des."

"So I am," said Cricket frankly. "Meanwhile you might be polite enough to offer me a drink."

"Help yourself."

"You wouldn't say that to Nira."

"Oh, don't be silly," Boyce said, his eyes dark and angry. He really couldn't be bothered with his exacting wife tonight, but he got up and poured her gin. "It's Nira who wants Rob on the holiday, I suppose," he grunted.

Cricket looked at him through her lashes. She felt suddenly spiteful.

"Well, she never does behave as though she is all out for moonlight shores *toute seule* with you, dear. Maybe she wants to initiate dear innocent old Rob into the sweet mysteries of life and love."

"Oh, shut up," said Boyce rudely.

"Diddums want his Nirry all to himself," cooed Cricket, who was feeling rather pleased with life, and still confident that she was going to have a good innings with Des out in Majorca—Rob or no Rob. It would amuse her to see Boyce fighting Rob desperately for pride of place with Nira. She admitted that Nira had a gorgeous figure and was very dignified and charming, but she didn't see what the men were so mad about. All that virtue! In Cricket's opinion—and she considered herself an expert in the matter—men wanted a bit more fire and excitement than Nira Curtis offered. A bit of holding back before the final surrender—yes. But in the long run Nira would be far too gentle and mild. However, although Cricket was bored with her own husband and mad about Des, she was maliciously pleased because Boyce was not getting all he wanted.

"Did Nira guess that we mightn't want Rob in the party?" asked Boyce in a sulky voice.

"Oh, she sort of suggested that if we objected she'd fob him off, but of course I couldn't say we did. The Curtises originally organised the holiday and I don't really mind old Rob. I think he's quite sweet in his way."

"There's too much sweetness being poured around here," said Boyce with an acidity he had been storing up all day. "You make me tired."

"Don't be stupid. I didn't say I wanted Rob on the party. I told you I was cross about it. Why don't you tell your darling Nira how you feel?"

"I can't very well. It's too late anyhow."

They wrangled until dinner time when their son joined them. Then Boyce complained of the meal— Cricket never had been a good cook. The beef was overdone, which Boyce disliked, and the roast potatoes were soft. He liked them crisp.

Simon seized his plateful and went back to the lounge to sit in front of the television in order to see a special crime play. Husband and wife started to bicker again, and this time Cricket had to climb down, Boyce held the financial reins. She wanted some extra cash for new holiday clothes. She knew she had to be careful to keep on Boyce's right side. She wanted to look particularly alluring in Majorca—for Des.

Finally she pretended to be on Boyce's side and to

sympathise about the Rob affair. But if she wanted fun with Des she'd better ensure that Boyce found some distraction. She, Cricket, would no doubt take Rob off all their hands sometimes. There was a band in The Formentor and a dance every night. Rob couldn't dance, so Boyce would keep his dear Nira for his partner. And Cricket didn't think Nira particularly wanted to chum up with Rob, anyway. It was just that she was sorry for him being so lonely, she told Boyce soothingly.

"Don't let's worry about it any more. I was angry at first but I'm not now. Give Cricket a kiss," and she went up to his chair and put her arms around his neck.

Boyce's humour was restored. He returned the kiss but his thoughts were still on Nira. Her continual cool rejection of him—unspoken but obvious—was getting on his nerves.

That very next evening he and Cricket went to dinner and bridge at the Curtises' house. The first thing Nira had to tell them was that Boyce's fears had been realised. There'd been a single-room cancellation at The Formentor and Rob had got it.

Cricket, her big blue eyes dancing, looked wickedly at her husband.

"Isn't that nice, Boyce?"

"It's okay by me," he said icily.

Nira, who felt relaxed and happy this evening, said, "I think Rob feels rather embarrassed about it all but I persuaded him we're pleased. I do think it'll be a real break for him. He must get terribly fed up with life at The Hollies with his old aunt."

"Yes," said Cricket, "after that wonderful life he led in Kenya. It was a sweet idea of yours, Nira."

Here Des cut in. "I was a bit worried that you two might mind," he said, looking from Boyce to Cricket.

"Of course we don't," said Cricket and gave him a look that set his pulses racing. She had a frightful effect on him, he reflected.

"Why should we?" asked Boyce, but he looked at Nira. She didn't notice it. She was busy with her entertaining. *Beautiful as ever,* Boyce thought moodily, *too damned superior and unattainable.* It drove him mad—

with a longing of which he was far too conscious. It wasn't like him to be so serious about girls. Most of them fell for him. Why must Nira be the exception?

He began to feel that Rob's presence in Majorca wouldn't really make the slightest difference. He wasn't in the running for Nira anyhow. He wouldn't need to battle with Rob. It was Nira, herself, he would have to fight.

He didn't get a chance to speak to her alone that evening. The bridge party went off as well as usual, although once or twice Boyce's cold shrewd mind became alive to the fact that Desmond was beginning to drink rather a lot. It reddened his face, made his voice louder. He blared, and he laughed a lot. Looking from him to Nira, Boyce also thought that he saw a slight look of disapproval in those wonderful eyes. He couldn't blame her. Boyce had a fondness for women but not for wine. He didn't think the two went well together and he preferred women.

Yes, he was sure Des was not only downing the whisky but throwing too many sidelong glances at Cricket. He wondered if Nira was conscious of this. She gave no sign of being the least upset so far as *that* was concerned, although she did at one juncture put a slim hand over Des's glass and say, "Easy, darling. You'll be trumping my aces in a moment." To which Des responded with one of his hearty laughs and promptly poured himself out another whisky.

The result was inevitable. Des began to play carelessly. As a rule he and Nira were the superior pair. Cricket was erratic and sometimes rather stupid about cards. Boyce was used to losing when he played in this house. Tonight Des overcalled and went down, doubled and vulnerable, on two occasions. He paid his losses—and Nira's—with his usual good humour, apologised to her, ruffled her hair gaily and said, "I don't think I was playing up to form, do you sweetie?"

The watchful Boyce now for the first time saw Nira's mouth tighten, and although she smiled, her voice was hard. "You weren't, were you?"

That was all but Boyce could sense the reproach be-

hind it. He really had to admire Nira as much for her
character as for her extreme beauty. She was so controlled. Cricket would have stormed at him and called
him an 'old boozer', or any other name she could think
of. Some of the women he played bridge with held post-
mortems and liked to prove that the heavy loss was all
their husband's fault. Nira said absolutely nothing to
Des while she collected the cards and tore up the used
markers. On the way home, Boyce mentioned this to his
wife. Cricket giggled.

"I bet there's a super post-mortem going on now. Des
really did play badly tonight. Did you think he was
drinking a teeny-weeny bit too much?"

"Teeny-weeny is a masterly understatement," said
Boyce.

"Well, I don't blame him. Nira's gorgeous but she
does rather expect a lot of a man, don't you think?"

Boyce put his tongue in his cheek. It wasn't unusual
for Cricket to try and disparage Nira. He held his
peace. But as they turned into the drive of their own
house he had one more thing to say on the subject of
Des and Nira.

"You're wrong about a post-mortem going on back
in the Curtises' home. I'll lay you a wager she won't say
a word to him about the game. She's a very diplomatic
sort of girl."

Cricket's blue eyes widened. She giggled again. Who
cared? Des could drink as much as he liked, so far as
she was concerned. She just doted on him. He was such
fun and so *passionate*. Boyce left her cold these days.
And as for Nira, let Boyce think her an angel. Who
cared? She, Cricket, didn't. And as Boyce fancied Nira,
Cricket didn't feel she need have much conscience
about taking Des as a lover.

Her parting shots were to make further disparaging
remarks about Nira. She couldn't cure herself of that
habit she had of pecking in a nasty little way at the
other women in the neighbourhood whom she thought
too attractive to men.

"I've never met a real angel, but I've a horrid suspicion that if I did, I'd find her an awful bore. Maybe

Des's drinking because he's bored with his angelic Nira."

Boyce continued to hold his peace. He let himself into the house with a cynical smile on his thin lips.

As he so rightly predicted, in the Curtis home, Nira was not reproaching her husband although she felt, for the first time during her marriage, the horrid sensation of having been let down.

Her love for her big, handsome, genial husband had always been so entire. She had never once doubted that it was deserved—and returned. He had his faults. She was not so stupid as to think that any man could be perfect. But Des had supplied all her needs so far.

She had perhaps always known in the depths of her heart that he was a little shallow and that there was something deeper in her own nature. He was a Philistine. She from her schooldays had been interested in art and philosophy, but after her marriage these things had taken second place to her love for Des and their children and the home.

She did not want her trust and happiness to subside in the smallest way. It must always be kept up to standard.

There was a stubborn streak in Nira and without being of a combative disposition, she was prepared to fight for things she believed in. However, there was going to be no open fight with Des on this question of drinking.

She remembered how, when she was a teenager, an uncle on her mother's side had come to live with them for a time, and was rarely sober. Her mother had reluctantly admitted that he drank too much.

Fresh, innocent, idealistic, the young Nira had expressed her indignation and announced that she couldn't understand why neither of her parents ever stopped Uncle Bill from drinking. When he wanted a whisky, they gave it to him. They should have made him take soft drinks, Nira said. She had then received her first lesson in how to deal with this human weakness. First and foremost, never to nag. Her mother told Nira that Aunt Jean, Uncle Bill's Scot's wife, had done too much of that. She hid the whisky—nagged at Bill every time he brought home a bottle—and this only drove him to drink more. He had been going through a bad time in the City and was harassed and very tired. Possibly he needed the extra stimulant, and if Jean had been sensible and not denied it to him, he might have got over the bad phase and settled down to the usual harmless glass or two, which the average man needed.

Nira had seen the wisdom in this, but she remembered telling her mother about a girl friend whose father never drank at all and was a teetotaller. Didn't Mummy believe that was best? Mummy had smiled and patted Nira's cheek and told her that she must learn to accept all kinds of people with all kinds of different ideas and principles. The great word—the operative word—to adhere to through life she declared was *tolerance*.

Nira never forgot that lesson. She could see for herself that Aunt Jean had been an intolerant woman. The young Nira had made a vow that she would never be like that. So now when it came to the test, and she had to face the fact that Des, for some reason best known to himself, was exceeding his ordinary quota of alcohol, she behaved with the diplomacy Boyce had attributed to her. It was Des, not Nira, who mentioned the alcoholic evening. First in bed, he watched Nira brush her long silky hair and in a mumbling voice suggested that she should hurry up and join him. It was midnight and he was sleepy, he said.

She put down her brush and turned to him smiling.

"Then go to sleep, darling. I'm not ready."

He blinked at her and held out a hand.

"Oh, come on—and while you're about it—how about getting me a drink? I'm damned thirsty."

Now she went back a little on her own philosophy.

"Haven't you had enough?"

"Possibly. But I like it. Don't try and ration me."

That stung her. She didn't think she deserved it. Her cheeks went hot and pink. She turned from him and continued to brush her hair.

The next thing she heard was a loud snore. When she looked at her husband again he was fast asleep. Mouth

open, grunting, he didn't really look as handsome or attractive as usual. Her heart suddenly sank low. She
slipped into bed beside him and switched off the light.
The sound of his snoring was not conducive to sleep.
He did snore sometimes and she usually managed to ignore it; snuggled up to him, warm and content. Tonight
she felt chilled and lonely. Contentment was far from
her heart. This Des was a stranger. With all her heart
she loved him but her idol was toppling a little on its
plinth, and she was horrified at the prospect of it crashing to the ground.

She could not bear the isolation. She put out a hand
and shook him, hot tears in her eyes.

"Des, Des, wake up. You haven't kissed me good
night."

He made no answer but edged away from her grunting again. The snores intensified.

For a moment she thought she was going to cry. On
second thoughts she decided that she was being stupid.
He had done nothing frightful. Let him have a few extra
drinks if he wanted. Everything would be all right in the
morning. She mustn't lose her sense of humour or expect too much. After a sleepless hour she was not very
happy and she put on a dressing-gown and retreated to
the spare bedroom where she curled up in a blanket and
soon was sound asleep.

As usual she was the first to get up. She woke Desmond with a cup of tea. He looked livery and obviously
had a hangover, but he was full of remorse.

"I drank too much, didn't I? Darling, I'm frightfully
sorry. I played ghastly bridge, too, I remember. I don't
know what came over me. And you had to go into the
spare room, poor sweet! I suppose I was snoring like
hell."

Nira gave him a faint smile.

"You were, and it's time you got going, darling, or
you'll miss your train."

He ate no breakfast but drank two large cups of coffee. Shaven and spruce, in his city suit, his thick brown
hair brushed and shining, he was her Des again, treating

her with the usual consideration and begging her to forgive him.

The unhappiness of the night was forgotten. They
embraced happily—close and normal again. Nira drove
the children to school and began to tackle the day's
work as usual. Only one awkward thought of last night's
bridge party troubled her. She hoped it wasn't going to
be repeated—at least not so that anyone would notice
it. If Des were to start to drink heavily, it would be too
awful, she reflected. She *couldn't* love a drunk. There
was something so repellent about being close and intimate with a man who was full of alcohol and whose
breath smelled and who didn't even behave in a civilised manner. The blaring voice, the boastful manner,
the rather idiotic grin, then the sudden aggressiveness—
all this would become unbearable. But at least he had
assured her it wouldn't happen again.

The next evening, he took her out to a film they had
both marked down as being worth seeing. They had a
pleasant time and he was once more the Des she knew
and was so dear to her. She went to sleep happily with
his arm around her in what she called their 'spoon and
fork' position—homely, comforting, married bliss.

During the few weeks that followed all seemed well.
Des certainly didn't disgrace himself by drinking over-
much, nor had Nira anything to complain of except that
once or twice, as the summer approached, he rang up
from the office at the last moment to say he couldn't be
home for dinner. As he never seemed able to let her
know his movements in advance, she couldn't make her
own plans so was left to spend the evenings alone.
When she asked him if it was going to be like this often,
he said that he didn't get any warning himself. It was
only when the senior partner asked him to stay on for
some conference connected with their business, that as
an executive in a big firm he couldn't very well say no.
Nira was determined to be patient and co-operative,
and tried not to grumble. If Des was working so hard
for her and the children, it was up to her to make things
easy for him.

Then one day early in June he phoned her from the

office just before five and told her it was going to be another late night in the office and suggested she ask someone to spend the evening with her, watch television or something.

"I shall begin to believe you've got a blonde up there," she teased him.

He gave one of his hearty laughs.

"I'm too busy and tired for lovely blondes, my darling. Look—why don't you ring up old Rob and get him to come round and have a chat with you? I won't be jealous."

"You don't have to be jealous of any man, and I'm quite sure I don't have to be jealous of any woman, joking apart."

"You couldn't be more right."

"I'll ring Rob. As a matter of fact I'd quite enjoy a chat with him and I know he gets enough of Aunt Ida."

Rob accepted Nira's invitation with alacrity. It would be a great treat, he said, to spend an evening with her and charming of her to think of asking him.

"Des is terribly busy these days," she sighed.

"Well, his misfortune is my good luck," came Rob's quiet friendly voice, "I'll be with you within the next half hour."

Chapter 6

ROB BROUGHT HER a large box of chocolates and she gave him coffee and a drink. They settled down in the drawing-room. But neither of them wanted to watch television. They were both good conversationalists and Nira, having got over her disappointment of having to spend another evening without Des, found herself well entertained by Rob. Not only was he a good talker, but a sympathetic listener. She could discuss almost anything with him.

She had always known that he was like that, and although she felt a small twinge of disloyalty, she had to admit that he was, strictly speaking, a man with more understanding than her dear Des. Of course Rob was older—more mature—Des was the eternal schoolboy. There was always a touch of sadness, too, about Rob which made her feel more warmth towards him than the average man she came across.

They only stopped talking to turn on the nine o'clock news. It was while they were listening to the latest story of the American astronauts soaring towards the moon, that the telephone bell rang.

Nira answered the call in the hall. To her surprise—and some irritation—it was Boyce.

"I really wanted to say a word to old Des—" he began, but Nira cut him short.

"He isn't here. He's working late tonight."

"In that case, would you be very bored if I ran round to see you?"

"I'm sorry, Boyce, I've already got a friend here—do forgive me." Then she added on a lighter note in order not to appear hostile, "What's Cricket doing?"

"Oh, I'm a grass-widower. She's away for the night in town staying with her aunt. She planned to do a day's shopping tomorrow and Aunty's off to South Africa. She wanted to see Cricket before she went."

"Oh!" said Nira, disinterested.

Boyce tried to keep her on the line, but she managed to make it clear that she was in a hurry to get away so he said goodbye, not forgetting to add that he was very disappointed.

She put down the receiver and stood for a moment, frowning, thinking.

Des and Cricket—both up in London tonight. Oh, but why not? There couldn't possibly be any sinister connection there.

She went back to Rob, who stood up in his courteous old-fashioned way as she entered the room.

"I've switched off the news. There was nothing interesting," he said smiling. "Let's go on with our chat. I am having such a lovely evening."

She warmed to the flattery in those words and knew that he really was enjoying himself. She could see it. She enjoyed having him there, too. He couldn't be nicer.

She forgot about Des and Cricket, and made fresh coffee for Rob and herself. They were still discussing life and the age they lived in when Rob suddenly looked at his watch and said, "Good lord—I must go! I do apologise for keeping you up so late. It's half-past eleven."

She found herself quick to suggest that he should stay.

"I don't want to go to bed early unless you do."

He gave her that charming smile that crinkled the corners of his eyes, and lent that fleeting glow of youthful happiness to a tired face.

"Not in the least," he said.

"Are you hungry? Can I make you a sandwich?" she asked.

He found her, as usual, completely disarming. She was married with two children, but she seemed to him so young at times, yet such a real woman. There was nothing silly or coy about her. She had a genius for friendship—for putting a man completely at his ease.

Tonight, looking at her, he realised to the full that she had become an essential part of his life. It was wrong and sometimes he wondered whether he ought to go on seeing her. But he could not tolerate the idea of cutting her out. He could not do without her. That he was fashioning a sword for his own heart, he could well imagine. But even that fear could not turn him away. And thinking of Des he wished Nira's husband was a better type—a bit more worthy of the quite extraordinary love and devotion that she squandered on him.

Des was gay and amusing, a man's man, and very attractive to women. But Nira was serious-minded, and in Rob's opinion, Des was shallow. Just how long it would be before she was disillusioned and the marriage deteriorated, Rob did not know. At the moment he did not want to think about it. It would hurt her too deeply. But it remained stubbornly at the back of his mind.

He stayed with her another hour, enjoying the ham sandwiches she brought him, and drinking one more whisky.

Reluctantly but inevitably, Nira compared her husband with this man who was strong-minded enough to stop her pouring a strong drink into his glass. "Only a weak one," he said. Why couldn't Des be as moderate? Deep down she was still sore about that unpleasant episode with Des on the night of Rob's party when he had taken Cricket home.

Just before Rob left, Nira remembered that she had some new photographs of the children. She delayed him in order to show them to him. He found them charming and remarked on the likeness between Jonathan and herself.

She said, "He has Des's gorgeous chestnut hair, but my eyes. I reckon he'll be just as handsome as his dad."

Rob smiled and laid the prints down.

"You're really very fond of that husband of yours, aren't you?"

"Very." Then she made him admire little Renira's photograph.

"She's a poppet," he nodded.

"She loves Uncle Rob. So does Jon. You're awfully good with children. You know, Rob, you ought to have been married."

Now he hastily said good night. She didn't notice the sudden look of pain that darkened his eyes, nor the fact that he made no comment on her remark. She was feeling relaxed and happy after a most pleasant evening. It was only when she put out a hand to say good night and he took it and kissed it, that she became aware not for the first time, how much she liked this man. Neither could she be blind to the fact that he more than liked her.

"We must have another evening together sometime when Desmond is away," she said involuntarily.

"I'd like that," said Rob, and turned away because he was suddenly sorely tempted to do more than kiss Nira's slim, friendly hand. He wanted with all his heart to take her in his arms and hold her against his heart, tell her that she was the sweetest thing on earth and that he worshipped her.

The idea of the holiday in Majorca began to assume tremendous proportions. To be able to see and talk to *her,* every day—what a dazzling prospect! He hadn't looked forward to anything so much since he left East Africa. He couldn't wait for it.

It was only when Nira was in bed winding up her little clock, that the lateness of the hour struck her. Surely by now Desmond ought to be home. Why on earth was he so late? She felt almost guilty because she had enjoyed herself so much talking to Rob and she had hardly noticed the time till now.

Rob had been very helpful about Jonathan. Des adored his son but he was not very scholastic and never went deeply into the question of Jonathan's schooling and future education. He knew that his mother would give him the money for the fees when the time came to send Jonathan to his public school. They had him down for Shrewsbury because that was where Des was educated, but it would have been much too expensive for them to send a boy there in these days without Gandy's help. Des as a child had not been too keen on his work; it had always been *games* with him. Although Nira tried to shut her eyes to the fact, Des could at times be rather stupid. He would never be much help to Jonathan, who even at ten was showing remarkable signs of being a brainy boy. Top of his class in quite a lot of subjects— particularly keen on history. Already he had acquired an astonishing fund of knowledge. History happened to be Rob's subject. He also had a very fine library of historical novels. He had mentioned more than once to Nira that as soon as Jonathan was a little older he could go and borrow any book that would help him, in whatever period he was studying at the time.

"I wish you had been his godfather," Nira had said one day, and then out of her innate loyalty to Des, added that of course Jonathan's own godfather was a terribly nice man—but he had unfortunately died not long ago on a racing-track, trying out a new car. While he had lived Jack had never talked to Jonathan about school—only about cars. Jonathan was mildly interested, but confided in his mother that he wished Uncle Jack had been interested in history. He hadn't seemed at all impressed when Jonathan told him about the essay he had written on Henry VIII. Jonathan had read it aloud to the whole school and was proud of the fact. But Uncle Jack (and Daddy) guffawed with laughter and just made silly jokes about the Merry Monarch and his wives.

Rob had won Jonathan's heart by doing exactly the opposite. He had asked to be allowed to read Jonathan's essay and commented on its excellence and originality.

Later Jonathan said to his mother, "Uncle Rob is super to talk to, isn't he, Mum? I think he's super altogether."

That was exactly what Nira felt while she waited for Des to come home. She even felt a trifle aggrieved because Des had become slightly scathing in his various comments on poor old Rob. He was neither poor nor old. The last person on earth who would wish to be pitied.

She read until her eyes blinked and she had to turn out her bedside lamp and sleep. She had given up waiting for Des. She began to wonder if he would come home at all. He could always, of course, find a bed in an emergency with Morris Fairway. Morris was one of Des's old school-friends, and the one whom Nira liked least. *He* certainly drank too much and seemed to think of and talk of nothing but girl-friends. He was still a bachelor and likely to remain one. The last time Nira saw him he annoyed her by openly denouncing marriage as a trap and jokingly sympathising with Des's position. Nira hadn't found it very funny. Still less had she liked it when Morris tried his wiles on her as the evening wore on. He was really a type she couldn't stand, but she supposed that Des liked him for old times' sake. And after all Morris's flat was a boon.

After this evening with Rob, feeling so cherished,

Nira decided not to worry any more about her husband.

When she next opened her eyes it was to hear the two children outside her door asking to be allowed to come in, and to see broad daylight. Rubbing the sleep from her eyes, she realised with a shock that it was seven o'clock. The pillow beside hers was untouched. Des had never come home.

Renira and Jonathan flung themselves on the bed and asked where Daddy was. Nira said, "You may well ask. Your dear Dad has deserted us. He's been up in London all night."

"Ooh!" exclaimed Renira.

"Jolly lucky!" said Jonathan.

Nira kissed them both and told them to go off and get dressed.

In the bath she was no longer smiling or joking. She felt thoroughly disturbed. Even if the business dinner had been prolonged against Des's will, he might at least have rung her up and let her know that he would be staying in town. Her feelings changed somewhat when by ten o'clock he had still neither telephoned nor come back. Aggravation gave place to anxiety. She telephoned Des's office. The telephonist, whom she knew, told her that Mr. Curtis hadn't yet arrived.

Nira's pulse-rate quickened and some of her colour faded. There must have been an accident. Whatever Des did, he never failed to turn up at the office at half-past nine. He had a conscience about that, because as he so often said, the young had no sense of time or discipline so it was up to the men of his age to set an example. One of Des's good qualities was his punctuality.

Nira left a message with the telephonist for Des to call his wife as soon as he arrived. For the next hour she tried to busy herself in the house. She was definitely worried now. She set to work to make a steak-and-kidney pudding which was one of Des's favourite dishes. Just as she was tying it up in the cloth, she heard a car in the drive. She wiped her hands and rushed to open the door.

At first she saw only Des's back. He was paying a

taxi. She supposed he had come from the station. But why hadn't he gone straight to his office?

A shock awaited her when Des turned round and walked slowly towards her—very slowly. He was limping and he had a piece of sticking plaster over his right eyebrow. The whole of the right side of his face looked red and bruised.

She felt sick. So there *had* been an accident. All her love and deep feeling for him surged up. She led him into the house.

"Des, my *darling,* what in God's name has happened?"

"Sorry if I've given you a fright," he mumbled the words. "I—let me sit down, sweetie, will you? And bring me a drink. I need one."

She helped him to an armchair in the lounge and threw open one of the windows to let in the air. She ran to fetch whisky bottle and glass without questioning his need for it.

He drank thirstily, then leaned back, closing his eyes.

"God, I feel lousy!"

"What's happened? For God's sake, tell me, Des. Why didn't you ring up? Why didn't you let me know? I'd have come up in the car to fetch you. Oh, Des, what *did* happen?"

He looked away from her.

"I was nearly run over coming out of the restaurant with old Steadman."

"But how? Where? *When?*"

"Just let me get my breath," he muttered, "I feel a bit sickish."

"The whisky will settle your stomach, my poor darling," she said tenderly, and filled his glass again.

He took it but he did not meet her gaze. He had too much on his conscience. He let her fuss over him. Talk about the whisky settling him, he reflected, he had nearly been settled for good and all last night, and he hadn't been with the senior partner when it happened, either. He had left old Steadman outside The Mirabelle where they had dined. After that he had gone on to Morris's flat where Cricket was waiting for him. Oh, it had all been so well organised and things had gone swimmingly. Boyce supposed that *she* was with her aunt and Des had meant just to borrow old Morris's flat for an hour or two in order to spend a few glamorous hours with Cricket. Then he meant to catch the last train home. But his plans had gone awry. His own fault, of course; he wouldn't deny it. Not that he had any intention of letting Nira know a thing.

After the second drink he opened his bloodshot eyes and gingerly touched the cut on his forehead. He began then to tell her a cock-and-bull story about Steadman dropping him outside Victoria Station and how, just as he was crossing the road, a car had backed into him and he had fallen down heavily. Hence the injured face and bruised shin.

"But how awful!" exclaimed Nira. "Oh, why didn't you let me *know*? What time was it?"

"It was only ten o'clock, but I was knocked unconscious. They took me to St. George's Casualty."

He had stayed there until he came out of his stupor this morning. The doctor had let him go in time for him to get the nine-ten train home. Des hadn't phoned her because he didn't want her to be worried.

"You'd have had a fit if you had heard I was in a hospital," he ended.

She knelt by his side, looking at him with lovely tender eyes, the colour gradually coming back into her face. She felt brimful of love and pity, and also of remorse, because she had been so suspicious and thought he had deliberately stayed away, or done something that he shouldn't do.

"I hope you took the name and address of the man who knocked you down," she said hotly.

Des ignored this.

"But why didn't the hospital let me know?" she persisted.

He continued to lie.

"My wallet dropped out of my pocket, when I fell, I suppose. Somebody pinched it, so there was nothing to identify me when they put me to bed. Don't look so tragic, darling. As you see, I am alive and kicking.

Luckily no bones were broken. It was just that I fell on the side of my face and one leg and so you see me now—looking *ever* so handsome!" He uttered the last words in an attempt to be jocular.

She took one of his hands and pressed it against her cheek.

"Oh, thank God you're all right, Des. I don't know what I'd have done if you'd been badly hurt!"

"You're sweet," he said mechanically. "And I'm sorry I couldn't contact you. Now be a good girl and help me up to bed. I feel a bit dizzy still and I could do with a sleep."

"Would you like another drink?"

"Hey! Who's encouraging me to take to the bottle? I thought you were on the war path about my boozing."

As he got up, she looked up at him with that tender and trusting gaze which he found rather awkward to accept.

"Under these circumstances, darling, of *course* you need a drink."

He didn't refuse. The whole bloody affair had resulted from too much champagne with Cricket. Damn Cricket *and* her sensuous little body. She bewitched him. She knew just how to drive a fellow wild, and she laced her kisses with alcohol, then the cycle started all over again.

After he put her in a taxi to go back to her aunt's house, he felt suddenly dizzy in the cool night air and the world had spun around him. He'd tripped and fallen into the gutter, hitting the side of his face and one leg against the kerb.

A passing policeman had helped him up and taken him back into the flat.

"Better get that cut over your eye seen to, sir," he had said.

Des had been just sober enough to make light of the affair and to assure the man that he had Elastoplast in the bathroom cupboard and he'd use that and some disinfectant and it would be okay. The whole story of his night in the hospital had been a fabrication but he didn't want Nira to know that he had spent those hectic hours in Morris's flat.

Nira was being particularly sweet and attentive but all he felt was a desire for sleep. His head hurt damnably and he was suffering as much from an appalling hangover as the effects of his fall. He was no lightweight and he had come down on that tarmac with one hell of a plonk, he recalled.

He was barely conscious once he got up to bed, but he heard Nira say, "I must get something to put on your eyebrow. It's swelling."

That irritated him and he couldn't stand one minute more of her tenderness and coddling. He wanted to be left alone.

"Oh, don't fuss so!" he muttered.

Hurt, she drew back from him. Then he was out like a light. She stood a moment staring down at the disfigured face and listening to a snoring that was becoming rather too familiar. All her tremendous feeling for him—the shock of his accident—the fear that he was really hurt—gradually diminished.

She pulled the curtains in order to darken the room and left him lying there, still dressed, having only taken off his collar and tie.

As she tiptoed from the darkened room the sound of his noisy breathing followed her. She went downstairs, a hollow sort of feeling inside. She was beginning to suspect that Des was stale drunk and that the whisky she had given him with so much sympathy had been little more that the 'hair of the dog that had bitten him'.

Later, after making the children's beds, she tidied up downstairs. When she looked in on Des, she found him still snoring. He had taken off his coat. On the carpet half under the bed, she suddenly saw his pocket-book. It must have fallen out of the pocket. Slowly she picked it up. There wasn't much money in it, only his driving licence, a bank credit-card, and a small black book of telephone numbers which she did not bother to investigate. Her mind concentrated on the fact that he had lied to her. He had told her that someone had pinched his wallet but he had had it all the time. Having lost the wallet was his explanation of why the hospital had not been able to contact her. But why? *Why?* Had he been with Steadman at all? *Or with Cricket?*

Once more Nira was tortured by doubt. But her practical side reminded her that she *must* get out and shop as it was early closing day in Ponders Heath. Des would sleep for at least another couple of hours. She had promised the children strawberry mousse for afters and she had only just discovered they were running out of cornflakes. She had to go now, at once. To add to her depression rain was beginning to pelt down. She found her waterproof jacket and an umbrella and tied a scarf over her hair.

Just as she was leaving the house the telephone-bell rang. Hastily she ran back and lifted the receiver. Rob's voice; thanking her for a lovely evening.

"You don't know how much I enjoyed it."

"I did, too," she said. But the sight of her own face in the hall mirror almost scared her, it was so grim. She had never seen herself look quite like that before.

Rob started to tell her something—she really couldn't concentrate and interrupted him.

"Do forgive me, Rob, I've got to go out before the shops shut."

The man at the other end of the wire was suddenly alive to the fact that all was not well with his Nira. Her voice sounded strange.

"Are you all right?"

"Yes, of course," she bit her lip and laughed. But the laugh did not convince him.

"You don't sound yourself this morning."

"Perhaps I'm not." She laughed again, a trifle too loudly.

"What time did Desmond get back?"

"He didn't. He stayed in town."

Silence. He waited for her to speak again.

She added, "He—he had a lot of work and he stayed the night with a friend."

"H'm," said Rob. But he didn't believe a thing about that work. "Well, well—let me know when you can have some lunch, or a game of golf," he added, "I won't keep you, my dear. Goodbye."

"Thanks awfully. Goodbye, Rob."

She turned from the telephone. Her lips were trembling. There were tears in her eyes. She felt somehow that her world was falling apart. Her faith in Des had been absolute during the eleven years of their marriage. But now—she wondered. Yet was she being unreasonable? What had he done except drink too much and stop the night in town? There was that stupid lie about his stolen wallet and not being able to get in touch with her. Why all *that*? She'd have to have it out with him.

She seized umbrella and shopping bag and hurried out into the pouring rain. Once in the High Street she had to dive suddenly into one or two shops to avoid meeting neighbours—women she knew. She was unwilling in her present state of mind to be forced into gossiping.

She bought what she wanted in the new big supermarket which had recently opened, then turned down Heath Hill which led to Nylands. Nylands—her home, the attractive house she loved so much and where she had been so happy. As she put the key in the front door this morning, she felt unbearably sad. She found herself wishing that the Bessiford's home was nearer so that she could run in and tell Rob all about things. He was wise and kind. She could confide in him and his advice would be good. Then she dismissed the idea.

The telephone-bell was ringing as she let herself into Nylands. She felt so tired she wished she did not have to answer it. This time it was Boyce.

"Hello, Beautiful," he said in the caressing voice which she was beginning to dislike, "I'm speaking from the office. I just felt I must have a word with you."

"Forgive me, I'm terribly busy this morning," she said coldly.

"I won't keep you a second. I just want to know what's wrong with old Des?"

"What should be?" she asked, startled.

"Well, I saw him getting off the London train just as

I was leaving the Heath this morning. He was limping."

Nira tried to calm down and collect her thoughts. She had to be careful what she said but she was not good at covering up—Des often said she was too honest. She had never found it easy to lie.

"Hello—are you there, Nira?"

"Yes. Nothing's wrong with Des except he hurt his leg slightly. He stayed the night with his friend Morris. He woke up with a ghastly headache and decided to come home instead of going to the office."

A little meaning laugh from Boyce.

"You and I are in the same boat. My dear wife was supposed to be staying with her aunt last night."

Nira snapped at him, "What's that meant to imply?"

"Well—she rang me first thing this morning and sounded as though she'd swallowed a magnum of champagne. She'd been out on a party and *not* with aunty. She even forgot she was supposed to take Simon to the dentist after lunch today. I can see I'll have to take a firm hand with her," Boyce ended with a laugh. "And you must do the same with old Des."

But Nira was not amused. Her face was hot, her thoughts confused.

"I don't get you, Boyce."

He ignored this.

"Cricket also complained of a frightful headache. Our better halves seem to have hangovers—the pair of them."

"Really, Boyce," Nira protested furiously.

He said, "Nira, my pet, aren't you thinking what *I* am thinking? Aren't we innocent victims of a great betrayal? Don't you twig that our devoted spouses were by some chance imbibing champagne *together*?"

Nira gasped. This was plain speaking now.

"I don't like your suggestions, Boyce." Her voice trembled.

He laughed. "Don't take me too seriously. But why didn't you let me come over and see you last night? You know I wanted to very much."

With her nerves in shreds, Nira was afraid she would break down unless she could get away from this man and his insinuations. She felt almost certain now that he was right. His wife and her husband had been together last night. Everything pointed to it. They had shared that champagne, and they both had hangovers this morning. Cricket had been away—with whom, if not with Des?

Nira put down the phone without even saying good-bye to Boyce. Her breathing was quick, her throat dry. She made up her mind then and there she must get the truth from Des. And another thing—she was determined now to make him cancel that party for Majorca. Nothing would induce her to face two weeks of Boyce, and his unwelcome attentions—not even though Rob was supposed to be with them. Neither would she stand by and watch Cricket's brazen attempts to seduce Des (or vice-versa, for all she knew).

It was no longer a compassionate loving wife but a jealous, angry woman who marched into the bedroom and roused her sleeping husband.

Chapter 7

"THE WHOLE THING is ridiculous. Why the hell should you take it for granted that Cricket and I spent a night together just because we'd both been to a champagne party. As for Boyce suggesting I'm having an affair with his wife—I've a good mind to go round and have it out with him."

Des spoke in a loud hectoring voice. Nira stood at the bottom of the bed looking at him. He was drinking a cup of strong black coffee that she had just made for him. She noted how the hand that held the cup was shaking. He didn't look very nice this morning. There was a bluish tinge to his unshaven chin. His eyes were red-rimmed and when she had bent over him she had to draw back quickly, repelled by his breath.

For the last half-hour they had been wrangling. Quarrels were something they had never before indulged in so long and so bitterly. She had had a few words with him over his drinking on the night the Hallings came to dinner but she had reproached herself after that for being intolerant and for nagging and all had been forgiven and forgotten.

This was different.

Des was trembling with temper and alcoholic excess. Nira was trembling because her whole nervous system was keyed up to a pitch she could hardly control. This was the husband she had always adored and believed in. It was ghastly to suspect that he had spent last night with Cricket—or any other woman. Over and over again he had fiercely denied it. He brushed off the incident of the wallet.

"I actually did think someone had whipped it," he said. "If it's still here so much the better. I admit I was drunk last night and that's why I fell down. It's the only thing I've been lying about. I just didn't want them to send for you from the hospital in case you saw me in that condition. I happen to love my wife and want to keep in her good books. Is that such a crime?"

Now Nira turned from the sight of his spoiled face and walked to the window. She opened it. The rain had stopped. The odours from the garden were sweet and fresh and the scent from the jasmine strong. The birds were singing madly and happily. The tears rushed to her eyes and she put her hands up to her face. She had been so madly happy, too. Was she really wronging Des by suspecting him? Was it just jealousy on her part? Was it coincidence that Cricket had been out all night drinking champagne as well as Des? She really had nothing concrete to confirm her suspicions. As for Boyce—she was fast coming to the conclusion that he was a nasty piece of work and no real friend either to Des or herself. He was also disgracefully disloyal to his wife. Of course he had a motive for wanting to link Des and Cricket. It was because *he* wanted to justify his pursuit of her, Nira.

He'd never get her—never as long as he lived. She wouldn't want to be touched by him—not if they were on a desert island and he the last man alive. She used once to think him quite attractive but now he stood for complete lack of moral scruple, for lies, for everything she disliked.

Des had never been like that. *Oh, Des, you couldn't have betrayed me!* Yet even as her mind dwelt on the word *betrayed* she wondered if she was an old-fashioned prig. She certainly wasn't 'with it'. So many couples were unfaithful to each other these days and thought nothing of it.

When she turned back to Des she was weeping.

"I don't want to think the worst. If you swear that all this was—was just because you were drunk, and you weren't with Cricket, I'll believe you."

The man in the bed put down his coffee cup and flung himself back on his pillow. His head ached abominably. He had never felt worse after any night out, and quite genuinely he was sorry about the whole thing. He was weak and he knew it. He'd let that little so-and-so, Cricket, get round him. Very exciting it had all been at the time, but he genuinely loved his wife. *In my fashion,* he thought. *Isn't there a song about it somewhere? I've been faithful in my fashion.*

He hated to hear Nira crying and to see the anguish on the face he had always found so sweet and lovable as well as lovely. He'd behaved vilely and he had been found out. That was the major crime—to be found out. But he had never had any intention of upsetting his marriage because of an affair with Cricket. He knew her—and himself—only too well. He soon tired of his girl-friends. There'd been a good many in his life. The only person he'd ever stood by and been faithful to (except for the few odd kisses and caresses in the corner) was Nira. And thinking over the last eleven years he began suddenly to admire his own fidelity. Eleven years of just making love to the odd girl or two! And until now he had kept Nira happy. Crikey! Not bad! He was really quite a fine fellow. There were lots worse including that ruddy fellow Boyce. He bet Boyce had not been as decent to Cricket. If only his head did not ache so badly, he'd get out of bed and take Nira in his arms and show her he still loved her. But there was no desire in him this morning for any woman, and all he could do was to stretch out a hand and say, "Nirry, my darling, come here."

She went over to her dressing-table, pulled out a couple of tissues, pressed them to her lips and wiped her streaming eyes. She felt dreadfully unhappy and still uncertain about the whole thing.

"Nirry," Des repeated, "come here, my pet. You can't just stand there howling like a kid. I won't have it. I can't bear you to be unhappy. You know I love you. You *know*."

All her old affection welled up. She rushed to the bed, sat down and buried her face against his shoulder. She sobbed, "I've never stopped loving *you*. I never thought anyone could come between us."

"They haven't. No one ever will. You're barking up the wrong tree, my angel." His fingers threaded through her hair and he caressed her neck and shoulders. "I swear I haven't been unfaithful to you, Nira. Now will you accept my word or do you *want* to go on believing the worst? If so, you're just a horrid jealous little thing!"

She sobbed and laughed in turn. His attempt to be jocular and the familiar touch of his big strong fingers began to reassure her. The ice round her heart cracked into a million pieces. The warmth seeped back. She was in the right place—in the circle of his arms—confident, secure again.

"If you give me your word of course I'll take it, Des," she whispered. "Forgive me for being so jealous and for accusing you, but it did all seem rather odd, didn't it?"

He agreed. "Certainly it seemed to add up to something against me and I'm the one who ought to ask for forgiveness—not you. I'm sorry I upset you so badly, darling."

He began to feel better now that she had said she believed him. He even began to believe in himself. He cut out the memory of that night's passion with Cricket. He went on stroking his wife's silky hair and dropping little kisses on her head. She must never suspect him again, he said. "And I won't drink or have any other woman in my life but you, which is as it has always been," he ended grandly.

Comforted, she pressed her cheek to his.

"Okay, Des, let's forget it. I'll run a bath for you, and, darling, do you feel fit enough to get up and dress and take me out in the car? Why don't we have lunch together somewhere? At The Rifleman where they have such good sandwiches, don't you think?"

He lied with a swagger. "I'd adore it—great idea. I'll feel myself again after a bath. They'll have to do without me in the office until tomorrow. I've still got a cracking head, you know."

"Are you sure you want to come out? Does the cut still hurt?"

"It's nothing," he lied again, thinking it best to do exactly as she wanted, and to make light of his accident. He'd had a nasty fall all right. But he was anxious to wipe this 'unfaithful with Cricket' fear right out of Nira's mind. He'd do anything to get back into her good books. As for Cricket, he'd tell the little devil as soon as he could get in touch with her, that their affair must stop. She was growing far too possessive and he knew that the next time—if he gave her cause—Nira would not only suspect but condemn him. Then the fat *would* be in the fire. It wasn't any use him wishing his wife was a bit less loyal and full of high principles. It wouldn't, of course, be Nira if she behaved like Cricket—or Maggie Wilson, whom he knew he could have an affair with any time he wanted. He honestly liked being married to Nira and adored the kids. They'd always had fun together. Better keep it that way.

So he bathed and dressed and after nailing down a horrid wish to take another drink in order to bolster himself up, he went out in the car with Nira.

She was happy again and ready to chat in the old gay

friendly way, but he barely listened to all the things she had to tell him about the children. He wasn't in the mood. The sun hurt his eyes. His leg ached. He put on dark glasses. Because he knew she liked it, he kept his hand on Nira's knee, pressed it now and again and gave her one or two of the long sidelong looks which had always thrilled her and made her feel they were still lovers.

The difficult moment came when they were seated up at the bar in the charming little pub ten miles out of Brighton eating cold turkey and salad. Once again Des closed his eyes to the sight of the bottles behind the bar.

"I want to discuss our holiday, darling," she said suddenly. "I know we're all booked up and so on, but I just *don't* want to go away with the Hallings now. I've *had* Boyce—and I don't think I could take two full weeks of watching Cricket flick her eyelashes at you."

"Darling, I thought you'd told me you weren't going to be jealous any more."

Nira flushed.

"I'm not. I just don't like her or her attitude to men and the way she behaves to other women's husbands. I can think of lots of other couples I'd rather we went away with. I made a bad mistake in ever thinking otherwise."

Des took off his dark glasses and put a tentative finger up to the sticking plaster. It was pretty obvious that Boyce had offended Nira, and he, Des, had decided to cut loose from Cricket; okay, but how were they going to get out of their commitments, when they were all supposed to go to Majorca together?

"Everything's booked, Nira darling," he reminded her.

"It can be cancelled. Anyhow, *they* can go if they still want to."

"What about Rob?"

"I'll be sorry about Rob, and he'll be disappointed but he'll understand."

The throbbing pain over Des's eyes added to a strong urge to get back to bed and sleep for another few hours began to make him feel irritable—despite his desire to placate his wife and get back on normal terms with her.

"I honestly don't see how you are going to explain it away. Rob will imagine all kinds of odd things. We don't want to start any sort of scandal."

Nira bit her lip.

"Of course it will be awkward. Can't we just say we've had a change of heart about our holiday and don't really want to go with Boyce and Cricket? That we don't want a communal holiday? Lots of things I could say. Rob doesn't like the Hallings anyhow, so he will sympathise, and I'll make it plain that it's best to cancel the plans," she ended rather sadly, thinking of Rob.

"Well, of course, as long as he doesn't get the wrong impression and think I am worried about you and Boyce—"

"Don't be funny!" Nira interrupted Des with a short laugh.

She was beginning to be impatient with her husband. Why didn't he see for himself that in the present circumstances it would be far too difficult for them all to go on holiday together—especially living in such close quarters, in the same hotel. As for what he had just said about Boyce and herself—her cheeks burned and she gave Des a reproachful look.

"Really! Why should Rob think there has been anything unusual between Boyce and me? Surely the boot is on the other foot. Quite a lot of people have probably seen you and Cricket dancing cheek to cheek in the Club and—and—all that," she finished lamely. Des quickly picked up the cudgels.

"My dear sweet Nira, when do people think the worst because they see a couple dancing cheek to cheek? You're being antediluvian."

"Well, anyhow," said Nira, "I refuse to have this crisis blamed on anything that has been going on between Boyce and myself because nothing *has*—as well you know."

"Don't you admit that he has got a thing about you?"

She waved a hand.

"Okay—so he has, but it is not serious and I don't take any notice—as you know."

"Well, I don't take much notice of Cricket," said Des blandly and pulled a packet of cigarettes out of his pocket.

"You're smoking too much," said Nira mechanically.

"And you're nagging."

She stared behind the bar at the shining glass case of lobsters—pink and inviting, on a nest of green salad. The little glow of happiness that had been warming her heart since her reconciliation with Des was rapidly fading. She looked around the attractive room. It was full of people. She always liked The Rifleman; the charming décor, yellow-buttoned sofas; the gay painting of a Victorian Rifleman in action; and the excellent cold buffet. This was one of their favourite places. But today it had lost all charm for Nira and the big handsome man beside her with his bruised face and cut eyebrow did not seem like her adored husband. He was a stranger and they were quarrelling again.

She didn't want to talk about the holiday any more. She slid off the stool and said, "Let's go."

Des paid the bill. They walked out to their car. The sun was shining. Several people were sitting at the little tables on the terrace. Taped music provided a suitable background and added to the clinking of glasses, gay voices and laughter. But Nira had seldom felt more depressed.

Neither one of them spoke until they had passed through the village of Warninglid and were well on the way back to Ponders Heath. Then Des pulled up the car, opened the door and got out.

"Drive the rest of the way, will you?" he asked. "I can hardly see out of my one good eye."

"I'm sorry," she said, and took his place.

For the rest of the way home Des folded his arms over his chest and stared gloomily ahead. He didn't much like this state of affairs. Her cool unfriendly attitude quite alarmed him. He was too used to her being the starry-eyed, tender-hearted girl who liked to say yes to everything he wanted. He supposed that he had only himself to blame, but he was going to stick to his role of injured innocence. He decided that he had a grudge against Nira.

"I don't know what all this bickering is about," he said, "but I wouldn't have bothered to get up and take you out to lunch if I'd thought you were going to start picking on me. Besides, you told me categorically that you had nothing against me and that you had been silly. Honestly, Nira, I don't think you are behaving very prettily."

She kept her eye on the road. Her lips were set and there was an expression on her face he had seen before—a stubborn look. Of course, Des reflected, he had always known his wife could be stubborn when she chose. He hated being criticised or frustrated. Damn it, Nira needed shaking sometimes. She was oddly old-fashioned in many ways—too set in her ideas.

They'd been happy and got on very well all these years but of course he reminded himself, she'd never had occasion to suspect him of infidelity. She'd only jokingly accused him of being a bit too keen on some girl or other. But up till now he hadn't felt such a strong craving for new excitement as he had experienced lately. Marriage was a trap, he told himself crossly. Men were different from women. They didn't always want to be pinned down to one woman, and most of them—most of the fellows he knew, anyhow—let their fancy stray now and again. He had better take a strong line with Nira or she'd take a new line with him and try to become the boss of the house, want to organise his whole life. That was something he wouldn't tolerate, even from her. Apart from her beauty, her sweetness, one of the reasons why he had been so fond of her in the past was because she seemed so pliant—easily taken in by him—so affectionate! He wouldn't enjoy married life if she started being a difficult wife.

He half decided to put her in coventry once they got home. Perhaps if he didn't speak to her for an hour or two, she would come to heel. And all he really wanted anyhow, was to be allowed to go back to bed and sleep.

As they reached their home they saw Rob. He was

standing beside his car which was parked in front of Nylands. What the hell was *he* doing here at this hour of the day, Des wondered fretfully.

Nira pulled up.

"Did you ask your boy-friend round?" Des growled in her ear. "If so you can send him away because I'm not in the mood for visitors, my dear."

Nira's colour rose.

"He's not my boy-friend," she whispered fiercely, "and I *didn't* invite him. And I'm not going to be rude to him now, even for you."

"Charming!" muttered Des.

Nira felt quite distraught. She was totally unused to such an atmosphere between her husband and herself. It destroyed her self-confidence. She didn't know who was in the wrong now—or how she was going to explain to Rob about cancelling the Majorcan holiday.

Before she could say anything, Rob walked up to them smiling. The very sight of his nice friendly face and those extremely kind eyes behind the tinted glasses warmed her heart. Her spirits rose a little.

"Oh, hello!" she said with a faint smile. "Have you been ringing the bell? Sorry we were out, Rob."

"No, I've only just got here," he said, and looked at Des who was edging himself stiffly out of the car. Des felt that his whole body hurt after last night's episode. He was in a poor temper. But he, too, tried to force a smile.

"Hi, Rob! Sorry we weren't at home."

"I didn't expect *you* to be," said Rob. "Is the commuter taking a day off?"

"No, I've had an accident," said Des briefly.

Rob now noticed the sticking plaster, the bruises, the limp and Desmond's generally poor condition. Quite unlike his usual hearty self.

Before Rob could sympathise, Nira said, "Do come in, please."

"No. I actually only came to ask if you had a brochure about that Majorcan hotel we are going to. Aunt Ida wanted to see one."

"Is she thinking of coming with us, too?" Des asked with an icy smile.

Nira felt that she was going to drop through the road. How *could* he? But Rob only laughed—charming and easy as ever.

"That I doubt. She wouldn't get much farther than the front door. The old lady never goes out, but she likes to see what's doing and where I'm going, and that sort of thing. But please don't worry about the brochure now. Any time will do."

"Well, I'm off to my bed. I'm not feeling so good," Des said. "Nira will look after you, Rob. Excuse me."

Rob and Nira were left alone on the pavement. Rob was now aware that something was very wrong. There was a distinct atmosphere between husband and wife. He said, "I've come at the wrong moment, do forgive me, Nira. Any time will do about the brochure, really."

But Nira had other ideas. She thought that this would be as good a time as any to try and tell Rob that their plans for the summer holiday must be cancelled.

"Please do come in, Rob. It's past three. I'll be making a cup of tea in a second. Des and I've just come back from The Rifleman. You've been there, haven't you? It's such good food."

She started to lead the way to the front door. Rob followed but with some reluctance.

"I don't want to intrude. I can come back any time and—"

"No, please come in. As Des said—he's going to lie down. He had an accident in town last night."

Rob said no more but he wondered very much what this was all about. He didn't remember ever having seen his lovely Nira look so grim.

"Go out in the garden and sit down by the pond," she added, "I'll join you in a moment."

Familiar with the house, Rob walked into the small study at the back and through the french windows into the small but attractive walled garden which Nira adored. She was only an amateur gardener and hadn't much time, busy as she was with her household chores and family, but she managed to produce some beautiful roses.

The sun was warm after the rainfall. The long bed beside the goldfish pool was brilliant with early roses. Rob stood looking down at the little golden fish darting in and out through the stones and green weeds in the cloudy water. As he knew, these fish were the children's pride and joy. Desmond had made the pool for them. He could be quite a useful chap when in the mood. Rob knew that too. What was happening between those two? She looked so pale, so strained.

When she joined him a minute later she had a cigarette between her fingers and she smiled. But he didn't think it was an easy smile.

He pulled up a canvas chair for her.

"Shall we sit?"

"Yes," she said, and looked down at the goldfish. They were coming up to the surface, mouths gaping, looking for food. She had forgotten to feed them this morning.

She felt so heavy-hearted and embarrassed about what she had to say to Rob, she didn't know how to begin. She fed the goldfish.

Once back with Rob, they both lit their cigarettes and she began to talk. He sat silent, listening. She stumbled over her first few words. "I—I don't know what— what you'll think—I'm so sorry—s-something has happened. I've got to ask you to cancel going to Majorca with us."

He looked at her. She was flushed and obviously disturbed. Just how bitterly disappointed he was, he had no intention of telling her, but he had begun to look forward very much—too much—to the prospect of a fortnight in Majorca with the Curtis family and particularly to being with *her*. Aunt Ida, only last night, had remarked that she hadn't for years seen him so keen on taking a holiday. Now *this* blow!

"What's happened, Nira?" he asked. His quiet voice gave her confidence, as it always did.

"Well, you know we were going with the Hallings?"

"Yes."

"Well, I—Des—there's been a sort of row with Cricket—I can't really explain—I mean we all still talk and that sort of thing but I—Des and I have decided we don't want to go away with them. They may go—if you'd like to join them, please don't feel—"

Rob interrupted. "I wouldn't dream of it. I assure you I was only going so as to be with you and Desmond."

"That's nice of you, but—"

"No buts. I'll just fade out—as you've done. After all I only booked my ticket over the phone and I can ring up and cancel it, as soon as I get home."

She did not look at him but stared at the water blindly, watching the little goldfish darting through the green plants. Her heart was heavy.

"It's all rather stupid, I suppose. I'm sorry, Rob."

"Don't keep apologising."

"But I am sorry—honestly."

"So am I, but it isn't the end of the world. Perhaps you'll fix another holiday one day and let me come with you."

Now she turned her earnest eyes—eyes that he always found so honest and beautiful—towards him.

"Of course. *Of course.* I'll look forward to it. There'll be another time."

He did not ask what had actually happened with the Hallings. He didn't really want to know. But he had a shrewd idea it was something to do with that fellow, Boyce. He also felt there was some mystery here, too. What about that accident to Des? He had looked pretty ghastly. And he had been all but rude—not as usual, charming, hail-fellow-well-met. When Rob looked at Nira again he felt dismayed. Her eyes were full of tears.

"What is it, my dear? Is it anything very wrong? Can I help?"

She would have given anything to unburden herself—to tell him the whole story of Boyce and Cricket, and all about Des's extraordinary behaviour, to say nothing of her own ugly suspicions. She couldn't get the words out. Loyalty to Des would not allow it. The worst of it was that she wasn't sure about *anything*. It was just all so unpleasant and depressing and it *might* be muddled thinking.

Her own tears horrified her. Hurriedly she got up and moved away from Rob under pretence of pulling some leaves out of the pond with the shrimping net which the children used to keep the water clear.

Rob also rose. He threw away a half-smoked cigarette and with hands in his pockets looked through his glasses at Nira's tall graceful figure. He had never thought her quite as vulnerable as this. Her tear-filled eyes upset him. Never a man of great conceit, he thought it better he should make an exit from the scene. If anything was wrong between Nira and Des they wouldn't want him hanging around. Des had, in fact, made that plain.

"I ought really to get home, Nira," he said, "and the sooner I make the hotel cancellation the better."

She didn't want him to go. More than ever before she needed the warmth and support of his friendship, but she said nothing. Only when they reached the front door she tried to be flippant. "Fine thing—inviting a friend to spend a holiday with you—then when he comes for the details about the place to be told we aren't going away."

Rob fully realised that the flippancy was a façade—she was nearer tears than smiles. He took his cue from her.

"It's the end of our friendship, madam," he announced.

Now she put both hands on his shoulders and looked up at him with an expression of tenderness which he found unbelievably thrilling.

"Don't you ever dare end it. I would hate to lose it. Goodbye, dear Rob, for the moment. See you!"

She walked slowly back into the house. She thought, *He never tried to get anything out of me. He just accepted what I said about cancelling the holiday and not a reproach. He really is a sweet man. Oh, damn, damn, why did Des have to muck it all up.*

But in a flash she realised that it wasn't only Des who

had mucked up the holiday. It was she herself who had told him she wouldn't go away with the Hallings.

Had she made a mistake? Was it all a storm in a teacup?

As she stood in the hall, ruminating, the bell rang.

She opened the front door. The last person in the world she wanted to see stood there—*Cricket*. Cricket looking a little less attractive than usual. Her pretty face, despite the make-up, was pale and puffy. She hadn't taken much trouble with her clothes. As a rule she was so carefully dressed and made-up. The blue trouser-suit today was crumpled. The silver-blonde hair untidy in need of setting. And she gave Nira a sullen look after the first "hello", and there was an ugly twist to her lips.

Nira froze.

"Come in," she said and stepped back, holding the door wide open.

Cricket walked in and followed Nira into the lounge.

Chapter 8

"HAVE I COME at an inconvenient time?" asked Cricket.

Nira avoided answering that question. Out of politeness she offered Cricket a cigarette, which was accepted. Both girls lit up and then Nira asked her uninvited guest to sit down. Cricket looked round rather nervously, Nira thought. She said, in her high, flute-like voice, "I was away for the night last night, you know."

"I do know. Boyce told me on the phone."

"Yes, he said he had phoned you and wanted to come round for a chat last night but you had someone else here. Was Des away?"

Nira thought, *She's been too clever. She knows per-*

fectly well that Des was away. Boyce must have told her by now.

"I came round to talk about our holiday." Cricket added the words somewhat lamely. She was wondering why Nira was being so stiff and unfriendly.

Nira said, "Des is upstairs in bed. He spent the night in a hospital. He had an accident."

Now Cricket, who wasn't really being clever about the whole affair, gave herself away before she could exercise restraint.

"An *accident*? But how? He was perfectly all right when he left me——" She broke off, her face suddenly scarlet and her long lashes fluttering. She took one or two deep breaths. Nira felt her heart go right down.

"When I last saw him, I mean," Cricket added, stuttering.

"You were together last night, weren't you?"

"No, of course not. I mean——what an idea——" Cricket laughed hysterically.

"Then tell me just *when* you thought him perfectly all right," Nira said, feeling merciless because she was now convinced she had been deceived by her husband and this woman. "When you said good night to him, I suppose. You'd both had too much champagne, of course."

Cricket sprang to her feet. She was white and there was a sick look in her large blue eyes, but she made a desperate struggle to right her mistake.

"I really don't know what you're talking about, Nira. I mean I thought he looked all right when I *last* saw him down here."

"That was some time ago, surely. Anyhow, what bearing does it have on the accident last night? Do let's be honest with each other. Des was drunk and fell down. He hurt his face and leg and cut an eyebrow and had to be taken to hospital, on his way back from a party—*a party with you*. Maybe Boyce isn't interested in what you do, but I am frightfully interested in what my husband does."

Cricket began to shake. The ash fell from her cigarette on to the carpet.

Nira, the tidy housewife, stooped automatically to brush it away.

"You were with him at Morris's flat, weren't you?" was her next question and she looked at Cricket with hard eyes. All the softness, the friendly sweetness, had gone right out of them.

Cricket suddenly began to realise that she had a formidable enemy in Des's wife. She hadn't expected to be found out—certainly never imagined Nira would hit on the truth like this. She could see it was her own fault. She really had made a frightful gaffe just now. She wished she hadn't come to see Nira. She wished she hadn't spent those hectic passionate hours with Des last night. She didn't want trouble. She didn't want to be so involved. She liked to be gay and happy—not worried. In this moment she felt horribly nervous. She didn't know how even Boyce, who was so permissive, would react to this.

She made a last desperate effort to allay Nira's suspicions.

"Of course I wasn't at Morris's flat—whoever Morris is. I stayed with my aunt."

"But I happen to know, because Boyce told me, that you'd been out at a party. Des was at a champagne party too."

"What are you trying to say—make out that Des and I are having a secret sordid sort of love affair?" asked Cricket and burst into tears. She covered her face with her hands and sobbed childishly. "I didn't know you could be so beastly—so suspicious. I think you're awful! I shall tell Boyce that I don't want to go away with you and Des if that's the sort of thing you're going to cook up about us."

Nira felt sick. She knew perfectly well now that Cricket and Des had been together last night. If Cricket wasn't guilty, why should she be crying and seem so scared. Besides, that half-finished sentence—*"An accident? But how? He was perfectly all right when he left me—"* And she had broken off. She couldn't go on, of course. She had been shocked to hear that Des had spent the night in a hospital—shocked into betraying herself—and him.

At this crucial point the door-bell rang. Nira was half tempted to leave it unanswered but now somebody tapped on the window and to her dismay she saw her mother-in-law standing outside. Gandy—neat, smart as ever, pale-blue dress and jacket, with a blue chiffon scarf tied over her waved white hair. Gandy never did have a hair out of place and always looked as though she had come straight from the beauty parlour; so well made up—and so young-looking for her age.

She was the last person on earth Nira wanted here now. But there was nothing for her to do but open the door. Gandy had waved a gay white glove at her. Nira gave a swift glance at Cricket whose face was still hidden in her hands.

"I've got to let my mother-in-law in. Perhaps you'd like to escape into the dining-room or go up to the children's bedroom. Susan isn't in. She's meeting them at school. You can be alone and put on some make-up and so forth—then slip out of the house."

Cricket sprang to her feet. She raised a very smudged, tear-wet face to Nira who felt not the slightest compassion for her. If Cricket was miserable she had no one but herself to blame.

"I'll hide in the dining-room, and dash off home without your guest knowing," Cricket said in a thick whisper.

"I don't suppose my mother-in-law will stay long if there's anything more you want to say to me."

"No, I don't, but I shall tell Boyce as soon as he gets back and he'll deal with your awful accusation—" Cricket gulped out the words then vanished.

Nira felt herself trembling as she opened the door to her mother-in-law. Mrs. Curtis came in, bringing with her as usual a delicious odour of the fresh lemon-scented toilet water she used.

"Can I come in?" (She was already in the drawing-room by now.) "I thought I'd drive over and see you as it's such a nice afternoon. Can I have tea with you and the children? Ought I to have let you know?"

Nira dutifully kissed the pale powdered cheek presented to her and assured her mother-in-law that she was delighted to see her. She wanted to tell her to go away and of course she couldn't. She mustn't risk her finding out that her son was upstairs, because she would insist on rushing up to see him. His bruised puffy face would both shock and alarm her. Besides, Gandy, of all people mustn't guess that anything was wrong between 'her young' as she called her son and his wife.

Nira made a desperate mental note that Susan should be back with Jonathan and Renira quite soon. She must act swiftly and suggest they all go out in the car. There was a pleasant little café not far from here where they could have tea. They would have a better one at home but the children would enjoy the change. The main thing was to get everyone out of this house. She would rush upstairs now to warn Des to keep out of the way.

Perforce she talked to Gandy for a moment. She only half heard all that the older woman had to say about the marvellous bridge she had been playing lately and how she had won a tournament with her friend, Lady Ansty, who had a flat near hers; yes, she, Gandy had won six no-trumps doubled and vulnerable, and on *two* occasions; fabulous bridge! Never stopping, she chattered on; then out from the brocade bag she carried, came a little box of sweets for each of the children, and one of bitter chocolate mints for Nira and Des who liked them.

She was a good, generous-hearted woman really, and never failed to bring little presents, but oh, thought Nira, what a moment to choose and how desperately boring it was to have to sit and listen to Gandy while her thoughts kept wandering first to Cricket (whom she hoped by now had made her exit), then to the room above where Des, she *hoped,* was still sound asleep.

After a moment she could no longer contain her impatience and with the excuse that Susan would be in any moment and she wanted to slip upstairs, Nira left Gandy to smoke her cigarette and wander around the room. She was an inquisitive woman and adored to quiz as she called it.

"Where did you buy this?" she'd ask, or *"Did I give*

you that?" or *"Oh, I wish I'd found a bargain like that!"* . . .

To Nira's relief, Cricket had left the house—as suggested. Nira found her husband sitting up in bed, wide awake. The face he turned to her was woeful; one eye almost closed. She would have been sorry for him but for the fact that she knew beyond doubt that he was guilty.

She spoke to him in a cold voice, her long lashes fluttering with nervousness. "Your mother's come unexpectedly. She mustn't see you."

"Why not?" began Des gruffly, "I could do with a little motherly love and attention. I'm not getting much from you."

She flashed a look of contempt at him.

"You know perfectly well you don't deserve it and I'm not going to stand by and hear you tell Gandy a lot of lies about your accident and how it happened because *you* know the truth and so do I now."

"What the hell do you mean—?" began Des more heatedly. He got out of bed and tried to look dignified, but failed. He was rather a sorry spectacle.

"I mean that just before Gandy turned up, Cricket—your dear little Cricket—paid me a visit. It's been quite a party. I only just managed to get *her* away in time, before Gandy saw her weeping."

Des felt suddenly very uncomfortable—in mind as well as body. He ruffled his thick chestnut hair and looked at Nira with alarm in his bloodshot eyes.

"What in the name of God was Cricket doing here?"

"She'd come back from town to take Simon to the dentist and thought she'd pop in here to have a nice chat with me about our holiday."

"So what?"

"She said just one or two things too many and confirmed my belief that the champagne party you had last night was with *her*. You were both at Morris's flat, weren't you, Des? And I won't believe you if you start telling me all you were doing was to make plans to join the Salvation Army."

Des looked at his wife aghast. He had never heard

her speak to him with such bitter sarcasm. God, he thought, what a mess he had made of things. Yet how could Nira be sure of her facts? *What had Cricket said?* When he started to bluster and assure Nira of his innocence, she cut him short.

"I've no time to talk now. All I ask is that you keep upstairs in this room. Lock your door—just in case Gandy comes up for any reason at all. Don't make a sound. You'll hear us drive off in the car. We're going to the Ponders Café for tea. I'm going to make an excuse not to offer your mother tea here, at home."

Before he could answer Nira was gone.

Susan's arrival with the two children made things a bit easier. In a high bright voice Nira informed all of them that she was about to treat Renira and Jonny to tea with Gandy at their favourite teashop.

Gandy seemed a little put out. She'd wanted to stay in the house but the children were unconsciously helpful to Nira. They seized their grandmother by the hand and began to scream their delight.

"I want one of those scrummy chocolate biscuits."

"I want the orange cake we had last time."

Nira bustled them out into the car and almost sobbed with relief once the front door closed behind them. Before leaving the house she had rushed into the kitchen to tell Susan to take some tea up to Mr. Curtis. She made up some story about his having been in an accident and didn't want his mother to know.

Susan, a placid, capable sort of girl, asked no questions but did as she was told.

Driving to the teashop, Nira asked herself bitterly why she had bothered about Des's tea—after all the misery he had caused her. Her head throbbed and her heart ached. She was nearer to tears than to smiles. She felt positively crushed. One thing she was thankful for during the tea party—she didn't have to exert herself to talk too much to Gandy because the children monopolised the conversation and soon afterwards Gandy said she must go back to Brighton. She never liked to stay out long.

As she kissed Nira goodbye, Mrs. Curtis suddenly

forgot her egotistical little self and noted that the tall, slim, beautiful girl who was her son's wife, looked unusually white and—now she came to think of it—Nira had been very silent—even odd—during tea.

"Aren't you well, dear?" she asked.

"Fine, thanks, Gandy."

"Nothing wrong?"

"Why should there be?" Nira gave a high-pitched laugh.

"You just don't look yourself, dear."

After Gandy had gone, Nira remembered those words and thought, *And I'm not myself. I'm a stranger and Des is a stranger. We aren't the same two people who loved each other so much and were so close. It's as though we'd both died and now we're in another awful world—a sort of hell—hating each other.*

Somehow Nira managed to get through the next hour, dutifully entertaining the children who always expected her to play with them before bedtime. Then she pleaded a headache and told them to let Susan give them their baths. She'd kiss them good night later on.

Heavy-hearted, with lagging footsteps, Nira then walked to her bedroom door and called out to Des.

He unlocked the door and returned to the little Victorian brocaded seat which stood under the window, where he had been sitting, smoking. Nira noted that he had finished the tea but left the cake Susan had brought up to him.

He stubbed his cigarette end in an ashtray, spread his legs out, put his hands in his pockets and glared at her. It was that glare that made her feel quite sick.

"Well, I hope you're pleased with yourself," he said. "You've mucked up everything properly, haven't you, with your idiotic suspicions."

Nira leaned her back against the door. Her eyes were as hard as his.

"Don't speak to me like that, Des. *I'm* not the one who's mucked things up."

"You made up that nonsense that Cricket said something to make you believe we'd been together last night."

"No—I caught her out. When I told her about your accident she said you were perfectly well when you left her. She was so shocked to learn that you'd had this accident, she just gave herself away. Then she tried to put it right and couldn't."

Now Des's bruised face flamed with anger—anger which was a part of guilt—of resentment because he had been found out. He spoke violently. "Since you want the truth you'd better hear it. I wouldn't have lied only I knew you'd be so bloody jealous. That's why I kept denying the truth, for your sake—to save *you*, my dear!"

Nira broke out into a cold sweat. She sat down on the edge of the bed. She thought she really was going to be sick, any moment. Her knees shook.

"My God, what a hero you are! What a noble motive for telling all those lies. Am I supposed to put a laurel wreath around your handsome head?"

"Oh, shut up."

"I want the truth and nothing but," she said, breathing noisily. "And as for my jealousy—I don't think it's altogether a question of that. A woman surely has a right to expect her husband to be faithful to her, hasn't she?"

"Aren't you exaggerating? Who said I'd been unfaithful? Cricket and I had dinner together."

"*And* went back to Morris's flat," Nira added.

"Okay. Okay. And we cracked a bottle of champagne."

"You cracked more than that. You've cracked up our marriage and done something absolutely awful to me!" she said hotly and began to cry.

He stared at her—his anger fading. He was right up to the neck now and he knew it. He didn't want this thing to go any further. He never had meant Nira to know about Cricket and he had certainly never had the slightest intention of cracking up their marriage. Never! But somehow her indignation and anger had infuriated him—made him beastly to her.

"You really are behind the times, my dear girl," he blustered. "Whatever you think happened in that flat—

even if we indulged in a bit of necking—what's the crime?"

"Were you just necking?" Nira repeated the word with an hysterical laugh. "I've never heard it called that before."

"Oh, for God's sake, let up. You seem to *want* to make the most of it."

She looked at him without understanding. "And you, I suppose, have done nothing wrong in your own opinion. You are *entitled* to lie and deceive me and make love to Cricket."

He scowled. "I'm sorry, Nira. I didn't want it to happen, honestly. It was just one of those things."

Nira was trembling from head to foot now. She dug her long fingers into the side of the bed.

"Are you going to try and make me believe it wasn't prearranged, that you and Cricket only met in town by accident? All the old stuff about staying late at the office, too."

He shifted from one foot to the other, uneasily. "What's the good of all these recriminations? You're my wife. You are supposed to love me and where there's love surely there's forgiveness," he said grandly.

Nira almost bit through her lip. She didn't know whether to laugh or to cry. When she had said that he had cracked up their marriage she had meant it. There was a great big fissure through the mountain of content and happiness—the joy she had known before last night. The memory of Cricket's pretty, vicious face and that kitten-quality that made her so treacherous and unattractive in Nira's sight, damped her spirits.

Des said, "You don't *want* to forgive me. Is that it? Perhaps you're not so fond of me after all? I always imagined you were full of high principles. You used to talk so much about fidelity and romantic love. Have *you* always been faithful to me? I'm beginning to wonder. What about that evening you spent with Rob—alone in this house except for the kids. Or are you going to go on telling me you're just good friends?"

Nira gasped. Her breath quickened. She looked at him with positive loathing.

"You dare say a thing like that; about Rob and *me?* You know perfectly well there's nothing like that between us and never has been. Nor have I had an affair with any other man. *You know it.* It's the most awful thing for you to suggest. You're absolutely contemptible."

Des cooled down. He realised he was playing a dangerous game. He didn't want to lose Nira. He seated himself on the bed beside her, picked up one of her hands and held on to it tightly, despite her efforts to drag it away. When he tried to kiss her she drew back. But he was all penitence now.

He said, "Oh, God, we mustn't go on like this, Nirry. It's crazy. Nira darling, darling Nira, I'm so terribly sorry. I was mad—drunk. I don't love Cricket. I swear I don't. She excites me but I don't love her. I love only you and our children."

At that moment there was no comfort for her in these words. She wrenched her fingers from his and covered her face with both hands.

"So you want to love me, and make love to her too. Well—you can't, and that's that," she said and the tears streamed down her face.

He was suddenly genuinely ashamed of himself. To see his beautiful Nira like this and because of him, stabbed his heart—Des had a heart although it was of the spongy kind. You could depress it but it bounced up again. Nothing much made a lasting impression. He had in fact been quite proud of the fact that for at least ten years of their marriage he had been more or less faithful to his wife. But there were times—such as now, when he really didn't think she should be quite so conventional. Of course he realised that he was more tolerant about his own sexual behaviour than he would be of *hers*. He wouldn't want her to be like Cricket, or even like Maggie Wilson who was pretty responsive—as well he knew. Perhaps he himself was being old-fashioned in thinking that there should be one law for the man, and another for the woman, and that a good wife should be good (so long as she was sexually appealing and sensually attractive to him) which Nira had always been

when it came to their intimate life. But hell! he didn't
want her to become too smug, either. He felt worried
and uncertain of his own feelings.

He took her hand and pressed it against his closed
eyes, flinching as he did so because the cut over his eyebrow hurt.

"Oh, darling, my darling, you're wrong. I certainly
don't want you *and* Cricket—only you. Last night was a
moment's folly. I swear it. For God's sake be your generous self and forget it. Wipe it right out of your memory."

For a moment she said nothing but sat motionless,
her face drawn with the pain of her thoughts. But for
the first time that day she began to feel a little better—a
little less anguished. She had despised Des for what he
had done to her glorious faith and love. Now the focus
was on herself. Perhaps she was being ungenerous—and
as far as Des's affair was concerned she was ready to
believe it *was* the first time. She was sure of that. She
must try to remember that if you loved a person you
didn't just wipe them out of existence because of one
lapse.

Soon she turned to him, melting, utterly feminine,
tender, jealous, reproachful yet still his woman, in love
with him. All the passionate moments they had known
together couldn't possibly be forgotten. Supposing this
thing had happened to her? Supposing *she* had had an
irresistible desire to make love to another man—she,
too, might have given way then regretted it bitterly and
hoped to be forgiven. She couldn't really imagine herself wanting any man but Des, but she felt that she
would be pompous, vain—even stupid—to suppose that
she never could surrender to the same sort of folly that
had led Des into such a situation. And, truly feminine
again, all her hatred and contempt became centred
upon the woman who had tempted him.

"You didn't mean to hurt me—I know you didn't!"
she broke out and sobbed the words, "You love me.
You don't love her. It's her fault. That's true. It *is* true,
isn't it, Des?"

"Absolutely true!" he said with an intensity that re-
assured her still further. "And it will never happen
again, my darling."

"I blame Cricket," she said with passion, and drew a
long slender hand across her nostrils, then got up to
find a tissue and blow her nose. Soon she calmed down
again and tried to be natural and laugh—crazily anxious to put things right. She belonged to Des and he to
her—she must wipe Cricket out of the picture. She
couldn't live with her husband in such a state of hostil-
ity. And she couldn't live without him. So she broke out
in denunciation of the other woman. "Cricket's a little
bitch. I hate her. I'll never, *never* willingly speak to her
again."

God, thought Des, *how do we get out of this? What'll
Boyce think? An open row between Nira and Cricket
will bring him round here in the role of injured husband, unless we're careful. But was that true?* Boyce
seemed not to mind what Cricket did or how she behaved. She had told him. It was only because of Nira
they had been so careful. They hadn't succeeded very
well. Damn Cricket for her stupidity!

He didn't think this was the time to talk too much
about Cricket. The position was much too delicate.
Above all he mustn't let Nira think he was in the least
anxious to continue seeing his girl-friend. He wasn't.
He'd had such a shock these last few hours that quite
frankly he had lost all desire for fun and games. Nira
was right. Cricket wasn't worth the loss of Nira and the
kids.

He took Nira into his arms and went through all the
old familiar motions of caressing her. He smoothed her
hair back from that lovely brow that was ordinarily so
serene; kissed her eyelids, drinking in her tears, repeating again and again that he was hellishly sorry he had
hurt her—he hadn't meant to do it. And then he tried
to lessen the blow he had given her by telling her that
although he and Cricket *had* spent a few hours together
in that flat—it hadn't really gone as far as Nira might
imagine.

But after returning his kisses and swearing that she would forgive and forget and give him another chance, she refused to accept any more lies from Des.

"Oh, don't try and make light of it! I'm not a fool, Des. Of course you—you and that little beast—oh, *God*!" She broke off, her tear-stained face flaming, pulled herself out of his arms, and clenched and unclenched her hands. He knew she was still tormented by jealousy.

He spent the next half-hour trying to convince her that she need have no such feelings and that this was only a nightmare—she would soon wake up and could feel that she was the only person in the world he really loved. *And* he was going to be a good boy for ever more—he swore it.

She listened and accepted the protests and promises and said little. But the one thing she didn't want to be was bitter. Having forgiven him she mustn't hold the affair against him. She mentioned the children.

"For their sake you wouldn't want to break up our home, would you?"

"Good lord no, nothing further from my mind. You know what a lot I think of them."

Nira gave a long sigh, walked to her dressing-table, sat down and started to repair her face. She dabbed cooling lotion on eyes that were pink and puffy with weeping. Funny, she thought, oh so funny that a man could love his wife and children (and she knew that Des did) yet find it so easy to go to bed with another woman. And he wasn't the only one. There were others—others in this town she and Des knew about. She'd always pitied the wives. Well, she didn't intend to join those who were in need of such pity. She tried to concentrate entirely on the thought of Renira and Jonathan.

"We must neither of us ever hurt those two. One's got to set an example. The world's in a pretty rotten state at the moment, Des. If we don't want our kids to grow up thinking nothing of sleeping around and behaving all anyhow, we've got to watch what we do ourselves!"

He agreed heartily. But his mind was more on the fact that he needed a strong drink than on the moral welfare of his growing children. He made an effort to accept Nira's little lecture with a meekness which he didn't often show, and went so far as to say, "It's not that I need any woman but you. It's this bloody drink that's responsible for my stupid behaviour. I don't deny it. I'll cut out the alcohol. I'll never have another gin—you'll see."

Nira laughed, and tears stung her eyelids at the same time. She took his arm between her hands, laid her cheek against it and murmured, "Oh, Des, darling, you're so like a naughty schoolboy. Who would be cross with you for long? I bet you don't give up the gin. But do remember it's the champagne that's *your* undoing, every time."

"Then I'll never have another glass of champagne."

"Tell that to the Marines, darling."

She laughed and cried again. In a state of nerves and tension unusual for her, she had lost her normal self-control. It had been a terrible thing to her, Cricket and Des's treachery. Her deep dislike of Cricket intensified.

The next thing they had to do was to decide how best to dispense with the Hallings. Cricket, thought Nira, was not going to come into this house again if *she* could help it. She didn't care what other people thought, and as for Boyce, he had been pressing her far too hard with his attentions lately and she didn't want *him*.

However, Nira and Des avoided this issue for the moment. They went together to say good night to the children. Renira was growing very observant. Nira didn't want the little girl to see that she had been crying. She put on dark glasses and pretended that her eyes were sore and that the light hurt them. Susan went home. Renira and Jon settled down. Soon it was time for Nira to cook Des's evening meal.

He said he couldn't eat a thing but that he wanted something to drink—coffee maybe. Nira said he looked so grim, he'd better make it a stronger one. He reminded her that he'd promised to go on the wagon to please her and only meant that he wanted coffee or orange-juice. She said he needn't go as far as that if he didn't want to. Anyhow, why couldn't he be moderate about drinking? She thought it would probably do him good to have a Scotch. Also to try and eat the steak she had bought for him.

"It's a ghastly price now but I thought you would enjoy it, so I was extravagant. You can't turn it down, darling."

He was hungry and gave in. Once supper was over, the subject of the Hallings and the cancellation of the holiday had to come up again, and about this they did not altogether agree.

"We all know each other at the golf club and it'll be so damned awkward if we have an open battle," Des said, although he looked at Nira anxiously because he did not want to upset her again. But she acceded in so far as she agreed that it was all very awkward *and* that they didn't want a scandal. But she wouldn't retract what she had said about not having Cricket in the house again. There was the business of Simon Halling which worried her, of course. Simon was Jonathan's best friend. That was more than awkward.

Des, feeling better now that he was back in favour and had both eaten and drunk, suggested cautiously that the boys should be allowed to carry on with their friendship and just the parents need not go on being so friendly. They could acknowledge each other at the Club—little matters of that kind, but no more dinners and bridge. And there was still the Majorcan bookings—plus Rob's holiday—to be considered.

"I've already told Rob that we're cancelling it," said Nira.

Des looked at her gloomily. She'd been a bit quick about it, he thought, but he supposed he couldn't blame her in the circumstances. Oh, the whole thing was hellishly embarrassing and he began to wish he'd never had that abortive affair with Cricket. It had spoiled everything.

Later that evening Rob's name was mentioned again.

"If we're not going to Majorca, I suppose we could

ask him to join us with the kids in Cornwall," Des said, wanting to be generous in the circumstances.

"Oh, he'd be delighted," said Nira, "but there's no necessity—he understands there's been some sort of crisis and is quite okay about it."

"Well, I'll leave it to you," Des said with more than his usual affability.

He was really anxious to get back on to the old good terms with his wife. Cricket and her luscious love-making had been all very well but the repercussions had been far too dangerous. A chap couldn't afford to make a muck of his whole married life just for the sake of a few hours in bed with a new and exciting woman. He must really take a hold on himself and not let it happen again. Nira was worth his consideration. She was a darling and it had hit him hard when she had turned on him. He'd had a ghastly fear that she might try to divorce him.

In the lounge, Nira switched on their colour television. She knew that there was a golf championship that Des particularly wanted to see, and she herself had no wish to enter into a lengthy conversation that might involve further recriminations and apologies—the wordy wreckage that a matrimonial storm so often washes up on the shore of two people's lives.

She closed her eyes to the golf match and thought about Rob and his immense kindliness. That sense of reliability he gave her. Integrity was a much-to-be admired virtue in any man, and growing more rare as time went on. Who, for instance, could depend on a man like Boyce, or several others she could name at the Club, although she tried hard to avoid putting her own husband into the category. Her feeling for Rob was strange—it almost amounted to a kind of childish hero-worship. Of him it could be said (as once indeed it had been said) of a great leader of the French Revolution: that he was *incorruptible*. She could imagine somehow that nothing could corrupt Rob. Yet there was nothing smug or sententious about him.

She knew he had been bitterly disappointed about the

holiday. He had looked forward to getting away from
Aunt Ida and life in The Hollies. Perhaps she would
take Des up on that offer to let Rob accompany them
on their holiday to Cornwall and so make up for his
disappointment over Formentor.

She felt herself to be in a rather queer mood tonight.
She still loved Des with all her heart, yet it was plain to
her that the tie which had once been so strong and complete between them, had in some way weakened.

He wanted to make love to her that night but she
rejected him—gently but firmly. She could not bear his
love-making while the slightest feeling of suspicion or
distrust existed. She must wait until she could get over
the whole thing.

She could be friendly with Des, and even tender, but
she could not measure his passion with hers. She even
fancied that he was relieved when she turned from him,
and was so soon asleep. After a moment she disengaged
herself from the arm which he had thrown across her,
and settled down on her own pillow. She found herself
thinking suddenly how much she would like Rob to be
with them on their Cornish holiday, even though they
had to wait till the end of July.

She loved Cornwall. She thought about it drowsily
before she slept. She had once discussed it with Rob.
He hadn't been there, but said he felt sure the awe-
inspiring splendour of the sea and the gigantic cliffs on
the north coast would appeal to him, as they did to her.

For Des, it had always been purely a parental duty to
swim in cold water, lie on the sands, or play cricket
with the children. He preferred their more sophisticated
exotic holidays abroad. But Nira loved her Cornish
coast as much as the children did. It would be nice if
Rob could come with them. She would try to arrange it
tomorrow.

Des was asleep—breathing noisily. Nira sighed and
shut her eyes. She felt very tired and most unusually
lonely.

Chapter 9

"I'D LOVE TO go down to Cornwall with you and the children if it can be arranged," Rob told Nira when she broached the subject of the family holiday at the Club the following day. "But I really feel I'd be gate-crashing—even more so than when I made a fivesome for Majorca. Des won't want me—just with his own family and—"

"He doesn't mind at all. *He* suggested it," interrupted Nira.

They were sitting in the sunshine on the veranda of the club house facing the first green. Des had insisted on going up to town. His eyebrow was healing and his limp less obvious, and they were short of staff at the office. Nira and Rob had arranged this game a week ago.

Rob was feeling good. What could be better than a fine morning in early summer and a game of golf with his adored Nira? But his feeling of pleasure began to evaporate as a definite change in her impressed itself upon him. He was sure something had happened to upset her—and badly. It puzzled him. She was nervy, unlike her usually tranquil self. She looked very pale, with dark smudges under the beautiful eyes.

He felt in the pocket of his suède waistcoat for a pipe.

"It's very decent of you both to offer to include me, and you know how fond I am of your young," he said.

"They are of you."

"What are your plans?"

"As a matter of fact," she said, "we aren't going to a

hotel in Mawgan Porth. We've booked rooms in a farm-house we know. It's a lovely little village."

"I've heard about it. They've got an airport there."

She nodded. "It's pretty crowded like all these holi-day resorts in the West, but much less so than places like Newquay. It still retains lots of its old charm. We were only going to have ten days but I am sure we can arrange to stay longer now that we are not going to Ma-jorca. Des will need a proper break from the City, and, of course, the children adore it. There are some lovely beaches around and the bathing can be super if we strike lucky with the weather. Trevarra Farm is an old stone-built house, owned by a retired couple—the Hos-kins—both very nice and she adores Renira and Jona-than. They don't farm any more but make quite a good bit of money in the summer letting rooms. The cook-ing's plain but quite decent. We've known the Hoskins for years. I'm quite sure they'll fix you up. She always keeps an extra room or two for her favorites. I'll phone her after six tonight. But you must remember it'll be just a children's holiday; nothing glamorous or as excit-ing as it might have been in Formentor."

"If you ask me," said Rob smiling his slow lazy smile, "I reckon I shall prefer Trevarra Farm to For-mentor, even if the kids don't get me into the icy water. After being so long in Kenya and the swimming out there, I'm spoilt for English sea-bathing. But I promise to play cricket with Jonathan."

Nira felt suddenly happier, less ill-at-ease. Grateful for this man's honesty and unfailing friendship. Nothing seemed to ruffle Rob. There were no awkward corners in him. *Dear* Rob! Not for the first time she thought what a fine husband he would have made. What a won-derful family man! It did seem a shame.

"Have you told the Hallings about Majorca yet?" he asked.

She bit her lip. She had not yet decided how best to deal with Boyce and Cricket. She said, "If Cricket turns up for golf I'll just tell her that the holiday's off and leave it at that. Maybe she'll understand," Nira added with a bitterness that was not lost on Rob.

"As we're such good friends, would it be impertinent of me to ask how this break has come about?" he asked gently.

The colour stained the creamy pallor of her face. She avoided his gaze. She was well aware that those kindly eyes had noticed that she was desperately worried.

She said, "Oh—it's something—rather personal. I—forgive me, Rob—I'd rather not discuss it."

Rob was sure now that the explanation for her present state of nerves lay with those two—Desmond and Cricket.

He'd bet his boots on it. He steered the conversation tactfully away from the subject and suggested that they fetched their clubs and started to play.

"I shall be awful today," Nira laughed. "Worse than usual. I've got a headache, so I'll slice every ball."

"I know what headaches are."

"Your kind must be worse than the one I've got today."

"Well, we'll play for a large sum of money so I'll win for a change."

She gave what he thought rather a hollow little laugh, but after playing for an hour in the fresh air and the sunshine, the delight of the game seemed to revive her spirits, and bring the sparkle back to her eyes.

He did beat her, but he was glad to see her relax, and whatever it was that had happened to upset her, it was obviously not troubling her too much just now. He rather hoped that Cricket Halling wouldn't come into the Club and distress her again.

A shock awaited them once they walked into the bar for a pre-lunch drink. Several of the members, drink in hand, were already there. Joyce Moffatt's voice, talking to Maggie Wilson and Colonel Moffatt could be heard above the rest.

"Isn't it *ghastly*! Poor wretched Boyce—he must be in a state."

No one could avoid hearing what Joyce said. Nira and Rob exchanged startled glances.

"What's happened?" Nira asked.

Those who were there, stopped talking and turned

and looked at Nira and Rob. Joyce was once more spokesman.

"These bloody car accidents," she said. "It happened at midnight, they say. I'd been expecting to see Cricket here. She was going to play a three-ball with Maggie and me and now we know why she didn't turn up."

"But what's happened?" demanded Nira. "Has Cricket had an accident?"

"Yes. It was on the early news. I suppose you missed it. She and Boyce were coming back from a party late last night and met a lorry at the corner of Sangster Road. You know that damned crossroads—I've always said there ought to be a sort of Give Way sign there."

Nira unzipped her jacket and threw it on the sofa. Her heart beating rapidly.

"What happened?" She turned to Maggie Wilson.

Maggie, like the others, looked pale and upset.

"The poor thing—she was driving. There was a lot on the radio about it—the ghastly tangle of wreckage and so on. The lorry driver was killed and they couldn't get poor little Cricket out for nearly an hour."

"Oh God," said Nira and sat down. Rob had drawn a stool close to her and helped her on it.

"Yes, she was driving," Maggie repeated, "and they say she was on the wrong side of the road. She was— she was—"

"Let's cut the details," put in Rob tersely. He could see that Nira was shivering. He understood her feelings. She and Cricket had quarrelled. She had been about to edge Cricket out of her life. But they had once been friendly and their two boys played together. Whatever had happened in the past must be forgotten now.

The next thing Nira did was to ask about Boyce. It appeared that he had come out of it miraculously unhurt except for minor cuts and bruises and a broken ankle. They were keeping him in hospital for twenty-four hours at least. Nira felt nothing but compassion.

"Poor, *poor* Boyce, what a hideous shock for him! And poor Cricket! So young to die like that."

It wasn't until much later when Rob was taking Nira home that he heard Nira voice a personal opinion that it may well have been after a champagne party that Cricket had driven so carelessly.

In due course this was expressed at the inquest. Boyce admitted that they had both exceeded the amount of alcohol a driver should permit himself. Because he had let Cricket drive, he felt doubly guilty. He made no effort to deny it.

As soon as they reached Nylands, Nira asked Rob to come in with her. They had meant to lunch at the Club but she couldn't stand all the crowd. They *would* keep harping back to the details of the accident and Cricket's death. Maggie had always been a dramatic sort of person. Her own husband had died in a car crash, so she revived *that* story and it all became too harrowing.

Rob stayed for a sandwich lunch with Nira, glad that he was there to look after her. She went straight to the telephone and got through to the local hospital. "I must speak to Boyce and see if I can do anything about Simon," she explained to Rob.

"Yes, of course, the poor little boy—grim for him."

He didn't hear the conversation between Nira and Boyce but she told him about it while she made the sandwiches. He watched her cutting the bread. He smoked his much-needed pipe. There were tears running down her cheeks.

"He seemed glad to talk to me," she said. "He's obviously suffering from shock as well as the broken ankle. Can't you imagine it? He keeps blaming himself for letting Cricket drive him back from that party. He says they had both had one or two over the odd but had been so near their home, they had somehow never dreamed they'd meet a lorry at that time of the morning and in Sangster Road of all places."

He also told Nira that he had no idea that Cricket had drunk quite so much. Much more than he had imagined. He went on and on, blaming himself. When Nira asked if she could do something about Simon, he said yes at once. He'd already phoned through to their daily who had been spending the night at their house which she often did when Mr. and Mrs. Halling were out late, so that Simon would not be alone. She was a nice woman and had children of her own and had been deeply shocked by the news. She had seen to it that Simon had had his breakfast and gone to school without letting him know why his parents had not come home last night.

"Let me help, too, if I can," put in Rob. "If the boy wants fetching, there's my car and I'm ready to do anything."

Nira threw him a grateful look. "I might keep you to that."

Boyce had told her that neither he nor Cricket had parents. His had been killed in an air raid during the war, and hers in a car crash, when Cricket was still at school.

"All these crashes," ended Nira. "God, Rob, it's a bit unnerving!"

"Agreed, but don't think about it too much if you can help it, darling."

The darling passed unnoticed. She went on telling him about Simon. "There's no one he can go and stay with, only some distant cousins and Boyce has a stepbrother in Kenya. He doesn't want Simon to go back to the house as there will be such an atmosphere there, bad for the child, with his mother dead and people ringing up, and flowers arriving and all the gruesome business—so I said he could come here. He adores Jonathan. Poor old Boyce has gone to pieces. He can't even face telling Simon about his mother—he wants me to."

Rob looked at her gravely. As she was about to lift the lunch tray from the table, he walked up to her and put an arm around her shoulders. He drew her close.

"You're all in, poor Nira. Just don't let that kind heart of yours run away with you. I know how you feel about helping Boyce out—but let me help *you*. I can fetch Simon from school. I'll even tell him about his mother, if you like. I'm rather good at talking to the young—so they tell me. I don't think I've ever mentioned it but I was a schoolteacher for a time after I left university. I didn't make a career of teaching but I did get on very well with the young ones. I think I'll know how to tackle the poor little chap."

Now Nira collapsed entirely. She put both arms around the tall man who was holding her and gave herself up to the blessed warmth and security of his embrace. Sobbing, she leaned her face against his shoulder, and between her sobs thanked him.

"You're such a dear, Rob, thank you awfully. No, I didn't know you'd ever been a schoolmaster but you're obviously just what Simon needs—a strong-minded understanding man. You'll be so much better for him than an emotional woman like myself."

Rob's pulses jerked as he felt the slim pliant body pressed against his own. He kissed her cheeks, brushing away the tears, knowing to his cost how desperately he loved her. To help her get through this crisis was vital. He was surprised to find how right she was, when she called herself an emotional woman. Of course he was an ignorant fool. She was highly-strung and vulnerable behind her cool façade. Hadn't she made it obvious what Des meant to her? He should have known.

He came dangerously close to kissing the beautiful mouth that was all too near his own, but realised that this was not the moment to swing from pity to passion. He pushed her hair back from her moist forehead, breathed in the odour of her hair, her scented skin, then gently released her from his arms. The sweat was breaking out on his own forehead now. He said, "That's settled, dear. You tell me what time to fetch Simon and exactly where his school is. I believe it's somewhere near the recreation park, isn't it? I've noticed the football-ground. Now come along and let's have that lunch and a stiff whisky and soda, too, if I might suggest it. I think we could both do with one."

At once Nira calmed down. Rob always had a soothing effect on her.

"I'm so sorry I'm behaving all anyhow. It would be wonderful if you'd collect Simon. Yes, do please tell him about his mother. Have a little talk with him, then bring him back here, by which time I'll have briefed Jonathan. They'll get together and have a game. In fact I'll go out and buy some new aircraft models. They both like doing those. Small boys are easily amused and thank God, at ten years old Simon can be managed more easily than if he were a couple of years older."

Rob agreed. Excusing herself, she went upstairs to fetch a clean handkerchief and make up her face, while he carried the tray through to the lounge.

During that meal Nira ate little. She hadn't the heart for it. She kept thinking about Cricket, broken and dying in her shattered car. What luck Boyce had had—if it could be called luck for a man to be left alive, knowing that he should never have allowed his wife to take the wheel.

Deliberately Rob avoided the subject of the crash. After lunch, he rang Simon's headmaster, who already knew the situation, and gave permission for him to fetch the boy whenever he chose.

Rob had a date with an old friend who was coming down to The Hollies for dinner, so he arranged to bring Simon back to Nira soon after five.

"You look all in—you really ought to have a rest before Simon comes, Nira," Rob said when she walked to the front door with him.

Nira was so unnerved that she burst into tears again. Unpopular though Cricket had been with Rob, he himself was upset enough. It was tragic that that pretty frivolous little creature had come to such a violent end. He could fully understand why Nira had lost her customary command of herself. Involuntarily he took her in his arms.

"Don't, darling, don't cry," he kept saying while he smoothed her hair and pressed her wet face against his shoulder.

"Oh, Rob," she sobbed, "Oh, *Rob*—poor little Simon—he adored his mother!"

"God knows why these things have to happen."

She clung to him for a moment, then remembered Des. *He* would have to be told. She wondered how it would affect him, but wondered it without bitterness or jealousy. She let Rob hold her and caress her in his tender way for a moment longer, then drew back and turned her face away.

"Do forgive me. I'm so sorry."

"'You know you needn't be formal with me, my love," he said.

His love—how curious that sounded, she thought, and how strangely it comforted her. Suddenly she went back to him, put her arms around his neck and kissed him on both cheeks.

"You are a darling, Rob. Thanks a thousand times. I don't know what I'd do without you—your friendship."

"And what would I do without yours." He smiled down at her.

At half-past five he brought Simon and Jonathan back together. Nira put her son into the picture and extracted a solemn promise from him to be particularly nice to Simon. Jonathan being a kindhearted boy, said that he would do his best and that he was "jolly pleased Simon could stay and sleep in the same room". It would be fun.

"It's tough for Simon losing his mother, isn't it, Mum?" he added.

"Very tough," said Nira who by this time was completely self-possessed again and ready for any emergency. "And don't take any notice if he cries a bit."

"Boys don't cry," said Jonathan gravely.

"I know they don't often," she agreed, "but this is a bit special, isn't it?"

He gave her a hug and said he'd hate to lose her and went off whistling. *How lucky children are,* Nira thought. The young—the ten-year-olds like Simon— were so gloriously remote from the agonies and ecstasies of the adult world. Nothing went too deep with them, fortunately. They couldn't grasp the full meaning of death. They were too far removed from it. Fortunately for them all, Simon took the news extraordinarily well. Nira never knew what Rob said to the boy or how he tackled him, but by the time he brought Simon into the lounge where Nira was waiting, the boy seemed quite calm. He had been crying, but now he was anxious to go off with his friend Jonathan and get away from the embarrassment of this terrible accident. Nira told him there was nothing for him to worry about— that his father would be out of hospital in a day or two.

Then they all drove round to the Hallings' house to fetch Simon's night bag. By the time they were back in Nylands, the two little boys were giggling about something that had happened at school. Once again Nira thanked heaven for the matter-of-fact outlook of children.

Finally there was Des to cope with. Rob had by this time gone home. When Nira met Des in the hall she could see from his face that he had already heard the news. Somebody he knew on the train must have told him. He looked quite ghastly, and he immediately launched into the subject.

"My God, isn't it grim news?"

"Appalling. We've got Simon here. Boyce is in hospital."

"Gerald Robinson told me. His wife phoned him up."

"I didn't phone you. I didn't think you'd want to hear like that."

Des made no answer but went straight to the dining-room and poured himself out a strong whisky. He remembered his promise to Nira and lifted the glass to her with a wry smile.

"I still mean to cut it out, but just tonight I really need this."

Nira's eyes softened. She slipped an arm through his affectionately. "Of course you do."

He sat down heavily, spilled some of the whisky on the table, mopped it up with his handkerchief and looked around for a cigarette which Nira found and lit for him. For a moment they discussed the details of the accident. Nira could see his big body trembling. She wondered vaguely if he had really loved Cricket in his way, but there was no room for jealousy in her mind. She tried to comfort him.

"You must feel particularly awful, poor Des."

"It isn't that I was really in love with her," he said awkwardly, "but we sort of got on very well. We had the same sense of humour. She was great fun—that's all."

Nira felt her colour rise. "Okay, Des."

He gulped down half the whisky. She could see that he was badly shaken. She put a hand on his knee.

"Don't take it too hard, Des."

"She was so full of life," he went on. "She had a lot of faults but she was a gay little thing."

"And very pretty," said Nira generously.

"And now she's lying in a mortuary."

"Des, don't dwell on it."

"I'll try not to. It isn't much use, is it?"

"The people to be sorry for are Boyce and Simon."

"Oh, I don't pretend it's a great personal loss for me but it's so shocking and I—I—"

"You were fond of her," broke in Nira. "I understand."

He took her hand and hid his face—still bruised and haggard—against the palm.

"You're a wonderful person, Nirry; too good for me."

"Oh, darling, don't be absurd. Sometimes you make me feel dreadfully smug when you talk about all this *goodness*. I'm not good. I'm just rather practical and not quite so up in the air as you are at times. I daresay I'm rather dull, really."

"Rubbish—you've never been dull in your life."

She closed her eyes. She had not been able to rest and she felt very tired.

"Death's so final, Des. Nothing can bring Cricket back so we must just try and do what we can for the two who are left."

Now Des put down his empty glass and grimaced at her.

"Don't let's be hypocritical and suggest that Boyce has lost the love of his life."

She got up, walked to the standard-lamp by the desk and switched it on. The room was flooded with amber light. She needed light, she thought. The whole day had seemed to her as though she were living in a black stifling cloud.

"Let's try not to talk about poor Cricket. I don't think I can take much more. I've had it all day. But I do want you to know that I'm full of sympathy for you, darling."

"I suppose everybody at the Club is in a state. Who have you seen?"

She sighed. He was determined to go on about the disaster. Better let him get it all off his chest. She was beginning to feel confused about the whole affair—about life and death—love and hate—everything. She wondered if ever she would feel happy and carefree again.

She let Des talk and answered all his questions. When Rob's name came up, remembering how wonderful he had been with Simon, she also remembered a moment in the hall when he had held her close in his arms. This was the second occasion. She had felt so safe and comforted—both times.

She had told him she didn't know what she'd do without his friendship, and she didn't know, she thought, while Des poured out his second whisky, and continued to harp on Cricket's death. *She just didn't know.*

Chapter 10

ANY HOPE THAT Nira might have entertained that Cricket's untimely death would solve her own marriage problem, was slowly but surely dashed. There was to be little peace in her life during the four months that followed the Hallings' accident.

First came Cricket's funeral. All who had known her, including her harshest critics in the neighbourhood, and at the golf club, went to the service, if not to the cremation. She was remembered kindly and mourned because of her youth and physical attractions and the sadness of her end. Immediately after the funeral, Nira had Boyce on her hands.

Glib-tongued, amusing, self-confident Boyce, underwent something of a metamorphosis following the horror of his wife's death. He exhibited a pathetic desire to be with Nira. He haunted Nylands and because of the circumstances, she hadn't the heart to reject him altogether. She and Des agreed that Simon, anyhow, should remain with them for the present. He was happy with Jonathan and rapidly accepted Nira as an adopted mother. But his presence in the house led to problems because the two boys paired off and little Renira often found herself an unwanted third. This made her fractious and difficult—which she had never been in the past. Susan, as ever, was a tower of strength, and kept the three amused. It was a help. But Nira's most embarrassing moments were spent with Boyce who all too often came round to see her and stared at her with his mournful eyes. He talked a great deal about his poor sweet dead wife. Although Nira was full of pity, she also was far too well aware that Boyce had been on poor terms with his wife for a long time before she died. Nira could not really relate this constant show of grief to his true feelings for Cricket. Being an honest person herself, his attitude began to irritate her.

When she told Des about it, his sole comment was, "Okay—so isn't it time you asked him to take Simon back to his own home. Boyce should be getting down to the task of making a new life for himself and that boy. We can't carry on with this Good Samaritan stuff for ever. I'm surprised he's so gutless."

Nira twisted her lips.

"Charitable Des! You're harder than I am, darling. Whatever I may think about Boyce, I haven't the heart to send Simon packing. He seems so happy with us."

"Well, it's up to you. You're the one who has to have him here," said Des, and shrugged. He was no longer interested.

At the end of June things changed for Boyce. His firm offered him a job with their company in Peru where they were about to engage on a new big business project. Boyce readily accepted. He came round to Ny-lands to tell Nira the news. She was alone. Boyce, who since Cricket's death had been genuinely grateful to her for all she had done for him and his son, reverted sud-denly to the man he had been in the past. He took both her long slim hands, pressed them against his cheek and looked at her with desirous eyes.

"Oh, Nira—lovely Nira, I shall always adore you. I'm likely to be away on this job for a couple of years. I shall only be able to see you when I come back on leave, and that won't be too often. I'm devastated, dar-ling."

She drew her fingers away and tried to ignore this emotional approach. She said lightly, "Boyce dear, I wish you the very best of luck, and every happiness in your new life and work. Peru sounds exciting."

"Not as exciting as you are, Nira," and Boyce's gaze strayed from her face to her long graceful throat, then her waist, her long tapering legs—all the beauty he found so irresistible.

She tried to pretend she hadn't heard what he said.

"What will you do about Simon?" she asked.

Reluctantly he let the sensual moment pass.

"I've arranged for him to be a boarder at his old school. He wants that. He's used to it there and gets on well with the boys and masters. Will I be asking too much if I suggest you take him out now and then?"

"Of course, Des and I will cherish him. We love him. And it'll be nice for Jonathan to go on seeing him at school, too. He'll always be welcome here."

"I can have him out in Peru during the holidays. An-other chap from my office is going out there with his wife and family. They say Simon can stay with them when he's on holiday. I shall be living with our assistant manager and he's a bachelor. We couldn't really do with a small boy in his flat."

Nira nodded. "Well, it all seems arranged and I hope your luck will change from now onwards, Boyce. You've been through a bad time."

"You're determined not to be anything more to me than a friend, aren't you?" he asked sadly.

"Boyce—*please*—*you* know that I—"

"That you're in love with your husband?" he broke in, "Nonsense, I'm not a fool. I don't want to refer to anything that happened in the past but I just can't believe you're as much in love with Des as you were."

Now she was angry.

"Boyce, *please,* I don't like what you infer and if we're to go on being friends you really mustn't say—or think—things like that."

"Certainly I shall go on thinking them," he said with a short laugh, and taking one of her hands again, kissed it from fingertips to wrist. "I adore you," he repeated, "Remember that."

The kissing left her cold. She did not find Boyce physically appealing. In any case it was Des she loved *that* way, and Boyce was all wrong about it.

But as he left the house she faced the fact that he had both confused and upset her. Why should he think that she didn't love Des as much as she used to? Why must he stir up the ghost of the past—especially now that Cricket was dead? And it wasn't true anyhow. She *did* love Des—just as much as ever.

But did he really love her? Could she really regain her old confidence in him, and could a woman, no matter how much in love, ever really forget a husband's infidelity, even if she forgave it?

One afternoon in July Des phoned to say he wouldn't be back for dinner that evening and might be late home.

"So sorry, darling, hope you haven't got my favourite dinner prepared."

Her spirits drooped.

"No, it's quite all right," she said. "I've got to help Susan sort out the children's clothes, anyhow. I never seem to get down to it when you're at home."

He told her that he loved her and hung up.

As Nira put down the telephone she found herself wondering . . . wondering if this late work at the office excuse was genuine, or if he was slipping again. Was he taking some girl out in town . . . *any girl?* . . .

She checked her thoughts, ashamed of them and remorseful. She had absolutely no reason to believe that Des was not to be trusted now. She was being absurd. But somehow the prospect of helping Susan sort the children's clothes bored her to death.

She rang up Rob.

His reaction was immediate and gratifying.

"Funny," he said, "I was going to ask you and Des if you'd seen that film at the local. It's an old one—*Dr. Zhivago*. Let me take you, will you?"

"I've seen it but I adored it. All that fantastic Russian scenery—that terrible train journey, and the marvellous way Omar Sharif played his part—all *her* love and self-sacrifice—oh, it was stupendous!"

"Then come and see it with me again."

Of course she went. She always enjoyed being with Rob. There was nothing awkward or difficult about their friendship, only the warmth that she valued so highly.

Des had begun to call him her boy-friend whenever he was mentioned. She accepted the term with good humour. That was all there was in it—Rob was her friend, nothing more. Des knew it.

She was once more enthralled by the great Zhivago film and sat eating the chocolates Rob bought for her, yet she could not quite forget Boyce's unwelcome allusion to the affair that had existed between Des and Cricket, or his suggestion that she and Des were not as much in love as they used to be.

The love element in the film appealed to her deeply emotional nature. When Rob glanced down at her he saw tears glistening on her cheeks. He felt more than a little distressed. He saw far too many signs these days that Nira was unhappy. He wished he knew more about it, so that he might be of more help. But when they parted she seemed composed—smiling again—full of warm gratitude for the evening's entertainment. Rob went home, still troubled.

Once Nira was back at Nylands, she determined to give Des a warm welcome when he returned. She remembered suddenly that it was over a month since he had held her in his arms like a lover. She felt a tremendous longing for their love to be as passionate tonight and complete as it used to be. She put on one of her newest, most attractive nightgowns and sprayed perfume over her throat. She would show him how much he meant to her and he would respond and dispel the shadows and make her feel safe and content again.

But Des came home flushed and talkative, bringing a very strong smell of drink and cigar smoke with him. He had obviously been to a party. He was certainly in high spirits, talking non-stop about his work and the Common Market and nothing she wanted to hear. She asked him what sort of work had kept him in town, and he told her it was the office—just something that had happened—a fault in the computer, and they had to have a conference and go further into the accounts. There was never enough time during the day, he said. Of course he wanted to be with her, Nira, but couldn't make it, etc.

She listened, wanting to believe, but with her heart full of disappointment and disbelief.

She couldn't accuse him of not trying to make love to her. He made every effort to do so—but he failed. Then he sheepishly kissed her good night and excused himself by saying he was over-tired.

"Sorry, darling, but you know I love you," he mumbled, and went to sleep.

Nira lay awake staring into the darkness. A depression descended upon her such as she had never before experienced. A lowering of her entire spirit, her moral, her fundamental belief that all was well between Des and herself.

She was too sensitive, she thought, perhaps psychic, for in the depths of her heart she *knew that Des had been with a woman tonight.* Who, God alone knew, possibly some girl in the office. *But she knew it.* She said nothing because she also knew that she could be wrong. And that next evening when he came back, he was his old gay attentive sober self, and she hoped to enjoy a pleasant evening. They were going to dinner at Maggie Wilson's. This would of course include the

American mother—Mrs. Kennett—and Rob had been asked as well.

They were late in reaching Maggie's attractive ultra-modern bungalow which had huge picture-windows facing the golf course. Rob was already there. Des nudged Nira and whispered, "I'll be darned well jealous soon. Wherever you are, your boy-friend follows."

She found his humour not very funny tonight—even annoying. She kept her lips tightly shut. During dinner she was quieter than usual. Rob glanced at her now and again and wondered what had happened to make his Nira so subdued. The look of strain that had been on her face quite often lately had returned. He was very aware of this. Des was slightly more boisterous than usual and talked a lot to Maggie. Rob noticed this, too, and felt more and more uneasy. What was happening between Nira and Des, he wondered.

Maggie's mother helped her daughter with the meal and kept up a flow of chatter. She was born and bred in California, and although in her sixties, still attractive. It wasn't the first time she had met the Curtises. She admired Nira immensely—found her both beautiful and charming.

Maggie was, as always, a good hostess and a Cordon Bleu cook. She produced an excellent dinner. As a rule Nira liked Maggie. She was sympathetic and good value. Tonight she looked particularly attractive in her long, pale-yellow organza hostess-gown. It had a low-cut neck which showed the curve of her beautiful white breasts, and went well with her red-bronzed hair which was her outstanding beauty. She wore it parted in the centre, looped back on either side and coiled in the nape of her neck—an old-fashioned style that suited her admirably.

Des sat on her left. Rob, the older man was on her right, but he was for the most part caught up with the conversation between the garrulous Mrs. Kennett and Nira, while Maggie concentrated on Des.

It was during the cheese course that Nira suddenly turned her head, glanced down the table towards her hostess, and noticed the way she and Des were looking at each other. In that split second they were not laughing, but staring intently into one another's eyes. Maggie's long-shaped eyes, brown, moist, thickly fringed, held an expression that no one—let alone Nira who was so perceptive—could mistake. It was the look of a woman in love and Des was returning it to the full. Nira knew *him* well enough to be sure of *that*, too.

For Nira, time seemed to stand still, then Des and Maggie both laughed, Maggie said something frivolous for everyone to hear, and the moment of revelation passed. But so revealing had it been that Nira experienced a sensation of hopeless loss. The repeated loss of her confidence in Des and the awful suspicion that now Cricket had gone and some weeks had passed, he was having another love affair; this time with Maggie.

Would Maggie do such a thing? Maggie, who was supposed to have been so devoted to her doctor-husband and so heart-broken when he died? Well, why not? Nira asked herself. She was lonely, hungry for love perhaps, after two years of widowhood. It was common talk that she wanted to marry again. And it was well known that she found Des attractive. Of course, Nira thought miserably, Des had a strong animal attraction for all women. *Didn't she know!*

Oh, God, she thought, *oh, God!*

Suddenly her gorge seemed to rise and she went ice-cold. She leaned across the table and spoke to Mrs. Kennett in a voice that could not be heard by the two at the top of the table.

"I suppose you and Maggie didn't see *Dr. Zhivago* last night at the local cinema, did you?"

"No, we didn't. We're going tomorrow night. Mag went up to town last night; to a party. Don't ask me where. I never know what my dear daughter does. She's a law unto herself, that baby. But aren't all girls the same these days."

Nira nodded. She couldn't speak. She locked her cold hands in her lap so tightly that the points of her nails grazed the palms. And she thought; *Maggie was in town last night, too. At a nameless party. So it's Maggie this time. It's Maggie.*

At once this thought was followed by self-reproach. She mustn't be stupid. She mustn't allow herself to become a jealous wife just because there had once been an affair. She had no real reason to suspect Maggie and her husband. Surely *this* wouldn't follow the Cricket pattern? It couldn't. Des wouldn't hurt her again in such a way so soon after *the other*. She, if she loved him, must trust him now.

Let Des and Maggie gaze into each other's eyes. As for Maggie being up in London (the Cricket pattern again), it was out of the question that he should have spent the evening with her and if he had, it mightn't be anything more than that they dined together, and he hadn't told her, Nira, because he knew she'd be upset. She had herself to blame. She never had been as free and easy with other men as Des was with women. He frequently teased her about her old-fashioned views.

On the way home she didn't even mention Maggie's name, but he did, and she thought he was so frank that either he was being very clever or was quite innocent.

"Mag looked terrific in that long yellow job she was wearing, don't you think, Nirry? What a dress and what a figure she's got!"

Nira sighed but she put a hand on his knee and pressed it lovingly.

"Better than your old woman's?"

He covered the hand with his. "No one's got a better figure than my old woman, if that's what you want to call yourself, my love."

Then rightly or wrongly she decided that she had just been idiotic about Maggie. So the night ended on a gay note. Des had certainly had plenty to drink but she couldn't accuse him of not being lover-like and once the new day dawned she had put the whole episode out of her mind. The only thing she did was to warn him with mock severity that she wouldn't stand for it if he kept on having late nights in town, and he could tell his boss so.

Des gave one of his hearty laughs, kissed her and assured her that there wouldn't be another late night at the office for some time to come so far as he could see, besides which they were off to Cornwall in a fortnight's time. And after that Nira was fully occupied getting everything ready for the holiday.

She saw Maggie and her mother once or twice up at the golf course and each time Maggie was warm and friendly and Nira began to feel that she had been quite on the wrong tack. She could cut out any idea that there was anything between Des and the attractive widow.

The holiday in Mawgan Porth was now arranged. There was room for Rob at Trevarra Farm. Poor little Simon had flown with his father to Peru a week ago. He was much missed by Jonathan but not at all by little Renira who openly expressed that she was glad she wouldn't have to be left out of everything by the two boys. Jon would be forced to play with *her* now.

Late in the afternoon before the Curtis family were due to set out for Mawgan Porth, Nira went to tea with Aunt Ida at The Hollies. The old lady had asked her long ago. Rob was at home. During the hour Nira spent with them, Miss Bessiford told her how pleased she was that her nephew was going away with the Curtis family tomorrow. The only thing that worried her was that he was driving his own car—they were going in convoy— setting out at seven in the morning. Aunt Ida was terrified of accidents.

"Mind you make him follow you, my dear, and don't let Mr. Curtis drive too fast. Rob will keep up with you and his eyesight isn't all that good these days."

"Nonsense, dear aunt," Rob grinned across the room at Nira. "She gets far too nervous about me, Nira. I've got to wear a scarf in case I get cold, and I've got to eat slowly because of my digestion and I take vitamin pills to please her every morning," he ended with a laugh.

Nira laughed. "I'll take care of him, Miss Bessiford," she said. "I never let Des drive too fast—especially when the children are in the car, I assure you. He's very good, anyhow."

"And my eyesight is perfectly all right now, otherwise I wouldn't be allowed to drive," put in Rob, patting his aunt's thin delicate hand.

She looked with great affection at him, then with

pleasure at the graceful girl sitting opposite them. Nira always seemed so young to the old lady, too young to be so long married and the mother of two big children. But then they all looked like that today with their trouser-suits or mini-skirts and their long hair. Not that Aunt Ida disapproved. She wished she had been a young girl herself during this period of history. She was not narrow-minded, neither had she joined the band of elderly people who disapproved of the young moderns.

She knew, of course, that her nephew had more than a special feeling for Nira Curtis and it grieved her sometimes to think that he would probably never marry now, and she would never see a child of his. She loved him very dearly. He was like a son to her, and Nira was just the sort of young woman she would have liked him to marry.

Nira went home in better spirits. Not only did she look forward to getting down to her beloved Cornish coast, but it would be extra nice this summer to have Rob with them.

She mentally enumerated the things she still had to do before they went off. Des would lock up the house and see to all that side. She would finish the last-minute packing and get the picnic together. She intended to take their lunch so that they could stop on the way and sit in the sun in some beauty spot rather than go to a crowded restaurant. She mustn't forget canned beer for Rob and Des, she reminded herself, and a Coke each for the children. Rob was bringing the usual box of chocolates for them. It really should be fun—especially as the weather this last week of July had been exceptionally warm and bright. That reminded Nira she mustn't forget her own swimsuit and cap. She and Susan had been so busy with all that the children wanted, they had left Mum out, *and* they must put a pack of cards in the car. The children sitting at the back liked to play games when they grew bored, although on the journey this time it had been promised they should ride some of the way in Uncle Rob's Rover.

Once home, Nira had half an hour in the children's bedroom with Susan and a wildly excited pair of children—too excited. It ended with Renira chasing her brother up and down the stairs trying to beat his bucket with the end of her wooden spade and never being able quite to get it and finally, tears.

Nira sent the screaming pair to bed an hour early and was secretly glad the punishment was justified by the fact that they needed the extra hour's sleep. They would have to be up tomorrow at half-past six. Susan was going away, too; not with them, but with her own family, on a package holiday to Torremolinos. She, like the children, was excited, too. Nira suddenly felt her age. It seemed sad yet it was a fact that often when you reach thirty you began to feel already approaching middle-age.

Des seemed quieter than usual. There was nothing very hearty or boisterous about him tonight. He went out to fill the car up for the journey tomorrow. When he came back, she teased him.

"And did my dear husband fill up too?"

He rounded on her and answered irritably, "If you want to know I stopped at The Rose and Crown for one—okay, I did. Was it a crime?"

She flushed hotly. Perhaps she'd been tactless but she used to be able to pull Des's leg and joke with him without his taking offence. Things between them were really changing and not for the best. A slow corrosion was weakening the whole structure of their marriage. It terrified her.

"Sorry," she said briefly. "Perhaps I'm envying you, darling. I've had rather a hard day and I'm exhausted. Let's have a drink together now. I wouldn't mind a soft one, and perhaps you'd fancy a beer."

He brought her the lime-juice she liked but didn't bother about a beer for himself. He said he needed a bath and an early night and was going up to pack his own case.

"I've just got one or two things to see to in the kitchen, then I'll be up too," she said.

Once in the kitchen by herself for no real reason she started to cry. A crushing sense of loneliness weighed her down. She and Des seemed so far apart. Inevitably her thoughts turned to Rob. It was pretty good to know there was at least one man she could depend on.

She was still depressed that next morning when she got up soon after six, to cook the breakfast and fill the Thermos flasks with coffee. It wasn't even fine enough to cheer her up. The sky was grey. It was definitely cloudy and cooler. She faced the unwelcome prospect of poor weather down in Cornwall—of a cold wind sweeping the beaches, of cold clammy swimsuits and the children getting chills. What a bore!

She hoped once they got off that Des would be his usual friendly affectionate self, but he seemed as quiet and preoccupied as he had been last night. Inevitably she thought, *He must be sorry he is leaving Maggie behind.*

Rob drove up on time. The children elected to sit in his car for the first lap of the journey. She let them go. She wanted to be alone with Des and try to talk to him.

He grumbled at the weather, and having to wear a pullover. Once out on the main road to the Winchester By-pass (they planned to stop at Exeter for lunch), Nira wondered why she had bothered to come and sit beside him. He was unresponsive to any of her attempts to discuss themselves and how they were feeling about things in general. He was obviously in no mood for that. He continued to grumble about the other drivers, then in due course, they met the holiday traffic which brought fresh complaints from Des. It was a slow almost bumper-to-bumper drive down the motorway. Nira, resigned, lapsed into silence. She felt shut out—rejected. Finally when they began to talk again, he snapped at her undeservedly. She snapped back at him.

"Oh, really, Des! You're so unpleasant this morning."

"I didn't know I was."

"What's biting you, anyhow?"

"Nothing."

"Well, you behave as though you've got a king-size chip on your shoulder."

"You're too imaginative. You're forever thinking things that aren't—well, they don't exist."

"Since when?" she asked indignantly, "Generally when I think things—they *do* exist."

He gave a quick look which she found nothing short of surly.

"A man can't always be at his best and particularly so early."

"It isn't all that early. We've been on the road for hours. Really, Des, I don't know what's come over you."

He opened his lips to speak and shut them again. He knew perfectly well what was wrong with him and it annoyed him because he also knew that Nira was right. She rarely did use her imagination without cause. She had an uncanny way of guessing the truth. Not that he imagined she had the least idea of what had been going on between Maggie and himself. He was sure he had managed to keep that from everybody. He had acted with absolute discretion. Lately he had wondered what had possessed him to start this affair with Maggie. He'd always had a bit of a yen for her, of course, and knew from the way she looked at him that she wasn't all that cold about him. But it wasn't until after Cricket's death that he felt the necessity to get on more intimate terms with her. Then, once it all began, and she had been warm and willing to respond, he was lost. He couldn't keep away from her.

It had always been the same with him. He couldn't withstand the lure of women as seductive as poor little Cricket, and now Maggie. He had even talked himself into believing that he was doing Maggie a good turn by becoming her lover. She was lonely and wanted a man in her life. They had actually agreed that it wouldn't hurt Nira so long as she didn't *know*.

He and Maggie had stolen some splendid passionate hours together.

He still loved his wife. Of course he did. He would never stop loving her and the kids. He wished he could be a better husband—but he just wasn't cut out to be faithful. But last night Maggie had given him a shock.

They had arranged to meet in Ponders Wood (it was during that hour that he had been busy filling up the car and having a drink). He had phoned her from the office earlier in the day and told her he must just kiss her goodbye. But there had been no kissing; no passionate farewells. Right from the start she stood aloof and told him that their affair had got to end.

"I've had a chat with Nira up at the Club," she said. "I know I've had lots of them but this was a particular talk. We just happened to be discussing marriage and she asked me if I would like to be married again and I said yes but that I didn't somehow think I would ever find the right person."

"Well, you know my position—I can't do anything about that," Des had said gloomily.

"That's not what I meant. I just meant that I don't think I would even marry you if you were free, Des. What I'm getting at is, Nira said if you died, she wouldn't know what to do because you've always been so close, and I can't tell you what she made me feel— too awful! She's really such a sweet person, and I can't go on having an affair with her husband. It may be awfully silly of me but I can't and won't be responsible for hurting her."

"Why should she be hurt if she doesn't *know*," he had tried to argue.

"She just might find out. I have an idea that she already guesses we have a thing about each other."

Des protested in vain. Maggie had been adamant. When he kissed her goodbye he had been forced to realise it was for the last time. And Maggie had a strong side to her—she wasn't as weak as Cricket—she wouldn't come back. He knew it. He knew also that she was right but he had gone home feeling gloomy and frustrated. It all had the effect of making him hostile in some funny way towards Nira. It was quite unjust, he admitted that. But he felt depressed about losing Maggie and quite frankly he was bored—for the moment anyhow—with domestic life. Possibly after a couple of weeks by the sea with the family he'd feel better. He'd try to dig in his heels and be a good boy but he couldn't even pretend this morning to act like a devoted husband.

Nira no longer tried to get nearer him or lighten the gloom between them. By the time they reached Exeter she felt as depressed as ever.

The picnic lunch was gay despite the grey coolness of the day, by virtue of the fact that the children were madly excited and talked non-stop, and at least Nira could feel glad half the long journey was over. It was more than trying for Renira and Jonathan, patient though they were, but they grew bored. On the whole they were good travellers and had never suffered from car-sickness like many of their friends.

Rob said they'd been splendid during the drive with him, but after Exeter they switched over to the family car. They would drive with Daddy, and Nira would keep Uncle Rob company.

Nira was relieved to find herself in Rob's comfortable car. It was good to talk to somebody who was completely responsive to everything she said and so anxious for her comfort. Beside which, he was never a bore. He always had plenty of things to talk about. She found him an excellent companion. But she was still subdued, and unlike herself, and Rob noticed it.

"You've been doing too much lately, haven't you? All those preparations for the holiday, and looking after everyone. I'm afraid it's tired you out," he said in his gentle way.

She denied this but suddenly asked him a question that confirmed the suspicions he had had for some time that things were not as right as they used to be between Nira and Des.

"Do you think a man needs more than one woman in his life?"

The question came as a slight shock. He didn't quite know the answer. He took his pipe from his mouth, put it in the glove-box and was silent for a moment or two, keeping his eyes on the tail-end of Des's car. Des was driving at a reasonable pace anybody could follow.

"Well, my dear," at length Rob answered, "that's not a subject on which one can generalise. Everything depends on the sort of man. Some men do need more than one woman. Some don't need *any* women in their lives at all. What sort are you referring to?"

She knew quite well but she wasn't going to tell Rob. She invented a fictitious character. "Oh, a friend of mine has a husband who seems to love her all right but also needs a new love from time to time. I just wondered what *you* think. I—I'm confused about it."

"Sounds like your friend's husband would like to go back to harem days," said Rob smiling. "The age-old necessity of man to renew the force of his sex-urge from time to time by planting a new young beauty in his home."

Nira laughed, too. "Oh, I don't think in this case that the man actually needs a *harem*, but don't you think that a man on the whole wants variety—he gets tired of the same old wife? He looks for fresh excitement."

"Perhaps—in order to bolster up the feeling of youth and vigour, and so on. But there are a lot of chaps who don't want anyone but the chosen wife. I tell you, it's all a question of temperament."

Nira kept her fingers locked together in her lap. She stared at the traffic ahead, then she said, "Perhaps it's a lot to do with the temperament of the women, too. Some wives become bored or love their husbands too much and show it too plainly. Men can get bogged down by too much adoration. Besides it's their nature to want what's hard to get. In fact I've often noticed that they seem to go for a girl who's undemonstrative and keeps them at arm's length."

Her sudden cynicism surprised him. He looked down at her uneasily. "I wouldn't exactly say that. I think what a man really needs is a warm, sweet, affectionate creature who is also a good friend to him—and a good cook," he added jokingly. "Of course she must be a good cook."

Nira was glad to laugh with him again. She decided not to continue the discussion. She was treading on dangerous ground. In another moment she'd be saying something that would leave no doubt in his mind that it was Des and herself she had been discussing.

She steered the conversation into a new channel.

Rob played along with her but he was troubled. Her attempt to philosophise over the matrimonial troubles of a 'friend' had been really rather pathetic. Of course she had been alluding to her own marriage. He was sure of it. Des had had an affair with Cricket Halling. And who else besides? *He* was the sort to need a harem. Rob thought he knew Des pretty well these days. Nira had become sad and disillusioned. Rob felt desperately upset, because he loved her with his whole heart and soul, and he knew he couldn't do a damned thing about it.

Chapter 11

THE ARRIVAL AT Mawgan Porth was nothing short of dramatic and quite different from anything Nira had expected. The weather was perfect. Hot sun and cloudless skies, quite different from when they left home. They made good time despite the slowish crawl, traffic jams, and frequent stops for the children. On the whole the journey was uneventful until they came to within four miles of Mawgan Porth. By this time the children were growing fretful and heartily sick of the long drive and Nira had a headache which was unusual for her. She presumed it was nerves as much as heat and dust, for it had been a close day as well as a fatiguing one. She cheered up at the first sight of the magnificent coast she knew so well—the dark purple-blue of the Atlantic— the creaming foam fringing the great breakers—the jutting rocks with their crusts of violet mussels—the gold of the wind-swept sand. Not even the march of time which had brought far too many little houses and kiosks and small shops to spoil the beauty of this place could destroy its intrinsic magic. Still sitting beside Rob, Nira enjoyed the sight doubly because he, too, was so enthusiastic. He had revived some of his youthful eagerness to take photographs and there were going to be some splendid opportunities down here. It couldn't be the sort of photography that had made him so successful in Nairobi, but there were wonderful colours along this coast. He was glad he had brought a special wide-angled lens.

"It makes one glad to be alive and very glad to be here," he said. He took off his glasses, shut his eyes and drew in a breath of the salty air. "Makes you feel better, doesn't it, Nira?"

She nodded. Now she had an idea. "Let's just hoot Des and the children to stop and tell them to take the road that leads to Sandy Beach."

"Is that very special?"

"It's the one with the least people on it because it's such a steep climb down and difficult for charabancs. I'd like to make sure it's still there," she smiled.

Des pulled his car up and waited for them to stop alongside. He had nothing against Nira's idea except that he thought perhaps it might have been best to get straight to Trevarra Farm.

"I don't know," said Nira, "it's just a feeling I have that I want first to catch a glimpse of Sandy Beach."

"So do I!" put in little Renira, jumping up and down in the car.

"So do I," echoed Jonathan. "It's where I first swam without my arm bands, isn't it, Mum? I want to see it."

So they all drove to Sandy Beach. And there the shock awaited them. A year ago it had been a lovely secluded spot—one of the few left. This afternoon it was unbelievably changed. Not only were there a mass of cars and caravans ranged along the top of the cliff, but a crowd of people were milling up and down the narrow zigzag path that led to the beach. In the hollow itself, encircled by a crowd of onlookers and obvious enthusiasts, were a party of cameramen with full equipment for shooting a movie. Nira, Rob, Des and the children got out of the two cars and stood staring. Now they could see a man standing on a promontory just below them shouting through a megaphone, "Cut! Cut—

for God's sake! I don't want any more of this. It's bloody awful. Start again, please, all of you—from the beginning—*all of you!"*

Dismayed yet fascinated, Nira shielded her eyes against the sun and went on staring at the crowded beach trying to make out what was happening. Des seemed to come alive. He had been moody and apathetic all during the journey. Now he was alert.

"Look at them. A film company on location—they're making a film down here. D'you see, Nira? Great fun!"

"It may be fun but bang goes our sleepy Sandy Beach," said Nira sadly.

"I'll trot down and see what they're shooting," said Des.

"Well, don't be long—we ought to get on," Nira reminded him.

He in turn reminded her that it had been *her* idea coming here, and started to make his way down the steep path. As he did so, a man and a girl climbing up to the top stopped just short of a collision with him. They seemed to be having an altercation. The man— young, bearded, burnt red by the sun, and looking decidedly harassed—was pleading with the girl.

"Now, Frankie, don't be awkward. You've got to let me shoot it again. It was all wrong. You know it was, darling."

The girl addressed as Frankie turned around to face him. She was sensationally beautiful, thought Nira. In a yellow bikini showing most of an exquisite slim brown body she had a huge peasant straw floppy hat on her head, and wore large round dark glasses. These she suddenly whipped off and pointed them accusingly at the man beside her, tossing back a mane of rich red hair.

"If you're trying to say that I'm the one who spoilt the scene, why not just say it? You can go to hell, Vince. I'm hot and I'm tired and I've had enough down on that god-damn beach. I want to rest and I want a drink, and I'm not staying below one moment longer. No more shooting today for little me."

"But Frankie, we haven't time to spare. You know we've got to get on with this sequence. We've only just started and we've a bare fortnight to finish the sequence. Be reasonable."

She screamed at him, "Go to hell!"

Nira exchanged glances with Rob. He smiled at her. He had been less interested in the row than in the camera equipment on the beach. That was more his line.

"Is this part of the act or what?" he asked Nira.

"I reckon it's a row between the director and the leading lady," she said.

Then something clicked in her brain. Frankie—of course—this was Frankie Motte, the famous new star who had made such a success in that big film last year—*Night of the Fifth*—(that's what it had been called), and there had been more than ordinary Guy Fawkes fireworks in it, too, she remembered. One of those fast-moving films with brittle witty dialogue and fantastic drama—and sex which suited Frankie, who was then only twenty. Nira remembered, too, how Des had tried to make her go up to London with him to the cinema, and how fascinated he had been by Frankie's photographs. He had been to see the film and come back raving about her. After that he used to talk about her fabulous red hair and figure and gorgeous long legs and jokingly call her his 'dolly-bird.'

Nira had taken it all lightly as a kind of joke. She was amused today to see the way he sprang to life when he actually saw his 'dolly-bird'. She seemed oblivious of him and the rest of the crowd on the cliff top who were watching and listening to the unrehearsed row. It was clear to Nira that she was exercising her right to be difficult and greatly embarrassing her harassed director.

Now Des suddenly became a participant in the scene because the fabulous Frankie wrenched off her dark glasses and threw them at her director. He ducked. The glasses landed on the turf at Des's feet.

He picked them up and handed them to her. He knew of course exactly who she was. He had so often made a study of that splendid body in pictures and now that he saw her in the flesh, he thought Frankie Motte attractive enough to stir any man's passions. She was heavily made-up. Her false lashes were incredibly long, but there was nothing unreal about the blue of the blazing eyes. They were magical. Des grinned at her, and when Des grinned like that, few women were ever unmoved by his charm. Even Frankie succumbed. She calmed down, and examined the tall handsome stranger through the glasses that were miraculously unbroken.

Her whipped-up rage evaporated. She drew nearer Des.

"Thanks awfully. I hope I didn't hit you."

"The glasses fell at my feet. All wrong—I ought to be falling at yours. Frankie Motte, I presume? You're my favourite film-star, d'you know that?"

She put a hand on her hip and gave him her most fascinating smile. A little studied, he decided, but most enticing, and he was enjoying the fact that the film director stood sullenly mopping his forehead, looking daggers at him.

Frankie asked Des for his name, then said, "You're sweet. Did you see *Night of the Fifth?*"

"Of course," he said, and made the two words sound like hot honey.

She cast a rather ugly look at the unfortunate Vince.

"I don't suppose you'll have a chance to see this new one we're supposed to be shooting in Cornwall because if Vince doesn't stop making me repeat and repeat and repeat, I'm quitting."

"Don't do that," said Des. "You'd rob the world of some worthwhile entertainment."

Vince looked at Des more kindly.

"You've said it, chum," he muttered.

"What I need is a drink and a rest," said Frankie, and stretched her arms above her head and stood there on the edge of the cliff like a nymph poised for flight, giving Des the works as she called it. She knew exactly how fabulous she looked.

Des was fascinated. He was well aware that she was the incarnation of artificial charm and that her looks were aided by every possible gadget. But nature had given her that superlative shape, and the blatant invitation in her marvellous eyes was more than enough to storm through Des's façade of the dutiful husband and father. He glanced toward his wife, and at the man standing with her, then at the children who were still in the car. If ever he'd wished he were a bachelor again he wished it now. Quickly he said, "My family and I are going to be down here for a couple of weeks, Miss Motte. Perhaps we shall see you again."

She smiled. It was a warm inviting smile, and Frankie had a big amusing mouth and exquisite teeth. She said, "Why not? We'll be on location here for another fortnight, I don't doubt—do you, Vince?" And she turned to her director, still smiling, for which he was devoutly thankful. Frankie in one of her tempers was unmanageable and he wanted to finish the Cornish scenes in his new film before the end of the month. They had plenty more stuff to shoot when they got back to the studio and one particular act due for a Rome setting.

"I'm sure we'll still be here," he said and ran a critical eye over Des—a fine-looking man. Photogenic, he'd wager. He added a few words to Des. "We want people who look good in the background for a couple of scenes. Come on down one morning and join the crowd."

Des's spirits, which had been rising ever since he saw his favourite film-star, rose a bit higher.

"I'd be amused," he said.

"Then we'll see you," said Frankie. "We're all staying at the Headland Hotel in Newquay. Come along one evening and have a drink with us." And with a friendly glance at Nira whom she thought a nice-looking but rather dull girl, she added, "And bring your wife."

Nira heard this. "I must say I'd adore to see Des—my husband—in a film—so thanks awfully." She smiled at Frankie.

Vince, watching, thought Nira rather lovely; very English, cool but attractive. He was experienced with women. In his job as a film director he met hundreds of seductive girls. There had been a time in his life when he had thought he would like to settle down with a woman like this one, and have two nice kids, like hers. He might make use of them, as well as Nira—put them all in the next scene. The public liked kids and animals.

When he looked at Frankie, he grimaced. She was enticing, amusing, all the things that could get a man—that was if he didn't need peace and quiet, but for the moment, Vince was thoroughly involved with his leading lady. He turned and put an arm around her shoulders. They were tanned and glistening with little drops of perspiration.

"Back to the job, sweetheart," he coaxed.

"Like you say," was her reply. She was not particularly concerned with grammar. She was in a better humour now. Her marvellous eyes still responded to the admiring glances Des was throwing in her direction.

She put an arm through Vince's and started to walk down the path—then she turned to wave at Des.

Vince growled, "Now, now, honey-girl, leave that nice guy alone. He's got a wife and kids and I know that look in your eyes."

She gave a low laugh. He knew that laughter, too. It was rather like the purring sound from a panther about to spring.

"I'm not so sure he's all that nice," she said lazily, "but he's got something for me, baby. Ring him up and ask him over to The Headland for drinks."

"Ask her, too, then. She's got something for me."

"Oh, she won't want to come. I know her type. I don't know who that older man is—her brother or something. Maybe he'll take care of her."

Vince looked down at the beach, crowded with the members of the cast plus the extras and all the paraphernalia of his film-making. "I don't think you've got one single moral, Frankie Motte," he said and stuck a cigar between his teeth.

She giggled. "Who wants morals? They're too deadly. Don't start preaching, baby. It doesn't suit you, and if I want a kiss from a stranger I'll have it. You still want *me* as your leading lady, don't you?"

He gave a sardonic grin. "You've got your contract."

"Okay, lover-boy, let's finish our scene and get back to the hotel. I'm fed up with the sand and the sea and the sweet pure air of Cornwall. Let's shoot the sequence where I've got to be carried into one of the caves by Chris."

Christopher Baker who was playing lead opposite Frankie was an actor of some note and a big draw with the slinky figure teenagers—long hair, side-burns, groovy outfit—all of it. He was as dark as if he had Mexican blood in him—a good foil for Frankie with that hair that held the burnished red-gold of satin in the light. But they fought like cat and dog. The trouble with Frankie was that she fought with everyone unless she happened to be going through a phase of what she called being 'loving and giving'. She seemed to be falling into one of these states at the moment. She said to Vince very softly, "Why can't you arrange for that gorgeous-looking man up on the cliff to carry me into the cave instead of Chris. Then I could play the giving part with genu-yne—feelings."

Up on the cliff the gorgeous-looking man stood watching the film-star walk on her sandalled feet with feline grace, slowly down the zigzag path until she reached the shore. He was quite sure he had not mistaken the message in her eyes. He had seen it so many times before in the eyes of other women. The memory of Maggie and the frustration he had felt at losing her before he left home vanished completely. He barely recalled the fact that she, too, had had a touch of red in her hair, and sweet invitation in her eyes.

He felt as excited about Frankie as a schoolboy. What luck, being able to muscle in on her and her film company, like this. Who would have dreamed they'd be on location so near Mawgan Porth. As for Frankie, he knew perfectly well he'd see her again because she wanted it that way. There was absolutely no room in his mind for compunction when he turned to his wife and children again. He only thought what a good thing it was that old Rob had come with them. No reason why he, Des, couldn't slip away discreetly whenever the occasion arose. He could leave Nira quite happily with her family and the boy-friend.

The two cars headed for Trevarra Farm. The children drove with Uncle Rob again. Nira sat with Des.

She said, "It looks as though it'll be quite an amusing holiday. It would be super if we could all be filmed together. Renira and Jonny are thrilled. Frankie Motte is quite a girl, isn't she? Terribly attractive—Miss World standard."

"She sure is," said Des, feeling in the best of humour.

And that was how it all started.

Chapter 12

THE FIRST WEEK of the holiday was hardly a success for anyone in the Curtis party—except Des. The weather changed again as so often happens on the Cornish coast even in the middle of summer. The wind blew from the south-west bringing heavy cloud and sharp storms of rain. The temperature dropped. The sands were deserted. The seagulls wheeled in towards land, crying desolately.

Trevarra Farm was not the big success it had seemed in former years. The Hoskins were as hospitable and amiable as ever but Nira noticed a decline in the general amenities of the place. The bathwater was never really hot—the food was uninspired, less lavish than it used to be, although there were plenty of eggs and milk for the children, and Mrs. Hoskins' saffron buns which they all enjoyed plus those little dishes of dark yellow Cornish cream with a thick crust on it which were so good to spread with jam or honey. But because of the cooler weather they all felt cheated.

Renira fretted because she wasn't allowed to wear her bikini. Jonathan was incensed because there was no swimming, no real fun on the beach. Not only was it cold but the wind whipped the sea into great breakers

and Des warned them all that it wasn't safe to swim.
Only twice during that first week were Renira and Jonathan able to find a pool in which they could paddle,
and take advantage of a sudden break in the sky when
the sun came through and it was warm enough.

Then Nira developed severe toothache and had to go
to a dentist who diagnosed an abscess. After unsuccessful treatment the tooth had to come out. A penicillin
injection did nothing to add to her comfort. She was, as
she admitted, a bit of a wreck at the end of it all—
disappointed not only for the children's sake—but for
Rob. She had praised life in Mawgan Porth so warmly
and knew he had looked forward to the sort of lazy life
in the sun one could lead down here in fine weather.

As usual, Nira was more than thankful for his presence and support. It was he who drove her into
Newquay to have the tooth out, because Des had been
called by Vince and asked to take part in the film. Nira
didn't want him to miss it. So it was Rob who took his
place—and amused the children when she felt too
miserably in pain to organise them and wanted only to
be allowed to lie down in a darkened room. Antibiotics
did not suit Nira.

As the days went by, Des became the one really
cheerful person in the party. He went around the place
whistling, saying that he didn't mind the rain or the
wind and he was always out walking or driving into
Newquay where the film crowd spent a lot of time in
their hotel, drinking away boredom, waiting for the sun
to come out again. They could only shoot the film spas-
modically.

Two days after Nira had had her tooth extracted, she
and Rob walked into the little village shop where one
could buy anything and everything. She needed more
Anadin. Her face hurt and her head ached. She felt
wretched, although she appreciated the fact that Renira
and Jonathan had gone out for the afternoon.

Rob looked at her anxiously. She looked white and
ill. Her eyes seemed to have sunk into her face.

"That damned tooth still hurting?" he asked.

"Yes—where the damned tooth *was,* it still hurts," she said with a faint laugh.

"Poor girl, it's a frightful bore for you and the last thing you needed on your holiday."

"Well, at least we've got rid of my darling children," she laughed again. "I love them to death but they've been so difficult because of this awful weather and having to stick indoors and amuse themselves—poor angels. And me being so off-colour, hasn't helped them. I'm glad we met those other people—the Wilsons. It's a godsend."

Wilson was a major in the Army. The family were on leave from Singapore and had met the Curtis family in the local. They had two children of their own, much the same age as Jonathan and Renira. They had all gone to see a Disney film in Newquay.

It wasn't that Rob found the children trying, but he hated to see Nira looking and feeling so ill and being constantly nagged at by the boisterous pair. At their age kids could be exacting and remorseless.

It was raining again. Where the devil was Des, Rob wondered, although he could guess. At The Headland again no doubt, with that film bunch, including Frankie. It was obvious to Rob that Des had gone off his head about the red-headed star. He had been behaving disgracefully—neglecting Nira shamefully. She never complained. She wouldn't, Rob thought, but he knew well how she must be feeling. Des spent far too much time with Frankie and her set. Nira went to one supper party with him, but never again, neither did she tell Rob much about it. Two nights ago, Des came back from one of his Newquay jaunts the worse for drink.

Whether there'd been a row between husband and wife, Rob did not know, but he imagined so because they were not on speaking terms when they all breakfasted in the big kitchen that next morning.

Rob was deeply disturbed. He didn't like the look of things for Nira. He could only guess what was going on in her mind, but he had little doubt that Des was no longer the faithful devoted husband Nira had always believed him to be. He made a great show of being devoted when he was with her. Rob was certain he was putting on an act for the family. He did a lot of laughing and joking. He bought the children toys, and gave Nira a large bottle of perfume, but the whole situation stank in Rob's nostrils. Des wanted both to eat his cake and have it. He was perhaps still fond of his charming wife but one woman wasn't enough for him. In the past there had been Cricket (perhaps even others). Now there was Frankie. A domestic storm was brewing. Rob felt that he would be involved. But he had no wish to go away and leave Nira, even if it meant unpleasantness for him. If she needed him, he was going to stay.

It was raining hard by the time they finished shopping and got back to the farm.

"I'd better change, I'm drenched," said Nira.

"Me, too," said Rob, "I'll meet you in ten minutes. Don't catch a chill now—you've had enough this last few days."

She left him standing in the Hoskins' parlour which had been given to them for their private use while they were here. There was only one small electric fire with a single bar—another sign of the Hoskins' new economy. It threw out little heat. The room was cold and dismal. Nira looked around and sighed. What a difference the weather could make. The last time they had been at Trevarra they had been out all day and it had seemed such fun.

As she put on dry jersey and slacks, she turned her thoughts to Des.

She had to face up to the fact that she'd hardly seen him this past week except when he had played the part of loving husband and father and joined them for an hour or two. And at night when they shared the big old-fashioned bed in the low-ceilinged room above the parlour, she had felt she might as well lie alone. A quick kiss and a 'Good night, sweetie' from Des—and he was fast asleep. They seemed no longer able to communicate.

While her tooth had been so bad she had felt too ill to protest much but now that she was beginning to feel better, she could see clearly what was happening. Her resentment was growing. The jealousy she used to feel over Cricket—her suspicions about Maggie—her fears for Des when he started to drink too much—all these things had accumulated and formed a black ugly picture in her mind.

They had quarrelled openly one night when he returned from Newquay in the early hours of the morning, so drunk that she wondered how he had driven back in the car without having an accident. It had set the seal on her unhappiness.

She had turned on him the next day. "It's that girl—your precious film-star who's been keeping you out—you call it a party with all the actors, et cetera, but it's a party with *her!*"

He made one or two feeble protests, then snarled at her, "Oh, shut up, Nira . . . I'm fed up with your nagging and possessiveness. You've got your dear Rob—let me alone—why don't you have a party with *him?*".

In her pain and bewilderment she had told him what she thought of him. "Don't dare try and bring Rob into this. You know perfectly well there's nothing between us."

"Don't tell me he isn't crazy about you!" he had retorted.

"If he is, it's in the nicest possible way. And if he was mad about me he'd keep it to himself. He isn't as unscrupulous as you are. Oh, Des, how you've changed!"

"We both have."

She had stared at him wild-eyed, her world falling apart.

"How have *I* changed?"

"Oh, I don't know—why don't you quit arguing. It's all this arguing that's driving me away from you."

"That's cowardly of you—you're just trying to put the blame on me. You're trying to say that it's because I've become a possessive sort of wife that you're fed up with me."

"I don't say anything of the sort, but I do say I'm a gay sort of chap and no saint and you knew it when you married me."

"I was gay too. We had wonderful times together, but always *together*."

"We're still together. What are you moaning about?"

With the back of her hand against her trembling lips, she looked up at his sullen, handsome face and shook her head, completely incredulous. He bore so little resemblance to the husband she had once adored. Her voice was broken as she said, "We were in love with each other for ages. Terribly happy—at least I thought so. It wasn't until I found out about Cricket I began to lose my faith in you and ever since then you've seemed to want to be what you call gay all the time."

"Why don't *you* try to be a bit more amusing for a change?"

Her head throbbed. The cavity in her mouth where the wretched wisdom tooth used to be, throbbed too, and she felt sick.

Suddenly Des noticed the way she put her hand against her cheek and how tired she looked. Weak character though he was, he had his kindly and gentle side. He took Nira in his arms, and tried to be nice to her.

"I'm a monster. I don't know what's come over me. Sorry, darling. You're the best girl in the world, and the only one I really love—honestly."

She pushed him away, her eyes blind with tears of sheer despair. "But I'm one of so many. I know it now. You can't leave the girls alone. And you'd like me to have an affair with Rob so that it would make *you* feel better. I can't accept that. Neither can I keep forgiving you for what you do. I *can't*."

"Hell! Who said there was anything to forgive at this moment?"

"You know there is. We came down here to have a lovely holiday and you've been out most of the time with Frankie Motte. You're absolutely fascinated by her, aren't you? *Aren't you?*"

"It doesn't say we're having an affair."

"But you are, aren't you? *Aren't you?*" she cried again, the tears pouring down her face.

He was fed up with having to lie and dissemble. The flame that had sprung up between him and the famous

Frankie had burned a little too swiftly and fiercely for him to resist. He never really wanted to resist. She was the most exciting and powerful magnet that had ever drawn him away from hearth and home, and she had told him that out of all the men she had made love to since she was sixteen, he was the greatest. She admitted she had a thing about him. His gaiety matched hers. She was bored by the film actors in her own profession and fed up with producers, managers and agents who followed her around, hoping to pick up money or bask in the reflection of her glory. Des was new and smart and he amused her. He was splendid to look at, wonderful to be with, and she had every intention of enjoying a swift affair with him. For the time being she wanted him, and what Frankie wanted, she got. The wife and children were a background nuisance and that was how she treated them.

While he was brooding about this, Nira shot another bitter unexpected question at him, taking him off his guard, giving him little time to think up any more lies.

"What about Maggie? It isn't just Frankie Motte. We've only just left Ponders Heath and I realised it was you and Maggie at home. You were after her. She was Cricket's successor. You take so many mistresses, don't you? And you tell me you don't love any of them, so you don't even betray my love for something real or big. I might try to understand and forgive if it was a real thing. But you have just little petty affairs. That's how you seem to like it. You don't deny it, do you?"

He made one feeble protest.

"I don't know why you're bringing up Maggie. We were attracted to each other, yes, but in actual fact she didn't think it fair to you and we ended it before we came away."

Nira gave a hard laugh. She sneered, "Charming! I'm glad she has that much conscience. Were her kisses better than mine and are Frankie's better than Maggie's? And when dear Frankie goes back to town, having enjoyed a little summer madness with a handsome stranger, will you find someone else and—"

He broke in, furious, on the defence; startled by the

fury of her outburst. He had never seen her like this before. It confused him.

"Look, Nira, I deny nothing. You have every right to be hurt and angry but it was only because I didn't *want* to hurt you. That's why I kept it all from you. If you had been a different sort of person, I'd have been much more honest."

Nira turned her eyes heavenwards.

"My God! So you wanted a halo of honesty to make things easier. It never entered your head that you not only dishonoured us—our love—our belief in each other—but our children. I can see from your face that you think that stuff old hat. You think I'm a prude—like your mother—or Aunt Ida. But you're wrong. I just won't admit that I'd have been a better wife if I'd let you do what you want and turned a blind eye until you got tired of your various girl-friends or they got tired of you."

Des kicked the toe of his shoe against the floor, hands in his pockets, eyes sullen. He didn't like what was happening between them. He hadn't meant it to turn out this way. But he was in the mood to feel himself aggrieved. She had become an over-possessive wife who, to use her own words, was as old-fashioned as his mother or Rob's aunt. Of course he was grateful to her for her fidelity and respected her for it in the depth of his heart, but with Cricket dead and Maggie backing out, Frankie remained a new powerful magnet—beautiful, famous, glittering. He was both dazzled and enslaved. Eventually he tried a new line with Nira.

"Don't let's split up over this. You know you're still number one with me. If I behave like a so-and-so, do try to turn a blind eye. You know I'll always come back."

She stormed at him, "No, I don't intend to sit back and wait for you to get tired of making love to other women. You can follow your fascinating Frankie back to London or New York or anywhere you like. You can ruin yourself for her, but first of all you'll get out of my life. I won't have you, and I won't let the children have you. I'll finish with you *absolutely*."

For a moment Des looked startled and apprehensive, then he laughed.

"You don't mean it, ducky, you're just being hysterical."

But after a few moments when she had proved to him that she did mean it, he climbed down. He hoped he could go on seeing Frankie in London anyhow. But divorce, no—he didn't want one.

"You know I'm devoted to you and the kids and I don't want to break up our home," he muttered.

"You've said that before. I don't believe one word and you're not going to have it both ways. I refuse to face that sort of life. I may be dull compared with your film-stars and I'm sure *she's* a big attraction, but I'm *me*. I want a decent husband and a decent life and if you can't give it to me any more you can go. I will divorce you."

The bitter fight continued for hours, leaving them both exhausted. It all began again the next day. Nira had been perfectly well aware that he was down on Sandy Beach watching them film Frankie, because the sun had come out again. That was yesterday and he had walked out of the farm this morning without even saying goodbye to her. They'd hardly spoken a word to each other last night. She had lain awake, her nerves jumping—feeling that the bottom had dropped out of her world. The clock merely ticked around, and she did the best she could to amuse the children and ignore the nagging pain in her face, and—with much more difficulty—the pain in her mind.

She had lost Des. He had lost her. It came to the same thing. Now this afternoon, sitting alone with Rob in the oak-beamed chintzy parlour at Trevarra Farm, she suddenly collapsed. She looked, Rob thought, terribly pale. He kept a close eye on her. After lunch he made some pretence of talking about a letter he had had from Aunt Ida this morning. "She doesn't seem too well at the moment. She's been in bed for a couple of days. What's the matter with my two best girls?" And he stretched out a hand to Nira, adding, "My ancient aunt and my young sweet friend."

"Oh, Rob," she said, "Oh, Rob, I'm a mess! I'm in an awful state. I feel so old it isn't true. If you're too nice to me I'll begin to cry. That would embarrass you terribly."

"I'd be upset but not embarrassed. And you needn't imagine I don't understand what's wrong. Of course I do. It's all too obvious."

She flushed, crouching there in front of the little electric fire, her cold hands spread to the inadequate warmth. She felt chilled right through her whole body, and inexpressibly sad.

"About Des, I mean. Have you—guessed about Des and me?"

He looked at the back of the dark silky head. She seemed so unsophisticated this afternoon. Her hair tied in a pony-tail and the slenderness of her neck made her somehow look so young. She had a fawn-like quality—a grace which he found both innocent and touching.

"I think I know. Do you want to tell me about it?" he asked gently.

She no longer felt she could put up even a small fight. Des mocked at Rob and tried to turn him into an image that made *him* feel less guilty. Rob seemed all that she had left of strength and security. The love she felt for Rob in this moment was sexless yet absolute. She knelt at his feet, folded her arms on his knees and cried until she could cry no more.

He took off his glasses and bent over her, embracing her shuddering body, stroking her head and the nape of her neck. He pressed his lips against her hair and did what he could to comfort her. To hear her uncontrolled sobs and to know the depth of the pain she was suffering went through his heart like a knife. He had seen it all coming and not been able to do a thing to help her, and while she had hidden behind pretence to save her pride—he had respected her wishes—but not now. Now that she was broken and turning to him for help. He said, "Oh, my darling, my poor darling, my poor love, don't cry like that. I can't bear it."

"I wish I were dead."

"No, you don't. You've got the children. Whatever

has happened between you and Desmond, you've always got Renira and Jonathan."

"I know and I oughtn't to want to die, but I do. We've been so close—Des and I and the children. We were such a happy family. I suppose I was just living in a world of romance. I was quite sure of him right up to the time that he and Cricket—"

"I know," Rob broke in, "I know."

She lifted a pitiful face, disfigured by grief yet still lovely to him. "I expect everybody knew but me." And down went her head again, hiding from Rob's compassionate gaze.

He pressed the fine bones of her skull between his warm hands. His own face was deeply grooved. His emotions ran high. He had not imagined that loving a woman as he loved this one, could be so agonising. He said, "Don't think I haven't noticed the change in you two and worried about it for a long time. But, my darling, even if Desmond has toppled off his pedestal, it needn't be the end of the world."

Up went her head, blue-grey eyes blazing through the tears. "How can you say that?"

He had to force the words now. "I mean that I haven't the slightest use for the way Desmond is behaving. In view of the fact that I love you very, very much; it doesn't make sense. I can't understand him, I'm sorry, but I'm close to hating him. It's murderous for me to know he's had the chance he's had with you and thrown it over. At the same time men don't love the way women do, of that I'm certain. Women like you give completely. There are men like Desmond who want love both in their home and out of it. But if you could accept the fact that he's no saint—and—"

"Rob," she broke in, speaking more calmly, "Are you trying to advise me to shut my eyes to Des's behaviour even though he'll keep on betraying me? If you are, I don't understand it. I should have thought that you of all people would realise I couldn't accept what Des is offering me in the future. Just one affair after another. No security—no trust—the sort of love-game some of the couples we know are playing—switching from one to another. It makes me sick—I couldn't do it. But he wants me to accept what he's done and carry on as though it hadn't happened."

Rob's face turned a dusky red.

"It makes me sick too, darling, but—"

"But you're trying to defend him because you are a man and men ought to stick together," she said with a cynicism he had never expected of her.

"Oh, Nira," he said, "forgive me, my dear, if I'm a bit off-beat but I really am shaken by all this."

"You're trying to be charitable to Des because you're fond of me and you want to do what you think best for me and my family."

A bit startled he acquiesced. "Very well, perhaps that's it."

Then she reached up her arms to him. "Rob, I think you're the most marvellous man in the world, and in my way I love you, Rob, very very much."

He felt a lurch of his heart—a throb of his pulses that threatened to break his control. He drew her up and held her against him. For the first time, with passion, he covered her face and throat with kisses. Then at last, her lips. Now it was her turn to be startled by the depth and significance of that long, long kiss. But almost immediately he pushed her away and stood up.

"I'm not being at all helpful to you, Nira," he said tensely, "The whole damn thing is getting too much for me. I love you and not only with affection and friendship. I'm heart and soul in love with you. All I can say is, please forgive me. We both seem to be letting down the defences. It's hopeless for me to pretend any more. I'm a man—a one-woman man if you like. It's *you*. It's been you for a long time and there'll never be another."

Her tears dried and her eyes shone suddenly with a joy she made no effort to conceal.

"Oh, Rob—darling Rob. I do thank you! I feel so proud—you're such a wonderful person. Rob—dear, *dear* Rob—"

She hid her face from him but clung tightly to him with both hands. He held her, in silence. In that complete silence and understanding they stayed close and warm, drawing comfort from each other.

He thought, *To her I am like an elder brother. She feels platonic affection for me, but I cannot feel only this for her. To me she is not a sister. She is the woman I love. I've never felt hatred for any human being before, but I hate Desmond Curtis. I loathe him for what he has done to her. And I hate myself because I want Nira—and I shouldn't. God, it's wrong!*

He was a man of principle. Whatever way the world was going at the moment, he had no use for married men who fooled around with other men's wives or indulged in promiscuous sordid little affairs just because they needed a new excitement to stimulate their appetites. Especially not men with wives like Nira. But while Rob held Nira close—Nira who was so unhappy, spiritually wounded, lost in her woe—he was all too conscious of the physical, as well as the spiritual side of things. He had never in his life before loved a woman seriously. There had been one or two brief affairs during those early days in Kenya, short-lived, half-hearted, almost forgotten.

One in particular with a girl older than himself. She worked in a big photographic centre in Nairobi which he visited regularly. When he had been shooting movies of big game he had seen her quite often and taken her out from time to time.

There had come a night when she had asked him back to the bungalow which she shared with her sister who was away. She was attractive, warm and enticing and had wanted him for her lover. He had learnt quite a lot about women during that brief hectic affair. He had not been the first with her and had no need for compunction, but he had felt remorseful because she had seemed to care a lot more than he did. It ended in them agreeing not to see each other again. He had been frank from the start that he didn't intend to marry but for a long time afterwards she had written him sad little letters. Not for a year had she found another man.

Then, happy and relieved, he sent her a wedding

present, and for her generosity and sweetness he had always been grateful. But it had made him careful not to become involved in the future. So the years for Rob had gone by, during which he made sure there were no more such episodes. He didn't like hurting anyone and he didn't want to be drawn into marriage before he was sure he could settle down to the domestic scene. By nature he was really a lone hand, until now. Nira was different. Now, especially when Desmond looked like breaking up their marriage, he was doubly conscious of the tremendous pull she had at his heartstrings. He wanted to swing from the brother-image to the lover. He felt the crazy beat of his pulses and with passion sweeping him up to heights he had never meant to climb, he began to kiss her madly. The slender vulnerable neck he had always admired so much, the soft pale face wet with tears, and then her lips again. But he put an end to it. He stood up, and taking her by the hand lifted her to her feet.

"I can hardly judge other men. You can see how I feel about you," he said huskily.

For a moment she stared at him with wide startled eyes. Her own blood was leaping *and she knew it*. It confused her and more still was she bewildered by the sudden change in Rob. Old Rob—great favourite at the Club—famous for his integrity, and his quiet authority and his interest in everything. Suddenly today Nira had felt the strength of passion in him. There was a definite vibration between them. Because she was so unhappy she wanted his kisses. But she steadied herself, taking it for granted that this storm had blown up only because he was sorry for her, full of the pity that is so near to love, and that she was in the emotional state to respond.

She thought it best to ignore what had happened, and it was in the old friendly voice that she said, "Thank you, darling, that was sweet of you. Sorry I've been such a drip. I ought to have more sense—and more courage. I'm not the first wife whose husband has gone astray—" she punctuated the last word with a laugh, "and I won't be the last. Here am I a woman of thirty with two children behaving like a teenager!"

Rob put on his glasses. He was alarmed by his own reactions. They were so conclusive. It had been proved to him that he was as vulnerable as any other man in the circumstances and that he was wide awake—in mind, body and spirit. In every way, as he had never been in his life before. It was quite obvious that he was capable of loving this girl—this married woman with her two children—with all the strength of his being. He was like a boy again—intoxicated by the rich promise of her lips. But he was not to allow himself to be led away by what he thought of as *promise*. She had only kissed him back in a sad very human moment of weakness. It promised nothing for the future. It mustn't. The one horrifying thought that followed was his fear that he might lose her altogether now that she *knew* he was in love with her.

But when she spoke again, she said, "I'll never forget all your goodness to me. You'll always be my dearest friend on earth," and she reached up and brushed his lips with the lightest kiss. It filled him with relief and gratitude. He had to exercise all his control as he lightly returned that caress, then gave her a brotherly hug.

"We understand each other completely, my dear. Forget my idiocy and remember only that anything I can do for you in this world I'll do. But what, *what?*"

She smoothed back her hair and put a handkerchief against her lips.

"I don't know." Looking at her reflection in the little mirror over the parlour fireplace she touched her lips with rouge, turned back to Rob and gave a long sigh. "We'll have to see how things work out. I suppose I've got to be sensible and not panic. As you and I once agreed, heaps of couples today have affairs on the side and think nothing of it. I could never lead my life that way, but perhaps Des will settle down in time. So the poignant question is, am I prepared to accept his present behaviour and wait for him to change—or part from him?"

Rob pulled his pipe from his pocket and stuck it between his teeth. He had never felt more inadequate—more reluctant to advise her in the right way. He would liked to have told her to leave Desmond and go away with *him*—just anywhere—yes—so that he could hold her loveliness in his arms for ever and for ever safeguard her from the sort of misery Desmond was causing her.

He forced himself to speak, "I think you should wait awhile as you suggest and perhaps Desmond will see what a fool he is and stop this nonsense. You don't want to break up your home—it wouldn't be good for the children. It never is."

"I agree. If it wasn't for Renira and Jonny perhaps I'd do it."

"I understand."

Not long after all this the children came back from Newquay full of the film they had seen, noisy and excited.

Nira felt a pang of conscience as she looked at her two. Whatever happened, she mustn't break up this marriage—the old charmed circle. It must return. She must think of Des as a boy who was sowing his wild oats and would get tired of the frolic and want to be his old self; the much more reliable and devoted Des she had married and who was father of the family.

Rob left them to go for a long walk by himself across the cliffs. At least the weather seemed more promising. The late afternoon was golden, beautiful; the sky, above a sea that was gradually settling down, blue, shot with green, looked like wrinkled silk with a long frill of cream as the breakers moved in to shore at ebb-tide.

After Rob had gone, Nira read to the children, gave them their milk and biscuits and put them to bed. Whatever the outcome of this holiday they, at least, looked radiant. The wind and the rain and the salt air beating against their little faces had made them as tanned as though they had basked in perpetual sunlight.

As Renira kissed her mother good night she nuzzled her cheek and giggled. "Mr. Wilson said I was a pwitty girl. Am I pwitty, Mummy?"

"Very, my darling."

"There!" said Renira defiantly to her brother, "I told you I was."

"Oh, but you mustn't be vain," Nira smiled, her arms around the small adorable figure in the short floral nightie.

"What's *vain* mean?"

"Too fond of yourself. You mustn't *ever* call yourself pretty. People won't think it nice. Let *them* always say it—never you."

"Why not?"

"Don't ask so many questions," Nira laughed again and pulled the blind down against the last red-gold rays from the setting sun.

Jonathan flung himself on his back, tossed his legs in the air, laughing loudly.

"I don't think she's pretty. She's hideous."

The corners of Renira's lips turned down. Nira hastened to kiss and console her and to tell them both to keep quiet. Then she left them before there could be any more trouble.

Once in her own bedroom she sat down on the edge of the bed and for a moment stared rather miserably around the room. She was so tired. The emotional scene with Rob had disturbed her even while it consoled. She had just told her small daughter not to be vain. Here was she, Nira, against her better judgment, proud and pleased because Rob had called her beautiful. *"You can see how I feel about you,"* he had said, and she had certainly felt the quick tell-tale throb of his heart against her breast. It hadn't left her cold nor had it irritated her, as Boyce's attentions had done. Yet while she analysed the whole situation she knew that she was still Des's wife—Des's girl—and the jealousy was still there, too, stabbing her while she imagined what he might be doing with Frankie Motte. How badly he behaved! Shamefully, *shamelessly* with Rob to see it, too. He had broken every promise he had made to her.

"Oh, what a muddle," she said the words aloud, and the tears pricked her eyelids, but she was determined not to cry again, and when Des came home she wouldn't say a reproachful word. She would pretend that it was quite in order that he should have walked out on his family all day and 'been on a party' as he called it, with that film crowd. Of course if it had been with the crowd it wouldn't have mattered. But Nira knew that Frankie, and Frankie alone, was the draw.

Chapter 13

WHILE THE RAIN continued to fall during the early part of that afternoon, the actors in Vince Lord's film, and the camera crew, had been forced to idle away the time in their hotel. Vince held a conference and informed them that the forecast was good so they would probably be able to shoot the rest of the beach scene tomorrow and get it finished. Then he went off to his own room to sulk. He hated bad weather interfering with his plans and he was more than a little annoyed that Frankie was showing such a marked interest in Desmond Curtis. When he had tackled her about it she had only laughed and said, "Don't be so stupid, darling. You know I hate my boy-friends to go all possessive and that's what you're trying to be. Besides, it's dull down here and Des is terribly good to look at, rather groovy altogether, don't you think? If I want fun and games with him, please shut your blood-shot eyes to it and stop nagging."

"Thanks very much," Vince had answered tartly and disappeared.

Des at her request drove Frankie away from Newquay and down the coast road towards Portreath. Just before they came in to Perranporth, they found an attractive roadhouse where they could have sandwiches and drinks. There was a small sitting-room at the back of the bar which they had to themselves. The landlord was only too pleased to accommodate them. He recognised the famous exciting-looking red-haired film star, and the gentleman was lavish with his money. Good enough! He ordered champagne instead of beer.

Inevitably there followed a session when Frankie, in the best of humours and fortified by the champagne and Des's companionship, ended up in his arms. He amused her. She adored his looks and his sense of humour. He was such a change from Vince. Vince was the clever one all right but she was sick of him *and* that crowd she worked with. They were all the same; weak-sycophantic. There was no such sick-worship in Des's handsome eyes. He asked for nothing. He just *took*— and she was in the mood to be taken—wooed out of her utter boredom.

Later while she dressed again, ran a comb through her glorious hair and put on the white anorak which she wore with white hipsters and long black shiny boots, she smiled at Des's reflection in the mirror.

"Well, lover-boy, are you going to follow me to Rome? You know we're shooting the end of this film there at the end of the week. I want you there with me, baby. What about it?"

Des, sitting on the sofa, a cigarette between his lips, looked at her provocative figure with narrowed eyes. He had had a lot of women in his life but never one quite like Frankie Motte. She was terrific.

He knew that he was behaving shockingly to Nira. Without doubt she *knew*—and old Rob guessed what was up and must think him pretty ghastly. But he couldn't help it. There had never been an opportunity such as this for him to have an affair with a girl like Frankie—an international star. She flattered his ego and made it almost impossible for him to say no to her. When all was said and done he couldn't really understand why she wanted him. She had her pick of so many men, some of them millionaires. But he took what the gods offered and enjoyed it.

Yet in his way, unstable—inconsistent—the image of his wife and children and the home they had built up together, prevailed. What conscience he had was uneasy.

Frankie smiled at him, moved close and rested her hands with their long silvered nails, on his shoulders.

"It was great just now, wasn't it, lover?" she whispered.

He seized one of the hands and kissed it. "You can say that again."

"We just—click—don't we?"

"As far as I'm concerned, you're a riot—a riot, my darling."

And now he pulled her down on the sofa beside him. But she didn't let him hold her for long. She moved away, shaking back her hair, her eyes mocking him under the long false lashes.

"Steady. I've just tidied up. What about Rome?"

He stubbed his cigarette end in an ashtray.

"Darling, I can't possibly. How can I? I'm a married man and I've got a job."

Frankie shrugged.

"You shouldn't have married. It's a stupid institution anyhow."

"I suppose so. You certainly make me feel it is. Like hell I'd like to be free to follow you to Italy."

"And you will, won't you?" she asked softly.

"It's tricky, darling. It's all very well for me to play truant and come over here like this, but to take a week off in Italy—that's not quite the same thing. I'd have frightful trouble with Nira."

Frankie yawned. "She's a nice girl, I'm sure, much nicer than me, but we've only got one life to live and I can't waste mine worrying about other men's wives. She's got her kids and she's got this fellow you call Rob, hasn't she?"

"Not in the way you think. It isn't as simple as all that. She still happens to be in love with me."

"Too bad for her. *I* want you in Rome, lover, and I'm used to getting what I want."

He glanced at his wristwatch, frowning. His brain was still a bit bemused with all the champagne and the events of the afternoon. But he realised that the kissing had got to stop. He must get back to Mawgan Porth, or he'd start a major row between Nira and himself which might have unfortunate results. He was not used to having to face serious decisions of the kind Frankie was trying to impose on him. He liked his affairs to be easy. Nipping in and out of somebody's bedroom was altogether different from throwing up wife and work in order to follow your girl-friend to Italy, even if she was Frankie Motte. *God,* he thought, *what a jungle I'm getting myself into. What's the answer?*

Now suddenly Frankie showed her other side. She went for him as she had gone for Vince when the Curtis family first saw her. She sprang to her feet in a rage and her huge eyes glared down in anger at the man who a few moments ago she had been smothering with kisses.

"Well, listen, baby, I'm not prepared to sit back and wait while you have fits of conscience about your wife and family. If that's the way it is you'd better go back to them right now. We could have had a marvellous time together in Italy—and after that. But your attitude bores me. Please drive me back to Newquay."

Des stood up, his pulses jerking and his face very red.

"Look, Frankie, you don't have to shout at me. Surely we can just talk things over."

"No, we can't. You're a drip. That's what you are. One of these creeps tied to a wife's apron-strings. No use to me—or anyone else who wants fun. Okay! I made a mistake ever thinking you different. But don't start trying to get what you can from both your wife *and* me. Frankie never takes second place to anyone. Just drive me home."

He looked at her. The fever that had crept into his blood for this girl began to simmer down. She was marvellous to look at and to make love to, but she'd be hell to live with, he thought, or to be with for long in any part of the world. Suddenly he remembered Nira—her cool sweetness—her tenderness—her trust in him. A trust that he had betrayed so often.

He felt sick and dispirited. He picked up his jacket and scarf.

"Okay," he said briefly. "Come on."

"No, I've changed my mind. I don't want to drive back with you. You bore me to sobs," she said with a venom that amazed him.

Her vanity, her greed and her belief that the world was her oyster and that she could do exactly what she wanted, was frightening, he decided.

While he struggled into his jacket, she dashed out of the room, crashing the door behind him. A few moments later she came back.

"I've phoned Vince. He's driving over to fetch me. *Goodbye.*"

This was a bit much even for Des. The sudden metamorphosis left him more than a little confused.

"Oh, hell, don't be like this. Can't we part friends? We've had such a wonderful few days together—" he began.

She broke in, "I'm off to the bar to buy myself a drink. I've *had* you, and you needn't bring your precious family down to join the crowd while we're shooting tomorrow. Stay at home and cherish them. That's what you really want to do, isn't it? *Goodbye.*"

She was out of the room again in a flash before he could answer.

He stood a moment lighting another cigarette with shaking fingers. He felt as though he had been swept off his feet in a tornado and he couldn't pick himself up again. Oh, well, let Vincent Lord comfort Frankie and keep her. It would obviously never have worked with him, Des. Unspeakable gloom encircled him as he left Frankie in the bar surrounded by admiring fans. He heard a champagne cork popping as he went out to his car.

God! he thought, and put a hand to his forehead. He was in a wave of perspiration. He had drunk far too much this afternoon. As for Frankie, she could drink him under the table.

He'd have to think of something on the way home that he could say in order to put things right with Nira. This time he really would try to play straight. Frankie had been a new experience and she had had him hypnotised. But there was a sort of corruption under her glamour and today it made him feel lower than he had ever felt in his life before.

Disgusted and remorseful, he climbed into his car and set out for Mawgan Porth. He felt a sharp reaction as the cool evening breeze blew against his hot face. A bit dazed. He must drive slowly, he told himself. He'd had a lot more than any test for alcohol content would permit. His eyes weren't focusing all that well, and these damn Cornish roads were narrow and winding. They could be tricky. He drove carefully for the first few miles then speeded up, anxious suddenly to get back to the wife he had treated so badly. He wanted to be in time to say good night to the kids. Poor old Jonathan— he hadn't played much cricket with the boy this holiday, but he'd make up for it tomorrow. It looked like being a fine day.

Just before he came into Newquay, Des was doing a steady sixty miles an hour in the Marina. His brain had not cleared. He felt suddenly sick and dizzy and afraid that he might pass out. He jammed his foot down on the brake and swerved across the road. It was at this point that an articulated lorry came round the corner on the wrong side. It hit the bonnet of the Marina with a sickening impact, buckling metal, shattering glass, and hurling Des from an instant of pain and panic into darkness and silence. For him it was the end not only of marriage but of life itself.

It took over an hour before a police car arrived on the scene followed by an ambulance. It took another half an hour before Des's body could be taken from the wreckage of the car. Then, with the lorry driver who was suffering from shock and cuts, they were taken to Newquay Hospital. There, a letter in the dead man's wallet, revealed his name and gave the police the information that he had booked rooms at Trevarra Farm in Mawgan Porth.

At seven o'clock a telephone call to the farm broke the news to Mrs. Curtis.

NIRA'S STORY

Chapter 1

WHEN YOU GET hit really hard, if it doesn't kill you it affects your mind. On the day that the police told me that Des had been killed on his way back from Newquay, I felt absolutely stunned and numb. I didn't feel any pain. I couldn't cry. I remember calling for Rob who came running down from his bedroom. He told me afterwards that when he saw me he was positively scared because I looked so ghastly. He took off his glasses and came up to me quickly.

"Nira, what is it? What's happened?"

"Des has been killed," I answered his question, and told him all that the police had told me. Rob looked quite blank at first then, as the truth broke over him, he was as shocked as I was. He took my hands, drew me to the sofa and told me to sit down while he fetched me a brandy. There wouldn't have been any in the farmhouse but dear Aunt Ida had packed a flask in Rob's case. She believed in using brandy medicinally in times of stress. "I can't believe it," I kept saying to Rob, my teeth chattering, "I can't."

"My God, how awful!" Rob said, staring down at me.

"History repeating itself," I said. "When are the horrors going to end? It isn't so long ago that Cricket died in almost the same way, crushed in the wreckage of her car."

The ever-resourceful Rob refused to let me talk about that.

"I'd better go to the police station at Newquay at once," he said. "Yes," I nodded.

He went off to fetch his car-keys. I found Mrs. Hoskin and told her what had happened.

"Oh my *gracious!*" exclaimed Mrs. Hoskin and put a hand up to her mouth. *"Never* such a thing! It can't be true. Oh, you poor dear, you do look bad!"

"I'm all right," I said. "But I've got to go and identify the body." It sounded crude, even callous, saying that, but there it was.

It was such a peaceful fine evening—never had the sea looked calmer or the sky more wonderful, full of amber and crimson light. The air was soft and gentle as it could so often be during a Cornish summer. One could never dream there were such things as storms or the havoc of gales—or the horror of sudden violent death.

Rob drove very quietly—out of consideration for me of course. I sat with one hand in his. He released it only now and again when he had to turn a corner.

I was haunted for ages by the memory of that grim session at Newquay police station. First the mortuary. A Des I just didn't recognise lay there on a slab, white and still, and quite remote from life. His face was extraordinarily untouched and handsome. It was his body that had received the full impact of the crash. I remember looking at my poor dead husband in a dazed sort of way, thinking how young he looked in death. He had recently been growing rather fleshy about the jowl, and was all too often flushed and rakish. But this was the Des I had married—or, at least a white marble image of him. I couldn't believe that he'd never laugh again—never again be the boisterous racy Des of former times—the good raconteur, the splendid lover I had loved so well.

Without Rob I couldn't have got through those dark hours. In the mortuary I held very tightly on to his hand. Before I left Des I leaned down and kissed his forehead, then turned away shuddering because it had so soon grown icy-cold. A kind policewoman took me away to have a cup of tea while Rob made all the necessary arrangements on my behalf.

I had told him that Gandy would never forgive me if

Des was buried down here. She wouldn't travel so far to the funeral. She would expect me to take Des back to Sussex, and possibly want him buried or cremated in Brighton, because it was her present home. I didn't care—it didn't seem to matter. Neither did I count the cost of it all. I was quite sure that when I came out of this stupor, this being what the Americans call 'in shock', I would start to cry and feel desperately sad— even though Des had betrayed me, and I was no longer his lover. But I was still his wife and he was the father of my children. Poor Renira and Jonathan—they had lost their father. That wasn't a good thing. It was only fortunate they were so young and wouldn't feel so upset as they might have been if they were older.

Gandy was the one I was sorry for. Des was the apple of her eye and her only child. I dreaded what it might do to her.

We went back to the farm. I eventually told the children that Daddy had gone away. I didn't want to tell them the truth just then, I couldn't, personally, stand any more emotional scenes. I just wanted them to go up to bed and to leave me alone. I didn't even want Rob at that time. I longed to be left quite by myself to think everything out, and to try to see the situation more clearly.

Des had left me for ever. I was his widow. I would never see him again. I stood in the same shoes that Boyce had worn when Cricket died. Funny that I kept thinking about Cricket. I even wondered crazily if they were now meeting each other in heaven—and what they would be saying. Or wouldn't they get to heaven? Hadn't they been good enough Christians?

In my nervous rather hysterical state I started to laugh. Rob was in the room and he immediately came and treated me quite roughly. He shook me and said, "Now stop it, Nira. *Stop it*. You've been marvellous up to now. Don't lose your grip."

I did stop laughing, I must say. I just felt desperately tired.

"Sorry," I said, "I think I had better go upstairs to bed. Tell Mrs. Hoskin that I don't want any supper.

You have yours, please. And thank you, dear, *dear* Rob for all you've done."

"I've done nothing," he said. "But I don't want you to go without supper. You can't afford to be ill. You'll need all your strength during these next few days."

Darling Rob, I am sure he was quoting Aunt Ida; as if going without my supper would make me ill! But I made no further protest when he said he would ask Mrs. Hoskin to take me up a tray, even if it was only a cup of tea and an egg.

"Oh, Rob," I said, "it's a sort of nightmare. Can you believe that Des is dead and never coming back—and that we'll never see him or speak to him again?"

"It must be terribly hard for you to accept," he said gently, then in his practical way, reminded me that I hadn't yet contacted Des's mother.

So before I could go to my room and shut myself in and give way to the tears that were beginning to burn against my eyelids, I had another miserable task to perform. Perhaps the hardest of them all. I had to break the awful news to Gandy. I didn't dare leave it, in case it was put in the newspapers and she'd see it like that. So many bad accidents are reported and Des worked for a very well-known firm, which reminded me that I had also to contact Mr. Steadman, Des's chief.

Oh, there were going to be so many things I must do—gruesome, ugly things. I was quite capable of carrying them out, but on that night I didn't feel I could face too much without cracking.

Rob offered to ring Gandy for me, but I wouldn't let him. I had to speak to her myself. How I managed to get the words out I don't know. She had answered my call so brightly, saying that she had been thinking of us all enjoying ourselves now that the weather was improving, and was Des brown and how were the darling babes? She even began to tell me what a big success she had had at bridge the night before and how she'd won a little slam, doubled, redoubled and vulnerable. Wasn't it thrilling?

Feeling sick, I then interrupted her chatter and told her about Des.

I must say she took it fairly well. She was quite a good person in her way, my mother-in-law, and of course, she knew absolutely nothing about the rift between Des and myself. She was for once decent enough to think of me before herself.

After she had groaned a little, she said, "Oh, my God, my God," and then, "Oh, my poor Nira and those poor children! What a terrible thing. Oh, *why* did it have to happen? I was afraid of it."

"Why?" I echoed her words.

I could hear her crying. I felt dreadfully sorry for her.

"Try not to be too sad, Gandy," I said. "At least we can be sure that he'll never grow old or have to bear a protracted illness or anything. He's at peace. They say he couldn't have known anything—just died instantly. He didn't suffer and he was having such a lovely time down here. He said it was the best holiday he'd ever had, with all that film crowd."

The words almost stuck in my throat. The telephone was in the parlour and Rob was there because I'd told him not to go. He had his back to me. I knew he was smoking his pipe and I wondered what he must have been thinking when he heard all the lies I had to tell. I had to make things as good as possible for poor Gandy. When she stopped crying and spoke to me again, I told her we would be coming home as soon as we could bring Des.

Then Gandy made the really big gesture. "That would be an awful business," she said. "Why not let our poor boy be buried in some nice little Cornish churchyard. I'll come down for the funeral. You arrange it and I'll get a hired car. I'll take the children back with me and I'll look after them while you are sorting things out. I know Susan's away," she went on, "so I'll be as helpful as I can, my dear," then she burst into tears again.

I comforted her and thanked her and told her we'd always stick together and all that sort of thing, then she thanked me and said she'd let me know when she'd arrive. I hung up. It was then the tears began to roll down my cheeks. I think I was so touched by the way Gandy had taken the news. I was sure she didn't really want to come all the way down to Cornwall. As a rule she was such a selfish, self-centred woman, but she had loved Des and she loved the children, and I made a vow that I'd always make it easy for her to see plenty of them.

When I put down the phone and turned to Rob, he took me gently in his arms and smoothed my hair as he had done so often. Once again he was the big brother I needed.

"There, there," he kept saying, "I know what you must be feeling."

So ended that tragic day.

Then came the funeral, Des was buried, as his mother wished, in a lovely little cemetery between Mawgan Porth and St. Columb, and the children and I were back in Nylands before I felt the full impact of what had happened. This time I wasn't stunned. I was cool, self-possessed and capable, even though fully alive to all the pain and trouble that followed Des's death.

Gandy kept her promise and took the children off my hands. Susan was due back in three days' time—we had all about reached the end of our holiday fortnight, but Gandy said she'd keep the children as long as I liked if Susan would take the train into Brighton every day to help her. The high-spirited pair were a bit much for a woman of Gandy's age and temperament, but she continued to be very unselfish about the whole thing.

The first week back in Ponders Heath was ghastly for me of course. The local paper was full of the accident. Pictures of Des and of me and the full story of the accident in Cornwall. There followed the usual spate of letters from friends and relations all of which had to be answered by me. A personal visit from Mr. Steadman who said the firm had lost an excellent man, much to be regretted. Flowers from dozens of my friends. Unexpected bouquets from people I hardly knew in Ponders Heath. It was amazing how much kindness one could be shown at such a time. Of course all the members of the Club were stunned by the news and although I didn't go up there at all, Rob, who came daily to see if he could do anything for me, said they all told him how sadly they would miss Des's cheerful attractive presence. Like me, they also looked back to poor Cricket's accident and the superstitious among them wondered gloomily if there would be a third accident among the members.

I told Rob that I'd received a huge bunch of roses—long-stemmed pink ones, with asparagus fern—from Maggie and her mother. A letter with it. Rob read it.

"My dear Nira,
You've no idea how grieved my mother and I were when we heard your dreadful news. It must have been a terrible shock for you and we send all our sympathies to you and your children. Des will never be forgotten by any of us. He was a great person. Please do let me come and see you one day.
Maggie."

Rob took off his glasses and met my gaze—a sort of understanding look passed between us. I gave what he must have thought a wintry smile.

"Nice letter," he said.

"Very nice," I said. "Poor Maggie."

"Why poor Maggie?"

"Never mind," I said, "death wipes out everything, doesn't it?"

And after those cryptic words I put on a coat and went out with him. I'd promised to have dinner at The Hollies. I was eating so little, Rob was worried about me. He said I looked like a ghost. Perhaps I did. I'm sure I'd lost weight, and that was only ten days after Des was laid to his last long rest.

Then came the business of sorting out all his things, most of which were his clothes which I gave away to the W.V.S. His personal valuables like his gold watch and his nice cuff links, of course I kept for Jonathan. It was a bleak job emptying his cupboards and drawers and still I couldn't quite believe he would never come back into his room, and this house. There would be no more love between us, and no more hate—which was the other side of love. I must let him remain in my memory not as the man who had made me so unhappy towards the end, but as the Des who had given me years of happiness when we first married.

Then there was all the legal business. Des had made a will. He left everything to me. Gandy came over to be present when the solicitor, Mr. Parsons, lunched with us and told us all about it.

Now came a fresh blow—a financial one for the children anyhow, although I didn't seem to mind much what it did to me. But Des, having left me everything, seemed to have borrowed so much in recent years without me knowing it, that most of his assets had already been swallowed up. The house was mortgaged, though not for much. I would at least have that to sell. All the shares his father had left him and which I thought were safely tucked away to bring in dividends and profits, had been sold. Bills came pouring in. I thought I used to know everything Des did, but I was wrong. He had his suits made by the most expensive tailors. He had ordered so much drink, and so many boxes of cigars and spent so much more in town than he ever did at home or on his family—it was little wonder he had accumulated big debts. Mr. Parsons said after they were paid there would be practically nothing left for me except Des's office pension and I'd have my widow's allowance, and something for the children. Obviously I should not be able to go on living at Nylands.

I didn't want Gandy to know all the things that Des had done but couldn't stop Mr. Parsons letting the cat out of the bag. He told her that Des had even borrowed on his life-insurance. I wouldn't get much of that.

Gandy's delicate powdered face turned quite red with anger and disbelief.

"But Des wasn't like that. He was a good-family man. I can't believe he has left his wife in such poor circumstances," she declared.

Mr. Parsons coughed and cleared his throat, and said he was sorry but those were the facts.

Gandy turned to me, utterly woebegone.

"Is it true, Nira? Had you any idea Des was being so extravagant?"

"No," I said, as steadily as I could.

"He was such a wonderful husband to you always."

"Yes," I said.

Gandy put a handkerchief to her eyes and her lips. "Oh, *dear!*" she wailed.

I looked at Mr. Parsons.

"I don't really understand what he spent all this money on, because we weren't so terribly free with it when Des was alive," I said. "How can he have spent it?"

"Gambling on the Stock Exchange, much of the time—that's how a lot of men lose their money," answered Mr. Parsons.

I nodded. It was possible. Des had always been unpredictable, and at times he used to rush into all kinds of projects without due thought.

So, to the list of his other follies—the ones I knew about—I must add gambling.

"Oh, well," I said, "I can always get a job. Anybody of my age with any intelligence can get a job these days. But it'll be hard on the children."

Gandy sniffed into her handkerchief.

"I shall still continue to make you a small allowance," she said, "but I haven't got so much money myself after paying tax and my own bills. I'll go on supplying the money for the children's education, but I couldn't begin to keep this home going for you. After all, I'm only in my sixties. I might live for a long time yet. I mustn't touch my capital."

"Very wise, Mrs. Curtis," said Mr. Parsons, whom I thought a rather smug stupid man. I wondered why Des had dealt with him, then remembered his father had dealt with Mr. Parsons' father—he was Gandy's solicitor as well. I said no more. I felt so tired. A feeling of absolute exhaustion weighed me down.

After Mr. Parsons had gone, Gandy went back to Brighton. She had left the children at the flat with Susan for the afternoon.

The *children,* I thought—I must have them home

this weekend. Gandy was looking weary and no doubt she would like some peace and quiet just now. I personally didn't think I would ever know peace or quiet again. I was living in a sort of cyclone that continued to whirl around me. On top of the horror of Des's death I now had to face the fact that I was going to be very badly off in future. Probably I'd make a profit on the sale of the house. But I would have to live on my investments. I began to see myself and Renira and Jonathan caged in a little place somewhere, counting every penny. I would certainly have to resign from the golf club. There would be no more golf parties or expensive holidays abroad.

It should all have been so different.

Oh, Des, I thought, *Oh, Des, what have you done to us?*

Yet I knew that what I was suffering today was as nothing—compared with the pain I had felt when I first learned that he had been unfaithful to me.

Without undue flattery to myself I think I had been a good wife to Des but I was never much of a hand with the accounts. That was something he always saw to. He used to pay the bills (so he said) and keep the receipts. I left the financial side to him. But I'd made a mistake. For here I was—each morning receiving another little bill—or a big one—for Mr. Desmond Curtis, and it all had to be sent to Mr. Parsons to be paid for out of Des's pitifully small estate.

I don't know what I'd have done without Gandy. Tiresome she used to be but now she was kind and sympathetic. Of course I bolstered up her image of her wonderful son. "He was a faithful devoted boy and we shall never see his like," she once said to me, weeping into her handkerchief. All I could do was to agree and try to remember the Des I had married.

Most of our old friends and acquaintances either called on me or phoned to say they wanted to come and see me. Lady Conniston stooped from her self-made pedestal and sent a gracious little note sympathising with my dreadful loss and begging me to take the children up to the Manor House any time I wanted. So once or twice I sent Jonathan up to play with the Conniston boy but I refused all invitations to meals with his parents. The Moffatts were very kind—Joyce having lost her twins in an accident, was swift to try and be a help and comfort, but I didn't feel close to her. Nor did I to any of my golfing friends. Strange and sad to say, it was Maggie I had liked best but she most of all I did not want to see. So I was very much alone and once the children were in bed I found myself wandering desolately from room to room and ending in my solitary bed, crying from fatigue, grief, all the emotions that could weigh a widow down. I didn't want to talk to anyone about Des and I didn't want to be the object of pity. Crushed though I was by this avalanche that had suddenly descended upon me, I had, as they say, my pride. I couldn't parade my sorrows. I devoted myself entirely to the children. Needless to say I had to send Susan packing. I couldn't possibly afford her now. She was very upset and even offered to take a lower salary in order to stay with us but of course I wouldn't let her. I could deal with driving the kids to and from school, and here, at home.

I could also afford to keep Mrs. Tulk, my daily, once a week, while I was selling up. I know I should have felt that losing my lovely home was a real tragedy but somehow I couldn't wait to get out. Everything reminded me of Des. Unfortunately I remembered all too vividly the rows we had had in recent months, and the tears I had shed, lying in that double bed of ours when he left me alone. The sooner I could make a new life for myself and the children elsewhere the better.

This sentiment was intensified after I received an express letter from Boyce from Peru (Jonathan would love all those huge exotic stamps) but the contents of the letter were slightly alarming. Boyce had heard about Des from Colonel Moffatt who corresponded with him. He said how shocked and distressed he was and sent his deepest sympathies, then added that he more than anyone could feel for me after what had happened to Cricket. The important line was to say he was coming back to England.

The job in Peru hadn't worked out. To begin with, Simon had perpetual sinus trouble since he arrived. He had also grown very thin and nervy and didn't seem to want to leave his father and fly back to England. Boyce disliked the set-up in Peru and had asked Head Office to send him home. It wasn't a good thing to do but Boyce didn't think the firm would sack him. He might just have to accept a lesser position. However, as a good research engineer he had no fears of not finding another job, even if he quit the firm. He ended by saying that he had booked a flight back to London on the 1st of October. He would bring Simon to Ponders Heath to his old school and he, himself, would look for a flat there. He had missed his old friends at the golf club and life in the Heath generally. He ended:

It seems years instead of months since I left England. It's you I miss most of all, dear lovely Nira. Maybe we shall be able to comfort each other a little. At least I can bring you my friendship.

He signed himself *Forever, Boyce.*

I could feel his presence as I read that letter and see those rather bold hazel eyes fixing me with a look that gave no room for doubt as to how he was feeling. *Comfort each other!* For heaven's sake! The last thing I wanted was to be comforted by Boyce or to renew that particular friendship. I had hoped I'd cut right away from him, or the memory of Cricket.

I took the letter up to The Hollies and showed it to Rob.

"I don't think I could take another session of Boyce. I think I'll sell Nylands at once. You know I've been putting it off because I just didn't feel I could tackle all that had to be done. But now I'm better. I *must* start sorting and packing. I did phone two agents who both said they were sure they could get me a handsome profit. Some of it of course will go toward settling overdrafts and bills, but Mr. Parsons thinks I'll have enough left to buy a nice flat somewhere for the children and myself."

We were sitting out in the small walled garden at the back of The Hollies, drinking our before-lunch sherries. Aunt Ida had been in bed for several days with one of her bronchial-asthma attacks.

I saw Rob's expression alter. He looked alarmed.

"But you're not going to leave Ponders Heath?"

"Everything's very expensive here," I sighed. "It's the commuters' paradise and Des's mother is terribly anxious for me to get a little place in Brighton so that we'd be near her."

Rob didn't answer for a moment, but he took off the tinted glasses and blinked his eyes at me.

"Shan't take kindly to that idea. I'd feel it an awful loss if you leave this vicinity."

As ever, my heart warmed to him but I was still uncertain as to whether I wanted to go on living in this town. It was so full of memories of Des—and Cricket—*and* Maggie. I'd be certain to meet *her*. Or would I soon stop letting anything upset me? Would I grow indifferent—even callous—reach a pitch where the name of Des would neither hurt nor distress?

Rob, his brows raised, handed me back Boyce's letter.

"Has this got you down? Because if you don't want to see Boyce we'll just make it plain to him. I can't say I'm all that pleased that he means to come back to the neighbourhood. Sorry about the little boy, of course, but I never did think Peru a good idea for Simon, even in the holidays."

"Oh, I could tackle Boyce—it isn't that—oh, Rob, I don't know *what* it is. I just want to get away."

"I understand," he said gently, "but would you be any happier in Brighton?"

"I don't know," I said, "I don't seem to know anything any more."

He picked up my right hand and touched it with his lips.

"Poor darling, it's all such a grim shake-up of your life. Everything seems to have happened within such a short time. I can't say I blame you for wanting to get away but I do feel while you are in the Heath I can keep an eye on you and the children and be of some help to you."

Now I took his hand and pressed it between my own. I felt the tears well in my eyes.

"Oh, you are marvellous to me. You've done everything so far. But I just honestly *don't* know what to do."

"Sell Nylands, and get what money you can," he said quietly. "Then why not store your things and take a little furnished flat or go into a small hotel until you've made up your mind where you do want to live permanently."

"You mean near my mother-in-law?"

I could see before he answered, that it wasn't at all what he meant or what he wanted. It was always a comfort to feel the warmth of Rob's tender affection for me. He was in love with me. I learned that from the passion of his kisses, his touch, down in Cornwall, on the day Des died. But he hadn't shown me that side since. He had been strictly controlled. He had given me just what I wanted—friendship and advice, and great kindness.

"I'll have a talk with my mother-in-law and see what evolves," I said.

The woman who came in to cook the hot midday meal for Rob and his aunt announced that lunch was ready. Rob pulled me up from my chair, tucked my arm through his and walked me into the dining-room.

"Now stop worrying and puzzling and planning. Just enjoy your meal. I've opened a half-bottle of claret. It's rather good, and it'll do *you* good!"

Later, after seeing the old lady, I went back to my home to prepare supper for the kids and then fetch them back from school. I looked with slightly worried eyes at the car. How much longer was I going to be able to run *that?* Despite Gandy's help I really had to cut down drastically. A car was a luxury even in this day and age when everybody seemed to have one. But, my goodness! I'd miss it, I'd be absolutely pinned wherever I was if I hadn't got a car. It wasn't all that old. No doubt I could sell it quite well, but I determined to keep it as long as I could.

I was glad there was no need for me to answer

Boyce's letter. He would be home almost as soon as a note would reach Peru. The irritation I had felt when I first learned that he intended to come back to the Heath—and pursue me again—soon faded. I had so much else to think of and do.

There were many more miserable moments ahead. So far, I hadn't begun to go through letters and papers except those Mr. Parsons had asked for and which were kept in Des's bureau. But suddenly I found a cigar-box in one of the drawers. I lifted up some of the cigars to see how many there were, wondering if I could give them to Rob. Underneath the bottom row lay a letter. Obviously he had put it there, in order to hide it.

My better self told me to tear it in half without reading it but I wasn't strong-minded enough to do this. I pulled the letter out of its envelope. It was written in a curly sort of feminine hand—vaguely familiar. I looked first at the signature. *Maggie.* I thought I'd recognised her writing! She had sent me a letter of sympathy after Des died. As I scanned it I began to feel sick and thoroughly resentful of this pretty dewey-eyed woman who had so ruthlessly taken Des's love from me. There it was for me to see in black and white and to make me all the more convinced that Des had been slightly sex-mad and ready to give way to his passions.

Maggie wrote like a lovesick schoolgirl. She mentioned that it was the first time she had dared write to him. He must have kept the letter out of sheer vanity because it was so full of praise for his looks, his strength, his wit, all the things that attracted her.

One paragraph stood out:

It was that first long kiss between us that decided me I couldn't say no to you any more. You were the lover I've always wanted. I've been so lonely since Bill died. I know you belong to Nira and I feel guilty but I must have you. Last night was marvellous. Oh, Lover, let us somehow perserve our feeling for each other. No one need ever know. I don't want to take you away from Nira but I do want your love. Oh, my darling—

I didn't read any more. I felt a sudden blind rage and tore that letter into shreds. How dared she? *How dared she* take what she called his love behind my back, even for a single night? She should have known better, seeing how she had loved Bill. How would she have liked it if I had tried to take him from *her?* Of course, she was lonely. So was I *right now* but I'm damned if I'd go and steal some other woman's man.

When had they spent this night together? I racked my brains and supposed it was any one of the nights when my dear hard-working husband said that he had to work at the office.

So when it was no longer Cricket, it was Maggie. Maggie was supposed to have given him up because of her conscience. But he had been her lover; and from her arms, he had come back to mine then to Frankie Motte's.

Suddenly hate surged over me. I literally sobbed in sheer anger and disgust. Then I rang up Gandy. I said, "I'm selling up Nylands as soon as I possibly can now. I don't want to do anything permanent in a hurry, but the children must go on with their schooling here, it suits them. So if you'll forgive me, Gandy, I'll just take a little furnished place or go into a small hotel like The Swan, outside Ponders Heath. They let rooms. No, I don't want to come to Brighton at the moment, Gandy. Forgive me and try to understand that there is so much for me to do here."

Gandy, kind and generous though she had been, did not quite understand and seemed upset. But that was her selfish side. She wanted the children to be near her no matter how awkward it made things for me. I managed to smooth her down and rang off. Her final words echoed in my ears:

"The tone of your voice tells me that you are changing, Nira dear. You mustn't let grief harden you."

I didn't know whether to laugh or cry about that. Hard! Yes, I had had to harden up. I wanted to. But my grief, if she but knew, was not so much because I had lost my husband as because I had lost my faith—

my intrinsic belief in goodness, in fidelity. Of course I had learnt what he was like before I ever came across that letter in the cigar box, but I admit that it upset me. It made me feel so utterly humiliated. I'd had to *share* Des. How horrible!

That night, when I was putting the children to bed I looked at Jonathan. How like his father he was growing, with that mop of chestnut hair, his fresh complexion and tall lanky body, and the cleft in his chin! Would he turn out to be a good stable kind of man or would he be another Des? Heaven forbid! I wouldn't want him to hurt any woman as Des had hurt me.

Jonny was putting on his pyjamas. He turned and gave me a roguish look.

"Renira and I have got a secret, Mum. We're not going to tell you."

I said nothing. That look was so like Desmond's and I'd had enough of secrets and things being kept from me. I suppose I was silly, but I just turned and ran out of the room, shut myself into my own bedroom and cried as I hadn't cried since Des's death.

Chapter 2

IT WAS JOYCE Moffatt who gave me the not unattractive idea for making a little money, and keeping Nylands a bit longer, which I now decided that I wanted—mainly because the children were so attached to it. They loved the garden in the summer. They had a fishpool and they each had a little plot of their own. They would be sad if they had to leave it at once. Then Joyce, who I met at the greengrocer's—it always seemed to be the meeting place for the shoppers in my circle—said, "Why don't you put an advertisement in the paper and take in two or three students? There's that new college that's opened in Reigate and everyone says that they can't get rooms for love or money. It isn't too far from Ponders Heath. Would you hate the thought?"

For the space of a minute I did hate it and said that I had made up my mind to leave Nylands, then Joyce embroidered on her theme. Some nice youngsters would undoubtedly help me in the evenings and I wouldn't feel so lonely, and they might baby-sit in Susan's place if I wanted to go out to a meal or a theatre or something. I'd get an income out of it even if only during the winter. I could sell the house next summer.

"I know how you feel—all at sixes and sevens," Joyce went on sympathetically, "but nice houses are so expensive—or even flats—and a friend of mine who has wanted to come to Ponders Heath for ages, hasn't been offered a thing worth having. You'd have a job getting fixed up."

I went home and brooded over this idea.

By this time—October—I'd told the children the truth about their Daddy. Jonathan, the older of the two and most sensitive, cried a bit. Renira looked puzzled, and pouted, but ended by saying with a cheerful smile, "I expect he's gone to heaven, don't you, Mummy, so he'll be able to make it all nice for us."

Whatever Des had done to me I couldn't feel hard or cynical in the face of that sort of remark. I just hugged Renira and hid her pretty face against my shoulder so that she shouldn't see that Mummy was crying. Lucky children! The thought of death held no sinister meaning for them. Almost as soon as they broke away from me they were giggling over some shared joke.

I wandered around my lonely house and felt it would be ghastly every night once the children had gone to bed. I wouldn't go out much in the winter, no matter where I lived, and if I got a smaller house or a flat, I wouldn't be able to have anyone to stay. If I let rooms here I'd have to cook a bit extra for the girls but no more than I used to cook for Des and myself.

Some gay teenagers!—the idea grew on me. Joyce had got something.

When I next saw Rob, I asked what he thought and he gave me that little enigmatic smile that grooved lines on either side of his mouth, and said, "A very good idea if it's going to keep you in Ponders Heath, my dear. I agree with Joyce. Don't be in too much hurry to sell till after Christmas, particularly if you can make a bit of money out of your lodgers."

I gave him a rather wintry smile in return. I knew of course that he wanted me to stay so the idea appealed to him. Strange to say, when I asked Gandy, *she* too agreed with Joyce. "I'd been thinking it over," she said, "and I actually talked to my lawyer about you yesterday. What with the mortgage you'd have to pay off, you wouldn't get all that much capital out of the sale and there'd be agent's fees and the expense of moving and getting a new place together. When you move, windows are always different and you can rarely use your old curtains—or carpets. You'd only have to give the students breakfast and an evening meal. Try it—see how it goes."

She added that she'd been concerned about the children moving so soon from their old home—especially as I didn't want to come to Brighton. I might as well stay at Nylands, she said.

"Are you very lonely, my poor Nira?" she then asked.

"Yes," I said flatly.

But I couldn't explain to her that it wasn't so much the loneliness that hurt me as the awful misery and resentment that kept sweeping over me at the thought that Des had never really belonged to me. *Never* in the way I had imagined. He had also blotted his copybook so badly during our last year together that he had destroyed the romantic love I had found so lovely. There was nothing left for me but bitterness and I didn't find it easy to get over it, despite the fact that I knew that sort of feeling gets you nowhere and only makes things worse.

I was very close to Rob during this crisis in my life.

He was my backbone. I often felt I'd have fallen right over, mentally, without his steady devotion. But I was also unable to forget that he was in love with me. It didn't worry me particularly except that I didn't want him to be hurt, and it was a dangerous situation because I was only human and the passion I had shared with my late husband was a passion not to be easily annihilated. Just because I was widowed and Des had behaved badly, it couldn't quite kill my longing for the warmth of a man's embrace and the touch of his lips on my mouth and all the shared ecstasy of the union between male and female which can be the most marvellous thing in the world. Bitter I might be, but I could not suddenly turn myself into a frigid cynical creature who found sex ugly and mistrusted all men.

I wasn't particularly ashamed of my natural inclinations, but I *was* rather ashamed because I didn't find my children enough. They were a tremendous comfort and a reason for living, but I was only just thirty. How was I going to live for so many more years being only a mother and a housewife? *How?*

The real danger lay in Rob's tremendous love for me. He said nothing, did nothing, but I always knew it was there. I was sure that I had only to hold out my arms and he'd take me in his. It wouldn't be fair, because I didn't want him as I had wanted Des—with *all* of me, and Rob was too good a person to be given short measure.

I was growing thin and nervy. The sooner I filled my house with people and tired myself out with work, the better. So I set out to get my students.

I had room for four and finally I took in four, despite Rob's fear that I might find it all too much with only Mrs. Tulk to help, and my two obstreperous children, plus the cooking and shopping.

"Let me get on with it, Rob," I told him. "I *need* to go to bed worn out. Just try and understand."

I think he did. He seemed to understand everything. He just patted my shoulder and said, "Okay, but try to take it a bit easier, darling."

I had learnt to be a careful shopper and I quite enjoyed giving the girls nice little meals when they came back from Reigate. Two of them were English—nineteen-year-old sisters named Moira and Jennifer Williams—from the Lake District. Nice quiet girls. One of them, obviously brilliant, was reading pure mathematics, the other history. They shared my spare room. Des's room I changed completely, steeling my heart against memories. The girls I put in there were both over twenty and foreigners—a fair-haired Danish beauty, Ingrid, and a petite dark little French girl from Boulogne. They were both reading English.

Ingrid was the star-turn.

She played a guitar and quite often entertained us in the evening, and of course the boy-friends began to arrive. I was determined not to be a difficult landlady. I gave the girls a key and told them to come in when they wanted and just not to make too much noise and wake the children.

I must admit some of the boy-friends were hardly my type—long hair, hairy faces, strange garments. One had a bushy beard and looked like a disciple. But they were all so nice, so interested in culture, in books or art or music—or in politics and events of the day. They treated me so sweetly—just as though I was their age. We had tremendous fun over our debates.

Renira attached herself fervently to the beautiful Ingrid and begged to be allowed to learn the guitar. Jonathan had a crush on Moira, because she was reading history and that was his subject at school. She couldn't have been nicer to him—treated him as though he were a fellow student, which thrilled him. So it worked out quite well and I suddenly found my life growing fuller. It had more purpose and it was almost as though the voices, the laughter, the music, the comings and goings of all these youngsters drove away the ghost of Des. My house was not now so full of painful memories.

I tried not to be extravagant and only at times gave the kids expensive food and had the odd bottle of wine. I made enough profit to satisfy me. My health and spirits improved. Rob was pleased about that.

"You're beginning to look your old self," he said.

"You might be one of the young students instead of the lady of the house."

He came in to see us several evenings. He admired Ingrid. Everybody did. She had long beautiful legs, long silky wheaten-coloured hair and eyes as blue as forget-me-nots; plus a dimple in one cheek. She laughed a lot and had an engaging broken accent. She talked enthusiastically to Rob because he had been to Norway in his youth and loved salmon fishing, so they found a lot in common. In fact Rob was very popular with all the girls who ended up by calling him Uncle Rob, as the children did.

"It makes me feel older than Abraham," Rob laughed on one occasion when we were talking.

"I don't think Ingrid looks on you as Abraham," I said a trifle drily. "She told me the other day that you were *too* charming—so English—so dignified."

"Dear, *dear!*" murmured Rob.

"Don't you think she's marvellous to look at and enchanting when she sings?" I asked.

"As a matter of fact I do," he nodded.

It was at that precise moment that I became conscious of jealousy. If Rob fell in love with some beautiful girl and tumbled into the marriage he had avoided for so long, I would definitely be upset. My heart-beats quickened. I felt my cheeks grow red. But I grinned at Rob.

"You ought to take her out one evening," I said deliberately.

"I'm sure she has plenty of boy-friends to do that."

"Her particular boy-friend has gone back to Norway," I persisted, "and she hasn't got another."

Looking up at him I saw him smiling—rather a mysterious little smile. I didn't know what it meant but I just went on attacking him. "Well, why *don't* you take her out? She doesn't think you old at all and she'd be thrilled."

He caught me suddenly by both my hands. "What's all this about? Are you match-making? Are you suggesting that I should start an affair of sorts with the beautiful Dane?"

I felt quite childishly annoyed with him. I pulled my hands away, and shrugged my shoulders.

"Well—why not?"

Then he grabbed hold of me and held me very tightly.

"There are moments," he said, "when I could beat you." And he kissed me on the mouth. It wasn't a light kiss. It was long, passionate and demanding—even more so than the ones he had given me down in Cornwall when I first realised how he felt about me.

When he lifted his head he was breathing very fast. He said, "Don't you dare try to pair me off with any of your students, and that goes for Ingrid or anyone else. You know perfectly well who attracts *me,* and now if you don't mind I've got to get home. Sorry if I lost my head. I'll be seeing you."

Just like that! And he went off before I could call him back or say another word to him.

He left me really confused. I didn't know what I felt about Rob, or what I wanted, or anything else. I just sat down and put my face in my hands and cried. But I couldn't even give way to the luxury of that for long because it was time to fetch the kids from school.

As I washed my face and hands, made up again and brushed my hair, I looked in the mirror. There were shadows under my eyes—lines, too. I needed more colour. I wanted a hair-do. Surely I wasn't beginning to let myself go just because I was running a guest-house for students and scarcely ever sat down. How could this woman in the mirror possibly line up in any man's eyes with a glowing exquisite young girl like Ingrid? She was all curves, and seduction, and I wasn't at all sure she wasn't in love with Uncle Rob. But he had just said I ought to know who really attracted him. His long deep kiss had left little room for doubt that he meant *me.* I had always known it. What I couldn't be sure of was how *I* felt about *him*. The need for kissing—the need for being held as he held me—was not enough. If there was ever to be another man in my life it would have to be because I loved him as wholly as I had loved Des. Besides, I'd only been a widow since August and this

was mid-December. Four months; it would have seemed disgraceful to the Victorians who considered there should always be a year's mourning for widows, if not two.

I really felt harassed and worried when that day ended. At times I was tempted to ring up Rob and tell him to come and see me. But *that* I didn't do. Whatever happened I wasn't going to be unfair to him.

All the same when I sat with my students that night I looked into the Danish girl's brilliant blue eyes, listened to her husky voice crooning folk-songs from her own land, and I was surprised that Rob didn't find her far more attractive than poor old haggard me!

That next morning I made a point of having my hair set. I even treated myself to a facial. The beautician found my skin much too dry and I surrendered to the luxury of being creamed and patted and soothed. Then I had a make-up and I had to admit I looked quite good.

Des used to think me beautiful. Apart from Rob, a lot of men in the past had admired me. As I came out of the shop, I began to feel much better. I decided that I must never let myself go down again or start imagining that at my age I was through with life. Also it was wrong to think that the extreme youth of girls like Ingrid was the only draw. Some men preferred older women. Age has its compensations. Besides, I wasn't even middle-aged yet.

Then Boyce came back into my life.

He had meant to return to Ponders Heath in time to bring Simon to school. But his plans had gone awry. First of all because he had contracted some strange virus which kept him in hospital in Peru. Simon had to travel to England with friends. We had already had the little boy out from school several times, which pleased Jonathan, and I was glad to see Simon, only there had been something about his face nowadays which reminded me painfully of his mother. Cricket was a person I'd sooner forget.

I heard from Boyce several times during the next few weeks. He was determined to keep in close touch with me but as soon as he recovered from his virus, he was persuaded by the firm to stay out in Peru till after the New Year. His replacement had not done too well. The affairs of the firm seemed to be in a bit of a muddle. Anyhow, Boyce's return was postponed until mid-January.

We all got through Christmas. Naturally I found myself looking back to a year ago when Des was with me and I hadn't known about his infidelities and we had seemed such a close-knit family. We always had such fun. Des and I used to hang up our stockings, like the children, then opened them with Renira and Jonathan who woke us at crack of dawn.

This year it was so different; so quiet. I didn't even have my students here to make the house gay because they all went back to their respective homes for the holiday.

The inimitable Miss Bessiford insisted on me and my family spending Christmas Day with her and Rob at The Hollies. I helped Rob decorate the house. There was someone to cook the turkey and wash up. Little Simon Halling was with us, too, because it wasn't expedient for him to go back to Peru. So there was a party—tree, crackers, and the spirit of Christmas prevailed.

Despite her great age, Aunt Ida enjoyed it all hugely. The children and I stayed to tea, then Rob drove us home. He said good night to me while the children were sorting their presents out in their own room. Dear Rob! He had been so good to us all—given such generous presents, including a beautiful scarlet leather shoulder bag for me—his own choice. Rob had good taste. And I'd given him a Dunhill pipe because I knew he always smoked that kind.

When we were alone in my drawing-room, he said, "I hope it hasn't been too bad a Christmas for you, my dear. I expect you've suffered from a few unhappy flashbacks, but that was inevitable."

"I'm okay," I said. "I've enjoyed my day with you and Aunt Ida."

"I'd have taken you out this evening only you said you couldn't get anyone to look after the children."

"I couldn't. Why don't you spend the evening with me?"

Abruptly, suddenly, he said, No,—he had to get back home because when I'd turned down his original invitation, he'd asked some old Kenya friends of his who were staying in Brighton to drive over and spend the evening with him.

The good humour I'd felt all day seeped away from me. I felt suddenly dreary—disappointed Rob wouldn't stay. Since that moment when he'd lost his head and kissed me again, he'd been his old friendly self and not shown one sign of wanting to touch me or kiss me again. I even wondered if he'd decided not to repeat it. So tonight we exchanged the usual sort of sister-brother peck on the cheek. Then he was gone.

Perhaps I was silly and over-sensitive, but when I lay in bed that night I began to wonder if I had shocked Rob by the intensity of my former response to his kisses. Would he think that I was insensitive, turning my back on the memory of Des so soon, even if he *had* killed my love for him? I didn't know. I was only aware that above all things I wanted to keep Rob's respect, affection and friendship. Those three things mattered vitally. All this going-to-bed-together which Des had thought nothing of, could only lead to disaster—or at least remorse. What was that poignant quotation I had read the other day? Something about *'No more passionate midnights and famishing tomorrows'*. Famishing means hungry—yes, one could give way to a bodily urge and after it was satisfied, feel hungrier and lonelier than ever unless the love was the kind to last for ever. But it wasn't always that sort of love.

I put my face against a pillow. I felt a sudden sense of despair and apprehension. And the worst thing of all was the hatred that would keep sweeping back into my mind and heart—hatred for Des who had destroyed even the memory of our former happiness.

When my children woke me up the next morning and, as usual, climbed into my bed, I put my arms around them and tried to make up my mind to think of nothing *but* them. I wouldn't make myself cheap with Rob again and kiss him wildly like an excited girl. Hadn't I sworn not to encourage him? I'd see less of him—that was it.

Being a Saturday, I drove the children out into Brighton to spend the day with Gandy who was never happier than when we were all with her. I steeled myself to listen to her repeated praise of her darling son. At least I could keep up that myth of the good faithful husband—allow *one* of us to retain her illusions.

Chapter 3

NEW YEAR APPROACHED. As was to be expected, Rob invited us all to The Hollies for lunch on New Year's Day, and suggested that I should go to a New Year's party with him at the hotel. However, having made up my mind not to live in his pocket, I thanked him gratefully, sent old Aunt Ida flowers, and accepted an invitation which came at the psychological moment from a married cousin who had just arrived in England from California.

I hadn't seen Penelope since I was a teenager. She had married an American and lived in Hollywood. Her husband was something to do with the film industry. I used to be rather fond of Penny as we called her. I remembered her as a petite fair-haired girl with a merry smile—a plump, cuddly little soul, always ready to be friendly. We had let our correspondence slide after my marriage to Des. I had not heard from her for years, until she received my notification of Des's death. Now her husband, Jack, had been called over to London suddenly on business. They rang me from their hotel in

London. Money was no object. Jack was a success.
Penny hired a car and came straight down to Nylands
to see me, and issued an invitation to me to go up to
town on New Year's Eve to a party at the Savoy with
her and Jack and some of her American friends, and
stay the night. I asked my Mrs. Tulk if she would look
after the children and sleep at Nylands with her husband (who was a retired gardener). They loved to
watch colour television, so that was arranged. Why not
go up to the party and stay with my cousin? I was so
tired of work and worry and of trying to reshape my
life. As Penny said, one shouldn't spend too much time
repining, and what was to be, was to be.

I shouldn't think Penny ever repined about anything.
At thirty she was as gay and amusing as she used to be
at seventeen. As I anticipated she had run to fat, which
made her look like a dumpling, she was so short, but
she was sweet and easy and as well-groomed and made-
up as most American women.

"You poor honey," she kept saying. "What a *thing*
for you to lose your nice husband so tragically. Jack
and I'll just cherish you while we're over here and I
only wish it was for longer than a week, but we've got
to fly back because Jack's doing the script for a new
film. Things aren't too good in Hollywood in the stu-
dios, but we hope to collaborate with an English producer."

Then she said how cute and pretty little Renira was,
and what a *darling* boy, Jonathan; but after a critical
look at me, shook her head, "Honey, you're as beautiful now as you were as a girl, but you're much too thin
and your eyes are sad. Why don't you all pack up and
come out to California to live?"

"I couldn't," I said, "there's my mother-in-law. She
dotes on the children and she has nothing now Des has
gone. I couldn't take them so far away from her."

Penny rolled her eyes upwards.

"Mothers-in-law!"

"Mine's not so bad," I said with a smile. "She's been
very good to me really."

Penny pushed a lock of fair hair (I swear it was a

wig) into place, and walked over to the bureau where a portrait of Des has always stood and which I kept there for the children. He had looked very young and so very handsome when it was taken. Penny raved about him, turned back to me and said, "Why I just break my heart for you, honey, you've lost a wonderful looking guy."

I said nothing, only nodded with a tight smile.

She was right. Only I'd lost him long before he died.

It all ended in me going up to the Savoy and staying the night as my generous cousin's guest. I felt rather guilty because I enjoyed myself—especially the dancing. I always did like that. I knew that I looked good in that dark violet dress with the long sleeves and high Russian collar which I'd worn at Rob's party at the Club. (Not so long ago, though it seemed a positive age.) I threw off all my cares and laughed and sparkled which I used to do in the good old days. Jack's English producer who was in our party—by name Roland Martin—seemed to take a special interest in me. He kept whisking me on to the floor before the others. We certainly danced well together. He was the exact antithesis of Des—not tall, with very dark hair, grey clever eyes and a lot of charm. He was gay and witty and Jack had told me he was a brilliant film producer.

Before the evening ended, Roland asked me when I could get up to town again as he'd like to take me out to dinner. He wasn't married. He was about my age, I should think, and Penny had whispered that he was very well-off and had a lovely little mews cottage in one of those streets leading off Park Lane.

I wasn't particularly thrilled by the thought that Roland was well-off and successful, but I liked his personality and it was good to be admired and wanted. What woman didn't like that? I didn't promise to meet him again but said I'd phone him. He gave me his office address and phone number. Our Savoy party ended hilariously with me putting an absolute blanket over creeping memories of last New Year's Eve at the golf club. Des had kissed me and whispered, "Happy New Year, my one and only sweetheart."

One and only—dear God! that hadn't been true, but I refused to let the thought do more than rear its head for a second, then I flung myself into the fun. At midnight I linked hands with Penny's nice husband, and Roland, and we kissed each other, wearing silly paper hats on our heads, and behaving like a lot of children.

It was great. When I left the Savoy, Penny remarked that I had made a terrific impression on Roland Martin.

"Don't you sit fretting, you follow your star, honey," she advised. "Roland's fallen for you. He says you're *so* distinguished, and he's just fine and I can't tell you how glad I am we asked him along."

Of course when I got back to Nylands, reaction set in. I'd lived for a few hours in a different world—the gay carefree world Jack and Penny always lived in and Roland Martin did, too. His hand had pressed mine very tightly when he had said good night and he had repeated his New Year's kiss in a way that left no doubt as to his sentiments. Yet I couldn't get up any real enthusiasm. In a funny way I was glad to be back in my home. The children were so ecstatically pleased to see me. Then I followed the old routine.

Mrs. Tulk and I had to get the house ready for my four students who were coming back in mid-January, so there was a lot to do. Gandy was coming for the weekend—just to make a change for her from her Brighton flat, *and* there was Rob.

My first thought after kissing the children had been to ring up The Hollies and tell Rob I was back. I wonder what made me resist that inclination. Just that feeling I'd had for a few days now, that I'd been seeing too much of him.

But *he* didn't feel the same way. Within twenty-four hours of me being home—on 2nd January in fact—he came round to Nylands bringing with him a huge pink and white cyclamen with lovely pale green variegated leaves.

"Just to say Happy New Year—a bit late, perhaps," he said.

He took off the tinted glasses for a second to smile at

me. I looked up into those very blue eyes and felt all the old warmth and affection envelop me. Oh, I loved Rob in my way (not that I knew what sort of way it was) but I *did* love him. He was so sweet to me. He couldn't dance. He wasn't brilliant. He was just *Rob* and the dearest thing on earth.

I took the cyclamen, put it on the table, lifted his right hand and held it against my cheek.

"You are an angel. Thanks awfully, Rob."

"Can I come in a moment?"

"You know you can."

In the sitting-room he sat and smoked with me. I made him a cup of coffee and he asked what sort of a party I'd had in town. So I told him all about it and rather wickedly added that a very fascinating film producer had fallen for me and invited me to dine with him in town any time I liked.

Rob didn't speak for a moment. He had put his glasses on again so I couldn't see his expression. But his lips smiled.

"Goings-on at the Savoy, eh? So that's what you do when you're let loose, and I'm not around to control you."

"Rob darling, I had a *wonderful* time—honestly, even if I did let myself go a bit. It was such a change. My cousin's a sweetie and it was all very expensive and lush and I had a super bedroom looking over the river, and one of those old-fashioned sunken marble baths of all things, can you believe it?"

"It sounds fine," said Rob, "and I'm very glad you enjoyed yourself."

"Have some more coffee," I said.

"Tell me more about this fascinating fellow. Is he married?"

"No."

"H'm," said Rob.

I could guess then exactly what he was feeling— thoroughly put out because I'd met an attractive bachelor. Jealous—darling old Rob! But he didn't say another word about it. He changed the conversation and asked me when I would be free to go and have lunch with him and bring the children. Aunt Ida, it appeared, was not quite as fit as usual. The doctor had warned him that it was on the cards she wouldn't leave her bedroom again. She was a great age and might become bedridden.

"I hope the poor old darling won't just fade away," Rob said with a sigh. "But I looked at her this morning and thought how frail she looks. Her little hand when you take it is quite brittle. I can't help wondering, will 1972 be her last year?"

"Oh, Rob!" I exclaimed. "Don't let's have any more dying. We've had enough."

"I'm feeling a bit depressed," he said. "Take no notice. The doctor hasn't given her a death-sentence, nothing like that. As he told me—these old ladies of around ninety sometimes go on and on, they have such strong hearts. God bless her, I wouldn't like to see her go. But you will come and eat with me, won't you?"

"Of course I will," I said.

At that moment I heard a car out in the drive. Then the front door bell rang. I opened the door and had quite a shock. There stood Boyce Halling. Rather a changed Boyce. He had lost some of his dashing looks; even though he had been away such a short time. I could see there was some grey in his hair and his face had a yellowish hue. Obviously he'd suffered from that virus quite considerably. He was a lot less bombastic, too.

"It's wonderful to see you, Nira," he said, and bent and touched my cheek with his lips. I felt suddenly sorry for him and kissed his cheek in return.

"Poor old Boyce, you've had a foul time."

"Yes, and whatever it was that hit me in Peru, hasn't altogether left me, either. They think now it was some sort of tropical bug. It's playing havoc with me. I haven't left the firm but I'm not going to take up my new post with them for another fortnight. I'm in town now. A friend of mine lent me a flat and I'm going to take Simon up there for the rest of the holidays. Then I don't know what I'll do, although I do want to come back to Ponders Heath and join the old commuters."

I took his coat and scarf and led the way into the sitting-room. "Rob's here," I said, "having a coffee. Can I get you one?"

"I can't drink coffee," he said. "Not allowed it."

"Tea?" I asked.

"Yes, I'd like a cup of weak tea very much. It's damned cold after Peru. I only landed yesterday. But your house is warm."

He didn't seem pleased to find Rob here with me and I don't think Rob was very pleased to see him. However, the two men were polite to each other. While I made the tea, they talked. When I took in the tray Boyce looked at me in the old familiar way and remarked that I'd lost a lot of weight.

"So have you," I said.

"I'm right off drink and cigarettes and rich food," he told me gloomily. "I saw a specialist yesterday afternoon as soon as I got back. A friend of mine arranged the interview for me. He said I'd got to go to The School of Tropical Medicine and have various tests."

"I'm sorry for you," said Rob. "Being well means such a lot in life. I've been through a bit of trouble myself in my time."

I, too, felt sorry for Boyce, but I didn't really want to be left alone with him. Rob, however, must have imagined that he was an unwanted third because soon after Boyce arrived, he departed. I asked him to stay but he said he had a prescription to pick up for Aunt Ida and had promised to get home.

Once Boyce and I were alone, he became a little more intimate. He moved to the sofa beside me and took my hand. "You look more beautiful than ever, Nira. Your gorgeous eyes are sad, but sorrow becomes you."

"Well, I wouldn't exactly *want* it as a beautifier," I said rather tartly and drew my hand away.

He said that he knew how I must have been feeling as he'd gone through it when Cricket was killed and how we ought to understand and comfort each other, both having lost the other half in a fatal accident and so

on and so on. I listened to it all patiently but of course
the moment came when he went too far.

He took my hand again and kissed it with passion.

"You know I've been in love with you for a long
time, Nira. This may not be the right time to say it—I
don't really know whether you've got over losing Des or
not but—"

I broke in, "I haven't been a widow more than five
months."

"Time enough," he said. "I'm quite sure you feel as I
do—that it isn't good to live alone."

"I've got the children," I said hurriedly.

"*And* Rob," said Boyce with a sarcasm that wasn't
lost on me.

I felt my cheeks grow hot. The old irritation Boyce
used to cause me returned.

"I don't know what you mean by that," I snapped.
"Rob has always been my greatest friend."

"Isn't he seizing his chance to step into Des's shoes?"

That was too crude for me. I got up. I felt my heart
beat fast with anger.

"Now look here, Boyce—" I began, but he interrupted.

"Don't be cross with me. Ever since I left England
I've had you in my thoughts. You've always driven me
mad, Nira. I'm sorry if I said the wrong thing about old
Rob. I don't suppose for a moment you'd marry him
even if he asked you."

That had the effect of making me indiscreet and
rash.

"How do you know I wouldn't?" I demanded.

"He's just not your type."

"And pray what is my type?"

"Des was, I suppose," said Boyce, then walked over
to me and put his hand on my shoulders. "Oh, Nira,
please give me a chance! We've both suffered. We're
both alone. I know you've got the children and I've got
Simon, but surely man needs woman and vice-versa.
No, don't move away from me. Tell me that you'll give
me a chance. Let me see a lot more of you. Perhaps by
the end of the summer you'll be thinking of remarrying.

You'll give me that chance, won't you? There's nothing on earth I wouldn't do for you and I swear I'll work hard to get a bit more money behind me so that I can offer you and the kids a really nice home."

Whatever I tried to say, he interrupted. Simon needed a mother. I would make the perfect one. Simon adored me. Our two boys got on so well. Wouldn't it be an ideal marriage? I'd never really given him the opportunity to show me the love he was sure I needed, and so on.

Love, I thought, *a man like Boyce doesn't know anything about real love. It means something quite different to him.* It was odd but all through this emotional assault and battery from Boyce, the image of Rob kept appearing in front of me. I could feel again as I had felt a short time ago, that once again I was clasped in his arms answering his kisses with mine. And each time I thought of it, I resented Boyce taking it for granted that I wouldn't *want* to marry Rob, if he asked me—and that he wasn't my type.

Of course Boyce eventually tried to kiss and embrace me—to make me feel warmer, more yielding through the force of sheer physical passion. But I'm afraid I disappointed him. I pushed him firmly away.

I said, "It's no use, Boyce. It never has been between us. Thanks awfully for asking me to marry you, but I just can't. I never could. We're not right for each other. I'd love to do anything I could for young Simon and he's always welcome to come here and stay with Jonathan—but that's all."

Boyce looked sick. When he left Nylands, I felt sorry for him. He really had changed, and whereas he used to inspire contempt in me, I now felt only pity—but that was as far as it went.

Standing in the doorway, putting on his gloves, he said, "I won't give up hope. I won't bother you—you obviously don't want to see me, but I have contacts at the golf club and I'll find out how you are and perhaps in a few months' time you might think differently."

"Sorry—I won't," I said firmly, but added, "Let us have Simon to stay sometimes if he'd like to come, and it suits you. I don't want to end the friendship between our boys."

"Thanks for so much," Boyce said rather bitterly and got into his car and drove away.

I hadn't asked whether he still intended to come and live down here but I rather thought that he wouldn't, after I had made it so plain that I had no intention of taking Cricket's place or letting him take Des's.

Once he had driven away and I was alone—Renira and Jonathan had gone in to the house next door to play with the children there—I began to prepare their lunch. But in the middle of it I had the most extraordinary wish to see the man who Boyce had said was not my type. Rob—I wanted to see *Rob*—my one great security—my one firm friend—*the one I loved*. Yes, I loved Rob. To hell with what Boyce had said. I loved Rob with all my heart. I couldn't bear my life unless I knew that he was somehow—somewhere—in it. But this new love must remain my secret. I would cherish the thought and say nothing. Life must go on just as it was. When I saw Rob again he must not know how I felt. So I didn't ring him. And he didn't ring me.

And that is the way my life continued—for quite a while.

Chapter 4

FEBRUARY CAME IN with snow, and with the first snowdrops blanching our walled garden in diamond brightness. Things suddenly changed disastrously for me, at first. The children were back at school, which was a help, and the students were back, too, and their presence in the evening gave me more freedom to go out. I had decided that I mustn't continue to refuse invitations

or nobody would bother even to ask Jonathan and Renira to their houses. So I went out to dinner with the
Moffatts, and even accepted an invitation to a women's
lunch-party at the Manor House, where I rather reluctantly received the gracious patronage and pity that
Lady Conniston bestowed on me in her subtle way. The
Parkinsons also asked me to a meal, and play bridge,
and invited Rob, too, tactfully, thinking, I suppose, that
I would like him as the fourth.

The party took place towards the end of the month.

The snow had begun to melt. Grey, stained-looking
slush bedevilled the streets of Ponders Heath. The ice-
cold winds gave way to a milder sou'-wester. It rained
furiously, while the first bulbs of the year tried bravely
to thrust their delicate yet fantastically strong green
spears through the sodden earth.

It was during that evening at the Parkinsons'—Rob
was my partner, husband and wife liked to play together—that I began to realise even more intensely how
much I loved him. I was frightfully careful not to show
it because I was still ashamed of loving any man quite
so soon. I think I behaved in the normal friendly manner and Rob was his usual charming self—until he
drove me home. Then when he stopped outside my
house and I asked him to come in for a night-cap, he
refused.

"No thank you, my dear. I meant to have an early
night really, and it's elevenish now. I've got some packing to finish."

I couldn't see his face clearly in the dim light inside
the car, but I sat very still. I felt a horrible sinking feeling.

"Packing?" I repeated. "Are you going away somewhere?"

"Yes," he said, "As a matter of fact things have
rather altered since you last came to The Hollies."

"What things?" I asked stupidly.

He explained that the doctor thought it best for Aunt
Ida to have a resident nurse-companion and although it
was about as much as they could afford, he had agreed
and managed to get hold of one. He needed a break,

Rob said—he was beginning to feel out of sorts. Fortunately he had been told by Aunt Ida's doctor about this very nice elderly woman who had been a nurse in her time. She took up residence at The Hollies yesterday. She was a bit slapdash and untidy, Rob ended with a laugh, but Aunt Ida quite liked her. They had the same sense of humour and got on well. She was good at taking care of the old lady and cooking for her which was all that mattered.

"It makes me feel I needn't worry about going away," Rob said.

I began to shiver—cold through and through. "I think it's a great idea for you," I said with false brightness. "Where are you going, Rob?"

"Well, you know that I told you about those Kenya friends of mine who arrived from Nairobi just before the New Year, well, they're staying on for a few weeks and they have asked me to go down for a bit to their place in Kent. They've got a lovely old farmhouse in Cowden which isn't very far from here, really. You go through East Grinstead."

"I see," I said in a small voice, "and maybe you'll fly back to Nairobi with these people."

"I think I'd like to," he said (to my dismay). "I'm so much better and my eyes are almost normal. I feel I could very well stand a few weeks in the old climate and enjoy seeing a lot of old friends who used to go on safari with me."

I didn't answer. He vouchsafed the further remark that he wouldn't have thought of going so far away if Aunt Ida's doctor hadn't assured him her heart was strong and her blood pressure not too bad and it was only that she was a bit frail. Age had sapped her natural vitality. But in these days, why worry, Rob ended, when one could fly home at a moment's notice. One needn't today have the same fears of leaving someone you loved for a short time.

Those last words somehow found a dismal echo in my mind. *Leaving someone you loved.* I had thought he loved *me,* but he was leaving me. I'd never doubted his love. Why had he suddenly changed his mind? *What had I done?* Was it because of me that he was going? I felt so desperate that I resorted to flippancy in order to cover up.

"Now don't tell me you're about to contract a secret wedding with beautiful Ingrid and take her out to Nairobi for your honeymoon."

That actually brought a chuckle from Rob.

"How ridiculous can you be?"

"Oh, well, I hope you'll have a wonderful time, and it'll be a splendid change for you," I exclaimed in a loud cheerful voice.

I really was so surprised by what he had just told me and so anguished by the thought that he was going to put thousands of miles between us—as from tomorrow, perhaps—that I couldn't think of another thing to say. A dozen burning questions were on the edge of my tongue and not one could I ask.

Were you shocked by the way I kissed you back the other night?

Has that driven you away?

Have you suddenly decided that you don't love me that way any more and you just want to go on being friends?

Have I done something or said something so that I've fallen short of your idea of me?

And a dozen more queries. I was hopelessly puzzled. I only knew that life had played a pretty scurvy trick. It was all very cynical now that I had made up my mind that I was in love with Rob, but it was too late. He didn't want me any more.

I was wretched but managed to pull myself together sufficiently to put on a nice brisk manner and thank him for all he had done for me and the children since Des died, also say that I would go and see Aunt Ida regularly and write to him, and all that. Then I felt his hand take mine. He lifted it to his lips and kissed it in the old delightful way, but let it drop again. He made no attempt to kiss me on the mouth. He just said in a gentle voice, "I've more need to thank *you,* Nira, believe me. I look on you and always will as the most wonderful friend in the world."

"And that's how I look on you," I said, trying not to sound absolutely desperate.

"I'm sure we'll always be close. I'll be back home very soon. The end of March at the latest—that is if nothing brings me back sooner. Write to me, won't you, dear?"

"You know I will," I whispered, but suddenly the enormity of the pain and the grief I was going to suffer once he had gone, struck me so forcibly that I couldn't stand sitting in that car with him a moment longer. I tried to lift the door handle of the car but it stuck and as I shook it Rob suddenly grabbed hold of me and pulled me against him. His long sensitive fingers passed over my face. The tears were pouring down my cheeks and he began to kiss me quite wildly. This was no grave, self-possessed man, no reluctant lover. This was a man who loved with passion and plenty and he kept saying, "Oh, God, I love you, Nira—*Nira,* my love! I don't know how I'm going to leave you but I know I've got to. Why are you crying? Oh, don't cry like that, it breaks my heart. You're everything in the world to me."

I drew away from him with a great gasping sigh. "Rob, I thought maybe you'd grown tired of me or didn't like me any more, or something. I thought you were running away from me."

"I was running away from myself," he said. "I've loved you a long time but I couldn't trust myself to go on being platonic, and anyhow I thought you were still in love with the memory of Des. Besides, I didn't imagine for a moment that you minded about me. And there's this Roland fellow."

"Idiot!" I laughed and cried together. "You must have known what *I* was feeling about you last time you took me in your arms. I was quite shameless. It's because of that I thought you were sort of put off."

"You're the idiotic one, my beloved *darling* Nira. Nothing on earth could put me off you. But I took it for granted you were only het-up after all the emotional storms you'd been through. Honestly, I know you kissed me with passion but I thought you were just momentarily stirred."

"Now you know the truth," I broke in, and put my face in my hands, not knowing whether I was the happiest girl on earth or the most miserable.

Very soon I knew that I was the happiest. Rob, my dear, dear Rob, gathered me in his embrace again. Later he said, "I'm still going to Nairobi. Not because I really need the holiday but just because I must give you more time to think things over."

"I don't want it," I said. "I know how I feel."

"All the same I think it would be right and proper for me to go away and come back as I've planned, towards the end of March, or beginning of April."

I found myself giggling like a schoolgirl with my face hidden against his shoulder—that strong wonderful shoulder that I seemed to have been leaning on for ages.

"You always do the right and proper thing."

"You make me sound a prig."

"You're not a prig," I said indignantly, "but you're different from so many men I've known. You have some splendid old-fashioned principles. We're neither of us very permissive. Des often used to call me a prude."

Rob laid his lips against mine and murmured, "The way you kiss doesn't suggest that."

"I hate you," I laughed, and we clung madly and stupidly like two young lovers in the darkness of the car. I became more and more convinced with every passing moment that I was in love again for the second time in my life—really and truly in love with Rob. I had loved Des, but with a sort of idolatrous passion because he was so handsome, so dashing and amusing. I was grateful to him, too. He had given me two lovely children and, up to a little while ago, a very happy life. I couldn't deny that, even though the happiness had at last been so badly tarnished.

Then in the midst of kissing Rob a distressing thought hit me. *What on earth would Gandy think?* But

I must leave that problem for the moment. I couldn't cope with it. Anyhow it was my life and not hers.

"You're going down to these people in Kent tomorrow—*tomorrow*. Oh, Rob!" I sighed.

"Dearest," he said, "I don't want to leave you but I think I must. You're altogether too much of a temptation. Your so-called right and proper Rob would like to pick you up this moment and carry you into the house and—" he broke off.

The significance of this was plain. I clung to him in silence for a moment, then, "All right," I said, "I understand. It might spoil things—I agree."

"You know of course that I'd rather marry you as soon as it could be arranged," he said, "but in my opinion, and providing you do still want to marry me—we should make it the late Spring. We could even go all conventional and announce our engagement in the papers just before I arrive back from East Africa. Then everyone in the Heath will know, and we can face the music together. Not that they don't all guess already I'm in love with you. I'm sure they do."

"But they don't know that *I'm* in love with you," I whispered, "and remember they don't know about Des and our marriage—the disastrous end. Only Maggie knows, and she no longer counts. They might think me beastly if I marry again *too* soon. Oh, I want you right now, darling, but I admit we ought to wait, so shall we?"

Rob answered my question with the wonderful words that I was convinced were the absolute truth.

"I shall always want you to do exactly what *you* want, my dearest dear. The choice is yours."

NIRA AND ROB

Chapter 1

DURING THE TIME Rob spent in Kenya he wrote to Nira every day. She answered. She loved to write. She had never found Des good at letters. His used to be rather immature scrawls—sometimes full of little intimacies which *could* be coarse, but Nira hadn't minded because she had loved him. She had smiled over them. But Rob was different. He was a great reader and thinker and his letters were quite literary. He said the most beautiful things in a beautiful way and never let Nira doubt that he was going to make her a wonderful husband as well as a tender lover.

By the middle of March, she and Rob had come to a full understanding. They agreed that she should give her students notice before Easter. She was to do no more slaving in order to augment her income. Rob didn't want it and they wouldn't need the money, he said. He had a small but adequate income and when dear old Aunt Ida passed on, he would have a little more. Aunt Ida was the only one in the Heath who already knew that he was going to marry Nira. It had been his wish that she should tell the old lady at once. She received the news with joy.

"It's nice that you've decided to wait a while, but I fully approve. My dear boy has always loved you and so have I, my dear."

Although Nira could not discuss the glowing future with anyone else in the Heath she could talk about it with Aunt Ida. The old lady's health improved while Rob was away, and Nira had an idea Miss Bessiford would reach her ninetieth birthday, even though she might spend it in bed.

Nira and Rob weren't going to rush into things, but for the time being, because of the children, Nira stayed at Nylands. She and Rob would marry at the end of April. They planned to spend their honeymoon in Corfu. Then she would sell Nylands and move to The Hollies. They'd pool resources. Aunt Ida wished them to redecorate the best bedroom and a small sitting-room for themselves.

The companion-nurse would stay on to look after the old lady as there was plenty of room, and the faithful Mrs. Tulk would help Nira by working full time at The Hollies. Despite protests from Rob, Nira volunteered to take on the cooking. She quite liked it.

There were so many plans and readjustments to make. Susan wasn't happy in her present job. She agreed to return to Nylands to look after Jonathan and Renira at least until Jonathan went to his public school.

So once more, Susan would take on the washing and ironing and help with the children and leave Nira free to be with her husband.

The week before Rob was due to fly home, Nira broke the news about her forthcoming marriage to the children. It would be nice, she said, if they would go on calling him Uncle Rob—not Daddy. They were delighted.

"Super!" said Jonathan. "Uncle Rob'll be able to play lots of cricket with me and help me with my prep."

"Super!" echoed little Renira. " 'Cos I love Uncle Rob."

"So do I!" Nira whispered and kissed them both on top of their heads.

Renira was growing more enchanting every day. She was going to be a real beauty. Jonny did look like his father at times but Nira adored him and he would have a wonderful example before him of what a man should be—once Uncle Rob started to live with them.

The hardest thing Nira had to do was to tell Gandy of her intended remarriage. To her it would surely seem too quick—an insult to her son's memory—all that sort of thing.

At first Gandy received Nira's confession (given

when she went over to Brighton to lunch) with dismay and even disapproval.

"It's *so soon*—barely nine months! I didn't expect it of you, dear. Of course I know you must have been lonely but I thought as you had the children," she broke off, in tears.

Nira's cheeks felt hot. She experienced a slight feeling of guilt but she tried to make Gandy see that a woman needed a man in her life and Rob after all was an old friend. She and Des had both known him for some time and grown very fond of him. He'd been the greatest help to Nira since Des died. The children loved him, too. She wouldn't need any financial help from Gandy in future because she and Rob had their own incomes. And so on. Nira talked rather quickly—trying to make the older woman understand.

It took a little time to thaw Gandy. Once she had softened up, she admitted she was glad to see Nira looking so happy again, and hoped she would put on weight now as she was far too skinny. She also generously announced that she would not back out of paying for the education of her grandchildren, and that she relied on Nira to let her see a lot of them.

Impulsively Nira hugged her mother-in-law—kissed the pale powdered cheek and told her she would always be just as welcome at The Hollies in the future as she had been at Nylands.

The sudden change in her life was so unexpected and exciting, that Nira often wondered if she would wake up and find either that it was a dream, or that something awful would happen to bring her fresh disaster. But nothing bad happened, and the day came when the announcement of her engagement to Rob was put in *The Telegraph*. After that, Nira's telephone never stopped ringing. Most of the members of the golf club who had known her when Des was alive seemed glad that she was marrying again, and especially that it was to Rob Bessiford. It was a genuine romance. The locals loved it. Maggie was the one person Nira heard nothing from, but that didn't surprise her. Anyhow, she'd been told by Joyce Moffatt that Maggie and her mother were selling up and leaving the district. Nira was glad. She didn't want to see Des's girl-friend again.

She started to go through her house and put away small personal things such as souvenirs and photographs relating to her first marriage. She had placed Des's nicest photograph in the children's bedroom. She would never disillusion them. They must always remember their father with love and respect.

It was rather a misty sunless April morning when Nira finally drove to Heathrow to meet the aircraft bringing Rob from Nairobi. All kinds of thoughts crowded through her mind while she sat in the Arrivals Lounge, waiting. Waiting for the man who had once been her dearest friend and was now her dearest love as well.

She recalled the many times during the past when she and Des used to drive down here, either when they were going abroad or in order to meet friends. Des used to like Heathrow—all the noise, the people, and the drama of the great airport attracted him.

Poor Des!—lying down there in his quiet grave in Cornwall. Nira no longer felt resentment or bitterness against him. She was grateful for the happiness she had once known with him, and had forgiven him for his betrayal. She hoped if he was anywhere around he would be glad about Rob and herself. She could almost see his mocking smile and hear his gay voice, "So after all you're hitching up with your boy-friend, your dear old Rob, eh?" Yet in spite of the mockery, he had admitted many times that he admired Rob—thought as many other people did in Ponders Heath, that he was one of the nicest of men. Perhaps Des would be pleased that Rob was to take his place in the family.

How different life would have been for her if Des had not been killed in that accident, Nira's thoughts continued. She had suffered so much before he died—she might have been forced to go on suffering. Now she wanted so desperately to be happy and to regain her joy in living and her faith in man.

The big graceful aircraft bringing Rob from Nairobi, touched down. Nira watched it, her heart beating madly fast and her cheeks pink. She was a little frightened yet absolutely happy. She couldn't wait to see him—to feel his arms around her.

She walked quickly out of the Arrivals Lounge and took up her position outside the door through which he would emerge from the Customs. She was glad that she had put on a little weight and looked better and younger than when he had left. She had bought a new suit for the occasion—a shortish skirt and jacket in fine cream jersey. A silk scarf, scarlet and blue, was knotted around her neck. Her dark silky hair—which Rob had personally forbidden her ever to cut short—fell to her shoulders. She really did look quite young and pretty today, she decided.

Rob thought so too, as he walked through the exit and saw her again. She appeared to him the most beautiful woman in the world. No woman of thirty this, but a young glowing girl—*his* girl—soon to be his wife. All the time he had been away in Kenya he had thought about her and their future. It had seemed miraculous that he, the confirmed bachelor was going to be married at last and to this glorious creature whom he had once thought utterly out of reach.

Nira moved toward him. He dropped the overnight bag he was carrying, and without inhibition, took her in his arms in front of the crowd at the barrier and kissed her on the lips.

"Nira—*Nira*—my love!"

"Oh, Rob." She could think of nothing more to say but just that. *"Oh, Rob."* The cry coming from the depths of her heart.

Then without speaking, their hands linked, they walked out to the front entrance . . .

The mists had cleared. The sun had come through, and suddenly it was Spring.

BOOK II

Climb to the Stars

Chapter 1·

A STREAMLINE car with a black shining body drew up outside the main entrance of the motor showrooms in Picadilly. The engine ticked over noiselessly. A tall young man, almost as spick-and-span as the car, stepped out of it; soft hat set a little jauntily on a smooth head as black, as shining, as the Royale "Victor", the newest, fastest thing in cars Royale had yet marketed.

Hands in his pockets, whistling under his breath, Pat Connel entered the showroom.

Through the glass windows of an office at the far end, a girl, seated at a desk, watched the young man walk toward her; watched him smile and exchange a few words with a salesman here and there.

Jane Daunt sighed a little, shook a drop of ink from her fountain-pen, and returned to the ledger in which she had been writing. She was John Royale's personal secretary, and, as such, one of the busiest young women in London. There was no time, she told herself, in her particular life, for romance. No use sighing because Pat Connel was not only one of the most efficient salesmen in Royale's service, but he had a pair of Irish blue eyes which were too handsome for any woman's peace of mind, and a mouth which suggested that the owner liked to get his own way.

And Pat Connel meant to get his own way. He had limitless ambition. One of these days it was his intention to enter a place like this as a buyer, not a salesman. He was going to make money, to be a power instead of one of the spokes in the wheel which turned

217

the fortunes of John Royale, whose name could be coupled with that of Henry Ford or Sir Herbert Austin.

In the pockets of Pat Connel there was very little cash. His elegant suit, his jaunty air, were all camouflage. He worked for a salary and commission. He could adopt a beguiling manner and rhapsodise with fervour on the perfections of the Royale motor-car. At times he was sick of the whole job and there was nothing but weariness and anxiety behind his smile. But he wasn't going to let anybody know that.

Jane Daunt knew it. And she wasn't going to let him know that *she* knew. But she did, because she was in love with him, had been so for over a year, ever since he had first become one of the Royale employees.

Pat was still whistling when he entered her office. It was a blithe sound. But Jane wondered just how tired he was and how far he had travelled in that car, which he had been trying to sell to others.

"Hullo!" she said.

" 'Morning, Miss Daunt."

"It was 'Jane' at the dance the other night," she reminded him.

Those very blue eyes of his looked at her with friendliness.

"Sure. . . ." His voice held the merest touch of a rich Irish brogue, no more. "And why shouldn't it be Jane now if you'd like it to be? I'm Pat to you. How's life?"

"Busy," she said. "It was a good dance, wasn't it?"

"Sure," he said again.

But while Jane remembered a waltz in the circle of his arms, when her heart had beaten much too fast, his thoughts turned to another girl who had danced at that ball, which was held annually by the firm for Royale employees. A much more important girl than Royale's secretary. John Royale's only daughter and heiress, Sonia.

Jane Daunt wondered suddenly if her nose was shining, and dived into her bag for a powder puff. She was glad that she had put on this new brown suit and the orange jumper with little brown leather buttons. She must have had a premonition that Pat Connel would be in town to-day.

Pat, sitting there on her desk, was hardly aware of the grace or slenderness of Jane in her tailored suit or of the attraction in her small pale face with the dark serious eyes and smooth brown head. Jane was meticulous in her work, meticulous about her personal appearance. One couldn't imagine those sleek brown waves of hair being ruffled or out of place. Nor could a man guess that there was a depth of passion in Jane Daunt which belied the tranquillity of her brows and the serene curve of her small mouth.

Pat Connel's imagination was full of the picture of Sonia Royale as he had last seen her. He had had a bet with another salesman that he would ask Miss Royale for a dance. And he had asked and got it. That was his way. He rushed in where angels feared to tread. She had treated him graciously, but with reserve, a hauteur that had annoyed and challenged him. But, God, she had looked marvellous in her shining silver dress . . . head so fair that it might almost have been silver, eyes of greenish-grey, the blackest, longest lashes he had ever seen, and a scarlet mouth which had haunted him long afterwards.

"Miss Royale looked grand that night, didn't she?" Pat Connel spoke his thoughts aloud.

Jane Daunt sat still a moment. So that was where his thoughts were! Something, perhaps her own feeling for this young man, provoked her to be sincere with him.

"Surely you aren't going to waste your time day-dreaming about Sonia?"

Pat's jaw stuck out.

"Why not?"

"She's the most sought-after girl in town—turning down big titles."

"Do you know her well?" asked Pat. "Tell me about her. Is she a snob?"

Jane's dark little head suddenly bent over her blotter. "I'm too busy to enlarge on my cousin's character."

"Your *cousin!* But I had no idea . . ."

"That I was part of the family? But I am, although

not many of the people here know it. The poor cousin."
Jane laughed a little. "But my mother was a Royale.
Both my parents died when I was seventeen, since when
I've lived in the Royale household. But I insisted on
working. I couldn't bear to be a dependent. So Uncle
John let me train in a secretarial college, and for the
last two years I've been his private secretary."

Pat looked at her with sudden interest. He admired
anybody who had an independent spirit.

"Well, you may be a member of the great family, but
you're not a snob, anyhow," he said. "And you've always been frightfully nice to me, too."

Her head bent low, so that he could not see the colour that rose to her cheeks.

"Why not?" Her voice was soft.

But Pat's thoughts turned to Sonia Royale again.

"How wonderful for you to live with the Royales. I
think that *she* is the loveliest thing on God's earth. Tell
me more about her. . . ."

But here the manager of the showrooms entered. Pat
slid off the desk and stood to attention.

"What have you done this week, Connel?" The manager was a brisk business man.

Pat handed him his notes for the week.

"Sold a sports-coupé at Basingstoke—a streamline at
Reading—that's all."

"Not bad, but not good enough."

Pat Connel, who had fought hard, using all his weap-
ons to achieve those sales, smiled grimly.

"People want to hand over their rubbish in part exchange. It isn't easy," he said.

Said the manager:

"You're the chap to do the job when things aren't
easy."

That was praise. But Pat Connel was not satisfied
and never would be until he had climbed to the top.
And the "top" was a long way out of the reach of a
young man who hadn't a penny in the world, only one
or two poor relations, and a room in Bloomsbury which
was a home.

"By the way, Connel," added the manager, "Miss

Royale is coming to look at that new Twenty Royale with the open green sports body. The Chief phoned from Coventry. He wants her to have it for a birthday present if she likes it. You'd better demonstrate it."

Jane Daunt looked up from her ledger and caught a glimpse of the light that sparkled in Pat's blue eyes.

"Certainly sir," he said.

"We'll go and have a look at it," said the manager.

Pat Connel picked up his hat. As he passed Jane's chair he bent over her a little.

"I'm in luck, aren't I?" he whispered.

She did not answer. She looked after his retreating figure and raised her brows.

"I wonder," she said aloud—"I wonder if any man is lucky who falls in love with my cousin Sonia."

At half-past three Sonia Royale came into the Royale showrooms. The manager was out on business. It was Pat Connel who received the Chief's daughter, and piloted her to the low green car.

Sonia Royale examined the car critically. But Pat Connel's criticism was of her.

The silver goddess of the other night was to-day an exquisite vision in a blue-and-white sports suit, a white coat, white beret set rakishly on a platinum head, white gauntlets on her hands.

"I like the look of this model," she said, and turned to him. "Let's take it out."

She was tall, and her manner was cool and superior. The touch of superiority irritated Pat Connel.

He unbuckled the strap around the bonnet of the car and displayed the engine.

"You'd like to see inside, wouldn't you?"

Sonia Royale knew nothing about the mechanism. She only knew that she liked the outside of the car because it looked very racy and very expensive. She said:

"Marvellous! Let's take it out."

"Certainly," he said.

"I'd like to try the gears," she said.

She was smiling. He could have sworn there was warmth, invitation, in the curve of that maddening scarlet mouth of hers, and yet he felt the command behind the smile, and rebelled against it. He would like to make this girl do something that *he* wanted. Of course he was crazy . . . but she had disturbed him from the moment he had first seen her and danced with her at the ball.

For years he had been too busy keeping the wolf from the door in the bitter struggle for a livelihood to think about marriage. He had flirted—his Irish temperament had led him to make love a little—lightly—in idle moments. But to-day he knew himself to be madly and unreasonably in love with the daughter of his Chief.

Later, as he steered the Twenty Royale out of the showrooms into the sunlit street, and Sonia, complacent and cool, was sitting beside him, he could smell the faint, lovely perfume which seemed a part of her. His heart seemed to beat in tune with the throb of the racing car.

"She runs sweetly, doesn't she?" murmured Sonia.

"A first-rate job," was his reply.

"Let's go to Richmond, and then I'll take over," said Sonia.

He guided the car out of the busy thoroughfare toward Richmond Park.

Sonia Royale sat back in the car, enjoying the sunlight of the April day, which was unusually warm, and the beautiful purring sound of the engine. Mr. Connel drove well, she thought. Glancing at him beneath her heavy lashes, she became more aware of the blackness of his hair and the blueness of his Irish eyes. A touch of the devil in that face, perhaps. She had thought him a good-looker at the staff ball. And she had heard her father say that Connel was one of his best salesmen. He had a charming voice, too. He was educated—a gentleman.

She found herself comparing him with the Hon. Francis Glyde. Francis had driven her down to Maidenhead yesterday. He was the son of an earl and had money to burn, and he was very much in love with her. But what a weakling he looked, and probably was, and what a bore, in comparison with this young motor-car salesman.

Something in Pat Connel's manner captured Sonia's imagination. She wished she had met him in her own social circle. They might have had some fun.

"Daddy says you're a wizard at getting people to forsake old favourites for the Royale," she said as they drove along.

"Praise indeed from the Chief," said Pat.

"It isn't easy to make people do things against their will, is it?" she said.

"No, but that's when a thing's worth doing."

"Do you always get your own way?" she asked with faint curiosity.

"I think I do."

"So do I," she said.

His heart suddenly leapt. So the hauteur, the superiority, had evaporated a little. She was becoming more human.

In Richmond Park he pulled up the car and said:

"Would you like to take the wheel now?"

She changed places with him. She put her foot on the clutch pedal. He looked down at that small foot and the slender ankle. The beauty of them made his senses swim. In a casual voice he warned her that the gear change was difficult and the acceleration very rapid.

"Oh, I know how to drive!" she said like a spoilt child.

But it only took him a minute to discover that she could not manage a car like the Twenty Royale. She would have been safer with something less responsive. He had no nerves. But he did not want, particularly, to lose his life or let her end her own violently. So he said:

"Not so fast."

Then Sonia Royale became very conscious of the young man at her side. Her lips took a mutinous curve. She was used to doing what she liked.

"I'm not going fast."

The car swerved. She slowed down a little, tried to change gear and missed it.

"Slow right down and get into neutral," he said.

"It isn't necessary."

"You'll find it is."

That carnation pink in her cheeks was lovely, he thought. She was not going to admit that she couldn't drive, and that amused him. But the fight had begun. The speedometer leapt up to fifty. Then sixty. A car came out of a side turning. Sonia swerved dangerously. Then Pat put a hand on the wheel and touched her slim gloved fingers. He was immensely thrilled by the contact, but she turned on him.

"I'm driving this car."

"You must slow down. It isn't safe, and there's a speed limit."

"I shall do what I like, Mr. Connel."

"In that case," he said, "if you'll forgive me, I'll get out and walk."

She was staggered. The insolence of it! She slowed down.

"I'll turn round and drive back," she said icily.

"Better let me take her through the traffic."

"I am driving."

"Miss Royale, for your own sake—"

"Don't be ridiculous," she snapped.

Their eyes met. His were intensely blue. To her intense astonishment he opened the door of the car and jumped out. And then, scarlet to the roots of her fair hair, Sonia put on the brakes. He took off his hat and bowed with cold courtesy.

Sonia's anger suddenly evaporated. She was immensely amused. She wondered what his reactions would be if she took a really high hand with him. A bit of an experimentalist with men was Sonia Royale. She looked him straight in the eyes.

"You're a coward as well as a cad, Mr. Connel. And you are a little ridiculous, exhibiting such fear."

That made him really angry.

He had not been afraid for himself, but for her. He wanted to prevent her from being such a little fool as to drive that car through traffic. He said through his teeth:

"Perhaps I won't take a bus back. Perhaps I'll insist on you giving me the wheel."

Sonia began to enjoy herself.

"And if I refuse?"

"I'll make it pretty difficult for you to drive."

He climbed into the car again, and with a quick movement switched off the engine, pulled out the key, and pocketed it.

Sonia said:

"You go too far. I shall see that you leave my father's employ."

Pat went white under his tan. So he was to be sacked at the whim of a spoilt child, a girl who wouldn't admit that she was in the wrong! And how lovely she was, sitting there, her strange grey-green eyes blazing at him!

"So I'm to lose my job, am I?" he said.

"I consider that you have been impertinent."

"I consider that I've been in my rights. I'm in charge of this car and responsible for you while you are in it. However, if you want to turn me out of the firm, no doubt you can manage it. And in that case, I must do something which will make me feel it worth while."

But his next gesture was unexpected, for Pat, blinded by her beauty and his own rage, caught her in his arms and kissed her on the lips.

For an instant the world seemed to rock about him. He felt exalted, ready to pay any price for that one touch of her lips. Then he sat back and said breathlessly:

"Now you're justified in getting me sacked. Go along. Drive on."

She sat stupefied, lifting one white-gloved hand to her lips. Nothing more astonishing had ever happened to her. She was furious, but she was intrigued. She managed to say:

"My father would kill you if I told him that."

"I doubt it," said Pat. "Now shall we get back? You can enjoy the thought of me searching London for a new job—minus references. That'll be difficult, but we agreed that the difficult things were the only ones worth getting."

She bent her head, hiding from him the tiny smile which lurked at the corner of her red lips. Really, he was marvellous. She got out of the car.

"Take my place and drive me home, please, Mr. Connel."

He smiled grimly and drove her home. He took it for granted that he had offended her beyond pardon and that he had lost his job. She had nothing to say to him when he left her at her home in Green Street. Quietly he raised his hat and moved away.

He was utterly and wholly in love with her now. Out of that brief, daring embrace had sprung a passion in Pat Connel that would not die easily.

But Sonia Royale watched the green racing car glitter in the sunshine and vanish round the corner with almost a thwarted look in her eyes.

He was marvellous. She had the strongest desire to see him again. He was the type of man who, having captured her, might have held her, even in marriage. But she knew, even as that thought ran through her mind, that she could not marry Patrick Connel any more than she could marry the Hon. Francis Glyde . . . or anybody else, because of that mad folly of hers in Paris two years ago.

Chapter 2

GLOOMILY Pat Connel walked into Jane Daunt's office.

Jane had finished work for the day. There was a small straw hat on the side of her dark little head, and she was drawing on a pair of gloves when the young salesman appeared. She looked at him inquiringly.

"Well? Enjoyed demonstrating the Victor?"

"Immensely," he said.

Jane's dark eyes narrowed a little. Something had happened . . . she could see that without being told. She said, casually:

"How was cousin Sonia?"

"Beautiful."

"You're looking tired. I suppose it's this spring day. It's so enervating."

"Possibly. Think I'll cut along home now."

"I'm going, too."

"I've got to take a car to the works first. Shall I drop you at Green Street?"

Her heart warmed to that. It was rarely that she had an opportunity of driving with this man who was the first, the only one, to go straight to her heart.

When they were moving along in the sunshine, Pat said:

"You may not be seeing much more of me."

She gave him a quick, anxious glance.

"Why ever not?"

"I think I'm leaving the firm."

"But for heaven's sake, why?"

"I expect to get the sack."

"Pat Connel, what have you done?" She shook her head at him.

He stared ahead of him grimly.

"Made a fool of myself, little Jane Daunt. Or perhaps I haven't. Perhaps it's never foolish to have courage. Anyhow, I behaved badly because I was angry. Miss Royale will tell you all about it."

Jane's heart sank. Perhaps never until now had she realised quite how much he had grown to mean . . . this handsome Irish boy with his purposeful chin and his gay insouciance.

Living in the Royale home, she met dozens of men, rich, titled, interesting, and otherwise. Naturally, her beautiful cousin was the flaming candle which attracted the moths, and they fluttered round her wildly. But there had been one or two who had paid attention to the quiet cousin and found a greater depth and a swee-

ter charm in her than in Sonia. Quite recently Jane had
had a proposal of marriage. Sonia had thought her mad
not to accept, as it had meant money. But Jane had no
intention of marrying without love. She preferred her
freedom and her job in her uncle's firm.

Recently that job had become even more precious
because it meant that she saw Pat Connel two or three
times a week when he was not away on demonstrating
tours. And if he left the firm, how would she feel about
it? Pretty badly. . . .

"What on earth *have* you been doing?" she asked
him.

But he avoided answering her. When he drew up before the big house in Green Street for the second time,
he was smiling.

"So long. See you to-morrow . . . *perhaps.*"

With many misgivings Jane Daunt walked up the
wide staircase of her uncle's beautiful house and went
straight to Sonia's bedroom. At this hour Sonia was
generally to be found in a cocktail suit lying on her
chaise-longue, resting before she changed for dinner.

And there she was, lovely, supine, fair head like silver upon a jade satin cushion, cigarette in a long holder
in the corner of her mouth, fingers twirling the stem of
an empty cocktail glass. She looked drowsy, luxurious.
She glanced out of the corners of her eyes at the small
brown figure of her cousin.

"Hullo! Isn't it muggy! It's the warmest April I've
ever known in town. I shall be glad to get out of it when
we go abroad next week."

Jane nodded. Then she went straight to the point.

"What happened during your drive with Mr. Connel
this afternoon?"

At once Sonia's eyes narrowed. She put down the
cocktail glass and sat up.

"He's an astounding young man."

"And how has he astounded you?"

There was more anxiety in Jane's brown eyes than
was apparent in her voice.

"My dear, he got annoyed with me because I
wouldn't let him drive. I admit I bungled the gears.

Then he tried to order me about . . . such a masterful young man! Then I told him he was impertinent and we had a row, and I ended by telling him I was going to get him sacked."

"So that's it!" said Jane.

"More than that. Listen to this . . ."

And Sonia, who had always made her cousin a confidante, because in some queer way she respected a wisdom, a capability, in Jane she knew was lacking in herself, then told Jane exactly what had happened in Richmond Park.

There rose before Jane's eyes a vivid picture of Pat Connel taking Sonia in his arms and kissing her. Typical of him to do a daring thing like that. But it hurt her . . . jarred all her sensibilities. She wished he hadn't done it. She said:

"Are you going to have him sacked?"

"Gracious, no! I want to see a bit more of him. He interests me!"

Jane was only temporarily relieved. Her straight dark brows drew together.

"Sonia, you can't fool round with a man like Pat Connel. Surely you don't intend to."

Sonia nestled luxuriously in her cushions.

"Have a cocktail, darling, and don't look so severe. I don't suppose I'll get much opportunity to break the young man's heart. But he might break mine with those eyes of his. He *is* a good-looker! Have you got a little crush on him yourself?"

Jane got up and moved away abruptly to the window.

"I like him," she said, "and I admire his work. He takes things seriously."

"I think I should take him seriously if I saw much of him. I get so sick of the men like Francis, who scrounge round for a stray word. If Pat Connel wants a thing, he gets it, doesn't he?"

Jane swung round.

"It's bad enough for you to fool around with people like Francis, but you ought to leave employees of the firm alone, Sonia. They've got their living to earn, and in any case it isn't fair of you to lead men on. You know why!"

Sonia got off her chaise-longue and stubbed her cigarette-end in an ash-tray.

"I suppose I'm never to be allowed to forget Paris," she said in a sullen voice.

Jane turned round to her. There was nothing but pity now in her eyes.

"My poor dear . . . how *can* you forget it?"

Silence a moment between them. A silence during which they both remembered that holiday in Paris in the spring of two years ago. John Royale had sent them over because Sonia had wanted some clothes. Sonia, aged twenty-two, Jane a year younger. Yet Jane seemed much older, accompanied Sonia in the light of a chaperone because she was to be relied upon to look after the daughter who was the apple of John Royale's eye.

Those two weeks in Paris had been a nightmare for Jane. The moment she got there she was plunged into drama . . . a drama which, unknown to the family in London, Sonia had been working up for herself. She had a lover. He, too, was in Paris. And one morning, unknown to Jane, Sonia slipped out of her hotel and married him. She was secretly married . . . John Royale's daughter and heiress.

It had been a shock to Jane, and she had never dared think what effect it would have upon her uncle. Ever since Sonia's mother died, the girl had meant everything to him.

The man was half-English, half-French on his mother's side. He had a job with an English firm in Paris. He had met Sonia at a cocktail party in London. He was aged about thirty, good-looking in a rather effeminate fashion, slender, blue-eyed, and almost as fair as Sonia. He had the merest trace of a French accent, which Sonia had found fascinating. And he was an adept lover.

She had asked him to the house, and John Royale had taken a violent dislike to him. Perhaps because he realised that Maurice Gardener was a wastrel, a sponger, one of those people who manage to move on the fringe of society, and a gambler by instinct. In no way the sort of companion whom John Royale desired for his young and impressionable daughter.

In Paris, Sonia had met and married Maurice Gardener. They were to keep it secret because Sonia knew that her father disliked Maurice, and she was afraid that he might visit his wrath upon her. He was a man of strong character and he idolised her, but how could she be sure that he would not tell her to go to Maurice and let him keep her, and that he would have nothing more to do with her? Sonia was in love, but she also prized her material comforts. She did not want to give up her cars, her trips to the South of France, her dozen and one luxuries. And Maurice was always hard up, always in debt.

Jane felt nausea even now, two years later, when she recalled that moment in the Paris hotel when her cousin had confronted her with the smiling Maurice and announced her marriage.

They had sworn her to secrecy. Nobody had ever known about that marriage except herself. She had done her utmost to persuade Sonia to make a clean breast of it to her father, but she had been forced to give that up as hopeless.

Sonia's passion for her husband lasted only a few days. It had taken no longer than that for her to discover that there was another girl . . . in Paris. A French girl to whom Maurice Gardener had made promises. And Sonia had found a letter in which Maurice protested undying passion for this Colette, who was a mannequin, and stated that he was marrying Sonia Royale entirely for her money.

Then there were scenes, reproaches, attempted explanations on the part of Maurice, and finally Sonia, her passion spent and dead, returned to London with her cousin—alone. Never again would she live with Maurice. Both she and Jane extracted from him an oath that he would not appear in England or interfere in her life, and in return Sonia would send him money when she could. So far, he had kept his promise. He had not worried her at all, and part of her allowance went to Paris regularly to keep him quiet.

That secret hung heavily upon Jane's conscience. She never thought of Maurice Gardener without wishing to God that she could make a clean breast of the marriage to her uncle. To-day, she said:

"Isn't it time you made some effort to get a divorce from Maurice? Why not rely on your father's devotion to you and let him help you out of this mess, so that you can think about marrying somebody else if you want to."

Sonia turned on her with the usual protest.

"I shall never tell father. I won't risk it. I couldn't bear to be thrown out and made to go to *him*."

So Jane, with the thought of Pat Connel uppermost in her mind, said:

"Then you must leave other men alone."

And that was the conclusion, with only one satisfaction for Jane. She learned from Sonia that Pat Connel was not to be dismissed from the firm.

Chapter 3

NOBODY was more astonished than Pat Connel when his expected notice to "quit" failed to come. He was fully prepared for it. But nothing happened. The manager saw him that next morning and sent him on one of his usual trips down to the West Country to demonstrate a Twenty Royale.

Pat saw Jane Daunt for a few minutes before he set off. He was touched when she said:

"So you're off on business! There was nothing in that sinister remark of yours about leaving the firm? I'm so glad."

She had seemed glad. He liked little Jane Daunt. She

would make a grand friend. And somehow he never connected her with the Royales, never felt that it was an impertinence to call her by her Christian name or treat her like a pal. Certainly she bore not the slightest resemblance to Sonia.

He did not see Sonia again until a week later, when he was driving one of the Royale saloons down Piccadilly. He was held up by a red signal and found himself alongside a big grey-and-silver Royale Victor which he knew at once belonged to the head of the firm.

The Chief, a grey-haired man with a rosy complexion and small twinkling eyes, was driving the car, and his daughter sat beside him. Pat Connel's heart raced. He stared in Sonia's direction. She turned her head and recognised him. She was lovely, he thought, in grey, toning with the car and wearing a chic mink cape, for there was a cold wind and the April day was not so warm.

He fancied that her cheeks reddened when she caught his eye, and he could have sworn that a smile lurked at the corner of her mouth, and there was direct challenge in the gaze she turned on him. Then the green lights flashed. They moved on and Pat lost sight of father and daughter in the big grey car.

Sudden depression seized him. He was a fool to feel this way about Sonia Royale. Obviously she was out of his reach. And yet, hadn't he refused a dozen times in his life to admit that anything was beyond the reach of a man who had the courage of his convictions and lived by them?

Sonia said to her father:

"That was one of our cars. Did you see it?"

"Yes, with young Connel."

"Do you like Mr. Connel?"

"First-rate salesman and an educated fellow into the bargain. Yes, I like him," was John Royale's reply.

Sonia shut her eyes and thought of a hot kiss which had been laid upon her lips and of Pat's Irish blue eyes burning down into her own. She must see him again. She didn't care what Jane had to say!

Later that day the London manager told Pat Connel that the Chief was going abroad. He was taking his daughter and his niece with him; the latter as his secretary. John Royale, apart from his business, was writing a book of travel for a hobby. Sonia had the fun of the trip, and Jane took down the notes and did the work.

"Connel, you're to take the grey saloon up to the works and get her overhauled," said the manager. "They're taking her through France, and possibly Spain."

"Is the Chief driving himself?" asked Pat.

"No, they're taking Woodham, their chauffeur."

Pat considered this gloomily. It meant that Sonia Royale would be away for weeks. He would have to just picture her being driven those hundreds of miles into the heart of Spain and North Africa, which would be enchanting now, perfect in the spring. Pat knew Morocco. In better days, when he was on holiday from school, he had gone to Tangier with his father.

Why couldn't he go now? Why must he stay behind just selling cars—selling cars—nothing else? As he took the big saloon out to the service depôt at Wembley, an overwhelming desire to accompany Sonia Royale on that trip seized him. It was, on the face of it, a desire as ridiculous and hopeless as the rest. But that night Pat's wild streak was uppermost.

He did not go straight back to his room in Bloomsbury that evening. He called at some Mews just behind the Royale house in Green Street, where Woodham, the chauffeur, lived with his wife and two children. Pat knew Woodham well. They had come up against each other on the question of cars and respected each other.

He found the chauffeur sitting in the kitchen with his eldest child on his lap, shirt-sleeves rolled up, pipe in his mouth. He had just finished washing down Miss Royale's green racer.

He greeted Pat pleasantly.

"I want to talk to you, Woodham," said Pat.

The chauffeur sent his small boy out of the kitchen.

"Anything I can do, Mr. Connel?"

Pat lit a cigarette and eyed the chauffeur through the smoke.

"Are you keen about this trip to Morocco?"

Woodham's face became downcast.

"Far from it, Mr. Connel. It's orders from headquarters and all that, but I never did care for foreign parts, and there's a lot of reason why I don't want to go just now. The missus is only just out of hospital, and not picking up very fast. She's fretting her heart out about me going abroad."

Pat bit his lip. He was sorry for Woodham, but the news was good from his own point of view. He sat talking to Woodham. Next Monday, Woodham was to take the car over to Dieppe on the night-boat. The others intended to fly to Paris the previous day, because the Chief had a business deal there, and the following morning were taking the train down to the coast, where they would meet Woodham and the car.

"Things ain't easy, Mr. Connel," the chauffeur finished. "But I don't see as how I can refuse to go without getting the sack."

Pat had a sudden vision of Sonia Royale in his arms, that provocative mouth of hers quivering under his.

"You're right," he said. "Things aren't at all easy. But I've got a proposition to make to you. If you like to agree to it, things might be less difficult for both of us."

The chauffeur took the pipe from his mouth and stared.

"How's that, Mr. Connel?"

"Look here, I saved twenty-five quid last year. Supposing you have it and take your wife away to the sea for a holiday, and *I* take the car over to Dieppe on Monday."

Woodham stared harder, then laughed.

"You're joking, Mr. Connel."

But Pat talked to him hard for ten minutes and managed to convince him that it was far from a joke.

"You're not going to lose your job," he finished, "and I shall tell the Chief when I get the other side, that your wife was taken bad and you couldn't leave her. So I, having heard about it, offered to go in your place.

You know how nervy he is about being driven by anybody but you, so a new chauffeur would cause the dickens of a fuss. But I've driven him, and he trusts me."

"But Mr. Connel—"

"Let me finish. I can wear your uniform—we're the
same height. And added to that, I happen to speak
Spanish, because when my father was alive I was going
to have a job in South America, and I learned the language. Then it all fell through, and so I became a salesman for Royale. But the Royale family will find me
pretty useful in Morocco, and you'd like to take the
wife to the sea, wouldn't you, Woodham?"

The chauffeur's honest face worked.

"By gum, I would, but it don't seem hardly right."

"On the other hand, it isn't very wrong, and if you'll
leave it to me—"

"But what on earth do you want to do a chauffeur's
job for, Mr. Connel?"

"Ah!" said Pat, and thought of a platinum head and
a pair of challenging green eyes. "Now, what about it,
Woodham? Are you on?"

A moment's hesitation. From upstairs came a baby's
wail and the sound of a woman's tired voice. Twenty-
five pounds to spend on a holiday, and Maggie ailing,
badly in need of it. Woodham squirmed.

"Gawd! It ain't easy to turn that down."

Pat's slim brown hand shot out and the chauffeur's
horny fingers closed over it.

Chapter 4

ONE week later, John Royale, his daughter Sonia, and
Jane Daunt were driven by Woodham to Croydon
Aerodrome, where they boarded an Imperial Airways
liner for Paris.

But it was not Woodham who drove the big grey saloon with the gleaming silver bonnet down to Newhaven and got on board the night-boat for Dieppe. It was Pat Connel. And now he stood on deck in the April starlight, looked across the rippling onyx water and thrilled at the prospect of meeting Sonia at the other side. He had left a note for the manager in London, telling him that he had been ordered abroad at the last moment with the Chief. It was an immense piece of cheek on his part, and he knew it. But the story he had ready for the Chief was watertight.

He was staking a lot on this, and he knew it. But wasn't it worth while? The possibility of six glorious weeks on the Continent beside *her*.

Little Jane Daunt would open her eyes wide when she saw him. She had taken special pains to say good-bye to him last night before she left the office. He had almost fancied that she was reluctant to say it. She was awfully nice to him, and he liked her. He wondered if there was some fellow that she cared about and if things were as difficult for her as for himself? She rather gave one that impression. There was always something a little wistful in those dark eyes of hers. But it never entered Pat Connel's head to associate that look with himself.

He slept soundly on board that night, and took the car off at Dieppe at eight o'clock the next morning.

At midday he was at the station to meet the boat-train from Paris.

A pulse beat rather thickly in Pat Connel's throat when he saw the Royale party descend from the train. Now for the fireworks, if any. There was Jane . . . the first to descend . . . neat and small in a tweed travelling coat and a beret. And then Sonia. His heart thrilled to the sight of her beauty. She was a peerless girl, wonderful in that silky mink coat, and a tiny green hat with a little lace veil across her eyes. Then finally John Royale directing porters and baggage.

Jane was the first to spot Pat. For a moment she thought her eyesight was playing tricks with her. It was Woodham who was expected to meet the train. But it wasn't Woodham who stood there in that olive-green uniform with the polished buttons, black glossy leggings, and a peaked cap at rakish angle on a handsome head. *That was Pat Connel.* As he neared her, he caught her eye and grinned like a truant schoolboy.

"Good heavens alive!" said Jane.

Then Sonia saw Pat. She, too, uttered an exclamation.

"Good lord!"

Pat Connel approached the Chief and touched his cap. He said in a clear voice:

"I have to report, sir, that I have come in Woodham's place. Woodham's wife was taken ill at the last moment and it was not advisable for him to leave her. He didn't want to let you down, so knowing how you dislike strange chauffeurs, I volunteered to come, and hope you don't mind, sir."

John Royale was surprised and a little put out. It had never entered his head that Woodham would not come, and it was somewhat disconcerting to find one of his salesmen in the chauffeur's place. He knew, however, that young Connel was an excellent driver, and, of course, an educated fellow. It wouldn't be unpleasant to have him on the tour. Pat made haste to add that he could speak a little Spanish.

"Well, well," said John Royale, "that'll be pretty useful. And if you don't mind the job, Connel, of course come along with us by all means."

He spoke in the kindly manner which endeared him to all his employees. There was no nicer man than John Royale. But Jane Daunt, her small mouth tightly closed, looked at Pat and entertained the serious suspicion that this was not all "on the level". She knew Pat only too well. She would not put it past him to have engineered this business. And if he had, and all for the sake of being with Sonia, then he was mad. And it would be a mad trip for all of them.

Pat was not looking at Jane. He was looking at Sonia. He moved forward and took a small suitcase out of her hand.

"Allow me, miss," he said.

Sonia looked straight up into his eyes and saw the devil lurking in them. He was amazingly attractive in that uniform. He looked more like a young Spanish officer than a chauffeur, she thought. She did not wonder how or why he had come. She merely knew that she was entranced to have him during this holiday. She had expected to be bored with just her father and her cousin. Pat Connel's company was worth having.

As Pat turned away to conduct them to the car, Sonia whispered to Jane:

"I say, what awful fun!"

Jane said stonily:

"Is it?"

"More than that, Jane. Do you know, I believe I'm really smitten with your Mr. Connel?"

Her Mr. Connel. How far from the truth that was! Jane looked at the back of the tall, graceful figure in the green uniform and clenched her small teeth.

"You fool, Pat Connel," she thought. *"You fool* to have done this."

The luggage was strapped on to the car. They were all travelling very light and had taken as little as possible.

Pat's heart sang as he took his place at the wheel. The gamble had come off! Everything was set fair for a marvellous time. The Chief had accepted him, and Sonia's wonderful eyes had even welcomed him . . . only little Jane Daunt looked as though she wasn't pleased. He couldn't think why.

"You'd better sit with Connel, Babe," John Royale addressed his daughter. "Jane and I will sit at the back, because I want her to take some notes on the scenery as we drive along."

And that was the way they set off down the straight road which led out of Dieppe toward Rouen. Sonia, warm and luxurious in her furs under a Jaeger rug, sat beside Pat—near—so near to him that he could detect that familiar heady perfume of hers. And his heart exulted at her nearness and the friendliness with which she now talked to him about the trip as they moved along. She appeared to have forgiven him completely

for that kiss the other day. But he knew she could not
have forgotten it, any more than he had done.

And Jane, trying hard not to feel absurdly jealous
and honest anxiety for Pat, jotted down in shorthand
the remarks which her uncle made about the route
which they traversed.

Every now and then Jane's brown eyes lifted from
her notebook, and she could see Sonia's fair head with
its impudent little hat, leaning closer and closer to the
shoulder of the handsome driver. How could she! It
made Jane writhe . . . how could she flirt like this,
knowing Pat's position . . . knowing her own?

It was a lovely day in spring. The French countryside
was looking its best. They passed through Rouen and
Evereux and by nightfall were at Chartres, where they
were to end the first day's journey. John Royale wanted
photographs and notes on the cathedral there, which
was the second most perfect example of Gothic architecture in France.

It was when they arrived at the Hôtel de Ville that
Jane felt most unhappy about Pat. For, of course, there
was no question of his being "one of the party". John
Royale took a handsome suite for his daughter and his
niece, and Pat went to the chauffeur's quarters.

There was one awkward moment when Pat carried
some of the luggage into the vestibule of the hotel.
Sonia, having thoroughly enjoyed her journey and
knowing full well what effect she had had upon Pat because she had chosen to be charming, whispered to her
father:

"He isn't like Woodham, Dad. . . . Don't you think
he ought to have a better room? . . . I mean, not be
boarded like a servant. . . ."

John Royale agreed. On the other hand, he found the
situation a little embarrassing. But it was Pat himself
who put an end to it.

"I've come in Woodham's place, and I must be
treated as Woodham," he announced. "I shall be perfectly happy. I shall wash down the car and be at your
disposal in the morning, sir."

Jane did not know whether to be glad or sorry. But

she lingered a moment by the car when Pat took his seat to drive round to the garage. Their gaze met. His smiling eyes were almost defiant. He could read disapproval in hers.

"Anything I can do, miss?"

"Pat Connel, you're a very unscrupulous young man," said Jane severely. "Drop this chauffeur business and tell me the truth. Was Woodham's wife so seriously ill that he couldn't come?"

"That's what I said."

"But it's not what I believe."

"You aren't trying to suggest that I manœuvred this, are you?" His smile mocked her.

"It was wrong. You've no right to be here, and it will only lead to trouble."

"Why should it? The Chief is very amiable, and *She* was angelic all day. I was half afraid she'd be so furious with me that she'd get me the sack on the spot."

"I almost wish she would," said Jane under her breath.

Then Pat ceased smiling.

"Don't damp my spirits, Jane. Can you blame me for wanting to be near her? It may be awful cheek on my part to even think about her, but I can't help it."

Jane stood motionless, the cool night wind blowing against her face. Her gaze turned from the serious, attractive face of the young Irishman to the glittering lights of the hotel wherein Sonia waited for her to come and help unpack . . . if not to do most of the unpacking. She felt wretched and helpless.

"It's a nice situation," she told herself gloomily, "to watch the man I'm in love with walking straight over a precipice, and not be able to pull him back."

Pat switched on the engine.

"You seem scared to death of me falling for your lovely cousin," he said. "But don't be. I can take care of myself, you know. Good night, little Jane Daunt."

Then he was gone, and she was left staring after the car helplessly.

Some hours later a slim, elegant girl in a white fur coat stole out of the Hôtel de Ville and stepped into a

grey-and-silver car which was drawn up at the entrance.
Immediately the door was shut and the car moved
away.

Sonia Royale loosened a big white fox collar, revealing a white throat and a glimpse of black velvet and
pearls, and gave a little laugh as she stretched slim an-
kles in tiny high-heeled shoes before her.

"What a marvellous night for a drive," she murmured.

Pat Connel nodded, but said nothing. Nobody had
been more surprised than himself when an order had
been sent to the servants' quarters that he was to take
the car round to the front entrance at nine o'clock.

Having spent an hour washing down the mud-
splashed body, which was no light job, and one to
which he was not accustomed, Pat had felt tired and
ready for bed. He had not bargained for night as well as
day work. But all feelings of fatigue or resentment vanished the moment he saw that it was Miss Royale who
wanted the car, and that she came alone.

There was magic in the night now, and in the presence of this bewitchingly lovely young woman who sat
beside him.

"Where do you want to go?" he asked.

"Nowhere in particular. Just drive a little way out
and then stop. I must get some fresh air. It's so stuffy in
these over-heated hotels. Daddy's immersed in writing,
and I told him I was going to bed, and Cousin Jane is
typing out her notes. She's very conscientious."

"I like Miss Daunt," said Pat. "I think she's a fine
girl."

Sonia made a little moue with her curved red lips.

"Oh, yes—she's a dear. But, of course, it's a little
boring sometimes to have a relation like that perpetually with one."

The cattiness in that remark escaped the young man,
who was so blindly enamoured. He said:

"Lucky relation to be near *you—perpetually*."

"The Irish have a wonderful faculty for saying nice
things. Drive faster," said Sonia.

Gravely Pat touched his peaked cap.

"Yes, miss."

"Don't call me that. You're not Woodham."

Jane had said that to him a few hours earlier, and it had merely amused him. But from Sonia it sounded different . . . it made his blood leap.

"You're very nice to me, Miss Royale."

"Do you know that my cousin Jane thinks that you did this on purpose . . . that Woodham's wife isn't so ill . . . in other words, that you engineered the whole thing?"

Pat squared his chin and looked ahead.

"That's a very serious allegation."

"I wouldn't put it past you, Pat Connel. You're rather an outrageous young man," said Sonia softly.

The red blood warmed his brown face.

"Am I?"

"Was this a plot?"

He did not answer. But she saw a smile lurking at the corner of his well-shaped mouth, and a warm little glow came over her as she remembered how those lips had claimed hers—in Richmond Park.

"Tell me," she said. "Come along . . . why keep the truth from me?"

"Very well. I did engineer it. I wanted to come, and it was the only way I could manage it."

"It was a very clever way. What did Woodham say about it?"

"He was a bit scared. You'll never, never blame him, will you?"

Sonia stifled a laugh.

"No; you're obviously the culprit. Did you bribe him?"

"Yes."

"Money to burn—eh?"

"Far from it. But it was worth everything I had to get out here."

Sonia thrilled. Her vanity was wholly satisfied by the thought of this impecunious young man throwing away his last penny in the effort to be near her. Of course it *was* that.

"Why were you so terribly anxious to join this party?" she asked him.

He wondered, suddenly, if this lovely girl, heiress to a fortune, was merely fooling with him. He froze at the thought. Abruptly he drew the car in to the side of the road, which was dark and lonely and a little way out of the town. The sky was brilliant with stars, but there was no moon, so he could not see more than the dim outline of her face. There was a rough note to his voice when he spoke again.

"I don't know why you want to know all these things, Miss Royale. I don't know why you should be interested—but if you want the truth—here it is. I came because I wanted to be near you. That may be an impertinence, but I'm not ashamed of saying it."

Sonia drew in a deep breath. She was nearer in that instant to feeling real sincere emotion than she had ever been in her life before. There was something about this forceful, impetuous young man which appealed to the feminine in her, bred in her a wholly feminine desire to conquer him utterly. He was the kind that would be worth conquering. It was partly her insatiable vanity and partly a desire for closer contact with him that led her to forget that she was not free and had no right to offer him even an instant's encouragement. She knew full well that whatever Pat Connel did would be in deadly earnest.

She leaned a little nearer him until a strand of her silver-fair hair touched his chin.

"You needn't be ashamed of saying anything—to me. And why shouldn't I be interested? Why shouldn't I be even flattered because you took so much trouble to come out here and be with me?"

"You can't mean that," he said.

But she put out a hand and felt for his. He crushed it in a grip that made her wince. She could feel his fingers shaking.

"And why do you think I didn't report you to my father when you behaved so badly in London?"

Pat's breath came unevenly.

"I consider *you* behaved rather badly too."

"Perhaps I realised that."

"And perhaps I ought to apologise for that kiss."

"Ought you?"

There was provocation in her voice and in her eyes. She meant him to lose his head, and he lost it. He said:

"God! You're the most beautiful, wonderful thing in the world!"

And then she was in his arms, and for the second time he kissed her. But this time her arm crept round his neck and she was responding to his caresses in a manner which set all the fires in Pat Connel's heart ablaze and made him wonder if this was a mad dream rather than reality.

Chapter 5

THE glamour of that starlit spring night on the Chartres road, and the warmth and beauty of Sonia in his arms, cast a spell upon Pat Connel which rendered him incapable of using his brain at all.

A little sane thought and he might have asked himself what possible wisdom lay in plunging into a hotly passionate love affair with the daughter of his Chief. He might have doubted his sanity in allowing himself to be so completely enslaved by the witchery of this girl. For although he was very man to her woman while his arms were about her and his lips against her mouth, nothing could alter the fact that he was an impecunious employee in her father's firm, and that she was heiress to a fortune.

He could be neither wise nor sane while her heart beat to the same mad glad tune as his. He could only whisper between his kisses:

"I love you . . . I love you . . . you know that I do!"

Sonia found herself slipping into an enchanted world. She had not meant to. She had wanted to be practical about this affair, and never for an instant to lose sight of the difference in their stations. But Pat was an ardent and charming lover, and his obvious adoration was most flattering. Added to which she was genuinely attracted by him. While she rested languorously in his embrace, her eyes shut, her fingers caressing the thickness of his black handsome head, she genuinely wished that she had met and loved him under very different circumstances to these.

"You're so lovely . . . you're like a flower . . . an angel . . ." Pat's husky Irish voice was pouring endearments into her ear.

The longer she listened and the closer she clung to him, the more sincerely did Sonia regret the impossibility of this situation. But she was too much of an egotist to allow herself to be conscience-stricken for long. Jane, of course, would tell her that she had no right to behave like this. Jane would say that it was grossly unfair to Pat Connel. Perhaps it was. He seemed so grave about it all. She sighed, and whispered:

"Oh, Pat!"

Then his arms slackened and he drew slightly back from her. His eyes probed deeply into hers.

"Why . . . why are you like this? Why are you being so sweet, so kind to me? I don't understand."

She smiled.

"Don't try. Put your arms around me again."

"But I must know. I want to understand. I've had the most colossal nerve, making love to you like this. . . ."

"Thank goodness you have."

"You wanted me to?"

"Isn't that obvious?"

"But, Sonia . . ." For the first time he was using her Christian name. His brain was hazy. He was like one drunk with love. "It's unbelievable . . . that you should feel like this about me."

"I'm not the first woman to feel like this about you,

Pat. You've got the devil in your eyes, and you know it."

"But, Sonia . . ." He stammered wildly, caught her other hand in his and kissed it. "You're so lovely, so wonderful."

She leaned toward him, sighing luxuriously.

"Am I!"

"Marvellous! . . . I could never tell you how marvellous! And I can't quite get accustomed to the thought that you want me to make love to you. . . ."

"Certainly I want you to."

"Do you love me?"

"Can't you guess?"

"But do you, *do you?*"

"Yes." She whispered the word with her lips against his ear. And again he kissed her with a passion that blinded her temporarily to everything on earth but the power of his personality and the sheer attractiveness of him as a lover.

His ardour moved her, called forth as much sincerity of feeling as she was capable of for any man. But she was frightened of that feeling. She did not want to love Pat Connel too much, otherwise she must necessarily think of his happiness before her own. And then she must inevitably end this affair speedily before it hurt him too much. There was nothing light or philandering about this young man's love for her. She knew it. It burned with a white-hot sincerity.

Now she drew away from him. She said:

"My sweet, we must be sensible."

He took a deep breath, like a man who has felt himself drowning and comes up to the surface again. He kept her hands fast in his.

"I adore you. You know that now, don't you?"

"Yes."

"I've always adored you. I fell in love with you that night at the ball when I first danced with you and you were so proud and aloof. You were just John Royale's daughter and heiress that night, being condescending to one of the lesser lights in the firm."

She laughed.

"That sounds awful. Was I so horrid?"

"You were wonderful. You always are."

"Even when I insisted on driving a car that I couldn't drive?"

"You were grand. That day at Richmond I fell more in love with you than ever."

"You were awfully daring, weren't you, my sweet? I might quite easily have had you turned out of the firm for kissing me."

"I don't know why you didn't. I expected you to."

"You know now why I didn't."

His heart beat hard and fast.

"Sonia, don't fool with me, will you? Don't lead me to believe that you were kind to me because you fell in love with me . . . unless it's true."

Her fingers stirred a trifle restlessly in his.

"It's quite true."

"But why . . . why . . . ?"

"You're not going to ask questions all over again, are you? Hush, my sweet . . . don't try to analyse it. Just be happy like I am."

"But I must analyse it. It's so frightfully important. Don't you see what it means? It might be the beginning . . . or the end of everything."

"That sounds cryptic!"

"But you must try and understand what I feel. I'm madly, desperately in love with you. For some reason which I shall never understand, you're being an angel to me and trying to make me believe that you love me too. Well, that *is* the beginning and the end of the world so far as I'm concerned."

"Why the end?"

"Just that there can never be anybody else but you."

A shadow crossed her face, but in the dim starlight he did not see it. She drew her hands away from his, found a flapjack in her evening bag, and automatically dusted her face with powder . . . a face that burned from Pat's impassioned kisses.

He went on speaking:

"I once had the impertinence to wonder whether I could ever make you love me. . . . I dreamed wild, impossible dreams about you. Yet now you're making them possible, and that's what makes my brain quite dizzy. It's too good to be true."

"Darling," she murmured, and wished for the first time in her life that she was not John Royale's heiress, but quite a poor, unknown girl who could have married this man.

"But you see," continued Pat, "now that you are making my dreams come true, I'm full of doubts and fears."

"About what?"

"Not about my love for you. That's indubitable. But about the future. What possible right have I got to propose marriage to you?"

Sonia frowned. She did not like that word "marriage". It made her feel much too uncomfortable. It reminded her much too painfully of the fact that she was not free to listen to a proposal from any man.

"Don't let's worry to-night about the future," she said in a low voice.

"But I must. I love you and I want to marry you. It may sound wildly impudent . . . for me to propose to you . . . but if you care for me . . . Sonia, darling, there isn't anything in the world I wouldn't do to try and win you. That look in your eyes just now when I kissed you . . . my God, that's sufficient to spur any man on to the most incredible victories. I feel I could scale mountains . . . swim oceans . . . conquer worlds. . . ."

"You say such marvellous things, my sweet."

"But I mean them. Only tell me that you love me and that you want to marry me, Sonia, and I'll start right now making myself worthy of you."

Sonia swallowed hard. For a little while she had been caught up in Pat's whirlwind of ardour and carried along despite herself. But now he was rushing beyond her. She could not, *must not* follow him. She said:

"Not so fast, darling, *please*. We can't talk of marriage just yet."

"But if I love you and you love me . . ."

"Darling, you're so impetuous! But we must be prudent. We must look at this thing from all angles—go carefully. There's my father . . ."

She broke off. But the expression in her voice was eloquent and had the desired effect of bringing Pat down from the pinnacle of rapture on which he had poised himself.

He lit a cigarette and smoked hard for an instant, his brows contracted. Of course, Sonia was right. He was a crazy fool to let his emotions run away with him like this. He could scarcely expect to propose marriage to Sonia and be accepted on the spot. There was her father to be reckoned with. And Sonia's position *and* his own.

"You do understand, don't you, darling?" came Sonia's soft voice. "It won't do to make our feelings for each other too public, at least not during this trip. You can see how awkward it would be. You've taken Woodham's place, and Daddy would be furious. He might throw up the whole trip and go straight back to London. Then instead of having a lovely few weeks together, there'd be rows and scenes. Oh, I don't want that. I don't want to spoil this holiday. If we're sensible and careful it can be so wonderful for us."

Pat reflected upon this. He had to admit that Sonia was justified in what she said. Obviously, the old man would be outraged at the thought that he, a mere salesman in the firm, acting as chauffeur, should have made love to his daughter. On the other hand, Pat was so much in love that he wanted to proclaim his passion for Sonia to the whole world. He was prepared to face even John Royale and say: "I adore her . . . I want to do something worthy . . . something to deserve her. . . ."

Fine, brave rhapsodies! But coming down to hard, cold facts, what *could* he do? How could he ever be in a position to marry Sonia? How could he expect her to lead the life of a poor man's wife? Or how could he stamp out all that was proud and independent in himself and take on a rich wife . . . even providing that John Royale chose to sanction the match?

"Don't look so worried, darling," said Sonia. "Things will work out, I dare say. Let's just be happy for the next few weeks and keep our love a secret, shall we?"

He threw away his cigarette and took her in his arms again.

"Anything that you say, but I want to do what's right. I don't want to be underhand about this love. . . . I should hate that. . . ."

She bit her lip. He was so very intense and sincere and she would really rather have kept this affair on a lighter basis. Pat Connel was rather a dangerous young man to trifle with. She was well aware of that. She shivered to think what he would say if he knew about Maurice. . . .

"I don't want anything underhand either," she tried to soothe him. "But obviously it will be disastrous if we give ourselves away at the beginning of this journey. We must keep it a secret until we get back to England, mustn't we?"

"Yes, I suppose so," he said reluctantly.

She sighed with relief.

"And then we'll talk about the future."

"There *will* be a future for us, Sonia, won't there? You do really care for me enough to contemplate some sort of life with me?"

Sonia tried to shut out the thought of Maurice . . . and Paris. She murmured:

"Of course. And meanwhile we'll just be frightfully happy and have a marvellous time. There'll be lots of moments when we can be together . . . steal away alone for an hour or two. . . . Daddy will never guess in a thousand years, and my Cousin Jane . . ." Sonia shrugged her shoulders. "We must just be careful of her."

"She's an awfully good sort, is little Jane Daunt," said Pat. "Even if she found out, she'd give us her blessing, don't you think so?"

Sonia gulped. There was an ironic humour in the idea of Jane giving them a blessing . . . Jane of all people in the world.

"M'm. We must go back now," she whispered.

"Tell me once more that you love me and that there's some hope for me . . . one day. . . ."

With his arms about her and his kisses on her lips, Sonia weakened and gave him a dozen promises that she could never keep, a dozen hopes which she knew would never be fulfilled.

Pat drove her back to the hotel feeling a god, a giant, deliriously in love, even ready to go against his better judgement and remain Sonia's lover in secret—because for this journey she wished it to be so.

Chapter 6

JANE DAUNT sat on the edge of her bed transcribing shorthand notes into longhand, which she liked to do while the dictation was still fresh in her memory.

With the shaded lamp by the bedside throwing a soft amber light upon the slight figure in the green silky wrapper, Jane looked more like a child intent upon a puzzle than John Royale's staid young secretary at work. For now the smooth brown hair, usually rolled so neatly at the nape of her neck, was loose and flowed softly almost to her shoulders, making a lovely frame for the pale oval of her face. She looked beautiful. But she looked tired and she felt it, too. She had been writing at her uncle's dictation most of the evening. Now it was ten o'clock, and after the long drive she felt an irresistible desire for sleep.

Where was Sonia? That was what troubled Jane. Her cousin had the room adjoining this one. The communicating door was ajar. Jane could see that Sonia's room was in darkness and knew that she had not come back. Her father thought she had gone to bed. Jane was quite sure that she had slipped out to meet somebody. And that somebody could be no other than Pat Connel.

A deep resentment burned in Jane's breast. It was a resentment that sprang not only from her intimate knowledge of Sonia's affairs, but her secret love for Pat, himself.

He was unattainable. She knew that, and he was madly in love with Sonia. And she, Jane, was sore and angry with him for having come out here like this. He was only making a fool of himself. There could be nothing but catastrophe at the end of it. Yet she could not stop loving him nor wishing with all her heart that she could avert disaster for him.

As for Sonia, no words could describe the sheer anger which Jane felt against her cousin to-night. Why must anybody so lovely be so heartless? Why couldn't she have learnt her lesson in Paris two years ago? And why must she fasten upon Pat Connel, a penniless young man who could never be anything to her, just to gratify her own insatiable vanity?

There could be only one excuse for her, and that was her upbringing. She had lost her mother at a young and impressionable age when she had most needed the guidance and good influence of that mother. And John Royale had spoilt her disgracefully. It was just that . . . she was spoilt . . . and she wanted her own way and cared little, or perhaps thought little, of how much she hurt others in attaining her own desires.

Jane found the thought of Pat and Sonia meeting somewhere out there in the spring starlight interfering badly with her work. She could no longer concentrate on her uncle's descriptions of the French countryside. She shut her notebook with an exasperated gesture and looked at her wristwatch. A quarter past ten. Where was that foolish girl?

Suddenly there came the sound of a door opening and shutting and a light flashed on. Jane swung round, went quickly to the communicating door and opened it wide. Sonia stood there, taking off her fur coat. Sonia with fair curls dishevelled, eyes shining, cheeks a richer

pink than usual. When she saw Jane she smiled. But
Jane met that smile with stern gravity.

"Where on earth have you been, Sonia?"

"Having a little fresh air, darling."

"But you've been gone hours."

"About an hour and a half to be exact, my love."

Jane's lips curved into a humourless smile.

"And I suppose you've been taking a brisk walk in
those—"

She pointed to Sonia's high-heeled satin shoes, which
showed no signs of stain or dust.

Sonia's smile vanished. She began to take off her
dress, yawning.

"Oh, my dear Jane, for heaven's sake don't consti-
tute yourself my keeper. You never have been, and I
don't see why you ever should be."

Jane coloured and came forward, nearer her cousin.

"I may not be your keeper, but I'm the best friend
you've got, Sonia, and you know it."

Sonia sat down, slender and exquisite in cami-
knickers of rich ivory satin and creamy lace. She unbuckled her shoes, still yawning. She was in too good a
humour to be really annoyed with Jane. Poor dear Jane
must deliver her little lecture and feel better, that was
all!

"You're always a dear to me, Janie. But don't interfere with me too much, darling. I don't like it."

"And I suppose," said Jane, with a direct look at her,
"you didn't like interference from me when I helped
you out of that mess with Maurice?"

"Why bring that up?"

"Because, you foolish girl, I know exactly where
you've been to-night, and I'm not going to bed until I
tell you what I think of you."

"And where *have* I been?" Sonia's grey-green eyes
shot a defiant look at her.

"Out with Pat Connel."

For an instant Sonia was tempted to break into angry
retort, to say: "And why shouldn't I . . .?" And to
taunt Jane with the fact that she was fonder of that
young man than she ought to be. But Sonia desisted.

She realised that it would be folly to attack Jane in such a manner. Unfortunately Jane had every right to try to stop her from indulging in an affair with Pat, for Jane alone knew about Maurice. On the other hand, Sonia imagined herself thoroughly in love with Pat—for the moment. She was not prepared to give anything up for his sake, but she was prepared to have a very wonderful holiday with him. And the only way to ensure it was to throw dust in Jane's eyes. So she lied coolly and deliberately. Sitting back in her chair, she smiled and shook her head at Jane.

"My dear old thing, you're perfectly right. But you've jumped to wrong conclusions. I went out into the grounds of the hotel and found Connel strolling about taking the air like I was. Naturally, we talked. As I told you this morning, I think he's a very attractive young man. But I did not have an assignation with him. I am *not* altogether forgetting my position—or his."

"You know quite well that he isn't like Woodham."

"On the other hand, he has put himself in Woodham's place and must be treated as such. As a matter of fact, he was inclined to be a little familiar, and that annoyed me, so I ordered him to get out the car and drive me through the town to see the sights. I think he was furious, but he had to do it, and here I am!"

Jane thought:

"My poor old Pat . . . how he must have hated being treated like that! But it's his own fault. . . ."

"I can see, darling," went on Sonia, "that you've taken it for granted that I'm out for a flirtation with Pat Connel. But I'm not. So stop worrying about either of us."

"Right," said Jane. "If that's really how you feel, I'm glad. I want you to leave him alone."

Sonia dabbed her face with cream.

"Why are *you* so interested in him, darling?" she asked casually.

But Jane was not giving herself away. She answered as casually:

"We're just good friends and always have been since he worked for the firm. I know how attractive you are,

Sonia, and how much he admires you. I don't think it
would be fair of you to fool round with him."

With slim finger-tips Sonia worked the cream into
her cheeks. Cheeks that were still stinging from the passionate kisses of her lover. And she was thinking:

"I don't want to fool round . . . I want Pat to love
me . . . I want to love him . . . and we're not going
to be stopped by Jane or anybody else."

Aloud she said:

"You needn't worry, Janie. I'm not going to hurt
your Irishman. Let's not harp on the subject, because
it's rather boring. I'm enjoying this tour, aren't you?"

Jane came behind her and dropped a kiss on the fair
head.

"Very much. But I'm tired. You look simply glowing. I don't know how you manage it. Good night, dear.
I'm off to sleep."

For an instant Sonia was tempted to turn round and
pour the whole of her heart out to her cousin. She was
really very devoted to Jane. Jane had been such a
stand-by, such a comfort, such a tower of strength all
through that awful Paris episode. And Sonia had her
good instincts. She was more thoughtless than unkind.
Most of her faults sprang from sheer egotism and vanity. She adored admiration and excitement. She needed
emotionalism. And she did not see why she should be
made to go on paying for ever for her folly with Maurice. Besides which, Pat Connel was desperately in love
with her. She wasn't hurting him. She was being very
kind and responsive. She was going to make him happy.

Her limpid eyes filled with sudden tears. They were
tears of self-pity. She was awfully sorry for herself because of Maurice. She wished she was free to return
Pat's love . . . had a right to accept him or any other
man as a lover.

Jane saw the flash of tears and was immediately
tender and solicitous. She put an arm round her cousin.

"What is it, honey?"

Sonia hid her eyes against Jane's shoulder.

"Nothing . . . but I was just thinking . . . how
cruel life has been. If only there wasn't Maurice. . . ."

"Poor darling. I know. I wish there was some way out."

"But there isn't," said Sonia in a muffled voice, "and so I must go on being good. Somehow, to-night, I've been thinking about Francis."

"Francis Glyde? But why?"

"Well, you know how much he's in love with me—wants to marry me. I'm afraid I was rather encouraging to him. Now I'm away from England I must write him a little note and tell him that it's hopeless."

Jane nodded. So it was of Francis Glyde that Sonia had been thinking . . . and of those shackles which were preventing her from accepting any offers of marriage . . . poor little Sonia! Jane stayed a while comforting her, talking to her. The memory of Pat Connel was forgotten. Jane was thrown completely off the scent and went to bed satisfied.

But after Jane had gone, Sonia wept again in secret. And the tears were not for Francis Glyde, but for Pat. She was genuinely miserable because she suddenly realised that the love which Pat was offering her differed from any of the other loves in her life. It was something big and enthralling, which she wanted badly and which she dared not take. And that did not suit Sonia Royale, who had had practically everything in the world that she wanted until now.

Jane, thinking things over in her own room, felt overwhelming relief, because Sonia had no real interest in Pat.

Perhaps the journey to Morocco would be a success after all. Not that her own position, so far as Pat was concerned, could alter in any way. But she could put up with that so long as she knew that he would not have his heart broken or his life ruined by Sonia.

Long before either her uncle or her cousin were up, Jane was dressed and downstairs and standing on the front steps of the hotel. The sky was clear and blue and the April morning fresh and exhilarating.

While she stood there, feeling suddenly hungry for her breakfast, she saw the Victor come into view round the corner of the garage. She watched it draw up at the

side of the steps. Pat, at the wheel, looking fresh and
attractive in his green uniform, caught sight of Jane and
saluted her. She went down the steps and greeted him.

"Good morning, Pat."

"Good morning, miss."

"Now, Pat, drop that."

He grinned at her like a boy.

"Top of the morning to you, then, mavourneen."

"And hardly *that*."

"Then, hullo to you, Jane."

"That's better." She smiled, and taking a cigarette-
case from the pocket of her short suède coat which she
wore over a polo jersey, she offered it to him. "Have
one?"

"And what will the head porter of the Hôtel de Ville
think if he sees one of the mademoiselles offering a cigarette in that familiar fashion to the chauffeur?"

Nevertheless, he took one and thanked her.

"You're a silly idiot to have come in Woodham's
place," Jane remarked in her blunt fashion.

"But I'm enjoying it thoroughly."

"You look as though you are."

"I am," he smiled gaily. "It's much more amusing
than trying to sell cars to people who haven't any
money."

"Well, so long as it amuses you . . ." She shrugged
her shoulders.

"Are you still cross with me for coming?"

"I still think it was a foolish thing for you to do."

"Ah, but you don't know how sensible it really
was!"

She looked at him steadily. She was not quite sure
why he was in such excellent spirits. Just for an instant
she had a faint, horrid little suspicion that what Sonia
had told her last night was not strictly true. Had she
really snubbed Pat and been indifferent to him? If so,
why wasn't he sunk in gloom, instead of sitting on top
of the world? Still, Pat was like that . . . always trying
to get on top of the world, if not actually achieving it.

"Aren't you enjoying the trip?" he asked her.

"I think so."

"It's sure to be marvellous driving through France this time of the year, and when we get to Spain it'll be hot and sunny, and in Morocco warmer still. By the way, Spain's a most romantic place."

"We've come for the purpose of giving my uncle a holiday rather than for romance," said Jane drily.

Pat looked at the point of his cigarette. He felt suddenly guilty. He would like to have told little Jane Daunt just how filled with wild romance this tour would be . . . for him . . . and for Sonia. But that was impossible. He had agreed that they must keep their love a secret . . . that for all their sakes he must say nothing until Sonia gave the word and the time be propitious for him to announce that they loved each other and that he had asked her to marry him.

The fact that their love needed all this secrecy was a fact to be deplored, but for Pat it could not destroy the essential thrill of it. He looked kindly upon Jane's pale young face and wondered suddenly what lay behind her gravity, her reserve.

"Do you never allow yourself a romantic thought?" he asked her. "Are you always so darned practical and efficient?"

Her brown eyes smouldered, but revealed nothing. And it was not given to him to know that in the very depths of her being Jane Daunt was essentially romantic . . . that her heart was starved for romance . . . that at the mere idea of the warm sunny days and the moonlit nights in Spain and in North Africa, so close to *him*, her whole soul was shaken, yes, shaken—but to no purpose. For this love that she bore him was to no purpose, and therefore must be concealed. She would have died before letting him guess what she felt, so she put up a bluff which he found impenetrable.

"I haven't time for romance," she said. "I'm much too busy, and I should imagine you are too."

"Oh, sure!" he laughed, but there was mockery in those very blue eyes of his. And he, too, was giving away nothing this morning.

Then the voice of John Royale interrupted their conversation.

"Ah! There you are, Jane. And Connel too. He's a bit early. We haven't had breakfast. But I prefer people to be too early than too late."

Pat Connel slipped back into Woodham's place. He touched his cap.

"Good morning, sir."

"Another half an hour and we'll push off," said John Royale, rubbing his hands. "Have you looked at the map, Connel? Do you know where we shall land next?"

"Yes, sir. We go about one hundred and thirty-nine kilometres to Tours, and then through to Poitiers, and with good luck and the Victor doing its best, we ought to be in Bordeaux to-night."

"Excellent," said Royale, "excellent!"

"Hullo, everybody," said a sweet, high voice.

Jane and the two men looked up. On the balcony of the first floor stood the figure of Sonia, fair as the spring morning in a daffodil-yellow dress of soft wool material, and a small Marina hat of the same colour at the side of her blonde curls.

She waved to them.

"All set for the day's journey?"

"All set, my dear," called back her father.

Jane looked at Pat. And her heart seemed suddenly to miss a beat when she saw the expression on his face. He was staring up at Sonia. In his eyes, so very blue under their thick black lashes, lay a passionate adoration which was horribly revealing to Jane. Equally revealing was the look which Sonia was giving him. Jane, intercepting it, felt the colour burn her cheeks and her heart sink. There was something more than instinct now to make her suspicious. She *knew* that Sonia had lied to her last night, and that there was *something* between those two. Something that was bound to destroy Pat in the end . . . Pat with all his ambitions, his gay courage, his ideals.

Jane turned and walked up the steps into the hotel. All the radiance of the morning had fled for her. She could only face a tangle of thoughts and ideas and emotions, ask herself what she could do, and know, even while she asked, that the answer was—*"Nothing!"*

Chapter 7

IT could not be said that Jane enjoyed the rest of that drive through France. By the time they reached the Spanish border, still less was she enjoying herself.

That look which she had intercepted between Sonia and Pat on the morning of their departure from Chartres was only the beginning of a dozen and one little incidents which strengthened her suspicions that these two were having a secret *affaire*.

Mile after mile through the radiant spring days Sonia would sit beside the driver of the big grey car, always a little closer than was necessary, never failing at intervals to give him the full benefit of her lovely eyes. Always Jane Daunt sat at the back of the car with her uncle, and, when she wasn't taking down notes, was forced to watch Pat, who, in his turn, glanced constantly at Sonia's exquisite profile. Such glances left Jane no room for doubt what lay in his mind. He was madly in love with Sonia.

But what game Sonia was playing, Jane could not guess. Sonia was so reticent nowadays. She lied—quite shamelessly, of course—whenever Jane questioned her.

Jane could hardly accuse her of lying, nor had she any real right to interfere, except that it was almost beyond her endurance to be a silent witness of Pat's downfall. For what else could it mean for him except a downfall? If Sonia was tempting him, playing with him, there must inevitably be a rude awakening for him.

John Royale, engrossed in his literary work, saw nothing of the little drama which was being performed under his very eyes. He presumed that the two girls were enjoying themselves, and Connel was a magnificent driver, more useful than Woodham could ever have been, so he was content.

They stayed a couple of days in Biarritz, where Mr. Royale abandoned his work for a game of golf on those famous and lovely links.

That was a particularly trying morning for Jane. Her uncle insisted upon taking her with him.

"You don't play golf, but you can be my caddy, and the exercise will do you good after all the driving and typing," he told her.

He wanted Sonia to go, too. But Sonia managed to have a "headache" and announced that she must lie down and rest. Later, she said, she would get Connel to drive her along the sea-front to see the sights of the gay, fashionable watering-place.

Jane knew what that meant! Sonia was planning a few hours alone with Pat. What could come of it, Jane dared not think. With a heavy heart she went off to the golf links with her uncle and left the other two behind.

Sonia spent that fresh sparkling morning in exactly the manner which Jane predicted. The moment her father and cousin were safely stowed away on the golf course and Pat had returned with the car, Sonia joined him and went out. There was no lying abed for her. In one of her most attractive outfits—grey flannel suit, white jersey, and spotted scarf—looking as radiant as a June rose, Sonia allowed Pat to drive her out of the town and a little way into the country, where they could talk.

The moment they were in a secluded spot, Pat, his handsome face quite pale with emotion, took the lovely figure in his arms and kissed her passionately on lips and throat.

"My sweet . . . my own sweet . . ."

She sighed languorously as she leaned against him. "I've needed this."

"So have I. Do you know, I haven't kissed you once since we left Bordeaux."

"And that seems a long time ago."

"It's an eternity between each time that I kiss you." She smiled.

"What a born lover you are."

"And you were born to be loved because you're so beautiful."

He kissed her again. Then, when the first ecstatic moments were fled, he drew away from her and grew sane again and suddenly grave.

"You know I don't like it, Sonia. All this secrecy worries me."

"Darling, aren't you getting used to it?"

"No, I don't think I ever shall. It doesn't suit my temperament. I'd far rather go straight to your father to-night, and tell him that I want to marry you—infernal, colossal impudence though it might seem."

Sonia's slim figure tautened.

"You can't do that. You mustn't."

"Oh, I know all the arguments," he said, frowning, "and I dare say it would break up everything; but I don't like going behind his back in this way."

"Neither do I, darling. But it would be mad to let conscience worry us too much and spoil our whole trip."

Her slim white hand stole up and caressed the black handsome head which attracted her so vitally. She tried to woo him from his feelings of guilt. But Pat was persistent this morning. It seemed that he worried much more about the situation than she did, although, she told herself, she had more cause to worry than he. For didn't she know that while that wretched Maurice existed, there could be no way out for her and for Pat.

"Are you sure your cousin Jane doesn't guess about us?" he asked her.

Sonia lit a cigarette and smoked it as she leaned back in the circle of his arm.

"I dare say—but what does it matter?"

With a half-humorous smile, he looked down at her perfect profile.

"Do you know, darling, I believe women are more unscrupulous than men. You don't worry that beautiful head of yours very much about this intrigue. But I do. Take Jane, for instance. She's always been a good friend to me. Sometimes she looks at me very reproachfully, as though she knows, and it makes me feel a bit of a cad. I suppose I *am* a cad, making love to my Chief's daughter behind his back."

"Not at all, since the Chief's daughter wishes you to do so and has asked you to say nothing about it," murmured Sonia. "And as for Jane, we really can't live our lives to please *her*."

"I suppose nothing matters so long as you really love me and will marry me one day and let me win the world for you," he said, intoxicated by the touch of her hand and the nearness of her.

Because a faint flush stole into her cheeks and a faint expression of dismay came into her eyes, she hid her face against his shoulder and embraced him mutely. Wherefore he took her silence to mean assent.

When they returned to the hotel after those few stolen hours, Pat was completely won over again, ready to do anything that Sonia commanded of him.

But Sonia in her queer way was not quite so pleased with life to-day. Once she was alone, she was pursued by her thoughts and memories. It was the memory of Maurice, her husband with whom she had lived for only a few days, which haunted her most persistently. Where was he now? How much longer would he insist on extorting money for her silence? And why, why couldn't she secure a divorce as secretly and effectively as she had effected that mad marriage?

Much as her father loved her, she knew that this thing, were it to come to his knowledge, would shock him horribly. He was the straightest man in the world, and he detested any kind of deception or underhand dealing. Sonia was beginning to be afraid . . . afraid, too, of Jane. Jane knew so much, and Jane was obviously attracted by Pat. Sonia could not but be aware that it was a very dangerous game which she was playing.

She had a little present waiting for Jane when she came back from the golf course. In a perverted fashion it salved her conscience a bit to be extra nice to Jane.

"Connel drove me into the town, and I found this for you, darling," she told her cousin languidly. She was lying on her bed, still keeping up the pretence of the headache.

Jane, brown and flushed after walking those eighteen holes in the wind and sun of the April morning, looked gravely at Sonia and then at the present—a blue-and-rose cashmere handkerchief-scarf.

"It's Molyneux, darling," murmured Sonia.

"It's lovely," said Jane, "and thanks awfully."

But her shrewd little brain knew perfectly well what this present meant. That mad girl had been out the whole morning with Pat, and this was a silent method of expressing remorse. If only she would *tell her* what she was doing . . . what she meant to do about Pat!

Jane could scarcely trust herself to stay in the room and speak to Sonia. Her nerves were jangling. And that was unusual for Jane, who was, as a rule, so cool and poised.

She was in a state of nerves for the rest of that day, and it culminated in an unhappy scene that night. She had known that it could only be a question of time before the intrigue between Sonia and Pat was discovered. Sonia was missing after dinner, and Jane was expected to do some work. But she was unable to put her mind to it. She was so worried about those two. And not only worried, but conscious of an entirely feminine jealousy. Why must Sonia, who could never marry any man till she was rid of Maurice, take the one man whom she, Jane, had ever loved? Why must Pat, who was so dear to her, have eyes and ears only for Sonia? It wasn't fair!

There was bitterness in Jane's heart as she excused herself from her uncle and walked out into the moonlit grounds of the big hotel in search of Sonia.

The luxuriant palms spread dark spiky shadows against the luminous sky and the air was rich and sweet with the scent of mimosa. Jane, with a short fur coat over her evening dress, wandered here and there, conscious in a queer, fatalistic fashion that she was going to find Sonia and Pat together. She did not want to find them . . . all that was most fastidious and proud in

her shrank from it . . . but she had to go on, pro-
pelled by something stronger than herself.

She came upon them, at length, sitting in an arbour
which looked upon a small Italian garden with stone-
paved pathways and white statues among the flowers.
She felt her heart flick and hurt horribly as she saw.
She stood stock-still.

Pat, wearing a grey suit instead of the chauffeur's uniform, was standing there, with Sonia in his arms. Sonia's white fur wrap barely concealed a glittering evening
dress which was made of some exquisite spun-gloss material. The moonlight seemed to radiate a million lights
from it. And only too plainly Jane saw those two faces,
both so beautiful in their own way, blurred into one
during that passionate embrace.

Then Pat caught sight of the watching figure, and
with an exclamation he released Sonia.

"God, there's Cousin Jane!" he said under his
breath.

Sonia swung round. For a moment she was speechless with dismay. How in heaven's name had Jane
found them here? Was it by mistake, or had she deliberately followed? For an instant anger surged through
Sonia. She was not going to be spied upon, no matter
whether Maurice existed or not . . . she was going to
tell Jane so. She was about to speak, but Jane turned
and ran away . . . ran as though the sight of the lovers was unbearable to her.

Pat drew a hand across his forehead.

"That's torn it," he said.

"Damn," said Sonia under her breath.

"I'm afraid there's no doubt in her mind about us
now. Sonia, I was a crazy fool to let you meet me like
this. I felt that we were taking an awful risk. And yet I
had to see you. . . . I wanted to . . ."

She flung herself back into his arms.

"Don't worry. I'll deal with Jane."

"What will you say?"

"Oh, something . . ."

"But you won't be able to deny it. . . ."

"No, I won't try, but I'll just tell Jane to mind her own business."

Pat released her.

"I told you this morning that I didn't like it, darling. It's all so secretive and . . ."

She stopped him with a fragrant hand against his lips.

"We've had that all out. You know why we must keep silence. It's for your sake as well as mine. I'll deal with Jane. Don't worry."

"Very well," he said wretchedly.

But the glamour of the evening had fled for Pat. He felt small and humiliated. He disliked having been seen by Jane Daunt like that. She must think him an awful bounder. She wasn't the kind of girl to countenance deceit, and he wouldn't blame her for despising him. But he must see her to-morrow and tell her frankly that he wanted to marry Sonia, and he was going to live and work with that one aim and object in his mind.

Surely she would admit that love gave him a certain right . . . real love such as this. She would forgive him when she knew that it wasn't just a passing passion . . . an ugly hole-and-corner temporary affair.

The lovers lingered for only another swift embrace, and then Sonia ran back to the hotel.

She went straight to Jane's bedroom and found the door locked.

"Jane," she called, "let me in."

Jane very reluctantly opened that door. Her face was pale and stern. Sonia avoided her gaze, but went straight to the point.

"I suppose you're furious with me. But you shouldn't have come spying. Then you wouldn't have known."

"I prefer to know," said Jane.

But even as she said the words, she wondered if that was true. She felt that she would be haunted night and day by the picture of those two figures merged into one, like a graceful statue of love out there in the Italian garden. Fine lovers, both of them. But Sonia was not for Pat, and Pat might have been *hers* if Sonia, with her cruel egotism and lack of regard for another's pain, hadn't drawn him into her own white arms.

"Well," said Sonia defiantly, "what about it?"

Chapter 8

THE long hateful scene was over. Sonia had gone and Jane was alone again.

She felt that as long as she lived she never wanted to see Biarritz again. She felt that it was a place in which she had been betrayed. Sonia was a traitor to her word, and Pat Connel to his own intelligence. Sonia was selfish and cruel. But Pat was crazy, blinded by this infatuation, enslaved by a woman's beauty and seductiveness. He must *know* that he could not play such a game with his Chief's daughter and get away with it. Even though he was serious—and Jane was sure that was so—it was all incredibly foolish of him. He could never hope to marry Sonia. It would have been difficult even if she had been free, but as things were it was impossible.

For two solid hours Jane had argued and protested with her cousin, used every ounce of strength that she possessed to try to make Sonia see that she could not, must not, let this affair continue. For two hours she had pleaded, begging Sonia to let Pat alone, if only for his sake.

And for two hours Sonia had listened and remained stubborn. From defiance she had changed to pathos. She had assured Jane that she was really in love with Pat Connel and wanted a little happiness in her life. And when Jane had pointed out that it was a gross injustice to Pat to take her happiness at the expense of his, Sonia had changed again. What sympathy she might have commanded she lost by becoming spiteful. She had ended by telling Jane that the main trouble with her was that she was *jealous*.

"You want him yourself!" she had said. "You're angry because I've got him—that's all."

It was those words which lingered to hurt Jane cruelly long after Sonia's exit from the room. It was a shaft that hit near the truth and yet was not quite true. She could not deny that she loved Pat Connel. But she did not deplore this affair because she, personally, wanted him. She would have tried to be glad about the affair had it been for his happiness. Or if Sonia had been honest, told him about Maurice, and he had still wanted to be her lover, she, Jane, might have deplored the folly of it; but she could have washed her hands of the business then and let them get on with it. But these circumstances were so different. Sonia was afraid to tell the truth, and Pat was being exalted crazily to a height from which he must inevitably crash. It was that thought which hit Jane so hard. She wanted so passionately to save him.

She could do nothing about it. Her hands were hopelessly tied. The last thing Sonia had done to-night was to remind her that she had taken a vow two years ago never to reveal the fact of her marriage to anybody on earth. Jane knew that she must keep silence; just stand by and see this affair continue and let Pat be dragged to his ruin.

Jane could understand Pat's attitude. He was a volatile, impressionable young Irishman with a terrific amount of vitality and enthusiasm for life, and Sonia was as beautiful as a poet's dream and kind to him . . . sweet and kind. Nobody knew better than Jane how adorable Sonia could be when she chose.

But what would he feel when he learned the truth, which he must eventually do? Sonia might imagine that he would be content to carry on with this intrigue, but Jane knew that such was not the case. He was straight, and he would want to put things on a straight and proper footing. Then Sonia would either have to tell him the facts about Maurice—or send him away.

Jane slept badly that night. She woke with a wretched little feeling that everything was spoilt now. There could be no further enjoyment for her during this tour. It would be nothing but an agony for her to sit in the background and watch Pat's reckless pursuit of Sonia.

It rained that day, and so John Royale abandoned his plans for spending another morning on the links, and they moved on from Biarritz through Saint Jean de Luz, and so to Hendaye and the Spanish frontier.

Here Pat Connel made himself very useful with his knowledge of Spain, the language, and people. With great ease he got them through the Spanish customs.

If it hadn't been for her worries, Jane would thoroughly have enjoyed this day which marked their entry into Spain. This was gorgeous country and wonderful weather. Spain was at her loveliest in the spring. White walls, blue skies, the verdant green of barley fields splashed with scarlet poppies, an occasional glimpse of sapphire sea. Picturesque peasants on their little grey donkeys, girls with coloured shawls and flowers. Black-eyed babies, beautiful as Murillo paintings, sprawling in the sunlit doorways of cottages which were half-covered with bright cerise bougainvillæa. An atmosphere which seemed utterly different from any other in the world.

In the afternoon they traversed a sinuous road flanked by woodlands, and so ascended through the violet-blue mountains, which were savage and splendid against the vivid sky. Through San Sebastian and Tolosa and Vittoria, they came at the setting of the sun to Burgos, where they spent the night.

It had been a day of driving which Pat had enjoyed more than anything. Especially those hairpin bends in the ascent of the Puerto de Echegarate. He was a little proud of his fine driving, and well rewarded when Sonia whispered:

"I wouldn't have had Woodham through this for anything. You're *marvellous*!"

Jane heard those words. They made her slightly sick. Resentment burned in her young breast.

"Why can't she leave him alone?" was her inward thought.

Later that evening Jane found the first opportunity since leaving Biarritz to speak alone with Pat.

She had dropped her favourite fountain-pen out of her bag in the back of the car. She went round to the hotel garage to find it. Pat, in his shirt-sleeves and gum-boots, was washing the dust and dirt off the big Victor. A cigarette was stuck on his lower lip, and he was whistling cheerfully. As he saw Jane approach, he took the cigarette from his lips and bowed from the waist.

"Buenos, Señorita."

"That," said Jane, "means 'Hail', or something, I suppose."

"It's an ordinary Spanish greeting."

"Very proud of yourself, aren't you?"

His blue eyes danced at her.

"Very."

She bit her lip. There flashed across her memory that unforgettable vision of Pat as she had seen him in the garden at Biarritz with Sonia in his arms. And some-how Pat's intuition told him what she was thinking. He, too, remembered. He ceased being flippant. A slow red crept up under the tan of his face. He came and stood beside her.

"Jane Daunt, are you thoroughly disgusted with me because of the other night? You look it."

She, too, flushed red and did not meet his gaze. Then before she could restrain herself, she said coldly:

"I came to fetch my fountain-pen. Have you seen it, Connel?"

The flush left his cheeks. He went rather white and immediately clicked his heels together.

"Yes, miss. I have it here."

He drew the pen from his pocket and handed it to her.

Immediately Jane regretted her tone and implication. It was mean of her to remind Pat that he had come as a chauffeur. She said impulsively:

"Oh, Pat, why are you being such a *fool*?"

He looked steadily down at her.

"Now, are we friends . . . or just Miss Daunt and servant?"

"You know we're friends."

"Sure, I thought so until you spoke just now."

"I was angry."

"I know. What you saw the other night upset you. Perhaps you have a right to be upset. You think it mean of me—beastly—to make love to Sonia behind her father's back."

"What do *you* think about it?"

His eyes glowed.

"I can think of nothing but her and the fact that I love her more than anything in the world."

Jane swallowed hard.

"You've always been ambitious, Pat. But isn't this a little *too* optimistic of you?"

"You mean because I'm a salesman without a sou and she's—Miss Royale?"

Jane nodded. She meant so much more than that . . . so much that she could not say.

"I admit that it sounds damned impudent, but she has given me the right to hope. You see, Jane, Sonia loves me as much as I do her."

Jane turned from him. For an instant she felt an absurd inclination to burst into tears. It was so hopeless and so pathetic. She was so terribly in love with him. It hurt like mad to hear him talk this way about another woman . . . and that woman one who could never be anything more to him than she was now.

"You might as well know about it," continued Pat. "Sonia won't mind me telling you. . . . I expect she's told you herself that we love each other. You can't doubt it after seeing us at Biarritz."

"Pat, Pat," said Jane in a low voice, "where can it all lead to?"

His gay, insouciant smile flashed out.

"The altar, I hope."

"You want to . . . marry her?"

"That is my one ambition . . . or one of my many,

shall I say? Sonia has asked me to keep all this secret from her father until we return to England because she is afraid that it might spoil the whole tour."

"Uncle John would never consent."

"Does money make all that difference, Jane? Or is it just that I'm not good enough for her?"

She swung round then, cheeks flaming.

"Of course you're good enough. . . . Why shouldn't you be? But it's all so difficult . . ."

"Don't fash yourself, little Jane Daunt," said Pat in his peculiarly tender Irish voice. "Don't worry. I can manage my own affairs, and I believe implicitly in Sonia. She has her reasons for not wanting me to be honest about my love for her for the moment."

"Yes," said Jane under her breath, "she has her reasons. . . ."

"I feel rotten about deceiving the old man, but it *would* spoil his holiday if I told him, wouldn't it?"

He caught Jane's eye and smiled whimsically. She tried to smile back.

"Undoubtedly."

"Then forgive me and don't be too hard on either of us. Just wish us luck."

She found it impossible to utter the words that he wanted to hear. He added:

"If I ever have the great good luck to make Sonia my wife, you and I will be sort of related, eh, mavourneen?"

She could bear no more. The desire to weep became too strong for her. She took the pen and turned and ran out of the garage.

For a moment she stood outside the hotel, trying to recover her composure before she joined her uncle and tackled her transcription.

What a lovely night, she thought! There was something about Spain which appealed vastly to Jane. She loved all that was uncivilised about it. She liked to see the women in their shawls with flowers behind their ears strolling with their lovers through the starry darkness. She liked to hear the faint sound of a tango rhythm, the click of a castanet, and the sweet tenor voice of some young singer chanting an old Spanish air with peculiar passion and melancholy.

She had never felt so sad in her life. Nothing seemed worth while. The man she loved was in love with somebody else, and he was going to be badly hurt at the end of it all.

Even while she stood there, sorrowfully contemplating the night, she saw a shadowy figure in white emerge from the hotel, hurry round the corner, and vanish. It was Sonia. Sonia stealing out to bid good night to her lover.

Jane's all too vivid imagination pictured the meeting between the two. Pat's gay face would become eager and passionate. He would open his arms and take Sonia into a close embrace. . . .

A little sob rose in Jane's throat. She turned and ran quickly into the hotel.

Chapter 9

AND so to Madrid!

The brilliant laughing capital of Spain was a little uneasy. The shadow of recent revolution lurked in the corners and unrest brooded over the people. But the place was still vivid enough and full of a careless charm which appealed in particular to Jane. Madrid was the very heart of the most romantic country in the world. In a way, it intensified her loneliness, for she had to stand by knowing that Pat and Sonia were absorbed in each other, ever wondering what the end would be.

The first night in Madrid marked a disaster. Jane, following much the same routine as usual, dined with her uncle and cousin. And after coffee had been served, she retreated with Mr. Royale to a quiet part of the lounge to take down notes of the day.

Sonia made the mistake of taking it for granted that these two would be nicely engrossed with work for the next hour or so and it never entered her head that her father would take it into his to go out again to-night.

But Mr. Royale, thoroughly interested in the Spanish capital, found himself bored with dictation, and after a brief spell of it, decided to put on his hat and go out for a walk.

If he wanted local colour he could get it strolling past the brightly lit cafés and shops. It was warm enough on this starry, windless night for Spanish folk to sit out under the striped awnings, sip their wine, smoke their cigarettes, and exchange endless philosophies and jests while the rest of their country fermented about their ears.

Mr. Royale suggested that Jane should put on a coat and accompany him, and she, feeling restless, was only too glad to do so.

She ran upstairs to her room to fetch the coat. So far as she knew Sonia had gone to bed, having pleaded a headache. She put her head inside Sonia's room to bid her good night and was surprised to find the room empty. The bed was turned down and a flowered chiffon nightgown spread in readiness, but no Sonia.

Jane went along to both the bathrooms on that floor. They were dark and empty. So Sonia was not having a bath. Therefore Sonia had not come upstairs at all although, after dinner, she had announced her intention of going straight to bed.

Now what was the foolish girl doing, Jane asked herself with set lips? She would certainly get herself entangled if she wasn't careful. However, there was no time for Jane to search farther for her cousin. Uncle John was waiting. Jane joined him and they went out together into the radiant night.

Sonia, meanwhile, walked arm-in-arm with her lover through the Puerta del Sol, the largest of the plazas in Madrid and through the Calle de Alcala toward the Buen Retrio park.

They walked gaily, happily like hundreds of other lovers who strolled through the Spanish streets, some of which were bordered with feathery acacias, silvered by moonlight, and great palms splaying fantastically against the luminous sky.

"You only want a shawl and I could address you as Señorita," said Pat. "Only you're a lot more attractive than any of these Spanish women."

"Some of them are supposed to be raving beauties."

"I can only see *you*," he said.

She pressed his arm to her side with a little murmur of appreciation. She had not yet grown tired of her lover's adulation. It was sweet food for her vanity.

"Aren't we quite mad to be doing this?" he asked her. "Are you quite sure you won't be missed?"

"No. I said good night to Daddy and left him working with Jane. He won't disturb me, and if Jane comes up and looks for me and doesn't find me there—well, she can think what she likes. I don't care."

Pat thought a moment of Jane Daunt's frank questioning eyes and that expression of disapproval which he had seen once or twice lately on her small face.

"Cousin Jane isn't at all pleased about us, is she?" he said.

Sonia made no reply, beyond a shrug of the shoulders. She knew so much better than Pat why Jane wasn't pleased. Jane had every right to be angry and disapproving, but Sonia could scarcely explain *that* to Pat!

They found a café, sat down at a little round marble-topped table, drank strong black coffee in tall glasses and watched the world go by.

It intrigued Sonia to hear Pat talking fluent Spanish to the waiters. He seemed to have forgotten none of the language which he had learnt in his youth. And it intrigued Pat to see the many devouring glances which his companion received from the Spaniards who passed her by.

"You're much too lovely to be safe," he told her, smiling. "I doubt if any of these fellows have seen anything look quite as angelic as you do in their lives before."

For a moment Sonia's conscience stabbed her, for tiny though it was, that conscience existed. She looked at him wistfully.

"I'm not really angelic, Pat."

"You are, my sweet."

"Do you really think I'm—so perfect?"

"Definitely. For how many girls are there in the world who are as good as they're beautiful?"

Sonia bit her lip.

"How do you know I'm so good, Pat?"

"I feel you are, darling."

"Don't you imagine I've ever had a love affair before?"

"I've never allowed myself to imagine anything about it. It's perfectly obvious that a girl who looks like you do and has had all the chances you've had, must also have had dozens of admirers."

"But you don't think I've ever admired anybody in my turn?"

"You're being very serious all of a sudden, Beautiful."

"I want to be," she persisted, urged by something unusually serious within herself. "I want to know if you think I've ever been in love before."

"I think that I'd rather not know. I might feel jealous," he said, "and in any case, whatever affair you've had is over, and you're going to marry me. That's all that matters."

Sonia felt her throat go dry. She dived in her bag for a little gold cigarette-case and put a cigarette between her lips. Pat leaned forward to light it for her and for an instant she saw the burning sincerity in those very blue eyes of his. It seemed to go straight to her heart. There arose in her the most genuine feeling of remorse which she had ever known . . . remorse that she should be deceiving a man who believed in her so implicitly . . . infinite regret that there had ever been a Maurice in her life.

"Pat," she said in a husky voice, "what would you do if I didn't mean to marry you and was just . . . having an affair?"

For an instant he looked startled, then sat back and laughed.

"Don't let's play about with suppositions like that. They're too unpleasant. I think it would just kill me, that's all. I've always been ambitious, but it's more than an ordinary ambition, my desire to make good some way and have you for my wife."

Sonia felt suddenly that she could not sit here and talk any more. All that was best in her seemed to be well to the surface to-night. She was afraid that she might break down and confess and tell Pat that she was already married. And that would be madness . . . that would take him right away from her. He would never understand. She was not brave enough to take the risk and perhaps lose what seemed at the moment so worth retaining . . . his love and his belief in her.

"Let's go back to the hotel," she said abruptly.

He looked at her with some consternation.

"Is there anything wrong, my darling?"

"No, nothing. I'm just tired."

They reached the hotel and stood a moment on the wide steps which led up to a kind of covered terrace where meals were served in the summer. Just for a moment Sonia cast discretion to the winds and flung herself into her lover's arms. She felt suddenly unutterably depressed. She had set out on this assignation in the highest of spirits. Now they had sunk to zero. She curved an arm about Pat's neck and drew his lips down to hers.

"Oh Pat, darling, I hate saying good night and good-bye."

He kissed the warm velvet mouth raised to his, his senses reeling. She had never seemed so close to him, so much in love.

At last she let him go, bade him a last good night and started to walk up the steps. He stood watching the slim figure in the fur coat, and was struck suddenly by something almost tragic in the droop of her head. She was unhappy, his adored love! The thought went through his heart like a knife. Incautiously he sprang up those steps after her and caught her in his arms.

"Darling . . . darling . . . wait . . . don't go. . . ."

And that was the precise moment in which John Royale and Jane chose to return to the hotel from their promenade.

Jane saw . . . and felt the colour scorch her cheeks, then drain away. Those two . . . ye gods, what utter folly . . . right in the front entrance! Mr. Royale saw and stood rooted to the ground.

"Good God!" he said.

His exclamation was loud enough to reach Pat, who released Sonia and swung round as though he had been shot.

"Oh, lord," he said under his breath. "That's done it!"

John Royale marched up the steps. He had but a confused impression of what he had seen. He just took it for granted that his chauffeur or salesman, or whatever he liked to call himself, was forcing his attentions upon Sonia. There was the poor child, struggling with him! They had only just come in time.

"Connel, what the devil does this mean?" he demanded, white with rage.

Pat straightened. The Irish fighting blood in him rose. If this was to be a battle he would plunge into it without fear. He would fight for Sonia, and she was worth fighting for. But her thoughts were not so brave. All her love and desire for Pat was submerged in fear . . . the fear of discovery.

Pat said:

"Look here, sir, I think I'd better tell you . . ."

"Wait!" interrupted Sonia breathlessly.

"Sonia, my darling girl," came from Mr. Royale, and put an arm about her. "What a fright this must have given you. I'm appalled . . . appalled to think that this young man should have taken such a liberty."

She looked at her father speechlessly. She realised that he had taken it for granted that Pat's advances were unwelcome. She also knew that Pat was on the

verge of making a full confession about their love for
each other. He was always wanting to do the straight
and honourable thing. But it could not be allowed to
happen. First of all, her father would never consent to
their union, but even if he did she, herself, could never
consent because of Maurice. Then that whole wretched
story would be revealed.

"How dared you, Connel!" thundered Mr. Royale.

Pat looked straight at him, then turned his head
slowly and looked at Sonia. Was she going to say anything? She was. She said:

"It wasn't altogether Connel's fault."

John Royale stared.

"What do you mean? Are you suggesting that you
encouraged such behaviour?"

Jane, standing in the background, waited breathlessly
for Sonia's next words. She, knowing so much, wondered whether her cousin would have the courage to
speak the truth. But Sonia was speaking half-truths—
anxious not to let all the blame fall upon Pat, and at the
same time not to incriminate herself too far.

"I—I wanted a little fresh air and I came out and
I—ran into Connel," she stammered. "We were talking,
and I . . ."

"And he took advantage and tried to kiss you. I tell
you I'm appalled!" said Mr. Royale, his temper well
roused.

"Now Daddy, don't jump to hasty conclusions," began Sonia, her lips trembling. "I—"

"You're just trying to excuse the fellow, because
you're soft-hearted," broke in her father. "No, Sonia,
I'm not going to have it." He turned on Pat, "I'll not
hear any excuses, young man. You've gone too far.
What you want is a good hiding and if I had a whip I'd
give it to you. You can consider yourself dismissed."

Pat went white. For the moment he was too dumb-
founded to reply. Sonia was near to fainting. She made
another desperate attempt to calm her father down, but
Mr. Royale in a temper was never a man to be argued
or reasoned with. He had taken it for granted that Con-

nel had behaved in a familiar fashion unwelcome to his daughter, and he passed sentence accordingly.

He pulled a case from his pocket, extracted a roll of notes and handed them to Pat.

"You're dismissed from the firm, Connel. This will pay your fare back to England. You can leave in the morning."

"I see," said Pat slowly, and mechanically his fingers closed round the roll of notes. He felt dazed, barely conscious that his world was crumbling to ruins around him. Sonia began to cry hysterically.

"You can't dismiss him . . . I tell you I was to blame as much as he was . . . Daddy . . . listen to me. . . ."

"Don't talk rubbish. How could you be as much to blame?" Mr. Royale thundered in upon her explanations. "At any rate I won't have him come with us one inch farther. He can go back to London and cool his heels. Come along in, Sonia."

She was drawn into the hotel protesting. Pat looked after her, his eyes dark and smouldering. In a way he wished that at this particular juncture of affairs they could have both told John Royale that they loved each other. But obviously it was not a tactful moment for confession. The old man would most certainly have cut up rough and denied them his blessing. But now what? He was disgraced and dismissed and the whole lovely, exciting journey with Sonia was ended.

He found himself confronted by Jane Daunt, Jane whose small face was as pale and set as his own.

"Hullo," he said dully, "are you in on this?"

"I was with Uncle John. Yes. We both saw you. Oh, you fool, Pat, you *fool*! Why do you take such risks?"

"Why do men ever take risks? Because they think them worth while, I suppose."

"Why kiss her good night in full view of the public?"

"I daresay it was mad, but there it is."

Jane beat one small fist on the other.

"It was all so unnecessary, and now you've lost your job!"

"It's pretty grim. But it would be worse if I'd lost Sonia."

Jane made a gesture of exasperation.

"What do you think you're doing, Pat Connel? How do you think all this is going to end? I knew it would only be a question of time before Uncle John found you two out—"

"He hasn't found us out," interrupted Pat. "He's just taken it for granted that I was attempting to be familiar with his daughter, and he won't accept her excuses for me, that's all."

"And how do you think he'd have reacted if you'd come forward with the announcement that your intentions were 'strictly honourable'?" Jane found herself asking with unusual bitterness.

Pat gave a short laugh.

"He'd have told me to go to hell, I daresay, and Sonia not to make a fool of herself. Perhaps she *is* making a fool of herself, falling for me."

"Perhaps you are the fool?" flashed Jane. "You make me sick and tired . . . both of you."

He stared at her. He had never seen Jane's soft brown eyes flash so furiously before. There was a kind of beauty in her angry young face which also struck him at that moment. Then he laughed again.

"My dear little Jane Daunt, I don't know why you should be so cross."

"Because you've made a mess of things."

"Temporarily, I admit it. But I'm not done—just because I've been sacked. I shall see Sonia before I go and—"

"And what good will that do you?"

"All the good in the world," he said softly. "So long as I know she still cares for me. And I know she does. She was marvellous—trying to take the blame tonight—but the old man was in such a rage it didn't work, and things would have been a bit worse if I'd done the 'intentions are honourable' business."

Jane set her teeth. She almost hated Sonia in this hour and hated Pat, too. This position of knowing everything and being able to say nothing was growing more bitter and difficult every day. She made a movement to pass Pat and go into the hotel. He gripped her arm.

"Don't you think Sonia really loves me, Jane?"

"Find that out for yourself," she flashed, and like a little whirlwind was gone, leaving him gaping after her.

Mr. Royale was still an angry and harassed man when Jane met him in the lounge.

"Here's a nice kettle of fish!" he said. "And the last person I'd have thought would behave in that fashion was Connel."

"And what are we going to do without a chauffeur?" asked Jane, feeling suddenly cold and tired.

"God knows. It's spoilt the whole trip. But I'm not going to have Connel with us. And I'd rather drive myself than engage one of these Spanish devils. Sonia's been making all sorts of excuses for the fellow, but I'd rather not hear them. If she *did* encourage such familiarity, she's a damned little fool and not what I always believed her to be. Personally I think she's just trying to excuse Connel because she's sorry for him. And I don't care if he did lose his head in the moonlight and that rubbish—chauffeurs are not supposed to lose their heads! Pah!"

He walked away from his niece, wiping the moisture from his forehead with a large pocket handkerchief.

Jane went upstairs. She found her cousin in her bedroom. Sonia had ceased weeping. With a sullen, tearstained face she regarded Jane.

"Well!" she said.

"Well," said Jane, "I hope you're satisfied."

"If you're going to start lecturing me you can get out."

"All right," said Jane. "I'll get out," and she moved toward the communicating-door.

Tears of self-pity sprang to Sonia's eyes again. She rushed after her cousin.

"No, don't go, stay and talk to me. Oh, Janie darling, I wish I'd never been born."

Jane turned and gave her a long disdainful look.

"My dear Sonia, I wonder how many times you say that, and yet you're luckier than millions of women in this world."

"Lucky!" repeated Sonia hysterically, "and what sort of break have I had recently?"

"You've always done what you wanted."

Sonia stamped her foot.

"Well, I didn't want *this* to happen," she said, and covered her face with her hands.

Jane felt suddenly cold. The whole affair was so obnoxious to her that she wished she could walk out of this hotel, become disembodied, and be wafted away somewhere into space up there with those large, clear stars. She was tired of loving hopelessly so much, giving so much and getting so little in return. Yet here was Sonia weeping noisily because she received everything and gave nothing that did not suit her.

"Why, why had Daddy got to come back just at that moment?" Sonia sobbed. "I didn't even know he'd gone out. I thought you were working."

"And what right had you to take Pat out and let him run such a risk? He's lost his job—everything. And you're supposed to love him."

Sonia flung herself face downwards on her bed.

"It's all very well for you. You're a strong fine character and I'm not, that's all. You may find it easy to be so noble, but I don't."

"Oh, Sonia," said Jane. "You're so wrong. I'm not fine and I'm not strong and I don't find it easy to be noble, but I think if I loved a man like Pat Connel I'd try to consider him as well as myself."

Sonia raised a disfigured face.

"What can I do now? I don't want Pat to go back to England. I want to go on seeing him. Oh, I'm so unhappy!"

"But where's it going to end? How can you go on like this, Sonia? You can't play with a man like Pat Connel. I swear you can't."

And the old arguments and protests followed until

late that night. They left Jane miserable, tormented with doubts and fears for *him*. They left Sonia with but one idea . . . and that was to prevent her thrilling, delirious love affair from coming to a speedy end.

Chapter 10

SONIA rose early and went round to the garage before anybody else was about. She found Pat standing by the car dressed in tweeds instead of the accustomed uniform. He looked pale and tired, as though he had not slept. But when he saw her his face became transfigured.

"Darling! I knew you'd come."

She rushed into his arms. He gave a deep sigh and let his cheek rest against her head. She was as brilliant and beautiful as the sunlit Spanish morning, he thought, and the warmth of her in his embrace was thrilling and comforting.

"What an awful night I've had!" she said. "I hardly closed my eyes."

"Same here, sweetheart. It was confounded bad luck those two turning up when they did."

"It was my mistake. I thought Daddy was in the hotel. I never dreamed he'd go out."

"I told you when we were sitting in that café I was afraid we'd get found out sooner or later, Sonia. And I don't think I'd have minded if we could have explained the whole position. But it obviously wasn't the moment to do so."

Sonia tightened her arms about him.

"You've never spoken a truer word, my dear. I think if we'd told Daddy last night that we were in love with each other, he'd have exploded. As it was, every time I tried to say that I'd led you on, he shut me up. At one point he said if it *was* true I ought to be thoroughly ashamed of myself."

Pat released her. He lit a cigarette and smoked it in silence for an instance, his face hardening.

"Which only shows that I'm not playing fair," he said. "I ought not to let you carry on like this. The Chief'll never consent to our marriage and I'll never have the right to ask you to leave everything for me."

That was a discussion which Sonia wished to avoid. The future did not concern her so vastly as the present. In her excitable, feckless fashion she lived for the day. She wanted Pat now, and now she must have him. She threw herself back into his arms.

"You're wrong about that. I'm not going to even allow you to get qualms. When we get back to England I can manage Daddy—talk him round. Only we can't spring it on him. It wants very careful slow manoeuvring. Last night has proved that. But you can't stop loving me . . . you *can't*."

He kissed her passionately on lips and throat.

"I know I can't, my sweet. I know it. But it's all gone wrong . . . and I don't quite see . . ."

"We must just go on loving each other!" she broke in breathlessly. "Oh, darling, you *can't* go back to England. I shall loathe every minute of the holiday without you. It will be too dreary for words with just Daddy and Jane."

He looked at her intently.

"Darling Sonia, do you really love me so much?"

She closed her eyes and swore that she did.

"I'll never leave you so long as you want me," he added. "But I've got the sack. I don't quite see what next I'm going to do."

She sighed.

"But what shall we do without you? Daddy's quite a good driver, but as you know, it was my uncle who's dead who designed the Victor, and Daddy knows nothing about the mechanism of it. He doesn't understand the inside of the car like you do, and if things went wrong we'd be stranded."

The thought of the Royales being stranded on some lonely foreign road was not too good. Pat caressed the fair silky head of his beloved and pictured a thousand awful things happening to her. It was typical of him when he said:

"Then I shall not go back to London. I shall follow you."

Sonia was thrilled.

"Darling, how can you?"

"Somehow or other. I know the route you're taking. I've studied it for hours. Somewhere in this city there must be a British motor-bike, or an old car. I've got enough money to buy something that will go, and even if I can't keep up with the Victor, I can trail along and eventually catch up with you. The Chief needn't know. I'll follow and keep out of sight."

"Pat, you're marvellous! What a marvellous idea!"

He kissed her on the lips.

"There isn't anything I won't do for you."

Sonia left that garage a good deal more contented than when she had entered it. And Pat went forth into the town prepared to spend the money that had been given him for his fare back to England on anything with two or four wheels that would go. He could imagine Jane Daunt calling him a fool. No doubt he was one. But when a man was in love and his lady loved him, what wouldn't he do for her sake?

Sonia said nothing to Jane when she returned to the hotel. Jane questioned her about Pat and Sonia answered guardedly:

"He hasn't made any definite plans."

For Jane, therefore, the whole trip was spoilt once they moved away from Madrid and traversed the route to Seville. For Jane the sun ceased to shine, the skies were no longer blue, and Spain became the dreariest place in the world. She sat alone in the back of the car and looked wretchedly at Sonia and her father, whose portly figure replaced the familiar handsome one of Connel in his olive-green uniform.

She wondered what on earth Pat meant to do when he got back to London, and how he would get a job

without a reference, for of course Uncle John would not
give him one. All Uncle John would say about Connel
was that it was a catastrophe that he had ever taken the
place of the trustworthy Woodham.

Every now and then Sonia turned her head and
looked behind her as though expecting to see Pat following in the distance. And whenever Jane caught sight
of that pretty, vivid face, she puzzled over it. She wondered just why Sonia appeared so full of suppressed excitement. She felt uneasy. She did not trust Sonia, and
one never knew what Pat Connel was going to do next.

They drove without mishap for about one hundred
and eighteen kilometres on the road to Seville. Some of
the scenery was uninspired straight, monotonous roads
flanked by brown, twisted cork trees and the dusty grey
of olives. But later they came to a marvellous range of
mountains, and the silver River Tajo winding through
the valleys.

It was when they were climbing the Puerto de Miravete that the Victor suddenly misbehaved itself and the
engine spat and stopped dead. Mr. Royale put on all
the brakes and drew the car in to the side of the road.

"Confound it!" he said.

"What is it, Daddy?" asked Sonia.

"I don't know, but it's a damned nuisance stopping
like this just on a hairpin bend and up this damned
mountain."

The two girls descended from the car and stretched
their limbs while Mr. Royale lifted the bonnet of the
car. The sun was setting. The view down the mountain-
side and into the valley was dazzling and splendid. But
it was Spain at her most rugged and lonely, and not at
all the right place for a breakdown.

Sonia and Jane exchanged glances.

"I knew this would happen the moment Daddy took
over the wheel," Sonia said in a low voice.

"It'll be fine if we get left here for the night," said
Jane drily.

Sonia looked anxiously down the steep road up
which they had been climbing.

For the first time she began to feel nervous and

strained. She wondered whether Pat was, indeed, following and would eventually reach them. Perhaps he hadn't been able to procure a vehicle. Perhaps he hadn't meant to come. It had been a crazy idea, anyhow.

Mr. Royale was fuming and swearing.

"I can't see what's wrong. Must be autovac trouble, I think. The petrol's not getting through."

Jane went to his side.

"I'm a good secretary, Uncle John, but I don't know anything about motor-cars, unfortunately. Can't we stop somebody?"

"But we don't speak Spanish, my dear girl."

"We might find somebody who understands English."

"And we might not! Be damned to that fellow Connel for his behaviour. He's got us into this mess."

Sonia stood by with downcast eyes and said nothing. Jane thought:

"If only Pat were here!"

A motor-bus came along. The driver was Spanish and all the people in it were of Spain. They stopped when they saw the big grey car and the trio of English tourists. They gathered round in their friendly fashion, babbled, gesticulated, understood nothing that Mr. Royale tried to say to them, and in the end climbed back into their bus and departed, shrugging their shoulders.

Mr. Royale mopped his forehead, scarlet and furious.

"You oughtn't to have sacked Connel, Daddy," Sonia said in a sweet, faintly malicious voice.

"Don't talk rubbish!" he snapped. "After what he did, how could I possibly have kept him?"

Sonia bit her red lips and said nothing.

The sun was rapidly disappearing behind the mountains. In another half-hour the heat of the day would be gone and the sudden chill of the spring night would descend upon them. The prospect of being hung up for hours and hours without much food, on the Puerto de Miravete was not to be relished by any of them.

And then came a sound for which Sonia had been listening and hoping all day. The honk-honk-honk of a British horn and a quick chug-chug-chug that could belong to nothing but a motor-bike. Eagerly she looked down the road. And yes, into view came a man on a motor-cycle leaving a trail of white dust behind him. Sonia knew, long before the features of the rider were discernible, that it was Pat.

Mr. Royale also watched the approaching vehicle. He said:

"The first motor-bike I've seen in Spain. It must be an Englishman."

Jane, her heart leaping, recognised the rider in spite of a strange check-cap, obviously of Spanish make, and a pair of goggles.

"It's Pat Connel!" she said impulsively.

"Connel!" repeated Mr. Royale, after which he remained speechless.

Thus Pat came back into his own. He had by no means expected to overtake the Victor. But then he had not expected anything so lucky to befall him as a breakdown of the Victor. He had been frankly dubious about the whole situation when he had first left Madrid on this disreputable old Sunbeam, which he had found for sale in an English garage. A little tinkering and it had been made roadworthy, but how long it would remain so he dared not think.

Without wondering what sort of reception he was going to get from the Chief, he pulled the motor-bike up beside the Victor, stepped from it and removed cap and goggles. His first glance was for Sonia, the next for Jane. His eyes twinkled at her. She flushed almost angrily and turned away. Pat saluted Mr. Royale.

"Can I be of any assistance, sir?" he asked with the utmost formality.

Mr. Royale gulped.

"What the devil are you doing here?"

"I just thought I might be of service, sir. I didn't like letting you all go on by yourselves and so I hope you'll forgive me, sir, but I bought this bike and followed."

Mr. Royale passed a handkerchief over his lips. He returned the young man's smiling gaze indignantly.

"The devil you did!" he said.

"Well, Daddy," said Sonia. "It's a terribly good thing he *did*. Now Connel will be able to see what's wrong with the car."

"He shan't touch it!" began Mr. Royale, but Sonia ran and clasped his arm.

"Don't be an idiot, Daddy," she whispered. "We don't want to be stuck here all night. And after all, I think it was marvellous of Connel to follow and not desert us."

"After what he did—" began Mr. Royale.

"I keep telling you," she interrupted, "it was as much my fault as Connel's. And he was dreadfully sorry the next morning—weren't you, Connel?"

"Terribly, sir," said Pat seriously. "Even if you chuck me out at the next town, I hope you'll let me help you now."

Mr. Royale was tired, worried, and longing for a drink. Against all his principles he caved in weakly. And he was a good deal more relieved than he intended to show, that the young puppy had had the audacity to follow them like this.

"Oh, very well," he said. "Get on with it, Connel, and see what's the matter."

Jane caught Pat's gaze again. Those vivid blue eyes of his were wickedly triumphant. He actually winked at her before he moved to the side of the Victor and began an examination of the engine. Jane pursed her lips.

"So *this* is what they arranged," she thought. "And this is why Sonia kept looking over her shoulder. She expected him!"

She refused to confess even to herself that she was thoroughly glad to see Pat again. Her pleasure would soon have evaporated before that look on Sonia's face. She had got what she wanted and was ill-disguising her feelings. Jane turned away from the pair of them feeling absolutely defeated. It was all such madness. Last night's disaster had not taught them a lesson. Other disasters would follow—she knew it.

Mr. Royale took his daughter's arm and walked her firmly down the road.

"I'm feeling stiff and a few steps will do us both good, my dear," he said. "Come along."

Sonia could not refuse. She knew perfectly well that her father was going to keep her well away from Connel even if he remained with them. But remain he must. She wheedled Mr. Royale in her most beguiling fashion.

"You must let Connel take us on to Seville, or even farther. Dismissing him that way was a mistake, Daddy."

"No mistake at all!" exploded Mr. Royale. "I can't have the man who acts as my chauffeur kissing my daughter in that familiar fashion . . . good heavens, what next? I don't care if the fellow *is* as well educated as we are."

"Spanish moons are very glamorous, Daddy," said Sonia in her silkiest voice, and rubbed her beautiful head against his shoulder. "And I'm *so* attractive, aren't I?"

"Attractive!" echoed Mr. Royale with a snort. "I think you're a baggage."

"What a lovely Victorian word, Daddy!"

"But seriously, Sonia, you don't want me to believe that you're on such terms with young Connel, do you?"

She bit her lip and crimsoned.

"I don't know what you mean by 'on such terms,' but he's a very nice young man, isn't he? You've always said so."

Mr. Royale became suddenly profoundly shocked and worried.

"Sonia, you're not suggesting . . ."

"Oh, Daddy, you're taking it all too solemnly," she broke in, terrified to pursue the conversation.

"My darling little girl," he said, "you're all I have. All I've had since your mother died. I've always wanted you to be happy, but at the same time, when you get married I want it to be to a man worthy of you. You have so much to offer . . . your beauty, your youth, my money when I'm gone. You could marry anybody. But it must be Somebody with a capital S."

She remained silent. Her heart was sinking very low. Pat Connel was not, in Mr. Royale's estimation, Somebody with a capital S. And as for Maurice, God . . . this discussion had only made her all the more aware that she dared not tell him the truth.

"Why discuss my marriage? It has nothing to do with Connel," she said as lightly as possible. "Take my advice, and forget that stupid incident last night, and take Connel on again. We'll never manage to drive through Morocco without him. Give him another chance."

"Then for heaven's sake, Sonia, be more decorous and see that Connel keeps his place."

While this argument was in progress, Jane stood watching Pat, who by now had the carburettor in pieces.

"Well," she said, "I suppose you think you've been very clever."

He glanced up at her.

"Don't be cross with me, little Jane Daunt. You were so very furious last night."

"I am—still."

"Because I followed?"

"Oh, because of so many things!" she said in a voice of exasperation.

"You don't like me any more, do you?"

Jane's dark eyes turned to the scarlet glow of the sun behind the sombre Spanish mountains. She felt suddenly cold and tired and annoyed with herself because she knew that she was glad, so much too glad to see this handsome impetuous young man who was unconsciously drawing ruin down upon himself.

If only she could have said to him:

"Follow us, do what you like, only *don't* pin your faith on Sonia or you will be hurt!"

But she could say nothing. So Pat took it for granted that he had lost some of that friendship which she had always given him in London. He was sorry because he admired Jane Daunt. He even had a curious kind of affection for her.

He returned to his work.

"I had the hell's own journey pursuing you," he said. "And I didn't dare stop for a meal in case I should never catch you up. But a motor-bike in the hot sunshine and dust after the comfort of the Victor . . . ye gods . . . can't you imagine it?"

She could, and she suddenly noticed that his face was livid with fatigue and streaked with grime. His forehead was drenched with perspiration.

"Look here," she said. "You're all in. Take a minute's rest and I'll give you a sip of tea from my flask."

He wiped his forehead and grinned at her.

"That's decent of you. You're always very nice to me really, although you don't approve of me."

The way he smiled down at her seemed to break her heart. Raw with pain she snapped at him:

"Oh, shut up! Sit down on the running-board and drink some tea."

But he refused to do anything until he had put the car in working order. It was a very small thing that was wrong and he soon found it. Suddenly the silence of the mountain road was broken by the deep-throated hum of the big Victor engine. A sound very welcome to Mr. Royale who heard it and came hurrying back with Sonia. Then, quite suddenly, Pat collapsed. He sat down on the running-board of the car. His head fell back.

"Want . . . food. . . ." he gasped heavily. "Sorry to be such a fool. . . ."

All that was tender in Jane surged to the surface. She forgot everybody else but Pat. In a moment she was at his side with a thermos of tea and some sandwiches from the luncheon basket which they had taken from Madrid. She could see that Pat was near to fainting. She put an arm about his shoulders and with her own handkerchief wiped his face, then lifted a cup of tea to his lips. He drank thirstily.

"That's . . . grand!"

Sonia, frightened at what she saw, rushed up.

"Oh . . . are you ill?"

Jane immediately moved away from Pat and made furious signs to Sonia to be quiet.

"Ssh . . . little idiot . . . do you want to give everything away?"

Sonia put a hand to her mouth and stood still. And now Pat's bloodshot eyes turned to her. She looked so beautiful standing there in the light of the setting sun that his heart seemed to melt at the sight of her, and his drooping spirits revived. Jane ceased to exist for him. But it was Jane who came back with more food and made him eat.

Mr. Royale looked on a trifle dubiously.

"Damn silly business doing all those miles on a motorcycle," he said. "Wonder you didn't kill yourself."

"I nearly did, sir," said Pat and stood up, feeling better after his refreshment.

Sonia gripped her father's arm.

"Go on, Daddy," she whispered. "Take him back. You said you would."

Mr. Royale, still under his daughter's influence, thereupon somewhat pompously announced words of pardon.

"You behaved badly last night, Connel, but on condition you keep in the position you took with us when you came in Woodham's shoes, you may continue with us to Morocco," he said.

Pat, exulting, saluted stiffly.

"Thank you very much indeed, sir."

Jane climbed back into the car feeling helpless and hopeless.

Mr. Royale, however, saw to it that Sonia sat in the back of the car with her cousin and that he, himself, took the place beside the prodigal driver.

The motor-bike was abandoned on the roadside. Pat bade farewell to it almost regretfully. It had made almost every bone in his body ache, but at least it had brought him to Sonia's rescue, so he felt a certain attachment for it. However, it was good to be back in the luxurious Victor, and he felt more relieved when they started up the mountain road again.

Chapter 11

Two more days of this journey and they were in Algeciras where they stayed a night at the Hôtel Reina Christina because Mr. Royale wished to make notes on the ruins of a Moorish aqueduct and take photographs of Ayuntamiento, where the Pact of Algeciras had been signed in 1906.

By this time he was quite restored to his good humour and had reinstated Connel into favour. The young man was invaluable. He had to admit it. And except for that one lapse had not shown further familiarity in his behaviour toward Sonia. He was formality itself. Neither had Mr. Royale further cause to feel uneasy about Sonia's attitude where Connel was concerned. She was obviously "putting him in his place". That Madrid affair was nothing to worry about.

They motored from Algeciras into Gibraltar, and thence journeyed by boat to Tangier.

As the boat moved away from Gibraltar Jane leaned over the rails and watched the mighty Rock gradually fade into the distance. She had left her uncle and cousin, feeling unlike Sonia's chatter, and relieved for half an hour of taking the incessant notes from her uncle. She felt solitary. She wanted to be alone. At the other end of the deck she could discern Pat's uniformed figure.

She felt a sudden loathing of the whole situation, and a curious growing distaste at the prospect of the weeks ahead of her in Morocco. Yet it was all wonderful. Everything around her was new and wonderful, full of vivid colour and romance. More than anything on earth she wanted to be with Pat Connel, and equally, under these circumstances, preferred not to be. She was so utterly removed from him.

They were passing so close to the coast that she could see the little Spanish farms nestling against the hillsides. The sea was blue-green, shimmering in the sunlight. Soon they were to leave Tarifa, the last port of Spain, behind them, and come to North Africa, where the rising mountains looked dark and sinister against a sky of purest blue.

The wind blew fresher and colder and now the mountains rose so high that the peaks were wreathed in the curling vapours. Over those mountains lay Tetuan and Pogador to which they would be journeying by car tomorrow.

Jane's gaze turned from the scenery toward Pat. He, too, was leaning over the rails staring beyond him, a cigarette in the corner of his mouth. She wondered if he was enjoying it as much as she. She would like to have gone to his side and talked to him. But she stayed where she was with that curious depression weighing down her heart.

Then suddenly even her enjoyment in the scenery was taken from her and her peace rudely shattered. She saw Sonia coming quickly toward her. Sonia with a chalk-white face and fear staring from her eyes.

"My dear, what on earth has happened?"

Sonia clutched her arm. Her teeth were chattering.

"Jane! Jane, something *awful!*"

"What?"

Jane had to put an arm around her because the girl was swaying, all her beauty wiped out by a ghastly look of terror. She had never seen Sonia look like that before.

"Tell me what's happened, quickly. . . ."

Sonia found her voice.

"Maurice," she said. *"Maurice. . . ."*

The colour rushed to Jane's cheeks.

"Maurice! Do you mean he's *here,* that you've seen him?"

"Yes. And he's seen me. Look . . . I've just rushed away from Daddy to you . . . *look!*"

Jane looked. And her own heart seemed to stand still. She saw a slightly built man who wore a black beret, French fashion, on the side of a fair head. The slim figure, just a shade too debonair, in a pin-striped suit and light check travelling coat, was all too familiar to Jane. It was Maurice Gardener, all right. Sonia's husband. Jane stared at him stupefied.

"What in the name of heaven is he doing here? Is he alone? Have you seen anyone with him?"

"No, he seems to be quite alone," said Sonia in a trembling voice. "Oh, my God, I suppose he's travelling, like we are, but why he should have chosen to come to Tangier at the same time as ourselves and be on *our* boat, I can't imagine! It's just a coincidence and the most appalling piece of bad luck for me!"

"Pull yourself together, and leave things to me," Jane said in her decisive manner.

"But what are we going to do?" wailed Sonia.

"Let me talk to him," said Jane.

But there was no chance for her to say anything to Maurice Gardener alone. At that precise moment he had turned and strolled along the deck to the two girls. Sonia was clinging on to Jane's arm in abject fear. The man's gaze fell upon them. His slightly bored expression altered to one of extreme interest and astonishment. The next minute he was there before them, sweeping off his beret with exaggerated courtesy.

"Hey! Of all the astonishing things. Sonia! And Cousin Jane!"

Sonia was incapable of answering. It seemed hard to her now to believe that she had ever fallen in love with Maurice. Much harder to credit that she had been fool enough to marry him. He was good-looking, yes. He had a gay, pleasant voice with the slightest foreign inflection. And she could remember that he had always made love divinely. But that she should have *married* him . . . heavens!

Jane did not lose her head. She said:

"Well, Maurice, you are the last person we expected to see."

"The world is full of lovely surprises," he said, and

added with a swift look of appreciation at the beautiful soignée figure of his wife . . . "And Sonia is surely the loveliest surprise of all."

Sonia remained mute. Said Jane drily:

"Don't let's waste time exchanging compliments. Are you staying in Tangier?"

He replaced his beret. His white teeth flashed in a smile.

"Surely! I'm on a little health trip. I've had a severe chill which almost turned to pneumonia, and in Paris the winds have been cold. My doctor ordered sunlight, and in Morocco I hope to find it. But I hope to find something even more delightful now that I've met you."

"What do you want, Maurice?" Sonia suddenly asked in a sharp frightened voice.

"It would take far too long for me to tell you that in detail," he smiled.

Sonia drew a sharp breath and looked in the direction of the glass loggia. Her father was still sitting there placidly smoking his cigar. But the sight of him struck fresh fear in her heart.

"Is it more money you want?" she whispered.

"Sonia, leave it to me," said Jane. "Maurice has had quite enough out of you. Why don't you go back to Uncle John and let me deal with this?"

Then Maurice coolly put his arm through Sonia's. He smiled at Jane, but the smile was defiant.

"I'm not so sure that I wish to be dealt with by you, little Cousin Jane. You interfered in Paris and broke things up between Sonia and me, and I'd rather not be interfered with any more."

Jane flushed.

"You wonder that I interfere? Did you expect me to go back to London and leave Sonia with you, after what she found out?"

Sonia looked round her wildly.

"Oh, be quiet, both of you. Somebody will hear!"

Maurice patted her hand.

"Nobody's going to hear, my dear. And don't be so foolish. I won't give you away if that's what you are afraid of. Nothing would give me greater pleasure than to announce to the whole boat that you are Mrs. Maurice Gardener. You are so chic—so good-looking. I always did think you were one of the loveliest girls I ever met. However . . ."

"You really mean you won't give me away?" she said hysterically.

"Not for the moment, anyhow."

"Then it is more money you want!"

"My dear child, I admit that one has to live," he drawled. "What you have been sending me lately hasn't been altogether adequate. And you know I lost my job at Christmas. I have been spending capital. If it hadn't been for your . . . shall we put it as kindness . . . I'd have had a bad time. Still, the old firm's taken me back now. So I'm not so hard hit. As a matter of fact I was going to write to you, Sonia, and ask you to meet me and talk things over."

She snatched her hand away from his. She was calmer now. Full of distaste she regarded him.

"What is there to talk about? Unless you're willing to set me free . . . let me divorce you. You refused to do so in Paris. You said you'd given up that other girl and that I couldn't find any evidence against you. That's why things have remained as they are. And of course I know perfectly well why. You prefer to keep me tied to you knowing that I shall never dare tell my father, and to get as much money out of me as you can! Oh, I despise you . . . !"

She broke off, panting.

"Sonia dear, don't get all worked up again," said Jane. "Much better to keep calm about it."

Maurice extracted a cigarette from a packet and lit it.

"Can't we dispense with the *duenna*?" he said. "I think it would be tactful if she left husband and wife to have a word together, alone."

Sonia turned pale at the words. But she said:

"Oh, all right. If you want to see me alone . . . perhaps it is better, Jane."

Jane shrugged her shoulders. She was quite sick and

tired of dragging Sonia out of difficulties. She had no desire whatsoever to remain. But she wondered what was at the back of Maurice Gardener's brain.

She could see Pat, still leaning up against the rails, enjoying the stern beauty of the mountains outlined against the gentian sky. Poor Pat! What disillusionment lay in store for him! Jane wondered what he would say if he knew that his idolised and idealised Sonia was now in conversation with *her husband*.

Sonia, in a panic, drew Maurice away to the farthest end of the boat, where she hoped she could not be seen by father or lover.

"Now, for God's sake tell me what you want, Maurice," she said.

"Who are you so nervous of? The old man . . .?"

She bit her lip. Maurice gave a low amused laugh.

"Don't tell me you've fallen for somebody else."

"You wouldn't have a right to criticize me if I have."

"Tut, tut, *cherie*; a husband's rights. . . ."

The French word of endearment brought the colour blazing to her cheeks. He had always called her *cherie*. Once she had thought it so sweet a word! How dead indeed is a dead love!

"You have no rights over me," she said. "And anyhow, even if you have, you swore you'd leave me alone as long as you got the money."

He shrugged his shoulders.

"This is all so crude! Let us be a little more delicate about it. Whether you believe me or not, I am not quite the mercenary fellow you think. I am human—with human impulses. Once I was very much in love . . ."

"With my money!" she cut in. "And my position as John Royale's daughter."

"I don't agree."

"I saw it in black and white in that letter to Colette. You told her that you loved her and that you married me entirely for my money."

"It wasn't altogether true, Sonia. I swear it. Colette was a little devil with a fiendish temper and I had to conciliate her somehow."

"That's a lie. And anyhow I don't see the use of raking up the past. Things were said which you can't deny and I told you I'd never willingly see you again."

He looked down at her. He had half forgotten that gold-and-white loveliness of hers. Perhaps in the first place he had never really loved her. He was a born gambler and it was a gambler's instinct which had made him elope with John Royale's daughter. He had made a muck of it. He had made a muck of that Colette business. But now he was not sure that he wouldn't like to settle down and be a good husband to lovely Sonia.

"Listen, *cherie,*" he said. "Don't be so bitter against me. Perhaps we both of us made mistakes, but it is never too late to mend."

"My dear Maurice, if you are trying to effect a touching reconciliation, you are making the biggest mistake of your life."

"Then you are in love with somebody else," he said.

She thought of Pat. And suddenly she said between her teeth:

"Yes, I am. What of it?"

"Oh, come!" he said, smiling, "I can't allow infidelity, it would be too heart-breaking!"

"For God's sake stop being flippant, and tell me what you want."

"That touching reconciliation which you speak of," he said coolly.

She stared at him in blank dismay. If he had wanted money she might have got some more for him. But he wanted *her,* that was very different.

"I really can't bear to see you look so unhappy," he added. "So don't let's talk about it any more. Where are you staying in Tangier?"

"El Minza," she said hopelessly.

"I, also."

"You're going to follow me?"

"Not at all. It is where I intended to stay. You will see my luggage is labelled. And you need not be afraid that I shall give away anything. If you are nice to me, I won't—for the moment, anyhow."

That sounded sinister to her. She said:

"Daddy knows you well enough, and he's bound to think it most peculiar, you being on the scene."

"My dear child, that's absurd. I've just as much right to stay at El Minza as you and your father. Now don't worry. I haven't the slightest desire to do you any harm, so take that frightened look off your lovely face. And here comes Cousin Jane in hot pursuit of us. So perhaps you'd better run along. We'll have a word to-night in the hotel."

Sonia turned away. She realised that there was nothing further to say at the moment. But her spirits were very low when she joined her cousin.

Sonia repeated the conversation.

"It's simply frightful," she said. "There is no question of us being reconciled. I hate him, and I love Pat. Jane, Jane, it's such a mess . . . and I don't know what to do."

Jane had little advice to offer. It was useless going over all the old ground. Useless pleading with Sonia to tell her father the truth and to give Pat a square deal. But if Maurice Gardener was to stay at their hotel and was going to assert himself, there was nothing so far as Jane could see to avert calamity.

Chapter 12

IN the Moorish court of the Hôtel El Minza, Jane sat alone smoking a cigarette and thinking about bed. She was tired after the day's journey and the strong sea air made her sleepy.

She decided regretfully that it would be a waste of time to go to bed and sleep, and waste of a glorious night. She had thought that nothing could be lovelier than the nights in Spain. But Morocco was unimaginably lovely. The whole place was like a tale from the *Arabian Nights*. Tangier, a fairy city with its white walls and slits of windows, its slender towers and minarets flooded in a splendour of moonlight.

Beauty and romance walked hand in hand in this place, and all that was romantic awoke in Jane's heart to-night. She was not ashamed of her emotions. She was as frank with herself as with others. She knew that she was tired of being practical and calm and efficient; tired of helping Sonia out of troubles and of typewriting Uncle John's dull notes. She wanted love and a lover . . . *the* lover. That meant, of course, that she wanted Pat.

Much as she appreciated this journey and, in particular this enchanting Morocco, she really dreaded the rest of the trip. It wasn't easy to be so near Pat day by day and to watch him wasting his time and affections on Sonia. It was an acute irritation. Deeper than that, it was sheer pain.

What a day it had been!

Uncle John had disliked the arrival at Tangier; the hideous upheaval on the quay, with masses of Arabs swarming, screaming, jostling. There had been feverish scenes in the custom house, lengthy examinations of the car, of the luggage; all the paraphernalia which wasted over an hour before the gates of Morocco were flung open to receive the battered travellers and their even more battered possessions.

It had amused Jane, but Uncle John preferred something more British and orderly. Pat had been a great help with his knowledge of Spanish. But Pat was not himself. He was depressed because he had not seen Sonia alone for a long while. And Sonia was even more depressed with the shadow of Maurice Gardener in the background.

Of course Maurice had to come face to face with the Royale party sooner or later and they met him in the lounge just before dinner. He passed by without any more recognition than a faint smile and nod at Sonia.

Where Sonia was just now Jane had no idea. She

presumed the foolish girl was indulging in one of her dangerous assignations with Pat.

She soon discovered that she was wrong on that score, for Pat himself made an appearance in the Moorish court, Pat in grey flannels looking worried and unhappy and obviously searching for somebody. Jane watched him make a nervous investigation of the various tables in and out the arches, then she called in a low voice:

"Pat!"

He hurried toward her. He seemed glad to see her.

"Hullo, Jane. Where's Sonia?"

She did not answer for a moment. But she thought with some bitterness what a little fool she was to have sat here in a state of romantic glamour thinking about this man whose first words to her were of desire for another woman.

"Where is Sonia?" he repeated.

"I don't know. I imagined she was with you."

"And where's the Chief? Dare I stay and yarn with you for a second?"

"If you want to. Uncle John's gone to bed."

Pat balanced himself on the arm of a basket-chair, hands thrust in his pockets, handsome face moody.

"I haven't had a chance to say a word to Sonia all day."

"Just as well."

"You would say that, of course. You don't realise how much we love each other."

"I realise quite how much *you* love *her!*"

Pat's chin shot up.

"Are you suggesting that she doesn't love me just as much?"

Jane flung away her cigarette.

"My dear Pat, I don't want to suggest anything. I don't really want to talk about it at all."

"Sorry if it bores you," he said huffily.

He was so like a spoiled little boy, she longed to put her arms around him in that moment and draw that attractive head close to her breast and tell him what a darling fool he was and how much she adored him. Instead of which, she said:

"Well, it is a bit boring . . . after a time. I've had it the whole trip."

His expression changed. He smiled at her. Little Jane was looking rather nice to-night, he thought, in her thin chiffon dress of palest yellow, with a black embroidered Spanish shawl over one shoulder. It made her face look piquant and vivid. She was utterly different to Sonia, and Pat's head was usually much too full of Sonia to think about Jane's physical attractions. But to-night suddenly he noticed them. He said:

"I daresay it bores you to death, Jane. And you've been damn good to both of us. Don't let's discuss her or myself. After all it's my own tangle and I've got to unwind it as best I can. Only I assure you she does love me, and that she wants just as much as I do for us to get married quickly."

Jane felt suddenly stubborn. She wasn't going to answer that indirect challenge and she wasn't going to put herself out to encourage him or allay his doubts and fears. He offered her a cigarette and she took it. As he lit it his hand touched hers and sent the blood racing through her body.

"How calm and poised you are, little Jane Daunt. I don't think I have ever met a woman so sure of herself."

Jane gave a quick, nervous laugh.

"Sure of myself!" she repeated. "But in what way?"

"Oh, lots of funny little ways. You are such a decisive character."

She laughed again and paid strict attention to her cigarette. This was the first time that Pat Connel had ever talked to her in quite such a personal strain. The first time for many long days, anyhow, that he had found time to discuss anything but Sonia. It was rather pleasant to have him standing here before her, leaning against one of the white arches, taking a sudden interest in her.

"My dear Pat," she said, "you make me sound as

though I were a prim and prudish school-marm briskly conducting classes."

"Not at all. . . ." Pat flicked the ash from his cigarette. The red point glowed in the darkness. "You look much too charming and you *are* much too charming to be a school-marm!"

She felt her cheeks scorch. Flattery from Pat! Heavens, what next? But it made her almost angry. She was not going to allow herself to be flattered just because Pat flung compliments at her in his facile Irish fashion. She almost snapped:

"Nonsense! That's a worn-out theory. Heaps of school mistresses these days are most attractive. And anyhow I'm *not* charming."

"Well, I think you've been terribly so—to both Sonia and myself."

Jane grit her teeth. Of course, Sonia must come into this!

"Well, I haven't felt charming," she said. "It's all upset me a lot."

"Now we are getting away from the subject of you."

"Why not?"

"I want to talk about you."

"Believe me, I'm a very dull subject."

"Sure and you're not!" drawled Pat's beguiling voice, and it made her feel suddenly helpless, powerless to put up too much of a fight against him in her heart, however much she fought against him on the surface. There were just times like these when she pitied Sonia from the bottom of her heart. It couldn't be easy for Sonia to relinquish Pat as a lover.

"May I just ask you one thing?" Pat went on.

"What?"

"Have *you* ever been in love?"

She tightened up. She dared not look in his direction. Pitching her half-smoked cigarette into the darkness, she stared after it.

"You don't think that's impertinent of me, do you?" added Pat in an apologetic voice.

Answering him, she managed to make her voice sound casual.

"Not at all, but why does it interest you?"

He sighed.

"I was just wondering whether you knew how these things affect one . . . I mean, really being in love does just eat one up . . . I wondered if you realised what it can be like."

She was silent an instant. She who knew so well that love could become an obsession. Sometimes it seemed to her that she was, indeed, being eaten up with love for Pat.

"That makes love sound a destructive thing," at length she said. "It shouldn't destroy . . . it should inspire and enrich . . ." she broke off abruptly. It was almost more than she could bear to sit here discussing love with Pat.

But he seemed enthusiastic to continue.

"Sure, and that's true, Jane. I agree with you. And I think that love *is* the greatest of all inspirations. But one can be consumed by it."

"One shouldn't allow oneself to be."

"There speaks the practical little Jane. No, I don't think that you have been in love."

She rose with an abrupt movement. Her shawl slid from her shoulder and trailed on the ground. Pat picked it up and placed it round her shoulders.

"You're not cold, are you? Why, you're shivering."

She wondered if he could be more maddening. And how dared he take it for granted that she had not been in love just because she was more in control of herself than he was, perhaps, and certainly more so than Sonia?

She came to the conclusion that if life had horrid little punishments in store for people who gave vent to their feelings, it imposed equal penalties on those who held themselves in check.

"I'm going in," she said. "I think I am a bit chilly."

"I'm sorry," he said, and meant it.

He would have liked to stay talking to Jane. She was a queer, reserved little thing, but he had a profound admiration for her. He knew that Sonia had also. A pity that Jane did not understand much about the "grand passion." He felt that it would soften and improve her. She was distinctly attractive physically. He had thought, when he had looked down at her just now, what marvellous eyes she had . . . wide-set, brown, velvety. She was not all hard, this little Jane!

Suddenly Pat said:

"Listen! Isn't that Sonia's voice? Is it herself that's coming? Ought I to bolt . . . I mean do you think the Chief will be with her?"

"No. Uncle John went to bed an hour ago."

They stood still together, side by side, half hidden by one of the white arches. Coming through the court toward them was Sonia and a man in evening clothes. To Pat he was a stranger. But Jane recognised that debonair figure and her heart gave a horrid little twist. Maurice! What on earth was Sonia doing with him? They had barely acknowledged each other just before dinner. But Jane knew that Maurice Gardener was not to be trusted. She had wondered ever since they had met on the boat what game he was up to now. Sonia had thought that he was trying to get her back. It looked like it. Jane felt suddenly nervous. It would not do for Pat to meet Maurice. The fat would be in the fire. She touched Pat's arm.

"I shouldn't stay if I were you."

But Pat's blue eyes were gazing in Sonia's direction. He had never seen her look more lovely than to-night in that black lace dinner dress which made her skin appear dazzling white. Her hair was silver fair, and she had put a red flower behind her ear as she had learned to do in Spain. His whole heart seemed to grow molten with love for her. He felt that he *must* see her to say good night, to hold her in his arms before he turned in for the night.

"Wait a second, Jane," he said.

Jane opened her lips to speak, then shut them again. She did not like the situation, but after all it was not her business. And why should she bother to drag Pat away from danger. He had been rushing into it from the first moment that he had declared his love for Sonia. It was his own funeral.

Sonia and Maurice had come to a standstill between the arches at right angles to Jane and Pat. It was obvious that Sonia had not seen them. She was talking very earnestly to Maurice and, although they could not hear what she said, her voice sounded urgent and slightly on the hysterical note.

Decidedly ill-at-ease, Jane glanced at Pat. His brows were knit.

"Who's that fellow with Sonia?"

Jane made no reply.

"I know," added Pat. "I noticed him on the boat coming over. He was wearing a beret. He isn't English, is he?"

Jane maintained silence. She felt quite powerless to answer any questions about Maurice Gardener. But there came across her in that instant a fateful sensation that this was a moment of crisis . . . a big crucial moment in all their lives.

Sonia, still unaware that she was being observed by her lover and her cousin, continued to argue with the man who was her husband.

Chapter 13

THE whole evening had seemed to Sonia one long argument. Whilst dressing for dinner she had argued with Jane, who had started all that old business about her making a clean breast of things to her father, instead of continuing a lot of lies and deception. Sonia had refused.

During dinner Mr. Royale, noticing Maurice Gardener at a table not far from them, had expressed his contempt of men of Maurice's type and of all spongers, finishing up with an onslaught against any young man who failed to get a job and hold it, and who took money from women. He had no use for them.

Jane, of course, had agreed. She, herself, was independent by nature and hated being beholden to anybody unless she gave something in exchange.

But Sonia, out of sheer perversity, argued in the opposite direction. She had every excuse for a poor fellow who couldn't get work or hadn't a penny, she declared. And why shouldn't he accept help or charity from those who could afford to give it? Where was the disgrace? Of course a hot argument ensued, and Mr. Royale made it quite clear that if ever a young gentleman of that type came after his daughter, he would be sent flying.

After dinner Sonia managed to whisper in Jane's ear:

"There! You see how impossible it would be for me to tell Daddy the truth about Maurice, or even about Pat being in love with me."

But Jane had no sympathy. She answered:

"You may be a coward about Maurice, but that doesn't excuse you for being cowardly about a man you are supposed to love."

Altogether a wretched evening for Sonia, and worse was to follow when, instead of being able to slip off and meet her lover, she was waylaid by Maurice, who insisted upon having a long discussion with her. Then followed the longest and fiercest of the arguments.

At the end of an hour of reproaches, bitterness, pleadings, protests, nothing had been settled between them. But the very fact that Sonia seemed disinclined to renew the old affections and bonds seemed to inflame Maurice to quite a sincere passion for her. A passion, however, which frightened far more than it flattered Sonia.

They had come finally to the Moorish court; Maurice still begging her to reconsider her decisions; Sonia imploring him to go away and leave her alone.

"I'll try and get you more money," she was saying now, raising a pale, distraught face to his. "Only go away, go away, *do!*"

He made an expressive foreign gesture with both hands.

"*Cherie,* you can't dislike me as much as this. Don't you remember our first wonderful night in Paris. . . ."

"And that third wonderful night when I found out what you really were!" she broke in hysterically.

"Couldn't you believe that I am sorry and let us begin again? I have a job, and if you care to live on what I earn, you need not trouble *cher* Papa at all."

"Don't you understand that I haven't the slightest wish to live with you again?"

"So! You must be very much in love with this other man. Who is he?"

"That's my affair."

"Mine also, surely."

"I refuse to stay here talking to you," she said, and turned to leave him.

Pat Connel, watching from the shadows, was then amazed to see the fair-haired man in the dinner jacket catch Sonia by the arm and pull her into his arms. Pat went white to the lips. His cigarette fell from his fingers.

"No, that's too much!" he said under his breath.

Jane, with very little colour in her own cheeks, caught his wrist.

"Wait, Pat. Jealousy is a dangerous thing. . . ."

"But she can't want . . ." he began.

Then he heard Sonia's raised voice, every word distinct:

"Cad . . . you *mean* cad! Don't touch me. . . ."

That was enough for Pat. He sprang forward, wrenching his wrist away from Jane's small nervous fingers.

"That's enough for me!" he said, between his teeth, and seizing Maurice by the shoulders, dragged him away from Sonia.

"You . . . !"

He never said the other word. But his clenched fist caught Maurice by surprise, a well-aimed blow on the jaw which sent the other man sprawling on the ground.

Sonia looked at him speechlessly. He was the last

person she had expected to see. The last one from whom she wanted support at this particular moment. She had an instant of agonising anxiety. What in heaven's name would Maurice do if he turned nasty about this? What would he say? She was to know soon enough.

Maurice had lost his balance, but the blow had not been hard enough to knock him out. He staggered on to his feet and stood there, a hand to his bruised cheek, staring a trifle dazedly at the man who had hit him.

Jane came slowly forward and stood apart from the trio, a tense quiet spectator of this drama. She knew quite well what was going to happen. This was the moment which she had anticipated ever since the affair between Sonia and Pat began. This would be the commencement of the little hell which Pat had unwittingly been storing up for himself.

Maurice spoke to Pat.

"Who the devil are you?"

His face was a mottled crimson. He breathed fast. Pat answered:

"That doesn't matter. But I might put the same question to you. *And* ask why the hell you laid a hand on Miss Royale."

"Wait, Pat . . ." began Sonia frenziedly.

But Maurice cut in.

"Miss Royale, eh? That's amusing. And so you think I have no right to lay a hand on her, do you?"

Pat blinked and stared. The man's significant words and attitude sent a horrible wave of nausea over him.

Maurice continued:

"Since you think I have not the right to touch Miss— er—Royale—perhaps I had better disillusion you as to your own right to knock me down for doing so. My name's Gardener. Maurice Gardener."

"I've never heard of you," rapped out Pat.

Maurice took a silk handkerchief from his pocket and wiped his lips.

"So! Then Sonia has kept very quiet about me."

Sonia stepped forward.

"Maurice!" her voice was full of wild entreaty.

He disregarded it.

"No, I'm not going to be treated like this . . . knocked down by anyone who thinks he has more right to you than I have."

He turned to Pat.

"Look here, young man. Let us make the introduction more thorough. I am Maurice Gardener and Sonia is Mrs. Maurice Gardener. In other words a gentleman has a perfectly good right to kiss his own wife good night."

Jane held her breath. So the truth was out at last! How would Pat take it? Poor Pat. She could pity him now. This was going to be a far bigger blow to him than the physical one he had dealt to the other man. Maurice was well revenged.

Pat stared dazedly first at Maurice and then at Sonia. Then he said:

"Tell me that is a lie."

She could not answer. She was tongue-tied. She looked as though she was going to faint. He seized her arm and shook her roughly.

"Go on! Tell me that man's lying. He *must* be!"

She shook her head wildly. In that moment, Sonia was punished a dozen times over for deceiving Pat Connel. All her weeks of scheming of hoping were being smashed in front of her eyes. She had played a losing game and now she knew it. She was lost.

Maurice said, with a more than usually strong foreign accent:

"Perhaps, *m'sieu,* you are to be excused, since you did not know that Sonia was married—and to me."

Pat ignored him. His gaze was riveted upon Sonia. His fingers still gripped her arm. His eyes looked like blue stones, clear, hard, pitiless.

"You tell me, *you* tell me! . . . Is it true? Are you married to this man?"

She collapsed and would have fallen if Jane had not hurried up and put a strong arm around her.

"Leave her alone, you two great bullies!" Jane said in a low tone. "Leave her alone. You're half killing her."

Sonia burst into tears and was led, or rather dragged, by Jane to a chair, in which she fell. She sat there, crumpled up, her fair head bowed on her arms. The two men looked down at her. Maurice shrugged his shoulders and nursed his injured cheek. He had broken all his promises not to betray Sonia, but after all, he did not relish being knocked down by a total stranger, and if Sonia was playing a double game it was time she was stopped.

But Pat Connel looked at Sonia with very different emotions. The sight of that bowed figure and the sound of her weeping hurt him unbelievably. All her pride and beauty were trailing in the dust. He knew that Maurice Gardener had not lied. Her silence and collapse were definite admissions of guilt. She *was* married to the man. *Married!* God, was it possible?

Pat had thought of her as having admirers, scores of them. A lover, perhaps. But a husband, never. She had promised to marry him. She had allowed him to build up a hundred wonderful dreams. He felt that she had committed an unforgivable sin in lying to him. All her love had been a lie. She had known all the way along that she could not marry him. She had taken his love only to satisfy her vanity. What an utter, utter fool he had been!

Jane, standing beside Sonia, trying without much success to calm her, looked up and spoke sharply to Maurice.

"You've done enough harm for to-night. Why don't you clear out?"

"*Eh bien.* I'm sorry," he said. "I didn't mean to do this. She drove me to it. Of course I won't say anything to the old man. . . ."

"Oh, go away!" said Jane.

Pat detained Maurice. Very white and set, he said stiffly:

"I apologise for knocking you down. I didn't know . . ."

Maurice put up a deprecating hand.

"But naturally. You have my sympathies. I do not know who you are, but my—er—charming wife is fortunate to have a champion with such a powerful right hand."

He bowed, and with a flashing smile made his exit.

"I almost wish you'd knocked him out for good and all," muttered Jane.

Pat sneered:

"Thanks. I'm not swinging in order to make a widow of Sonia."

Sonia darted up wildly, her face blotched and tear-stained.

"Pat . . . don't . . . don't be too hard . . . if you knew everything. . . ."

"I don't want to know anything," he cut in. "Enough lies have been told."

"Well, I daresay you'll get the truth now," said Jane.

"*You* knew," Pat said, his eyes flashing at Jane. "You knew she was married and didn't warn me. . . ."

"My dear Pat," she said coldly. "I don't give away other people's secrets. It was not my place to warn you, neither was it my story to tell."

He flushed a dark crimson.

"Perhaps not. And you would be loyal. It's just as well there is some loyalty left in the world."

Sonia put the back of her hand against her mouth and looked at him piteously.

"Pat, how can you be so hard?"

"Do you blame me? Can't you see what you've done to me? You should have told me the truth long ago. It's you who have been hard—and cruel."

Jane, her heart pounding, hurting, measured *his* hurt, his broken faith, his wounded pride, and could have wept for him. But she felt there was nothing for her to do but to go out and leave these two alone.

She went up to her bedroom. She did not switch on the light, but stood a moment by the window. She could see nothing but Pat's face, white, hurt, bitterly angry. She suffered for and with him. She would have given much to spare him this knowledge and this pain. Yet she could do nothing. All her love for him was useless. She could not even comfort him. It was the realisation that her love was so futile that defeated Jane to-night. When she turned away from the window, the tears were pouring down her cheeks.

In the deserted Moorish Court, Sonia and Pat talked together. But not for long. Feeling was too high on both sides and although Sonia, womanlike, half enjoyed a big dramatic scene, Pat wanted to fly from it.

He would have left her when Jane did, but she caught his hand, and implored him hysterically to stay and listen to her.

"What is there to be said?" he asked her roughly. "Unless you want to give me all the lurid details of your marriage with this Frenchman."

"He isn't altogether French—he's half-English."

"All the same to me if he's Portuguese."

Sonia stopped crying. She gave Pat a resentful look from under long wet lashes.

"I thought you loved me . . . if you did, you couldn't be so brutal. . . ."

He stared at her incredulously.

"Brutal! I? And how about you? Could anything have been more brutal than your treatment of me? I believed in you. I loved you so much that I would have staked my life on you. And I would have lost it. Well, I *have* lost all that really counted."

"It's just as hard on me."

"I deny that. You haven't suddenly discovered *my* wife, in my arms."

"I never wanted to be in Maurice's arms. It's the last thing I wanted."

He gave her another incredulous look.

"I just don't understand you, Sonia. How could you have imagined that you'd keep me by leading me on with all sorts of hopes you knew must inevitably be wrecked? I presume the Chief doesn't know either."

"No," she whispered. "Nobody does—except Jane."

The story poured out then. As far as Pat could tell, he was hearing the truth now, when he learned of the foolish infatuation which had led Sonia into the crazy marriage with Maurice Gardener in Paris, two years ago. She excused herself on every score. She had been young, impressionable, spoiled, she said. And he was ready to believe her and to credit that the whole thing had been a mad mistake which many another lovely, foolish girl might have made.

But there seemed to him nothing to excuse her cowardice in keeping the story from him. Even if she had, justifiably, been too frightened to confess to her father, she should never have withheld facts from him, Pat. For he had truly loved her, and true love, surely, deserves fair and courageous treatment.

"You let me think that I was going to marry you—work for you—and it wasn't true. You just made a fool of me!" he reproached her bitterly.

"But I wanted to marry you. Pat, don't you love me enough even now to wait until I can get a divorce?"

He was silent a moment. He had been so shocked by the discovery that Sonia was married that his brain had scarcely had time to smooth things out, or analyse his emotions. But as he looked down at her, his beloved one, who was fair as a lily, beautiful as a poem, his heart gave a great jerk of red-hot pain. He had loved her so very much. Too much! The goddess had tumbled from her pedestal and lay shattered at his feet. How could he ever feel the same about her again?

She caught his arm and looked up at him with swimming eyes.

"Pat, Pat, don't be too hard on me. . . ."

He found himself shaking.

"You don't understand what this has done to me, Sonia. I absolutely counted on you and your love?"

"But I do love you . . . I swear it."

"Do you? How much? So much that you'd come with me this very moment to your father and tell him the truth? So much that you'd tell him everything that you've told me and then go away with me and let Gardener divorce you, and start life with me somewhere? Would you do that? Would you, Sonia?"

For an instant she stared at him wildly. Then her lashes drooped, her cheeks scorched.

"Daddy would chuck me straight out and you too, and we wouldn't have a cent. . . ."

"Ah! You're being cautious. The financial side comes into it, does it? It wouldn't appeal to you to take my hand and wander with me like a gypsy, away over the hills? That would be too sentimental, too romantic. You'd rather have the Victor to drive you to the stars, eh?"

She snatched her hand away.

"Now you're being melodramatic and hateful."

"No, I'm being honest with myself and trying to make you honest, too. But you don't love me enough to be chucked out with me, do you? You want a water-tight position before you tell your father anything about your husband—or your lover!"

She flared into temper like a spoiled child.

"Pat, you're just being a fool! Don't you see that if we handle things carefully we can still have a wonderful time, and there wouldn't be any need to face poverty or disgrace?"

Silence between them. In that instant the last shred of faith in her seemed to be torn from his heart by the very roots. He felt sick with disappointment. Then she made the final mistake. She came close to him, put her arms about his neck and strove by sheer physical allure to win back his admiration.

For a fraction of a minute all his senses stirred in response. His arms went round her savagely. He had never been more in love with any woman in his life than with this one, never wanted anything as madly as possession of her—complete possession.

Then he saw something unbeautiful, distorted in her mind which blotted out the beauty of her face and form. She loved him, but not enough to make a sacrifice for him. That wasn't love as he understood it. That wasn't what he was going to accept, no matter how attractive it seemed on the surface.

Speechlessly he thrust her away from him, turned and rushed away, out of her sight.

Chapter 14

JANE went in search of Sonia.

Jane had had her "cry" and finished with it. Now, anxious for her cousin, she went through the hotel to look for her. She found her still sitting there in the Moorish court.

"Hadn't you better go to bed?" Jane said kindly. "It's been a horrible evening for all of us, and it's no good talking about it now. We must wait and see what happens in the morning. You've got Maurice to deal with. I presume you still don't intend to tell Uncle John."

"I do not. I've had enough for the time being," said Sonia bitterly. "I'm more than ever determined not to tell Daddy."

Jane said nothing. She felt that it was hopeless to try to argue with Sonia. Glancing at her wristwatch, she saw that it was nearly eleven. Where was Pat? She felt ill-at-ease and miserable at the memory of his stricken face. She said:

"Where did Pat go?"

"I don't know," said Sonia, and began to cry again.

Jane took her firmly to her bedroom and left her there. She could see perfectly well that Sonia was not going to tackle any of the problems with either courage or sense. She must just remain what she was—a supreme egotist. She, Jane, would have to see Maurice in the morning. She would have to talk to him and try to induce him to let Sonia alone, or arrange a quiet divorce.

Meanwhile she found it impossible to go to bed until she had made sure that Pat was all right. She knew that

he had been hit hard by to-night's revelation and that it
might go badly with one of his hot Irish temperament.

With her Spanish shawl around her shoulders, Jane
searched El Minza for Pat. But Pat was nowhere to be
found. She telephoned to the servants' quarters and was
told that Mr. Royale's chauffeur was not in his room.

After that Jane began to be afraid. Where *was* Pat?
What had he done when he had left Sonia? How far
had he been affected by the discovery of the truth about
her? Perhaps it had just driven him wild, and he was in
the mood not to care what he did.

A dozen alarming conjectures shaped themselves in
Jane's mind. And the knowledge came to her that she
had really never loved until to-night. But to-night she
loved Pat Connel with all that was fierce and passionate
and, simultaneously, protective and maternal in her.
She was conscious of nothing but the overwhelming desire to help him, and if necessary, save him from himself.

She knew that she must find him before she closed
her eyes in sleep to-night.

The hotel guide, a brown-skinned, dark-eyed Algerian with a red fez at an insolent angle on his sleek
black head, was lounging on the entrance steps, arms
folded, a cigarette between his lips.

Jane addressed him. Immediately the figure in the
luminous white robes leaped to attention.

"Lady?"

She asked him if he had seen a young Englishman in
a grey flannel suit . . . blue eyes, black hair . . . he
was wearing a green chauffeur's uniform when he arrived at the hotel this afternoon.

The guide gave Jane a flashing smile.

Yes, he had seen the gentleman. In fact, half an hour
ago he had been in conversation with him. The gentleman had wanted distraction and had asked where he
might find gaiety and music in the town.

"Where did you send him?" she asked the guide.

"To Lotus Café, lady. Very gay there! Moorish girls
dancing . . . Moorish music . . . best in Morocco."

Jane stared in front of her. It did not take her long to make up her mind what she was going to do. She said promptly:

"Take me there."

The guide stared. His eyes expressed horror.

"Lotus Café not for lady. Only for gentleman."

Jane's lips tightened.

"You can look after me. I wish to go there."

The guide salaamed.

"If lady pleases . . . shall I order conveyance?"

"How far is it?"

"Way down hill. Near main street."

"Then get the hotel car."

The guide hastened to do her bidding. He saw money in it and that was all that mattered to him. If the pretty little English lady, who held her shawl firmly about her as though to hide her charms rather than flaunt them in the manner of his own women, wished to go to the infamous café, she must do so. After all he was used to receiving queer orders . . . particularly from American ladies, who found these placed of entertainment "all too cute".

The car drew up outside a narrow white house with green shutters. From the lower windows came an orange glow of light, and a noise which seemed to Jane to have a close association with the wailing of cats on the roof tops. It was the shrill incantation to the accompaniment of pipes, known as Moorish music.

The guide helped Jane out of the car.

"Lotus Café, lady."

"Wait for me here one moment," she said.

She pushed aside the striped curtain and looked into the room. For a moment she saw nothing clearly. The café was veiled in a thick haze of smoke. It was unbearably hot.

Then Jane's blinking eyes focused upon three half-naked girls with brown glistening bodies performing some kind of slow dance in the centre of the floor. Around them, at little tables, sat a motley crowd. Mostly Arabs with white or striped burnous, Algerians with the red fez, Spanish uniformed police, and one or two English or American men.

Jane quailed at the idea of entering. It was only her violent desire to save Pat that kept her standing there at all, because she had an instinctive desire to hide herself from the bold gazes that were directed at her once her presence was noticed in the doorway.

Then her heart gave a great leap. She saw the man for whom she was searching. Pat was sitting alone at one of the tables, a glass in his hand. Quite plainly now she saw his face. It looked very white, glistening as though with sweat in the garish light. A profoundly tragic face, all the humour and boyishness wiped from it. He stared without any particular interest at the undulating figures of the Moorish girls.

And this was the gaiety which he was seeking, this the oblivion from that searing pain of having loved somebody who wasn't worthy. . . .

Suddenly Jane called his name, loudly and clearly, so that her voice carried above the wailing chant of the native musician.

"Pat!"

His head shot up. He looked in her direction. With immense astonishment he recognised that small figure in the light camels'-hair coat, belted round the waist, small hands thrust in the pockets.

"Jane," he said stupidly.

She beckoned to him. He rose to his feet. He was a little drunk, but not very. He paid his bill, quite aware that he was being charged three times more than the drinks were worth and in no mood to dispute it. He came straight through the smoke-thickened café, took Jane's arm, led her outside, and let the striped curtain fall behind them.

"What the hell are you doing here?" he asked.

His voice was like his eyes, rather blurred. But Jane looked at him with profound relief, a relief so great that she could have wept. If nothing more than this had happened to him—she need not have worried her head off about him.

"You idiot, Pat Connel!" she said in a furious little voice. "You prize idiot!"

"Why, may I ask?"

"Coming down to a place like this and getting tight."

"I'm not tight."

"Not very," admitted. "But if you'd sat there much longer you'd have been *very* . . . then anything might have happened to you in that thieving, pock-marked crowd."

He dropped her arm, pulled a cigarette from his pocket and lit it. As he flung away the burnt match he stared down at her flushed angry young face.

"Who told you I was here?"

"I asked the hotel guide."

"How indiscreet of him!" said Pat, and laughed, but the laugh was not a blithe sound.

"Perhaps it was indiscreet of me to come and look for you, but I'm glad I did."

"What did you suppose was going to happen to me?"

Her lashes drooped. She felt suddenly embarrassed.

"Oh, I don't know. I daresay I've been a fool. . . ."

His mind, which had been fogged by the fumes of bad alcohol, began to clear. Out here where it was fresh, cool, crystal clear in the spring moonlight, he could breath again, think again. He didn't want to think. He had gone there into that rotten stupefying place of amusement for the express purpose of being stupefied. That was what he wanted . . . something that would stop him remembering Sonia and what she had done to him.

"You should have left me alone," he said.

Jane's breath came more quickly. With all her heart she longed to put an arm about him and tell him not to suffer like this about Sonia, to assure him that it wasn't worth it. But she could do nothing but feel hurt and foolish because she had made a blunder in following him.

"I know I had no right to interfere," she said. "I don't know what made me come. I'll go back."

She turned to the car and the guide opened the door for her. Pat followed.

"I might as well come too."

"Do as you wish," she said coldly. "But I don't advise you to swallow any more of that synthetic whisky. It will make you feel awful in the morning."

He gave a brief laugh, and swung himself into the car beside her.

"Dear little Jane, I've never known you not to have a sensible word ready for an emergency. And you're always right. That's the worst of it. You've been right all the way along. Only I haven't believed you. I didn't want to . . . oh, *hell*!"

He suddenly sat back in the corner of the car and put the back of his hand across his eyes.

The guide discreetly slammed the door.

"I walk back, lady."

The car moved on. Jane sat still, conscious of little satisfaction because she had "always been right."

Pat said:

"You were darned right about that whisky. God, it was foul! The whole café was foul."

"Yes," said Jane.

"I felt crazy. I wanted to get tight. I was for a bit, but I'm not now. I see it's no use. Good old Dowson knew all about it. 'I called for madder music, stronger wine, hoping to put thy pale lost lilies out of sight . . .' "

"Please," interrupted Jane. "Don't quote *Cynara* to me."

"No, it's cheap, isn't it? I feel a bit cheap."

Her love and pity for him battled with the desire to be intensely angry with him. Impulsively she put out her hand. He clung to the small cool fingers as a drowning man clutches at a straw.

"I'm not cross, really," said Jane. "I'm dreadfully grieved for you."

"Sure and I've been a double-dyed ass," he said, his rich Irish voice breaking suddenly. "But I loved her so much, Jane. I adored her!"

"I know."

"She shouldn't have let me go on believing I had a right to her love."

"She's a queer girl, Pat. She's been so spoiled all her

life, I suppose one must try to make excuses if she isn't as rational as other people."

"You can excuse her. I can't. I shall never forgive her for not telling me that she was married."

"It's been a frightful position for me. I wanted to warn you. I couldn't."

"You've been mighty loyal to her."

"You wouldn't have expected me to betray her."

He looked down at the small firm little hand which he was holding, and then up at Jane. Her face was pale and tender in the moonlight. And her eyes were very sad. He had been struck once or twice by the sadness in Jane's eyes. He was conscious of a great warmth of admiration and respect and liking for her.

"I wouldn't expect *you* to betray anybody," he said. "Although at one time to-night I felt I had no faith left in anyone."

She thrilled to his praise.

"You must keep faith with yourself, Pat—that's all that matters."

"Why do you bother about me? Why have you ever bothered about me?"

She sat very still, scarcely daring to breathe. This was where she must guard her secret very well indeed. At length she said:

"I suppose it's because I like you—because I've always liked you."

He looked down at her. She was looking straight up at him. Her eyes seemed very clear and bright and beautiful. Even in the midst of his misery, his furious resentment against Sonia, the lies which had smashed his faith and his ideals, he was still man enough to be conscious of Jane Daunt's attractions. He put an arm about her shoulder, drew her to his side and said:

"Thank you, Jane. Thank you, my dear."

Her eyes suddenly closed in a frightened way. She sat very still, not daring to move. She felt both bitterness and rapture in the circle of his arm. His head was resting against her shoulder in a weary dejected way. He was rather like a tired, dispirited little boy. There was no question of sex in that embrace. Her own blood might be leaping wildly because of his proximity, but she knew that there was no passion in him—only a craving for comfort, for sanctuary, somebody to help him bear the intense pain of his disillusionment.

All that was proud and reserved in Jane made her want to push him away, to cry out sharply:

"Don't! Don't touch me. I'm not here ready for the asking, just because Sonia has failed you!"

But there was something deeper, warmer, and much more human than that which made her oblivious of her own feelings to-night. She was concentrating on him. She put both arms around him and said:

"Poor dear! Poor dear Pat!"

Neither of them spoke again. But they sat like that with their arms clasped about each other, while the hotel car climbed the steep hill towards El Minza.

During those few moments Jane was absurdly, wildly happy. And he was absurdly, wildly unhappy. But the comfort and security of their embrace seemed to draw the sting out of things, or at least made them more bearable for him.

Just before they reached the hotel, they drew apart again, but he kept hold of her hands.

"I can't pretend to thank you," he said huskily. "I don't suppose I shall ever be able to tell you how much you've done for me to-night."

Now that his arms were no longer around her she was filled with sudden embarrassment. A hot blush enveloped her whole body.

"There's nothing to thank me for, Pat," she said; but did not look at him.

"Plenty," he said. "To begin with, I expect you saved me from making a complete fool of myself."

She tried to laugh.

"Glad I was of some use, Pat. I know how badly you feel. But don't let it sink you. You're much too good a fellow for that. And don't let Sonia have the satisfaction of thinking she can break you."

With a quick nervous gesture, Pat smoothed his hair

back from his forehead, then took a packet of cigarettes from his pocket. He offered Jane one but she refused. He lit one for himself. As he put it between his lips, he said:

"Believe me, I'm not interested in what Sonia thinks."

"That may or may not be true," said Jane. "You feel that way to-night, but——"

He turned on her.

"Do you think I could ever forget——"

She interrupted:

"I don't say that at all. But naturally you're feeling raw to-night."

"And I shall feel raw to-morrow," he said. "And the next day and the next."

Jane felt unutterably tender toward him. Poor hurt Pat! Funny how like a small hurt boy he seemed to her to-night.

She said:

"It'll get better, Pat. These things do, you know."

He shrugged his shoulders. The car was drawing up outside the hotel entrance. Pat stepped out, helped Jane, then paid the man.

The car moved away, and left them standing there on the hotel steps. The moonlight was still flooding Tangier with that bright unearthly splendour. It was growing colder. Jane shivered as she looked at her watch.

"It's late," she said. "I think we'd both better go to bed, don't you?"

"You ought to have been in bed long ago," he said. "I feel frightfully guilty about it . . . I had no idea you'd worry about me . . . for me . . . it was sweet of you, Jane!"

She turned away and began moving to the hotel.

"See you in the morning, Pat. Try and sleep now, won't you?"

"Wait a moment," he said.

She turned back and smiled. "Yes?"

"I'm not going on with this trip."

She looked him straight in the eyes.

"Yes, you are, Pat," she said.

"I'm not! Do you think I could stand hours and days of this journey with *her* . . . never getting away from her . . . after all that's happened . . . it would be a bit too much!"

"Pat," said Jane quietly, "I've always thought Sonia an egotist—and—I think you're one, too."

"What is egotistical in it?"

"You are concentrating on yourself and your own reactions. But I think you have my uncle to consider, too. In that rather mad fashion of yours, you took Woodham's place. You volunteered to be our chauffeur. Then you got yourself into a row, and upset everything and everybody, after which Uncle John forgave you and took you back. Now you're going to walk out on him. You know that he's been looking forward to driving over the mountains more than anything. You don't hesitate to land him in difficulties, do you? He won't tolerate strange drivers. He's depending on you; must *he* suffer because of this mess? I admit that most of it is Sonia's fault. But you're a bit to blame too, Pat, for rushing into the affair, aren't you? From the beginning it was bound to be disastrous!"

He had listened to her speech, smoking quickly, his eyes fixed on the luminous distance. Then he said:

"If Sonia had been free to marry me, as I thought she was, it wouldn't have been a disaster."

"Even so, I fail to see why Uncle John should suffer for it!"

Pat bit his lips.

"Yes, you're right about that."

"You say I'm always right, don't you?" she asked, with a sudden humorous smile.

"But, Jane, I don't want to go on! I want to get back to London. I want to forget Sonia. I want to put this thing behind me and start again."

"You can do that when the trip's over, Pat. You won't feel better for letting everybody down, will you?"

"Oh, confound you, Jane Daunt!" he said angrily. "Why the dickens must you always be right?"

"Stick it, Pat!" she said. "Don't go back on us now. Make yourself carry on in spite of what has happened. In spite of Sonia."

"And how do you think she's going to feel about it? What's she going to do? What's that miserable husband of hers going to do?"

"I don't know. He's a nuisance and always has been one."

"Why did she ever marry him—" he began, then he stopped and set his teeth. "No, I don't want to begin thinking about that. It's been circling round and round my head ever since I found out . . . it has driven me mad."

"I think money may settle him," said Jane. "It always has done in the past. Certainly, I want her to tell her father, and get the thing over and done with. I always have wanted her to do that, but she won't. She's afraid."

"I would never have thought her capable—" began Pat, but stopped himself again. It was too awful that love . . . such love as he had felt for Sonia should turn to bitterness . . . to contempt. Once he had felt so unworthy of her love. Horrible now to feel that *she* was unworthy to be loved!

"I daresay there'll be trouble," said Jane. "But I'll see Maurice in the morning and try to make him more reasonable. He gave her away to you to-night. But I think he's too much of a coward to do so to Uncle John. He knows perfectly well that he wouldn't get another penny."

Pat looked at her with horror in his eyes.

Sonia had been sending Maurice Gardener money . . . blackmailed by her own husband. It was beastly, beastly!

"Stop thinking about it, Pat. Go to bed and forget," said Jane.

He pitched his cigarette into the darkness.

"Very well."

She came nearer to him and touched his arm.

"And Pat, be big," she said. "Big enough to help Un-

cle John. I know it won't be easy if you have to see
Sonia every day. But you can do anything if you make
up your mind to it."

"I believe you could, Jane Daunt!" he said.

"You, too."

"Oh, very well, since you've decided everything for
me, I'll try not to walk out."

"I don't want to make your decisions for you, Pat.
It's nothing to do with me really. But I'm your friend
. . ." her voice choked a little on that word ". . . As
a friend, I ask you to stay and see the trip through."

"I will, Jane," he said. "Good night, my dear. Good
night, and thank you again."

She held out her hand. He took it and raised it to his
lips. It was a gesture of homage and gratitude. But it
shook Jane's nerve. She longed to cry out:

"Oh Pat, Pat, I love you so! So desperately! Pat,
don't let the thought of Sonia hurt you any more. Let
me love you . . . *let me!*"

But she did nothing of the sort. She drew her hand
away, turned, and walked into the hotel.

Chapter 15

JANE awakened that next morning to find Sonia standing by her bedside, and the sunlight streaming bril-
liantly into the room. She sat up and rubbed her eyes.

"Hullo! Is it very late?"

"No, it's quite early," said Sonia. "But I had to come
and talk to you. Look."

She held out a sheet of notepaper, scribbled over in a
slanting untidy hand.

"From Maurice. Pushed under my door."

Jane pushed her dark tumbled hair out of her eyes and, hunching her knees, took the note that Sonia handed her. She yawned.

"Gosh! I'm tired!"

"Haven't you slept? I haven't! Not a wink!"

"I slept like a horse, but I was pretty late getting to bed."

"Where were you last night?" asked Sonia, regarding Jane curiously. "I felt frightfully worried and miserable after I got to bed so I came along to talk to you, but you weren't here."

"No," said Jane, without meeting her cousin's gaze. "I was out."

"Out! Who with? What were you doing out at that time of night?"

"I was with Pat," said Jane abruptly.

"With Pat, were you? And what had he to say to you?"

"Quite a lot," answered Jane.

"Aren't you going to tell me?"

"Let me read this letter first of all."

"Well, that solves one difficulty anyhow," said Sonia. "In fact it solves quite a good many. Maurice has gone. He left after an early breakfast."

"We're leaving too."

"But he didn't know that. He just thought he'd be doing me a good turn by clearing out. I think he was sorry for last night."

Jane was wide awake now. She read what Maurice had written, and with considerable relief. Certainly he was saving them all a lot of trouble.

"DEAR SONIA,

"On thinking things over I have decided that I behaved like a cad to-night. I had no right to break my word and give you away. I suppose I was a cad ever to marry you. I see it is useless trying to effect any sort of reconciliation between us since you're in love with this other fellow and you don't want me. I only hope I haven't upset your apple-cart too badly. Anyhow, I'm not going to make trouble between you and your father. I'll clear out of the hotel and disappear. Don't worry about me any more.

"I hate to mention money but things are rather bad with me and so if you can send me a little now and again, do so for old time's sake, *cherie*.

"I think it's more than possible that I may give you grounds for divorce in the near future. You may communicate with me at my old address in Paris.

"Yours,

"MAURICE."

Jane looked up at her cousin.

"Well, that's the best thing he's ever done."

"Having done the worst last night," said Sonia bitterly. "He came between me and Pat. That's all that really matters to me."

Jane reached for a cigarette, lit it, picked up the telephone and ordered a cup of tea, then lay back on her pillow and smoked thoughtfully.

"Thank God, there won't have to be a scene or argument with Maurice. He's come to his senses at last. I think it scared him . . . being knocked down by Pat in that way. Of course he knows perfectly well, too, if he gave you away to Uncle John, he'd never get another shilling. It's money that really counts with Maurice."

Sonia got up and began to pace the room restlessly. She looked haggard and wretched. The sleepless nights had marred her loveliness. She said:

"Maurice may be out of the way, and it may even look as though he'll give me a divorce. That would be pretty wonderful, but I've lost Pat. I have lost him, haven't I?" She turned and faced Jane. "I suppose you know all there is to know. He talked to you, didn't he? Go on, Jane. Tell me what he said. Tell me. I've got a right to know."

"Sonia," said Jane, "I'm not going to tell you anything about last night except that Pat very nearly made a fool of himself because he was so unhappy about you, and I stepped in and stopped him. That's all. It's been a ghastly shock to him and you can't be surprised. You can take it for granted things are over between you two."

"Why should they be?" Sonia suddenly flashed, cheeks crimson, eyes blazing. "Why should they if I can get my freedom? If Pat really loves me, he'll forgive me. You can't wipe out love all in a minute like that."

"Oh yes you can!" said Jane grimly. "And I think you wiped it out last night very thoroughly."

Sonia drew near the bed, her small hands clenched to her sides.

"Has he told you that he'll never forgive me?"

"Yes," said Jane quietly.

"I don't see why he shouldn't."

"You may have no pride, Sonia. He has plenty, and in spite of this hole-in-the-corner affair with you, he has a sense of honour and straightness. He never could forgive you for leading him on and encouraging him to love you when you knew the position you were in."

Sonia raised her head, a handkerchief to her quivering lips.

"And are we all continuing the trip in this atmosphere?" she demanded. "It'll be charming, won't it? So friendly, so smooth!" she ended, with an hysterical laugh.

"As far as I know we're continuing," Jane said. "You've considered yourself since this holiday began. Now you must think of Uncle John. He's frightfully keen on it all and he's enjoying the rest, looking forward to writing his book. We needn't all get dramatic and break up the party and worry him to death, need we?"

"I suppose not."

"I daresay it won't be pleasant. But you'll just have to make the best of it."

"With Pat and myself not on speaking terms, eh?" said Sonia. "That will be fun!"

"You've had your fun."

"Oh, how cruel you are!" said Sonia, breaking into fresh sobbing.

"I don't mean to be cruel," said Jane. "But you

would have this affair, now you must put up with the results. It will be just as unpleasant for Pat. Only for God's sake *leave him alone.*"

Sonia did not reply. She sat with hunched-up shoulders in an attitude that suggested defiance. Her thoughts ran on indiscriminately. In her fashion she was still in love with Pat. The very fact that she had lost him made her want him more. She was not going to give him up without a struggle. She foresaw that if they did all go on with this journey across the Riff mountains, she would be in daily contact with Pat. Well, he had loved her madly. She was not prepared to believe that all that feeling was dead and gone.

She still had her youth and beauty and brilliance. He could not be blind to it all. Surely, in time, he would fall under the spell of her charm once more. He would forgive her. They could begin again. And this time she would be free. Maurice was going to set her free.

The tears dried on Sonia's lashes then. Hope sprang anew in her heart. She was undefeated. And as usual she was thinking of nobody's point of view save her own.

She rose from the bed and stretched herself.

"Oh, well, I suppose we'd better get dressed. Daddy will want to get on. Thank God, Maurice has gone. That's lifted a weight off my shoulders. Now we're going into the wilderness, aren't we? I believe these mountains are terribly lonely and primitive."

"Terribly," echoed Jane.

Sonia went out. Jane lay still after she had gone. She, too, was thinking. Sonia's swift change from despair to cheerfulness worried her not a little. She knew her cousin so well. She half guessed what lay at the back of her mind. Sonia meant to try to win Pat back again. Well, did that matter to her, Jane? It never entered her head to try to win Pat on the rebound. She wasn't made that way. On the other hand, she did think of him. Would it be for his happiness, his ultimate good, if he succumbed to Sonia's charms again?

The memory of the deception Sonia had practised upon him and all the lies she had told, could never wholly be wiped out. He would never love her again in the same idealistic, whole-hearted fashion. It was Jane's belief that he would never love Sonia again at all. In any case, the prospect of watching Sonia make a fight for him, of Pat being hurt all over again, did not appeal to Jane.

She got up, put on her dressing-gown, and went along to the bathroom in a mood of depression. She thought with a wry smile how lucky her uncle was. He was the only person who looked forward to this journey with any real pleasure, blissfully ignorant as he was of all the trouble going on around him. Dear old Uncle John!

At ten o'clock Mr. Royale emerged from the hotel ready for the day's journey. The Victor was there, sleek and shining for them, with Pat at the wheel. Jane and Sonia followed Mr. Royale to the car. Pat gave them all a cold, detached look, touched his cap and said:

"Good morning!"

For a fraction of an instant Pat's gaze rested upon the figure of Sonia. Beautiful and desirable as ever. But this morning, desire seemed cold in Pat's heart. He was conscious only of bitterness. With icy politeness he touched his cap, said "Good morning," and set about helping with the luggage.

Mr. Royale—no longer worried by the thought that there was a "flirtation" going on between his daughter and young Connel—all that nonsense, he imagined, had been left behind them—seated himself in the back of his car with his niece, who was to take notes of their travels.

Sonia took her accustomed seat beside the driver. She stole a look at him. She had taken special pains with her toilet this morning. She had touched up eyes and cheeks, removed the traces of her sleepless night, and put on a new and attractive suit of almond green, with a thin Hungarian blouse exquisitely embroidered.

But Pat did not turn his head to look at her. He drove away from El Minza with a stony face, his gaze fixed on the road before him. He was conscious only of that fierce resentment against Sonia. He almost hated

her because of her grace, her beauty, all that had ever
fired his imagination, all that had made a fool of him.
The familiar, intoxicating perfume which emanated
from her was an irritation now rather than a stimulant.

Jane, taking shorthand notes at her uncle's dictation,
glanced up now and then at the two in front of her. She
could hear Sonia making an attempt at conversation,
which was responded to by Pat only with cold formality. Not once did he look at her. Little doubt Sonia
must feel chagrined and thwarted. But it was Pat whom
Jane pitied. She knew of those two it was Pat who
really suffered.

Jane found it hard to concentrate on her work. Several times she had to interrupt her uncle and ask what
he had said.

"What's the matter with you, my dear?" he said, surprised by her unusual inaccuracy.

She had no excuse to offer. She only knew that she
found it hard to concentrate. She kept thinking about
last night—last night when the hotel car had driven Pat
and herself back to El Minza, and they had clung close
to each other. He, blind with pain and misery, seeking
desperately for comfort. She, only too ready to give it,
loving him with all her soul. This love business wasn't
fair, Jane cried to herself. *It wasn't fair*. It hurt far too
much.

Pat went on answering Sonia's artless questions
abruptly—almost rudely. He would have given anything
to find that it was all a nightmare; to wake up, be able
to look into Sonia's large shining eyes and know that
she spoke the truth, and had always spoken the truth,
know that she loved him and he could rely upon her
love; that one day he would make her his wife.

There were grim difficulties ahead of him. He knew
that well enough. As soon as they got back to London
he must leave John Royale's service. He would not stay
in the Victor Company, nor see anybody that reminded
him of Sonia. Life stretched before him a blank—just a
blank—nothing more.

They left Tangier behind them. The white minarets,
the mosaic mosque, faded into a blue distance. They

were on the dusty, winding road which led to the mountains—those sinister ranges where there had been so much fighting amongst the Riffs.

Sonia looked about her gloomily. She did not care much for the aspect of those dark remote peaks and this rough territory. She was miserable. The savage country made her more miserable.

But it appealed to Jane. This was real Morocco. It had a fierce, proud beauty of its own. It appealed to all that was remote and proud in her.

It did not seem long before they were swallowed up in the dark valleys between the mountains. The road grew more lonely; the surface stony and the ground on either side of them was a greenish brown, dotted with stunted palms and shrubs. In the distance, through a mist of blue, the mountain peaks were veiled in low-lying rain clouds. But above them the heavens were clear and the sunshine brilliant.

It looked as though at any moment they might plunge into a storm of rain. The big black storm clouds rolling up on the horizon were grand and awe-inspiring.

Everywhere grew the little purple ground irises, fields of them, the spring flowers of Morocco.

Now and then they passed a solitary Arab on foot, or riding a donkey. Sometimes women padded along on bare feet, wearing shawls and striped petticoats, and these unveiled women of the hills inspired John Royale to make copious notes. It was all amazingly like a scene from ancient Jerusalem, he announced.

But Sonia was not interested. She turned round to her father and said:

"Where are we getting to? It's horribly lonely. I'm sure we'll be attacked and robbed."

"I doubt that, my dear," said Mr. Royale. "Mind you, there was a case of kidnapping not so very long ago—an English newspaper correspondent was carried off and held for ransom. But I don't see why we should be. We're not important enough."

Sonia glanced at Pat.

"I might be carried off and sold in a slave market," she said childishly.

Pat's face did not move a muscle. But he was thinking:

"Yes, that's what you would deserve. To be sold as a slave . . . to be whipped . . . to be made to suffer as you make men suffer. . . ."

When they had been driving a couple of hours, they stopped for a breathing space and had the drinks and sandwiches from the lunch basket which they had brought from El Minza.

Mr. Royale and Pat examined the map between them. They had left the main road which leads from Tangier to Ceuta. They had taken a less sophisticated route which Mr. Royale chose because it would eventually land them at Pogador—a Moorish town in the valley said to contain relics of architecture dating back from thousands of years B.C.

"We should reach Pogador before dark, shouldn't we?" inquired Mr. Royale.

Pat nodded. "Yes, sir."

"What sort of place is Pogador?" queried Sonia pettishly. "Sounds awful to me."

"Aren't you enjoying it, Babe?" asked her father.

"No," she said abruptly.

"But you've been in such high spirits all the way along," he said, and eyed her a trifle anxiously. "Feeling quite fit, aren't you, darling?"

"Quite, thanks, Daddy."

Mr. Royale turned to his niece.

"What's wrong with her, Jane?"

"Oh, just a little bored with it, perhaps," said Jane, hedging.

But Sonia looked at Pat and this time Pat looked straight back at her. Into her large limpid eyes came a look of pleading. But his were dark and bitter. She took a sudden step towards him.

"Pat," she whispered under her breath.

"Can I do anything for you, miss?" he asked in a cold, deliberate voice.

She turned away, scarlet and furious.

When they moved on Mr. Royale suggested that his daughter should sit beside him.

"Come and hold your old Daddy's hand, Babe," he said affectionately, "and let Jane have a rest from work."

Sonia had no other choice but to fall in with his suggestion. But looking at the back of Pat's handsome head, she swore to herself that she would make him change his feelings before this journey ended. He should not look at her like that, coldly, dispassionately. He *should* not.

Jane, seated beside Pat, maintained a silence which he eventually broke.

"Jolly little journey, isn't it?"

"It's such a pity," said Jane, "that we have to concentrate upon our personal emotions. There's so much to be got out of everything else. Look at the grandeur of this scenery. Don't the mountains make you feel that all our dramas are petty and futile?"

Pat's set face relaxed a little.

"Not so much petty as futile, Jane. Love, hatred, all the emotions are *quite* futile!"

She winced.

"As I told you last night, my dear, you mustn't let it hurt you too badly."

"Ah, but you don't know what it is to love, Jane."

She was on the point of denying that violently and saying to him:

"It isn't true! I *do* know what it is to love . . . suffer . . . to watch the man I love being hurt by another woman! Isn't that bad enough?"

But she said nothing. After the pause Pat added:

"How completely circumstances can alter one's outlook! This time yesterday I was glad to be alive, there was so much to look forward to. To-day, I don't really feel I'd care if we were set upon by a lot of cut-throats and finished off."

Jane smiled grimly.

"Speak for yourself, Mr. Connel. I don't want my throat slit, thank you."

"It's much too nice a throat to slit, anyhow," he said, with a flash of his old gallantry.

Jane actually blushed.

"Idiot!" she said.

Suddenly he felt the warmth of her friendship flowing to him. It pulled him out of the darkness, the almost suicidal mood in which he had set forth from Tangier. She was great, this Jane, she was fine and strong. Any fellow on earth would feel glad of her friendship.

Chapter 16

THEY came to Pogador after what seemed an interminable run of two hundred miles across the mountains. Sonia was depressed and bad tempered and did not join in the general enthusiasm as they drove down a steep hill and sighted the lovely old town.

The big Victor purred slowly and smoothly through narrow streets that were cobbled and indescribably filthy; nevertheless the white walls, the blue arches, the old Eastern houses crowding one upon the other crazily, with little space for air, presented a picture of purest beauty.

Across heavily latticed, barred windows, climbed masses of flowering creeper. Gardens were gay with cerise geraniums, and the delicate pink of almond blossom now in full bloom.

"Oh, it's marvellous!" cried Jane, looking to the right and left of her.

"I don't suppose you'll ever see anything more really Moorish than Pogador," said Pat. "I've been here once before. The hotel is only barely fit for tourists, and that's about all I can say, but I think the Chief will get enough copy here."

Mr. Royale was already in raptures. Sonia said nothing. She was nursing a grievance against Jane. Jane could make Pat speak to her. Why should he smile and talk to her like that? Sonia hated Pogador. She complained of the unsavoury odours. She refused to see the fairy-tale fascination of the place.

Pat had to drive very slowly. On either side of the car flowed continual streams of humanity and animals. Donkeys, goats, swarms of half-naked children with enormous black eyes and lovely mischievous faces.

The big English car was regarded with great curiosity. Not many tourists came to Pogador. It was too far out of the usual route. Swarms of little Arab boys rushed after them screaming for *backsheesh*.

Pat guided them at last into a kind of square which was cleaner and more civilised. And here they found their hotel, and it was with some relief that they disembarked from the car and stretched cramped limbs after the long drive.

There was no question in Pogador of chauffeur's quarters. Pat was given a room with the rest of them. And Mr. Royale, in cheerful mood, invited him to dine with the party.

"You brought us here splendidly, Connel. We'll drop the chauffeur business this evening, shall we? Join us for the evening meal."

Pat wanted to refuse. He had not the slightest desire to see so much of Sonia. He tried to escape, but Mr. Royale would have none of it.

"Get out of your uniform, my boy, and then come along and have food with us," he said in his genial fashion.

Pat had no other course but to accept. An invitation from the Chief was, after all, as good as a command.

Sonia cheered up. Pat was going to spend the evening with them in a friendly way and there might be a chance for her to see him alone. She would only have to be alone with him for a few moments. They would talk, and then she would soon make him understand how much she loved him and how sorry she was for what she had done. He *must* be made to look at her again as though he loved her. All day long she had missed that look in Pat's eyes. She was hungry for it.

Jane regarded the evening with some misgivings. She

knew perfectly well what lay at the back of her cousin's mind. And she knew, too, that Pat was still feeling raw and bitter and not likely to enjoy his dinner.

The bedrooms were primitive but clean. There was plenty of hot bath water. Presently, refreshed and changed, the little party foregathered in the dining-room for the evening meal.

Sonia appeared somewhat over-dressed for the occasion in evening toilette, black chiffon, which always suited her fair slender beauty, and with a small Spanish mantilla draped over her head. Through the black lace her golden hair gleamed charmingly, and in that dark delicate frame her face looked a little pale and sad. It gave her a haunting look.

"You're like a Goya picture, my dear," her father remarked gallantly.

Sonia glanced through her long lashes at Pat, who had put on a grey lounge suit and just joined the party. He did not return her gaze.

Jane, watching, wondered grimly how this evening would end. The mantilla, the tragic air, the black dress showing the warm white beauty of Sonia's throat and shoulders, were all to attract *him*. Jane knew it. Pat must know it, too. Was this going to be another sleepless night for everybody?

The dinner was poor, the worst they had had on this journey so far. They were the only guests in the hotel. The Algerian waiter who attended them was anxious to please, and they managed to find some sherry which was drinkable. But that was about all.

"I shall be glad to leave Pogador!" said Sonia as they lit their cigarettes. "It's foul!"

"My dear Babe," said her father, "you haven't the right spirit of adventure. If you want the luxury of civilisation you should have remained behind in a place like El Minza. We're going into the wilderness. It will be a wilder and more primitive journey to-morrow, won't it, Connel?" he addressed Pat.

"Much more so, I believe, sir," he said. "Although as a matter of fact I haven't been farther than Pogador myself."

"I think it should be thrilling," said Jane.

"It might be," said Sonia, and looked through her lashes at Pat.

They had black coffee—the best part of the meal—in the one and only lounge, which contained a couple of divans piled with striped cushions, white walls hung with Eastern rugs, little inlaid Moorish tables and a jewelled lamp hanging on chains from the ceiling, which gave a rich subdued light.

"It's quite Oriental and romantic, isn't it?" remarked Sonia, with a rather high-pitched laugh.

"Those rugs are worth some money," murmured Mr. Royale. "Jane, my dear, if you've finished your coffee, how about coming along to my room and taking some dictation? I've a good deal to say about this place."

"I'm ready," said Jane.

She caught Pat's gaze as she rose. She had been quiet and nervy all evening. And Pat was obviously in a state of nerves. It was equally obvious that he did not want to be left alone with Sonia. His eyes half pleaded to Jane to stay. But she had to go. Reluctantly she followed her uncle out of the lounge.

Sonia sat back against one of the cushions on one of the divans. The hour for which she had been waiting had come. Her heart beat fast. Her cheeks were delicately pink. She said:

"Have you a cigarette, Pat?"

Immediately he rose to his feet and offered her his cigarette-case. Courteously he lit a match and applied it to the cigarette for her. But he avoided looking into her eyes. He said in a chilly voice:

"If you'll excuse me, Miss Royale—or should I say *Mrs. Gardener*—I'll get off to bed. I'm rather tired."

Sonia sat bolt upright. Her face scorched with burning colour, her eyes furious.

"How dare you!" she asked under her breath. "Oh, how *dare* you!"

Pat put his heels together and bowed.

"I beg your pardon. *Miss Royale,* if you prefer it."

"You know that I prefer it. You know that nobody else dreams . . ."

"I won't make the mistake again," he cut in.

"It wasn't a mistake. You did it on purpose . . . to hurt me. . . ." she panted.

Pat clenched his hands. He was conscious of strong emotions tearing through his body. And now he looked down at her. He was well aware of the haunting loveliness of that cameo-like face framed by the black lace mantilla. He could feel all the allure of her red amorous lips, her limpid, asking eyes. Yet he was conscious of one outstanding fact. He no longer loved Sonia. He no longer respected her, therefore he no longer loved her. Desire without love . . . that was nothing . . . worse than nothing. He could not enter into it. He could not even be sorry that he had hurt her by using her married name.

"If you don't mind I'll go to my room," he said.

"Is that all you're going to say to me?" she asked in a trembling voice.

"I don't think there's anything else to say."

"There is . . . there are thousands of things."

"Then they're better left unsaid."

She put out a hand and caught at his arm.

"Pat, don't be like this . . . I know I've been rotten to you . . . that I've lied . . . that I was a coward . . . anything that you like . . . only don't be like this. Let's talk it out . . . we can't go on this way . . . after all we've been to each other."

For an instant Pat looked down at her incredulously. Then he said:

"You don't understand. It's because of all we've been to each other that I am through . . . absolutely through, Sonia."

"You mean you don't want to . . . make it up?"

"Make it up!" he echoed. "How can one *make up* a thing like this, Sonia? It isn't just a quarrel . . . a dispute that can be settled."

"But supposing I tell you that I'm going to get my divorce and be free?"

"That doesn't concern me."

"But it does, Pat. It *must*! Oh, surely you haven't lost all your love for me . . . my dear . . . it's all

been horrible . . . beastly . . . and I'm to blame,
I realise, but there's happiness ahead of us . . . if
you'll only try not to be so bitter."

He was stirred by her as he always had been. He
knew that she was his for the asking. But when he remembered all that she had done, her cowardice, her
dishonesty, those other feelings died in him.

"No, Sonia," he said. "No. There can be no possible
happiness ahead of us. We're through. I told you that
last night."

"But Pat," she cried. "You can't have stopped loving
me altogether. . . ."

"I'm not going to discuss what I feel for you," he
said roughly. "I only ask you to leave me alone."

Her face went white. Her eyes looked abnormally
large and wild. She was sinking all her pride—ready to
stoop to any levels to get him back.

"Then doesn't it mean anything to you that I can get
my freedom?"

"It would have done," he said, "if you'd been willing
to go away with me last night . . . face poverty and
disgrace, anything, as long as we had each other. But
I refuse to hang round and just wait till you think that
you've got me, plus everything else that you want out
of life."

She put the back of her hand against her lips.

"Oh!" she whispered. "You *beast!*"

"I'm sorry," he said, and felt himself shaking.

"I don't believe that you *ever* loved me. . . ."

"You're not capable of judging," he said.

She threw him a speechless look, then rushed out of
the room through the striped curtains which led into the
hotel entrance. She ran straight into the arms of Jane,
who, cigarette between her lips and a fountain-pen in
her hand, had come down to find some ink. Sonia
knocked the fountain-pen out of her hand, and Jane
stooped to pick it up.

Sonia was in a white-hot passion, and as the two girls
stood there staring at each other, the last shreds of Sonia's control snapped. She said through her teeth:

"You've done this, *you* . . . !"

"Done what?" demanded Jane, taking the cigarette from her lips.

"You've taken my place with Pat. He believes in you. He likes you. And he just loathes me now. *Loathes* me, I tell you. He hasn't a kind word to say . . . oh, my God, I wish I'd never been born!"

Jane flushed to the roots of her hair. She caught Sonia's arm and shook her a little.

"Be quiet. For heaven's sake, be quiet! . . ."

"You said something to him last night . . . you made things worse, I know you did. . . ."

Jane shook her cousin again. She was quite aware that Sonia was hysterical and not responsible for what she said, but her gaze sped in terror to the striped curtain. If Pat was through there, he would hear every word that Sonia was screaming. Thank goodness nobody else was about. The dimly lit mosaic hall was deserted.

"Sonia, you must be quiet. You know it's not true. I've always tried to help you."

"But you're in love with Pat yourself. You can't deny it. You're glad Maurice ruined things between me and Pat. You want Pat for yourself . . . you can't deny that you're in love with him. . . ."

Jane was as white now as she had been red. She found herself shaking. She dropped Sonia's arm as though she could not bear to touch her. Under her breath she said:

"Sonia, I'll never forgive you for this . . . never!"

"I don't care!"

"But you will," interrupted Jane, "because if you don't control yourself this instant I shall go straight upstairs and tell Uncle John everything."

That brought Sonia to her senses. Panting, wild-eyed, she stared at Jane, then began to whimper.

"Well, it's true. Why shouldn't I say it? Jane . . ."

"I don't want to talk to you," broke in Jane. "I think you're off your head. And I'm sorry for any help I've ever given you."

Sonia flung up her arms with a dramatic gesture of despair. The black lace mantilla slipped from her head.

She caught it in her hand and turning, rushed speech-lessly up the stairs to her own room.

Jane stood motionless. She felt quite sick. It wasn't so much that she resented what Sonia had said. She was not ashamed of loving Pat. But to have the thing screamed aloud . . . her well-guarded secret exposed in that way, possibly to *him* . . . that was unbearable!

In a dazed way she looked at the fountain-pen in her hand and remembered that her uncle was waiting for her to go back with some ink. She was not by nature melodramatic or hysterical like Sonia. When there was something to be done she did it, no matter how un-pleasant. If she had to face Pat in that lounge she would face him. The ink was there, on the one and only writing desk. She had seen it. She only hoped desper-ately that Pat had *not* heard.

Then the striped curtains parted. Pat walked through and they came face to face. He had, of course, been an unwilling listener to the scene which Sonia had made. He, too, was white, and there was a sick look in his eyes. His gaze met and held Jane's for an instant. Then, to her dismay, a burning tell-tale flush spread over her face and throat. She could not speak. She walked straight past him into the lounge.

He looked after her, his emotions chaotic. But he was more conscious of shame than anything else in this hour. Shame at Sonia's treachery to the cousin who had always been so loyal to her.

He knew that to-night's events had torn the last roots of infatuation from his heart. In a way it was a relief, because he could not suffer about Sonia any more. He could not even hate her. He only felt indifferent. And indifference is the final nail in the coffin of love.

He would like to have said something to Jane, tried to have helped her, make things easier for her. He knew perfectly well what agonies of embarrassment and hu-miliation she must be enduring. She, who was so proud. She was the last girl in the world to want any man to know that she cared for him under such conditions as these. And it had never entered his head until Sonia's words had put it there, that Jane was in love with him. She had been a fine friend, and a hard critic. But he had never suspected that she entertained more intimate feelings for him.

He might have doubted the truth of what Sonia had said had it not been for that burning revealing colour on Jane's face just now. That had betrayed her. For an instant he put a hand up to his eyes. God! What a mess! But whatever he did in the future he must try not to let her see that he *knew*. He was so grateful to her for all that she had done for him. He owed her so much. And he felt so completely unworthy of her love, if indeed, she had honoured him with it.

Jane came through with the ink. They avoided looking at each other this time. But Pat said, with a deliberate attempt at casualness:

"What's our Jane doing snooping round with pen and ink and that determined expression? On business bent for the Chief?"

"Yes. We're working. You're the one that's snooping round."

She passed him, her heart-beats hurting her, dark lashes hiding the distress in her eyes. As she reached the staircase, Pat threw a swift, unhappy look at her back.

"Good night, Jane."

"Good night," she said, without looking round, and went upstairs and passed out of sight.

She was more wretched than she had ever been in her life. Pat's casual treatment of her downstairs just now had raised a doubt in her mind as to whether he *had* heard what Sonia had said. There was no definite need for her to feel quite so outraged or ashamed. But she did and she was *miserable*.

It would be a good thing, she thought bitterly, when this trip ended. There seemed no hope now of happiness or peace for any of them. As far as she could see, tomorrow's advance into the wilderness, where they would be flung more than ever upon each other's company, would be sheer purgatory. And she dreaded it.

Chapter 17

IT was, as Jane had anticipated, another sleepless night. Sonia shared a double room with her and spent most of the night crying from sheer self-pity. And then when Jane was at last allowed to go to sleep, her rest was curtailed by the early and unexpected appearance of Mr. Royale. He came into their room in his dressing-gown, his genial face downcast.

"Rather unfortunate news, you girls," he said. "We shan't be able to leave the hotel this morning. Our chauffeur's indisposed."

Sonia said nothing. As far as she was concerned Pat could be ill and stay so. Her humiliation last night at his hands had been so complete that she almost hated him.

But Jane rubbed her tired eyes and was immediately anxious on Pat's behalf.

"What's wrong with him, Uncle John?"

Mr. Royale thought it was a touch of 'flu. At any rate Connel had sent a message to him this morning and asked him to go along and see him. He had found the young man looking pretty cheap, had taken his temperature—Mr. Royale always carried a thermometer—and it was well up. Pat also complained of headache and pains, which had come on suddenly in the night. He was covered with confusion and full of apologies, but thought it unwise to tackle the day's journey.

"To which I agreed," finished Mr. Royale. "Of course he must stay in bed. No doubt he'll be all right in the morning."

When breakfast was over Jane went along to Pat's room. In answer to her knock a voice said: *"Entrada."* She walked in. The curtains were drawn. In the shadows Pat lay in bed, shivering with fever under a thin blanket.

He looked at Jane with over-bright eyes and groaned.

"Oh, so it's you! Welcome, Jane. I thought it was that greasy, fat, unattractive woman who calls herself the chambermaid."

Jane walked to the bedside.

"Never you mind about attractive women. You just hurry up and get well," she said in her brusque way, but her brown eyes were soft and anxious for him.

He blinked at her.

"I feel like hell, Jane Daunt. Can't think what's wrong. Came on so suddenly in the night."

"It's a visitation on you for your sins. Have you taken some aspirin?"

"One."

"Ridiculous. You want three at least. I'll crush some and get you some warm milk.

Pat groaned again and turned his back on her.

"Warm milk! Sure, and I'd be sick as a dog. Jane— don't start bullying me when I'm ill."

She looked at the black tousled head on the white pillow . . . such a darling boyish head, she thought. And she loved him so frightfully! But she kept up her stern demeanour, made one or two practical suggestions, carried them out, and then left him, promising to look at him again later.

She joined her uncle and cousin, who were down in the lounge.

"Well, what do you think of him?" asked Mr. Royale.

"He looks rotten," said Jane. "But I don't suppose it's anything but 'flu."

"Get a doctor," said Sonia pettishly.

"My dear!" expostulated her father, "there won't be an English doctor in Pogador. A Spanish 'medico', perhaps, but you might as well consign yourself to the grave straight away as send for one of them."

"A nice place you've brought us to, Daddy."

"Come, come, Babe. Look at the sunshine, and that

glorious collection of palm trees out there. You've got your tail down for some reason or other. Not sickening for 'flu too, are you, darling?"

"No," said Sonia, and lapsed into sullen silence.

The three of them spent the morning inspecting the fine old architecture in the Arab quarter of Pogador. Mr. Royale enjoyed himself. He did not mind the delay. Jane took notes diligently, but Sonia was bored and had little to say. She was not amused by the bazaars. She was never really amused unless she was being the centre of interest herself, or some attractive man was making love to her. Now that she had lost Pat she had lost all interest in this holiday. The relationship between herself and Jane was strained, too. She had said more than she intended last night and she knew that Jane was angry with her.

But there was more trouble in store for the Royale party than any of them had bargained for. When they reached the hotel they found it in chaos. The servants were tearing about with scared faces and the stout blackbearded gentleman in the red fez who called himself the manager, immediately rushed to Mr. Royale and began to babble incoherently.

The two girls stared at each other.

"What's he saying?" demanded Sonia.

"I don't know," said Mr. Royale. "It's all in Spanish, and I can't understand when they speak at that speed. Something has happened, anyhow. The whole place seems to be fermenting. Jane, my dear, run up and see if Connel's any better, and if he knows what the trouble is. He's our only interpreter."

Jane started to walk across the hall, but there was no need for her to go farther. Pat, himself, appeared. He was in pyjamas and dressing-gown. He was holloweyed and his cheeks were scarlet with fever.

"What on earth are you doing out of bed?" cried Jane.

Pat was shivering visibly.

"Have you heard?" he said.

"Heard what?" asked Mr. Royale. "What the deuce

is all this about, Connel? Everybody's tearing about like a lot of lunatics."

"They're packing up to get out, sir. In about half an hour there won't be a soul left in this place."

"But why? What's happened?"

And then Pat's lips formed and uttered the dreaded word . . . just one small word, but sufficient to make the faces of his listeners blanch.

"Smallpox," he said.

Sonia immediately screamed.

"Oh!" and her hands flew up to her delicate pink-and-white cheeks as though, in an instant, she visualised her loveliness being destroyed by that most dreaded scourge of the East.

Mr. Royale said:

"Good God!"

Jane stood still, her gaze fixed on Pat.

No word came from her. Following instantly upon the shock of what Pat had said there came to her the fearful suspicion:

"Pat . . . has he got it?"

Pat was telling the Chief what he knew.

During the morning nobody had been near him, in spite of the fact that he had rung his bell constantly. Then he got up and walked into the corridor and saw the Algerian who had waited on them last night, carrying a bundle of clothes down the stairs. He had questioned the fellow, who had told him that four of the staff had gone down suddenly with smallpox. Nobody intended to stay except a kitchen-boy and an old Arab who washed dishes, both of whom had had the disease.

"But they can't abandon the hotel," protested Mr. Royale. "It's preposterous."

"They're a lot of cowards," said Pat. "And it's just what they will do."

"Well, whoever wants to stay in it?" said Sonia in a high-pitched voice. "We must get away ourselves at once—at once!"

"Of course," said her father. "I ought never to have brought you here, but it never entered my head that there'd be an outbreak like this . . . it's terrible, terrible!"

Then Jane, whose dark eyes had never wavered from Pat's feverish face, said sharply:

"But what about Connel? He can't travel. He's in a high temperature. He might get pneumonia."

"I'll be all right," said Pat.

But even as he spoke he felt deadly faint and swayed on his feet.

Jane dropped a parcel which she had bought in the bazaar that morning, sprang to his side and put a supporting arm around him.

"No . . . you're far from all right!"

Sonia clutched her father's arm.

"Daddy . . . *daddy* . . . *he's* probably got it."

Mr. Royale's cheeks lost all their healthy colour.

"My dear . . . what an idea. . . ."

"But it may be true!" panted Sonia. "It probably is. Jane, come away from him, don't touch him!"

Jane threw her a look of withering contempt.

"What shall I do . . . just let him drop?"

"But, my dear, if he has got it . . ." began her uncle.

"Well, if he has, he isn't going to be left to it like an animal on a bundle of straw, is he?" Jane asked furiously.

Pat only half-heard the little storm which was raging over his head. All the faces, the Chief's, Sonia's, Jane's, were revolving round him. The pain in his head was excruciating. But he was conscious of Jane's protective arm, of her defending voice, and he knew suddenly that she *did* love him and that it was love in the real sense of the word.

He laughed stupidly, swaying on his feet.

"Sonia's wise . . . not to touch me . . . mustn't risk anything . . . but I . . . I haven't got it . . . only vaccinated . . . little while ago. . . ."

Then the world blacked out and he went down like a stone at Jane's feet, almost dragging her with him.

Sonia refused to let go of her father's arm.

"Daddy, don't touch him, you mustn't. Let Jane be a fool if she wants."

"What in God's name shall we do?" said Mr. Royale weakly. "We were wrong, very wrong, Babe, not to be vaccinated before we came out to Morocco. I shall never forgive myself it I've brought you into danger."

"We must go away at once!" said Sonia.

"Sonia's right, Jane. We must get out of this immediately and drive straight back to Tangier."

"And take Pat with us?" asked Jane, looking up, the Christian name slipping unconsciously from her lips.

"That's impossible," said Sonia. She was trembling with fright. "If he's got it, we'll all get it. We daren't risk that."

"Very well," said Jane. "If he stays here I stay with him."

"My dear Jane—" began Mr. Royale.

"It's unthinkable that we should all leave him here to die if he is really ill," cut in Jane. "You can see for yourself that these rats are all leaving the sinking ship and soon there won't be a soul in the hotel. I can't let Pat lie here and starve. He ought to be in bed now. Uncle John, you must help me carry him in to the divan in the lounge. We can drag him there between us and I'll get some blankets from upstairs."

"It isn't fair to make Daddy touch him . . ." began Sonia.

Then Jane turned on her.

"Oh—you make me sick. And after all . . ."

She choked and paused. She was going to say: "After all your protestation of loving him. . . ." But she dared not give Sonia away in front of her father.

Sonia was thinking of nothing but that awful word *smallpox*. In her estimation it was not the time for romance, or for remembering that she had ever been in love with Pat. She looked at his unconscious figure with horror, all her anxiety for herself.

Mr. Royale, in a state of nerves and slightly dazed by the whole thing, allowed his niece to take command of the situation. It seemed to him a critical one and there

was no time for him to wonder why Jane should be so
concerned about young Connel. He just did what she
asked. Together they managed to drag Pat into the
Moorish lounge and got him on to the divan. Jane tore
upstairs and came down again with blankets, which she
piled over the sick man. Then, with a white set face, she
faced her uncle and cousin.

"Now listen," she said, "there's no time to argue or
dither. Pat's very ill. He says that he was only vaccinated the other day so I don't suppose he's got smallpox, and *I'm* not going to worry. I was vaccinated myself not so many years ago. The main thing is that he
mustn't be moved at the moment. Drive him out in the
car now and he'll certainly get pneumonia and die. But
you two have got to get away. Uncle John, you must
take the Victor and drive back to Tangier. You won't
get there till midnight, but it's the only thing to do.
Then you can send an ambulance out from the clinic
for Pat. I'll stay here and nurse him until you come. It's
only a question of twenty-four hours."

"My dear, it's very noble——" began Mr. Royale.

"It's nothing of the kind," she interrupted. "I want to
do it. But you and Sonia mustn't stay."

Mr. Royale turned helplessly to his daughter.

She took his arm and clung to it, avoiding Jane's
clear stern gaze.

"Yes, Daddy, Jane's right. Let's get off quickly. It
doesn't matter about food. We daren't touch any food
from this place. Oh, *come on*, quickly . . . they can
bring our luggage back in the ambulance. Don't let's
wait for it."

For an instant Mr. Royale hesitated. He eyed his
niece with misgiving.

"I don't feel I should leave you, my dear. . . ."

Jane, wasting no time, was crushing some aspirin in a
slip of white paper.

"I shall be quite all right, Uncle John. And the
sooner you reach Tangier, the sooner we'll have help."

"God bless you, my dear," said Mr. Royale, with the
suspicion of a break in his voice. "You're like your
mother was before you . . . a very brave woman."

Jane shook her head and smiled. Uncle John didn't understand. It wasn't brave to stay behind with the man you loved, and face danger with him. She would have had to have much more courage to leave Pat lying here alone.

She went out into the sunlit street and saw them off. Sonia, now in the car, was still jittering, but bade Jane good-bye and was seized with sudden remorse at the sight of her small solitary figure standing there on the doorstep.

"Will you be all right, Janie? Hadn't you better come with us?"

"No," said Jane coldly.

"Don't think too badly of me, Jane. I know I'm a coward . . . but *smallpox*."

"We don't know that he's got it yet," snapped Jane. "Good-bye."

Chapter 18

A FEW moments later Jane watched the big shining Victor disappear in a cloud of dust. Perhaps then her heart quailed a very little. Uncle John had gone . . . and she was alone with a very sick man in a practically deserted hotel, in an isolated Moorish town full of thieving natives and the lowest type of Spaniard. Not pleasant! Then the thought of Pat and her love for him overwhelmed her and cast out all fear.

Quickly she went back into the lounge. Pat's eyes were wide open now and he was muttering under his breath and obviously delirious. She took his hot hand and held it a moment, looking anxiously down at him. She had no particular knowledge of nursing, only practical common sense and that mother instinct which is in

every woman who loves. She could only do what she
thought best. She had not the slightest idea how long
smallpox took to develop or what the symptoms would
be. But somehow she did not think that Pat had got it.
They might, of course, both catch it just through staying here, but there was no alternative.

She decided that it would be wise to try and get hold
of the local "medico". At least he would know how to
deal with the illnesses of his own country. She found
her pocket-dictionary and prepared a question in Spanish, and then tried to find somebody who would listen
to her.

The manager himself had seized his things and departed. He did not intend to risk anything. Jane, wandering from room to room, found nobody in the hotel
except the old Arab and the boy in the kitchen. She
tried to make them understand what she wanted. But it
was hopeless. They were both willing and eager to help
her, but could do nothing but look at her like uncomprehending animals, roll their eyes, gesticulate, and
pour torrents of bastard Spanish and Arabic into her
ears.

The kitchen was in chaos. The cooks had departed in
the middle of preparing the midday meal. Jane, although she was healthily hungry, decided that she
would not eat any of the food, in case it was infected.
She must go hungry for twenty-four hours. And it
would not matter if Pat had nothing to-day but drinks.
She found a saucepan, poured some water into it,
boiled it and took it upstairs to the lounge. She could
give Pat sips of that when it cooled down.

Pat tossed and moaned and muttered on his pillows.
Jane left him again and hurried out into the street. The
little square was deserted. Pogador appeared to give no
sign of life. The rabbits had scuttled into their warrens.
A rumour had been spread by an ignorant member of
the hotel staff that the English chauffeur had brought a
mysterious plague to Pogador . . . an illness resulting
in rapid death. Already two of the hotel servants had
succumbed, not from smallpox, the tale-bearer said, but
this plague. The English gentleman and the golden-

haired *señorita* had already fled from the town in their car. Nobody, therefore, would go near the hotel. Small-pox was bad enough, but the thought of an unknown plague spread terror through the superstitious natives in all quarters.

When Jane appeared, anybody that saw her scuttled away from her, believing her also to be a carrier of the fatal malady.

She found it hopeless to try to approach anybody or to find the medical man. So at length she returned to the abandoned hotel and to Pat's side.

She sat down beside him, wiped her burning face with a handkerchief and closed her eyes. Heavens! she was tired and hot. This was a bad business and quite frankly she could not look forward to the long hours in front of her. Hours of anxiety over Pat's condition and without food for herself, without even daring to make herself a cup of tea down in that filthy kitchen.

Pat threw up an arm and moaned.

"Sonia!"

Jane's lips tightened. So he was still thinking of *her* . . . Sonia who would have abandoned him to his fate this day! Not very jolly for her to sit here and listen to him raving about another woman.

Then Pat looked straight at her with his glazed eyes and muttered.

"You're vile . . . you're *vile* . . . !"

Jane laid a hand on his forehead and stroked back the thick dark hair.

"You're not talking to me, I hope," she said, with a flash of her old humour.

"Go away," said Pat. "Don't try and get me back this way, Sonia. Despicable . . . hate you. . . ."

Jane lifted her brows. So that was how he felt about Sonia! Well, it wasn't anything for her to be jealous of! She went on smoothing his forehead. He thrust her away and babbled about his love and his hate.

She went upstairs to her bedroom and brought down a bowl of cold water, a sponge, and towel. The only thing that she could do was to bathe him and try to lower his temperature. So she tucked up her sleeves and set to work on him in her practical way. He moved fretfully under her touch, but she managed to cool him down a little, wiping him carefully with a towel, like a mother with a sick child.

An hour or two passed. Pat grew delirious again, and she gave him some of the boiled water which had grown cool. He gulped it thirstily and then lay back on the cushions, gasping.

"Lie still," she begged. "Lie still and try to sleep."

Pat stared up at her without consciousness.

"Devil," he said through his teeth.

She gave a weak laugh.

"My dear Pat . . ."

"Cruel as hell," he said, and putting up an arm suddenly, caught her slim, small body and pulled her down against him.

"I loved you once," he muttered. "I adored you . . . believed in you. . . ."

Jane struggled in his hold. Her whole body was hot and resentful because she knew that to him she was Sonia, the phantom of his sick ravings.

"Stop that, Pat. Let me go."

He covered her hair with wild kisses.

"You're so lovely . . . so sweet. . . ."

"Let me go, I tell you . . ." said Jane.

She made desperate efforts to get away from him, but in his delirium he was too strong for her and suddenly she felt sick and faint. She struggled no more but lay still, her face buried against his shoulder. He, too, was quiet. For a moment Jane could think of nothing except her hopeless love for this man. The tears sprang to her eyes and scorched her burning face. But she thought:

"I wish I could die . . . like this . . . with him!"

Pat's eyes shut as though he were asleep. For a time neither of them stirred. At length some of the rolling mists cleared from the sick man's brain and he grew suddenly aware of real things. His lashes lifted, saw, hazily, the striped silk curtains and mosaic walls of the Moorish lounge; became conscious of the divan on which he was lying, and conscious, too, that a girl . . .

a slim girl was lying in the crook of his arm crying as though her heart would break.

For a few moments, weak and dizzy, he made neither movement nor did he speak. But he looked stupidly at the girl's dark ruffled head and her prostrate figure in the thin blue linen dress, beside him. Then he knew who it was. With a sense of shock he spoke her name.

"Jane!"

Instantly she drew away from him and sprang to her feet. Gasping, drawing a hand across her wet eyes like an ashamed boy, she looked down at him.

"Jane," he whispered again. "What the devil . . . ?"

"So you're sane again," she broke in.

He knit his brows.

"Sane? What's been happening? What am I doing here? And why were you . . ."

She interrupted him, her cheeks scorching with embarrassment.

"You were delirious. Old idiot, you pulled me down and I couldn't get away . . . raving you were!"

He looked up at her, growing every instant clearer and more fully conscious of things. And very conscious indeed of the memory of Jane lying there sobbing beside him.

"My dear," he said. "Why were you crying?"

"I wasn't!" she said angrily. "And don't talk. You've got to lie quiet. You've been like a madman with fever, but I suppose the aspirin's done the trick. I bunged about half the bottle into you, trying to get your temperature down. I gave you a sponge bath as good as any hospital nurse, too. Here . . . drink some of this. . . ."

She picked up a cup, knelt beside him, and raised it to his lips.

He sipped the water gratefully.

"Thanks, Jane. But sure and I don't understand . . . what's the matter . . . where's everybody?"

Before she could answer remembrance flashed back into his mind. A look of horror came into his eyes.

"Good God . . . *the smallpox* . . . !"

"Oh, do be quiet, Pat. You aren't fit to talk."

"But, Jane," he gasped. "Jane, you oughtn't to be here . . . I might have it. . . ."

"You said you've been vaccinated."

"So I have, but there's a risk."

"I don't think so. I was vaccinated, too. But Sonia wasn't, and she and Uncle John have gone back to Tangier. They'll send an ambulance out from the clinic for you."

"Good God!" he said again. "They left you here?"

"They had to. I wanted to stay."

He lay still, breathing quickly. He wished he did not feel so sick and weak. But he looked at Jane speechless with gratitude. It seemed to him the most wonderful thing in the world that she should have volunteered to stay and take such an appalling risk, no matter how slender the chances of either of them being stricken down. Jane felt suddenly shy of that look in his eyes and turned away from it.

"I'm not worrying," she said briskly.

"But I am," he whispered. "For you . . . you oughtn't to have stayed . . . I can never thank you. . . ."

"There's nothing to thank me for. I only want you to be quiet."

"I will be, Jane, but tell me . . . who else is in the hotel?"

She gave a nervous little laugh.

"Only us, as far as I can see. But what's it matter? We wouldn't dare eat the food even if it was served to us. Anyway it's best for you to keep on water, and I shan't starve. It's all good for the slimming."

"What time is it?"

"About four. Uncle John won't get to Tangier much before midnight because he drives slower than you do. And then if they send the ambulance out straight away it should reach us by ten or eleven to-morrow morning. It isn't so bad."

He lay still again. He had never known anything finer than this girl's pluck. He said huskily:

"Why didn't you go with them? God, Jane, it was swell of you, but you shouldn't . . ."

"Don't say any more. Go to sleep."

"I've been a nice fool, playing this trick on you all, but I think I know what it is. It's a touch of the sun. It affects me that way sometimes. I did this on my father when I was a boy, when we were in Morocco. My temperature plays odd games with me and flies up sky-high for nothing. That's what it is . . . a touch of the sun."

Her heart went out to him in a great rush. Dear God, that was all that mattered to her, to know that there was nothing more wrong with him than that. Out of sheer weakness the tears came into her eyes again and rolled down her cheeks.

"That's grand, Pat."

"*You're* grand," he said. "And Jane, I'm damned sorry if I did or said anything rotten, just now . . . when I was delirious . . . I made you cry . . . and now you're crying again . . . Jane, mavourneen. . . ."

She choked back a sob fiercely. She *would not* make a fool of herself just because she had been through a trying time and her nerves were frayed and her emotions all stirred. But when Pat said "mavourneen" in that devastating voice of his, what was any girl to do . . . any girl who loved him?

"For heaven's sake stop talking and go to sleep," she gasped through her sobs, and terrified of herself, rushed out of the lounge and up to her bedroom.

When she came back to Pat she had herself well in control again. She had taken off her dress, which had been badly crumpled by the tussle with Pat, and put on a dressing-gown of orange Turkish towelling, tied with a cord round the waist. She used it for sea-bathing, as a rule, and as it had sleeves only to the elbows, it was quite a cool thing to wear. It also seemed to her a practical garment in which to nurse Pat. If his temperature went up later on, she would probably have to sluice him down again.

The swift Eastern darkness fell upon them. While it was yet light Jane had taken the precaution of finding a lamp and some matches, for there was no other form of illumination in this primitive hotel. She also had a queer feeling against leaving the place open all night,

and so she went firmly round the hotel and shut and
barred all the doors. She had no wish to be set upon by
a band of desperadoes from the mountains, or some
thieving natives of the town who were willing to risk
"the plague" for what valuables there were to steal. And
by now she knew that she and Pat were utterly alone.
The stricken servants lay in their quarters, which were
in a separate building through a courtyard. And the old
Arab and the kitchen-boy had abandoned their posts.

Pat slept on, for which Jane was profoundly thankful, for it showed an improvement in his condition. By
now she was terribly hungry. She had boiled some more
water and drank plenty of that, but the long day without any nourishment was beginning to tell on her. Also
her nerve was shaken. She sat close to Pat's side, huddled in a chair with a blanket over her knees, for it was
growing cold now that the sun had set. The single oil
lamp shed an eerie light in the Oriental lounge and
flung strange shadows against the walls. It was quiet,
much too quiet. An almost uncanny silence brooded
over Pogador. The only sound to be heard was the distant throb of drums and the thin wail of some Eastern
instrument from the native quarter. That in itself made
sinister hearing.

The worst of Jane's troubles was that she had run out
of cigarettes. She needed one badly to calm her nerves
just now. Her eyelids grew hot and heavy. She longed
for sleep, but dared not close her eyes. Somebody might
break open a window or get into the hotel. She must
keep guard over her patient. After that high fever he
would be very weak and unable to protect himself.

Of course, she was just being a nervous little idiot,
she told herself. Nobody was likely to come near this
place to-night. And to-morrow help would come from
Tangier.

But supposing her uncle and cousin never reached
Tangier? Dear old Uncle John was so unintelligent
about motor mechanism, and if there was a breakdown
he would never be able to put things right. He would
have to wait for help. A delay like that and it would

perhaps mean forty-eight hours before they could send the ambulance to Pogador.

Pat awoke about half-past eleven. Jane gave a little sigh of relief as he opened his eyes. These chill, dark hours, huddled up in her chair, trying to keep awake, had seemed unending.

She lifted the cup of water to his lips, supporting him with an arm.

"Feeling better?"

"M'm," he said drowsily.

She put her fingers on his pulse. It seemed to her a good deal slower. His eyes looked sunken, but there was no longer that hectic flush on his cheeks.

"You *are* better, I believe," she said. "Let's take your temperature."

She could have wept with joy to find that it was just below 100°. Earlier in the day it had been over 103°. She took the thermometer and smiled at him.

"It's well down. You're all right, Pat. I think you're right about the sunstroke. That's all it is. If it had been the *other* you'd have had all sorts of horrid symptoms by now."

He stretched his arms above his head, yawned, and looked round at the lamp-lit lounge.

"Gosh! I feel I've been asleep for years. What have you been doing?"

"Just sitting here."

He looked at the slim young figure in the orange dressing-gown and became aware of the pallor and tension in her face. And he realised suddenly what a strain she had been through.

"Aren't you a marvel," he said. "Just a marvel!"

Jane blushed, and immediately snapped:

"Rot!"

"And are we still ship-wrecked, so to speak, on a desert island?"

"We are. Not a soul in the hotel. I went round before dark. I thought it better to shut ourselves in."

"Much better," he agreed. "Is it late?"

"Getting on for twelve."

"Have you had any sleep?"

"I don't want any."

"That's rubbish. You've been watching me. I'm all right now. You go to sleep now—wrap yourself up on that other sofa over there."

"No, *you* should sleep again."

"I don't want to."

"Pat, you're weak as a rat, and whatever you've got, it's important for you to sleep."

He fixed his blue heavy eyes upon her.

"Do you never think of yourself?"

"Certainly. But I'm not tired. And you're my patient, and you've got to do what the nurse says."

"What a grand nurse she is, too."

Suddenly her head lifted and her eyes widened.

"Listen!"

"What to?"

She didn't answer for a moment. Then she walked to the striped curtains and parted them. After a pause she let them fall again and turned back to him with a half-shamed laugh.

"It's nothing. I just thought I heard . . ."

"You've got the jimjams," he broke in. "And I don't wonder. It's all been an awful strain on you. You're tired out. You've got to sleep now, Jane, and if there's anything to listen for, I'll do the listening for the next few hours."

She walked back to his bedside and was furious with herself because the tears welled into her eyes. She was weak from lack of food, and after the heat, exertion and tension of the day. He saw those tears glittering on her lashes and was filled with indescribable tenderness for her. Until now he had felt too ill to think much about her, but in this hour the full realisation of her courage and what she had done for him came upon him. He held out a hand.

"Come here, Jane."

She obeyed, and found herself placing her fingers in his.

"Now, Pat, be good and sleep again," she began, and made an effort to blink back those tears which she felt were ridiculous.

He said:

"I want to tell you that I think you're the grandest girl I've ever known. Not one in a thousand would have risked smallpox like this. I wish to God I thought I could do something to repay you. If I grow to be a million I shall never forget that you stayed behind in this infernal place with me."

She shook her head mutely, and stood there speechlessly with her hand locked in his. And the sight of Jane Daunt, who had always been so practical, so poised, so cool, looking like a child in her dressing-gown, with her dark, ruffled hair and with those tears streaming down her cheeks, was infinitely moving to him. It was impossible for him not to remember what he had heard last night . . . remember that Sonia had accused Jane of being in love with him. Well, what more could any woman have done for any man, than Jane had done for him this day? And how in God's name was he ever going to repay such a debt?

Suddenly he drew her hand against his cheeks with a caressing movement and then kissed it.

"The grandest girl I've ever known," he repeated. "Thank you, dear, and . . . bless you!"

It took Jane her last ounce of pride and pluck to withstand that stirring tenderness from him. She could so easily have broken down and flung herself straight into his arms. But somehow she managed to laugh helplessly, drag her fingers away and say:

"I'm just the world's idiot. Don't mind me, Pat. It's the diet. I don't think slimming agrees with me."

Then she went back to the chair and drew the blanket firmly round her.

"A few more hours of sleep and you'll be a different man," she added. "And in the morning . . . sing hey for the rescue party!"

"You're an obstinate child," he said. "But I'm obstinate, too, and I am *not* going to sleep until you've had some rest. I can't really think why we don't both go to sleep."

Jane blew her small nose violently.

"Just in case of robbers and thieves."

"Well, I daresay we'll wake up if they come, and as long as they leave us alone they're welcome to take anything they see."

"Quite," said Jane with a laugh that had a break in it.

"Well, I'll make a bargain. I'll go to sleep if you do."

She agreed to that. And once her heavy eyelids closed she was soon fast asleep because she was really worn out. But Pat had no intention of sleeping. It was he who watched over her during the rest of that sinister night, and during that silent watch, the knowledge came to him that all these weeks and months he had been a blind fool. Jane had loved him and he had loved Sonia. And therein he had made the biggest mistake of his life. For it was Jane Daunt and not Sonia who was worth a man's loving, and for Jane, with her grand character and that adorable mixture that was in her of soft femininity and courageous boy, who could fashion the ladder on which a man might indeed, climb to the stars!

Chapter 19

HAD Jane and Pat sat down and thought about it, they might have named a dozen people who would come to their rescue; authorities of the English clinic in Tangier heading the list. But never would they have hit upon the person who was eventually responsible for putting an end to that nightmare scare in Pogador.

Soon after dawn broke over the Moorish town, flushing the white minarets and shuttered houses with rose and opalescent light, a little bus rattled over the cobbled street and pulled up in the square. It was the fortnightly bus from Tetuan, and Pogador's one method of communication with the outer world.

Out of this bus stepped two or three superior Arab merchants, a dark-skinned soldier of the Foreign Legion, the driver with his mail bag, and—a slim, blue-eyed man—who might be English or American—who wore a check suit and a black beret at a rakish angle on his fair head.

He was not surprised by the deserted appearance of the square, for it was still very early in the morning. He found the main entrance barred, and knocked upon it loudly. They should be open to meet the bus, he thought crossly, and stood there in the fresh cool morning yawning and stretching his limbs.

Nobody answered his summons. He knocked again loudly and called in Spanish.

"*Oiga! Dega!*"

It was that call which roused Jane from her slumbers. She started up violently. The little lounge was still dim, for the sunlight had not penetrated through the thick curtains. She looked down at Pat. He was awake and had raised himself on one elbow.

"Somebody at the door. It can't be . . ."

"Not our rescue party, no—" she broke in. "They've scarcely had time to get back from Tangier. It's only five o'clock in the morning."

Fresh banging and roaring at the barred door. An explosive voice making demands in French, Spanish, and English. And it was at the sound of the English that Jane leapt to the door.

"Pat, listen. It'll be help of some kind, anyhow!"

With a fast-beating heart, Jane unbarred the front door of the hotel and flung it open. And the next moment she found herself staring, stupefied, at the fair-haired man in the beret.

"*Maurice!*" she gasped.

Maurice Gardener stared back at her. His face was a study in bewilderment, as he took in the sight of the small girlish figure in the orange dressing-gown, the ruffled hair, and pale little face. Then he took off his beret, blinking hard.

"*Mon Dieu!* Cousin Jane! Am I mad, or is it you?"

At any other time than this Jane would not have

béen pleased to see Sonia's husband. But at the moment
he seemed an angel in disguise, and she straightway began to cry with sheer relief from the nervous tension
which she had passed through since yesterday. She
sobbed:

"Oh, Maurice, but I'm glad to see you."

He came into the hall, shaking his head in bewilderment.

"But, Jane, what does this mean? Why the tears?
Why have you opened the door to me? Is the place bewitched? Are there no servants. . .?"

Jane tried to stop crying.

"No. Nobody. Everyone's gone . . . oh, where have
you come from?"

"On the bus from Tetuan. When I left Tangier I
went straight to Tetuan and was so bored I couldn't remain. I heard there was a night bus leaving for this out-
landish spot. Someone told me it was worth seeing and
that the mountain air would do me good, so along I
came. And *sapristi,* what a journey!"

He broke off and stared at Jane.

"Why are you crying? Where is . . . Sonia?"

Out tumbled Jane's story. Maurice dropped his bag,
lit a cigarette, and listened in amazement. His face
changed colour somewhat when the word "smallpox"
fell from her lips. He clicked his tongue.

"But this is serious. You poor little thing! What an
experience for you. Why in heaven's name didn't you
go with Sonia and Mr. Royale?"

"Because," said Jane in a low voice, "I wouldn't
leave . . . Mr. Connel."

Maurice Gardener pulled his lips down in a grimace.

"The gentleman with the strong right arm, *hein*? But
I thought my charming wife was interested in him."

"I'm afraid you finished all that, Maurice."

"Well, this is no time to discuss such things. Here I
am, a solitary visitor to a stricken town, and your Mr.
Connel . . . has he the smallpox?"

"No, we are both convinced he has not. He had sunstroke. But Sonia was afraid that it was the other thing,

and anyhow his temperature was so high yesterday we dared not move him."

Maurice nodded.

"So like Sonia. She would risk nothing for anybody. But you, Cousin Jane, I have always had a great admiration for you. I'm not surprised you stayed behind."

"Oh, give me a cigarette," said Jane, in confusion. "I've been dying for one."

He handed her his case.

"And I'm dying for food."

"You're not likely to get that . . . the infection. . . ."

"My dear Jane, I have the honour to inform you that I am immune from this plague. I had smallpox as a boy in France. It means nothing to me."

"Then doubtless you'll find something in the kitchen. But you'll have to find it for yourself," said Jane, half-laughing, half-crying.

"I will," he said. "But obviously it is essential for you and Mr. Connel to get away from this place. When do you expect the ambulance?"

"Not for hours. And anyhow we don't need it now. Pat's almost well again—only he's too weak to walk far."

Maurice reflected, biting his lips.

"Then get him dressed, Jane, and I will commandeer the bus."

"The *bus*!" repeated Jane.

"Why not? The driver is a Spaniard. I can tackle him. He expects to remain here until the afternoon, and I can get you and Mr. Connel halfway to Tangier, and we will probably meet the rescue party. I am a good driver—then I will return home with the bus. Much better to get you away at once, isn't it so?"

"It would be a terrific relief," she said. "And, Maurice, it would be wonderful of you. . . ."

He bowed as she paused.

"It will be a pleasure to me to be of some use in this world. My existence is generally futile. You have said hard words to me, Cousin Jane, on one or two occa-

sions, but perhaps maybe you will give me this chance
to show you that I am still—a gentleman!"

Jane wiped her eyes. It was typical of Maurice to be
showy and grandiloquent, but she knew that he was
coming up to the scratch as far as he could do. She said
huskily:

"Thanks, Maurice. You're a brick."

He bowed again.

"From *petite* Cousin Jane that is flattery indeed!"
He went out into the sunlight, prepared to bribe the
driver, commandeer the bus, and take charge of the situation. Jane rushed back to Pat and told him the sur-
prising news.

"Good lord!" said Pat. "What a queer state of affairs . . . Sonia's husband coming to the rescue. Decent of him, Jane—after I've knocked the fellow down,
too!"

"I think he has a good side to him, Pat."

Suddenly he held out a hand to her.

"And you, you've got something in you, Jane, that
would bring out the best in any man."

She clung to his hand for a moment, her tears falling
again.

"Sorry . . . for being . . . so stupid . . . I think
it's just lack of food."

He drew the small hand to his lips.

"As long as I live I shall remember that you risked
sheer horror in order to stay behind and look after me,
Jane. Dear, dear Jane!"

"Oh, don't say nice things to me . . . I'm really not
in the right state of mind to stand it, Pat," she said, her
face puckered and wet with tears. "I'm going upstairs to
dress, and bring down your things. Then we must get
you up. You do feel strong enough?"

"Sure . . . another twenty-four hours and I'll be
myself again. I reckon it's been a bit of fright about
nothing."

She nodded, smiling at him through her tears.

And an hour later they were on the road to Tangier
in that badly sprung, draughty, rattling little bus. Maurice sat at the wheel in excellent spirits, between his lips

a cigarette, which he removed only to utter imprecations against the steering and the gears, which were, he informed his passengers, of pre-historic design.

The passengers themselves sat on their hard seats fully conscious of the luck which had come to them in the shape of Maurice Gardener.

It was good to be away from that hotel and the sinister atmosphere, and much of the discomfort of the bus was mitigated by the cushions and rugs which they had brought with them. Jane, still in her rôle of nurse, had wrapped Pat in blankets and filled a hot-water bottle for his feet, determined that he should not catch cold after the fever. And Maurice had rummaged the kitchens and found tinned biscuits which they could eat without fear and which assuaged some of the pangs of hunger now assailing both patient and nurse.

A never-to-be-forgotten journey!

Jane had little to say. But now and then her soft brown eyes rested upon Pat with a tenderness which she could barely conceal and an immense thankfulness that there was no need to be anxious about his condition.

As for Pat, it was to Jane rather than the passing scenery that his gaze frequently wandered. Gallant Jane, before whom mentally he bent his knee.

As for Maurice Gardener, Pat could only regard the gay, insolent figure at the wheel with a feeling of friendliness. It didn't seem to matter at all that he was Sonia's husband, and that it was he who had shattered the romance which Pat had woven so wildly around her. That all seemed long ago, another life. This was a new life in which reality had replaced romance. And nothing was so real or so important as the friendship which Jane had given him and the love which she had proven up to the hilt.

The sun rose higher as they journeyed along retracing the road which they had taken only two days ago. Soon it grew so hot that Pat was able to dispense with his two layers of blankets and rugs and his hot-water bottle. But Jane fussed over him.

"You're not to catch cold," she kept saying.

He smiled at her and answered:

"All right nurse. I'll be good."

It was not an ambulance which met them two hours later on that remote, sun-baked mountain road. It was the Victor driven by Mr. Royale, with an elderly man wearing glasses seated beside him. Jane and Pat recognised the shining bonnet of the car long before they came alongside. Maurice pulled up with a jerk and Jane climbed down from the bus and ran to Mr. Royale.

"Uncle John!"

He looked at her with amazement. His face was pale and drawn and his eyes bloodshot. He was deadly tired.

"Good heavens!" he exclaimed. "What are you doing in *that*. . . ." he pointed to the queer little bus which had the names of "Tetuan" "Pogador" painted upon it.

Jane explained. She told her uncle all that had happened since yesterday.

"Pat hasn't got smallpox at all," she finished breathlessly. "And I don't seem to be developing it, either. But, oh, Uncle John, we were glad to see Maurice Gardener, I can tell you!"

Mr. Royale drew a hand across his eyes. He had been much more worried about his niece than he cared to admit, and very conscience-stricken at having left her behind him.

"Well, thank God for that!" he said. "It's been a business, I tell you, my dear! I couldn't get an ambulance, and the clinic won't accept smallpox suspects, but I eventually found this extremely kind friend . . ." he indicated the man beside him, ". . . Dr. Pollock. He has a villa in Tangier, and he volunteered to come with me."

Jane greeted the doctor, who said:

"I might as well get out and take a look at the patient."

Whereupon he moved from the Victor into the bus and sat down beside Pat.

"You must be exhausted, Uncle John" said Jane, looking compassionately at Mr. Royale's haggard face.

He wiped his forehead with a handkerchief.

"A bit played out, my dear. I'm too old for these

excitements. As for writing a book on Morocco . . . I'd as soon go home and never set eyes on the infernal country again. This night has taken the spirit of adventure from me, all right."

"I think it's encouraged one in me," said Jane, with a funny little smile.

Mr. Royale looked at the driver of the bus and shook his head.

"Fancy that fellow Gardener turning up! I've never liked him, but I suppose we owe him something for this."

"I think we do," said Jane.

"Have you had anything to eat?" her uncle asked, conscious now that Jane's face was pinched and hollow-eyed.

"Only biscuits," she confessed.

"Well, we've brought hot drinks in thermos flasks, and food," he said. "And before I drive a step farther I'm going to take a cushion and a rug and sleep."

"We might all do the same," said Jane.

Dr. Pollock emerged from the bus and approached them.

"Nothing much wrong with that young fellow except a touch of the sun," he said.

"And I don't think there's much wrong with me except hunger," said Jane.

"You're a lot of frauds," said Dr. Pollock. "But it's just as well you're out of Pogador. It's about the most uncivilised spot in Morocco."

There followed a strange picnic; all of them sitting in the bus. Pat, Jane, and Maurice Gardener drank hot coffee and ate hard-boiled eggs and bread-and-butter ravenously. Never had food tasted so good. Mr. Royale and the doctor joined in the repast, and they might all have been old, attached friends. This queer encounter had brought them in close contact. They found themselves exchanging stories and jokes, laughing helplessly, quarrelling gaily over the last crumb of food and the last drop of coffee.

And after that they slept . . . all of them, including Maurice.

"They'll be raising blue murder in Pogador if I get back late with their bus," he said, "but, *mon Dieu,* I must have my piece of rest as well."

Later, when the afternoon had grown cooler and Pat had been transferred into the Victor, Maurice prepared to make the homeward journey. Jane shook hands with him and said:

"You've been grand to us, Maurice. I'm going to tell Sonia."

He shrugged his shoulders and pulled the beret more rakishly on the side of his head.

"The charming Sonia has no use for me, and I haven't much for her now. She has played the coward in this game."

"One must make allowances for Sonia," said Jane.

"I shall do what she has wanted me to do for so long," he said. "I shall set her free. Good-bye, Cousin Jane. We are not likely to meet again."

Driving back to Tangier in the Victor, Mr. Royale said:

"Not such a bad chap after all, Gardener. Very decent of him to collect that old bus and bring you young people out here. I felt I ought to do something in return, so I told him to look us up next time he was in London."

Pat and Jane exchanged glances. They both knew, somehow, that Maurice Gardener was not likely to call at the Royale house in London.

And John Royale was never to know that it was Sonia's husband to whom he had extended that invitation, for the divorce which set Sonia free later in the year was so discreetly manœuvred that Mr. Royale remained in ignorance of it and of the whole of that disastrous folly which had almost ruined his daughter in Paris two years ago.

Chapter 20

ABOUT a month later Jane Daunt sat in her accustomed place at her desk in the office of the big Royale showrooms in Piccadilly.

She had had a busy day. It was a fine May, and in London there was plenty of business doing in the car world.

Jane, tired and hot, wiped the nib of her pen, sat back in her chair, and lit a cigarette.

It was half-past four. An hour which she had been eagerly awaiting ever since she started work to-day. Pat was coming to see her. There was a letter in her bag from him received this morning, telling her to expect him at this time. He had been away on one of his usual jobs on behalf of the Royale motor company, and Jane had not seen him for a week. A very long week it had seemed, for ever since their return from abroad they had been in contact almost daily. If he didn't catch a glimpse of her here in the office he rang her up at home or took her out for a meal or a picture. Since their adventures in Morocco, and in particular that sinister night together in Pogador, there had existed between them a comradeship and understanding that had been infinitely satisfying to Jane. As far as she could see it had been equally satisfying to Pat.

He had been a changed man since his return to London. The wild, irresponsible, impulsive Irishman had given place to a steadier man; a man still ambitious and hard-working, but with a more fully developed sense of proportion, one who could put a true value on things and did not waste his days in dreaming.

She had heard from everybody in the firm that he had been working furiously, and her uncle had personally expressed himself "pleased with young Connel".

The break between Sonia and Pat was final and absolute. They had not even had to endure each other's company on the return journey from Tangier, because Sonia, once she got back to El Minza, removed herself from the little party. Pat was finished with her, therefore she was finished with him. She had had a letter from an old school friend in Majorca, inviting her to stay out there, and she accepted. She left her father and cousin, pleading as an excuse that the horrible adventure in Pogador had completely destroyed her nerve, and she would not go a mile farther in the car. So Mr. Royale packed her off by sea to Majorca and he, his niece, and Connel returned to England alone.

As far as Jane could judge, Pat had put the past behind him very thoroughly.

During the journey back to England, and in the days that followed, Jane was no longer forced to undergo the torture of seeing the man she loved interest himself in another woman. She might not count in his life except as a friend, as she wanted to, but at least she was spared the misery of watching him head straight for disaster.

Jane looked at her watch. A quarter-to-five. Pat was late. He was coming up from the West country. Probably he was jammed in a traffic block. It was awful driving in London these days, she thought, what with all the heavy vehicles, private cars, all the irritating signals, and the Belisha beacons.

Sonia was coming back from Majorca to-morrow. She had met a marvellous young man out there in whom she was interested, so she had told Jane in the last letter received.

Well, whatever future troubles assailed Sonia, next time Jane was determined not to be mixed up in them. It was quite obvious that Sonia could not be happy unless she had a lover and was satisfying her personal vanity, and equally obvious that no disaster would ever teach her a lesson. One day, no doubt, when she was free, she would marry again, and then some unfortunate man as her husband would have to try to control her.

A voice behind Jane said:

"Hullo!"

Jane, in the act of dusting her small nose and smoothing an unruly lock of hair, swivelled round in her chair.

"Oh! Hullo, Pat. It's you."

Pat Connel came into the office and shut the frosted-glass door behind him. He looked brown and well and was wearing the grey flannels in which Jane always liked him. His blue eyes were brilliant and his voice held a note of excitement as he said:

"Great news, little Jane! G-r-e-a-t news!"

Jane blinked up at him.

"My dear Pat, what's happened?"

He balanced himself on the edge of the desk and handed her his cigarette-case.

"First of all, how's Jane?"

"Fine. And what mischief are you up to, Pat Connel?"

"No mischief at all. Sure and I'm a hard-working devil these days, and you know it. I've just sold two Victors in Devon and Cornwall."

Her brown eyes rested on him with a softness which was for him alone. He was such a boy, this "hard-working devil", and she wished she was not in love with him and that she could just feel in a platonic way about him as he did about her.

"Well," she said. "Come on—out with the news."

"I had a long-distance call from our manager last night. He thought I'd like to know that I'd been promoted."

"Promoted!" repeated Jane. "What to?"

"Sales manager in France, little Jane. Not just salesman in England, but *manager* of the Continental depôt. I hear the Chief was impressed by my knowledge of languages when we were abroad, and they've offered me this job at a salary of one thousand pounds and commission. Jane, it's *grand.*"

She sat still. She wanted to congratulate him. It *was* grand . . . a big job, and it would satisfy quite a few of Pat's ambitions. But it was going to take him away from London . . . from her. With a sinking heart she said:

"How splendid, Pat. No wonder you're excited. I suppose it means you . . . will live in Paris."

"Of course. I love Paris, don't you?"

"Love it," she echoed.

"Won't you smoke?"

"No, thank you."

"And there's some talk of me going to Madrid later on, as well, and trying to interest the Spaniards in our cars."

"Madrid, eh?" said Jane.

Their eyes met. Her lashes lowered nervously, and he suddenly flushed under his tan. They were both remembering that first fatal night they had spent in Madrid, the night when Mr. Royale had found his "chauffeur" kissing his daughter and had dismissed him. That night when Jane had suffered agonies of mind only a shade worse than she suffered now when there was no Sonia, but she was still no more than Pat's friend.

Pat said:

"I'm to start in June—two weeks' time."

Jane drummed her fingers on her blotter.

"So we shan't be seeing much more of you here."

He did not answer for a moment. He looked at her bent dark head. All remembrance of the folly of Madrid and of his infatuation for Sonia Royale was wiped out by another memory . . . one which he regarded as almost sacred . . . a slim young figure in an orange dressing-gown huddled beside him in the shadows in a Moorish hotel lounge; a gallant young figure keeping guard over him . . . a very gallant girl who had stayed behind in a fever-stricken town to nurse him and had taken an appalling risk for him.

He had realised that night that she loved him. He realised this afternoon that he loved her. And he did not know what to say, he, who was usually so ready with speeches, with an Irishman's faculty for making love to a pretty woman. But this was different, this profound feeling which welled up in him for Jane Daunt and brought a lump to his throat.

She looked up at him, her eyes bright and rather hard.

"You'll have to write occasionally and tell me how you're getting on."

"Will you miss me, Jane?"

She blushed to the roots of her hair.

"What a conceited question!"

"Well, will you? Tell me."

"Certainly not."

"You mean you won't miss me?"

"Why should I?"

"You're hedging."

"Oh, don't be so silly, Pat."

"Perhaps I am silly," he said. "But I've a notion that I'm going to miss you . . . just like hell!"

Her heart raced.

"Oh, no you won't."

"But I will, Jane, because your friendship means so much to me."

"You'll make new friends . . . in Paris."

"Maybe. And fall in love with a gay Parisienne, eh?"

Jane met his gaze unflinchingly.

"I wouldn't be at all surprised."

"Well, I would," he said roughly, "because I don't like Frenchwomen. And I'm not likely to fall in love with anybody. I'm much too much in love with you."

That staggered Jane so completely that she could only stare up at him speechlessly, her face changing from red to white. Then she gasped:

"Pat!"

He seized both her hands and wrung them.

"But it's true, Jane, mavourneen. I'm hopelessly in love with you. And it isn't a light, frivolous sort of love, nor an infatuation. I just adore you. I've been at your feet ever since that night in Pogador. I knew then that you were the grandest girl in the world."

"But—how absurd!"

"You mean you don't believe me. You have doubts of me? You think I change my feelings easily and quickly? But you've got to try and understand that that experience with Sonia *was* only an experience which just took all the scales from my eyes and taught me facts. And you . . . you've taught me all that I ever want to know. You've been so good to me, Jane. I suppose it's too much for me to expect you to go on being good . . . to ask you to try to believe me when I tell you that I love you better than anyone, anything in the world."

She shook her head dumbly, her fingers trembling in his.

"I don't know what to believe," she said weakly:

"But you must. I couldn't go on if you didn't. And that job in Paris won't mean a thing to me unless you'll come with me, Jane."

"Come with you!" she repeated.

"Yes. Marry me and come and live with me in Paris, my dear. I feel I've got something to offer you. A good job and a good screw. Of course the Chief may chuck me out for daring to propose to his niece. But as you've told me in the past, I've got plenty of nerve. Jane, *darling,* won't you marry me?"

"I . . . I can't think."

"I'll go to the Chief to-night and ask permission."

"Certainly not!" cried Jane. "Uncle John has no say at all in my private affairs. I shall marry whom I choose."

"But supposing he chucks me out?"

"He won't. I won't let him."

Pat drew a deep breath.

"Then you mean you *will* marry me?"

"I suppose so," said Jane weakly. "I expect I'm mad as a hatter. But I must . . . I must come with you, Pat. I love you so much! Life doesn't mean a thing to me either, without you."

He pulled her out of the chair into his arms.

"You're too good for me, Jane, but if you'll take me as I am . . . there's nothing I won't do to justify your trust in me."

Her arms were about his neck, and her cheeks, wet with tears, pressed against his. She whispered:

"If you love me, that's enough."

"Ah, *you* know how to love, Jane, my dearest. Haven't you proved it . . . a dozen times? Jane, you must teach me something about it, too. I want to learn all over again. And I swear you won't have to pull me out of Moorish cafés, or lecture me . . ."

"More than once a year?" she finished for him, half-laughing, half-crying.

"Never," he said, smoothing the dark hair back from her forehead. "Never, my sweetheart, if I have you. You're so *very* sweet!"

An office boy opened the door and peered in; Jane, with Pat's lips upon hers, was not aware of the fact. The boy gave one look at the Chief's secretary and the young Irish salesman locked in each other's arms, then went out again, mischievously whistling: "Love in Bloom."

BOOK III

Sweet Cassandra

For
"Burney" and Peggy

Chapter 1

IT was Cassandra's habit to get up in the morning and switch on her little radio so that she could hear some dance music and perform one or two neat steps across her bedroom while she pulled on her tights and put on her bra, then sluiced her face madly in cold water. She had always had a lovely skin and believed it was because she washed with soap and water. She used creams only as a foundation for make-up.

It was a misty May day, with the golden promise of sunshine. Cassandra (nobody ever called her that except her stepfather who was an appalling egotist and in her estimation spent his time in trying to be different from everybody else) was better known as Cass. She loved light music and was naturally of a cheerful disposition; in her way quite a philosopher for all her youth. She believed in the saying: *Laugh and the world laughs with you.* At the same time she was practical and had a strong streak of common sense. This had always been of great help to her—a sensible and cheerful person was better able to cope with life and Cass's life, ever since her well-loved father died, had been far from happy.

This room, which was really a large attic with sloping roof on one side, and a dormer window, was to her more of a home than the rest of the house. The one room in which she could keep her own treasures; do as she liked; get away from the overbearing influence of the General—General Miles Woodbeare, D.S.O., whom her mother had married a year after Cass's father died; that was ten years ago. And Cass might well have grown gloomy and discontented. Nothing had gone her way since she was adolescent, and she wasn't altogether sure it had gone Mummy's way; yet Mummy had seemed deeply in love with Miles Woodbeare at first. Even Cass who disliked him, could not deny that he was exceedingly handsome—all six foot two of him. Straight, soldierly, with thick prematurely grey hair, and still young-looking for his fifty years. But as Cass often thought with some bitterness, nobody knew what a supremely self-centred and even heartless being existed behind that classic face. Kevin—Cass's boy-friend, who didn't like the General any more than she did—said that he had seen through him right away; those blue eyes were so glacial and the lips, half-hidden by the thick grey moustache, too thin—almost cruel.

However, it was not of her stepfather Cass was thinking this morning as she danced around her little room—her holy-of-holies as she called it. Sometimes Cass had to admit that Mummy wasn't interested in anybody but the General, and that *she* had taken second place to her stepfather during the last ten years. Before that, the family—Mummy, Daddy and herself, had seemed gloriously united.

At this moment it was Kevin who occupied all of Cass's mind and heart. Kevin she was thinking of while she listened to a woman on the radio crooning that haunting Irish folksong:

> *I know where I'm going*
> *And I know who'll go with me*
> *I know who I love*
> *But the de'il knows who I'll marry.*

"But it's not only the devil—it's me. *I know who I'll marry,*" Cass muttered and stopped dancing around. She was wasting time. She quickly outlined her rather sweet full mouth with a new pale lipstick. It toned well with her caramel-coloured mini-skirt. With it she wore a white shirt and cardigan which Mummy had chosen and the General paid for (reluctantly, Cass was sure). He gave it to her for her twentieth birthday, a week ago. She liked herself in this caramel shade. It suited her long silky gold brown hair which she wore parted in the middle, and it fell on either side her oval face.

Mummy did not mind this long hair. She and Cass were a bit alike, although Mummy was over forty now and her hair was cut short and curled.

Poor Mummy! Cass was sure she was scared of the General. He could be difficult when he was crossed. Cass, who still wanted to love her mother, was ashamed of her because she was so weak. Kevin had lately taken to calling her *'Yes-dear'* because she seemed to spend her life being servile to the General.

"How's *'Yes-dear'* today?" Kevin would ask Cass when they met, and she would answer:

"Now, Kev, don't be beastly. Mum can't help it. If she said 'No dear', to him, he'd create."

When Cass and Kevin fell in love, at a Charity Ball where they first met and danced together, Cass broke through the wall of reserve she had built around herself, and confided all her troubles to Kevin. His extraordinary gifts for listening with sympathy and understanding drew her to him. It was wonderful—after her life with a stepfather who neither listened nor sympathised with anyone.

Yes, Cass reflected this morning, *I do know where I'm going now and I know who I'll marry. It'll be Kevin or nobody.*

But when? How? With *him,* that wretched General, so dead against them. Now because she knew that it was expected of her, she ran down a flight of stairs and knocked on the door of *their* bedroom.

Her natural high spirits evaporated as she walked into the room. There was her stepfather in a smart dressing-gown in the centre of the double bed, spruce, shaved, full of dignity, while Mummy sat at a table beside him fully dressed and looking a little wan and tired. She had been up earlier to get the breakfast and carry up the tray. As usual, the General was 'creating'. What about Cass did not know but outside the door she had heard the loud voice of authority declaiming.

"Good morning, darling," Dorothy Woodbeare said timidly, as she turned what Cass called 'her pathetic spaniel look' upon her daughter.

The General did not waste time. As a military man he favoured direct attack. He removed his horn-rimmed glasses, stared at Cass with his cold blue eyes, and barked:

"I have been telling your mother finally and definitely, Cassandra, that I will not agree to this ridiculous marriage you want. I do not approve of your young man."

Cass felt the hot colour scorch her cheeks then drain away. Her hands, clutching her white plastic bag, trembled suddenly. She no longer felt gay. This awful man seemed to have the knack of reducing her in a flash to depression and antipathy. Before she could control herself, she rose to the defence of Kevin.

"Well, *really*—what a beginning to anybody's day! Why must you be so unpleasant about my future husband?"

"Future husband!" The General bellowed the words. "Did you hear that, Dorothy? She speaks of him as her *future husband.*"

"Oh, dear," whispered Mrs. Woodbeare.

She was, as everybody knew, a weak character. With Cass's father it had been all right because he was a kindly, charming man, who had managed to carry her along on the wings of his love. She had been happy with him. And they had both adored their little daughter. When poor David was alive, they had lived in the country near Brighton, where once David worked as a dental surgeon. They had led a peaceful sort of existence. There were never any fireworks or disputes. Now there seemed to be at least one, daily.

She had never meant it to be like this. After poor David died suddenly of a heart condition and left her badly off, she had thought it wonderful to have met and married a fine splendid-looking man like General Woodbeare. At the time of their meeting when they were all on holiday in Majorca, staying at the same hotel, Miles had seemed to adore her, and he had been so nice to little Cass. Dorothy felt sure he would make her a good father. He had been a confirmed bachelor. He was still in the Army. He seemed delighted with his attractive wife and a home life instead of barracks or Clubs. But it didn't work out that way. Almost as soon as they returned from the honeymoon, Miles exhibited that other side of his nature. Dorothy soon learned that the handsome hearty soldier could also be a tyrant and a bully. A man of set ideas who wanted to rule the roost, found Cass a nuisance and was jealous of the time and love his wife gave to the child.

So it had ended in Cass and her mother gradually being separated from each other. Cass was sent to boarding-school and kept there whether she liked it or not. The General always upset or scared her and she was not as ready and willing as her mother to be bullied. She had more spirit. The two had clashed from the start.

When the General retired from the Army and bought this house in Putney, Cass during the holidays never really relaxed or was left alone with her mother. The General expected her to follow the strict routine he set for her, and to obey him. Dorothy knew full well that she had failed her daughter, but she could not bear scenes and kept out of the rows. Besides, she, too, was an egotist at heart. *She* wanted to keep her husband's love and attention. In a cowardly way she sided with him against the young girl.

"Oh, dear," she whispered again this morning, then, as usual, appealed to Cass: "Try and do as your father wants, dear, please."

That put Cass into a resentful mood. She never did look on the General as her father. She addressed him by his military prefix.

"I'm sorry, General, sorry, that is, that you don't like Kevin, but you are not fair to him—honestly!"

"Oh, he's a nice enough boy, but I don't think he's what Father and I really want for you—" began Mrs. Woodbeare. The General waved a silencing hand in his wife's direction, without looking at her, and interrupted:

"I'll deal with this, Dorothy."

Cass stood rigid and still while her stepfather loudly listed all the things he had against Kevin Martin.

He was only twenty-three—too young to marry. He hadn't established himself anywhere in the world at *anything*. True he had a degree in English for which he had worked at Bristol University—but the lowest possible one. He was without real ambition, had so far taken only odd jobs—like being a salesman in a bookshop or some other temporary work, and now he thought he was a writer, the General added scathingly. No settled career or income. And what with that hair that needed cutting and the careless way he dressed, he was all that the General detested. He could not actually call Kevin a beatnik but he had no background, no prospects. How the devil did Cass think that he could support a wife?

Cass listened to all this, and more. Her lips took a mutinous curve down, but she stared back bravely at her stepfather's scowling face.

She said:

"I haven't much time to tell you what *I* really think of Kev. I've got a job and it takes me a long time to get to the Strand. But you really don't know Kevin. He's unusually clever. He gained an honours degree at Bristol University and he worked for it, didn't he?"

"His aunt had to subsidise him from the time he left school," argued the General. "And he hasn't settled down to a proper regular job."

"That isn't his fault," explained Cass, her eyes flashing indignantly. "We've had this all out before, and as I've told you, General, it's unfair to criticize Kevin as you do. His parents were killed in an air crash. They didn't leave him a sou. His aunt believed in him enough to help him over his education. And I believe in him enough to want to marry him. He *has* got ambition, and he *will* make a writer one day. He doesn't want a settled job till he's found his feet in the literary world. He writes good articles and he intends finally to write a book."

"The rubbish they publish today," sneered the General, putting on his glasses again and grimacing.

"Oh, you're so prejudiced against Kev. I hate you!" cried Cass with unaccustomed heat. Her mother gasped.

"Cass!"

"It's just as I would expect," said the General, snorting. "Thanks to your upbringing, Dorothy, your daughter is not only impertinent to me but hopelessly prejudiced in favour of all the wrong things and the wrong people in the world today. These young upstarts think they know everything. They lack morals and manners and they—"

Cass, still daring, broke in:

"I haven't time to listen to a diatribe against modern youth. If I miss my bus, I'll lose my job."

"Oh, Cass, do tell your stepfather you did not mean to be rude!" implored Mrs. Woodbeare.

Cass looked at her mother with a mixture of pity and scorn.

"I'd just like to say, Mummy, that I am what I am today scarcely because of *your* upbringing. For the last ten years I've been dictated to either by the headmistress of my school or by General Miles Woodbeare, D.S.O."

"I will *not* have this impertinence!" thundered the General, and glared at the slim defiant young girl. Her beauty and grace and natural sweetness completely escaped him. He hated her for the way in which she stood up to him and what little money she had cost him over the years. He was a mean man and defiance was a thing Miles Woodbeare had never been able to tolerate.

After Cass swept out of the room, he turned upon his wife, who had risen to her feet and gone to search for a face tissue in order to wipe away her tears.

"For God's sake, don't start snivelling, Dorothy, you know how it annoys me. Do something more constructive than cry. Make that daughter of yours see sense."

Mrs. Woodbeare came back, tissue pressed to her lips.

"Miles, you must remember, dear, that you can't easily control a girl of Cass's age. She's twenty and has been earning her living for the last eighteen months, and she does give us a few pounds a week towards her keep, and after all, Mrs. Taylor's girl, next door, is allowed to keep all her earnings for herself."

"I don't care a damn about the Taylors. Anyhow, Taylor is in the City, earning quite a bit of money and their house is twice as big as ours. They can afford a full-time gardener, instead of which I have to do all the mowing, etc. I have only my pension and small private means and you know what my taxation is."

Dorothy sat down by the bed and tried to smile a

little timid smile in order to soften up her exacting and frightening husband.

"Darling, you know how much I admire you and I hardly ever take Cass's part, but these days girls and boys do seem to make their own lives. Parents can't choose their daughter's husband."

"Do you want her to marry that mixed-up youth then? Do you call *him* a suitable husband in any way for your daughter? *My* step-daughter? I wouldn't want to introduce Kevin Martin to anybody in my Club, or acknowledge him as a son-in-law."

Mrs. Woodbeare felt compelled to protest.

"Darling, he isn't as bad as that. He hasn't got long hair like some—it's only a *bit* long at the back, and they all wear it that way now, and even if he doesn't dress like a military man, he isn't *freakish* like some of them, is he?"

"Maybe not, but he has little to recommend him. Cass hinted last night that they don't intend to wait. It's outrageous—not even an engagement; no announcement in the *Telegraph;* no proper procedure; and no money. As I said just now, he hasn't even got a proper job."

"Oh, I agree with you, Miles, that it would be foolish, but—"

"But what?" he cut in irritably.

"They seem very much in love."

"Oh, don't be asinine, Dorothy; *in love!*"

She gave him a wistful look from large eyes that had lost much of their brilliance.

"We were once very much in love in Majorca, weren't we?"

The General coughed, cleared his throat and crackled the pages of his daily paper.

"I dare say. I dare say. But we are at least sensible people who knew their own minds. These two are idiots. Anyhow I am not prepared to sit and listen to sentimental reminiscences at this time of the morning. All I can say is that it's a pity Kevin Martin can't be put into uniform and sent to the battlefront."

"What battlefront, dear?" asked Mrs. Woodbeare unhappily.

"Oh, I don't know. Let's talk of something else. We will have nothing more to do with her. She is behaving very stupidly. Most ungrateful after all *I've* done for her."

Mrs. Woodbeare was near to tears again. With sudden uneasiness she cried:

"Whatever we do, don't let's drive her into leaving home and eloping with him."

The General glared at her.

"Now, you're not going to suggest Gretna Green or some such idiocy."

"No, that's out of date, but young people today do get married willy-nilly and magistrates let them. Cass hasn't got my soft nature, really, Miles. She's like her father. He was soft in one way but very determined in another and she's the same. I'd hate her to leave home in anger."

"She can go to the devil," said the General whose temper this morning was at its worst. "And if she is foolish enough to defy us, she won't see either of us again."

Dorothy Woodbeare sat silent now, completely crushed. She supposed she had brought all this on herself by her second marriage. She could hardly bear the idea of seeing Cass go right out of her life. She wouldn't see her grandchildren, if they had any, either. She would have *nothing* in her old age.

Now her tears really fell thick and fast, and in order not to anger Miles, she picked up the breakfast-tray and hurried out of the room.

Chapter 2

"I JUST don't think I can stand life at home much longer."

Cass made this announcement after taking a long drink of Coke through a straw, straight from the tin she was holding. It was an exceptionally warm day now that the mists had cleared. She sat on a bench in Temple Gardens, with Kevin beside her, eating the remains of his ham roll. They often met and lunched here like this when the weather was fine. It was lovely near the shining Thames, and the song of the birds in the trees made them feel that they were in the country rather than the City of London. It was an easy meeeting-place for both of them. Kevin at the moment was doing a temporary job in an advertising firm with offices in Chancery Lane. Cassandra worked for a goldsmith and silversmith firm in the Strand.

This was, for Cass, the loveliest hour of the day, but just now she looked rather mournfully at the sparrows hopping on the grass in front of them picking up the crumbs. She dabbed her lips with a tissue and sighed deeply.

"It's always been the same since I grew up. My life's been ruined by the General. If only darling Daddy hadn't died and Mum hadn't married that ghastly man."

"I must say he *is* pretty ghastly," agreed the young man beside her. "Perfect gentleman, ever-so-military and all correct, but there's a nasty bit of flint where his heart ought to be."

"Pity we can't arrange a transplant for him," said Cass with a sudden return of her old humour.

Kevin put an arm round her shoulders. She felt a lot

better under that warm pressure, and better still when she heard him murmur:

"Poor sweet Cass—you've had one hell of a time! I lost my own parents when I was young but Aunt Millie was always good to me and I still miss the old girl. It's just a pity she was living on an annuity which, of course, ended with her death. She always told me she would have nothing to leave—even the house she lived in was only rented. I might in ordinary circumstances have had the furniture and effects, but we talked it over and I said I wanted to stand on my own feet, and anyhow she wanted to leave what was in the house to an old woman who had looked after her for twenty years. I think she needed it more than I did. A bachelor of my age should ask nothing of anybody really. I have never approved of inherited wealth."

"I think that's great," said Cass, "I admire your outlook, darling. I want to make my own way, too. Why not?" and she threw back her head defiantly.

He liked to see that swift graceful defiant gesture. He liked the way Cass's long leaf-brown hair tossed about her bare slender neck as she moved it. He liked everything about her. It had been a question of love at first sight with him. There had been a series of girlfriends before but none of them serious. Cass was the one.

"The fact is," he said, "I know you live quite comfortably in the Putney house and so on, and if we get married now, it'll be a good old sit-in with no money for theatre tickets or flicks or anything I'd like to buy you, etc." And he flung the final remains of his roll on to the grass. The sparrows, already satiated, despised it and flew away.

"Lucky brutes," Kevin added, "they've got nice warm nests and they can sit on them and bill and coo, and they have no rates or taxes or any restrictions. Why aren't we birds?"

"I'm your bird, darling," said Cass rather flippantly, for she wasn't feeling flippant today. She still carried an ugly memory of what the General had said this morning. She continued: "Seriously speaking, Kev, I couldn't care less about having to economise if I could be with you. I don't have all that much of a good time in Putney I assure you. The General just kills me. And it kills me to see my poor weak Mama giving in to him like she does."

Kevin folded his arms across his chest and frowned.

"Your mother is very sweet and all that but I don't think much of the way she's neglected you all these years for that foul fellow."

"I suppose she was in love. *I* ought to understand about love," said Cass feelingly.

"Don't line me up alongside General Miles Woodbeare, for Pete's sake!" exclaimed Kevin, grimacing at her. "Falling in love with me is quite different."

Her warm hazel eyes smiled at him.

"You mean you aren't a foul fellow?"

"Certainly not, I'm a brilliant young writer in the making, I'm honest and I've got a kind heart and the girls queue for me."

"And you're disgustingly vain."

"Oh, *darling*, I'm *not!*" he protested.

Then they laughed at each other.

"I don't think you are really," she complied. "You're the reverse. You know what I think of you, Kev. To me you're marvellous."

"The Lord knows why," he said, "but I'm grateful." And he bent and quickly touched her warm cheek with his lips.

She felt nearer to him than she had ever done and full of love—a love that was fast becoming like a shining armour against the sorrows and misfortunes of the world. She had not really known how lonely she was until she met Kevin. She had had to live her life in a solitary sort of way apart from her mother and stepfather even though she was under the same roof with them. She had one or two good friends and she had gone out with boys now and then, but when Kevin came along it was different. He was so special. He was right when he said he had a warm heart and complete honesty. He was a bit of a visionary, too. At times, perhaps, inclined to dream, to theorise rather than put his best ideas into firm practice; and he was hopeless about money. He had spent a lot on her since they met—much against her wishes. Without actually having to borrow he nearly always seemed in debt and having to work extra hard at night, writing articles to make a bit of cash, instead of getting on with the book he was always talking about.

He was certainly not as practical as Cass, but she kept telling herself that he was a creative artist, and people like that were not the plodders and savers of this world. It did not make her love him any the less—on the contrary, his artistic qualities, and his knowledge, and the interesting way he talked and debated with their young friends, fascinated her.

The man with whom he shared a flat had told Cass only the other day that he thought Kevin would go far and that he had such 'a damned good brain'. Cass believed that once she was his wife she could look after him and leave him free to write as he wanted to. He was so sure he would make the grade one day as a novelist.

Now she felt the pressure of his arm around her again.

"Look at me, Cass," he said.

She turned to him. She adored his eyes—they were so blue under their thick black lashes. He looked rather Irish. His mother had come from Connemara. Kevin was the name of his uncle who had been killed during one of the Irish uprisings.

The longish hair that the General deplored was thick and dark with a wave in it. Kevin's face was too thin and haggard for classic good looks. But Cass thought him terribly interesting to look at. With those high cheekbones, his was an arresting face. He had a warm expressive voice. It she admitted he had faults, egotism was the worst; too much concentration on self. He became so absorbed in whatever he was saying or doing he was sometimes quite impatient with her for distracting his thoughts. She was sure this was all part of his creative subconscious mind. An egotism that might lead to big things. Besides, when he was concentrating on *her* as he was doing now, who could be more wonderful, or make a girl feel more deeply loved? Yes, she was sure of his love and that they were right for each other.

"I am looking at you, Kev," she said in a voice of make-believe meekness. "What do you want from your slave?"

"Slave be damned," he said, and kissed the tip of her ear, "*I'm* the slave. I just want to say that as you're so unhappy at home, I refuse to leave you there a day longer. You've given them a chance to say yes, and to help fix up a nice little conventional wedding. Well—we don't want it. Whoever wants a sort of 'do' with you in white satin, veil and orange blossom, and me in a morning coat, and all that Edwardian nonsense of a reception afterwards? We can do better than that."

Cass bit her lips. She had long since realised that the average man did not perhaps share the average girl's enthusiasm for conventional weddings. She rather fancied a bit of what Kevin called 'frightfulness'. But during these last few months, constantly in Kevin's company, she herself had changed. He was making her feel that in this difficult turbulent world, it was simple down-to-earth action that people needed. But she would never have dreamed of telling anybody, especially not her mother, that they had once discussed the idea of living together without getting married. But Cass had felt glad when Kevin himself decided it would not be a good idea. One or two of his friends had done this sort of thing, then parted from the girl, and set up house with someone else. Kevin was 'with it' but he did believe firmly in marriage and fidelity and having a family. They were agreed on that.

"What have you in mind, Kev?" she asked. He moved away from her, took a packet of cigarettes from his pocket, then put it back, and leaning forward, glanced over his shoulder at her and gave a wry smile.

"Better cut the gaspers out, eh? I'll have to save some money now."

Her heart jerked. That remark had only one implication.

"You really mean you want us to get married straight away?"

"If *you* want to."

"Do *you* really want to?" she parried.

"You don't know how much," he answered with an

emotion that stirred her whole heart and brought the flaming colour to her cheeks.

"Oh, Kev—*darling* Kevin, do we dare?"

"I'm a free man. I can do what I want. You're the one's who's got to face the music."

"Darling, it would be lovely music and I wouldn't mind. The General said categorically this morning that he would not agree to our marrying, and Mummy does exactly what *he* says. But there is little they can do about it."

"Quite!" agreed Kevin.

He stared at a solitary sparrow which had come back to peck at the end of his roll. His mind was pushing ahead as it often did into a far-distant future when he would be a famous writer and he and Cass would live in a super house with a garden, in the country which they both liked. They would have a big car and he'd take Cass on the Continent for holidays; and in time they'd have a couple of kids. It would be an improvement on life. He had enjoyed his years at university with Barney Dixon, with whom he now shared a flat. But Barney, who was in an architect's office as a trainee, was off to his first job in Scotland. There had been some talk about a fellow they knew taking his place, but Kevin had not been keen on the idea. Besides, he disliked that two-roomed flat with the bath in the kitchen and windows at the back of a tall house that faced a noisy garage, not far from Russell Square. It was all right for two chaps but Kevin couldn't imagine taking Cass there. Somehow he'd have to find a more suitable place for her.

When he spoke, his voice was abrupt.

"Let's get married first, Cass, and cry about it afterwards."

She gripped his hand, put it against her cheek, then laughed.

"What a thing to say! We won't cry about it ever. We'll celebrate permanently."

"Okay," he said. "We'll celebrate. Let's make our plans."

She drew breath. She was enormously flattered because this wonderful young man wanted to marry her instead of thinking it a good plan to remain single. Oh, she loved him so much, she wouldn't want to be an encumbrance.

"We can both keep our jobs for the time being," she said eagerly, "and we'll find somewhere nice to live and share expenses. Everyone does now."

"Well, Barney's moving out the first week in June. I don't want you to live there. It's pretty ropy. But you've seen it—that day you came to the drink party and met Barney. You didn't like it, did you?"

"No, but if I were your wife and it was our home I'd soon make it quite different!" she said, flushed with enthusiasm. "It's only a question of a little painting or papering, and making it all nice and cosy, which two men haven't got it in them to do."

"The woman's touch, you mean," Kevin smiled.

"It'll be heaven after Putney," she assured him. "But do you *really* want to give up your freedom for me, Kev? Wouldn't you rather wait?"

"And have you bullied by that arrogant ape who expects you to dance to his tune all the time? To hell with that, my love."

"Okay, to hell with that," Cass echoed cheerfully, "I'll tell them at home tonight."

"You will?" He took both her hands and looked deeply into her eyes. "Cass, you're a super person. You're really great."

"I'll adore to face whatever comes with you, Kev," she whispered.

So they made their plans.

Chapter 3

THE storm that broke that same evening in the usually
quiet sedate Putney home of General Miles Woodbeare,
D.S.O., was a major one. At first Cass had told Kevin
to leave her to manage it alone, but he insisted on being
with her. This, of course, enhanced him in her eyes.
Poet, artist, whatever he was, Kevin Martin was no
coward and he wasn't going to let Cass take the full
force of the General's ire on her slim shoulders alone.

Kevin followed Cass into the sitting-room where the
Woodbeares were just about to switch from T.V. News
to *All Our Yesterdays* which was the General's favourite. All guns and men in uniform and pictures of a past
in which he felt himself to have been the greatest of all
heroes and the one who most deserved his medals.

He did not get up as his stepdaughter walked in, but
glared at the tall thin young man behind her. The long-
haired untidy-looking Mr. Martin, who looked as
though he needed a bath, the General thought, forgetful
of the fact that he had not had any time to wash or
change since he had done a full day's work in the heat
of the City.

He addressed Cass.

"I thought I told you that your—er—*friend* . . .
was not welcome in this house, Cassandra."

Mrs. Woodbeare looked nervously from her husband
to the young couple. She pretended not to have heard
what Miles said.

"Oh—er—come in, er—you both look as though
you would like a nice cool drink—" she began.

The General held up a hand, his eyes as usual like
blue stones behind the horn-rimmed glasses.

"Just a moment, Dorothy."

As her mother stood to attention, Cass felt the usual pity for her, yet wished, passionately, that she had been the sort of woman that would be strong and maternal and ready to take her daughter's part: like Mrs. Burnham, the mother of Cass's best friend, Elizabeth, who was always called Liz. There had been a crisis in Liz's life over some young man her father hadn't wanted her to marry, and Mrs. Burnham had been absolutely super and stood by Liz all the time. How she wished that Liz wasn't going to be married at the end of the summer. She would miss her.

Now the General fixed his gaze upon Kevin.

"When I was a young man of your age, I was a subaltern in the Army and accustomed to discipline, and, I *hope*, one who respected the wishes of his seniors. I made it clear to you when we last met that I did not wish Cassandra to associate with you."

Kevin froze. He pushed a lock of dark hair back from his forehead and stood looking mutinously at the detestable man whom Cass had the misfortune to own as stepfather.

"First of all, sir, you may be senior to me but I do not consider you my *superior*—certainly not in the way a subaltern thinks of his commanding officer, neither do I think you have any justifiable reason in forbidding Cass to associate with me."

The General glared.

"That, sir, is for me to decide."

Here Cass broke in:

"I really must remind you, General, that you are *not* my father. I know I've been brought up with you but it doesn't give you the right to control my life."

He glared at her.

"You have always been ungrateful, Cassandra, for all that I have done for you—and your mother."

Mrs. Woodbeare blinked her weak eyes. She wasn't really certain what her second husband *had*, in fact, done for her or Cass except make them both unhappy, but she was far too timid to say so. She kept telling herself how splendid Miles was, how *distinguished*. Although in her heart of hearts she rather liked Kevin

Martin. She could feel his charm. She was feminine enough for that.

Cass continued to speak:

"As I told you this morning, you have nothing really against Kevin, but we've had all this out before. What we've come to tell you tonight is that we intend to get married the first week in June."

The silence that followed this brave speech froze the atmosphere completely. But Kevin did not let any time elapse before he added:

"Exactly so. And I have dared to darken your threshold tonight, General Woodbeare, because I consider it up to me to inform you face to face that whatever you say or do, I shall marry Cass. So that is *that*."

The General rose to his feet, buttoned up his jacket and straightened his striped regimental tie. Dorothy Woodbeare sat down because her legs refused to support her. Her face puckered in preparation of tears, but no tears came. Dry-eyed and fearful she looked at her daughter. Cass, who had a very soft side to her, went to her, and put an arm around the slight shoulders, noting not for the first time how much older her mother was beginning to look—quite a lot of grey in the brown hair and far too many lines around her eyes. It almost frightened Cass to think that love could end like this . . . the woman who had once been madly in love, discovering that her choice was the type the General had turned out to be; yet still struggling pathetically after long years to preserve her romantic belief that she still loved him. Poor Mummy!

Once Cass had felt a little scared of taking this vastly important step. She was fully aware that she would probably be 'thrown out' by the General. But she had overcome those doubts and fears. She was sure that she would be terribly happy with Kevin, no matter how poor they would be or how much of a struggle faced them. She felt full of confidence that she would never share her mother's fate and live to regret her marriage.

"Don't be too upset, Mummy," she whispered, while the General and Kevin continued to exchange decidedly acrimonious words, neither giving way an inch. "I do love Kevin so much and it's no good my going on living here like this, making you miserable as well as myself."

Mrs. Woodbeare bowed her head.

"Don't do it, Cass. It'll be worse when you've gone."

Cass felt uncomfortable.

"You mean he'll take it out on you if I defy him?"

"Oh, Cass, you may be right, but how can you live on what you two earn and with no capital—nothing behind you?"

"We young ones don't need capital—we're not like you," said Cass bravely.

The General caught these words. He had been keeping an ear open to what his wife and stepdaughter were saying. He snapped:

"And more's the pity. If you behaved as decently and properly as your mother's generation, you'd be the better for it."

"I doubt if there's any use our bickering like this," said Kevin abruptly. "Our generation is not at all like yours, and I don't suppose yours was like *your* father's."

"I beg to differ," the General thundered, scowling at Kevin over his glasses. "My father and I were alike, both soldiers—decent men with standards. And with us there was none of this permissive society—and all this fancy dress, drug-taking and so on—" and the General waved an arm in the air, then added: "But you're right. There *is* no use in our continuing this discussion. Kindly leave the house. If Cassandra wishes to wreck her life, then she must leave it with you."

This for Cass was not unexpected. She had discussed every eventuality on the way home with Kevin. But her heart sank a little as she saw the way her mother seemed to go to pieces. Dorothy Woodbeare sat there shaking, sudden tears pouring down her cheeks.

Cass swung round to her stepfather.

"I hope you think it right and proper to bully Mummy and everyone the way you do, and make Mummy miserable!" she said furiously.

The General did not answer. He seated himself, picked up a *Country Life* and started to read it.

Kevin held out a hand to Cass.

"Come on, let's go. It's his sort of intolerance, and

lack of understanding that causes student revolts, and our desire to change the world. But a man like General Woodbeare would never see it."

The General did not move an inch but continued his reading. Mrs. Woodbeare made a feeble effort to intervene.

"Miles, dear, you can't let Cass go like this, surely. I mean she must have time to pack and so forth. You can't want to turn her out at a moment's notice. What would people think?"

"I have no interest in what your friends think. The people whose esteem I value would agree with me."

"Anyhow, don't worry about me, Mummy," said Cass, "I was prepared for this. I phoned Liz from the office and she said her mother would be happy for me to stay with her until I'm married."

Dorothy Woodbeare stared at her daughter.

"How can you rush into marriage at a moment's notice like this. It's most unwise and—and stupid."

"Only in your eyes, Mum. It's a terrific thrill for Kev and me— a super adventure. He'll get a special licence so we can get married when we like."

Mrs. Woodbeare gulped. She looked, Kevin thought, rather like a sad fish in a tank from which the water was gradually being drained. A fish who would shortly be left floundering. Poor silly creature! Somehow it annoyed him that she looked a bit like Cass, although only a *little* bit. But she had none of Cass's youth or courage or real beauty.

The General now deigned to raise his voice.

"I suggest we do not waste any more time. I have no further interest in my stepdaughter or her future husband. She must pay for her stupidity and for defying me. One thing is certain. This will no longer be her home. Let her stay the night and pack her things, and be gone in the morning."

Dorothy Woodbeare started to cry in earnest. She was genuinely upset. Yet true to her nature, she began to feel a creeping satisfaction in the thought that Cass's marriage would leave the field *quite* clear at home for her. For years she had tried to keep the peace between the two of them. Now she would be alone with her smart handsome soldier-husband. He was frequently irritated by poor David's daughter now, just as he had been when she was still a child. Everything might turn out for the best.

Cass and Kevin exchanged glances. Cass, for all her bravado, had been feeling a trifle choked, particularly at the sight of her weeping mother. But that long steady intimate look from Kevin's blue eyes hardened her resolve to get out of this house as quickly as she could. Besides, it meant being with *him* and much sooner than she had dared hope for. His decision to marry her at once meant that he was not the type interested in casual kisses and vain promises. He was genuine—the Kevin she had believed in and adored since their first meeting.

"It suits me to go, General," she said coldly without even glancing in his direction. "Don't worry about any food for me, Mum, I'll have a bite somewhere with Kev, then come back and go up and pack. I won't come into your room again. I shall be as glad to say goodbye to the General as he is to sign a permanent leave-warrant for me."

This sarcasm passed over the General's head. He interested himself more deeply in his *Country Life* and felt as he had done for years that Dorothy's daughter had bad blood in her. She was a little no-good. Damned ungrateful when one thought what a nice home she had always had and how proud she should have been to introduce *him* to people as her stepfather. How abysmally lacking in discipline and common sense all these youngsters were today. Anyhow, he need have no conscience about turning her out. Let that young ape of a journalist, or whatever he called himself, keep her in future. He never wanted to see her again and he was going to make sure she didn't get round Dorothy if and when she came crawling back for help. Why, she was behaving like a lunatic—marrying a fellow without a spare cent in his pocket.

Once the young lovers had left the house, the General thought it time to call his wife to attention. At times she was only one whit better than her daughter, he reflected. But she was good-tempered and affectionate and an excellent cook. Under his command she had also become an economical housewife. It was a lot cheaper and more comfortable keeping a wife and home like this than staying at his expensive Club.

"Now, my dear, pull yourself together and dry your eyes and let's see what's left of *All Our Yesterdays*. I'm damned annoyed that I've been done out of it so far."

Mrs. Woodbeare blew her nose, put away her handkerchief and rose meekly to her husband's command.

"Yes, all right, dear, although I do hope you haven't been too hard on her. After all this *is* her home."

"*My* home," corrected the General.

"Well, ours," said Mrs. Woodbeare weakly. "And the only one Cass has had since her father—"

"I'm not concerned with her father—let us not discuss him," cut in the General, switching on the television and returning to his chair, "and no more talk about Cassandra, please. She's made her own bed and must lie on it."

"Supposing that young man *doesn't* marry her?"

"That might well be, but I'm not concerned."

"I shall be so anxious."

"You're permanently anxious. Now please be quiet, Dorothy. Go and mix the salad or something and let me see my programme in peace."

"Yes, dear," said Dorothy. But before she left him, she put a box of the small cigars he liked to smoke near to hand. He took one and conceded her a smile. The General's smiles were like electric flashes; they came on and went off with such rapidity that she hadn't the time to appreciate the first flash.

"It'll be nice to have you to myself," he said.

This unusual concession filled Mrs. Woodbeare with such joy that her tear-stained face suffused with colour and her eyes shone. She looked almost pretty again, and became as coy as a girl.

"That's how *I* feel, too, Miles, darling. I know what you do is always right. I won't be anxious any more. But there is just one question I must ask you, dear."

He scowled instead of frowned, and perforce turned the television volume down, but his gaze hungrily followed a battery attack. The Gunners! Wonderful lot— he had served with them. Pity long-haired idiots like

Kevin Martin hadn't been in the last war. How he hated this generation!

"Well, well, what is it, Dorothy?" he asked.

"About m-money," she stammered. "Oughtn't we to give Cass a little financial help just to start her off?"

The General turned his eyes on her, staring.

"*Give her money*—when she's defied us both and is marrying against our wishes?"

Dorothy bit her lip and pulled nervously at a button on her cardigan.

"I just thought—"

"Well, stop thinking, my dear, and stop talking about your daughter *if* you please. She won't get a penny out of me and I forbid you to give her any. Do you hear me?"

"Yes, dear," said Mrs. Woodbeare.

In a café in the town down at the bottom of Putney Hill, Cass and Kevin sat at the bar, ate ham omelettes and drank several cups of coffee while they discussed the exciting plans for their marriage.

If Kevin had had a single doubt about the wisdom of what he was doing in taking this girl away from her home, it vanished while he listened to her gay sweet voice and looked at her radiant face. She was really beautiful, he thought. He loved her hands. She used them a lot and he liked the jingle of the little gold bracelet with charms which she generally wore. He had bought it for her last Christmas and got into fresh debt because of it. He realised that he would have to watch the money now and go steady. He was a little surprised at what he was doing because he and Barney had so often discussed girls and marriage and both agreed that it was a damned good thing for a chap to wait until he was at least twenty-five before tying himself up. *And* until he was in a settled job. And here he was, barely twenty-three. Wouldn't marriage mean that he would have to give up his ambition to write? Kevin gulped down half a cup of coffee and his lean intense face took on a worried look. Cass immediately noticed it. She pressed his long thin fingers under the table.

"Kev, darling . . . you're not regretting what we've decided on, are you?"

A moment's silence, then he thrust out his lower lip.

"Not on your life. I'm tickled pink at the idea you'll be living with me and we'll be married, this time three more weeks. But we've both got to do a lot of thinking . . . I mean, the financial position is tricky."

"Darling, you're in your advertising job for another three months, and you're making eighteen pounds a week and I made twelve—that's thirty between us, twenty-four after tax. We can't starve on *that*."

"Okay," he nodded and tossed back that lock of black springy hair that would keep falling across one cheek, "but I don't like that job and never will. I'm no good in the advertising world really. I find it dull. I couldn't stick it for long. And I *don't* want my wife to do a permanent job. It's not my idea of marriage."

Her brow wrinkled.

"Oh, Kev, darling, whatever happens at first it will only be to start with. Things will change. I know you don't want to go on sitting in an office. I *know* you ought to be writing. And I'd leave my job tomorrow if I could. But I can't. One day we'll both stay at home and we'll have gorgeous children and lots of dogs and—"

"Don't mention children, it frightens me," he broke in laughing.

"Darling, all in *time*," she said. "Family-planning and all that."

Overcome suddenly by her nearness, her fervent beautiful eyes and the hunger for her that was truly in his heart, he answered the pressure of her fingers with a convulsive grip.

"You're angelic. I'm nuts about you."

"And I dig you, oh, Kev, how I dig you," she whispered.

The café was full now; girls in mini-skirts, in jeans, or gay dresses, most of them with long flowing hair, eyes thickly, falsely, lashed; boys in open-neck shirts and bright coloured pants or hipsters; young men, some with side-burns and beards; others with shaven, eager young faces. It was a favourite place for the young. The air was cloudy with cigarette-smoke, gay with laughter, the sound of piped music, the tinkling of cups, clatter of plates and utensils, the hiss of the Espresso machine.

The May evening was as hot as a summer's night and the sweat was rolling down the faces of the two white-coated men who were serving food and soft drinks at top speed.

Cass and Kevin saw nobody, heard nothing. They were too absorbed in each other. For over an hour they sat there suggesting this way and that for running their lives, finally concluding that for the moment they must both go on working and wait to see what evolved. Once Barney Dixon had gone and Cass was living with Kevin in the little back-flat, life, they agreed, would be much richer and fuller than it was now. Together they would be ready and willing to face any troubles that came along. One couldn't get married on two small combined salaries and a lot of hope, and not expect trouble. *But I'll get clear of debt before I marry her,* Kevin thought. Certainly he'd manage that.

"As a matter of fact," he said, "I've been saving up the best bit of news until the end of the evening, Cass."

Now he told her that one of the weeklies had read and approved his suggestion for a series of articles entitled *Living It Up.* He had written the first one—they would touch on all the subjects dear to the hearts of modern youth. People like themselves—facing the stupendous changes in this permissive age, having broken loose from the shackles of parents and teachers, etc. In fact, Kevin went on, coming events had cast their shadows before with a vengeance. Now he could write the rest of the articles with experience and personal emotion. And she could supply the feminine slant. He could make a couple of hundred pounds. This particular magazine had a big circulation. Paid well. The editor had told Kevin on the phone yesterday he wrote just the stuff they needed.

"He even hinted that he would later commission a further series on another subject. I've got to go and see him when I can get an hour off," Kevin finished.

Cass's eyes gleamed.

"Oh, Kev, how *fabulous!*"

"It's a new market for me and I should find myself solvent before I slip the ring on your finger, honey."

"What terrific news. Fancy you keeping it from me all this time. But I knew you'd do something big."

"It isn't my first sale," Kevin reminded her grandly.

"Of course it isn't, darling, and it won't be your last. Oh, we must hope that you'll be able to chuck the office and do nothing but write very soon."

Kevin looked at his watch.

"Nearly ten—I ought to take you home. Silly to annoy that ruddy old General into insulting you some more when you get back."

She laughed.

"Don't worry, he won't speak to me again—ever, but I'll manage to say a few words to poor Mummy."

"If she hadn't been so busy pleasing herself, and done more to help you, this business wouldn't have happened, and she might have acted the conventional mother weeping in the pew, sad to lose her darling daughter—all dewy, amongst the orange-blossoms."

They laughed together. On that note Kevin paid the bill and walked Cass home through the fine starry night.

In the garden near the Woodbeares' front door, where it was dark, they held each other close and kissed. Cass felt herself trembling suddenly—all flippancy, all lightness of heart vanishing, replaced by fervent desire. A more primitive hunger—a deep physical need suddenly weaving into the pattern of her emotions. No man in the world could make her feel as Kevin did, she thought in this moment of enchantment. She burned her boats and arranged to hand the whole of her life over to him.

"I love you. Oh, *I love you*," she breathed the words, pressing her cheek against his, both hands feverishly caressing his head.

With equal passion he responded to her, holding her so tightly that her whole body seemed to ache under the pressure of his strong hands. One thing she adored about Kevin was his strength, unexpected in a man of his slight build. But in this hour his eyes were full of fire that until tonight she had only guessed at. She felt burned up—feverish with expectation of the glorious future. The memory of that hateful old man in that house, with her ineffectual mother, could not rouse the faintest apprehension in her tonight.

Chapter 4

THE next three weeks in Cass's life seemed to rush by. But her departure from the Putney house that had been her home for the last ten years could not be called pleasant.

She did not see her mother alone again, although she tried to do so. The General, aware that his wife inclined towards Cass, stayed firmly at her side, until Cass and her luggage—an old school trunk and two suitcases— were safely in the taxi which was to take her to Liz's home in Richmond.

The General did not say one word, nor did he deign to look at Cass's slim defiant figure and even more defiant face. He stared fiercely at his wife, stroking his moustache with one forefinger, a smirk on his face which, Cass later told Kevin, expressed his extreme satisfaction that he must be upsetting both the women by *not* leaving them alone.

"If ever there was a sadist, he's one!" Cass declared.

Mrs. Woodbeare, looking rather tired, as though she had had a sleepless night (and she always had to put up with the General's snoring), did what talking had to be done. It was Cass's opinion that *he* put most of her words into her mouth. When Cass mentioned that she hadn't room to pack all her books (she had accumulated several shelves-full, being an ardent reader) or her knick-knacks and she would send for them, Mrs. Woodbeare said:

"I'm afraid your stepfather feels, as I do, dear . . ." an apologetic cough . . . "that it's entirely your fault that you're going off like this at a moment's notice, and what you can't take must be left behind."

"That," said Cass, "is nonsense. *My* things are *mine*. What does the General want to do with them? Sell them?"

The General remained icily silent. Mrs. Woodbeare said nervously:

"Try not to be unpleasant, Cass, it won't do any good."

"It's the General who's being unpleasant—not me. Anyhow once I've left this house I shall feel no further obligation to do what *he* wants and neither can he legally keep my possessions. Even a landlady in a cheap boarding-house can't do that unless the rent is owing. Well, I have paid my rent regularly. He's had something towards the bills ever since I started earning."

Mrs. Woodbeare, who had been well primed, had an answer for that:

"Yes, dear, but it was only right and proper as we are *not* well off."

Cass interrupted:

"The taxi's waiting, Mummy. Prices are all up and *I'm* not well off. I shall send for my books and for that stool I made at school and covered myself, and for my two lampshades which I bought with my own money *and* my carpet. I saved up for that and it cost ten pounds at that sale we went to, remember? So if you'd please have it taken up I'll pay for the man's time and I'll ask Pickfords to collect my stuff as soon as I'm in my flat. I've left the address on my mantelpiece. You can get me there after the 6th June, when Kev and I intend to get married. Meanwhile, you know Liz's phone number."

Mrs. Woodbeare cast another nervous glance at her husband and continued with what she had been told to say.

"I don't think we shall be corresponding for the *moment*, Cass."

Now the General looked up and added:

"Or at *all*, Dorothy. You will have no further communication with Cassandra."

Cass gave a scornful laugh.

"How stupid can you be? This is 1970. You can't start aping Mr. Barratt of Wimpole Street. Neither can you stop Mummy writing or phoning me if she wants to."

Mrs. Woodbeare now made a frantic attempt to catch her daughter's eye and convey that she would find some way of evading the extreme dictatorship, but please not to make trouble now.

Cass, somewhat sick at heart, stepped forward, kissed her mother on both cheeks, and whispered:

"Cheer up—it'll be better when I've really left, and I'll keep in touch with you. I'm not afraid of *him*."

She picked up her cases, walked to the door and called the driver in to take her trunk.

She had a heart-warming reception from the Burnhams. Liz, a short fair rather plump girl with endearing dimples and a happy optimistic nature like Cass's, told her she could share her bedroom until she, Cass, was married. Mrs. Burnham kissed her warmly and left no doubt in Cass's mind that she was welcome. She had always got on well with the Burnhams and secretly envied her friend the warmth and friendliness of this home. They were such a united family. Mr. Burnham was the manager in a local bank. Liz's brother Nigel, aged nineteen, was articled to a firm of solicitors—a nice boy, not particularly brainy, not perhaps as clever as his sister who had three A Levels, but Liz was not going to make use of her learning. She would soon be married to her doctor who had a practice in the Midlands, and settle down to a domestic routine. Mrs. Burnham was all that Cass might have wished her own mother to be—a big-bosomed, amiable, thoroughly maternal woman; not good-looking, but most attractive with the dimples Liz had inherited, a fine pink skin and eyes that twinkled behind horn-rimmed glasses. Nobody had ever heard Violet Burnham say a word against anybody, nor did she think much about herself. She was entirely devoted to her family and friends, and when she wasn't looking after them, she was busy with 'Meals On Wheels' or sitting on Charity Committees.

From her early schooldays when Cass used to come here to tea with her friend or sometimes, when the General wanted to be rid of her, stayed at night, she had felt this home to be more hers than her own.

Suddenly she found herself not smiling but crying silently, clasped to Mrs. Burnham's ample bosom.

"There, dear, don't be upset. Come and have a nice cup of tea and let's talk things over," Mrs. Burnham said in her soothing voice, and motioned Liz to leave them alone.

And when Cass had talked things over with Mrs. Burnham she was all the more certain she was doing the right thing. The family knew Kevin. She had brought him here once or twice. Mr. Burnham liked him and that meant a lot to Cass who had always found Bob Burnham a steady sensible sort of man. Naturally, as a banker, he wished frankly that young Martin had more money-sense, but excused him on the grounds that he was artistic and clever and such people were generally a bit highly strung and impulsive and not too sagacious about the way they conducted their finances.

But Violet Burnham comforted Cass on that day of her arrival by assuring her that both she and Bob believed in Kevin and were positive that he would succeed. Liz, of course, liked him enormously. She had always said that any girl would fall for Kev's Irish blue eyes, that rather lean hungry look of his and the charm of his smile.

By the time the family had finished comforting her, Cass was smiling again—radiantly happy.

"It's all been a bit of a shock to you, leaving home so abruptly," Mrs. Burnham remarked, "and we didn't expect you to get married this way but things will fall into place, ducky, don't be upset. I understand how you feel. I'm afraid your poor mother isn't very strong-minded and the General has made a great mistake. I'm quite shocked, but I'm sure he'll regret it and it'll all blow over."

Cass did not argue. Dear Mrs. B. as usual being kind about people, but she could not see the General ever climbing down, neither did she want to go back to that beastly house, *ever*. But she'd telephone Mummy when she wanted to, and he couldn't *always* be there to answer the phone first. She knew roughly the times he went out. For instance, on a Friday he always played bridge at his Club. She could phone Mummy then. Meanwhile Cass did not even want to see *her*. She just wanted to concentrate on Kevin and their future.

That night the Burnhams planned more of a real wedding for their dear Cass than either she or Kevin anticipated. They would all go along to the Richmond Register Office, Mrs. Burnham announced, then come back here for a 'spread'—wedding-cake and all.

Liz added:

"And you say that Barney Dixon moves out of that little flat on the 4th June. Where will you have your honeymoon?"

"We can't afford one," Cass said promptly and quite happily.

After that life became hectic.

Cass felt as though she was in a kind of hiatus, suspended between two worlds—one of glorious liberty and one in which, perversely, she kept casting backward glances at the old prison. She could do without the General, but she worried about her mother. One phone call had proved unsuccessful. Unfortunately the General answered. When he heard her voice he hung up. At the second call she got Mrs. Fuller, the daily. Mrs. Fuller said that Mrs. Woodbeare was laid up in her bed with a touch of 'flu and couldn't come down to speak to her.

"Is she really ill?" Cass asked anxiously.

Mrs. Fuller said she'd ask. She returned with the message that Mrs. Woodbeare would be up in a day or two and that Miss Hayes was not to worry about her.

Cass had never changed her name, and was now profoundly glad that she was Miss Hayes. She would have hated to have been a Woodbeare. But even the name Hayes would soon be a thing of the past and she would be Cassandra Martin (glorious thought!). Nevertheless she continued to worry a bit about her mother. The next two calls were abortive—both times the General was in. On the last occasion he snarled at her:

"I must ask you not to keep calling this number. Your mother is quite well and extremely happy. She is now having some peace, so please do not pester her—or me."

When Cass repeated this incident to Kevin, his nostrils flared a little. He grunted:

"What a shocker that fellow is, but I shouldn't worry about your mother—she never worried about *you!*"

"Oh, Kevin, don't be so hard," said Cass suddenly and it was the first time she had ever criticised him. He looked quite ruthless. Then he became the Kevin she knew. His hardness rolled away, and he kissed her.

"You've got such a kind heart, my love. You must be a bit tougher. It's a rough world. I'm quite sure *'Yes-dear'* will be all right. I suppose you don't by any chance remember your 'daily's' home address?"

"Yes, I do, I had to borrow the car and go and fetch her twice."

"Drop her a line, enclose a stamped addressed envelope with the Burnham's address. Ask her to scribble you a line, or even phone your office, if at any time she thinks poor *'Yes-dear'* is really ill."

Cass thought that a marvellous idea and was duly grateful to Kevin, and in due course a scribble arrived from the 'daily' to tell Miss Cass that Mrs. Woodbeare had quite recovered and was hoping to go on holiday soon.

Cass worried no more about her mother. She turned all her thoughts now to her own life.

She and Kevin had both asked to be allowed to go on their summer holiday now so that they could spend the time putting their little flat in order. It was all right for Kevin who had only a temporary job. They would let him off, anyhow, for the first week after their marriage. But Cass's employers were short-handed and far too busy. They specialised in antique silver. At the moment the market was doing a roaring trade. They were sympathetic over Miss Hayes getting married but sorry . . .

Kevin, sitting with Cass in their favourite City sandwich bar—for it was a wet day and they were denied the pleasure of their picnic in Temple Gardens—was all for her handing in her cards.

"I think it's the *end*," he said hotly. "You must give notice."

"Darling, I can't. Miss Williams who used to work with me has just left on account of illness, and isn't coming back, and although I'm a junior, I do quite a lot of specialised work. I've been training under her and I can help with repairs on delicate jewellery. They can't easily replace me. And we do need my salary now."

"Blast!" muttered Kevin, then grinned at her. "My Irish blood is obviously going to be tempered by the sound common sense of my English wife."

Chapter 5

FOR Cass the first big set-back occurred before her Register Office wedding which was arranged for Saturday, 6th June. Fate seemed against Kevin and herself. First of all Kevin's firm, which was launching a huge publicity campaign on the Continent, asked him to go with another young man in his department, to Brussels. They were holding an exhibition in which the London firm was interested. Kevin happened to speak good French and because of that plus his attractive looks and personality, they thought him just the right one to send.

He did not want to go. It was the wrong time to enjoy ten days in Belgium, he said gloomily. When Cass heard about it, she said that of course he must go, but it seemed such a shame that it couldn't have been *after* rather than before their wedding, so that she could have gone with him.

Kevin agreed but it was a lovely dream—quite beyond reality.

"It'll be good business experience for me—something to write articles about perhaps," he said, "they've even hinted that they might ask me to stay on in the firm.

But I don't want to—you know how I feel, Cass, I must get down to my writing."

She was full of sympathy but a little depressed. This would mean that Kevin would be out of England right up to the day before Barny Dixon moved out of the flat; there would be absolutely no time for them to get it ready, as they had planned.

The kindly Burnhams suggested that they should stay with them until their flat was fit to go to but Cass refused the invitation. It would mean Nigel turning out of his own room and a lot of extra work for 'Mum', and anyhow they wanted to be *alone* after their wedding. Cass was too fond of Mrs. Burnham to say that but Mrs. Burnham understood.

Cass went on with her own job, quite lost without her Kevin. The only compensations were the letters he sent, full of love and longing. One she particularly treasured said:

"Brussels is a fine city and it's all very interesting but since I've been away from you I realise you are part of my life, if not all of it. I can't live without you much longer. Darling Cass, don't let any other fellow take you from me while I'm away."

Cass read that paragraph several times. She wrote back to him and assured him there *could* never be another man for her. Later she thought what a lot poor little Liz missed by being so moderate—so practical in her approach to Richard. She, Cass, meant to sink or swim with Kevin. And she refused to entertain the idea of a possible sinking.

She did not get in touch with her mother for the next ten days of her exile from home. Then when she did telephone and contact her, she found that, in her weak way, Dorothy Woodbeare was once more the woman who had originally married the General and who had allowed her child to slip into a very secondary place in her life. They were going down to Poole for a holiday, she said. The General had friends there with a boat and liked sailing. But when Cass said she would like to have seen her mother once before the wedding,

Mrs. Woodbeare said it was impossible. She 'must do what Miles wanted'.

"I'm sure *you* will do what Kevin wants, Cass, Mrs. Woodbeare ended on a somewhat caustic note.

Abruptly Cass said:

"I will, but not if I think that what he wants me to do is wrong. Anyhow, Mummy, we'll say goodbye."

"Of course I wish you the best of luck—" began Mrs. Woodbeare.

But Cass had put down the receiver. She had no further wish to speak to her mother.

Now, during this last week before the wedding, in spite of all the warmth and affection she received from the Burnhams she felt somehow a little lost and lonely. Kevin seemed far away. Just a little of Cass's gaiety and self-confidence deserted her.

When she had first seen Kevin's flat, she had been appalled by its shabbiness and lack of modern equipment. An age-old dirty gas-stove (as far as she could remember); small dark rooms; a dingy loo. She couldn't get in to do a thing until two days before her wedding. Meanwhile she was frantically dress-making with Mrs. Burnham's help. They made two cotton frocks and the dress and jacket for the wedding—pale blue silk with gilt buttons. Liz had given her a hat as a wedding present—white straw with a big floppy brim, and a white bag. Mr. Burnham had come up with a generous cheque of twenty pounds which would be more than useful.

Cass had to admit that it was all a bit of a rush. She only had her weekends free. It took so long to get to the Strand from Richmond and back again, and she was often tired in the evening. Her eyes ached what with the close work at the goldsmith's, the constant use of magnifying glasses—and her sewing.

She was depressed, too, because when she had asked for her holiday on the grounds that she was getting married, Mr. Mannstein, one of the directors, after refusing with regrets, had asked her quite jovially what sort of engagement ring her boyfriend had given her. But Cass had been at a loss to answer.

The fact was that she *had* no engagement ring. She

had begged Kevin not to spend the money. There was the wedding ring to buy—already measured for and ordered, and it was silly to spend money they could ill-afford, she agreed. Yet somehow she had begun to feel that an engagement ring *was* necessary. A girl liked to show it off to her friends. Truly feminine—now, she wished they hadn't agreed not to buy a ring.

She was waking up fast to the fact that one couldn't sail along in enchanted space expecting everything to be marvellous, even when a girl was so much in love. Life and the world, as Kevin had told her, were 'rough'. All kinds of problems cropped up and had to be faced. A check had to be kept on one's emotions. Above all she told herself, she must never become too critical. Many modern marriages fell down because a couple could be too frank, too outspoken, and often prejudiced in their opinions.

She wanted above all things for life with Kevin to remain romantic. While he was away she went on working feverishly to that end.

Two days before her wedding she felt her optimistic self again, tense and excited. In the passage outside the room she shared with Liz were her two suitcases ready and packed. Yesterday she had added a pair of bell-bottomed trousers—black—to wear with a white frilly blouse, in case she and Kev had time (and cash) to go to a party. And, of course, one particularly delicious filmy nightgown—a shortie, with frills.

She made an appointment to have her hair washed and set early on *the* morning. They did not have to be at the Register Office until eleven o'clock.

This afternoon (her firm had given her from Thursday till Monday) she intended to go and work in the flat in Groom Street off Russell Square. She must clean it up before Kev got back from Brussels tomorrow. Barney had phoned to say he was leaving the key with a Mr. Brewer—an elderly bachelor who occupied the two rooms below. Mrs. Burnham, without whom Cass did not know how she could have managed, lent her Mini car. Liz was driving her there, plus Hoover, brush and pan, detergents and dusters.

This morning Cass received a letter from her mother. In it was a five pound note.

"I'm sorry this is all I can send you. Buy yourself something for the wedding, but as you know Miles and I find it hard to acknowledge the whole affair. At least I wish you luck, darling, and hope you won't regret it. But Miles is quite sure you will. You can send for your possessions after you've settled down. I have made your stepfather agree to this."

Cass read this brief note somewhat cynically to Liz as they drove to Russell Square.

"Charming! Just the sort of letter a girl needs from her mother at a time like this."

"I don't understand her. I think it's awful!" said Liz.

"Oh, she's Miles-mad and has been ever since she met him. You've no idea how sweet she was when Daddy was alive. I can remember it. It's awful the way people can change when they're influenced like that."

"Ought a woman to allow her husband to influence her so completely?"

That started off another of the debates the two girls were so fond of. In the end Cass said that no living woman could stand up against the General, particularly not Mummy. *She* had stood up to him, but then she wasn't emotionally involved. When a relationship had no sex in it, it was much easier to be strong-minded and independent.

This brought a giggle from Liz.

"Don't tell me your mother ever felt sexy about the General. You have to be joking!"

"Oh, well, I shall buy something for my new kitchen," was Cass's final comment, thinking of Mummy's pathetic fiver. "At least His Highness is allowing me to collect my stool, my books, my carpet and my other bits and pieces which include quite a valuable little painting Daddy left me. The General always had his eye on it but he didn't dare snatch it. Even Mummy would have stopped that."

When the two girls reached the flat now belonging to Kevin alone, they were both shocked into a grim silence as they stared around. For all Cass's gay eager zest in life and love, this was enough to strike chill in her heart.

Cass had never much liked Barney Dixon—even Kevin had complained that he had to be 'nagged' into a bath—and once Kevin had gone to Belgium it would seem that he had done little either to clean the flat or leave it habitable.

Cass tried with a Christian spirit to excuse him on the grounds that he had had to rush off at short notice but *really*, the place was deplorable. A film of dust lay over everything. Bits of paper and string, old newspapers and periodicals littered the floors. The girls looked, wide-eyed, at the shrunken grubby curtains; the carpets stained with marks of spilled drink; the cheap furniture. Unemptied ash-trays, used glasses, everywhere. A loose cover on the divan did not match the curtains, and, as Liz remarked, even the clock on the mantlepiece had stopped and the glass was cracked.

As for the kitchen, with that awful rusted-up bath in it—this brought an exclamation of despair from Cass. It was even grubbier than the other two rooms. On the small draining board lay a pile of dirty crockery. Flies buzzed madly around a half-opened tin of condensed milk and one half filled with baked beans. There were empty bottles in the sink.

If Cass had not been the type of girl she was, she would have burst into tears then and there and rushed out of the flat; *her future home*.

"Blimey!" she said under her breath. Then she looked at Liz and they both burst out laughing. The situation was saved, but as long as she lived, Cass would never forget her repugnance at the sight of Kevin's home.

"This needs a regimental labour-corps," said Liz with a shudder. "Let's send for the General."

They laughed again. Then Cass shook her head.

"Where do we start?"

"In the kitchen, getting *that* and the bath clean," said Liz promptly. "Thank goodness Mum didn't come with us. She'd have been shaken. She's such a stickler for hygiene."

"So am I," said Cass, "and I can't understand Kev. He always looks so nice, himself. His shirts are spotless. He's such a *clean* man—how can he *live* in this place?"

The kindly Liz tried to console her.

"We're seeing it at its worst. That awful friend of Kev's must have been on a drinking session during the last week. You said he drank too much."

"Yes, I'm glad he's going out of Kev's life—not that Kev takes more than the odd glass of beer. But he said Barney was amusing and generous and they got on, and I suppose two bachelors shacking up together don't notice the details like women do. Both Kev and Barney are so masculine—none of the pansy touch. But I know Kev would be appalled to think I've got to cope with this. He told me to leave it all until he got back."

"He wouldn't have had time to do a thing," said Liz. "You're supposed to be coming here directly after the lunch in our house, my *poor* darling!"

Immediately Cass recovered her spirits and became defiant. "*Not* poor! I've got Kev so I've got everything. It's just a matter now of spit and polish. As you say, I wish we could send for the General and put him 'on fatigue', to use a good old Army term."

They worked for three hours without stopping. They swept, they scrubbed, they rehung the curtains, they even polished the window-panes. Cass hastily decided that she must buy some cheap net and put it across these back windows to hide those awful ashcans in the dismal yard below. She must shut out the sight of the neighbours' sooty washing-line, too. It would be more difficult to deaden the noise of those urchins screaming below. Thank goodness, at least this was a top-floor flat. They could get more air. The whole house was so stuffy. It reeked of cabbage-water.

Romance with a capital 'R', Cass smiled to herself wryly, but with the thought of Kevin as a talisman and Liz's loyal support, she achieved a transformation in the flat. No doubt, as she said, Barney would not have recognized the ghastly mess he had left behind and it would please Kevin to find things looking so neat, so shining clean.

They then rushed out before the shops closed, and

Mrs. Woodbeare's fiver disappeared rapidly in payment for the long list of 'musts' in Cass's basket. Groceries, cleaning materials, vegetables. Liz dived into her purse and insisted on buying two beautiful scarlet geranium plants to cheer up the sitting-room window sill.

When Kev came back, Cass said, he would have to buy a new electric light bulb or two and she would be able to exchange the sordid stained carpet in the sitting-room for her own attractive green one from her old room at Putney. She'd soon make a real home of the flat.

Both girls were exhausted as they drove away but Cass was full of the joy of life again.

"It looked quite attractive, didn't it?" she asked her friend.

"It sure did," said Liz in pseudo-American, but in her heart she wondered if she loved even her dear Richard enough to live in a 'dump' like that flat. Her close association with Cass was beginning to make her feel nervous about her personal attitude towards Richard. Was she as much in love with him as she had thought? Did Cass love Kev in the right way? Ready to accept *anything*, no matter how unappetising, so long as she could be with him?

Liz thought:

Poor darling Cass, I only hope he's worth it and will never let you down.

Time rushed by. Then it was the wedding eve, and Kev came home.

This time fate had a real blow in store for Cass. She had wanted to meet Kevin at the airport—he was flying back to Heathrow—but she had had an unexpected telegram telling her not to do so and that he would come straight to Richmond. He expected to get there before supper.

It rained all day. She didn't care. It would be nice if they had it fine tomorrow, but she was so wildly excited at the thought of Kev's return and their marriage, that she didn't care about anything. The Burnham family were all sitting around the television, watching the News, when they heard the sound of a taxi coming up to the door. *A taxi!* That *must* be Kevin, Cass thought, but it wasn't like him to be so extravagant. He usually came by Underground.

Mrs. Burnham looked at Cass's glowing face as the girl sprang up. How beautiful she was, bless her. Like Liz, Violet inwardly prayed that Kevin would never disappoint their dear Cass.

She'd been so starved of love, all her life, poor angel, now she was hungry for it—concentrating on this young man. Mrs. Burnham wished, perhaps, that she was not such a *'giver'*. Kevin, like any other man, might find it hard not to take too much.

They heard the front door shut, then silence outside. Obviously the young couple were embracing. When the door opened, they saw a worried-looking unsmiling Cass, leading Kevin in by the right arm; the left one jutted out at an unnatural angle, set in plaster. He looked paler than usual; quite ill. Mrs. Burnham got up and gave a shocked exclamation.

"My dear, what on earth's happened?"

"I've been imbecile enough to break my arm," he said.

Cass added:

"Isn't it *grim?* He had an accident yesterday morning, crossing the road in a busy street in Brussels. Some silly idiot was going too fast, pulled up suddenly and skidded into him and knocked him down. He had to go to hospital and stay and have the arm set. Lucky he wasn't killed. I feel quite sick!"

"Oh, you poor lamb! And poor Kev! Come and sit down at once and Dad can get you a drink. We've got some whisky. You look as though you need it, Kev."

"I'm all right," he said wearily, "only still a bit shocked, I think. I didn't feel too good in the aircraft, but I'm fine now."

Cass sat beside him, holding his free hand, her eyes full of love and compassion. *He looked awful,* she thought, so drawn and hollow-eyed. He couldn't have slept last night.

Kevin pressed her fingers and smiled at her.

"Don't look so tragic, darling, I'm still breathing. At least my firm will have to give me some sick leave now—and I'll get sick benefit, too," he laughed. "That's something."

A dread thought struck Cass.

"You won't be fit for our wedding."

"Nonsense," said Kevin, "I'm not missing the greatest event in history just because I've got a fractured arm."

She could not remove her warm gaze from him.

Her cheeks were hot and pink—her eyes troubled and her heart beating fast with emotion. It had been a shock to her to see Kevin standing there on the doorstep looking so ill and with his broken arm.

"I'll hurry on supper. I dare say you'd like a bit, Kevin," said Mrs. Burnham.

"Actually I don't want anything," he said. "I couldn't eat."

"Oh, darling, you must—" Cass began.

Then to her horror, Kevin slid sideways a little, and with his head resting on her shoulder, he quietly fainted.

Chapter 6

The Burnhams' doctor, a charming man of Polish origin, who used the English name of Smith, was hastily summoned because Kevin did not recover consciousness immediately. He must have hit his head when he fell in that accident.

"We'll have to see how things go," said Dr. Smith as he put away his stethoscope.

Cass looked down at Kevin. He was lying on the sofa by a wide-open window while Mrs. Burnham fanned him. She was a great believer in open air at times like this. Cass's spirits had dropped to zero. What a calamity! Kevin looked so *ill*. His eyes had only opened once, then he just smiled at her, murmured her name and closed his eyes again.

She looked in an agonised way at the doctor.

"We're supposed to be getting married tomorrow morning."

"That, I am afraid, won't be possible," he said sympathetically. "It would be very unwise even if Mr. Martin improves and could get on his feet. He might well faint again. You'll have to postpone the wedding."

Mrs. Burnham and Cass exchanged glances. Liz put a hand against her lips and whispered:

"Oh, *dear!*"

Nigel, who had only just come in, thought it best to make himself scarce. His father had the same idea. The two men walked out into the kitchen where Mr. Burnham fancied he smelt burning. Poor Vi had just been about to dish up supper—a small joint. Mr. Burnham gingerly took it out of the oven.

"Bad business—rotten luck for those young things," he said.

"A brand saved from the burning—Kev's in luck. I just don't believe in marriage," announced Nigel.

"Fancy that," said his father mildly. "What *do* you believe in?"

"Freedom," said Nigel promptly.

He was a tall boy with glasses, serious face, and thick fair hair which he was forced by his employer to keep shorter than he liked. He belonged to the set that believed in freedom of thought, action—and dress. At weekends he wore fancy shirts, jeans and sandals. But he was a lovable good-hearted young man, and his father understood him. He looked at him now and smiled amiably.

"You'll change, old son. Wait till you meet someone you really fall for—not these 'mini-minors' you go out with now. I was all for being a bachelor until I met your mother and it took a sweet girl like Cass to turn Kevin to a marrying man. From what he told me when we chatted, he isn't any more fundamentally domesticated than you are. You'll be snatched in time."

In the lounge Mrs. Burnham, Liz and Cass were

talking to the doctor. When he suggested that he might 'pop' young Martin into hospital for a check-up and keep him under observation for a day or two, Mrs. Burnham agreed; this would be sensible. Cass protested.

"Oh, *no!* Surely I could nurse him?"

Mrs. Burnham said on a doubtful note:

"Well, I suppose we could send Nigel next door—I know the Wheelers would give him a room but—"

"No," Cass shook her head. "You've done quite enough with me here all this time. I know Kevin wouldn't dream of taking Nigel's room. But we could go to our flat—it's all ready. We've even got the food in. I could take care of him there. After all, we're *nearly* married."

"Well, only 'nearly'," said Violet Burnham with a little smile.

"Doctor, couldn't I *possibly* look after him?" Cass appealed to the physician.

It was his opinion, however, that it would be wiser for Kevin if he were under observation in the local hospital for at least twenty-four hours. Then if nothing troublesome evolved, they could do as they pleased. But no wedding tomorrow—definitely not.

Cass, the tears springing to her eyes, had to bow to authority. Anyhow she wanted to do what was best for Kev. But it was all most worrying, and a bitter disappointment.

She did not share the Burnhams' evening meal. She insisted on travelling in the ambulance with Kevin who continually opened his eyes and seemed to want to hold on to her hand. An hour later he was safely tucked up in bed in the Observation Ward and she, miserable and lonely, was back in her temporary home.

The Burnhams did all they could to comfort her. When she refused to eat Mrs. Burnham insisted on her drinking a cup of hot chocolate. She told the girl that it wouldn't be sensible to get all 'het up' and make herself ill. There was little doubt that Kevin would soon be out of the hospital, then she could look after him. She *must*—Mrs. Burnham could see that. He had no relatives—no one but Cass.

"And I couldn't care less what people think—I shall stay in the flat with him and nurse him until he's fit again!" Cass announced.

"Why not?" put in Liz.

Mrs. Burnham said dryly:

"I don't suppose anybody will think the worst of you, dear. We certainly won't."

"I think we know how to behave," said Cass a trifle primly, "and we can get married the moment he's fit."

"You poor lamb!" said Mrs. Burnham, her warm dimpled cheeks pink with compassion.

"I only hope," she said to her husband later that night, "that it *is* all shock and nerves with Kev, and so on, and not his head. Still John Smith didn't seem too worried. He always plays it safe, and it's best Kevin should be watched and X-rayed. I expect they'll make sure that arm's all right, too. You never know how these foreign doctors have set it."

Cass wept herself to sleep on the night that should have been so full of thrilling promise. She kept thinking of Kevin's white gaunt face and fractured arm. It had been *awful* when he fainted, leaning against her shoulder like that—such a shock! But thank goodness it had happened once he got back and not on the flight. Thank goodness, too, that she and Liz had worked so hard at the flat so she and Kev *could* live in it. All she wanted to do now was to take some bed-linen along. When for a second she turned her thoughts to Mummy and the General, she blew her nose and sniffed a little. She could imagine what they'd say if she occupied the flat with Kev before they were man and wife. Well, *if* they heard about it, let them think the worst. She wouldn't care.

After a wretched night she telephoned the hospital and at last was relieved to hear that Kevin was better. He had slept well. He had no temperature and his arm didn't ache so much. He had eaten some breakfast. The doctors were making some tests today. She would visit him this evening between seven and eight p.m.

Once again Liz came to the rescue, drove her to the hospital and said she would wait for her, sit in the car and read. The faithful friend, thought Cass. She had be-

come fonder of Liz than ever since she had lived with
the Burnhams. She wasn't an exciting girl but so affectionate and steadfast. And Cass admired the way she
remained unruffled in times of crisis. Cass was beginning to fear that she, herself, was none too placid. She
swung, perhaps rather too rapidly, from joy to misery—
from confidence to anxiety—a little like Kevin himself.
They would have to be careful, when married, not to be
too neurotic. It was the placid people who had the
happiest marriages, she was sure. Kevin with all his
writer's sensitivity and creative spirit was mercurial
enough. She must learn to keep calm.

She repressed her emotions when at last she sat at his
bedside in the ward and tried to model herself on the
maternal and sensible Mrs. Burnham.

"You look fine, darling. You're going to be quite all
right. You've nothing to worry about any more," she
said cheerfully.

"Oh yes, I have," said Kevin. "Plenty," and he
looked at her with some resentment in his blue handsome eyes, she thought. He was still very pale but then
Kevin never did have much colour and at least he no
longer looked as ghastly as he did last night. He sat up
in bed, alert and normal, his black hair ruffled over his
head like a small boy's, the usual wave falling over one
eyebrow.

"You *mustn't* worry, Kev—you must get well," she
said.

"You're very cool all of a sudden," he said, and his
lower lip jutted out—a sign with Kevin that he was not
pleased.

She thought:

*Whatever a girl does, she can't win. If I'd started to
sob he'd have told me not to be such an emotional little
idiot.*

Then with the old humour, she laughed.

"Don't let's be miserable. We're together again—
that's all that matters and you're looking heaps better
and I'm sure I'll be able to fetch you home tomorrow."

"I hope so. I loathe hospitals. They're very decent
here but I can't stand the smells, the sights, or the
sounds."

She sympathised. There were two old men on either side of Kevin who looked as though they were half-dead already. Poor darling Kev; a sick-ward certainly wasn't the place for *him*.

"Now," she said, "don't get into one of your Irish-rebellion moods, and put on your things and walk out or anything like that. Give them a chance to make sure you're okay."

"You *are* being the little philosopher, aren't you? Do you realise, my sweet Cassandra, that if things had gone right, you and I would have been married by this time and having our wedding sausage and mash together."

She seized his left hand in both of hers, and pressed it. With eyes full of worship and sympathy, she exclaimed:

"Oh, my darling, you *know* I realise it! I've thought about it all day. It's been grim."

Now his thin face softened. He bent quickly and kissed her.

"I do love you. I'm just sore because of what's happened—fed up to the teeth. Can't even use my arm to hold you as I want to. And I've still got a swimmy head. Worst of all I'm still a bachelor. It's the *end*. I owe you an apology. What a way for a man to treat his bride."

"Kev, *darling*, it wasn't your fault."

"To hell with that imbecile who skidded into me," he muttered, and leaned back against his pillows. Then he sat up again and added: "I've been so busy here, what with crowds of doctors and nurses round my bed, trolleys being wheeled in and out, the Red Cross coming along with books and tobacco and sweets, and a trip to the X-ray Department. It's been a sort of circus. Meanwhile I suppose you've had to cancel everything we'd fixed, poor darling."

She nodded, feeling her heart overflowing with love and concern for him.

But there hadn't been all that much to cancel, she said, only the Register Office. And Mrs. Burnham's arrangements for the luncheon. Dear old Bob Burnham, unbeknown to them, had apparently booked a table for dinner for them at the Savoy of all places, and was going to foot the bill. He thought it would be so splendid for them to start life with a super meal in a super place. But it was only postponed, of course. If Kev was discharged on Monday and all went well, they could get married. The Sister had told her they never discharged patients on Sunday. They might well book the Registrar for Tuesday or Wednesday.

"Liz said she'll drive us to the flat on Monday," Cass finished.

That brought the light back to Kevin's eyes, and he began to tease her which was a good sign she thought. It meant that he was definitely better.

"Don't tell me we're going to live in sin!"

"Not at all," she said, her cheeks hot and pink. "Only in the eyes of those who evil think. Anyway you'll have to keep pretty quiet until you're absolutely okay again."

Now with his left hand he took a strand of her silky hair, drew it across his lips and gave her a long intimate look.

"I don't know if I'll want to keep quiet. Maybe you'd better stay away and send a pretty little nurse to the flat. Some of them here are smashers."

"You're getting ideas. The sooner you come home the better," said Cass severely.

"I don't want anybody but you, my true love," he whispered, and suddenly all her cares and disappointments fell away. She was enveloped in the cloak of his love, and felt infinitely close to him. She even forgot how the tears had fallen down her cheeks when she telephoned the Register of Births, Deaths and Marriages to postpone the wedding.

"Oh, Kev," she said, "it'll be such bliss to be alone together and you won't recognize the flat."

"I hope old Barney cleaned it up before he left."

She forebore to answer, not wanting to worry him, and turned the conversation to his business affairs. She wanted to know how he got on in Brussels. She told him how marvellous his letters had been. He told her all about the Exhibition and how much he liked Brussels and how pleased the firm seemed about the work he had done there.

"You know I told you they want me to stay on," he added.

"And will you?"

"I ought to, I suppose," he said sighing, "now that I've nearly got a wife to support—"

She interrupted:

"Don't worry about it now. We'll sort it all out later. And, Kev, I don't *want* security and money if it means you not having time to write. You *must* write."

"You're an angel," he said.

She added that she must go now as Liz was sitting outside waiting.

His lips were eager and demanding as she kissed him.

She whispered:

"Good-night, my darling, *darling* Kev. We'll both think about each other tonight and pretend that it *is* our wedding night."

He grinned up at her.

"We'll want a bit of imagination, won't we?"

"Oh I love you!" she said fervently.

"I love *you*," he said.

On that happy note they separated.

Another twenty-four hours—Sunday night—and Cass felt that an avalanche of worry and misfortune slid away, leaving her high on the radiant peaks of happiness. Kevin's X-rays had shown no serious damage to the arm, but there was nasty bruising to the head, and they had had to give Kevin tablets for constant headache. He was sufficiently improved to be allowed home but only on condition that he went straight to bed and rested for at least forty-eight hours. After this his own doctor should see him again. Contrary to Mrs. Burnham's patriotic expectations, the Belgian doctor had set the fracture very nicely. Cass was allowed to fetch him as early as she liked on Monday.

"About time," Cass told Liz, laughing, "there's a little nurse in his ward I could be very jealous of. She spoke to me as I went out—Irish as you make them and very glam-huge blue eyes, rather like Kevin's. They've all got these fabulous eyes. And do you know she admitted quite blatantly that she's sorry to be losing her good-looking countryman. I bet she is! And he's an awful flirt. But I told her that only one half of him came from Ireland and that's the half I mean to cultivate, otherwise I can see myself having to ward off all the girls who fall for him."

"He doesn't care about anybody but you," said Liz loyally, "and he's far too busy trying to make his way in life to worry about other females."

"You're dead right," said Cass happily.

Then it seemed no time before she and Liz borrowed Mrs. Burnham's little car for the last time, and fetched Kevin from the hospital. Her employers had given her another twenty-four hours' leave, being sorry for poor little Miss Hayes whose wedding had been so sadly delayed.

Kevin still looked pale but much more his old self. His fine drawn intelligent face was alert and keen-eyed again. He made light of the outstretched arm in its plaster cast and held Cass's hand with his right one as they sat in the back of the car, close together. Liz kept looking at them in her driving mirror and grinning.

"Hi, you two! I can see you—none of this back-of-the-car nonsense."

"You're just jealous!" said Cass.

Yes, Liz thought, as she drove carefully through the heavy traffic towards Central London, maybe I am. Kevin is really very amusing and attractive, and I can see why Cass feels she can't do enough for him. Maybe I'll never be as crazy as this about my Richard, but he *is* a doctor—quieter and more thoughtful—and I don't think I could really deal with a man like Kev. I'd get too confused and anxious. Cass seems to understand him and takes everything that comes so calmly."

That was what Kevin was thinking in this very moment. He kept lifting Cass's hand to his lips and kissing it. A fine strong young hand, and she used very pale varnish on her nails which made the skin look tanned. She had in fact been sitting out in the Burnhams' garden and achieved a tan that suited her. As they turned into Russell Square and then down the narrow 'No-through road' called Groom Street where he lived, he suddenly lifted a strand of her hair and murmured:

"Suddenly aware
That the autumn leaves were turning to
the colour of her hair."

Cass pressed her cheek against his shoulder.

"Our tune—I adore *Windmills Of Your Mind*. Mine
has been like a windmill lately, turning and turning. It's
been hectic really, Kev, ever since I left home."

Kevin pointed to the tall ugly Victorian house in
front of which Liz was now neatly parking the Mini
Minor.

"Welcome to your new and very temporary home,
my love, and I'll make sure it won't be for long. I'll
work like a lunatic and get enough money to buy you a
house worthy of you."

When they stepped out of the car, it was hardly into
a blaze of sunshine. The June sky was overcast. A slight
drizzle was falling, and it was very close. There was
thunder in the air. Kevin was forced to stand by helplessly while the two girls pulled out the suitcases.

"As a one-armed bandit character, I don't feel at all
helpful," he grumbled.

Cass said:

"Never mind, darling—I'm as strong as a horse and
Liz won't mind taking up one of the cases."

They climbed the odorous and unattractive staircase
with its worn linoleum steps and finally reached the flat
which had a card marked *Kevin Martin and Barnard
Dixon* above the letter-box.

Kevin promptly pulled that out.

"That must be changed."

"When do you think you'll be able to get married?"
Liz suddenly asked. Because of her upbringing, she felt
just a twinge of uneasiness because to begin with Cass
must live with Kev, unmarried.

"I'll get on to the Registrar and fix it up for tomorrow," said Kevin.

Liz took the key and unlocked the front door and
they all walked into the tiny hall.

Cass protested:

"Out of the question. Sister made me promise to
keep you in bed for at least forty-eight hours. I've al-

ready overstepped my leave of absence and must go
back to work tomorrow or lose my job. No, my boy, it's
bed for you with Sister Cassandra Hayes in charge to
keep you pinned down."

Kevin grimaced and grinned at Liz.

"Witness? I'm being bullied before even we're married."

"Well, you've still got time to walk out," Liz grinned
back at him.

"Just let him try," said Cass, "I'll feed him arsenic if
he tries to walk out on me."

All three were laughing as they entered the flat.

The lounge looked as neat and clean as the two girls
had left it, with the scarlet of the geraniums bravely
shining in the grey light of the cloudy day. But it was
stuffy and Liz rushed to open the window. There was a
surprise for both Cass and Kevin, although Liz already
knew about it. A gay blue and white check cloth on the
table; a bottle of champagne with two wine glasses; a
cold roast chicken; salad; a crusty loaf, butter and
cheese; fresh fruit; *and* a basket of strawberries with a
carton of cream.

Cass, her eyes enormous, stared.

"Look! Oh, Kevin, *Liz*, how *super!* A banquet all
ready, and champaggers too."

Before Kevin could add his word of praise, Cass
turned to Liz.

"This is your doing—or your mother's."

"Well, it was Mum's idea of a surprise," said Liz.

"It's absolutely super," Cass repeated, her eyes now
full of tears.

Kevin ran his fingers through his rather untidy black
hair.

"It really is great. Your mother is the most generous
woman I've ever met, Liz."

"She was glad to be able to do it. She came along
here early this morning. Luckily I still had the key in
my bag so didn't have to ask Cass. She'd prepared it all
last night. Well, folks, now I must get back. Mum wants
the car."

"Oh, but you must stay and have a glass of champagne with us," began Kevin.

"I can't. I must go. And besides it's all for you two.
You can have a feast by yourselves, whether Kev's in
his bed or out of it. But I dare say Sister Hayes will
allow him to stay up for his midday meal."

She embraced them both and wished them luck.

Then she was gone and the young couple were alone.

Chapter 7

ARM in arm Kevin and Cass went through the little flat.
It still looked dingy and second-rate after the Burnhams' home, but Kevin was impressed by the new shining cleanliness and the changes Cass had made.

"I can see a man really does need feminine influence," he observed.

"Well, it *is* a bit improved, I admit," laughed Cass.
"After lunch, bed for you. I promised them at the hos-
pital and I *don't* want your bad headache to come back.
You haven't got one now, have you?"

He hadn't the heart to tell her that there was a nagging pain in his temples; that his whole skull felt sore,
and that he was still suffering from the shock of the
accident. When they were in the bedroom he put his left
arm around Cass's slim waist and held her close for a
moment.

"I don't feel anything but an overwhelming passion
for you. God knows I love you, Cass. Although while I
was in Brussels I had all kinds of inhibitions about
marrying you, me being so hard up and with so little to
offer and all that but—"

She broke in:

"I'd rather be married to you on nothing than be the
wife of any millionaire you care to name. It's you I
love," and she put both hands around his neck and
kissed him back with a warmth that matched his. They

trembled in each other's embrace, kissing wildly, urgently, until Cass suddenly noticed the little beads of perspiration on Kevin's forehead, and his cheeks felt cold rather than hot, like her own.

"You're not well yet, not totally well. We must be sensible, darling," she whispered and drew away from him.

He found a handkerchief, wiped his forehead and suddenly lay down on the bed and closed his eyes.

In sudden terror she ran to him.

"Kev, Kev, are you all right?"

Those marvellous blue eyes, which were to her the mirrors of her heart's desire, opened again. He smiled and held out his uninjured arm.

"I'm okay, my love. It's just I felt a bit giddy. Sister said I might. I suppose I *couldn't* face a wedding tomorrow even if it were possible."

"You're dead right, darling."

Relieved to see him smiling again and with a more normal look, Cass put a pillow under his head and another under the bad arm.

"Lie quiet, darling. Don't get up again. We'll celebrate later. You'll feel better tonight. We'll have our feast in here—I'll fix it. You'll see. It's just reaction, and you really must have gone through hell on that flight, plus the journey down to Richmond so soon after the accident."

He pressed the palm of her hand against his lips.

"It's superb, here in my flat—and with my wife to look after me. You see—I look on you as my wife already, Cass."

"I will be, too, on Saturday," she whispered. "Now do shut your eyes, angel, while I make you a nice cup of Nescafé. You like that better than tea, don't you? And shall I light you a cigarette?"

"I gave up smoking while I was in Brussels. It's a pernicious habit and I want to save cash for you."

Cass looked down at him, wide-eyed.

"We-ell! That is something; You adored smoking."

"Bad for the lungs," he grinned.

"Well, it's sweet of you to want to give it up for me, and I'll give up something, too."

"I'd like to know what," he said. "You haven't got a single vice."

"Yes, I have—*you*—but I don't intend to give *you* up."

As she flirted with this man whom she was so soon to marry, she unpacked his case, pulled out his pyjamas and dressing-grown and a few other things he would need tonight. She found one pair of clean cotton sheets and a pillow-case, in the cupboard. She'd fix his bed while he was washing. She'd tuck herself up on the divan in the lounge. Then she'd go and buy some more linen and a few towels. She had Bob Burnham's twenty pounds in her bag. How useful it would be! The things they'd need—bare necessities—would take every penny. Thank goodness they were both earning.

The bedroom was long and narrow but had two windows which she opened wide. The outlook was not attractive. It was all chimney-tops and near-placed houses, as gloomy and depressing as their own, and this morning it was darker than ever because of the gathering thunder clouds.

She wished for Kev's sake that she could have taken him today to convalesce in a beautiful hotel overlooking the sea or a lake—or anything but the backs of buildings in Russell Square with the roar of London traffic to disturb the peace.

But she was satisfied that Kevin had quite recovered from his temporary giddiness. Then she busied herself in the kitchen, found a round Woolworth's tray and placed two blue and white striped Woolworth's cups, saucers and spoons on it. Goodness, they'd need more crockery, *and* knives and forks. Kev and Barney must have done all their eating out. Having made the coffee, she took it to Kev, and sat talking to him.

They discussed their appreciation of the kindly Burnhams. There was a call-box in the main hall downstairs. She'd phone Mrs. Burnham tonight and thank her. This afternoon while he dozed, she'd pop out. There were quite a few shops at the end of Groom Street. They needed more milk and eggs and coffee. She'd make a list. Kevin teased her. He was sitting up now, more himself.

"Quite the little housewife, aren't we?"

"I'm learning," she laughed. "I've never done much of this sort of thing because Mummy did it all at home, but I've been watching dear Mrs. Burnham and gained quite a bit of experience from her."

"I shall appreciate all you do, my love. I've never been really looked after since Aunt Millie died and that was some time ago."

"Well, you know how unhappy I've been since Daddy died, so we're both rather two little orphans of the storm, so we'll love each other like anything, and look after each other," said Cass.

"You bet we will. I only wish Aunt Millie could have met you. She'd have approved. She was a nice person, rather of the Mrs. Burnham type, only thin instead of fat but she had the same generous kindly qualities. I was only thinking the other day that I ought to try and look up my other aunt, her sister Cynthia. I never met her. She married a South African and went to live in Capetown when I was infant. For all I know she might be dead too."

"Well, it's always nice to find a *nice* relation. I haven't got anybody in the world except Mummy and that ghastly man she married."

"I must sieve through some of Aunt Millie's letters which are in an old trunk down in the basement. They allow you to put luggage in one of those iron-barred prisons they used to call kitchens—no longer used as such."

"Do you think you might find your aunt still alive?"

"Should do. Aunt Cynthia was older than Aunt Mill. I often heard stories of how pretty she was and considered naughty. Fast they called it in those days. I'm sure I would have liked her."

"Do you know her married name?"

"Mrs. de Groot—yes, she married a Dutchman."

"Oh, Kev, do try and contact her. They might have a gorgeous ranch in South Africa and we could go out and stay with them."

"You're an optimist, sweetie. Anyhow, when would *we* be rich enough to afford the fare to the Cape?"

"Yes, there is that about it," sighed Cass.

"Added to which Aunt Mill told me, if I remember right, in a letter while I was still at university, that she'd heard that Aunt Cynthia and her husband were in England. But she never saw them. There was one of these old-fashioned feuds between the sisters. Aunt Mill was a spinster, and I believe she was once in love with this Dutch fellow but the lovely Cynthia stole him away so poor Mill wouldn't ever speak to her again. My mother used to keep in touch with Cynthia when *she* was alive, but I know nothing more."

"I'll still stick to my belief that you should try to find Aunt Cynthia," said Cass. "Now I'm going out to look at the local shops and you're to have a nap."

When Cass returned with her shopping bag full, she felt a bit anxious about the amount she had spent, and on so few things. It was the first time she had really come up against the rising prices for a housewife. She would have to be careful.

She found Kevin asleep. She looked down at the dark hair ruffled on the pillow and the fine-drawn face, rather pathetically young in repose. Of course he was twenty-three—quite an age for a man these days but they would have a tough financial fight, she thought, sighing, despite any allowances or 'perks' to be got from the Welfare State.

She moved softly round the flat during the next hour or two, rearranging furniture, forming plans to make it all look better in time. She decided eventually to get somebody to help her move the divan from the sitting-room into the bedroom so that they could put the two mattresses across, and make a double bed of them. At the thought of her forthcoming wedding and how close, how splendidly warm and close, they would be then in each other's arms, her heart beat fast and furiously.

She began to feel hungry. As soon as Kev woke they would have their chicken and open the champagne. Why not? It was half-past one before Kevin surfaced and joined her in the sitting-room. He insisted on getting up for lunch with her. She was delighted to see him looking so much brighter. He seemed in high spirits. He opened the champagne, and they toasted each other.

"To my near-wife of the very, very, *very* near future!" he said, his warm blue eyes caressing her.

"To my very, very, *very* near-husband!" she answered blissfully.

They laughed, kissed and drank their champagne. The scene was somewhat rudely interrupted by the sound of the front door bell.

"That might be one of Barney's creditors," said Kevin dryly.

"Don't move, I'll see," said Cass.

She was astonished and not a little perturbed when she opened the front door to disclose the all-too familiar figure of her mother, Mrs. Woodbeare, in the light blue raincoat which she always wore when it was raining, and with a scarf tied over her head. In her arms she carried a large box. She looked very friendly and smiling.

"Heavens, Mummy, I never expected to see *you!*" exclaimed Cass.

"Well, here I am. Aren't you going to invite me in?" asked Mrs. Woodbeare pleasantly, and added: "What a *dreadful* approach to your new home, dear. The taxi hardly knew where to come. I've told him to wait for me. I can't stay more than a few moments."

Somewhat reluctantly, Cass let her mother into the flat. She was apprehensive. She saw danger ahead and the red light flashed even more ominously when Mrs. Woodbeare went on:

"Your stepfather and I are going down to Poole tomorrow. I just felt I couldn't leave without seeing you even though he wouldn't let me go to your wedding. But now you're married, I felt it would relieve my mind to see you and wish you both happiness. I've brought you a nice large cake, my dear, and a few scones."

Cass led her mother into the small sitting-room. Those words *Now that you're married,* had made her heart sink. Of course Mummy didn't know about the present situation.

Mrs. Woodbeare placed her box on the table and stared around her, obviously none too impressed by what she saw. Shabby and common, she thought. What *would* Miles have said if he'd seen it? But determined to be friendly, she held out a hand to Kevin.

"Congratulations, Kevin," she said, with a little cough.

He looked at the woman who was virtually his mother-in-law. He did not actively dislike her. He felt indifferent to poor '*Yes-dear*'. A weak and stupid creature in his opinion, yet in that blue mac, with the scarf over her hair, she looked more youthful than usual and he had to admit that like this she bore a distinct resemblance to his adored Cass. She must have been pretty at Cass's age, he thought. But that was as far as the resemblance went.

"I agree, I'm a lucky man to have Cass," he said.

Mrs. Woodbeare loosened her scarf and pushed back her hair. Cass who knew her so well could read the contempt in the expression with which she examined her surroundings. It wasn't only the approach to the flat she despised. A few more shocks awaited her, Cass thought grimly.

"May I sit down?" asked Mrs. Woodbeare.

"Of course," Kevin answered.

Now they both sat down, but Cass remained standing—at a loss for words.

"Well, you two, I can't pretend to approve, but there it is! I've been very naughty and gone behind my husband's back. I didn't tell him I was coming to see you. It's the only time I've ever deceived him, but after all, Cass, you *are* my daughter, dear, and I suppose you must in these days be allowed to marry who you wish. Oh, well, show me your wedding ring and tell me all about the affair. I presume it was at the Register Office. Did your friend Mrs. Burnham hold a little reception for you afterwards? She seems a very good friend."

Cass and Kevin exchanged agonised glances. Perhaps if Cass had been left to answer, she might have prevaricated in order to save trouble. But Kevin, with his burning sense of honesty, his refusal to accept any form of lying or hypocrisy, was the first to retort:

"We can't tell you about the wedding, because it hasn't taken place."

Mrs. Woodbeare's forced smile vanished. She looked so surprised and horrified that Cass had an hysterical desire to laugh; instead of which she coughed and blurted out:

"Kevin had an accident. He was run over. You can see his arm—I only fetched him from hospital this morning."

Dorothy Woodbeare looked from the arm encased in plaster, back to her daughter's face. Her own was scarlet.

"I see—I'm sorry—I mean about the accident. So your wedding was *postponed*. How unfortunate. Oh, well, would you care to share my taxi to the Underground, Cass? I expect you're still living at Richmond."

But Cass was ready and willing now to be honest. Why *should* they dissemble, or allow her mother to wallow in her respectable conjectures.

"No, Mummy," she said, "I'm *living here*. We moved in today. Kevin has nobody else to look after him. He's no longer a hospital case, but he can't do a thing for himself with only one arm now, can he?"

Silence. Mrs. Woodbeare tied on her scarf again.

"You are living here—without being married?"

"Yes," said Cass.

"This is a shock to me," said Mrs. Woodbeare in a whisper.

"Not so much a shock as it was to me when I was knocked down in the Grande Place of Brussels," said Kevin cheerfully. "But don't worry, Mrs. Woodbeare, if it's your daughter's honour you're concerned about, I'll hold up my right hand, and swear to preserve that honour until such time as we can get to the Registrar, which will, I hope, be on Saturday morning."

Dorothy Woodbeare sat silent. Her air of *bonhomie* had completely disappeared. She looked so upset that Cass started to feel sorry for her because she knew the older generation had set ideas about these things. But pity quickly changed to anger. Mrs. Woodbeare rose to her feet, buttoned up her raincoat, and said:

"Your stepfather was right. He said you had no principles, Cass, and no gratitude to us, considering how good we've been to you. I agree with him. I'm sorry I bothered to go behind his back and come here. I didn't really think I'd find you in, you know. I thought you'd be at work and I intended to leave your cake with a neighbour, or some sort of caretaker. Then when I saw a hall-light through the glass in your front door I realised someone was in, so I knocked. But I'm *sorry*. It was a mistake."

"Now look here, Mummy, what's all this imply?" asked Cass, her cheeks flaming. "Hasn't Kevin just told you that you need not worry about my *honour?*"

"That's as it may be," broke in her mother, "but I'm afraid my outlook—like your stepfather's—is different from yours. Or from that of any of you young people today. You all lack a sense of decency."

"One moment, Mrs. Woodbeare, that's rather a strong word," broke in Kevin sharply.

She swung round on him.

"I have nothing to say to *you*. I'm sorry about your accident and I'm sure it was a disappointment to you both that you had to postpone the wedding. But when Cass says she is already *living* here in this—this *awful* flat with you and people thinking you're married when you're *not,* I find it most distasteful. I can't get over it! I did think, Cass—" she turned back to her daughter— "that you wouldn't do a thing like *this*."

Cass felt maddened.

"A thing like *what?*"

"Living with Kevin, people thinking you're husband and wife. I met some old man in the main hall just now. I asked him which flat Mrs. and Mrs. Martin had and he said the top one. *He* thought you were Mr. and Mrs."

"Good for him," snapped Kevin. "I repeat what I said to you just now—we intend to get married on Saturday. Cass is not able to get any more time off so it couldn't be before."

"Did you expect me to let Kevin, with only one arm in use, look after himself?" demanded Cass.

"I don't want to discuss it," said Mrs. Woodbeare. "Whatever excuse you make, you know quite well you ought not to be sharing a flat alone with a man until you *are* married."

Kevin stood up.

"I don't wish to be rude to you, Mrs. Woodbeare, because whether you like it or not you are about to become my mother-in-law. And whether you like it or not Cass is very sweetly making a home with me here until such time as I can place the ring on her finger. And if you and the General wish to think of us as wicked sinners leading a disreputable life for a few days, you are welcome to your thoughts."

"And at least," put in Cass, "there are people like Mr. and Mrs. Burnham who are the same generation as you and the General, but who don't immediately place the worst construction on things. They take it for granted that we have *some* standards, even if they are not as high as yours. Now, Mummy, I am not going to have Kevin upset any more. He isn't at all well yet. You'd better go."

Mrs. Woodbeare's face puckered. She pulled a handkerchief from her bag and placed it to her lips.

"I wish I had never come. I'll have to keep it to myself. I certainly dare not tell Miles."

"What would the General do if he did know—court-martial me?" asked Kevin flippantly, and sat down again because Cass was right. His head *was* swimming a little. Why in the name of fortune did '*Yes-dear*' want to come and upset them like this? Poor sweet Cass! How did she put up with this intolerant prude for so long?

Cass, soft-hearted as usual, followed her mother into the hall.

"Now, don't cry and upset yourself, Mummy, it's all so silly. I'm *not* going to disgrace you. I shall remain pure as the driven snow until Saturday. Is that any consolation to you?"

"No, it's not—the whole thing—the way you ran away from home—marrying against our wishes—this sordid place—everything is dreadful. Your father would have been heart-broken."

Impulsively Cass said:

"I'm not at all sure he would. He thought the best of people. You told me so, and if Daddy had lived, I wouldn't have run away. The General chucked me out, anyhow, and told me not to darken his doorstep again,

didn't he?" Then Cass added in an exasperated way:
"Oh, *do* stop crying, Mummy. I'll be all right. I'll write
to Poole, if you'll give me the address, and let you
know I'm safely married."

. "I don't think I want to hear from you," said Mrs.
Woodbeare in a smothered voice. "It would be better if
we don't have any contact for the present."

She was down the first staircase now. Cass, full of
resentment, leaned over the banisters and called out:

"Well, you can't stop me from collecting all my bits
and pieces. I need them, as no doubt your eagle-eye
was quick to notice, Mummy. And I'm madly happy—
just being able to look after Kev. And in the future I
shall be happier than I *ever* was at Putney, so that's
that."

A pause, then a faint—very faint—gesture from
Mrs. Woodbeare who called up:

"Let me know when you intend to send for your
things, please. I'd rather *you* did not come yourself.
We'll only quarrel."

"Married or single," said Cass humorously. "Okay,
I'll send someone else. Goodbye, Mummy."

"Goodbye, Cass."

Slowly the girl turned and walked back into the flat.
Her eyelids were smarting. This, she felt, might indeed
be a long farewell to her mother. The mother who,
years ago, Cass had loved and whom poor Daddy had
once loved, too. What a sad sorry woman she had
grown into after ten years with General Woodbeare.
And how completely she had blighted the innocent little
party that Cass and Kevin had been having. But she
wasn't going to let Kev see she was upset. It was just
unpleasant. A waste, too, that her mother, having come
with good intentions, should have gone away feeling angry and shocked, without reason.

Kevin, with difficulty, and one hand, was trying to
slice a piece of chicken with a not-very-sharp kitchen
knife. He grinned at her.

"Hardly a cheerful interlude, I fear. Hope it hasn't
upset you, darling."

"I hope it hasn't upset *you*, Kev."

"Not at all. But oh, my Cass, I hate smug respectable

people who place the worst construction on things and I think poor '*Yes-dear*' really does believe our being here together is imperilling our immortal souls."

"Let's try and forget her and have our lunch in peace," said Cass in a low voice.

"I love you," said Kevin. "Don't be sorry you've come to look after me so sinfully, will you?"

"You know I won't. I adore you. Are you sure you are well enough to have this meal, or shall I bring it to you in bed?"

He made a clicking noise with his tongue.

"What a *disgraceful* suggestion, my dear Miss Hayes."

Now they laughed again. Cass cheered up enormously.

"Poor old Mum—I only wish she were as happy as we are and it's really rather sad, her bringing up a wedding cake, too."

"Is that what it is? Let's open the box and have a slice," said Kevin cheerfully. "I'm keen on cake."

"You don't think you ought to go back to bed?"

"No, I'm all right. My head's clear again. I feel miles better, and as soon as we've had lunch, darling, we'll ring up the Registrar's Office and see if we can't make a firm date for Saturday."

"Will do," said Cass.

He moved his body, touched his injured arm and grimaced as though he had a sudden pain, she thought.

Her flippancy vanished and gave way to distress.

"Oh, Kev—what's the matter?"

"The damned old arm is aching."

"Is that by any chance an understatement?"

"Not at all—let's eat," said Kevin.

But it wasn't true . . . the arm was hurting badly and so was his head. He ate nothing and before the afternoon ended was back in bed with a slight temperature. Cass panicked. The old gentleman below recommended the nearest National Health doctor. When he came it was to kill any hopes Cass and Kevin had entertained of being married on Saturday morning.

Dr. Mackenzie was a nice, fresh-faced, bespectacled young Scot, thoroughly overworked but still smiling. He was also intelligent. He got into touch with the hospital that had recently discharged Kevin, made sure from the X-rays that there was no infection in the bone and satisfied himself that Kevin's condition was due only to a too-quick discharge from the ward, and strain. Kevin could not altogether conceal his nervous, highly strung disposition from the shrewd Scot. After cautioning him to stay in bed for at least another week and get as much sleep as possible, he took Cass into the sitting-room and gave her a few instructions.

"I'm sure you'll be capable of looking after your husband, Mrs. Martin," he said, tearing a slip off his prescription pad and handing it to her: "As I've said, keep him quiet. He'll be fine. But one must remember he was knocked down and it was a real shock. They should never have let him out of that hospital in Brussels. He's got guts. He managed to fly home. But now he's paying for the effort. No going back to work for at least ten days."

Cass's face burned as she heard those words 'Mrs. Martin'. She looked down at the prescription, her heart sinking. No *wedding*—well, what did anything matter now except that Kevin should get well.

"I can look after him," she said.

"There won't be anything much to do but feed him and give him these tablets. His temperature will probably be down in the morning. You haven't been married very long, have you?" the doctor added, smiling at her over his glasses. He was thinking that she looked more like a little girl than a married woman—all that soft brown hair falling around her flushed face; so slim; a charming girl.

Cass managed to stammer:

"N-no, not long, doctor."

"You know my number now. Ring me if you want me," he said, and was gone.

Cass went back to Kevin's bedside.

"I must leave you for a moment, love. I've just got to get this prescription made up. He says it will relieve your head and bring down the temp."

Kevin looked up at her, groaning.

"What a useless so-and-so I am to you. Sorry, my Cass."

She knelt beside him, took his uninjured hand and put it against her cheek.

"You know you're not useless and you couldn't help your accident."

"I'll make up for it when I'm better," he whispered.

"I'm thrilled to be able to look after you in our own flat, you know that."

"Well, *you* must go to work tomorrow, whatever happens. I won't want food until you come home. Just get me a few oranges."

"If only I could stay with you, but we *must* have money. I daren't lose my job."

"I won't need ten days' convalescence. The doctor was playing it safe. I'll be right as rain by the week-end."

"Wait and see."

He tried to laugh.

"Think what '*Yes-dear*' would say. Her daughter leading a dishonourable life for at least another week."

That made her smile. Life with Kevin was good even when things were difficult. She felt suddenly blissfully happy again.

Chapter 8

KEVIN had youth, plus an indomitable spirit on his side. He was not going to allow life to get him down for long. He made a more rapid recovery than Dr. Mackenzie had prophesied. Within twenty-four hours of the set-back he had recovered from the fever. There were no more headaches. The aching arm seemed to be settling down.

It became a tussle for Cass to keep him in bed. She

threatened to walk out of the flat and leave him to his fate if he disobeyed her and got up.

"I'll get back on you for all this bullying once you're my wife," he threatened in return. She laughed and stopped the rest of the threats with kisses. But after a night's rest he seemed so much better she let him get up, and by Friday, Kevin was really well again.

On the Friday evening they went out for a short stroll around Russell Square, through the warm summer evening. Cass liked the fresh air and the star-bright sky and felt undeniably happy. How she loved him! Despite the disfigurement of that arm jutting out on its splint, she adored the swagger of his thin, lean, tall figure, with those loose, thin, high, thin shoulders. They were just *Kevin*. Like his Irish eyes. She was never tired of looking at him.

When they were up in the flat again she asked anxiously if he felt at all tired. Tongue in cheek, he answered:

"Still doing the big wife act, hey? You're the sort of girl that likes having a man under her thumb."

"You know I'm not at all like that!" she protested indignantly. "But the doctor said you needed at least ten days' convalescence."

They were in the kitchen. Cass was about to take a couple of steaks (which she had bought extravagantly), out of the fridge. But Kevin, with his good arm, pulled her away and up against him.

"I'm pretty mad about you, you know," he said in a low tone.

"Oh, Kev!" Her eyes shone. "You know I am, too, about you. It's been so wonderful looking after you like this."

He continued to hold her fast while she laced her fingers behind his neck.

"Okay, but listen, honey. I don't dig the idea of ten days' convalescence and I don't intend to pay the slightest attention to the doctor. I'll ask you a question. How do you suppose I'm going to stand it if I'm forced to live here alone with you in what you call 'our flat' much longer? All this brother and sister act and what have you?"

She knew exactly what he meant. She felt exactly the same. It was not an easy situation. It had been all right while he was 'her invalid', 'her patient', but there was no more nursing to be done. He was feeling good, and he was, as he said, *mad about her*.

She hid a burning face against his shoulder.

"Kev . . . all the time we've been together here since I joined you, you've been great to me. Life has been great. But I agree with what you say. Only—"

"Okay," he broke in, "what do you propose we should do about it?"

She refused to look at him. After a second she began:

"Well, I know it's a bind but—"

He interrupted again:

"Masterly understatement."

"Okay. I'd better go away until we *can* be married," she whispered.

"And leave me—the one-armed man—to look after myself," he jeered. "*There's* mad love for you!"

She lifted a flushed, embarrassed face.

"Don't tease me. What can I do about it, Kev? We agreed, didn't we—?"

He let her get no further. He kissed her on the mouth.

"Sweet, *sweet* Cassandra—okay! I won't pull your leg any more. But I'm not going to let you walk out on me—or those principles you cherish. I wouldn't be able to look '*Yes-dear*' in the face again if I did. (Not that I anticipate that she'll ever give me the chance.) So I'll tell you what's going to happen to you. You'll go to bed early. You'll have a nice long sleep, and tomorrow morning I, with my one good hand, will make you a cup of tea and bring it to you and wake you up and say: 'Good morning, Miss Hayes. It's a fine day.' (It's going to be, you know, because the forecast's good.) Then I'll say 'Happy the bride the sun shines on' and you'll ask me what I mean and I'll tell you. I'm telling you now. At eleven a.m. tomorrow the marriage between Kevin Martin and Cassandra Hayes will take place at the Register Office in Richmond, after which Mr. Martin will give Mrs. Martin a damned good lunch, after which they will call on the Burnhams to receive congratulations and a few savouries that the said Mrs. Burnham has made for the Martins to take home. After *that*, sweet Cass, you won't be able to walk out on me. If you do, I'll have the marriage annulled."

Cass listened to this speech in utter confusion and with a breathless mounting excitement. Her mouth opened wide, then she gasped:

"Kevin! Have you gone quite crazy? Do you really mean we're going to be married *tomorrow?* Have you really made all these *arrangements?"*

He nodded, kissed her again and sat on the edge of the kitchen table, grinning. She loved that grin. Sometimes in repose Kevin's face looked sad, even gloomy. When it was like that she left him alone. She took it for granted that the creative spirit was working in him— troubling his mind. But such moods were over quickly and then he would laugh again and joke and all would be well. But now she was rapturous with happiness and gratitude.

"You've kept it a secret from me! You must have phoned the Registrar and the Burnhams and fixed it all behind my back, when I was out."

"My love, I had to. I was just about frenzied. Besides I felt that damned silly accident in Brussels spoilt all your fun—all the preparations you'd made for our wedding. I also knew you wouldn't be able to get any more time off from the shop. You said so. So it had to be tomorrow or wait another whole week. And I couldn't face that."

Her heart swelled with pride. Who else could have been so marvellous or considerate as Kev? She wanted to cry. Instead, she turned away from him so that he shouldn't see her brimming eyes.

"Well, really! How could you be sure you were going to be fit enough to be married? You've made a terrifically quick recovery. But oh, Kev, I'm so thrilled. You don't *know!"*

"I do know," he said. "Come back to me."

She turned. He was holding out the good hand. She placed hers in it and gave a small nervous laugh.

"I can't believe this is the last day I shall be Cassandra Hayes," she said huskily. "It's fantastic."

"You've been fantastic to me, darling. Thanks for all you've done. It hasn't been much of a start for you in this sordid flat, but as I sold those articles, I swear I'll write something terrific soon and make piles of money for you. You'll see."

"I know you will," she said fervently.

"You're so sweet, the way you believe in me."

"*You* believe in *me*, or you wouldn't be marrying me."

"I think we get on well, don't you?"

"Putting it mildly," she laughed up at him.

"I hope you agree that it's best for us just to slide into the Registrar's alone and get the marriage over, without the friends or limelight."

"I absolutely agree."

He lifted her hand and kissed the palm.

"To tell you the truth, I don't think I've ever been so thrilled in the whole of my hard-working life, though I doubt if I shall be as happy tomorrow."

"You mean just because then you'll be legally tied up to me?" she asked indignantly.

He laughed.

"I'm pulling your leg again, angel. Let's have our feast."

Radiant, heart beating so quickly that she hardly knew how to control her breathing, Cassandra returned to her domestic chores.

Darling, *darling* Kevin—this last week had taught her a lot more about him than she had known before. She was sure some men in the same situation might not have behaved nearly as well as he had done these last few days. She thought of her mother and the General, and wished that they could be told how right she had been about Kev, and how wrong *they* were. Later that evening, with her arms around him and her cheek pressed to his strongly-beating heart, she crooned a few words from her favourite song:

I know where I'm going and I know who'll come with me. I know who I love and . . .

She paraphrased the next line:

I DO know who I'll marry!

The great wedding day dawned. At last Cass put on the attractive blue outfit that Mrs. Burnham had helped her make, and Liz's big white hat.

It was all very brief and cut and dried, with two of the staff to witness the marriage. Then they were on their way to the Burnhams.

As Cass drove away from the Register Office with Kevin, she looked down at her narrow gold wedding ring and felt breathless with happiness.

"Here comes the bride," said Kevin and kissed her sweet, pale pink mouth. "You've got eyes like saucers," he teased her, "and may I say you're just my 'cup', love. You look delicious."

"The right cup for the right saucer," she giggled.

They sat with their arms around each other, driving to the Burnhams' house.

For Cass, this was the fulfillment of a dream. Penniless they might be, but at least they were *together*. In the real big meaning of 'togetherness', she decided with deep sentiment. She had once coveted a 'white wedding' in a little church somewhere, but things hadn't worked out that way. Because of their virtual elopement, of course. While she had looked after Kevin in the flat, she had felt already that she was a married woman. Did the words and the certificate and this darling ring on her finger make all that difference? Yes, she knew that they did. Marriage would always mean something. She must write to her mother today. She would sign the letter *'Cassandra'* and relieve *her* anxiety.

Kevin's thoughts were much the same as his wife's, but with just that masculine difference. He felt sentimental but he was thinking about his temporary job, and whether or not he ought to keep it, so as to be sure of bringing home the pay-packet. He was thinking also of his talent as an author. Life was odd, he reflected. A short time ago he was a bachelor, telling his friends he didn't intend to get married for years. He used to be quite scared of being tied up to any girl.

But he had met Cassandra. And here he was, a married man. She was a darling, and he knew that he was a lucky chap.

The Burnhams received the young couple with open arms. There were kisses and hugs and congratulations all round. Mr. Burnham had wanted to stand them a dinner, but understood when Kevin told him that it was his special wish to take his wife to a restaurant and be madly extravagant, himself, on this great day. Nevertheless, Mr. Burnham had a bottle of champagne ready in their own home, first of all. The family drank toasts and fussed over Kevin's broken arm, over Cass because she looked so beautiful—and over the pair of them. And finally they were driven by Liz to the flat there they deposited the huge box of food for the rest of the week which Violet Burnham had, in her generous way, packed up for them. Afterwards Cass and Kevin went on to the Savoy. In the Grill Room, when the menu was handed to Cass, Kevin leaned across the table and whispered:

"Don't look at the prices. Order exactly what you want, Mrs. Martin. And make the best of it, because I don't suppose I'll ever be able to afford to bring you here again; at least not for years and years."

"Gloomy prospect," said Cass, and sniffed.

"If you're not satisfied, honey, we can have the marriage annulled."

"Just try," said Cass. "What *I* want, Mr. Martin, is a prawn cocktail, then roast duckling—then we'll see if I've any room left for a sweet."

"Madness," said Kevin. "You'll die of indigestion. I'll have the same."

They shared a half bottle of white wine and raised their glasses to each other.

"To my wife," said Kevin, and gave her the sort of look that make her heart turn over.

"To my husband," she whispered. She suddenly wanted to cry and that was the last thing a bride should do. Why was it, she wondered, that tremendous happiness should make you feel tearful? It was so silly. The difficulties of her childhood, with her stepfather, seemed in this golden hour to drift away like phantoms of the night, dispelled by the sunlight. She could deal with any troubles ahead. All she wanted was to be a good wife to Kevin. He must never *never* feel that he had been too hasty and quixotic, carrying her off like this; marrying her against her family's wishes. Neither must he ever be allowed to get bored, and sink in those sombre moods that she dreaded. Today, at least, held nothing but glorious promise. She loved him, *loved* him, and felt herself equally loved.

That night in the little flat, the twin beds were put side by side and the mattresses made into one and there was no longer a wall between them. They had an awful lot of fun making up that bed. Kevin kept saying:

"Damn this abominable arm. I want to be more help to you and I want to hold you with both of my arms. It's maddening."

She kept assuring him that one arm was quite enough, quite strong enough, too. So finally they lay close to each other, and it was an enchanted night, and the sordid little room seemed as near heaven as they could get.

They were blissfully happy on the Monday morning. Kevin, however, was frustrated because he could not carry on with his work until his arm was out of its splint. If he wanted to use his typewriter, he could use one finger, but at slow speed, and he hated writing with a pen. That was slow, too. His thoughts ran so quickly. But he hated to see Cass, his newly-made wife, going off to work and leaving him behind.

"I feel what they call in Yorkshire 'right daft'," he grumbled. "Staying here like a female and you going off to the job. What am I going to do till you come back?"

"Read and rest and *don't* attempt the chores—leave them," she said. "I'll do them when I get back. Just be here—that's all I ask."

He smiled down at her. She was so glowing, so warm and sweet, and so full of love for him, he could only adore her.

"I'll be waiting for you. I'll live for the moment," he said and held her very close.

Cass remained ecstatically happy all through the summer months. It was hot and stuffy up in that flat, noisy and soul-destroying at times because of the impossibility of keeping anything clean. She had no washing-machine, no spin-dryer, no luxuries. It was all hard work in the old-fashioned sense of the word. They just couldn't afford modern gadgets. They had both begun to put by every penny they could afford out of their joint incomes, determined not to stay too long in Groom Street, but to look for another smaller flat if need be so long as it had the tiniest garden, or a back yard where they could get some fresh air, and not feel so stifled.

Cass had never admired Kevin more than during these early stages of their marriage. She knew how passionately he wanted to find time to write. Once he returned to his job he was only able to turn out a few articles, working at weekends, and sometimes late into the night. Then Cass would lie alone in their big home-made bed and listen to the tap-tap of the machine and feel her heart sink, because he looked so tired and she didn't think he was getting enough sleep. As soon as his head touched the pillow he was lost to her, and she had to shake him awake to get him off to the office in time. As usual she was the cheerful one, ready to gloss over difficulties. He was a good husband—never allowed her to wash up unless he dried, and helped her clean the flat on Saturday mornings. He cut out his drinks as well as cigarettes, in order to put more into the 'kitty'. He wanted to supply more than *she* did, he told her. She thought that so sweet of him; but she still had his dark moods to contend with. But if ever he was terse or being difficult, he quickly repented and within a matter of minutes was taking her in his arms, kissing her with a lover's passionate warmth, making her feel that all was well again.

By the time the summer ended Cass had grown used to her status as Kevin's wife, but she had the curious feeling that she was in a kind of hiatus—suspended through space. Every day was the same. They went to work, they came back, they tried to save. Often they couldn't. They loved, laughed, and sometimes fought, but always with love. Not once did she regret leaving home. If she found having a temperamental husband who was like a square peg in a round hole difficult, she managed him. She managed her own life too. Her natural optimism remained uppermost—even when she, herself suffered from moments of depression. But she never let Kevin know.

"I can see when Kev's upset but I don't think he notices when I am. Men are very different," she remarked to Liz after one awkward session with her moody husband.

Liz, who was practically putting the needle and thread into the last article for her trousseau, smiled at her friend.

"Men *are* different," she echoed, "*and* how! Wonder how I'll cope after the marriage bells stop ringing. Not as well as you, I bet!"

To Cass, the loss of Liz once she married her doctor and flew off to Sydney where he had been offered a good job, was considerable. Liz was her one really close and dear girl-friend. They had shared so much since they left school.

But it had to be. Cass knew that Mrs. Burnham missed her daughter almost unbearably at times. The distance between them now was very great. So Cass saw Mrs. Burnham whenever she could and grew closer to both Liz's parents as time went on. She and Kevin were always welcome at the house in Richmond. Violet Burnham now called Cass 'my little second daughter', and cherished her accordingly.

They had been worried about Liz before her marriage, but now all seemed well. Cass felt that Liz, herself, had been unduly anxious about making the grade as Richard's wife. Her letters from Australia, once she settled down, came regularly and were ecstatic.

In the January of the succeeding year a very important coming event was announced.

Liz was going to have a baby.

When Cass was told she looked at Mrs. Burnham with eyes full of tears.

"Oh, I'm thrilled for her! How absolutely *incred-*

ible—Liz a mother! My goodness it makes me feel a childless old woman!"

"Don't be silly, dear," said Mrs. Burnham with her throaty laugh. "Neither of you girls have been married five minutes. There's plenty of time for babies, and *you* certainly can't think of having one until Kev's more settled. Bob and I are afraid he thoroughly dislikes that advertising job. Something must happen so that he can get down to his literary work. As for my Liz, well, she's in a different position. She's got a lovely home, and sunshine; and now a baby will crown her happiness."

"And you," said Cass, "will get down to some more knitting—*Granny!*"

"Do you know, I like the sound of that name!" said Mrs. Burnham proudly.

It was a wet, cold January.

Life wasn't as easy for Cass during the rest of that winter as it had been in the warm days.

They had to economise on the electricity and it was often bitterly cold up in that top flat. Cass felt she was never really warm unless tucked up snugly in bed with her adored husband. She remained well enough but Kev was addicted to colds. He had three bad ones in succession and in early February had to take a week off because of 'flu. Cass nursed him (as she had done before so successfully), switched on all fires, insisted on keeping him warm, and announced that the economising would have to stop for a week. Finally Kevin got up and went back to work looking thinner and paler than ever.

Then it was her turn. There came a night when her temperature was so high and she was so drenched with fever, that Kevin took fright. He was not used to seeing his pretty vivacious adored wife laid low like this. He stayed at home to feed her properly, nurse her up—and clean the flat that suffered from the temporary loss of its dedicated housewife. Unfortunately at this moment the Burnhams were all away. They had taken a winter holiday instead of a summer one and gone to relatives in Jersey. Kevin was finally reduced to asking Cass whether she would like him to telephone for her mother.

With fever-glazed eyes and splitting headache, Cass sat up in bed and screamed a protest.

"No, no, a *thousand* times no! I don't care how high my temperature is. I won't die. The doctor said so. He swore these antibiotic pills would put me right, and I think I *am* feeling a bit better tonight. For God's sake don't send for Mummy."

Kevin, wilting under the pressure of Cass's illness, his own work, and the general rat-race of life—particularly life without any money—acquiesced. He didn't really think he could stand '*Yes-dear*' around the place but if Cass wanted her—he'd stand aside. Cass didn't want her mother and she managed alone. Eventually she crawled out of her bed feeling ghastly—hollow-eyed and thinner. But she was on the mend.

She had had several letters from her mother during the last eight months but no visits—no invitations to the old home, even if Cass had wanted to go there. Fatuous letters, Kevin called them, typical of his mother-in-law, who wrote such things as:

> *I would come and see you, my dear, but the General doesn't want me to as he thinks it would only upset me.*

There seemed little chance of a reconciliation between Cass and her former family. She no longer belonged to them. She had become Kevin's 'family'. She wanted nothing, no one else. Youth and strength were on her side and she recovered from the nasty bout of flu even more rapidly than Kevin who coughed his way through February into March.

Their happiest times were the weekends when they went by coach down to Brighton. It was cold enough still and the winds were rough but the sea air was exhilarating after London and Russell Square. So in time Kevin pulled up, too, and with the advent of April they both felt back to their old form and able to work with energy again.

Cass was a careful housewife and Kevin was economising so they managed to add to their little pile of savings. In addition, Kevin, at intervals, sold his articles and even one short story which was a new venture. When Cass first saw his name in print her pride and pleasure knew no bounds. He found it touching because he knew he had been very short-tempered while he was writing the story. But if Cass was hurt when he snapped at her, she tried not to mind too much. She had married a budding genius, she told herself with humour, and must put up with his moods.

Came a night when they looked at their Savings Book and saw the total amounted to nearly four hundred pounds.

"Only a small proportion is out of my job, it's mainly your writing," Cass announced, her eyes shining.

He dropped a kiss on her hair and patted her flushed cheek.

"You're a darling and thanks for being so patient with me. I couldn't have saved a cent, living with any other girl, I swear it."

Cass rubbed her face against his.

"Well, you're not going to live with any other girl *ever*, so you're okay. Let's take out the whole four hundred pounds and squander it."

"You have to be joking," said Kevin, "but what I'd like to do is to take out a hundred and us go abroad on a package deal this summer. You look fantastically tired sometimes and I feel like death warmed up. Why don't we give ourselves a proper holiday?'

"Let's think about it," said the practical Cass.

There was no knowing what might have come out of this suggestion if that next day there hadn't come a sudden break in their fortunes which put the idea of a summer holiday abroad right out of the picture, and it came in the shape of a long white envelope—a letter addressed to *Kevin Martin, Esq*.

Cass, who was home first, saw it, and put it on the kitchen table. She didn't really think much about it. She was too engrossed in trying to make a new dish of kedgeree with soy sauce to give it some extra flavour which would be good for Kevin's supper. While she worked, it suddenly struck her that she had been married to Kevin for nearly a whole year—unbelievable, but true. This was the first day of May—in six weeks' time they would be celebrating their first wedding anniversary. What bliss it had been!

Kevin came home.

"I feel grubby and look it," he said. "I must wash. What's this?" he picked the envelope up from the kitchen table.

"Don't know," said Cass bending over her stove and stirring the rice.

He slit the envelope, read in silence for a moment, and then Cass heard a gasp that made her lift her head and look at him.

"You look loopy," she said affectionately, "what's the news?"

"I feel loopy," he exclaimed. "Oh, *my giddy aunt!*"

And 'giddy-aunt' was the right words as Cass soon discovered, for he pulled her into the next room, sat her down on the sofa and thrust the letter into her hands.

"Read this, sweet, sweet Cassandra. Do you know I'm *flabbergasted*. I don't believe I ever told you but there's been so much on my mind these last few months I darned well forgot. Do you remember suggesting I should write to my Aunt Cynthia?"

Cass nodded. She was busy digesting the contents of the letter, only half hearing what Kevin was saying as he enlarged on the fact that he had told his aunt about his wedding and hoped that one day they might go out to South Africa and visit her. Then as the weeks went by and he did not get an answer, the whole matter slipped from his mind. But that casual letter to Aunt Cynthia had borne fruit. Thank God, he said, that he had found Aunt Cynthia's address in Capetown when he went through Aunt Millie's papers. Cass had suggested he should do so. He owed it all to *her*, he said.

Cass hardly heard the praise. She was engrossed in the letter.

"Dear Mr. Martin,
    I have to inform you that your letter to Mrs. Cynthia de Groot has been forwarded to us from Capetown. I must also, with deep regret, inform you that your aunt is no longer alive. She died just over a

*month ago, in Essex, where she has been living for
the last twelve years. Mr. de Groot predeceased her
five years before that. My firm has acted for both
Mr. and Mrs. de Groot since their arrival in England, when Mr. de Groot retired and purchased a
property in the village of Cold Dutton, six miles from
Chelmsford.*

*Fortunately your letter finally reached Mr. de
Groot's bank, and they forwarded it to us. It is
equally fortunate that we are not now put to the task
of having to try and trace you, because you were
mentioned in Mrs. de Groot's Will, but she gave only
the address of her sister, the late Miss Millicent
Brown. On making enquiries we learned that Miss
Brown also died some while ago and the present tenant in her house had no address, so we could not
contact you.*

*We were just about to put an advertisement in the
papers but now it is no longer necessary. It will be to
your advantage if you would come to our office as
soon as you can with papers of identification.*

Very truly yours,
Best, Compton and Withers, solicitors."

Cass raised starry eyes to her husband.

"Be to your advantage," she repeated. "Oh, *Kev!"*

Kevin, walking up and down with that graceful swagger of his tall thin figure, pushing back the disobedient
lock of hair, grinned at her:

"Sounds a bit of orr-right, and obviously means that
Aunt Cynthia, bless her, had a change of heart before
she made her Will, and decided to leave her nephew
something. But don't let's run away with the idea that
there's a fortune in it, sweety-pie, because she never
had a penny of her own and I dare say her Dutchman
left her money to her own kith and kin in South Africa.
We just don't know till we're told."

Cass sprang to her feet.

"You'll go on Monday morning, won't you? You'll
have to phone the office and say that you have had an
urgent summons from some solicitors."

SWEET CASSANDRA

"I'll do just that, your ladyship," said Kevin with a mock bow.

"Kev, it *might* be a fortune!"

"Somehow I doubt it, but at least whatever it is it seems to be 'to my advantage'."

Cass put the letter on the table and drew the back of her hand across her camp forehead.

"I must go and have a cold bath. Oh, Kev, it *does* sound exciting."

"All the more so, because so unexpected. I wrote to Aunt Cynthia because you suggested we might eventually find our way to South Africa. But I felt it was a forlorn hope because I did hear she'd come back to England, and that's about all. The feud between those two old women lasted until they both died. Sad, don't you think?"

"Very. And Aunt Cynthia couldn't have been all that old when she died, could she?"

"Well, she was a year or two older than Aunt Millie and she would have been about sixty now. No, she couldn't have been all that old, as you say."

"I shan't sleep a wink tonight, will you?" Cass, now in the kitchen, sang the words above the sound of running water.

In truth neither of them slept much. They kept waking up, arms around each other, cheek to cheek, trying to guess what the 'benefit' would be. Money, no doubt—*but how much?* Oh, what a thing to have happened!

They switched the light on and off. They threw off one blanket because it was so hot, and so little air came through the small windows on what was a warm May night. They gulped down glasses of cold water. They kissed, then slept again; but it was certainly a disturbed night.

Sunday was just as bad. They could settle down to nothing. They telephoned the Burnhams and told them about it. They shared the excitement.

Monday morning came. Cass could hardly bear to leave Kevin and go to her job.

"I'm so het up, I shall be swallowing the precious stones instead of polishing them."

"Can I ring you and tell you the worst, after I've been to the lawyers?"

"Oh *do*, I'll tell the girl who answers the phone to let me speak to you and she'll play. We're rather friendly."

When that phone call finally came, however, Kevin told her so little that Cass felt frustrated. It was all rather complicated, he said. He couldn't begin to explain. He'd save it all up for this evening. Cass was distraught because this was one of the few days that she and Kev could not even share the usual lunch in their Gardens. For business reasons he would be occupied during the lunch hour. So that meant the whole long afternoon for Cass in an agony of suspense.

"Oh, Kev, just tell me one thing—*is* it a fortune?"

"No," he said. "Bye-bye, sweetie," and rang off.

That subdued Cass a little. But she was still in a welter of excitement as she journeyed home. She had reached Groom Street before she realised that she had forgotten to buy the cold ham and salad she meant to give Kev for their supper. She had to go all the way back to the little grocer's shop they patronised. Then she raced home, up the stairs and into the flat.

She was thankful to find Kevin there waiting for her; at the typewriter, of course, by the open window, wearing cotton jeans and no shirt. It was another stifling day.

He looked up as she entered.

"Hi!"

"Hi!" she answered. They had adopted this American form of greeting each other.

Cass laid her parcels on the table, threw off her jacket and rushed at him.

"Tell me. *Tell me.* It's been beastly you not telling me anything. I've been having kittens all afternoon."

He hugged and kissed her.

"I'm sure they'd be awfully pretty kittens, love."

"Oh, shut up. *Tell me!*"

"Sit down then."

"I'd better wash first, I'm so sticky."

"Never mind—look at me! Listen!" he tapped his bare chest.

So she listened. Her large hazel eyes concentrated

upon him while he unfolded the strange story of his un-expected legacy.

Mr. Best, of Best, Compton and Withers, turned out to be a nice old boy—so Kevin described him. He accepted Kevin's passport and a couple of Aunt Millie's letters as proof that he was indeed Kevin Martin. He then gave Kevin a brief outline of what had taken place in Aunt Cynthia's life during the past ten years.

Bernard de Groot had been a good deal older than his wife. He was a widower when he married her and of his first marriage there was a daughter, Natasha.

Mr. Best made it plain to Kevin that Aunt Cynthia had been devoted to her Dutch husband but found her stepdaughter extremely difficult. The girl eventually married and went away and never bothered to return to see her stepmother after her father's death. So Aunt Cynthia decided to leave her personal possessions—the house and its contents—to her only nephew. With it, there also was a legacy amounting to roughly five thousand pounds' worth of shares.

"That was all she had of her own. Mr. de Groot's money was left in trust for his daughter. Aunt Cynthia lived on the interest but could not touch the capital, after she was widowed."

"How involved!" exclaimed Cass.

"I was touched," Kevin continued, "because old Best said my aunt spoke of me quite kindly before the end and wished she had known me. She never quarrelled with my mother, of course. But once Millie adopted me after my parents were killed, Aunt Cynthia cut away from us all. These silly old girls enjoyed keeping up their quarrel. I'm really amazed Aunt Cynthia remembered me in the end."

"And won't this daughter, Natasha, put in a claim for the house?"

"She can't. It was given to my aunt absolutely years before de Groot died. There's been something of a drama around this young girl apparently."

Cass listened breathlessly to the 'drama'. She had to concentrate in order not to feel confused—there was so much to absorb—so much to think about.

The first Mrs. de Groot appeared to have had Russian blood in her veins. From her Russian grandmother, Natasha inherited great beauty plus a fiery temperament. After she left school she quarrelled continually with her father and stepmother and later ran away with a medical student in Liverpool whom the de Groots had never met. Her father had obviously been distressed by this but taken it calmly in his stoic Dutch way.

Mr. Best, who had been a personal friend as well as lawyer to the de Groots, was able to give Kevin quite a few details. Kevin gathered that Aunt Cynthia had been none too keen on her stepdaughter ever returning to Pond House. Only when Mr. de Groot's death was announced in the paper did Natasha contact her again. Then a rather stilted letter of condolence came from Paris. Natasha gave few details about herself but made it plain that her marriage to her medical student had not lasted, and that she was married again—this time to a French pianist; and that her name was now Madame Maurice Courraine.

"Oh," said Cass, "then we're not likely to be troubled by *her*."

"No, I shouldn't think so. She has nothing to come home for. What was left of Mr. de Groot's capital, less death duties, amounted to precious little. Natasha got it after Aunt Cynthia died."

Cass drew breath.

"So my Kev has got a house, and five thousand pounds' worth of shares."

"Your Kev has, but Mr. Best advised me not to touch the capital. The dividends from the shares should bring us in about a couple of hundred a year. The real trouble, Cass, seems that if this house is all that big, we won't be able to afford to live in it."

"On the other hand," said Cass, "we could try, and it would mean you could write—*really* get down to your writing in a quiet country house like that."

"And what would we do for money, love?"

"Oh perhaps I could take up market gardening or something; learn about mushrooms, or we might take in paying guests," she suggested vaguely.

"That's the last thing," broke in Kevin on a warning note.

She hugged him.

"Okay. Anything you say. But if it's a place we want to live in, Kev, don't let's mind what sort of repair it's in. I don't care myself if there are bats in the belfry—or a horrid ghost or even a nice one."

He burst out laughing.

"Sweet, *sweet* Cass, that's you all over. You certainly aren't a defeatist."

"I believe in trying everything," she declared.

He looked into the glowing eyes that were as bright as jewels and with a forefinger touched the softness of her hot cheeks. There was something brave and beautiful about this wife of his, he thought.

He said:

"Let's have our meal and talk while we eat. I'm pretty excited myself, you know. It's sure going to make all the difference to us. But let me correct you on one point, my love. We can't sell the house even if we want to. My funny old aunt seems to have been quite dotty about the place and because her husband adored it, too, she was reluctant for it to pass into strangers' hands. So she made it a condition that we didn't sell the property to anybody else for at least five years."

"Aren't people odd about their Wills," sighed Cass, then added brightly: "Oh, well—maybe it's all for the best. It'll sort of help us to make a decision. If we must live in it, we *must*."

"We'll wait for the end of the week then go down to Essex on Saturday. There seems to be an old gardener chap called William who lives in Cold Dutton and does a bit of work in the kitchen garden. He worked for Aunty in her palmy days. Mr. Best says he grows vegetables for himself now—of course only until the place is occupied again. We get the keys from him."

"He might grow vegetables for us," said Cass thoughtfully.

Kevin made her a sweeping bow.

"Already I hail you as Lady Martin of Pond House."

"Is that what it's called?"

"Yep. Rather attractive, don't you think?"

"Pond House," said Cass slowly, savouring the words. "It sounds absolutely *super*. Oh, dear, now we've got to wait for Saturday before we see it."

"We spend our lives waiting for something."

"Like we waited for each other," she reminded him, and stretched her arms above her head, shut her eyes, and let out a long sigh. "Oh, Kev, maybe this is the beginning of an absolutely new life for us. How wonderful, wonderful, *wonderful,* for you to have inherited a house and even the teeniest bit of money."

"You're getting big ideas," he smiled at her. "Since when have *you*—or I— ever been in a position to look upon five thousand pounds as 'teeny'? Off with you to the kitchen, Mrs. Martin, and toss a salad. I'll make the dressing."

"Oh, I do love you!" she exclaimed as she vanished.

"I love you," he shouted.

That supper was the happiest, most exciting meal they had shared for a long time.

Chapter 9

CASS and Kevin sat in the taxi taking them from Cold Dutton station to Pond House, staring out of each window, engrossed in what they saw. They were in possession of the keys which Kevin had collected in the village from the old gardener, William.

Soon they came to the long curving drive leading up to the house that had once belonged to Aunt Cynthia and which was now Kevin's. It still seemed to the young people like a dream.

"My property! *My God!*" Kevin kept muttering, to which Cass, pink-cheeked and excited, added with her infectious laugh:

"*Our* property, if you please! Don't be so egotistical."

Although this was May, it was by no means the best of days to be seeing the place. It had rained steadily since they left London and although the skies were clearing now, there seemed more rain to come. The forecast had been bad. Everything was wet, dripping and dismal. The drive was overgrown with weeds. The whole place bore an air of neglect. It was obvious from the start that Mrs. de Groot, once her husband died, had found it difficult to maintain the place with the sole aid of an ageing gardener on half-time employ. But it must once have been beautiful. Cass pointed out great clumps of dark rain-washed rhododendron bushes, and a tangle of flowering shrubs struggling against the creeping paralysis of the weeds threatening to destroy civilisation. The sinister spiral of the bindweed looked viciously triumphant, choking and clinging to the pink and yellow azaleas.

The taxi drove them up to the house and here the formal garden looked little better. Some attempt had been made to look after one bed of tulips in the circular drive. These gave the only touch of colour.

The house itself was shadowed by a great monkey-puzzle tree which, like the rest, was sodden and dripping.

As they got out of the taxi, Cass and Kevin stared speechlessly in front of them.

Pond House bore no resemblance to anything they had anticipated. Certainly it was no dream-house. A big rambling Victorian building of reddish brick, hidden behind Virginia creeper and every kind of climbing shrub including a beautiful old wistaria over a white porch which looked like a later addition to the house, and bore the inscription 1887.

White shutters (even though grey with dirt) had also been added and detracted from some of the ugliness of the building. The windows had not been cleaned. They were closed and shuttered. To the right of the house there was one remarkable elevation—a belfry containing a bell. On top of this structure there sat a weather-cock.

The fascinated gaze of the young couple, turning to the left, now saw what was very definitely the feature of the house and must have been an inspiration from Aunt Cynthia's Dutch husband: an essentially Dutch-looking, glass-covered verandah, running the length of the house. Below lay the pond that had given the house its name. With awe, Kevin and Cass regarded this size-able stretch of water. It could almost have been called a lake. In fine weather it must be glorious; that was their first reaction. On this gloomy morning it had a slightly sinister aspect. The water was a leaden, muddy grey. Below the verandah, the mere was dark with a tangle of bulrushes, irises and water-lily leaves. The opposite bank was darkly fringed with beech trees, silver birches and alders; on the right a weeping willow, dip-ping into the water, brought an exclamation of delight from Cass.

"Oh, how *lovely!*"

"I take it one can walk right around the pond. And isn't that a sort of boat-house affair on the other side, Cass?"

"Yes, it is," she agreed.

"Then there might be a boat in it," said Kevin.

"Congratulations my dear Maigret," said Cass.

"Unbelievable," said Kevin, shaking his head. "Drop down this green grassy bank, my dear, and you're in the water. I imagine when you're in the house, it's like being in a boat—the verandah practically overhangs the pond."

"Oh, Kev, it's divine! *So* unique!"

"You can say that again and you'll want a unique income to keep the damn place going."

"Nobody *has* kept it going—you can see it's all gone kind of wild. Look—there are masses of queer birds on the water—*Look!* All sorts of ducks, even a pair of geese flapping about on that bank. Do you see, Kev? It's a paradise for bird watchers. This is why your uncle must have bought the place—not for the ugly house, but for the lake. I *refuse* to call it a pond."

"Call it what you like, sweet. We're stuck with it," said Kevin feeling and looking a trifle shaken.

"After the flat!" exclaimed Cass, unbuttoning her

short waterproof jacket, and throwing her hands dramatically above her head, "Oh, gosh, it'll be worth fighting for and working for!"

"Starving for and dying for too," he added dryly.

"Oh, Kev don't be morbid. Let's look inside. We haven't seen inside yet, you know."

"Hold on to me, I feel giddy," he said, and pretended to totter as he grabbed her.

The taxi driver, who had lit a cigarette, and was watching the young couple, threw them a cryptic look.

"How long will you be wanting me? Am I to wait?"

"No, don't wait," said Kevin, diving into his pocket, "I'll pay you now. We can walk back to the station."

"We can *walk?*" repeated Cass. "Six and a half miles?"

"Do us good," he said.

"Okay," she laughed.

The driver took his fare and the tip, and eyed the young couple with kindly humour.

"Rather you than me in this old place. Bit too out of the world, isn't it?"

"We don't mind that," said Kevin and added: "Did you know my aunt, Mrs. de Groot?"

"Yes, I knew both of them. She was a very nice lady—used to be fond of her garden. Got some sort of leg trouble the last two years and couldn't do much active work and used to sit all day in that glass room watching the birds. See them geese?" He pointed to a pair of birds waddling nearer the house.

Cass and Kevin now became aware of the beauty of the long glistening blue necks, and the gold and white plumage of the birds.

"Chinese geese they call 'em. Mr. de Groot, he put a lot of such stuff on the water. He liked to see the goslings hatched. Them mallard ducks too—and there's a pair of birds out yonder with sort of crests on their heads, grebes they call 'em. They've been there nigh on eight years to the best of my knowledge."

"It looks to me," said Kevin, "as though we'll either love the birds, or quit."

The driver looked curiously at the tall lanky young man in the blue denims and jacket. Not a bad looking young chap, he thought. His hair on the long side but not as long as most of 'em, and the young lady was very pleasant—a good-looker, too.

"You the new owners?" he asked.

"We are," said Kevin and felt for the first time the thrill of ownership.

That thrill diminished somewhat as he and Cass walked slowly through the house.

The size was alarming and for many reasons—the sight of it. It didn't take long, thought Cass, to assess the character of a person if you examined a house they'd once lived in. The Dutchman was obviously responsible for the structural alterations, the concentration on scenery and the wild fowl; also for much of the ponderous dark oak furniture which included one or two good pieces of marquetry.

The dining-room in particular had a Dutch flavour—particularly the big oil paintings of fat smiling rosy-cheeked women wearing national costume, and of red-nosed gentlemen smoking Meerschaum pipes, sitting by their firesides in tiled kitchens. Kevin's vivid imagination and creative brain was quick to imagine what Aunt Cynthia's husband must have been like—fat, double-chinned, kindly, like the men in the portraits.

Most of the main rooms were little short of twenty feet long. The double drawing-room had three glass doors opening on to the verandah. They had to undo the shutters and open the windows before they could see the pond. It was very impressive out there. But once the light filtered into the room, it showed up the dust and sad neglect. Aunt Cynthia might have left instructions that the house was to be kept in order, but little appeared to have been done, and her lawyers had had neither time nor, perhaps, inclination, to look into the matter too closely.

Cass was vastly intrigued by this 'salon' as she called it. So utterly different from the flat. So different, too, from her old home with Mummy and the General. It was huge and overpoweringly full of things. The wall-paper must once have been an expensive one—pale blue, heavily embossed. The colour was now faded and discoloured in patches. The pictures were far too numerous, mainly water-colours of scenes in Capetown by local artists, with conventional gilt frames. There was only one striking picture over the mantelpiece which Kevin immediately fell in love with—a vivid painting of Table Mountain by a Capetown artist.

"I'll have that," he said nodding, "and you can take the rest."

Cass, looking around her, blinked. What did she want? Poor Aunt Cynthia had definitely been a collector of small unimportant objects. No heavy Dutch furniture in here. One nice satinwood writing bureau. The rest of the furniture could be found in any big furniture stores. Varnished wood of no particular period; little tables, cabinets full of china objects picked up from numerous travels; rows of carved wood animals from Africa: giraffes, elephants, antelopes; beaded mats, brass trays; masses of framed photographs Cass hadn't time to examine now. Painted shelves filled with novels. A wrought-iron stand bearing a dejected row of plants that had long since died from lack of water. And a boudoir grand piano occupying one entire corner of the room.

"Somebody played," said Cass. "Who do you suppose?"

"Well, there was no musical talent in my family as far as I know. And I can't imagine the Dutch gentleman playing."

"I expect it was the daughter with Russian blood in her—the fair Natasha."

"Who knows?" shrugged Kevin.

"Well, if the piano belongs to her she may turn up one day and ask for it."

"Well, we don't play, so she can have it," said Kevin. "Personally I'd like to give away or sell most of the things in here."

"That'll be the day," said Cass. "The place is the size of Buckingham Palace and fully furnished. Let's stick to what we've got. Anyhow I don't really dislike some of these curios. They're quaint and homely."

"An apt description of my wife," said Kevin.

Cass who had opened the piano lid, struck one or

two out-of-tune notes, banged down the lid, rushed to him and set her teeth.

"You call me quaint and homely again and that'll be the end of our marriage. I won't come down and dust this mausoleum *or* cook your food, and you can go swim in the lake with the wild geese."

They kissed, laughing, and continued their tour.

There was yet another living-room on the ground floor. This, undoubtedly, had been Mr. de Groot's sanctum. Old pistols and guns on the walls, dozens of framed photographs, mostly enlargements, of bird-life, and a huge cabinet full of reference books in both Dutch and English. The big flat desk bearing a bronzed inkstand and a portable typewriter, made instant appeal to Kevin.

"This is a sign—ready-made for an author."

"Oh, darling, how splendid!"

"A better machine than mine, too. One of those nice little Olympias. That *does* gladden my anguished heart."

Cass looked at her husband as he opened the machine; at the bent thin back she loved so well. Her heart swelled with pride. He was coming into his own. She knew he was. Life had suddenly become rich with promise for them both. This extraordinary house—so full of character—*so fantastic*—ready-made study and all—seemed to her the answer to all their prayers and the beginning of the life they had both wanted. But they had expected to have to wait and work for years and years before it could become so much as a probability.

What was the snag here? The longer she was in Pond House the more she became aware of its dimensions *and* the lack of the right sort of money that was needed for its upkeep. What poor Aunt Cynthia had left Kev— the whole five thousand pounds—could vanish in one year in a place like this. To Cass it seemed probable that they would never be able to take over Pond House.

Later on she began to feel optimistic again. The kitchen was a pleasant surprise. Obviously Aunt Cynthia in recent years had felt the need to modernise. Although there was no central heating—and the thought of Pond House in the winter without it made Cass shiver—there was at least a good electric hot water system, plus a steel sink and modern unit, and a corner table and chairs.

"That's where you and I will be eating *our* sardines," said Cass. "No dining-room for us."

"Let's see the upstairs," said Kev impatiently.

There were two floors, approached by a wide staircase with a half landing. One tremendously long window was decorated with stained-glass panes at the top. They hated it. The top floor could be shut off. It was unnecessary.

All the main rooms on the first floor overlooked the pond. She and Kevin would have the huge double bedroom with its own bathroom; a suite on its own. The other rooms could be shut up, unless friends came to stay.

Cass teased Kevin.

"Honestly, with a place like this I'll have to bury my pride and send Mummy and the General an invitation to spend a cultural weekend, bird-watching at the country home of Mr. and Mrs. Kevin Martin."

Kevin turned on her:

"Don't you dare bring '*Yes-dear*' and that Army computer down to my house or I'll shoot them both with one of Mr. de Groot's pistols and throw their bodies into the lake and you can call in *all* your Maigrets."

"Really, Kev!"

Now his handsome Irish eyes glowered at her, half in fun, half-serious.

"Sweet Cass, I'm deadly serious when I say I must be left in peace if we do come down here, otherwise I'll never write a line and we won't be able to afford to buy even one sardine."

"Nobody shall interfere with your writing, Kev. I promise. I'll guard you like a tiger. Oh, Kev, I can't wait for us to take over and I don't mind how much work it means for me."

"Are you sure you won't find it too much, and too lonely?"

"Lonely with *you*?"

"Well, once I start writing, I may go on and on."

Her eyes sparkled at him.

"Won't you even have a coffee break or spend the night with me?"

He swung her into his arms.

"Darling, I will. You know I will, and I think it's marvellous of you to be so interested in this funny old place. Some girls would have loathed it. I'm sure it isn't every housewife's cup of tea."

Cass shrugged her shoulders. They were standing in the middle of Aunt Cynthia's bedroom. How easy to guess what *she* had been like, Cass thought. Very feminine, very domesticated, meticulously tidy. Dusty the place might be after this month of mourning, but everything was in order. White lace over pink silk on the twin beds which had painted headboards; a table beside each bed; gilded lamps with pink silk shades; white striped satin wallpaper; white painted double wardrobe with drawers and hanging cupboards; spindly white chairs with satin seats; a day-couch with cushions.

Cass could imagine old Mrs. de Groot sitting there as her final illness overtook her, watching the gardener feed the geese. Neat rows of crystal bottles still stood on the glass-covered dressing-table; the triple mirror had one side glass cracked.

Sadly Cass looked at this.

"I wonder if it broke in her lifetime? If so she must have felt it meant bad luck—the end for her. Oh, Kev, how sad it is that people have to grow old and die and leave all the things they've collected and loved behind them. I must take care of this even if it's old-fashioned."

"M'm," said Kevin but he was not interested. He was looking at the crested grebes the taxi man had pointed out, beginning to think that if he wasn't careful he would be distracted from his writing by the fascination of these birds. They looked so proud and graceful with their tiny coronets—sailing like miniature ships across the water.

"Just look at these windows. You can step out on the balcony in the morning when it's fine and dive down into the lake," said Cass.

"That'll be the day," said Kevin.

"Well, *I* can swim!" said Cass tossing her head.

"I'm too thin, I feel the cold," said Kevin, and walked to the bathroom. That at least made them both giggle. It was more than twice the size of their bedroom in town. The floor was covered in pink carpet. The bath was enormous. Pink tiles glistened half way up the walls. There was a shower in one corner encased in transparent sheeting.

"Lord-love-a-duck!" exclaimed Kevin.

"Think on these things," said Cass solemnly. "While I lie gleaming in the water, you can stand under your shower singing your madrigals."

"Under *cold* water?"

"Certainly not. We have a very good water system—an electric immersion heater, so William told me when we collected the keys; remember?"

"We shall be totally unable to pay big electricity bills. Our water will stay cold except what you boil to wash up with," said Kevin promptly.

"Killjoy!" she flung at him.

He took another look around the pink bathroom and the pink bedroom, then sobered, admired Mr. de Groot's dressing-room, next door. It was strictly masculine with cream coloured walls, dark green curtains and mahogany furniture.

"I shall sleep in here when you annoy me," he said, "and enjoy peace, masculinity and sanity as I'm quite sure my aunt's Dutch husband fled at times from her nattering."

Cass sniffed:

"How do you know she nattered?"

"It's in the family. Aunt Millie used to natter at me. I expect Cynthia drove him crazy every night by referring to the feud between her and poor Aunt Millie, to whom this house should have belonged because Mr. de Groot nearly married *her;* only Aunt Cynthia was prettier and she snaffled him."

Cass firmly shut the door between Cynthia's pink bedroom and Mr. de Groot's gloomy dressing-room.

"The first night you shut yourself in *there* away from me marks the end of our marriage, and I *don't* natter!"

"You don't, darling," he said, more seriously.

Suddenly he took her in his arms and pushed the leaf brown hair back from her excited young face.

"You don't regret marrying me, do you?"

She tried to joke.

"Now that you're the wealthy owner of five thousand pounds and this crazy old house on the water? I'll say I don't."

"No, I mean—you're always so gay and happy and you take everything in your stride, darling, and I'm so moody and not nearly nice enough for you."

Her own face was moulded now in graver lines. She laced her hands behind his head.

"Darling Kev, you've never said anything like that before. You needn't worry, because I like your moods. I understand them and I adore you. How could I possibly regret leaving that awful house with poor Mummy and the General? Life's been one long thrill since you took me away."

"A thrill in Groom Street?" he grimaced.

"Yes, even there, and just think of the life we'll lead here. It'll be *fun*. It'll be worth all the work and effort. You'll write your epic and it will sell in millions all over the world."

Suddenly he found her love and her infinite faith in him very touching. He began to kiss her with the long hungry kisses of a lover. She lost count of time. She was in complete accord with him, and smiled, a woman's secret enigmatic little smile when he walked with her to one of the twin beds, pulled off the lace spread and drew her down beside him. Her heart hammered and her lips were hungry for his.

He whispered:

"Let's make love to each other here for the first time in *our* house. Quite alone, Cass, in our big lonely house. We'll be happy here, I know we will. You're dead right about it. Oh, Cass, sweet *sweet* Cassandra!"

After that they stopped talking. The room was quiet. Through the windows that Kev had opened came the queer harsh sound of wild geese flying across the water.

To Cass, lying there on one of Aunt Cynthia's beds in the pink and white room, it was an hour of enchantment, of poignancy that went deep into her heart.

She never forgot it.

Chapter 10

So the lives of Kevin and Cass, who had married without a penny in the world, with uncertain jobs and with no clear idea of what might happen in the future, suddenly completely changed.

Another discussion with Aunt Cynthia's solicitor decided them that the best thing they could do was to leave London at the earliest opportunity and take possession of Pond House.

There was no difficulty in disposing of the flat. It was a reasonable rent and the agent who had originally let it to Kevin and his friend found a suitable tenant within forty-eight hours.

Cass, much to Kevin's surprise and delight, proved herself quite a business woman. For it was she who set a price on the 'bits and pieces' in the flat, none of which they would need now they had all their new grand possessions. And Cass got what she asked for. It had been agreed with Kev's friend, Barney, that if Kev ever wished to sell up he could, and send Barney half the proceeds. Times being as they were, Cass did not find it difficult to make a profit. It seemed awful, she said to Kevin, to ask so much for rubbish, but lucky for them the incoming 'young marrieds', wanted all they were offered. In the end, after the share-out with Barney, Kevin had yet another two hundred pounds to add to their savings.

They decided to move on June 14th, the day after their wedding anniversary and *that*, Kevin said, must not be a day of hard work but of glorious celebration. A double celebration—of the wedding and of Kevin's good fortune. They would start their second year in their very own country house.

"All the same," Cass said on the morning they finally left the flat, "I feel a bit sentimental about never climbing those stairs again. I shall never forget that horrid grubby flat. It was our first home."

" '*Living in sin*,' as '*Yes-dear*' would say," Kevin reminded her wickedly.

They made one or two interesting discoveries during the second interview with Mr. Best. For the first time, Kevin saw the deeds of the house, and the plan of the alterations Mr. de Groot had made. It was all as Kevin had imagined; de Groot had built on that superb verandah and Aunt Cynthia had modernised the kitchen and the original bathrooms. In all, there were seven acres of land belonging to Pond House. Only half an acre could be called cultivated garden. There was a small kitchen garden and orchard. The orchard was good. There were some fine fruit trees. And there were two fields let out to local farmers. These should bring Kevin in nearly thirty pounds a year. On the debit side, the rates and taxes would amount to about eighty pounds a half year.

Armed with this knowledge, the young Martins travelled down to their property.

There were two people to welcome them at Pond House. Old William the gardener, nearly eighty, rheumy-eyed, wearing a straw hat which Cass adored and firmly decided to borrow—and Mrs. Pinner, the former 'daily' who had 'done for' Mrs. de Groot. She was what Kevin called a 'know-all', the bossy type he never could bear. She had a habit of looking over her glasses and staring, marble-eyed, which made Cass feel nervous. From the start Mrs. Pinner wanted to control Cass. While William and Kevin strolled around the grounds, Mrs. Pinner tried to establish her authority over Cass who was given little opportunity to tell the woman that she didn't want her.

Mrs. Pinner stood in the kitchen, arms folded tightly across her withered bosom, describing the hours she'd spent trying to clean this huge house single-handed;

how she'd helped to nurse the poor lady in her last
months before she was taken to a nursing home, and
how the solicitors had asked her to clean up (alone and
all!) after the funeral.

Goggle-eyed, Cass tried in vain to stem the torrent of
words—all ringing with self-praise and ending with
baleful suggestions that she had been 'put upon' by
everyone.

"There's more to do here than one can rightly manage, and I'm sure you'll agree. Someone like myself
should not be asked to tackle it alone *and* I've only
been getting five shillings an hour here and in Cold
Dutton now they're asking six, so I hope we shall be
able to come to an arrangement, Mrs. Martin."

When at last she drew breath, Cass exhausted but
determined not to be swept away by Mrs. Pinner, put in
her own spoke. If she had liked anything about Mrs.
Pinner she might have suggested that she 'saw them in'.
But she not only mistrusted the woman but wondered
how much praise was really due to her. The dust and
dirt that hung around Pond House did not suggest that
Mrs. Pinner had earned her five shillings an hour—or
half of it.

Cass described the scene afterwards to Kevin as
being somewhat embarrassing. When Mrs. Pinner heard
that she was not going to be 'took on' she was at first
stunned, then vicious. She began to attack Cass, looking
the young girl up and down with that terrible stony
stare.

"Well, I never! I'm sure nobody can have told you
I'm a poor worker and didn't give satisfaction to Mrs.
de Groot. Some women would have walked out, but I
didn't. I know the place and where everything's kept,
and you'll have a time finding someone to come in my
place. *And* take the bus from the village and walk down
this long drive in all weathers."

Cass then showed her spirit and rather acidly informed Mrs. Pinner that nobody was going to be asked
to walk down the drive because she did not intend to
have domestic help.

"And so I must say good morning, Mrs. Pinner, because I'm very busy," she ended.

Further stunned, Mrs. Pinner removed her glasses, polished them, placed them back on her nose and left the house.

"No doubt," Cass told Kevin, "it will go round the village that there's something queer about the Martins because they don't want domestic help, but I can tell you here and now I *don't want Mrs. Pinner*. She isn't like Mummy's nice daily. I was rather fond of her. Poor Aunt Cynthia must have had a time with this old witch—maybe she was too old and ill in the end to argue with her. And she had to have someone. But *I* don't need anybody."

"You're really rather a masterpiece," was Kevin's answer to that. "My respect for you grows daily. As for William—he's a nice old boy and he's going to come at least once a week to help keep the front in order, and if we let him carry on with his kitchen produce, he'll give us a bean, or a row of peas, etc. But he agreed with me that the place is so overgrown now there's little we can do but keep it scythed down."

Cass nodded but her mind wasn't on the garden. It was on the domestic scene. She was excited and pleased to be in their new magnificent home (for magnificent it was, despite its forlorn air and genteel decay). But her heart was beginning to sink just a little as she wondered what to tackle first. How lucky to be young and strong. The best thing she could do was to put on old slacks and a shirt and start in the kitchen. Kev must throw open every window and get some air through the house, for it really smelled stuffy.

The next thing was to put hot water bottles in the pink and white beds and push *them* together. (They seemed to spend their lives dragging mattresses the wrong way round and trying to make two into one, she thought deliriously.) At least they had stopped the taxi in Cold Dutton and brought back enough tinned food and necessities to last them for a few days—apart from the things they had brought down from the flat. Then they must get unpacked, and oh; there was so much to see to—both inside the house and out. The day wouldn't be long enough. And such a day! Warm and sunny—it was grand to be alive, not like that wet dreary morning when they first saw the place.

When they finally stopped work for a sandwich and cup of coffee, they sat on the verandah for their first meal in Pond House. They feasted their eyes on the pond. The water was looking exquisite today, shimmering in the heat.

"God bless Aunt Cynthia is what I say," announced Kevin as he drained his coffee cup and handed it to Cass for more.

"God bless Aunt Cynthia," she repeated solemnly.

The telephone bell rang. A strange sound to them—strident, echoing through the empty house. Very empty, they agreed, except for themselves, and very quiet, and far away from the rest of the world.

"It's for you, Cass."

Cass wiped the crumbs from her mouth.

"For *me*—whoever can know I'm *here*?"

"Who do you suppose? You only gave the address to your mother. It's the General himself calling."

"You have to be joking," said Cass. "He'd perish rather than telephone to me unless—" a frightening thought struck her—"unless something's happened to Mummy."

Kevin looked gloomily at the radiant water. The blue and gold geese were in view, cruising around the margin of the pond, pecking at the kingcups and the duck weed. He hated Miles Woodbeare. He was the serpent in paradise, he thought, dramatically. As soon as they got here he, of *all men* in the world, had to ferret out poor Cass.

Cass's dialogue with the General was short and alarming. In his staccato voice, he announced that he had managed to find her new address in her mother's desk and phoned in the hope of finding her. Dorothy had been taken ill—very ill—yesterday. She wanted to see Cassandra. (He said this as though the words were forced out of him.)

"I cannot believe that bringing you here will make her any better," he went on, "but as she wishes it—well, I felt I must approach you."

"How bad is she?" asked Cass. Her heart was sinking. She had quarrelled with her mother but she *was*, after all, her mother, and once Cass had loved her before the General had influenced and dominated her and finally separated them.

Cass returned to Kevin, her face grave.

"Oh, Kev—isn't it awful—I've got to go straight up to London," she said in a shaken voice.

Kevin looked horrified.

"Up to London? *Now?* But you *can't!* We've only just come down. We haven't been here more than a few hours and—"

"Kevin, I'm sorry, I've got to go. Mummy may die."

She explained that even the General, who never admitted that anything was wrong with anybody, had announced that his wife had had a stroke and it was serious. He had rarely allowed her to send for a doctor, and they had had no idea her blood-pressure was dangerously high.

"If she dies, he'll have murdered her," Cass announced with melodrama.

Kevin despite the fact that he had little use for his mother-in-law, became sympathetic.

"A stroke! That's bad. What else did he say?"

"The doctor has sent in a nurse. They don't think she'll live, Kev. Even the General is anxious. Yes, he actually said he was. So Mummy must be very bad. I must go to her."

"Did she say she wanted you?"

"Apparently, yes. She recovered consciousness for a few moments and asked for me."

Kevin twisted his lips. Poor old *'Yes-dear's* conscience had worked at last. It took the fear of death to make some people realise how rottenly they had behaved, he thought. But in the circumstances he must let Cass go.

He sent for the station taxi.

"I can cope alone," he said. "Don't worry about me. I've found a Hoover—I'll get cracking on the carpets when you've gone and at least have the place a bit cleaner before you get back."

She threw her arms around his neck and hugged him.

"You're angelic. I'm so sorry—you *know* I don't

want to leave you, darling, but I may have to stay in Putney the night."

"I suppose so," said Kevin gloomily.

He had looked forward to the 'take-over' down here, with Cass. What a life! You had a spot of good fortune on one hand, then it was wiped out on the other.

Cass changed into her town suit and caught the first quick train from Cold Dutton to Liverpool Street.

She found it strange and sad, when she walked down the familiar acacia-lined road leading on to Putney Common. She arrived at the front door of the suburban house that bore the unsuitable name *TOBRUK*. The General had given it that name because he had fought in Tobruk with the Eighth Army against Rommel—in 1942. It was a whole year, she reflected, since she had left *TOBRUK* having been told she was never to enter it again.

The General opened the front door. Impeccably dressed as ever in one of his light-weight Middle East suits, wearing his horn-rimmed glasses, and his sternest expression. He looked at Cass without the smallest affection but said, politely:

"Ah! Thank you for coming."

He had never thanked her for anything before. Cass felt that her mother must be very bad.

Dorothy Woodbeare was, indeed, a dying woman. Since the General had telephoned Cass, she had drifted into unconsciousness. The doctor did not expect her to last the night.

The General told Cass this, coughing and with none of his usual hectoring manner. If Cass could have believed that he had a heart, he looked really upset today. He said that her mother's fatal illness had come as a great shock. She had been out shopping, came back with her parcels and collapsed. Perhaps it was the sudden heat. At first they had thought she would recover, but she had not rallied—as the doctor hoped.

Cass, listening to the details, felt a little sick. She drew off her gloves and after a swift look round the familiar sitting-room, said:

"I'll go up to her."

"Yes, do," said the General.

Cass met a uniformed nurse coming out of her mother's bedroom.

"I'm Cass Martin, Mrs. Woodbeare's daughter. How is my mother?" asked Cass nervously.

"I'm sorry—but the news is bad, Mrs. Martin," said the woman gently, "I expect General Woodbeare warned you."

"Yes," said Cass, and walked into the room, immediately sensing the depressing atmosphere. The blinds were half down. In the middle of the double bed her mother lay very still, looking strangely small and shrunken and pathetic, her pretty brown head sunk in the pillow, her face greyish-white. But she did not look old. She seemed to Cass to look extraordinarily young.

A great lump rose to her throat. The years rolled away with all grievances, differences of opinion and resentments. She was a little girl again. This was Mummy.

"Oh!" from Cass, the tears brimming into her eyes. "Oh, you *poor* darling!"

And she sat down by the bed and took one of her mother's inert hands and pressed it against her warm cheek. It was much too cold—too fragile.

For a couple of seconds only, Dorothy Woodbeare seemed aware of Cass's presence. She opened her eyes and smiled.

"Hello, Cass-Cass," she whispered.

That choked the girl. She hadn't heard that name for so many long years. Why, not since she was a little thing of five or six when Daddy was still alive. The small boy next door used to come in and play with her. *He* had given her the nickname, Cass-Cass.

"Dear, dear Mummy. You're going to get quite well now that I'm here," she said with an attempt at gaiety.

But the hand within hers gave no answering pressure, and Dorothy Woodbeare's eyelids closed again. The nurse approached the bed, looked at her patient, then turned to Cass.

"I think you'd better ask your father to come up," she whispered.

Dorothy Woodbeare never recovered consciousness. With the awful realisation that there was such a narrow margin between life and death, Cass went to her old bedroom and wept bitterly.

Later that night she faced her stepfather in the dining-room for the evening meal.

She telephoned Kevin and told him that she could not get back tonight, but would be with him early in the morning.

"Isn't it awful, Mummy dying so suddenly," she said.

"Grim," was Kevin's reply, "and pretty dreary for you, my poor sweet."

"As a matter of fact," Cass went on, half-whispering into the receiver so that she couldn't be overheard, "I'm really quite sorry for the old boy. He's doing the soldier's-courage act; squaring his shoulders, brushing up his moustache and talking about 'We must try to behave as *she* would have wished'. I think he feels it. He made a slave of her but he cared for her in his way, I suppose."

"Don't waste too much pity on him. Come back to me, I need you," said Kevin.

Cass's heart warmed. She had indeed felt the coldness of death itself during the last few hours. Passionately she wanted to be back in Kevin's arms—passionately was she in need of his warm vibrant presence. She couldn't bear him to be sleeping alone in their big house tonight—without her.

The General, with immaculate efficiency, paid off the nurse, made all necessary arrangements for his wife's body to be taken to the funeral parlour, then ate the scrambled eggs and bacon that Cass served up to him, with a cup of strong black coffee. He seemed not to wish to discuss his wife's death. He talked politics. So Cass, although deeply depressed—grieving for the mother she had loved in her childhood—made no reference to her. Later the General announced that the funeral would be in three days' time.

"Then I'm afraid I must go home first, General," said Cass, "but of course, I'll come back for poor Mummy's funeral and I'd like to have my husband with me."

The General brushed up his moustache with his table napkin and stared stonily ahead.

"As you wish," he said grudgingly.

"I do want to say," went on Cass, "or perhaps I don't *need* to say, that I'm dreadfully upset about Mummy— all the more so because we didn't see eye to eye over my marriage and hadn't seen anything of each other for so long."

"That was no fault of hers," said the General coldly.

Cass declined to argue at a time like this. Let the old man stew in the juice of his acrimonious and intolerant attitude towards her. She felt that it was fantastic that there should ever have come a day when she would cook his supper and eat it alone with him. Suddenly she felt very tired and weepy again. She wanted to go to bed.

She tried to make conversation with the General but he maintained a grim silence. What, she finally asked him, did he intend to do in the future?

"It's too early for me to say," was his stiff answer, "I shall probably sell up and live at my Club. I shall not attempt to stay here without your mother." He then added the only word of praise that Cass had ever heard from him. "Poor Dorothy—she was a good woman and she looked after me very well."

Yes, thought Cass, you old brute, and *you* never looked after *her* at all.

Or was she prejudiced? The longer she lived, the more forcibly it struck her that all human beings had different ways of living—and of loving. Perhaps he *had* loved her mother in his odd way. But looking after a wife to *him* meant paying bills and ruling the roost.

How could a man like Miles Woodbeare know what a woman really needed—what *every* wife needed? Just love—the warmth and affection, the closeness that made every trouble seem negligible. The sort of love she was getting from Kevin. Suddenly Cass said:

"I know you never thought much of my husband but he's been marvellous to me. I'm very happy with him."

The General turned a jaundiced eye upon her.

"Oh, well, I can't say you look as though you've been either starved or beaten," he said with unaccustomed humour.

Cass warmed to this and began to enlarge on Kevin's

good points, until an extra loud cough from the General warned her that he was bored. But on the whole he had tried to be friendly. She began to feel that it was a pity Mummy couldn't know how well she had got on with the old boy, tonight. He was at last showing *some* signs of being human. He *would* be lonely without his wife. He wasn't all that young any more. Cass softened towards him.

She was still further surprised when he remarked that he had 'no objection' to her taking away a few things that had belonged to her mother; such as her tortoise-shell and silver-backed toilet set, or her leather bags or any 'articles' as the General called them, that might be useful to Cass. She could also take the opal ring and brooch to match that had been given to her mother by Cass's father.

Cass stared at the General in amazement.

"Well, thank you," she said in a low voice, "I think Mummy would like that."

The General added:

"I take it that you have fallen on your feet—ahem—ahem—insomuch as your husband has been left this country place."

"Yes, by one of his aunts, and it's absolutely gorgeous although it's much too big and we'll have to find some way of making plenty of money so we can keep it up."

The General looked at her over his glasses.

"No money with the estate, eh? Not much good to you," he barked, then: "What sort of house is it?"

"Victorian—right on a lovely piece of water with lots of wild birds, and a few ornamental geese and so on, that were bred by Mr. de Groot."

Miles Woodbeare became quite interested.

"Any shooting around, eh, what?" he asked. "I used to be fond of a bit of duck-shooting. Did a lot in Norfolk when I was a young officer. And more when I was stationed in Kenya."

As Cass afterwards told her husband, this was the moment when she saw the warning light. Having never expected to see her stepfather again and with her poor mother not yet buried, she had a ghastly feeling that the General was fishing for an invitation to stay with her, Cass, at the Pond House.

She made haste to tell her stepfather that they had only taken possession of the place this morning and there was a great deal to do before they could have guests, but of course, if he cared to come down one weekend later on, they'd be delighted. Having said these words in her impulsive and generous way, she immediately regretted them. Heaven knew what Kevin would say if he thought that the General was likely to disturb his new-found peace.

However, there was nothing to be done about it now and nothing was likely to come of it.

The next morning Cass and her stepfather parted on more amicable terms than might have been expected. The General managed even one more word of praise—this time for Cass.

"Marriage has improved you, I think. You're turning into quite a sensible young woman."

"Thanks a lot, General," said Cass and rushed away.

Chapter 11

ONE morning in December, Cass put on her gum boots, ski trousers and a thick-knitted jersey with polo collar and went out to the kitchen garden to see old William who was busy digging.

Cass and William had established a firm alliance. Kevin was not really garden or produce minded; he left most of what he called 'the great out-of-doors' to Cass. But he was far from lazy. He spent the greater part of the day in his study (it was now firmly established as his and little was left of Mr. de Groot's influence).

Sometimes he would find a table, put his typewriter on it and work on the verandah. The pond and all the fascinating wild life gave him, he said, inspiration.

He was trying his hand at a serious novel. Every night he read a little of it to Cass who sat at his feet, a dedicated listener. She devoutly believed that his hard work must inevitably bring him fame and money. Six months of life at Pond House had taught her that quite a lot of money was necessary if they wanted to stay here.

They lived humbly enough. They deliberately made no friends in the neighbourhood because they could not afford to entertain. They worked most of the time. The interest on Kevin's five thousand pounds could not go far. Their savings were dwindling. So far, Kevin had only been commissioned to write one more series of articles, with the hope of a further order.

He was counting a lot on his book. It was a suspense story with a thread of espionage in it. A great deal of it took place in West Berlin. Not that Kevin had ever been there but he had a vivid imagination, devoured books on the subject that Cass found for him in the Public Library at Chelmsford, and was using copious notes taken when he was at University where he had shared a room with a young German student. From this boy he had learned much about life in Berlin before and after 'The Wall' went up.

In Cass's opinion the story was tremendously interesting and Kevin wrote well. His English was beautiful, much better in her opinion than that of the average writer. He had not wasted his time at Bristol.

Cass never spent a penny on herself. She was wearing out all her old clothes. She didn't need much down here. But their electricity bill was big. It was necessary that Kevin should be warm while he worked.

His best present to Cass out of his legacy had been an Aga cooker—that gave them heat in the kitchen and could be used for cooking.

At night, they sat by one small electric fire and watched their television—left behind by poor Aunt Cynthia and much appreciated. It was their one amusement.

Next year Kevin was determined to organise a method of cutting logs from the 'estate', so they could have a wood-fire to sit by.

Pond House, to him, in the golden light of summer proved more stimulating and welcoming than in midwinter. It was so cold this month; the water froze at the margin of the pond. The trees, stripped bare, were rimed with frost. It was desolate out there on the water. Even the geese seemed disinclined to swim, although they came faithfully up to the house for their feed.

Cass had tried to establish a regular sale for her vegetables. Old William worked, with and for her, and took half the profits. His sixteen year old grandson, Bert, had left school and was working with him. There should be plenty of fresh vegetables this spring that Cass could market. She had also bought a dozen chickens which she looked after. Kevin loathed chickens. But he liked the eggs. Cass was more often out of doors than in.

She also had a bright idea of planting one field with baby Christmas trees and selling them.

Old William, who had developed a healthy respect for young Mrs. Martin, chatted with her this morning in his amicable fashion. His strong Essex dialect also fascinated Cass.

At the start he had expected her to be a typical city lady who knew nothing about kitchen gardens or anything on the land. But she had proved a willing learner and a good worker and didn't argue with him which pleased the old man! They got on well together. He knew, that, despite his age, he could get a bigger wage elsewhere, but he preferred to stay on at Pond House with the new owners.

Cass trudged beside the old fellow across the hard frozen earth, the north wind whipping the blood into her cheeks. She felt happy. She adored this life. She had taken to the country in a big way. She went to bed at times feeling so tired that every bone in her body ached, but she still liked it. It was healthy. It was good. The old life with poor Mummy and the General seemed a long long time ago and poor by comparison.

She had her worries over Kevin; he did not think he
was earning money quickly enough, couldn't get on as
fast as he should with his book, and so the black moods
would descend like a fog. He wanted to give her the
earth, she knew that. But on the whole he was happy
and proud of his inheritance. He, too, was benefiting by
the fresh air. Cass had to bully him but she made him
take at least one walk a day. They would trudge round
the pond together, examining their wild fowl. Cass
loved it all as much now that the waters were icy and
the wind so sharp as during the warmth and gold of the
summer.

Last night when they were in bed, he had wakened
her from her first deep sleep by kissing her eyelids
open. He whispered:

"Talk to me. I can't sleep. I'm so worried."

At once she threw off her stupor of exhaustion,
wreathed her arms around him and whispered back:

"Why? What is it, my darling?"

"I'm worried about you."

"Why about me?"

"You work so hard."

"So do you."

"I sit at a ruddy desk. You're always on your feet—
indoors or out. You've lost weight."

She took both his hands and placed them on either
side of her narrow waist.

"Hi! You said you liked me this way."

"But you don't want to overdo it."

At once she was warm and dewy-eyed with her passionate love for him, forgetful of the times he snapped
at her or troubled her with his depressions.

"Oh, Kev, you're so sweet. *Do* stop worrying. I'm fit
as a fiddle. I was getting too plump in town. Why, when
the Burnhams came down last Sunday, they said how
well and brown I looked. I adore the outside work. I'm
afraid I rather neglect my cooking sometimes, but I do
want to get the market gardening going, and make William feel that what he makes is worth while. We could
never afford a proper, highly paid gardener."

"I was talking to a chap in the pub the other night
and he said there was nothing much in what you're

doing," said Kevin gloomily. "Anyhow, I'm the man of the house and it's up to me to bring in the dibs."

She laughed and nuzzled his neck with her lips.

"Don't be archaic, angel."

"You are happy, aren't you?"

"Fantastically. I adore you. I adore Pond House, and I've only one fear."

Kevin switched on a table-lamp and reached for a packet of cigarettes. Then he drew in his hand again, sheepishly remembering that he had given up smoking and that anyhow it was one o'clock in the morning and they ought both be asleep.

"What's your fear, honey?" he yawned.

"That the General might keep his word and come down for a weekend."

Kevin snorted.

"He won't be welcome. He may be all melting now that he's alone and poor old '*Yes-dear*' isn't alive to leap to his orders, but I'm darned if I'll have him here trying to regimentate *us*. You might find him out in the yard square-bashing William." That made her rock with laughter.

They were both asleep within a few minutes and it was Kevin who got up and went down to make the early tea and bring her up a cup because he said he had woken her up and, through him, she'd missed her full quota of sleep.

She could forgive him anything.

She was out for a couple of hours before she began to feel the cold was too intense and the sky was darkening. She wanted a cup of hot coffee.

There was a flurry of snow. The first of the year. Cass looked up at the dark billow of clouds with some interest. It might be rather beautiful here in the snow; and if the pond froze over, it would be *super*—they would have to buy skates.

She got back to the house to find a large grey Citroën car parked in front of the entrance. Pulling off her gauntlets she rubbed her cold hands together and stared at the handsome car.

Who on *earth* was calling at this hour? Who owned a Citroën? She and Kev were not really on visiting terms with 'the neighbourhood' but she knew who most of the people were, and what cars they had. One saw them in the village, and heard about them from gossips in the pubs and shops. And old William was a fount of knowledge.

There was the Vicar of Cold Dutton—they had, in fact, been called upon by him. A rather dull young man with a dull wife and four plain children. There were what William called 'the gentry' up at Fairmyle Hall, the grounds of which adjoined the boundaries of Pond House. Titled people, Sir Gerald and Lady Winn-Kerr. Once or twice Cass had seen Sir Gerald out riding. He reminded her of the General; old school type; white moustache; a lot of dignity. Lady Winn-Kerr was on all the committees and had already tried to drag Cass into the Women's Institute, but she had had to refuse; she had so much to do at home she couldn't cope with local affairs. There were various farms and their owners around and, of course, all the inhabitants of the new Council houses that had been put up to the west of old Cold Dutton.

But she didn't remember ever having seen a grey Citroën.

She opened the front door.

The first sound she heard was that of a piano being played—extraordinarily well, too. Cass was not a musical scholar, but she remembered this from her schooldays—a Chopin Scherzo. Well, who could imagine that so much sound could be beaten out of that old Broadwood in Aunt Cynthia's drawing-room?

The she heard men's voices. The next moment Kevin appeared in the hall, holding a glass in one hand and a cigarette in the other. The cigarette struck her more forcibly than the drink. At midday sometimes, when Kev was working, he had a glass of beer but she had not seen him smoke a cigarette for almost a year. The second thing was that he looked less haggard than usual. Untidy, of course, in his old corduroys and the thick blue jersey which, she thought sadly, needed mending and washing. He insisted on wearing it while he worked. But he looked alert and in the best of humours.

"Ah, you're back, sweet," he said. "We've been waiting for you."

"Who's *'we'?*" asked Cass, and took off the woolly beret she wore when she was out of doors and ran her fingers through her long, wind-blown hair.

"Natasha's husband is playing the piano—can't you hear?"

"Natasha's husband?" she echoed and gaped at him.

"Yes, Aunt Cynthia's step-daughter and her husband have just arrived. They flew over from France this morning, plus Citroën. They phoned from Lydd about two minutes after you left the house this morning and said they were on their way. It's taken them two hours getting here."

"Natasha and her husband," said Cass slowly, both looking and feeling a trifle confused. "Good lord!"

The piano stopped then started again. And now Cass, considerably shaken, heard a low and attractive feminine voice singing a French song.

Cass gripped Kevin's arm so fiercely that she split the drink.

"Mind out," he hissed.

"That's *gin!*" she whispered. "Where did you get it?"

"They brought it, out-of-bond stuff."

"You're *smoking.*"

"I couldn't resist it. They gave me one of those big cartons. My nerves were screaming for a smoke. Do you mind?"

"No, not a bit . . ." Cass had taken off her coat now and was brushing the mud off the hems of her ski-trousers. "But Kev—there's nothing but sausages for lunch. We can't entertain them."

"They're going to take us out. I told them we could get quite a good grill at the Queen's Head."

Cass blinked at him.

"You *have* been busy organising! How long have they been here?"

"Only about twenty minutes."

"But they're in the sitting room—it's icy in there."

"Natasha said that her husband wanted to play. It *is* her piano, anyhow."

"Is she going to put it in the boot of the Citroën when she leaves?" asked Cass with sudden sarcasm.

"Don't be idiotic."

"I admit he plays well," added Cass. "They might have let us know they were about to descend on us. They don't expect to be put up for the night, do they?"

"Yes, they do," said Kevin, and put an arm around his wife's shoulder. "Don't be peevish. I just had to say *yes*. Natasha said she was dying to spend a night in her old home."

"And who's going to cook the evening meal *and* the breakfast *and* do all the work?" asked Cass with a sudden smile and one of her quick giggles. *"You?"*

"Oh, she said she'd help," said Kevin vaguely.

"What's she like?"

"A smasher."

"Cripes!" said Cass, "and *he?* What' his name?"

"Maurice Courraine; she pronounces it *Maureece*."

"Ever so French," said Cass.

"Darling, you must come and be nice to them."

"Well, of course," said Cass, "but it's all a bit of a surprise."

Still with his arm around Cass's slim shoulders, Kevin led her into the salon which they never used. She was thankful that she had actually dusted it yesterday. Kevin seemed to have collected all the electric fires in the house. There were two burning at each end.

Natasha, who was standing by the grand piano singing, stopped abruptly and turned as the pair entered.

Cass was at once aware that Kevin had been justified in calling Mr. de Groot's daughter a 'smasher'. She had seldom seen a more beautiful girl. At twenty-four, at her best, she was tall and slim, with narrow hips, and beautiful breasts, high and tilted under a very short white dress made of some attractive woollen material. The smallness of her waist was accentuated by a broad chain belt. There were several gold and beaded necklaces twined around her throat. Over her shoulders hung a light golden brown fur coat.

Mink, thought Cass, *my gawd, it's mink!* And that hair—what wonderful hair, pinkish auburn—the colour almost of coral; brushed severely from a delicately-boned face, tied with a huge rakish bow. Cass had never seen such beautiful hair. It shone in the dusk on this winter's day. Her eyes shone, too. They looked enormous, dark chestnut brown, heavily-lashed. The one flaw was her nose. The nostrils were a trifle too broad.

Model-girl, thought Cass, *clothes straight out of Harper's Bazaar. And that is going to help me in the house and do the washing-up, is it?*

Kevin introduced the two girls.

"Natasha, this is my wife, Cassandra. We call her Cass. Cass, this is Natasha, who was brought up in this house. She says it's hardly changed."

"Hullo!" said Cass, and held out a friendly hand which Natasha took but dropped again quickly. It struck Cass in that second that she didn't like Natasha. She had one of those limp handshakes that Cass detested—no strength, no warmth from those long, thin, beautifully manicured fingers.

Cass looked at her own hands, red from the cold, nails breaking, no varnish. She put her tongue in her cheek and glanced out of the corners of her eyes at Kevin. It struck her suddenly that she must appear like a beatnik to him, beside Natasha.

You can't work on the land and look as though you've stepped out of a glossy magazine, she thought. *I hope Kev realises that.*

Now Natasha was speaking:

"You must meet my husband, Maurice—" she pronounced it *Maureece* as Kevin had said. Cass looked with curiosity and some surprise at the Frenchman who was Natasha's second husband.

Maurice Courraine was at least a head shorter than his tall graceful wife, thick-set and unglamorous. Cass judged that he must be at least ten years older than Natasha. Large black glasses hid his eyes. His podgy face was boyish in a way, with round cheeks and a big, generous mouth. But his face had the waxen pallor of one who spent too much time indoors. A small pointed black beard added to his years. But the most startling thing was his hair, which, Cass thought, must at one time have been as black as the beard. There was masses of it—now silver grey, thick, upspringing, waving back from an intellectual forehead.

He moved towards her slowly and Cass's quick eye noted that Natasha handed him an ebony stick on which he leaned. He was an invalid, she thought. He could not have been a more unsuitable husband for the glowing, glamorous Natasha. Yet those podgy fingers of his had extracted such rich brilliant sounds from that old piano.

"This is Cassandra," said Natasha in a languid voice and using Cass's full name, "Kevin's wife. They've only been married a year and a half."

Maurice Courraine extended his right hand to Cass. From him, the grasp was warm and friendly. She responded to it and gave him one of her big smiles.

"Hullo, how are you? I heard you playing as I came in. It was fabulous. I wish you hadn't stopped."

"You like music?" he asked. He spoke excellent English with only a faint, attractive accent.

She felt his gaze examining her closely through the dark glasses, but somehow that look was friendly. He did not make her feel uncomfortable as Natasha had done.

"Not much. I mean, I don't know much about classical music," she said, blushing, "but I adore hearing it—I mean, when the piano's played as *you* play it. And of course, it was super to hear Natasha singing," she added politely, glancing at the girl.

"Maurice doesn't think I *sing*. He calls it crooning," said Natasha with her low husky laugh—a laugh with which Cass was to become all too familiar. For some strange reason it gave her the shivers. It had a sinister, suggestive quality.

Soon they were all four sitting by the window, looking out at the pond. Kevin poured out more drinks and lit more cigarettes, including one for Natasha who was resting her slim willowy body comfortably in one of the armchairs. Kevin began to talk with enthusiasm about the pond and pointed out the Chinese geese that were swimming slowly over the cold grey water toward the tangles of bulrushes just below the verandah.

"Mr. de Groot, your father, bred all these odd creatures, we're told. He seems to have been a great bird fancier. And Aunt Cynthia was mad about them too, wasn't she? So are we, now—Cass and I—we feed them every day. They're quite tame. They know us. We've christened them Margot and Rudolf."

Natasha gave a soft laugh.

"Ah! Because they're so graceful, after Fonteyn and Nureyev. What fun!"

"I wish I could see them," said Maurice Courraine suddenly.

With a shock Cass suddenly realised that the trouble with Natasha's French husband was that he *could not see*. He was obviously not totally blind but must be very nearly so. Her heart was suddenly wrung with pity. Then Natasha explained—speaking, Cass thought, with a cool indifference which did not somehow fit the occasion.

"Poor Maurice—he was so unlucky. He's had about six operations lately, but his right eye has gone altogether and there's some trouble with the left. He can see a bit but not far and he can never read music any more which is a bit devastating for him."

"Don't let's talk about it please," said Maurice in a low tone.

Cass and Kevin exchanged glances. Kevin looked at his wrist watch.

"Cass and I had better freshen up," he said. "We ought to be getting along to Cold Dutton. It's a quarter to one."

Natasha turned to Cass, her curving lips, glistening silvery pink, sensuous, smiled. It was a smile, Cass felt instinctively, with a touch of cruelty in it. Yes—that was what spoilt her beauty. She was cruel. Even after so brief an acquaintance Cass felt this strongly. Suddenly she sympathised with Aunt Cynthia who had not liked her stepdaughter.

"Are you sure you don't mind us putting up at Pond House for a few days?" Natasha asked her.

A few days! That made Cass's heart sink, but she answered gaily enough:

"Of course not. Stay as long as you like. After all, it's your old home."

"I think it's an imposition," put in Maurice. "I know

Kevin suggested it, but we men are like that—we do not always see the housewife's point of view. How do we know, Natasha, that Mrs. Martin—or may I call her Cassandra, which is a most beautiful name—wishes to have us here."

"Dear Maurice," murmured Natasha, "always so thoughtful for others, aren't you, dearest?"

Very thoughtful, Cass decided, and liked Maurice and detested Natasha. Of course Cass was always too impulsive. Kev said so. She had a habit of making up her mind too quickly about things and people.

It was Cass who took the semi-blind man by the arm and led him up the stairs to the spare room. Here again, she thanked heaven that she had taken it upon herself to dust and tidy it yesterday because it had been so neglected. It was very cold in the big room and she saw Natasha shiver and slide both arms into her mink coat.

"I hope she freezes," Cass muttered to herself. "I wonder why she wants to stay in this cold, draughty, old house. It can't be just sentiment. She isn't the sentimental type."

Cass apologised for the cold room, called Kevin to find another electric fire and apologised also because nothing had been prepared. She then made a note of all the things she would have to do after lunch. A nuisance. She wanted to work a bit longer in the kitchen garden, but now she would have to go shopping—buy food—air some sheets (thank goodness Aunt Cynthia had left a cupboard full of decent linen) and make this room more welcoming.

She saw Natasha's long lovely eyes, with critical gaze, travel around the room, examining everything.

"I remember this so well. My stepmother used to use it for her special friends because it has that nice tallboy, and those brass bedheads. The beds are so high and old-fashioned, aren't they? No doubt, comfortable. My stepmother liked her comforts; but she had such suburban taste. I hate this floral carpet and those awful blue curtains."

"You must tell us more about Mrs. de Groot tonight. Kev didn't really know her," said Cass.

She resented Natasha's unkind remarks.

"*Kev*—you mean Kevin?" asked Natasha, wandering around the room, examining everything.

"Yes; I call him *Kev,*" said Cass coldly.

Natasha looked through her lashes.

"He's simply charming, isn't he? So intelligent. It's fascinating—meeting a real live author."

Watch it, thought Cass grimly, *this girl may be the nympho type. She's had two husbands already and if I'm not careful she'll go after mine.*

Then she noticed Maurice. He had seated his short plump body on the edge of one of the beds, taken off his glasses and was wiping his eyes with a large white handkerchief. The poor little bearded man looked so forlorn somehow on the edge of that bed, wiping his eyes as though he were crying. Cass saw those eyes for the first time. They looked sore and he blinked at her, but he smiled. They were beautiful eyes—grey, like his hair. She could almost believe that he had once been quite attractive. But now he looked ill and sad and old.

"Did Kev show you the bathroom, Mr. Courraine?" she asked gently.

He put the dark glasses on again and smiled at her.

"Thank you, yes."

"Well, we'll all meet downstairs in a few moments," said Cass.

The lunch that followed at the Queen's Head in Cold Dutton was revealing to Cass. As they ate the typically English lunch—soup, choice of chicken or lamb, apple tart and cream—they talked in a general way. About Paris, Germany, politics, the situation in England, the Common Market, and, of course, the weather. How cold it was, but it was even colder in Paris. The Courraines had an apartment in Neuilly but they were selling the lease because it was too expensive, with the rising cost of living in France.

Cass learned more about Maurice. Up to a few months ago he had been a busy, successful pianist. As an accompanist he had achieved considerable fame on the Continent. He used to play for some of the most famous singers in the world. His ability to read difficult music at sight had been one of his greatest assets. But his ruined eyesight meant that he could no longer do this. Hence the sudden considerable drop in his income and the need to cut down expenses.

"Tough luck," was Kevin's comment, with a genuine note of sympathy.

He could imagine his own frustration if he could no longer write or even dictate. It must be very galling to a man to feel that his life's work was being stripped away from him through no fault of his own. Cass thought that it was more than tough. It was a real tragedy for Maurice Courraine. What had he left now but his wife's sympathy and understanding? But Natasha for some extraordinary reason seemed to give him neither. She grumbled all through the meal.

It was ghastly having to give up her beautiful apartment. Ghastly having to come back to England which she had always hated. It meant the end of entertaining. They used to have fabulous evenings with famous people. Maurice often flew suddenly to Vienna or West Berlin, always in demand because of his faultless playing. Natasha used to go with him. They stayed in fabulous hotels and had a wonderful life. How mean of her, Cass thought, to keep referring to past glories. How uncomfortable it must make her husband feel that her present discontent was his fault. She noticed that he remained silent. Only once he turned on Natasha.

"Please, *chérie,* let us not talk about me or what has happened to my eyes any more," he said in a voice of such pain that it almost hurt Cass physically.

When they returned to Pond House, Kevin offered to take Natasha for a quick walk around the pond. Cass could lend her some boots. Natasha had said that she had warm slacks in her luggage and a thick jersey. She would unpack and put them on. Finally she went off with Kevin still wearing the mink and still looking beautiful and without a hair out of place, thought Cass who watched them go.

Kev had said that he wanted to write all day today so that he could finish a chapter. He seemed to have forgotten that, she thought.

Before the front door closed on the two, she had heard him laughing—one of those gay spontaneous bursts of laughter which meant that he was in the best of moods. So . . . no doubt he enjoyed the prospect of a walk with the beautiful Natasha who, when she finished grumbling continually, gave Kevin the full rich benefit of her swimming gaze under those long false lashes. She had openly remarked at lunch that she thought Kevin looked like Peter O'Toole who was her favourite film star.

"Well, I think Kev looks just like *Kev*—" Cass capped this bluntly.

Kevin had looked at Natasha and grinned.

Anyhow, it was obvious to Cass that Mr. de Groot's daughter was quite taken by Kevin and blatantly, callously, bored by Maurice—the man she had married when he was a famous pianist. No doubt she had thought she would lead an exciting life with him for ever.

Now the excitement was over.

Well, she's not going to find it fun here—no matter how hard she flirts with my husband. He'll soon see through her, Cass told herself.

But would he?

Did men see through lovely girls like Natasha who flattered them? she wondered.

Chapter 12

THE evening that followed was what Cass described to herself as 'pleasant enough but madly extravagant'. Once more the salon was occupied. Kevin didn't seem to think they could ask Natasha and her husband to sit in the kitchen, or his study, as they, the Martins, so often did. So two electric fires burned merrily for hours, and they had had to warm up the dining-room as well. Cass found herself giving a real dinner party. She had never been a good cook but once again, with extravagance, she bought steaks and grilled them, and followed it with a cherry tart (thank goodness for bought pastry!)

Natasha ate little—obviously one of those girls who considered her figure, but Maurice—true to France—enjoyed his food, and congratulated the chef.

"Sweet of you," Cass said, "but I'm afraid I'm pretty poor at the job, really."

Kevin defended her.

"My wife has become an outdoor girl and she's doing ruddy well with her vegetables, I may say."

Natasha, who had changed into a becoming violet and gold caftan, which looked quite out of place in Cass's opinion, gave her throaty laugh.

"How amusing that sounds. How do you do well with a vegetable?"

Everybody laughed except Cass.

"I don't suppose you found it amusing, seeing all the winter sprouts, cabbages and savoys," she said.

Natasha looked at her hostess through her long lashes.

"I admire your energy. Actually, I've never been interested in the great out-of-doors. I used to get into trouble with Daddy and Cynthia, because I hated gardening. But then I'm definitely an indoor girl."

"Quite," said Cass caustically.

Natasha continued:

"It was wonderful walking around the lake with Kev showing me all the work you've done. Imagine clearing all those rushes and weeds away from the boathouse landing stage, for instance. And Kev says he's going to get that boat mended so that you can use it in the summer."

"If I ever get time," put in Kevin hastily.

Cass thought: So it's *Kev* now. Only a few hours ago she was critical because I called him that. Well, *well!*

She recalled Kevin's high spirits when he returned from that walk. He had talked to her quite frankly of Natasha's intelligence and charm.

Cass laughed and joked a little less than usual.

They had music after the meal. Natasha offered to

help wash up but Cass firmly refused. *She* would be more trouble than anything.

"I'd rather do it myself," Cass said. "Thanks all the same."

"But you must not," Maurice had said with kindliness. "Please let us help."

Kevin settled the matter. The guests were to go into the salon and have their coffee, he said, while he and Cass 'did the job'. They were used to washing up together and would be quick about it.

Finally the evening developed into a 'concert', with Maurice playing the piano, to which Cass listened with pleasure. She was tired; it was good to lean back in her chair, shut her eyes and enjoy the music. Now and again she opened them and saw Kevin and Natasha sitting side by side on the sofa. They were talking in undertones.

When she was alone with Kevin that night, Cass said:

"I thought it was rude of that girl to natter while her husband was playing."

Kev pulled his shirt over his head and answered casually:

"Oh, I don't suppose Maurice minded. We were whispering really. Anyhow you can't expect her to treat it so religiously. She's had plenty of it all their married life."

"Doesn't she like music then?"

"Yes, but you can get too much of it, can't you?"

"Well, I thought her rude," said Cass.

Kevin sat on the edge of the bed and lit a cigarette. "It's not like you to be so hypercritical, sweet."

Not for the world was Cass going to admit that she was overtired, feeling rather stupid, and definitely jealous of Natasha. That would be a really idiotic thing to do.

"What time are they leaving?" she asked Kev after a pause.

"There's no rush, is there?"

Now Cass stopped brushing her hair and looked into Kevin's handsome blue eyes with amazement.

"You don't want them to *stay on,* do you?" she asked aghast.

He frowned.

"What's bitten you? Have you taken a violent dislike to them or something?"

Cass stammered:

"N-no, I mean I'd rather be alone with you, that's all."

"Sweet of you, honey, but do remember that this was Natasha's old home."

"I've *been* remembering it, but I don't see why it entitles her to live here now." Then before Kevin could answer, she added: "And as long as they're here, *you* won't do any work."

"Of course I will," he said irritably.

"Well, you haven't done much today."

"They've only just arrived. I had to be around."

"Well, how long *are* they staying?"

He was still sitting on the bed smoking. The sight of the cigarette did little to comfort Cass. Madame Natasha Courraine was definitely a poor influence. Not only had she made him smoke again but drink. Only a little, of course—wine during the meal and two liqueurs. They had brought the brandy over from France. But as she saw him sitting there yawning and smoking, she came to the conclusion that he would hardly start work in the morning with his usual energy. Then she reproached herself for becoming exactly as he had accused her—hypercritical. Of course she had nothing against poor, nearly blind Maurice, but somehow Natasha put her hackles up.

She sat down on the bed beside Kevin and laid her cheek against his shoulder.

"How long do you want them to stay, darling? It's your home and, as you say, she was born here. It's not for me to dictate. Just *you* say."

Kevin cheered up.

"Now you're being sensible, darling. It isn't like you to be so unfriendly. I think he's a bit of a bore except for his music, but she is most entertaining. She's led a fantastic life since she ran away from here, I assure you."

"I believe you," said Cass, with her tongue in her cheek. "But I don't agree that Maurice is a bore. He's a very cultured sweet man, and what does it matter that he's short and podgy and unglamorous?"

"My kind little Cass," said Kev and dropped a kiss on her hair. "I do love you, you know, my darling," he added. "I thought you put up a damned good meal, too. That steak was perfect."

"Thanks, pal."

She felt light-hearted again, and the somewhat sinister shadow of Natasha slipped away. Unfortunately it slipped back all too quickly and much too overpoweringly, for now Kevin came out with the thing that had been on his mind all evening.

While Cass was busy in the kitchen, he had had a long talk with the guests. They had come to England because the financial situation was getting tricky. Maurice had once made a lot of money but relied on making more and lived above his income. He still had a certain amount of capital but not enough for the sort of life Natasha wanted. Added to her money which she had inherited from her father, they could manage only simply. What they intended to do was to find a cottage and live quietly. This had been Maurice's idea, of course. Natasha was a town girl and adored a gay Continental life. The loss of Maurice's eyesight and his career had been a terrible blow to her, Kevin remarked. Cass silently wondered whether it had not been a bigger blow to poor Maurice, but Kevin seemed to be sympathetic only with *her*. He went on to say that since the Courraines had arrived at Pond House they had realised how difficult things were for Kevin and how much too big the house was for them. Then Natasha had suddenly had the wonderful idea of living here at Pond House and sharing expenses.

"They could have the guest wing and bathroom and not interfere with us at all," Kevin ended, lighting the second cigarette since he came to bed, "and they'd halve the bills, light and fuel, rates and so on—and of course, food. It would make a huge difference to us, Cass."

She sat very still as though frozen into immobility.

All the way through Kevin's story her heart had been
sinking lower and lower. Now at last she spoke.

"I must say I'm a bit stupefied. *You* suggest that we
should let the Courraines come here and share our
home. You who warned me off because I dared talk
about 'paying guests' just in fun. Why, you said that
you'd murder me if I let the General live with us."

Kevin got up and began to walk around the room
with that graceful swaggering walk of his.

"Hell, it's hardly the same having the Courraines as
your cantankerous stepfather, my dear."

"No doubt Natasha is a lot more attractive even
though you find *Monsieur* a bore," said Cass and bit
hard at her lips, hoping she was not going to be stupid
enough to cry.

She had never been more surprised than when Kevin
broached the possibility of sharing his house with the
Courraines. She felt resentful and unco-operative and in
her frank, impulsive fashion, she showed it.

"I would hate to share Pond House with anyone. I'd
rather work twice as hard and twice as long and do
without the financial help, thanks very much."

"But it's a sensible proposition—" he began.

"It isn't, it's against everything we planned and
against your own idea," she interrupted. "You said you
must be left alone to work in peace."

"Okay. I could shut myself in my study as usual,
couldn't I?"

She looked up at him indignantly.

"With Natasha knocking on the door asking to be
taken for little walks round the pond."

"Oh, Cass, darling, don't be fatuous."

"Or Maurice playing the piano right next door to
you. You who always tell me you must have quiet."

"Darling, beggars can't be choosers. Obviously I'd
rather have the place to ourselves but this seems a way
for us to get on to our feet during our first year. Halv-
ing the expenses will be a colossal help."

Cass stood up, her heart beating fast and furiously.

"And am I to cook for four instead of two and to
give nice dinners every night and alter our whole way of

living? I can only just manage when we muck in—the two of us, and picnic, but—"

"Natasha says she'll help," broke in Kevin.

Now Cass gave a loud long laugh.

"How can you be so naïve, my *darling?* That beauty-queen with her long pointed nails and her Continental lazy ways—I bet she *is* lazy—why, she's never had to lift a saucepan on to a stove in her life. She told me that even when she was married to her number one she had domestic help."

"We'll be able to afford a daily, with them footing the bills," argued Kevin. "In fact Maurice was very decent and said that he knew that despite their present embarrassment, they were much better off than we are and he offered to pay entirely for a domestic help."

"If we can find one," muttered Cass.

"You seem to have taken against Natasha for some reason," Kevin said suddenly and resentfully.

Cass was on the verge of saying *yes*—that she thoroughly disliked Mr. de Groot's 'difficult daughter'—but refrained. Something warned her that it might be foolish to show open animosity towards this girl who her husband was finding an intelligent and attractive companion. Cass had always despised jealous wives. It meant a lack of trust. She trusted Kev. She did not for a moment think he was attracted by Natasha *that way.* All the same he was a man and human and Natasha was very beautiful and glamorous.

And I, thought Cass, *had better watch my step and not go round all the time in awful old slacks and jerseys. Or stop varnishing my nails, or say I haven't time to get my hair done.*

Why was she thinking this way? Oh, were they really going to stay on here indefinitely?

Kevin came up and put an arm around her.

"Darling, don't look so tragic. If you really don't want the Courraines, say so, and I'll veto the whole plan. I can always say we don't think it'll work."

Cass had difficulty now in not bursting into tears but she managed to smile.

"I'm not against it if you're keen, darling. As I've said before, it is *your* house."

"Darling, that's rubbish; it's yours too. I regard it as *ours*. But I did think it a way for us to save a bit. This place is very expensive to run."

"Won't a couple like the Courraines mean that the whole cost of living will go up and we'll be all square in the end anyhow?"

"No. Maurice is very generous and said they'd personally buy a lot of things to eat, and all the drinks and extras, and so on, and they'll also be away quite a bit as Maurice has musical friends in London. Already they've been invited to stay."

"I see," said Cass in a low voice.

"Well, don't you think it could work?"

She lifted large and suddenly sad eyes to his. She felt sad somehow, yet had no real cause to. But she couldn't help thinking that it was Natasha's charm and beauty rather than Maurice's money that was the big temptation for Kevin. And because she felt that way she was ready to show her love and trust by sacrificing her own wishes and falling in with him. She *had* to have faith in Kev. It was true that the expenses here were pretty grim, and they needed help. And if they could get a daily to take all the housework in this big place off her shoulders, she could surely manage the cooking.

"Yes, it might work," she answered Kevin's question at last and patted his cheek, then kissed the tip of his nose, "By all means let's try it. I'd like to feel some of the financial burden was being lifted from you, my pet."

Kevin looked relieved.

"Good," he said. "We'll tell them in the morning."

Cass left Kevin to do the 'telling'. After a night's rest she felt better able to cope with the situation. She just hoped that it *would* work out satisfactorily, not only for herself, but for Kevin. He had been so adamant about allowing no one to disturb his work.

Before she went out to her usual early meeting with old William, and to feed the chickens, she gave Kevin one word of caution.

"I'll do my best, Kev, but you must make it plain to Natasha and Maurice that they can't interrupt you once you start writing."

"Of course, darling." He was in a good humour. "And I'm not having *you* do too much extra work—you do enough. You're friendly with your grocer—old Notman. Try and see him as soon as you can and ask if he could find you a daily."

Before they parted she had said:

"It won't be a *permanent* arrangement, will it? I mean, Natasha is sure to get bored down here even if poor old Maurice doesn't. There's not much he can do with those wretched eyes of his."

"Oh, it won't be for ever, of course not! Maurice is going to see a big oculist at Moorfields. You never know, someone might work magic for him."

So Cass went off on her day's work worried but resigned and didn't see Natasha or Maurice till lunch time. She had taken them up a tray with their breakfast toast and coffee. She found it less bother than getting them up and downstairs. Natasha was not an early riser.

When she returned to the house at midday she was relieved to find that neither Natasha nor Maurice was there. They were in London for the day. Cass felt a lot better when she was eating an omelette alone, as usual, with her beloved Kev in the kitchen.

They had news for each other.

Kev had done a good morning's work and was on the verge of completing his novel. He was excited and pleased.

"The next thing for me to do is to find a Chelmsford typing bureau and get the manuscript properly typed."

"Oh Kev, how marvellous!" Her eyes shone at him.

"Mind you, I shall need at least another month's work on it but I could get the first part typed."

"Has it got a title?"

"Yes—*Nightmare in Berlin.*"

"That's terrific," she said.

He scraped the last vestige of omelette from his plate and grinned at her.

"Always my little booster. I hope the chaps who read it will feel the same as you."

"Well, we've been so busy and tired at night, you

haven't read me the last few chapters. I'm dying to hear them."

Kevin now turned to the subject of the Courraines.

"They've gone up to see some French friends of Maurice's—they've a flat in town—and to make an appointment with Maurice's eye-specialist."

"I'd better think about dinner for tonight," said Cass. "Did you see Mr. Notman?"

"Yes, and there's hope. He said dailies were terribly hard to come by in this district and heaps of people are waiting for them but he seems to rather 'dig' me and he's full of sympathy about me not liking that awful Mrs. Pinner. She's no pal of his. He's even hinted that she had poor Aunt Cynthia right under her thumb when she was so much of an invalid, and had done her wrong."

"Is he going to find you somebody?"

"Yes—he has a niece whose husband works for the telephone company and they live on the new Council estate here. He says she's got one child at school, but could get to me by bus, and work all morning, and they're in need of money because there's some long story about them having to have his old mother to live with them now she's a widow, and their expenses are going up, etc."

"So is she coming?"

"He thinks she will because she mentioned that she must take a job. There's an infant, too. But mother-in-law will look after it."

"How much will it cost?"

"Three hours a morning, sixteen and six—and her bus fare."

"This is where the Courraines will come in," said Kevin, with a grin. "They'll pay, and you won't have to do another day's dusting."

It seemed to Cass that Kevin was well satisfied by the new arrangement. Perhaps, she thought regretfully, men were so much less sentimental than women, that they did not set the store on 'togetherness' that women did. But unless the Courraines were out during the day, she would never have Kev to herself, until they went to bed. For her, things seemed suddenly spoiled.

Chapter 13.

IF Cass had entertained a hope that the Courraines would only be temporary residents at the Pond House, she was doomed to disappointment.

They stayed on and on.

Almost as soon as their luggage arrived and they settled in their wing, Christmas was upon them all.

It was a very different Christmas from the first that Cass and Kevin had shared after their marriage—less intimate. In a remarkably short time it seemed to Cass that her life completely changed—and so far as she was concerned not for the better, although she could not complain that her actual lot had been made harder by the presence of the Courraines.

Mr. Notman's niece, Joyce, arrived and became a faithful and reliable helper, a capable and cheerful young woman who put in a really good three hours' work and, surprisingly enough, kept the big house clean and shining. Natasha said it had returned to the meticulous orderliness of the days when her father and stepmother lived here. The furniture was well polished, the silver shone, the carpets were Hoovered, and Cass found she had nothing to do but cook an evening meal, except on Sundays when Joyce had her husband home and did not go out to work. Joyce became a firm friend although she showed from the start that she had no liking for Madame Courraine.

"She's not like you, Mrs. Martin," Joyce remarked on one occasion when she had just finished turning out 'the guest wing'. "She's that untidy and careless. Nail varnish on that nice silk eiderdown—stains on the carpet where she's dropped her make-up—never puts away anything. Thinks I'm here to do it, I s'pose. I don't hold with these beauty queens."

Cass laughed but inwardly sympathised. She'd got to know Natasha well enough now to realise that the girl was, as she had anticipated, lazy, undomesticated, and unbelievably selfish. With honeyed words and a dozen excuses, Natasha managed to get out of helping whenever it was possible. She even made a 'thing' about shopping for Cass, and if she did, she nearly always bought the wrong article at the highest price. It was death to Cass's careful housekeeping.

The thing Cass most disliked was Natasha's casual and sometime blatant unkindness to her husband. Cass had developed a real affection for the poor little bearded man with his tragic eyes and unfailing courtesy. She had never heard him say one unpleasant thing to Natasha, even when she was nagging and complaining. He obviously adored her. He was patient and, in Cass's opinion, foolishly adoring.

But how Maurice chose to behave to his wife was one thing; how Kevin behaved was another. And this aspect caused Cass quite a few disagreeable moments.

Christmas was gay and really quite fun. Cass enjoyed it. Natasha had made another alteration in their lives which, to Cass's surprise, did not seem to worry Kevin. Her one-time Hermit-Kev, as she used to call him, seemed to be coming out of his shell, willing to be drawn into a much more social existence. Obviously Natasha could not live without people and parties and Natasha was able to influence Kevin. Maurice wanted to lead a quiet life. Cass knew that he was secretly grieving for his lost sight and his ruined career and that it cost him a lot to appear happy and talkative in public. But he was sociable for Natasha's sake.

She revived few of the old friendships the de Groots had once made when Natasha was young. But now that she was Madame Courraine, she made new contacts wherever a little excitement was offered. Cass now found herself on visiting terms with Sir Gerald and Lady Winn-Kerr. It was to their Christmas dinner and dance that the Martins and the Courraines were invited. The daughter of the house had married a well-known director of the B.B.C. They filled the house at Christmas time with amusing people; actors, actresses, producers, with one or two film-stars thrown in.

Natasha was almost the most beautiful and outstanding girl in the room and this gave her enormous pleasure. Kevin turned gradually into a man Cass scarcely recognised. There were many parties in the New Year, and afterwards Natasha cunningly infiltrated herself into the well-off hunting set. She even talked of buying a horse—of hunting next winter, which gave Cass deep concern. It was positively frightening to her the way Natasha was 'digging in'—behaving as though she meant Pond House to be her home for ever.

Kevin no longer suffered from gloomy moods or seemed worried about his work. To Cass's concern, he failed to put in the usual number of hours at his writing. But when Natasha was at home, he was in good spirits. Cass sometimes told herself unhappily that he was more tolerant of the things Natasha liked to do and that he had never cared for. The dedicated Kevin was well on the way to becoming a playboy. After four months of sharing her home with the Courraines, Cass knew that she was bitterly jealous of Natasha; afraid for Kevin as well as for herself.

He was still her affectionate and devoted husband. But to her it was with a difference. It was as though the deep passionate love and understanding that once existed between them had become something lighter—less intense. There were longer intervals between their love-making and even when she did lie in his arms, shut away from the rest of the world, she sensed a change in him. Not an indifference—never that—but it was as though his moments of passionate need for her were as swiftly over as they were diminishing in ardour.

Cass, more in love with her husband than ever, was conscious of a growing need for his love. But she said nothing. She was wise enough to keep her fears entirely to herself. She was very unhappy. But nobody knew it. She went on with her market gardening, her chickens, the eggs, and all the things she found essential if she was to help Kevin with the finances.

There was no marked improvement in her cooking.

Natasha showed openly that she did not enjoy home food. But Maurice was sweet to Cass and even sat in the kitchen at times talking to her about French dishes, encouraging her efforts. His mother used to cook superbly, it appeared. He remembered the wonderful sauces she made. He even remembered some of the recipes and Cass had quite a lot of fun trying her hand at these. If Natasha did not like them, Maurice would. Cass had a firm ally in him. He also talked to her about himself. She knew now that he was a very unhappy man not only because of his infirmity (and the oculist at Moorfields had not been able to do anything more for him than had been done in Paris), but about his personal life.

He adored his beautiful young wife but was fully conscious that she was not in love with him.

"I'm too old for her," he told Cass one evening in early April, "I never should have let her marry me."

Cass was making a Hollandaise sauce with instructions from Maurice. He had bought a special piece of salmon because it was Kevin's birthday and they were having a little private celebration tonight—with champagne.

She stopped stirring, took the pan off the stove, and shook her head at Maurice.

He was stroking his beard with a reflective gesture and had taken off his glasses. The sore grey eyes looked terribly sad, she thought, and suddenly her whole gorge rose against Natasha. Natasha, who was so charming to Kev and so very different to her husband.

"Dear Maurice," she said gently, "Don't say things like that. You are not too old for Natasha or any girl."

He smiled at her, peering short-sightedly.

"You are sweet and kind, *ma petite*. Kevin is a lucky man. I, too, am lucky, but my Natasha's patience is being sorely tried. I used to be a vigorous, successful musician, able to give her a wonderful life. Now I can give her little except the task of taking care of me. To be nearly blind is a great drawback, for I can be of such little help to her or anybody else. Only when I play my piano do I feel consoled."

Cass's anger against Natasha did not diminish. She

thought it so generous and selfless of the little man to bemoan his affliction for his *wife's* sake. Not one word of complaint because *he* could no longer see well, or enjoy reading, or any of the benefits enjoyed by a man with good sight.

She returned to her cooking, sighing.

"Don't let it get you down, Maurice," she said. "One day I am sure some specialist will turn up and cure you. Anyhow, Natasha will grow used to the change of circumstances. She loves you very much, you know."

It was a great effort on Cass's part to utter this lie because she didn't think anything of the kind. But she felt that she must try and comfort the kindly Frenchman if she could.

Now he turned the conversation to Cass.

"You—you are always cheerful and happy, *mon enfant*. Forgive me if I call you that. You seem such a child to me. You are so much less *femme du monde*—woman of the world—than my Natasha."

Cass laughed gaily.

"The idiot child, Cassandra."

"Very far from *idiot*."

"I bet Kev would tell you I'm a bit of a bore at times. In fact I think he appreciates Natasha's sophistication."

She spoke without rancour. But Maurice Courraine looked with slight concern at the slim girl with the long silky untidy hair falling around her flushed young face. She was wearing what she, herself, called her most disreputable pair of slacks and a striped short-sleeved pullover. He had never known a girl quite so hard-working, so uncomplaining, as Cass, or a wife so loyal to her husband. He had grown to like and admire her. He found her not only sympathetic but brave and good. A girl without affectations or pretensions—a girl whom a man could make a friend of; but being French, Maurice Courraine was well aware of that other side to Cass—the attractive feminine side. He could imagine a man loving her with deep passion. And he was not quite sure that Kevin gave her all that she deserved. On the other hand he had nothing against the young Englishman. Kevin himself was a hard worker, and what Maurice called typically English in his outlook. But Maurice was afraid at times for Cass. He was not so blind that he could fail to see the way Kev looked at Natasha. And how *she* responded.

A week later—when the sun was out and the old winds had been replaced by the first warm breath of spring—Maurice saw more than he wanted.

He was strolling around the pond—walking with care because, with his failing sight, he was apt to stumble. He paused now and then to listen to the wild plaintive cry of the geese across the water. At length he came to the boathouse and stood a moment leaning on his stick, peering, wishing that he could see plainly the beautiful birds which had been so often described to him in detail by Cass.

Suddenly through the broken-paned, dusty window of the boathouse he heard a familiar sound. Low husky laughter—Natasha's! His blood chilled as he heard it. His sensitive ears *knew* that it was not exactly the laugh of a woman sharing a joke with a friend. This was the woman he knew intimately, a woman sharing a breathless sensual experience. There followed the sound of Kevin's voice. So the two of them were in there, thought Maurice, his heart sinking. In that deserted boathouse, unaware of eavesdroppers, they had not heard his footsteps on the soft mossy ground.

"Oh my God, Natasha, Natasha, you are driving me mad!" Kevin cried these words.

Maurice, rooted to the spot, listened, and longed to turn—quickly, quickly, before they became aware of him. But now he heard his wife speak in her turn:

"Darling Kevin—I *want* to drive you mad. I've been feeling a bit mad myself for days—for weeks. Oh, *Kevin!*"

"Natasha, don't look at me like that. Don't touch me—don't let me kiss you—please. I couldn't stand it."

"But I want you, Kevin. You're the most attractive man I've met for years. There's something terrifically exciting about you. Something I've been looking for all my life, perhaps."

Maurice trembled violently. He was cold yet the sweat poured down his forehead. He groaned. It was as though a knife had been thrust into his heart—then turned—and he was dying out here in the beautiful woodland fringing the pond; but the voices inside the boathouse continued to carry, and to destroy him. Destroy his peace—his faith in Natasha—his whole happiness.

Kevin again:

"It's only a 'thing' with you—darling, beautiful Natasha. You can't possibly want me seriously. What have I got to offer?"

"What has Maurice got to offer?" came her brutal question.

"Oh, I know the poor fellow is a bit of a wreck now, but he's a damned nice chap and—"

"Please don't preach to me about Maurice," she interrupted, "Oh, I don't mean I'll leave him now that he's incapacitated and all that, but we're living here together, you and I. We see each other morning, noon and night. How can we help it if we feel this incredible longing for each other?"

"I don't deny that you attract me—and that's putting it mildly. You're the loveliest, most glamorous creature I've ever known. You're utterly feminine—a living temptation—but paradoxically there's an odd masculine side to you, an oddly ruthless side. Most women are just a mass of emotion. They haven't a clue as to how a man feels, but *you* know. You are the same. You want something—you take it. God, I find you almost irresistible."

"Then don't try to resist, darling Kevin. Hold me. Kiss me. Forget everything else."

Maurice Courraine hung his head. He felt sheer physical pain convulsing his whole being. Irresistible—yes, Natasha could be that—it was how she had been to him. He had never meant to marry—he had been dedicated to his piano—his career. But she had swept him off his feet, just as she was trying to sweep Kevin now.

That poor young man! Maurice felt little resentment against Kevin. He was a boy; clever, literary, ambitious—but no man of the world, able to cope with a glorious compelling female creature like Natasha. He could hardly imagine all that Kevin must have been experiencing lately. He had unhappily forgotten what he owed to his wife who did so much for him (and for everybody)—too much. At times Maurice used to feel quite cross with Kevin for not treating her with more gratitude. Yet as he had got to know the Martins better, Maurice had also learned to understand them and their English ultramodern way of behaving. The young people today were not given to flattering each other—to idolising a woman as he, Maurice, idolised and pampered Natasha. They were in love but were less intense and more practical. Yet they seemed to understand each other. Maurice, from time to time, used to be touched by the way Kevin teased Cass, then praised her, and kissed her. Obviously there was genuine warmth behind his curt and sometimes selfish behaviour. A look in his eyes that suggested that he was Cass's lover as well as her husband.

Now this . . .

God, how could Natasha be so ruthless, so utterly cruel as to try and seduce a man away from a wife like Cassandra? Maurice choked, trembled, felt suddenly a sick man as well as a half-blind one.

He did not want to hear any more—he could not bear it. Whether Kevin succumbed in the end to Natasha's attempt to draw him into her siren's web remained to be seen; Maurice did not want to know. Never, never would he tell either of those young people in the boathouse what he had overheard. And *never* would he tell little Cass.

Maybe this affair would pass. Natasha had not been very kind about him, her husband, but at least she had told Kevin she did not mean to leave him. Maybe this was just a madness burning up between them fiercely, and as swiftly and fiercely it might burn itself out.

For all their sakes, Maurice hoped so.

So he turned and walked silently away. Before he reached the house he caught his foot in the tangled undergrowth and pitched headlong against a bush, scratching his face and hands badly. He limped back to the house and lay down, feeling faint and wretched.

The scratches were noticed when they all met for drinks before the evening meal. He laughed and told the others that they were 'nothing', and that he had fallen against a thorn bush coming down the drive.

Natasha with her usual lack of sympathy said:

"How silly of you, Maurice."

It was Cass who at once showed concern and offered to find him some healing cream.

He accepted her offer, smiling at her with his unfailing courtesy. He did not think the others could guess at the agony of his heartbreak. He even sat at the piano and played some Mozart, gaily, to hide his misery. He tried to pretend even to himself that he had never heard those two in the boathouse; that he had imagined it.

Kevin seemed quite normal. A little quiet perhaps, but he ignored Natasha and addressed himself frequently to Cass. Natasha seemed in high spirits. Finally she told Maurice to stop playing Mozart and to accompany her. She wanted to sing a Russian folk song she had just learned.

Maurice listened to that haunting voice while he played for her and thought desolately how much he still loved this beautiful wife of his, and how terrible it would be if she would never lie in his arms again because she loved another man.

What had happened between those two?

He wished now that he knew, because of the terrible driving anguish within him. If Kevin had been weak, would he, Maurice, ever know? Or would Natasha with all her experience of men and the world—and she had had many love affairs—amuse herself with Kevin for a short time, then turn to pastures new? He knew her light nature. But he had believed her when she told him before their marriage that she meant to settle down with him. Well, whatever had happened, he must try somehow to turn himself into a buffer between Cass and those two, Kevin and Natasha. He could not endure the young girl who loved her husband, to be disillusioned. It would be too utterly unjust.

That night, when Maurice and Natasha were alone in their bedroom, she offered to rub his back—he suffered from acute backache at times these days—particularly at the nape of the neck. She was, in fact, quite sweet and attentive.

"Silly old thing—falling about—where did you fall?" she asked and hummed the melody of the folk-song she had sung downstairs.

"I told you—in the drive," Maurice lied again.

Then suddenly while her hands smoothed his back, he hid his face in the pillow, hid his tortured feelings and said:

"Natasha, I think we have lived here long enough. I want to leave Pond House now. We must find a home of our own."

The fingers massaging him stayed still. He felt her move away, turned his head, and saw her standing at the window looking out at the dark April night. The wind was rising. He could hear, as he so often heard, the lap-lap of the water below the windows.

"No," Natasha answered calmly but with determination, "I don't want to leave. I like it here."

Maurice sat up now, clenching his hands.

"When we agreed to share with the young pair, we also agreed that it was to be just a temporary affair while we sorted out our lives."

"Why do you keep calling them *the young pair?*" she asked impatiently. "I am only a very little older than Cass. *You* are the old one."

He winced.

"I know it, my dear, but let us keep to the point. It is time we had a home of our own."

He could not see her well enough to mark any change in her expression but he heard the sharpness of her next remark.

"Don't be silly, Maurice. We are helping what you call 'the young couple'. We pay half the bills—often more. Until Kevin's book is accepted and he can make money, they would be embarrassed financially if we walked out. Your dear Cass would lose her 'daily' and so on. We would not be doing them a service."

"That is one way of looking at it," said Maurice patiently, "but there is another. I—" he cleared his throat—"I would like to return to living with my wife alone."

She did not answer but began to walk up and down the room and he could see the flick of her head—he knew that irritable flick—tossing back the wonderful auburn hair—as she moved around.

"I think it's more fun with the four of us," she said in a low tone.

Maurice closed his eyes.—

Oh God, he thought, *I know too well what she means. She does not want the four of us. Just the two of them. He has become her lover, I would swear it. But I don't know—perhaps I shall never know.*

He got no more satisfaction out of Natasha that night. She said little more but put her foot down firmly on the idea of leaving Pond House. He dared not insist, in case it brought matters to a head. His only thought was to save Cass from finding out about Kevin's growing passion for Natasha.

But things didn't work out that way.

Chapter 14

LIFE at Pond House continued much as usual for another month. During this time Cass was so busy with her market gardening and her cooking that she had little time for self analysis; for wondering whether she was really content living like this or not. She was so tired at night she would often fall asleep while Maurice played the piano, or she sat still in a basket chair by the open windows in the verandah, listening to the night calls of the birds across the water.

But she did sense a change in Kevin.

He was rarely irritable or thoughtless with her now. When she had time to think about their relationship, it seemed these days that for some reason best known to himself he was putting up a special show of affection. Naturally she liked it and was always quick to respond. The fact that they rarely made love she tried to explain.

They were both so exhausted these days. But dear kind Maurice was talking about giving them a break—taking them to the sea somewhere for a week's holiday. Cass felt well enough. She was thin but brown, and better than she used to be when she worked in the City (that life, polishing precious stones, or doing odd jobs for the firm, seemed like another one far removed from Cold Dutton). But she was miserable. She could not help it.

Natasha, too, had changed in Cass's opinion and for the better. Perhaps she had misjudged her. She was trying to be more helpful, insisted on drying the dishes after every evening meal nowadays. She took Cass out in the car to shop in Chelmsford, and was generally co-operative.

Ond day Cass remarked upon this to Maurice.

"Some beautiful girls like Natasha would be thoroughly spoiled, and lazy, but your wife is really quite a help."

This piece of innocent generosity positively hurt Maurice. *Mon Dieu,* he thought, *this nice child is no psychologist, neither does she know my cruel Natasha. Of course she is being nice and helpful. She is pulling the wool over Cass's eyes. She doesn't want to leave her lover. If he is her lover!*

That question remained in Maurice's mind as a constant, hateful doubt.

Whatever they were, the two concerned did not show their feelings in public. Maurice, through his tinted glasses, often watched them. They were quite casual with each other. They were being clever—that was Maurice's opinion.

But what if Cass found out?

The affair continued in a kind of behind-the-scenes way until the end of the summer.

Early in September things changed. Financially, Kevin was on the up grade. His novel had been accepted though not yet published. But he received one cheque for royalties in advance. Both the publishers and Kevin, himself, were confident of success. The readers' opinion had been that *Nightmare in Berlin* had the right ingredients for a best-selling thriller. They likened Kevin's work to that of Ian Fleming, or John Creasey.

But meanwhile the Martins had to live, and neither one of them wished to make the Courraines pay more than their fair share for the upkeep of the home. So Kevin, out of sheer pride, accepted a regular job which he did not really care for, a job which Cass thought very second-class and certainly not good enough for her clever husband. He had met the editor of a small local Essex paper, and became friendly with him. The sub-editor had had a serious operation and might not be able to return to the paper for some time. The editor-in-chief found Kevin highly intelligent and what he called 'on the ball'. He offered him the job. The money was not good—not as good, indeed, as Kevin had received while with the advertising firm when he first met Cass. And it was not a whole-time job. He was only in the Chelmsford office for three days a week. But it was all grist to the mill, as he told Cass when she first questioned his wisdom in accepting the offer. He must pull his weight until he was an established writer, and when he wasn't working on the paper, he could write more articles. He could always sell them.

Cass was proud of this. She admired his motives for joining the local paper.

When Natasha offered to fetch him by car on the days he was in Chelmsford, Cass was delighted for Kevin's sake, and said so. He had to get there by bus—or walk. She thought it kind of Natasha. Her early jealousy of the other girl had long since evaporated.

It was left to Maurice, in his misery, to wonder how early Kevin really left his office—and how long Natasha took to bring him back.

Cass's trust in her husband and her love for him seemed infinitely touching to the Frenchman—and infinitely dangerous.

All was going well with Cass's market-gardening until old William fell and broke a hip and was told he would probably have to stay in hospital for some long time. His grandson said that he doubted whether Granddad would ever be able to come back. Cass stepped up the boy's wage and worked harder with him in order to cope with the situation. But at times she was reduced to tears by sheer weariness and frustration. She just didn't have old William's knowledge, and the boy often had to waste valuable time going to the hospital in Chelmsford to ask his grandfather how to do certain things that defeated him—and his employer.

Then catastrophe befell the chickens that Cass had reared and was proud of. They were attacked by a fox one misty September night. Everybody in the house heard the squawking of the mother and the barking of the fox. Kevin and Cass got up, took torches and went down to the chicken house. But they were too late. There was nothing much left of Cass's brood but a few pathetic little corpses, their heads bitten off, and a heap of half-dead hens that had to be destroyed.

Cass wept indignantly.

"That cruel beastly fox! It isn't even as though he was hungry. It was just a wanton killing."

She said those words in front of the Courraines who had come downstairs in their dressing-gowns, wondering what the disturbance was about. It was one in the morning.

Maurice, ever sympathetic, patted Cass's shoulder and murmured:

"*Pauvre petite*—poor little Cass, you loved your *poussins*. I shall buy you some more."

Now Natasha showed her old form.

"Really! All this about a few chickens. I think they're such stupid things and I hate eggs. Why does Cass bother?"

Kevin, who could never bear to see Cass cry because she did it so rarely, defended her now.

"Well, I like eggs and so does Maurice, if I'm not wrong. We both wallop those super omelettes Cass makes. And it wasn't very nice—what we found in the run, I assure you. Cass was upset."

Cass looked at him gratefully, dried her tears, and suggested they should go to bed.

"I'll be up in a minute," Kevin called after her, as she went, followed by Maurice. "I just want one cigarette."

"Me, too," said Natasha boldly.

Kevin looked at his wife's back. She was climbing the stairs with more than a suggestion of weariness. He rarely saw those slim shoulders so bowed. She was damned tired these days, he thought. And she never seemed to have any fun. It was all work and no play for her.

"Kevin!" said Natasha softly.

He turned to her. She was incredibly beautiful, in a pale apricot-hued negligée—short nightgown, with transparent coat tied at the throat with an enormous satin bow. It was almost the colour of her hair. She was the most delectable woman he had ever known. Her steady pursuit of him certainly flattered his ego—as it might have done any man's. He read the invitation in those huge dark eyes and the upward lift of her red sensual mouth. But he looked up the stairs again. Cass had gone. But he still saw that tired little figure and remembered her distress when they first found the carnage left by the fox.

Not for the first time, he felt bitterly ashamed of his liaison with Natasha and disgusted with himself.

"Kevin," Natasha repeated his name, put down the cigarette she had been smoking and came towards him. He shook a warning finger at her.

"No—not here or now, please."

Natasha was unused to rejection. Her expression changed.

"What's bitten you? There's no one around. I heard both Maurice and Cass shut their doors."

"I'm not suggesting that they'll rush down the stairs and find us in a clinch," he said roughly. "I just don't want—"

"Don't want to kiss me good-morning?" she put in with a twist of her lips. Such exciting lips, Kevin knew it only too well. The physical side of him was stirred, yet his mind still rebelled.

"Look, Tasha—" he had shortened her name to that. She liked it because nobody else used it—"It's my day at the office tomorrow, and I'm tired. Let's say goodnight and be sensible about—about this thing between us."

"Are *you* so sensible? I've not seen much signs of it."

He clenched his hands—fighting down the desire to grab hold of her and crush that lissom figure in the

apricot-coloured negligée—cover that tempting face
with kisses; the violent sort of kisses she liked and returned.

"There's a time and a place for everything," he
snapped the words.

"Well, well," she drawled, and looked at him through
her lashes. "Being around so early in the morning
doesn't suit you, lover."

He kept silent, staring not at her but at the floor. He
was conscious after these long months of association
with Natasha that she was not only beautiful and alluring but shamelessly immoral. She had absolutely no
sense of loyalty either to that wretched afflicted French
husband of hers—nor any feeling for Cass. Kevin knew
it and as a rule didn't care. He only wanted to make
love to Natasha. But tonight he felt different. Cass was
his wife and one of the best. It was because of her that
he hated himself. Suddenly he knew that he wanted to
end the intrigue with Natasha. But not here and now.
He couldn't cope with Natasha tonight. She was beginning to look annoyed. He didn't want a scene.

"Well, this is great!" she said. "My charming Kevin
has suddenly developed a conscience. And all because
of a few dead chickens! Cass is so sentimental—it sick-
ens me."

"Look!" he said in a low voice, "you are Helen of
Troy, Cleopatra, Lady Hamilton—the whole lot rolled
into one. Okay. And I don't deny that I want you. Nor
do I deny that I've been stabbing that nice husband of
yours in the back all summer. But I'm not going to let
you criticise Cass. Now, leave me alone and go to bed,
for God's sake."

Natasha went white. Her heart pounded with a mixture of fury and chagrin. She had never loved anybody
in her life and she didn't really love Kevin, but she
found that lean graceful body of his extraordinarily attractive and still more did she like his strength of will
and purpose. He didn't grovel like Maurice. She
couldn't ever be sure of him. He was a moody devil.
That challenged Natasha and excited her. As for his
defence of Cass, what did it matter? But if he wanted to

put an end to their affair he would have to think twice, she told herself furiously.

She looked into Kevin's blue, stormy eyes and suddenly gave her low provocative laugh.

"What a storm in a teacup—or should I say what a fox in a hen coop," she laughed again. "You're rather like a fox, Kevin—powerful and handsome. I'm the poor little bird, and you've bitten off my head. Aren't you sorry?"

"Go to hell," said Kevin and turned and left her.

She stubbed her cigarette end in an ashtray, and followed, not even bothering to turn out the light. She didn't have to pay the electricity bills anyhow.

Cass was fast asleep when Kevin got to bed. Before he switched off the lamp, he looked down at the smudged tear-stained face, and the silky tangle of her hair. He thought of the words he had once quoted to her:

"Suddenly aware that the autumn leaves are turning to the colour of your hair."

Sweet, sweet Cassandra. And he had betrayed her. *I'm a bastard,* he thought. *I don't deserve Cass.*

The cold ruthless band of egotism that had been clamping down his conscience was snapping. He had never felt more wretched. He longed to wake Cass, tell her everything, ask her forgiveness and feel absolved.

He could not bring himself to do it. It would hurt her too much. But he must put an end to the Natasha episode, no matter how much he desired her. She would have to leave Pond House—the pair of them must go, even if he, Kevin, and Cass suffered grave financial loss.

If Natasha stayed with all her wiles, her absorbing desire to make him her property, something worse might happen. They would all lose—lose everything.

Kevin could not get to sleep. He lay battling with himself and his desires and his sincere wish not to hurt Cass. She had been his first love. He had meant her to be his only love. Now he wanted her to be that again. Just after dawn—a misty golden September morning with the lake veiled and the trees sad and spectral—

Cass woke up. Half drugged with sleep she smiled at Kevin, put her arms around him and hugged him.

"Darling," she said drowsily.

"Cass, I love you. I do love you," he said in a choked voice.

"I know you do," she said, and sighed with content.

He held her close, caressing her with a passion more intense than he had shown for many long months. She did not altogether understand but if he said he loved her, that was all she wanted. The wonderful return to their 'togetherness' compensated her for the sad events of last night.

In the morning she went out to her work on the allotment with young Bert, feeling fine and happy. Before Kevin left the house he had kissed her goodbye with much of the old warmth. She knew that something had been missing between them lately, but whatever it was, no matter—it had come back.

The following week brought a more serious state of affairs.

Kevin failed to return home at the usual time from Chelmsford. He was so late that Cass questioned Maurice, who said that he knew Natasha had gone in to fetch him. The weather looked bad and Kevin would appreciate the lift.

Cass, who was basting a joint of beef, turned a flushed face to Maurice.

"What time is it now?"

"A quarter past seven."

"Oh, dear, the meat will be overdone and you and Kev both like it so red. What *can* have happened? When Natasha fetches him they are usually back long before six."

Yes, what can have happened, Maurice asked himself uneasily. But he spoke cheerfully.

"They've eloped," he said, trying to be jocular.

Cass laughed too, with such genuine humour that Maurice flinched.

"I bet! Can't you see your Natasha living in a back room with my Kev, cooking eggs and bacon—putting up with *that* sort of life."

"No, I can't see it," said Maurice in intensity, "but you put up with it, didn't you?"

"I did when we had our London flat and when we first came down here, but thanks to you and your help and having Joyce for the housework and all that, I'm very well off now."

"Natasha does not think you are," said Maurice. "I know of no two more different women. You ask for exactly the opposite things out of life."

Cass put the joint back in the oven and stood up.

"Oh, well," she smiled, "that's okay. Natasha is hardly likely to elope with Kev, is she?"

Maurice turned away, went to the piano and consoled himself in the only way left to him—by playing. The piano these days was well-tuned and not a bad instrument—he could make it sing.

Eight o'clock came and half past eight, and no sign of the Citroën.

By this time Maurice was alarmed and Cass kept nervously looking at the clock.

"Honestly, what can have happened?"

He peered at her through his glasses.

"Is it possible they have met with an accident?"

Under her warm tan Cass's face paled.

"Don't!"

"Oh, it isn't really likely," Maurice made haste to add. "Natasha is an excellent driver. Did you know she once partnered one of the Monte Carlo Rally drivers and took over in her turn? She really is expert."

"All the same, they should have been here two hours ago."

"Did Kevin mention that he might pay a visit to anybody on the way home?"

"No, he just said 'see you at six as usual'. Do you think we should ring up the local hospital and ask—"

"It's an idea," said Maurice.

"I'll ring," said Cass and walked out of the kitchen.

Maurice stood silent. He had an inexplicable feeling that there had not been an accident, that Natasha, ever resourceful and cunning *and* determined, had manoeuvred this length of absence because she wanted to be alone with Kevin. It was disgraceful of course. But then Natasha had behaved disgracefully ever since they left Paris. The husband who loved her so deeply felt crushed by the weight of his thoughts. It wasn't pleasant to be made aware that the object of your devotion is unscrupulous—oblivious of everybody else's feelings.

Then Cass rushed into the kitchen, her face radiant. "They're back. It's okay. I've just heard the car."

Maurice took his stick and walked slowly, heavily into the hall.

They heard the Citroën engine stop. Cass flung open the front door.

"Oh, it's pelting!" she exclaimed.

Maurice could not see through the darkness but he could hear the rain, and the night air felt damp and cold.

Natasha was the first to walk into the brightly-lit hall.

"Hullo, folks, sorry we're late. We had a bit of trouble with the car."

Kevin appeared. He looked haggard and gloomy but muttered an apology for being so late.

"Oh, it doesn't matter, darling," said Cass. "But I was absolutely terrified you'd had an accident."

"I'll go up and wash," said Kevin abruptly.

Maurice drew near to his wife, near enough to see her more plainly. He, like Cass, had dreaded an accident. He could not have borne his beautiful Natasha to be found in a mangled wreck if the Citroën had been hit by a heavy lorry or some such terrible thing. He knew her so well. *He knew that expression on her face.* The look of a sensual, demanding woman who has been left unsatisfied. A terrible look that he had seen far too often lately.

She ignored Maurice and announced that she, too, must go up and tidy.

"But what was wrong with the car?" Maurice called after her.

"Oh—the car petered out—midway between Chelmsford and Cold Dutton. We're both soaked. It was so wet—ugh! I need a hot bath if Cass doesn't mind keeping my food warm."

"But what was *wrong?*" persisted Maurice, hoping at least that her answer would allay his fears.

But she lied. Somehow he knew that she lied. She called down in a casual way:

"The engine just wouldn't start again. We had to send a passer-by to Pilkington's garage and it was an hour before they turned up. We just sat there. It was infuriating. Something to do with the carburettor. He got it going after ages. Kev will tell you later." And she disappeared.

Maurice felt a sudden choking mistrust—a hatred of what she was doing—to Cass—to Kevin—let alone to himself. He knew that he could check up. Ring up Pikingtons and ask about the car. Perhaps what she said was true but he didn't believe it and if ever he had seen a man look upset and nervous, it was Kevin.

What had happened out there on this dark night?

Oh, Natasha, thought Maurice, *Natasha!*

Chapter 15

THAT night, Cass, despite the usual cloak of weariness weighing her down, found it hard to sleep. Kevin had given her a quick kiss, then turned over. His back was rigid. She made no attempt to touch him, but suddenly for the first time she experienced an almost psychic sense that something was wrong—very wrong with him.

Afterwards she wondered how she could have been so blind or trusting, but just now she did not attribute his extraordinary change of manner to an emotional crisis. True, he had been very quiet, even morose, this evening, but she had put that down to his being 'fed up' because the car had let them down, or he was in one of his moods. She could imagine how maddening it must have been for him sitting waiting for the breakdown van to arrive in the pouring rain.

If, of course, she had known what was passing through his mind now this moment, she would have been horrified, to say nothing of astonished. For Kevin was not, as she imagined, asleep. He was wide awake, haggard, trying to control the rage and frustration that threatened to overwhelm him. Rage against Natasha and himself. Rigid he lay there with his back to the one being in the world whom he most deeply respected and did not want to hurt, knowing that it was inevitable now that she should suffer.

There had been no breakdown or trouble with the carburettor. He had deplored Natasha's idea of trumping up such a tale. But she laughed and accused him of being chicken-hearted. Nobody could find out the truth unless they made inquiries. He had always maintained that Cass was not a jealous person and would never check up on him—she would be the last to suspect the truth.

The truth was not attractive. Kevin went back in his mind, over and over again, those two hours in the Citroën, parked on a lane two miles out of Chelmsford.

Natasha had stopped the car and put the key in her pocket.

"Why have you done that?" he asked, quietly at first. Then on an angry note: "Start her up and drive on, please, Tasha."

Her huge magnificent eyes gleamed at him through the darkness. He could smell the perfume that she used. He felt her long thin fingers touch his cheek.

"Don't be like this, Kevin," she whispered. "It's not you. What's happened? Why have you changed? Are you one of these men who just make love to a woman, then get tired of her and walk out?"

"This is no time or place for a discourse on my behaviour."

"Oh, yes it is. It's got to be. I can't stand you ignoring me. Why are you so stand-offish and *different?* You were beastly to me that night when the fox got the chickens. You've been horrid the whole of this week.

You make excuses not to meet me in the boathouse or anywhere else, and I want to know *why*."

He tried to argue and protest that they would be noticeably late if they stayed here to talk this thing out. Her nearness, the fact that they were alone in the car on this wild autumn night, had no sensual impact upon him this evening. He knew now beyond doubt that it was not this girl who really mattered to him—but his wife.

He tried to be patient. Natasha was growing hysterical. He could see that he must calm her down. She drew away from him and started to sob.

"You are my life now—my world. The only lover I've ever cared two damns about for more than five minutes."

"I'm flattered but it can't go on, Tasha. We've both of us been pretty unscrupulous—both to Maurice and Cass. Well, let's face it, we were crazy about each other, but it can't go on."

"Why not? I've been half mad all this week, wanting you so much."

Those words drove him to cynical response.

"Weren't you half mad about the other men in your life? Isn't it all part of the pattern? You're a very beautiful and alluring creature and men do fall for you and you for them. You've said so. But it's you who often get fed up, my dear. However, let's be factual. Our affair has never been on a permanent basis either side, and you said that was how you wanted it."

She caught hold of his arm with both her hands and leaned against him, moaning:

"Kevin, Kevin, don't be so callous. You know what we've shared. We're unusually well-matched—we adore our times together. You can't put an end to it—just like this!" She snapped her fingers.

He softened sufficiently to touch her hair with his hand.

"Sorry, darling, but it's got to end. I can't go on risking spoiling Cass's life—or your husband's. At the moment they don't know—but they're bound to find out if we carry on. Haven't you *any* feeling for poor old Maurice?"

"Don't talk to me of Maurice."

"Well, haven't you?" he persisted.

She answered angrily:

"Yes, I'm sorry about his eyes and all that but I'm only human. I need a different man—a man like you. Besides, I'm not the martyr type. I can't spend the rest of my life leading him around."

Kevin, remembering this dialogue, felt his face burn at the memory. He had felt ashamed of her, and of himself for having betrayed Cass's love and faith because of such a girl. God alone knew *he* was an egotist. He had broken his vows, and had nothing to boast about, but he wasn't as totally blind and deaf to other people's sufferings as Natasha. He had had a quick mental picture of how Cass would have behaved in similar circumstances had *he* lost his eyesight. He could see her cherishing him—leading him if need be to the ends of the earth if she had to, without complaint.

Suddenly he pushed Natasha away from him.

"Pack it in for God's sake, and let's go home. I can't take any more."

He heard the indrawn hiss of her breath.

"So you've had your fun and just want to 'pack it in' as you call it."

"I didn't regard our affair exactly as *fun*. You attracted me terribly and I admit it. But I'm not going on with it, that's all. Ever since we came to Pond House Cass has half killed herself in the effort to keep things going and help me, and I refuse to take away what illusions she's got about me. I'm equally sure that poor old Maurice trusts you, and that makes me feel even more damnable about it. I can't think why *you* don't."

She burst out:

"You're a hypocrite—a humbug—trying to pretend that I'm a wicked sinner and you're an angel of mercy, sacrificing yourself for your wife."

"It's about time I did," he said with cold scorn.

"Well, it's not going to be as easy as that. If you think we're going to live at Pond House and see each other every day and never go back to our boathouse, you're wrong."

"I'm not, you know," he said grimly. "We're washed

up, Tasha. Look, my dear, sorry, but—" he added more gently—"you've been marvellous to me and I thank you for all the hours we've had together. I'm no damned angel, and if what we did can be called sin, then I sinned with you willingly. I just want to stop it all now."

"Because of Cass?"

"Yes—and Maurice."

He heard her give an hysterical laugh that ended in tears.

"God, how you've changed. I hate you! And I hate Cass. She's too good to live. I won't accept what you say about us ending. I won't. *I won't.*"

"My dear girl, you'll have to. It takes two to play at the love game and I'm opting out."

"So you think. But don't tell me you won't want me again once this little session of 'holier-than-thou' has blown over."

Her sarcasm was lost on him. He said:

"I'm not such a hypocrite as you think. I admit I might want you again if I saw too much of you in the future but I'm going to ask you and Maurice to leave Pond House. I want to be alone with Cass, no matter what it costs us."

"You're a fool," cried Natasha, then dragged his head down to hers and fastened her lips to his. She was trembling with anger and passion—and a sudden feeling of despair. For the first time in her life she was afraid—she found herself dealing with a man who was stronger than she was, and she didn't like it.

"You can't get away from me—we're made for each other," she sobbed.

Only for an instant Kevin felt the old devilish flame of desire for that lovely passionate body and the pink lustre of her wanton lips opening to his. Then he pushed her roughly away.

"Start the car up. Drive me home—please," he said harshly. "This sort of thing can't do any good. I've made up my mind."

"Well, I haven't!" she cried. "I still want you. I won't leave Pond House with Maurice. If I leave, it's going to be with you."

Now he laughed.

"You know damn well, because I've always told you, I have no intention of leaving my wife. And I don't want to break up your marriage either. We've gone too far already, but the only harm that's been done so far is to ourselves. Let's keep it that way."

"I—won't—stand—for—it—Kevin." She whispered the words between great sobbing intakes of her breath.

"Give me the key of the car," he said.

"I shall tell Cass what's happened," she choked. "I swear I will. Then we'll see if she's so angelic. She'll pack up and leave you if I know her."

Kevin's hands clenched. He stared through the darkness into Natasha's gleaming eyes. Her beauty suddenly seemed vicious and cruel.

He hated her. It was the aftermath of a passion that has died, a passion that had always been rootless and ephemeral—only he had found it out too late.

He said in a quiet measured voice:

"If you upset Cass I'll—" he stopped, gulping.

"What'll you do?" broke in Natasha. *"Kill me?"*

"I'd want to," he said. "But you wouldn't be worth life imprisonment."

Natasha laughed and cried and raged. The ugly scene went on until Kevin was worn down. He knew that the time was passing and that questions would be asked at home. His only fear now was that Cass might be hurt and that poor man, Maurice, who couldn't see, might find out what had been going on. His conscience was so battered that he felt an actual physical pain. His head was splitting. He had always realised, of course, that Natasha had bad blood in her. She was bad—yes, that was the word. Poor Aunt Cynthia had known it. How well did Kevin understand now why the de Groots had been glad to see the back of this girl.

Finally, when Natasha's storm of passion and fury died down, he said:

"Do up your face and comb your hair and drive back, or I'll get out of the car and walk."

She had no more arguments, no more protests left. She had said about everything, alternating between declaring passionate love for him and sneering at his new-found conscience. It was plain to Kevin that it didn't matter to her what happened to her husband. But what happened to Cass had become of vital importance to him.

So she had driven the Citroën back to Cold Dutton.

Now he lay sleepless, horribly aware that he was in a most invidious, dangerous position. Natasha would be revengeful. She had been cool, if friendly all evening. But he could well believe that she was inwardly smouldering and would do her best to come between him and Cass. She would hurt Cass out of sheer jealousy.

What in the name of God could he do? He had looked at himself—into the very mirror of his soul—and found himself wanting. What he had done had put Cass in mortal danger and he was bitterly remorseful. Nor could he ever excuse himself for having had a love-affair with the wife of a man who lived beneath his roof.

Far into the early hours of the morning, Kev wrestled with himself and his unhappy thoughts. Once Cass stirred, and in her sleep put an arm across him and murmured: *"Darling."* He did not wake her but gently took that hand between his. It was rough and the nails were short and it wasn't at all like Natasha's tapering fingers with their long, silvered nails. But in this moment desire was not in him—only love—a new and boundless love for Cass.

In the morning he was no nearer finding a solution to his problem. He only knew one thing—that he must talk to Maurice, and ask him in the nicest possible way to terminate their stay at Pond House. Maurice would understand—he had often said, himself, that he felt they ought not to stay here permanently. But the burning question was what Natasha meant to do and whether she would carry out her damnable threat to open Cass's eyes to the truth.

The household woke to a dry day. The rain had petered out during the night. But the morning was grey and cool; everything was very damp and the vegetation on the fringe of the pond looked rank; drooped unhappily. The birds did not sing. The water was shrouded in a sad autumn mist. Cass had to switch on the lights in the kitchen because it was so dark. She glanced with some concern at Kevin's face while he ate his breakfast. He did not seem to be enjoying that nice brown egg she had given him. He drank his tea in gloomy silence.

"Aren't you well, sweetie?" she asked him.

"Perfectly," he answered without looking at her.

"What are you going to do today?"

"Write," he said. "I'm on an article about the Crested Grebes. I think it'll sell to a magazine like *Country Life* or some such periodical. See you at lunch," and he disappeared.

Cass finished her own breakfast with a slight feeling of unease. What on earth was biting poor Kev? Had that girl, Natasha, done or said something to annoy him? Cass wasn't really sure he liked Natasha as a person although she knew he admired her physical beauty greatly. Or had he said something to her about them leaving Pond House. Perhaps poor Natasha was offended, and they were quarrelling. Cass didn't know.

This was a Saturday morning. Joyce had sent her lad on a bike to say that she was laid up with a chill and temperature and couldn't come, and would Mrs. Martin please send her money.

Cass had a lot to do out of doors, but she had to leave it now to Bert. She started the less attractive round indoors—bed-making, dusting and tidying up.

She dragged the Hoover up the staircase. She was still feeling rather concerned about Kevin and his odd conduct. She began to unwind the Hoover lead and plugged it it. The carpet in the passage outside all the bedrooms badly needed attention—Joyce hadn't had time to do that yesterday.

Cass was the last person to approve of listening behind closed doors, but on this particular occasion the temptation was thrust upon her. She was just about to switch the Hoover on outside the Courraines' door. It wouldn't disturb them. She had already taken in their breakfast trays. Natasha never woke up early and although Maurice often offered to go down and breakfast with Kevin, Cass would not let him. Apart from his eyes, she did not think the poor man was very well.

There was some talk of him going to Vienna in the near future to see a world famous oculist.

Natasha must be very much awake, Cass decided, because she could hear her voice, loud—less caressing than usual.

"Oh, shut up, Maurice. I don't want to listen to any more lectures and I am *not* leaving Pond House."

"But you are, *ma chère petite*. You're leaving with me in a week's time. We will go together to Austria and perhaps even settle over there instead of in England. I do not think you like England."

"But I like Pond House!" exclaimed Natasha. "And I'm staying here while you go to Vienna."

"To make more trouble?"

"I don't know what you mean," Natasha almost shouted the words.

In the corridor Cass stood as though she couldn't move, both hands clutching the handle of the Hoover. Indeed, she felt as though she were about to drown, and must hang on to something if she were to save her life. A terrible feeling of impending disaster froze her into immobility. The voices of the Courraines went on. They were having a desperate row, but it wasn't until the name *Kevin* was actually mentioned by Maurice that the avalanche really began to fall upon Cass.

"While I am here in the house, Natasha, I feel a sort of deterrent to your shameless pursuit of Kevin. If you are left alone you will act without a curb and that poor little wife of his will find out."

Cass closed both eyes as though trying to shut out understanding of what she was listening to. Natasha gave what Cass described to herself as a horrid laugh, full of ugly meaning.

"Kevin's wife—Kevin's dear little loving trusting wife—I really am getting sick of hearing her praises. You and Kevin seem to share the belief that she's heaven-sent. Well *I* may not be, my dear Maurice, but you've enjoyed my hellish charms, haven't you?"

"I still love you, unfortunately," came Maurice's voice on a low note, "but I despise you for what you are doing to these young people who have given us a home."

"Oh, shut up," she said. "Don't preach. And what have I done, anyhow?"

"Natasha, I am not as blind as I appear. There was no genuine breakdown in the Citroën. You kept Kevin out for the same reason you kept him in the boathouse that day when I overheard you trying to induce him to make love to you."

"And supposing he did?" Natasha retaliated with a wild disregard of consequences.

"You're shameless, my dear," said Maurice, "but I think I have always known that. I've forgiven much, but this affair with Kevin I will not tolerate."

"Stop it then if you can!" she screamed. "Kevin's mad about me."

Then Cass opened her eyes and stared at the door of the Courraines' room as though she could see through it, see some terrible apparition—the ghost of her love and her faith, which had been torn from her body and dragged into that room, and was now trailing abjectly away. She left Hoover and ran—ran as fast as she could into her own bedroom and flung herself on to her bed. She had heard enough, far too much.

Kevin and Natasha—Kevin was mad about her— Natasha had said so. And they were having an affair. Poor Maurice knew about it. He had seen—and heard. He was trying to make her leave the house and she wouldn't go.

Cass dug her short nails into the palms of her hands. She did not cry. She lay there breathing very fast, trying to control herself. The shock was bad—very bad. What an idiot she'd been—an innocent, ignorant fool, not to have suspected those two. But she had never dreamed Kevin was *that* sort of man. He had his faults—she knew them all—but he was, nevertheless, she believed, her loyal lovable Kev. How could *he* be carrying on an intrigue with another man's wife under his own roof?

In the boathouse—Cass's imagination was vivid enough to make her whole body shudder with revulsion. She began to beat her fists against the pillow. She whispered: "You shouldn't have done it, Kev. You shouldn't. *You shouldn't!*"

Then the tears came raining down her cheeks and

she passed from horror and indignation to intense anger against Natasha, and even more particularly against Kev.

I shall never be happy again, she thought.

She wanted to rush down the passage, burst into the Courraines' room and attack Natasha—attack her physically. Hit her. Yes, she could hit her, willingly, across that lovely sensual face. To have done so much harm to the other two people in this house, and to be as Maurice described it, so *shameless*. She wasn't fit to live.

And she isn't going to live one day longer in this house, Cass told herself, and suddenly she sat up, shivering with nerves and with an increasing sense of devastating resentment.

I'm going to tell her to go. She is to pack up at once. Maurice is to take her away. Poor Maurice, he can't be very happy either!

Then a terrible thought struck her. Thinking things over more calmly, it might be, she decided, that Kev was not just infatuated—or seduced—by Natasha's beauty and fascination. He might be serious about her. And if she left Pond House, he might go with her.

Once again the avalanche descended upon Cass. She was suffocated. All her belief, her hopes for the future, her whole life's happiness, were smothered. She could no longer breathe.

She ran to the window which she had closed against the early morning mist and flung it open. She put out her face and shut her eyes and drew in long draughts of air. She remained like that, blindly weeping. When she heard the familiar call of the lovely birds they had christened Margot and Rudolf—sailing majestically over the pond towards her—she turned away. Everything was spoilt. Everything that she had helped Kev build up. He did not love her. He loved Natasha.

She walked to her mirror and stared at her reflection. What a wild face! Her hair falling around her neck, her cheeks hot and crimson. There was a hole in her jersey and the knees of her slacks were stained—she had fallen down in the turnip field yesterday. She looked ghastly, she thought. What man would be in love with a girl who looked like that? How could she blame Kevin for turning to a sleek, chic, fabulous woman like Natasha?

"All the same," Cass said aloud, "you shouldn't have done it, Kev. You shouldn't. *You shouldn't!*"

The desire to run to the Courraines' room and strike at Natasha died. As for going into the study to tell Kev what she'd heard—that she couldn't face. Every bit of her was hurt—body and mind. She felt rejected—rejected by her lover, her husband, the man she had lived with, worked for and adored. It's grim, she thought, to feel rejected, and to imagine another girl in your husband's arms. She felt sick. She began to wonder, too, if she was doomed. She had believed she had found true and lasting happiness in this marriage; that she had put all the trials and tribulations of her rather unhappy childhood behind her for ever. But she wasn't destined to be happy.

Now there came a sudden queer mental flashback to another day when she had been rejected: by her own mother. It had been at the beginning of the school holidays about a year after Mummy married the General. All during the term Cass had looked forward, like the other girls, to going home and being taken to the seaside by her mother, for it was the summer holidays. She had even hoped the General would let them go alone as she was away from Mummy so much. But her mother had told her (quite kindly and nicely, of course) that the General wished to spend his holiday in France visiting the war cemeteries and taking his wife to see some of the towns and villages in which he had fought and where he had won his D.S.O.

Mrs. Woodbeare had said:

"I've arranged to send you down to Devonshire, dear, to a sort of holiday hotel where a lot of girls go whose mothers live abroad. They have riding and tennis and parties and you'll have a lovely time."

What Kev would describe as the typical *'Yes-dear'* remark—from a selfish woman who was completely under the thumb of her second husband and oblivious to her child's hurt.

It's queer, Cass thought, as she stood there in her

bedroom this morning, how that old episode came to mind. Cass, the child, had gone down to Devonshire and, in a way, she had had quite a nice time. But she had still felt rejected—cheated—thrown aside for the General—robbed of her rightful holiday with her mother. The wound had stayed open for a very long time.

What of this new wound? It would never heal. It would go on hurting, *hurting*.

Suddenly she felt the need to get out of the house.

She brushed her hair, tied it back, put on a short leather jacket which she wore when she was working in this kind of weather, and joined Bert who was still hoeing his way through the turnip field.

Chapter 16

ALL through the cold damp hours of that autumn morning, after hoeing was finished Cass worked with Bert, helping to plant seedlings, yet wondering in a dull hopeless fashion whether she would be here to see their fruition. Almost with horror she contemplated this fact. How could it be possible that less than two and a half years after her marriage, another girl could come and take her husband away from her?

She stood a moment resting one hand on a spade, while she wiped the perspiration from her forehead.

Grimy, dusty Cass in mud-caked Wellington boots; beautiful enticing Natasha in mink, she thought. What had *she* worn down there in the boathouse? Something filmy and seductive, of course—or nothing!

A ghastly desire to laugh shook Cass's whole body. It was all so cynical. Anyhow, the Cass Kevin had married used not to look as she did today. She used to go to the office pretty and fresh—as smartly dressed as she could afford. She remembered those days when she sat with Kevin in Temple Gardens and they fed the birds with sandwich crumbs. How he used to draw a strand of her long silky hair through his lips and tell her she was as fresh and perfumed as the spring.

Was that the sort of thing he whispered to Natasha?

Cass dropped the spade suddenly, told Bert she had finished for the morning and walked away. She crossed the meadow that had been leased out to one of the farmers. As she neared the house, she saw a hawk hovering near by in its dark sinister fashion. It had marked out a helpless, less combative sort of bird, she supposed, and was about to pounce on it. Life was cruel. Nature was cruel. And love was cruel—crueller than death in the ultimate betrayal.

She stifled the desire to cry and set her teeth. She admonished herself aloud:

"Pack it in, Cass. Snivelling around the place won't help you, nor will hating Natasha and agonising over Kev. Fight for your man. That's the answer. Don't be a coward. Go in right now, face Kev and tell him that you know but that you will never let that witch have him."

Why should she let him go? He had brought her here. They had started this life on the land together. Here, in this house he had become a writer. The novel in which he had put his heart and soul and most of his time was due for publication.

Then she laughed a little hysterically for the second time. Don't go and let him see you looking like a peasant. Change into one of your most attractive outfits. Drench yourself in scent. Use the whole damn bottle. Get him back. *Get him back.*

What might have happened if she had been able to carry out this dramatic bid for repossession of her husband, she was never to know.

An unexpected and astonishing thing happened.

She reached the front door just in time to see a station taxi draw up in front of the house. Out of it stepped the tall familiar figure of her stepfather. She stared and gaped. *The General himself!* What next was going to happen in her life? What on earth was *he* doing here? He had never come down before. He hadn't invited himself, and they hadn't asked him. But he remembered to send her his Army crested Christmas cards from the Club, and she, because she felt her mother would have liked it, always sent him a card on his birthday as well as at Christmas. But only the other day she had been telling Kev it was time they did something about the old boy and got in touch with him. For all they knew he might be dead.

Here was General Miles Woodbeare looking far from dead. In fact, he had put on considerable weight and was no longer lean—he had a stomach. She recognised the grey tweed coat. The buttons were strained. He wore a striped silk muffler—his regimental colours, as always. He also wore the customary green pork-pie hat.

He finished paying off the taxi and turned her way.

"Good heavens!" he said, peering over his glasses. "Is that *you?* I didn't recognise you at first."

"No, I expect I look rather odd. I'm a market gardener," she said with a giggle that had little humour behind it, and then: *"Hullo!* I didn't expect to see you. I must say it's given me quite a shock."

Unfailingly polite, he removed his hat in greeting, then put it on again.

"How do, Cassandra."

She stood silent. The years rolled back. Cass Martin was Cassandra Hayes again. Mummy was alive. There was no Kevin—no Pond House—only the three of them living in *Tobruk.*

Suddenly, quite idiotically, Cass lost control of herself. All the time she had been out on the land, working, she had been keyed up, fighting the inclination to shout her sorrows to the world, and winning the battle. Now, tension relaxed and she felt a fantastic pleasure at seeing the old man. She barely listened as he began to explain that he had come down uninvited because he felt he owed it to her mother (whose memory he cherished) to make sure Cassandra was 'still alive and kicking'. He was sure she'd be kicking—she always was, he added with sarcasm, but brushed up his moustache and smiled in quite a friendly way. He thought he'd cadge a spot of lunch from them, he added, and get them to

show him their estate. He was still interested in the
duck shooting. (Cough! Cough!)

Then he saw that Cass had hidden her face in her
hands and was sobbing. Actually crying like a child.

The sight was so extraordinary that the General was
reduced to silence. He could hardly tolerate poor Dorothy's tears—or any woman's, but Cass was one who
never used to cry. He used to tell Dorothy that her
daughter was a hard little devil because she never wept,
even when she was punished. He had at times in his
peculiar way admired Cass's fighting spirit. One should
never surrender. That was the first thing a soldier
learned.

Now Cass was crying so bitterly, and standing there
looking so forlorn in her muddy boots and shabby
leather coat, the old man felt more than uncomfortable.
It was really foreign to his nature to show sympathy for
what he would term 'weakness'. He had always been
annoyed when Dorothy whined. But this girl wasn't
whining. She was just obviously desperately unhappy.

A sudden thought struck the General.

*That fellow she's married hasn't turned out any bet-
ter than I thought he would—that's what's happened!*

Somewhat victoriously he advanced upon Cass. He
said: "Come, come, my dear—what is all this? I expected to find you the lady of the manor—flourishing
—full of beans, eh, what?"

She did not answer but kept her face hidden, and
shook her head desolately.

He took her arm.

"Can't stand out here. Wind's cold and my chest isn't
too good these days. Aren't you going to ask me indoors?"

To his horror, albeit his satisfaction, Cass thereupon
flung herself into his arms which had to open wide to
catch her. She stuttered:

"Oh, G-General, G-General, I wish I were d-dead—
buried with Mummy."

That really shocked him. He cleared his throat.

"Good heavens. You mustn't talk like that. Never
heard such a thing. Not like you, Cassandra—you're a
fighter—always were."

Cass choked and suddenly came to her senses. She was shaken to find herself being pressed to the General's bosom and patted on the head. Yet it comforted her. She was in such a muddle in her mind she really did not know what she felt. It was a queer thing—this reunion with her stepfather. She stopped crying, began to wipe her smudged face and giggled.

"You must think I'm round the bend—so sorry. I don't know what came over me. I do feel a bit off-beat."

The General took a large handkerchief from his coat pocket and handed it to her.

"Here—you're making a mess of your face. Blow your nose and take me indoors and tell me all about it."

She took him indoors. She hastily passed Kevin's closed door. She could hear the tap-tap of the typewriter and was thankful he was still at work. She was afraid of running into Maurice and Natasha but the Citroën was missing so Natasha must be out. Possibly Maurice had gone with her.

Satisfied that nobody was in the sitting-room, Cass drew the General in and found him a basket chair on the verandah. Having blown her nose on the welcome handkerchief, she said:

"I'll wash it and send it back."

"Nonsense, I'll want it on the journey home."

"I'll wash it before you go."

"Always one for an argument," he said with a twist of his lips, but his eyes were still friendly as they looked up at her from under their bushy brows.

Cass grew calm. Her desire to dress up for a big seduction scene with Kevin faded. She seated herself opposite her stepfather and kept thinking how extraordinary it was that she should be so pleased to see him.

"General," she said, "you've been good enough to come all this way; of course you must stay to lunch. I'll give you a sherry, then if you don't mind I'll make you an omelette. I can fry some bacon with it and you can have a salad, too. I'm afraid it's all I have. Kev and I never eat at midday."

"It'll suit me. My digestion isn't what it was. But

don't make me an omelette. Poach my egg for me, please."

'Okay," she said meekly, and added: "There are two other people here. He's French—a Monsieur Courraine—she, Natasha is the stepdaughter of the aunt who left this property to Kevin."

"Ah, yes," said the General, but he wasn't really paying attention. He was leaning back in his chair looking out at the sheet of water, sincere admiration in his eyes.

"Very attractive surroundings," he said. "Don't care for the style of the house but this glass place, hanging right over the water so to speak—most original. Must be wonderful on a fine day. Not bad even now. Bit foggy on the way down. Clearing up, don't you think?"

She nodded. It was a good deal finer than it had been. There were still patches of mist on the water but now one could see the beauty of the red and gold autumn trees on the opposite bank. There was no sun but the sky was lighter. Some of the birds, so well known to her, and come out and were sailing across the water. When the crested grebes appeared, the General became excited.

"I say! Rare type of birds, those. Got a pair of binoculars? I'd like to look at them."

She fetched the pair that Mr. de Groot had left in his study and which she and Kevin used. They kept them in a cupboard behind an old screen on the verandah itself. The General twirled the viewfinder around to suit his sight. Cass watched, marvelling at the change in him. A pleasant change; perhaps he had been lonely and miserable since Mummy died. Perhaps life had become less worth living with his advancing years, the deterioration of his health (he was to tell them later that he had had a major operation and nearly died a year ago), and certainly he must miss Mummy who had done everything for him—and adored him. Cass couldn't imagine anybody in the Club which was now his home taking the slightest interest in the old thing. Basically he was a bore.

Once more she was glad he had come. She poured him out a sherry which he accepted. He even raised the glass and said: "Cheers" in his brisk military voice.

Then he added: "And where's this husband of yours?"

"Working."

"At what?"

She gave him a brief resumé of the writing that Kevin had stuck at so indefatigably; praised his efforts and his book; and praised *him*. Nothing would induce her to tell the General what she had just discovered. She said in the most cheerful voice:

"Kevin's a marvellous husband and we're just as happy ever. I made an ass of myself just now because I was terribly tired. I've been over-doing it."

The General was no psychologist and did not disbelieve her. He just raised his brows.

"I see. Well, I came down to find out if you were all right and I must say I was a bit put out when you—er—broke down."

Then Cass silently begged heaven to forgive her and uttered a shameless lie.

"I was so pleased to see you, General—I think it was the shock."

She was rewarded by the pathetic sight of the General's mask-like face breaking up, and the ice-blue eyes melting. In quite an emotional voice he said:

"Really? Really? After all our differences, eh what? When I first married your mother and you were a mite I was very fond of you, Cassandra, yer know. We rubbed each other up the wrong way when you grew up, I grant you. But I've often thought about you and hoped for your dear mother's sake that your marriage had prospered."

"Oh, it has," said Cass gaily, "and we won't rub each other up the wrong way any more, will we?"

"No need to, my dear, no need to. I'm pleased to be in touch with you again. After all, you are my stepdaughter . . . I've nobody else in the world, yer know."

Cass felt the tears sting her eyelids. The misery of her deepest feelings returned with a rush. She hastily handed the sherry bottle to her stepfather, and said that she must go and cook. As she went, she added that she would tell Kev he was here and he'd come and talk to him.

It was only when she was standing outside Kevin's door that she suddenly remembered how ghastly she must look with her tear-smudged face and dirt-stained hands. She didn't mind Kevin seeing the marks of her labours, but she did mind him seeing the traces of her tears. She was not going to let him *know*. . . .

She turned and ran upstairs. A few minutes later, nose powdered, hair brushed, and hands clean, she faced her husband.

He was bent over his desk scribbling. She wrinkled her nose. The atmosphere was thick with cigarette smoke and seemed too hot.

"You've got a good old fug going in here," she said.

She spoke as though nothing whatsoever had happened to break her heart, but that heart hurt as though a cruel hand was squeezing it when he turned his face to her; the lean attractive face she had so adored, with the blue Irish eyes and the big curly mouth and the black truant lock of hair falling across his brow. He was smiling, then frowning, as though he didn't know which to do.

Suddenly in a state of confusion she broke into a hurried explanation of her stepfather's arrival and before Kevin could comment, added:

"I know he's the uninvited, unwanted guest and all that, but don't be cross about it and make him feel unwelcome. The poor old thing's changed quite a bit and I think he's lonely. I've asked him to lunch."

Kevin began to speak but she broke in again:

"It's no worse than having the Courraines here and they were not invited either, but they stayed. Now it's my side of the family."

She ended with a high-pitched laugh which made Kevin open his eyes very wide and stare. What in the name of fortune was the matter with Cass, he wondered. She was being most odd. But he didn't argue or protest. After all, it ill behooved him to put up a defence on behalf of the Courraines, seeing how things had turned out. He was still feeling madly remorseful and worried almost to death about the whole situation with Natasha.

Damn Natasha!

Husband and wife looked at each other, both feeling that they were strangers; uncomprehending of the other's mental state. Then Kevin said:

"Okay! Okay! I'll go and give the old boy a drink. Fancy him coming all the way down here like this."

"He's on the verandah looking at the birds and talking about shooting wild duck in Kenya," said Cass with a nervous laugh. "I'm off to knock up some sort of meal. I presume the Courraines are not in for lunch. Now I come to think of it, Maurice did say something about Natasha driving him up to town to see that eyeman again because of his headaches."

Without waiting for a reply she made her exit.

She took it for granted that Kevin would be polite to the General. She was a little surprised, that he hadn't grumbled about this intrusion upon his peace, *but,* she thought bitterly, as she took some eggs out of the basket Bert had brought in early that morning, it was just as well he didn't exhibit 'a mood'. She would have found it difficult not to tell him what she had heard this morning. Confused and upset as she was, Kevin's friendly attitude to the General made things little better in the depths of her suffering mind, when finally she called the two men in to lunch.

She had hastily laid lunch on the table in the big Dutch dining-room. She knew that the General would not appreciate eating in the kitchen. She found the men drinking together, and carrying on quite a lively discussion about wild fowl. It was phenomenal she thought, to find Kevin being so talkative to her stepfather. The General too was treating Kevin as an equal. It should have made her very happy. Yet somehow she felt suspicious of Kevin. *Why* was he being so pleasant? Wasn't it a horrid sign that he had a guilty conscience?

She was glad she was not expected to join in the conversation during lunch. She sat quiet, trying to eat her omelette without her usual hearty appetite; she had that sick empty feeling still inside her; that *crushed* feeling. Once or twice when she caught Kevin's gaze, he looked away again quickly. Then she shut her eyes and clasped her fingers furiously together in order to keep her control.

Oh, God, God, I loved you so much, Kev. I loved you so much.

Loved! That was in the past tense. Could it all be past? All their years together, their battles for survival, their shared passion and companionship, were they to be thrown on to the dust heap? She dared not look into the future—a future which he might wish to share with *Natasha.* She found it hard to be controlled but managed it somehow. Finally after biscuits, cheese and some celery which she had pulled out of the fridge, she asked the two men to go back to the verandah while she made coffee.

"Thanks for an excellent lunch, Cassandra. Perfectly poached, my eggs," the General said briskly as he walked out of the dining-room. "I must say this is a very pleasant room; fine old Dutch furniture. I like it."

Kevin made pretence of following the General's tall figure, then hurried back to the kitchen where Cass was squirting liquid soap into the washing-up bowl.

"How long have I got to play the host?" he asked in a fierce whisper.

"Until after the coffee."

"Can't you leave the washing-up? I can't go on making conversation by myself."

She didn't turn to look at him but stirred the water angrily into bubbles.

"You don't usually find that so hard. Anyhow, I thought you two were getting on very nicely."

"I admit he's better than he was in the old days but I'll never really like him."

Before she could restrain herself, Cass swung round and flashed at him:

"At least he looked after my mother until she died."

Now Kevin because conscious that something was very wrong indeed with his wife. His sense of guilt fermented into positive despair.

"What do you mean by that?"

"What I say. He made my mother *happy*—in her own way—until she died."

Kevin positively jittered.

"And do I make *you* so *unhappy?*"

It was on the tip of her tongue to tell him just how wretched he had indeed made her; to accuse him of flagrant infidelity. Yet in this instant of tension of unspoken enmity between them, she knew that she still loved him with all her heart. She couldn't *bear* it. She wouldn't. Neither could she make a scene now, while her stepfather was in the house.

She swung round again and splashed at the washing-up water, conscious that the tears were pouring down her face. Through her teeth, she said:

"Oh go back to the General, for God's sake, and leave me alone with my work."

"But what's the matter—" he began.

She broke in:

"Nothing. I'm not well and I'm tired—that's all."

Kevin ruffled the back of his hair. He did not know whether he believed her or not. He walked out of the kitchen and shut the door rather loudly behind him.

The Cass pulled her hands out of the water, wiped them and covered her face. She choked and sobbed for a full moment as though the anguish of her thoughts had become intolerable.

I can't bear it, she thought, *I can't! Oh, God, let me go back to when I first woke up this morning and I didn't know about Natasha.*

When eventually she carried the coffee tray out to the verandah, she was more composed. She did not look at Kevin, but smiled at the General, who actually screwed his own rigid features into the semblance of a smile back at her.

"Ah! Coffee! Nothing like a good strong cup after a meal. I remember, you can make good coffee, Cassandra. Your poor mother did, too. Used to drink gallons of it when I was stationed in Egypt. Damned good Turkish coffee."

He launched into a lengthy description of the way in which the Egyptians made their thick, sweet, ground-filled beverage. Cass and Kevin sat rigid, silent, not looking at each other. Both felt on the edge of a precipice, wondering when they would fall in.

It was not until the coffee had been finished to the

last drop that the General, more considerate than he used to be, suggested that he might be keeping both of them from their work.

"Ought to get off. I know I didn't give you warning. Good of you to have me to lunch. Feel I ought to be making a move."

Kevin, still avoiding Cass's eyes, said:

"Well, I must admit I've got to finish my article. On the phone this morning, my editor said he'd like it up by the first post."

"Quite so," said the General. "Glad you're pulling in cash. Must read this book of yours when it comes out."

Suddenly Cass felt a strange wish to keep her step-father here. She didn't want to be left alone with Kevin, and those other two. It was nonsense, of course, but she said:

"Don't go if you don't want, General. I know it's raining again but if you'd like to walk round the pond, I'll take you, and you could stay on to dinner."

"No thanks, my dear," he said, "I really ought to get off. If Kevin'll ring for a taxi I'll catch the next train back to town. I get chills rather too easily these days and it's a poor day for walking. Very damp—weather's changed again. Never mind—seen your home and like it and I'll come again. Perhaps you'd ask me to stay one weekend."

"Of course," said Kevin politely.

"If we're still here," added Cass.

The General stared.

"Don't tell me you two are thinking of leaving. You've only just settled in."

She did not answer. Kevin also stared. She was flushed and her lips were mutinous. He'd never seen her look like that. And what she had just said had shocked him.

"I don't know what Cass means," he told the General with a brief laugh. "Of course we'll still be here."

"Oh, will we? I thought you said the other day we mightn't be able to afford to keep Pond House up," said Cass in a high over-bright voice, and giving him a glacial smile as she added: "We can't afford it, can we, unless we replace the Courraines and *they're* leaving."

It was Kevin's turn to lapse into silence. Now he was very conscious of an undercurrent—a dark sinister undercurrent which he neither liked nor understood. But no more was said.

The General rose.

"If you don't mind I'll just run along to the cloakroom. Ring for that cab, Kevin, like a good chap."

After the old man had gone, Kevin gave Cass a long questioning look.

"What was all that about, Cass? Who said the Courraines were leaving?"

"Well, if they don't go, I will," said Cass in a cold hard voice.

That flung Kevin completely off balance. When he began to ask for an explanation, she frustrated him.

"Don't let's talk about it now—go and ring for Mr. Potter. Please, Kev, don't argue. There are things to sort out but they can't be sorted out now."

Then he knew that she knew.

Chapter 17

Cass insisted on driving into Chelmsford with the General.

"Mr. Potter knows us well. He'll give me a lift back to Cold Dutton. I want to go and buy some fish in Chelmsford. Then I'll catch a bus halfway back from the village to our place. We're not too far away from the stop."

The General looked pleased. Kevin was less pleased.

"I rather want to talk to you, Cass."

"I want to talk to you," she said coolly, "but it can wait."

They were in the study. The General was still on the verandah waiting for Mr. Potter's taxi. Kevin and Cass glared at each other. They were both at fever-pitch, ready to break into a violent storm yet suspended in space, unable to make a move of their own volition. Suddenly Kevin felt an agonised wish to come down to earth—to find himself once more on the same wavelength as Cass. He saw a yawning chasm ever widening between them and it horrified him. He wished that he had never been born; that Natasha had never been born; that this ghastly affair had never taken place. It was like a poisonous growth that he had not been able to check and now it was spreading, threatening to destroy them all. He didn't care whether he lived or not but he didn't want Cass to die. His sweet Cassandra! God, how he hated to see that glacial, meaning look on her face. The expression that said *I know and I hate you..*

For so long he had found nothing in those golden hazel, honest eyes save love and trust. It was a grim metamorphosis.

Cass left the house with her stepfather and without saying another word to Kevin.

After she had gone, Kevin suffered as he had never thought possible. He began to realise at last that he had always been too self-centred and casual. He had truly loved Cass. That was why he had married her. But what manner of man was he that he could have betrayed her with Natasha? And the memory of Natasha was now so abhorrent to him that he could hardly think of her calmly; in fact he did not know how he was going to get through this evening—or any other evening, behaving normally with the Courraines—and Cass.

Of course such a situation couldn't go on. The gathering storm would break, and put an end to all pretence.

He tried to work but couldn't write another line. His mind seethed with horrible possibilities—and the worst of them was that Cass might leave him.

He wondered how she had found out. He wouldn't put it past Natasha to have told her. He couldn't bear it if Cass left him; or if she wouldn't forgive him.

He walked like a lost soul from room to room in the

big empty house. Finally, up in their bedroom he stood
with his hands in his pockets staring around him. It
wasn't a tidy room. Cass's socks which she wore under
her farm boots had been thrown on the floor, with an
old pair of shoes. Mud-caked ski-pants and jersey lay
on the bed. Powder had been spilt on the dressing-
table. A comb had fallen on the carpet. Kevin picked it
up. Cass must have changed hastily to go into Chelmsford. He remembered how bravely she had stood up to
the General during those days (so long ago now) when
her mother had been alive; when she had defied both of
them in order to marry *him*. How good she had been
about the filthy little flat in Groom Street, too. Yet they
had been very happy there. They had known real closeness and contentment even though they were poor and
struggling.

Kevin sat on the edge of the bed and put his head
between his hands. Suddenly he wished to God that
Aunt Cynthia had never left him this house and the
money. If they hadn't come here, the Courraines
couldn't have come either. Natasha wouldn't have returned to her old home and found him, and cast her
damnable spell over him. Not that he blamed her more
than himself for what had happened. He knew that he
had been weak as putty in her hands. And he had
wanted her. But only for the moment. He'd known it all
the way along. It had been a flare-up of sheer animal
passion between Natasha and himself. He was well
aware that she was not worth the smallest of Cass's fingers.

How the hell was he going to get out of this mess
without hurting Cass? That was all that mattered to him
now. He wondered how long she would be in Chelmsford and whether the volcano would erupt between
them once she got back, and if so what the result would
be.

Suddenly he could no longer bear to stay in Pond
House alone. He decided to walk to Cold Dutton
Woods, a mile and a half up the main road, and wrestle
with his conscience alone, right away from home.

As he trudged down the road through the rain in his
old macintosh, head bare, face set and grim, he tried to

think sensibly. Yet somehow his tormented conscience
kept leading him down this ugly tunnel of memory to
that first time with Natasha in the boathouse.

He remembered that he had shut out all conscience
then, as he held that voluptuous beautiful body in his
arms. He had forgotten Cass, his wife. That was what
passion without love could do to a man. The sort of
passion that was a killer. But in that hour he had felt
himself to be a conqueror because Natasha had surrendered to him. She had laughed up at him with her wonderful witch's eyes, and whispered:

"I'm crazy about you. Tell me you love me, lover."

Yet somehow he had not been able to say those
words: *I love you.* He had just told her he was crazy
about her, too. But even in his delirium he had felt that
the word *love* belonged to Cass alone.

Funny thing, he thought this afternoon, with the rain
beating against his face. Two years of fidelity, friendship and happiness could be wiped out in one hour of
insanity.

He thought:

*I want my brains examined, to have done what I've
done to Cass.*

He walked until he was soaked through and dog-
tired. Then he turned back to Pond House.

He felt only a little better but at least he had reached
a decision. He would tell Cass. He would not wait for
her to tell him. He must convince her that he hadn't
meant it to happen and that he truly loved her and
wanted her forgiveness.

It was nearly five when he opened the front door.
Dusk was creeping over the house and pond. He threw
off his coat and called out:

"Cass!"

There was no answer. The place seemed dark and
silent. Immediately fear shook Kevin. The fear that
Cass had gone to London with her stepfather and did
not mean to come back.

"Cass!" he called the name again, urgently.

Then he saw a light up on the landing and the figure
of Maurice Courraine at the top of the staircase. He

was wearing a coat and silk scarf and looked as though
he had only just come in. Kevin said:

"So you're just back, Maurice."

With one hand on the banister and the other on his
stick, Maurice came slowly down the stairs—one at a
time.

"Yes, I am back."

"And Natasha?" Somehow the name stuck in Kevin's
throat.

"No. She has not come with me."

Maurice was on the bottom stair now. For once he
stood level with Kevin who thought the little Frenchman looked ashy pale. His usually well-brushed grey
hair was untidy. He took off his tinted glasses and
Kevin could see that his eyes were more than usually
inflamed. He passed a hand wearily across them, then
replaced the glasses.

"Natasha is never coming back," he said in a low,
slow voice.

If Kevin's first thought was one of relief, it speedily
changed to concern, for it was obvious that Maurice
was a sick, sorrowful man.

"I say—look here—what's all this about? Come
along and have a Cognac or something," he said with
embarrassment.

"Yes," said Maurice in a sombre voice and with a
deep sigh. "Thank you. Cognac would be very accepta-
ble."

"You haven't seen Cass, have you?" asked Kevin as
they walked to the salon where he switched on the
lights and an electric fire. It was very cold and he had
felt Maurice shivering.

"No, she's not in. I could not find her."

Kevin's heart sank.

"She went out two hours ago to take her stepfather
into Chelmsford."

"Her stepfather?" repeated Maurice. He spoke in a
slow rather dull voice as though he attached little importance to anything.

Kevin explained about the General, then brought the
brandy. He made Maurice sit down and drink it.

"You came home by train?"

"No. I fear I was extravagant," said Maurice with the ghost of a smile, "I was feeling ill. I hired a car in London."

Kevin suddenly felt in need of a nip of brandy for himself. He pulled one of the electric fires near them and looked with still more concern at the Frenchman. Maurice lay back in an armchair with closed eyes. He really looked ghastly, Kevin reflected.

"What's happened to Natasha?" At last he blurted out the question.

"She has left me," said Maurice, opening his eyes. "She has left you, too, Kevin."

The younger man felt his pulses jerk unpleasantly. The hot colour flamed into his face. Maurice did not give him an opportunity to speak.

"I know all, Kevin," he added quietly. "Do not worry, please. But I repeat that she has left both of us. It is of course of much more importance to me, since I am her husband."

Kevin, speechless—stricken and feeling the lowest thing on earth—tossed down his drink. He was in need of that fiery liquid. He, too, had begun to shake.

"Look, Maurice," he said, "I—"

"You were in love with my wife," broke in Maurice. "Yes, I know."

"No," said Kevin violently, "I can't excuse myself even on those grounds. I was never really in love with her. Oh God, I don't understand myself," he added violently, "and I don't know what you must think of me or why you speak to me so kindly. Why aren't you telling me I'm a bastard?"

The Frenchman drew a long, deep sigh.

"I do not feel that you are one, *mon pauvre*. I only pity you. You have been a foolish boy. But I should have had more sense. Natasha is a wicked girl. Very wicked indeed. She has no heart. She has only a beautiful face and the sort of body that drives a man to frenzy."

"How did you find out?" Kevin asked, miserably.

"I have known for some time. I heard—and I saw—one day. Do not let us go into details that can only distress us both."

"But my God, what can I say? I feel such a damned awful so-and-so. *I am one.* I ought to be grovelling. What I've done is unpardonable."

"To me there is nothing that cannot be forgiven in the name of genuine emotion, even if it is not absolute love," said Maurice Courraine. "You are young and strong and vigorous-minded and a creative artist. Such men are sensitive to great beauty—open to extreme temptation. Everything was made so easy for you. This haunting place with all its atmosphere; the fact that Natasha was sick of me, and that your wife was always busy. So Natasha had every opportunity to pursue you. Yes, pursue. You need not tell me, Kevin, for I *know*. Me, too, she pursued in the days when she first wanted me. It was the same with her first husband, and with her many lovers. For she had many, Kevin. She was insatiable. Never is she faithful to any one man. I tried to find sympathy for her because the catastrophe of my eyesight meant the end of any glamour I used to have as a once famous accompanist. She was not the type to make a nurse for an invalid. I was crippled because of the failure of my eyesight. Then she met you here and decided to stay, and play her usual game. You have no money, no, but you are an exciting young man who resisted her at first, and that alone was a challenge to Natasha. She could not stand resistance."

"We were both to blame," said Kevin. "I had no right—"

"Right?" Maurice broke in. "There's no such thing as right or wrong in a case like this. There are morals and principles—laws set down by man. There are *dos* and *don'ts* and *shoulds* and *shouldn'ts,* but human beings remain human. Fundamentally they are primitive beings with primitive feelings. All right—use the conventional argument if you prefer it. You had no right to deceive your wife and to dishonour me but I forgive you freely, my friend, because Natasha was like a panther—a really beautiful cruel panther. She steals up on her victims, mauls them, then leaves them to die in torment. She finished with me. But she didn't yet want to end the affair with you. It was not time for the kill. Then you turned your back on her, so if she had stayed here she would eventually have left you. I loved her once. I was foolish enough to think she needed my love and protection. Now I know better. You, too, *mon pauvre* Kevin, you have learned better. I can see it—feel it—I have watched you. I know you have wanted to get away."

Kevin buried his face in his hands.

"I've no defence," he said huskily. "I'm totally ashamed. You're being unbearably decent about it."

"Decent," said Maurice, and laughed sadly, "what a truly English word!"

"I don't know what to say next."

"Say nothing. Perhaps I'd better explain that when I set out for London with my wife, she spoken openly of her passion for you but said she had come to the conclusion that life was not as attractive in this house as it used to be. The hunt was over and the prey was about to escape. She would, I think, have hurt Cass if she could, but I warned her that if she did so, I would not only cut her out of my life but out of my Will. I have some money in France. Natasha loves money. I made the Will in favour of her. She asked for her freedom. I told her she could have it—plus the money. But not unless she left Pond House without telling your wife what had been going on."

Kevin raised his head sharply. He stared at Maurice.

"But I don't understand."

"It is as I say. I like and admire your young wife, my dear Kevin, as I have never liked any woman before. She is a very wonderful person—brave and good, adorably feminine, as well. And she loves you devotedly. I would prefer to see all my money go to my faithless wife rather than let your Cassandra be hurt."

"I appreciate it, Maurice. It's a terrific tribute to Cass. But she knows. *She knows.*"

Now it was Maurice's turn to raise his head and stare.

"How does she know? Who told her?"

"I don't know. I've got to find that out. I'm still in the dark about it."

"Are you sure?"

"As sure as I can be. By everything she said while

her stepfather was here and what she said just before she went to Chelmsford."

"If it is true, then it is a real tragedy. I wanted to spare her," said Maurice.

"God knows *I* never wanted her to suffer," said Kevin miserably. "Oh, God, *God!* . . ." He beat his clenched fist on the arm of his chair. "I'd give my life for it not to have turned out like this. I've injured you, who I like and respect, and Cass, too. I can never forgive myself."

Maurice stared ahead of him. He said:

"Let us not talk of no forgiveness. Natasha wants a divorce. She decided not to return here and asked that I send her things on to her. She took with her a case of jewellery and, of course, her mink coat. Tonight she stays in London with friends. Tomorrow she will fly to Paris. When we lived there, she was once offered a modelling job in one of the biggest *haute couture* houses— I forget which. But she has such startling good looks and such a perfect figure, she can easily get work. And of course there will be another man very soon," ended Maurice with a tired cynical laugh.

Kevin, his face haggard, looked at his watch.

"What's happened to Cass—where's she got to?" he grunted and knew that he was wildly anxious.

He left Maurice sitting, brooding and silent. He rang the station taxi. Mr. Potter himself, answered. On being questioned the man said he had brought Mrs. Martin back from Chelmsford at about half past three and she asked him to drop her in the village.

Kevin put down the telephone. He reckoned that Cass should have been home long before now, even if she walked all the way from Cold Dutton. Often she hitchhiked if she saw a car coming in the direction of Pond House. Where could she be? He could only suppose that she had dropped in at the house of their local doctor, Philip Alderson, and was still there. Cass had become rather friendly with the wife, Stella; a tall graceful girl with a nice smile, who had recently had twin sons.

Worried to death though he was, Kevin could not help remembering the day Cass came back from seeing

the new-born twins. She had leaned her cheek against
his shoulder in that confiding way of hers and said:

"Don't let *us* put off having children too long, Kev. I
know you want to get established but I'd adore to have
a family—an infant of yours. I really envied Stella today. She looked so blissful and the twins are fabulous."

He had laughed and teased her.

"Well, so long as it's an infant of mine and no one
else's—okay."

Yes, she might have dropped in for what she called
'a natter' with Stella Alderson.

Should he ring the doctor's house and find out? It
was not in Kevin's nature to root around, trying to
track his wife down unless there was an emergency. In
his mind this *was* an emergency, but perhaps in no one
else's, and if Cass didn't want to come home yet, that
was her affair. After all she never tried to track him
when he was late home.

Feeling dejected beyond words, he sauntered back
into the room that Cass called her 'salon'. He was about
to speak to Maurice when he became aware that the
Frenchman was no longer in the room. At once a cold
draught of air smote him and he noticed that one of the
verandah doors was swinging in the wind. A sudden
feeling of horror possessed Kevin. He ran out on to the
verandah. He saw that one of the sliding windows
which were removable in summer had been pulled
back. The wind was blowing in from the pond bringing the rain with it, spattering over the chairs and
tables. At the same time he fancied he heard the sound
of splashing and of a faint voice calling: *"Help!"*

Maurice, Kevin thought and his feeling of horror
grew. *Maurice had fallen through that window into the
water.*

He rushed out into the night. The light was almost
gone but through the grey dusk he could just see a
shape struggling in the water. He called hoarsely:

"Maurice . . . Maurice . . . I'm here. Hold on
. . . I'm coming . . ."

The next moment he had jumped down into the tangle of water weeds and rushes. Almost immediately he
was submerged up to the neck. He knew how deep it

was—much deeper than he and Cass had imagined at first, for during their first summer here they had thought they might be able to wade in but they sank. They had come spluttering and laughing.

But this was no occasion for laughter. Maurice was out there and Kevin could see his head going down. He was bubbling and sinking. His cries were no longer distinguishable.

Kevin was not a strong swimmer. He was not, in fact, much of a swimmer at all, but he knew that he must try to save the drowning man. Whether this had been an accident or intentional he did not know and had no time to decide.

"Maurice—hold on for God's sake." He shouted the words as he struck out gasping from the icy impact of the water—conscious that he was wearing far too many clothes. It didn't make swimming easy. He wanted to tread water and take off his coat but he knew that there wasn't time. The little Frenchman was drowning, dying, there in front of his eyes.

"Maur-rice!" he yelled the name again desperately.

There was no answer from Natasha's husband. Only silence except for the splashing of Kevin's arms and legs in the dank unpleasant water and the taste of mud and slime in his mouth. And suddenly, sorrowfully, there came a long-drawn-out cry from one of the Chinese geese across the darkening water.

Chapter 18

AT this moment, Cass was seated opposite Stella Alderson in the doctor's warm, comfortable little house which was right on the High Street at Cold Dutton.

The doctor was still taking surgery. The twins had been bathed and put to bed, watched by a sad and envious Cass. Cass who with her naturally gay optimistic nature rarely envied anybody anything.

But at the end of this black day in her life she wished she could be Stella Alderson—content, fulfilled as a wife and mother, and secure. Yes, it was the loss of strength and comfort and the security that she used to feel with Kevin that affected her most deeply.

After she had finished her shopping in Chelmsford, buying several things that they needed in the house and couldn't get in the village, she had returned to Cold Dutton in a miserable mood, unwilling to go home to face the misery that awaited her. Especially she dreaded facing Kevin with all defences down on both sides. She dared not even think how it might end. Above all, she dreaded having to confront Natasha and watch her horrid triumph.

So she had stalled—decided to spend an hour with her friend. They liked each other and got on well. Stella was the one real friend Cass had made since her marriage and Kevin did not get on badly with Philip Alderson. Phil was a hard-working G.P. dedicated to his profession and not disinterested in books, which appealed to Kevin. The four of them had occasional meals in each other's houses. During the last six months their friendship had developed.

Stella, of course, knew all about Cass's 'paying guests' and thought it a good plan that somebody should help with the expenses of the big place. But she did not particularly care for Natasha Courraine. And living as she did right in the heart of the village Stella had heard several rumours about Natasha from the older people in the parish who used to know the de Groots. There were quite a few unflattering stories going around about Natasha's conduct as a young girl. The old people seemed to have few good words for her; Dr. Alderson, himself, was anti-Natasha because she had, so he had found out, done a great deal of harm to the son of the man whose practice Philip had originally taken over.

It wasn't difficult to believe now, Cass told herself bitterly this evening. Natasha was evil and predatory. She had even fooled around with his boy of nineteen while he was sitting his exams in accountancy. He fell madly in love with the beautiful girl who offered so much glamour and unusual excitement in an otherwise dull community. She had led him on without remorse and distracted him from his studies. When he had failed she had quit—and found another, more successful boyfriend. She had done a lot of harm to the old doctor's son and it was the sort of thing that Philip Alderson despised.

No, Natasha was not popular in the Alderson household.

Cass was tempted to open up and tell Stella what had happened at home. But in the end she couldn't bring herself to run Kevin down—no matter what he had done. So, when Stella at last noticed Cass's unusual depression and questioned her, Cass laughed it off as 'just a liver attack', and drew the conversation away from herself.

"When do you plan to have nice twins like mine?" Stella asked cheerfully now as she sat opposite Cass, busily knitting, waiting for the doctor to join them. Cass had promised to stay for a drink.

Cass flinched and did not meet Stella's gaze.

"Oh, some day no doubt," she answered lightly.

"How is your handsome Kev?"

"Still handsome," laughed Cass.

"You must have been surprised to see your stepfather after so long?"

"I was, and it's funny what time can do. I used to hate him because he came between me and my mother. But when I saw him again today somehow I quite liked him. He was a link with the old days."

Stella looked up at the clock.

"I understand. It's natural. Excuse me a moment, I must go and switch on my oven."

Suddenly Cass felt she could no longer sit here in the bright little room talking to happy Stella and she did not want to face Dr. Alderson who had a sharp pair of eyes and might notice how she looked, and guess how she felt. He was more observant than Stella.

"I must get back," she said rising, and reaching for her coat.

"Oh, Phil will be disappointed if you don't stay and have a sherry with him."

"Forgive me—I really ought to go. I've been away longer than I meant. Kevin might be worrying."

She said the words mechanically but Stella laughed.

"He won't worry. He's much too sure of you. I don't know that it's good for husbands to be too sure of us girls. What do you say?"

Cass turned away.

Dear God, she thought, *I'm the one who isn't sure any longer.*

"Wouldn't you like to wait and let Phil drive you home? It's such a dirty night."

"No, I'm okay. I can pick up that 127 bus to the corner and I don't mind the rain."

"You're tough," smiled Stella, looking with affection at Cass's face which was still brown from the summer's sun and the long hours she spent in the open air. She and Phil adored Cass. She really was the nicest person, and she did so love that husband of hers. Stella thought him a bit of an egotist, but Phil said he thought him a good chap at heart and Phil was rarely wrong.

Cass missed the bus by half a minute and stood in the rain miserably watching the red tail-lamps disappear down the road. Now she could only hope to hitch a lift. She did not fancy walking the whole mile and a quarter to the Pond House. She had suddenly 'gone exhausted' as she told herself. Physically and mentally 'done in'.

Nobody stopped to give her a lift so walk she did. Finally she opened her front door and dragged her footsteps across the hall, rain dripping from her coat. Her headscarf and hair were soaked. She pulled off the scarf and stood a moment shaking it, staring around. The house seemed very quiet. No voices. Only one light coming from under the door of Kevin's study.

Now she came to think of it, she hadn't seen the Citroën. Maybe the Courraines were still out. She hoped so fervently. She pushed back her wet hair and looked again at Kevin's door. *Oh well,* she thought, *here goes!*

Kevin was not at his desk. His fire was on and the room was warm and he was walking up and down, a drink in one hand and a cigarette in the other. When he saw Cass he put down both cigarette and glass and spoke to her in a harsh almost unrecognisable voice. In fact she thought him altogether unrecognisable. He looked ghastly and dishevelled.

He said:

"Where the hell have you been?"

She stiffened.

"What's it matter?" she asked resentfully.

"I've been worrying—"

"You have to be joking," she broke in. "Why should *you* worry about me?"

Now he gripped her by both arms and shook her.

"Be quiet. Don't talk to me like that or look at me like that. I can't stand it. I'm nearly out of my mind."

"And what about my mind—" she began. Then she stopped. For if ever she saw naked pain and misery in a man's eyes they lay in Kevin's and suddenly she was reduced to silence.

"Let go of my arms," she whispered. "You're hurting me."

He let her go. Weakly she sank into the chair by the electric fire and held her chilled hands out to the glow.

"I need something strong to drink," she said. "I'm all in."

"Where have you been?"

"To the Aldersons."

"You've been the hell of a long time."

"Why should that matter to you? Your time has been your own—now mine is going to be my own."

"Oh, shut up, Cass, *shut up*. Don't keep narking at me hinting all kinds of dark things. Say them—be done with it. But no—first of all I want to tell you what's happened here."

Cass had an hysterical desire to laugh and only just managed to restrain it.

"Are you going to stage a touching confession? If so, I don't think I want to hear it until I've had my drink."

He swore under his breath, poured a whisky from a bottle in his cupboard and handed it to her. He had never felt so glad to see anybody as he was to see her—little Cass with her long wet hair, looking like a half-drowned nymph. Then the mere thought of the word drowned brought sickness to his stomach. He felt speechless—paralysed—unable to take her in his arms and hold her close, *close,* as he really wanted to do.

"Something terrible has happened while you've been gone," he said hoarsely.

The bitterness and resentment in her gave place to the sensation that something had indeed happened; something very sinister.

"What, Kev? What's happened? Where are the Courraines?"

"I don't know where Natasha is and I don't care. I only hope she's in hell," he said harshly.

Cass stared up at his ghastly face. She was half glad to hear him say such a thing but half suspicious of what it might mean. He did not give her time to comment. He went on:

"Maurice . . . poor Maurice . . . is dead."

Cass, who held an unlighted cigarette in her hand, dropped it. She looked up at Kevin with enormous eyes.

"Oh, *no!*"

"I need another drink," he said.

She touched his hand.

"Are you all right? You're like ice. Your lips look blue."

"I've been in the water."

"What water—*where?*"

He brushed the hair, black and still damp, back from his forehead.

"In the pond. I came out smelling—oh, Cass, it's all rotting in there—beastly. I've just had a hot bath but I can't get warm or get the stench out of my nostrils."

All that had happened between them, all Cass's grief and suffering and bitterness, were forgotten. He looked so awful she only wanted to help and comfort him—whatever he needed. She pressed his bluish red hands between her own which, in contrast, were warm. She gasped:

"*Kev.* For God's sake what's been going on? Why were you in the pond?"

He poured out a drop of whisky, tossed it down and wiped his lips with the back of his hand. He made an effort to pull himself together. He hadn't stopped shaking or feeling sick since he had brought Maurice's unconscious body out of the water and dragged it with superhuman strength up the bank and into the house.

Now he related the whole story from the beginning; how Maurice had come back from London and told him that Natasha had walked out on him, how they had talked together; how utterly crushed and miserable Maurice had seemed—and ill. The oculist had warned him that the Viennese he meant to consult would not be able to help him. His eye trouble was incurable. Soon he would be completely blind. That, Kevin told Cass, did not seem as big a tragedy to Maurice as the fact that Natasha had left him, and shaken his whole belief in woman-kind. She had betrayed him right from the beginning of their life together. Taunted him with stories of her conquests, her wretched infidelities even when she was in France; when they were first married.

"Then," Kevin finished, "of course there was *me*. I joined the gang. I helped to hit Maurice down, along with the rest of them. I feel the lowest thing on earth."

Cass sat absolutely silent. This was the moment of truth—the first time he had actually admitted his betrayal of her, his wife. She could not speak. She could not even go on holding his hand. She dropped it and bent down to pick up her cigarette. Mechanically Kevin reached for a match and lit the cigarette. He went on with his story. He begged Cass to be patient and for the moment not to make him say any more about his affair with Natasha. He must tell her the rest about Maurice. He described the hour he had spent talking to him, then how worried he was because Cass had not come home, and so he went out into the hall and telephoned Mr. Potter to make sure that she had come back from Chelmsford Station.

"I even thought you might have gone to London with the General," Kevin said with a cracked laugh. "I wouldn't have blamed you."

Cass did not speak. Her throat was dry and her thoughts confused.

Kevin went on telling his story. How on the verandah he found the sliding doors open and the rain blowing in and Maurice struggling in the water. So he jumped in and tried to save the Frenchman.

"But you know I'm a ruddy awful swimmer," he went on hoarsely, "always have been—and I don't suppose I managed too well. I wasn't quick enough. By the time I got out to him and pulled him in, I'd gone down once or twice myself, and oh God, I was frightfully sick. I was half crazy with fear for Maurice. I tried lifesaving, you know—pressing on his lungs and all that, but I couldn't bring him round so I phoned for Philip Alderson. The line was continually engaged and I thought the matter so serious I got on to that Dr. Cowan at Chelmsford whom Lady Winn-Kerr thinks so much of. He came straight out. Maurice was still breathing, but after a bit he died. Cowan couldn't save him. He said it was his heart. He sent for an ambulance. They took him away. Of course there'll be an inquest. Cass, Cass—I did all I could. I tried to save him, Cass. I tried, *oh God*—I wanted to do something for him—something good because I felt so guilty. I *was* guilty!"

Now Kevin was on his knees before her, collapsed, with his face buried on his folded arms, leaning against her knees. He was sobbing—great convulsive sobs that shook the tall lean body she had loved so much, and *still loved*. She knew it beyond doubt, with every drop of blood in her veins. She still loved—and must forgive him.

She wrapped her arms around him and held him close as though trying to infuse him with some of her warmth. Then she pulled his head up and brought his cold wet face down against her neck. She wept with him.

"I understand—I know how you must feel—I won't hold it against you, Kev. Natasha was a fiend. I knew it all the way along. And poor Maurice knew it. He used to talk to me sometimes. I knew how wretched she made him. She was a fiend—I wouldn't blame you or any man. She could be so damnably attractive when she wanted."

Kevin beat the air with his fists.

"Don't be too decent to me for God's sake. I don't deserve it."

"Oh, Kev," Cass moaned, "I understand. It was just a crazy infatuation. I forgive you. I want to. I love you. I won't let it make any difference, I swear it. Please stop feeling so badly."

"But Maurice is dead and I helped to kill him."

"That's just dramatic nonsense. You always exaggerate things, Kev. I know you did him wrong and you shouldn't have had the affair, but you were only one of dozens. You can't pick yourself out as a *killer*. Anyhow, it's no use looking back. It can't help any of us."

Kevin gave a great tearing sob that ended in a laugh and she felt the pressure of his forehead against her knees.

"How like you to be so practical even in a moment like this."

She threaded her fingers through his hair. The tears went on running blindly down her cheeks but she was calming down.

"Someone's got to be practical. We can't act like a Greek chorus. It's over. I can't bear the idea that Maurice is dead. It's too awful. It's tragic. Yet in a way it's good that he's at peace. He would never have been happy with that woman and what did he face but loneliness and total blindness? It's awful to think that he'll never play our piano or any piano again, but it's better this way. If you want to look at things really sensibly."

Kevin kept silent, his hands gripping her; pressing his head against her lap as though terrified to let her go. He said then how nice Dr. Cowan had been and how sympathetic. Cowan had asked Kevin how the thing had come about and Kevin had told him that he had just come back into the room and found the Frenchman in the water. Cowan had taken Kevin upstairs afterwards and made him get out of his wet clothes, and into a bath because he was so cold. He had kept telling Kevin that he had done his best.

"That's what *I* tell you," said Cass.

"But it'll haunt me," said Kevin, "for the rest of my life."

"You mustn't let it, darling. You'll have to try and forget. Does Dr. Cowan think it was an accident?"

Kevin lifted his head and looked at Cass with tormented eyes.

"He thinks as I did—Maurice needed some air, and slid the window back and leaned out—then because he couldn't see properly, he went right through—rolled down into the water. Poor chap, poor old Maurice!"

"Then you mustn't think anything else."

"But I begin to wonder—" began Kevin hoarsely.

She interrupted:

"Don't say it, *don't say what you think*. Maybe I think it too, but I won't allow myself to. Anyhow he would have been dreadfully unhappy if he'd gone on living, and if he did it on purpose he must be forgiven. It's best for him."

Kevin stood up—he pulled her into his arms and pressed his cheek to hers. He said:

"Darling, darling, I dreaded you'd come back and tell me to get the hell out—or quit, yourself."

She shook her head.

"I was terribly upset at first. I felt murderous—dreadfully let down."

"So you were. I'm so ashamed of myself. I swear I regret it—I hate having been so weak. Why should you be sorry for me?"

"I'm sorry for myself," she whispered. "I can't live without you."

"Oh, Cass, my sweet, *sweet* Cassandra, you're more than any man deserves."

"I don't think infidelity is so important if it's just a sort of crazy passion a person regrets. What I couldn't forgive is a cold-blooded sort of long-drawn-out affair where the wife is continually humiliated."

"God forgive me if I've humiliated you, Cass. I swear I never meant to. And what I felt for Natasha is exactly what you said—a crazy passion. I actually told her on that night when the car was supposed to have broken down that I wanted to end it but she threatened to tell you. I wanted to tell you, too, but I dreaded hurting you. I tried to think of a way out—of saving you. Then poor old Maurice offered her all his money to leave you alone—she accepted. It was so mean and callous."

Cass drew back and stared up at Kevin incredulously.

"He did *what?*"

Kevin repeated what Maurice had told him.

"He had a tremendous respect and admiration for you. He said he'd rather give Natasha her freedom *and* the money than see you hurt. But I knew by then that *you* already knew. How, Cass—tell me *how?*"

She told him, and ended with sad humour:

"There I was, all domesticated, going to Hoover the landing and instead I heard the whole story and reckoned I'd lost my husband. Shows one shouldn't be so keen to clean up the place. Oh, Kev, *Kev* . . ." and then she was crying, holding on to him, "I'll never forget Maurice. It was wonderful of him to be so good to me."

Kevin drew away from her and lit a cigarette.

"I haven't been too good, have I?"

"I don't mind if you still love me."

"I never really stopped," he said, "and if you'll trust me in spite of what I've done I swear I'll never let you down again."

"I'll trust you," she whispered. "Honest, I will."

"We've still got a bit to go through, Cass, the inquest; the publicity; and I expect people will talk and wonder . . ."

"Let them. They'll never know what really happened any more than we do. They'll just think it was a tragic accident."

"I wish I'd been able to save him, Cass."

"Of course you do, but I keep telling you, he's happier this way."

Kevin dropped the unlighted cigarette, pulled her back into his arms and kissed her upturned mouth.

"Cass—you've been fabulous over this, I'll never forget it. I'll make up to you for everything. I'll never get into another mood to upset you."

She smiled and drew a hand across her tired eyes.

"I bet you will. Now let me go, darling. Isn't it time I got you something to eat?"

Popular Romances
from
BALLANTINE

Bestsellers from BALLANTINE